Hello, I am Prime Minister, President and I am open to the world.

Hello, I am Prostitute Linda and I am open to the world.

Prime Minister, President and Prostitute all start with the letter 'P'

I love my Pussy.

NO SEX
NO LIFE

Linda Li

Publisher: Inspiring Publishers,
P.O. Box 159, Calwell, ACT Australia 2905
Email: publishaspg@gmail.com
http://www.inspiringpublishers.com

 A catalogue record for this book is available from the National Library of Australia

NATIONAL LIBRARY OF AUSTRALIA

National Library of Australia The Prepublication Data Service

Author: Linda Li
Title: No Sex No Life
Genre: Nonfiction / Memoir

Paperback ISBN: 978-1-922920-49-2
eBook ISBN: 978-1-922920-50-8

The Number One Prostitute (Part I)

Chapter One
The Number One Prostitute

In this chapter, I present sex as the most essential nature of human beings that exists at almost any place and any time, and humans as vicars of Bray; two-faced people who dress immaculately and behave decently enough when they appear in public places such as offices, meetings or parties, but have no scruples about their words and deeds when they give rein to their lust's imagination. I illustrate, with a lot of vivid and factual episodes that different people have different attitudes toward sex and therefore have different habitual practices or even extraordinary sexual illusions and fantasies in their sexual lives. In narrating my personal experiences as a prostitute, I demonstrate a comprehensive review of lovemaking and how to make it more satisfying for both sides. At the end of this chapter, I illustrateV why we should discriminate, or rather separate sex from love.

Chapter Two
Goddess on Earth

I have found the soul, which has been disputed for thousands of years. Soul is a flow of consciousness you can't see or feel but it can get in or out of your body. It is something that is living, thinking and has a memory. I believe everybody (except a maniac or a blockhead) has a soul inside himself. My soul has told me about the existence of God and that the world was created by Him, as well as all the souls. I have used my thirteen days' narration to illustrate my pilgrimage of struggling between being an ordinary woman and a goddess.

Contents

Chapter One
The Number One Prostitute

Introduction

My description of a prostitute's life is a presentation of real scenes, figures and episodes combined with artistic recreation and reconstruction. (All the characters in this narrative are based on real people but I have changed all the descriptions of the original prototypes: their heights, their skin colors, their nationalities or the size of their organs. For example, I will remodel a tall figure in my novel into a short one, a fat figure into a thin one, a black figure into a white one, an American figure into an English one, a French figure into a German one, an Italian figure into a Canadian one or a big-cocked one into a small-cocked one. I have even edited the episodes of two figures into a single story.) If any gentleman happens to find that he is similar to one of the characters in my narrative, it must be a sheer coincidence. And ladies, you should have no reason to suspect your husbands, lovers or boyfriends. I'm only telling my life experiences and stories in order to illustrate four things: First, whenever and wherever there are humans, there is sex, just as the Chinese ancient philosopher Confucius put it: the desire for food and the desire for sex are two essential, inherent desires of humans.

Second, sex is a part of our everyday lives. Everyone has sex in an individual way and has his or her own, unique understanding of the meaning of sex. To me, sex is quite different in essence from love.

Third, every man has two sides just as a coin does. He will dress immaculately and behave decently enough when he appears in public places such as offices, meetings or parties but he will have no scruples about his words and deeds and behave wantonly when he gives rein to his lust. The two sides combine to make an integral person; and years of my experience as a prostitute has granted me a subtle ability to see through to the other side of men.

Fourth, every man has some secrets which he will not disclose to anybody in his life. It's universally true and it's the same with women. If I had not taken on this occupation, I would have, like any ordinary woman, brought to the grave all my sexual privacy and my secrets in life. In that case, my autobiography would have been written otherwise. Now that I've been a professional prostitute for nearly ten years and witnessed this side of humanity so thoroughly, I regard cocks, cunts or asses as ordinary human organs just like noses or mouths. So why can't we demonstrate or comment on them in public? In the civilizations of ancient Greece and Rome, nudes were among the most important genres in sculpture. The nude statues of the Greeks were so realistic that they even displayed characteristic physical features of men, like for instance that one of their testicles was usually higher than the other. I'd like to write an unprecedentedly indecent book about these things in an effort to win a Nobel Prize for Indecency Literature, if such a Prize existed.

And last but not least, whatever job you're doing, you must put your heart and soul into it and do it studiously and ardently, in order to gain your own experience and develop your own methods that distinguish you from your peers so you can survive in this highly competitive society. As Charles Darwin put it, the fittest survive.

As a sex worker in prostitution, I have witnessed and appreciated thousands and thousands of cocks of many different sizes and shapes; cocks and cocks galore. So why can't I describe this spectrum of cocks in detail and visualize them into "statues" with my pen so as to let my readers witness the vigorous totem of human life? As the Greek philosopher Socrates put it, to be full of life is to be characterized by an appearance of the most intense, visual appeal.

My name is Linda and I'm a Chinese Australian. I am a sex worker, commonly referred to as a prostitute. I live in Canberra, where I have lived and worked for many years. I love this city, I love my occupation, I love my clients and I love my home.

Prostitution is a legal occupation here in Australia and it is also protected by the law in most countries except China. I'm a licensed prostitute and I pay taxes to the government accordingly. My advertisement appears every day in the newspaper, *Canberra Daily.*

My house is near the downtown of Canberra and it is also my workplace. Eight years ago, I bought the house in the name of my limited company. Most of my friends said I must have gone mad because should something happen to the company, the house under its name would become the assets of the Australian government or the Taxation Office. Yet my instinct told me my future was based on this house, which would be the start and the foundation stone of my career. I know myself only too well. I will not base my business solely on selling my flesh, but I will also use my wisdom, resolution and vision to create a brave new future.

A series of dreams will stem from here and the accumulation of wealth will start from here as well. As is usually said by the Chinese, a spark can start a prairie fire. Given enough time, my fond dream is sure to become a reality.

Mine is a typical European-style house. My dealer told me it was designed by an Italian architect and it was rated as a four- star house in Australia, combining modern sense and classical grace. The house's north-facing wall near the street is solemnly brown grey in color and the other three walls are a lively cream. There are black security mesh on all the doors and windows, through which the bright Australian sunlight sifts in to flood the floor, adding a hazy beauty to the house.

The house faces north. In Chinese tradition, good residential houses are supposed to face south so as to let in as much sunlight as possible. But since Australia is an antipode and lies in the

Southern Hemisphere, a house facing north is just as ideal for a Chinese hostess. Conveniently located on the north and west, it is adjacent to a street lined with verdurous bushes and cypress trees. With beautiful gardens in front and at the rear, it is a really reclusive residence within the bustle of downtown. When the sun rises in the morning, the first gleams stream in exhilaratingly; at noon the sunlight spills through the north window, making everything in the room glitter; in the evening, the glow of the sunset through the windows floods the floor of the living room, bringing you into a blissful wonderland.

East of the yard is a tree about six feet high, forming a partition between my neighbor's driveway and my sixteen-foot- wide parking space. A garage adjacent to the parking space is attached to the house proper. On the north, street-facing wall, three, floor-to-ceiling glass doors stand side by side. A French window, about three feet wide, is about five feet away from these doors. On the west side is a Victorian-styled room, with an arch window closely resembling the shape of a semi-ellipse and a roof similar to that of a church.

The layout of the house is like a huge, asymmetric "U". The front door is on the left side of the "U" and faces east, which coincides with *fengshui* (a Chinese term for architectural geometry): that in construction, first priority should be given to the East. Opposite the front door is the west wall of the garage, which is actually the extension of the house proper. The garage is three feet longer than the west-end living room, with three, floor-to-ceiling doors and a French window at the bottom of the "U" In a word, the design adequately serves a modern family's purpose for style and utility.

Two cypress trees stand before the front door, as tall as the gables and west of the doorstep is a garden in which roses are in full bloom. The rear garden is as attractive as the front one. Living amid the flowers of all kinds, I can't help taking even more of a fancy to my house.

The sunlit dining room is about 860 square feet in size and connects to an open kitchen with huge cabinets serving as a partition between the two rooms. This allows me to entertain my clients at the dining table with casual chats and funny jokes while I am cooking in the kitchen. Walking across the dining room, you will reach the garage. I have converted the garage into a storage room arrayed with rows of wooden shelves and installed a powerful, Japanese-made air conditioner to preserve thousands of dollars' worth of wines, ports, beers and drinks of all brands, with which I entertain my clients.

The spacious dining room sits on the west side of the garage, with a six-foot-tall, luxury four-door silver refrigerator in the northeast corner. A huge dining table about seven feet long and five feet wide stands in the middle of the dining room, surrounded by six, high-back, black leather chairs. In addition to the alcohol and soft drinks in the refrigerator, which can be replenished from the garage stock at any time, my cabinets and dining table are also stacked with bags of chips, cashews, almonds, walnuts and chocolates. These, of course, are also prepared for the guests and clients.

The east and south walls of the dining room are each adorned with oil paintings, which were painted by Lily; a girl I struck up an acquaintance with ten years ago at the brothel. She said it had taken her more than a month to finish them and I paid her 2,500 dollars for them. The painting on the east wall depicts a typical Australian autumn scene: the undulating pastoral hills are covered by green grasses with bright, red leaves dotted among them as if a breeze were singing a pastoral song about the leisurely pace of the seasons. The other oil painting on the south wall illustrates another equally common scene of the Australian countryside: against a background of the cold glow of the rising Moon, bright light glitters in the reflection of the golden cypress trees in the dark, green river under a misty blue bridge, intoxicating you in a moonlit dream. The two landscape oil paintings, so different in styles and color tones, enliven my house harmoniously.

Directly above the painting hangs a circular clock with a black dial plate and alternating gold and silver dial numbers, from which I check the time when I am cooking in the kitchen or eating in the dining room. I need a good sense of time every day to know exactly when clients have called and make necessary arrangements for appointments. In fact, I keep a clock in every room so I will know the time regardless of where I am in the house (I do not keep personal watches since it might hurt my clients during my work).

Below the paintings is a television shelf made of silver and black aluminum alloys, which holds a sixty-inch television. The location of the television is very convenient, since I can watch it from either the kitchen or the dining room.

On the wall between the door and the French windows hangs a photograph about twenty-four inches by forty-eight inches; Glade Creek Grist Mill by Ken Duncan. It depicts a thatched cottage and a foot bridge over a creek in an Australian autumn countryside. A huge, twenty-inch by twenty-eight-inch mirror adorns the wall under the painting. My clients and I often enjoy ourselves looking in the mirror, commenting on our figures and clothing and talking about any other topic under the sun.

Connecting to the dining room is the kitchen; a forbidden place of mine. Usually no clients are allowed in there. Although I sell my own body and my body belongs to whichever man that comes for me, my kitchen is my own reclusive space. Equipped with a luxurious double-door refrigerator, a famous-brand microwave oven and modern gas stoves, the kitchen serves me quite well. I need adequate energy and nutrition to be refreshed and strong enough to receive my next client, especially when I feel exhausted sometimes, after work.

Alongside the kitchen, near the front door is a huge living room about 645 square feet in size. The furnishings and atmosphere of the living room match up nicely with the Victorian style of the building: the semi-elliptic room is shrouded in the sun beams that shimmer through the French windows. A Korean-made, red-brown grand piano sits directly in front of the four French windows, while on the northern side of the room; a 3D sixty- five-inch flat screen television is positioned on a dark-brown desk. A wall clock with a white dial and decorative silver rings hangs above the television set. A large, black treadmill and an exercise machine of the same color stand in the middle of the room, facing the television.

On the southeast side of the room, there is a writing table with a panel of blue glass about half an inch thick. On it are my personal phones and fax machine. A black leather revolving chair is by the writing table. A set of cream-colored corner lounges are presented in the southwest side of the living room with two horseshoe-shaped coffee tables beside them and a floor lamp with a white lampshade. When the night falls, the soft light will spill across the floor.

As my clients never stop frequenting me, I spend most of my time on the bed in the working room. When I have no clients to serve, I will sit down at the grand piano and play some of my favorite tunes. Having experienced all kinds of joys and sorrows in life, I have finally found my preferred job and lifestyle. Owning a nice, cozy house and having a satisfying job makes me feel content and I have nothing much to complain about.

Coming out of the living room and across the kitchen and dining room, you will find three bedrooms, side by side on the south side of the house. East of the bedrooms is the laundry room, the back door of which leads out to the backyard. Adjacent to the laundry is the first bedroom which covers an area of 194 square feet and includes a very spacious en suite bathroom tiled with full-length, white-frosted mosaic. The bathtub, toilet and vanity are all made of quality Italian porcelain and the bath cubicle is partitioned with large glass panes, half an inch thick.

Two fifty-inch Panasonic television sets hang on both the north and east walls so that my patrons can watch top-notch porn videos from almost any angle. An imaginative oil painting depicting a lovely girl squatting with a very alluring black cat between her thighs hangs nearby. The painting is titled "I Love My Pussy." "Pussy" is a pun, as the word "pussy" in English can denote either a cat or a girl's cunt. Fixed above the oil painting is a round clock, which allows me to keep track of the working hours. Opposite the single-door fridge beside the south window is a cream-colored double bed and its bedside tables. A huge, Chinese artistic fan about five feet across overlooks the bed, with peony flowers blooming in a riot in the season of spring.

The second bedroom is about 139 square feet in size and contains a king-size bed covered with comfortable bedding, a cream-colored bedside table and a forty-six-inch flat screen television, which hangs on the window-facing wall. This is my own bedroom. Only after I knock off work in the early hours of the morning do I indulge myself in a sound sleep on this king- size bed.

The 269-square-foot master bedroom is the largest of the three bedrooms and serves as my working room. When you enter this room, you will see a mirrored cabinet on your right with four, floor-to-ceiling-high sliding doors, opposite a huge mirror on the south wall, about six feet tall and six feet wide. The reflection of light between the parallel mirrors makes the room look brighter and more spacious than it really is.

On your left, a cream wooden bedside table and a king-size bed face the east wall with matching sheets and pillows. As in the other two bedrooms, all the furniture here is cream-colored. This is my favorite color and it turns out that most of my clients feel this color choice renders the bedroom unique and elegant.

Two twin sixty-inch Japanese Hitachi television sets are installed separately on the east and west walls of the working room. Under the television sets lies a black leather massage table. Beside the other end of the table is a wooden chair.

On the right of the west window hangs an interesting painting with dimensions of forty by fifty inches, realistically illustrating the fifty-six different positions of sexual intercourse. The strenuous worker depicted in this painting must be an expert at this art.

On the left of the window stands a stereo sound system and video recorder with four black Boss loudspeakers the size of fists hanging in the top corners of the room. The audio-visual system is always ready to play beautiful music and top-notch porn videos, which together not only help whet my clients' lust but also fill the room with an atmosphere of romanticism and tenderness.

The en suite to the master bedroom is spacious and bright. The sanitary ware is also made of quality Italian porcelain and the showerhead is of high-grade stainless steel. This is part of the luxurious life I enjoy, as a spacious, comfortable and elegant bathroom is extremely important to me and also for my job. My emphasis on cleanliness and elegance stem from the great respect and ardent love I have for my own profession.

Someone may well ask, "Why are you dwelling at such length upon such trifling things as the furnishings, color pattern or garden layout of your house? Do they have anything to do with your story? The answer is, definitely yes. Because this background clearly indicates my adherence to my professional code and my fastidiousness about my working conditions. Supposing my house is a dirty, messy and vulgar place, how can we distinguish it from any ordinary brothel in the world? That's why I am the only one among so many prostitutes who is unanimously praised as the number-one prostitute.

My house is my workplace. It covers an area of more than 2000 square feet and is therefore spacious enough for me to walk around to breathe in the fresh air and feast my eyes on my treasured garden landscape. The house is a precious fruit of my life-long efforts.

The bed sheets, pillow cases and towels used in these three bedrooms are all snow white in color. That is because the color of white allows for no laziness. Whenever the sheets and towels get a little dirty, it becomes conspicuous and thus I will give them a thorough clean. My practice is one towel for each individual client without any exception so as to ensure the highest level of hygiene for my clients. And secondly but no less importantly, I'm hoping to show everybody that although I'm a prostitute, I'm a very clean person to the extent of having an obsession for cleanliness.

Either my living habits or my inner soul is almost immaculate and transparent. I am a good, honest citizen, have never broken any laws or regulations and conduct business honestly. I mean no evil to anyone and I have my own principles.

I'm contributing to Australia not only by paying taxes in accordance with my profession but also by comforting my clients through integrating with them physically and mentally, thus finding the right way to solve all the perplexing problems relating to "sex." For all these years, my clients have never stopped frequenting me and most of them have become regular patrons. I am well worthy of being the number-one prostitute. I think I deserve the reputation.

September 25, 2010

September may be the most beautiful season in Canberra, when spring has returned to this world-famous garden city. A variety of unnamed flowers are in full bloom with birds galore chirping away in the trees. The verdure meets the eye everywhere and the warm breeze brings in the fresh and intoxicating scent of nature. It's so wonderful a scene!

On the fine morning of the twenty-fifth of September, 2010, I got up at eight o'clock and after washing up, put on a long, sexy, rose- colored dress with my back wholly exposed. I looked in the mirror and scrutinized myself carefully. During my latest trip to China, I underwent some operations of cosmetic surgery of my brows, eyelashes and lips and on my return many of my regular patrons complimented me on my younger appearance. I myself also had a complacent feeling about the effect of the surgery: my eyes became much brighter and under a nice nose, my lips were seductively red without the help of any lipstick. My oval face, with its becoming black brows, big eyes and red lips, looked more smooth and tender. I wore a thick, glittering, silvery alloy necklace around my shapely neck and a pair of shining, platinum earrings against a background of freshly-dyed hair; a black cascade over my shoulders. I stood five foot four, neither too lanky nor too plump. Looking into the mirror, I found myself much younger. I couldn't help smiling to myself: from now on, I would pretend to be younger, just as a popular Chinese wisecrack put it: paint an old cucumber green to make it look ripe. Everyone would regard me as a lady of twenty-eight, almost twenty years younger than I actually was, so I, like an old cucumber painted green, could go on serving my customers for another twenty years.

I went to the kitchen and boiled two eggs and poured myself two cups of milk and emptied them with a gulp. Then, putting on a navy-blue wool coat, I opened the door to the laundry and threw all the towels used the night before into the washer and turned it on. I pushed open the back door and went into the rear garden to admire the yellow, pink, red, white and orange roses that were in full bloom. The verdant magnolia trees were in buds while the cypress trees were lush and green on the west side of the street.

A couple of bright-colored parrots hopped with joy in the trees as if they were to usher in the coming spring. I looked up at them and they tweeted back at me friendlily. Suddenly, a female parrot landed on the lawn and a male one followed her. The male jumped onto the back of the female and picked her comb between his beak, as if flirting with her. The couple of little creatures made a lot of noise, twittering and chattering. I giggled out, "Enjoy yourselves," and went on toward the front garden.

The two tall peach trees, burdened with so many pink flowers, stood by the pathway. The house looked so picturesque with the blooming peach flowers as its background. Looking down, I saw all the roses in the front garden trembling in the breeze and couldn't resist the temptation to squat down before a huge purple rose and have a deep sniffle."Ah,"I thought to myself,"What an intoxicating smell!" The roses in my garden really smell much better than most perfumes and feel much smoother than the most beautiful silks in the world. I could do nothing but admire the beauty of spring.

Faced with this most beautiful scene, I couldn't help heaving a long, happy sigh. How hard it was indeed to earn all that belonged to me! I'm no longer a woman who has nothing to her name. I am now a well-known prostitute who owns three properties in Australia. Working as a prostitute has made me realize my value of life – I have become richer and younger. When called a "girl" by a boy in his twenties, I feel ten or twenty years younger and when reminded of my properties, I feel much assured.

Mention of properties suddenly reminded me that I had not been updated in several days regarding two of my houses up for sale on Sydney's real estate market and that I'd better give Peter, my real-estate agent a ring, to ask how things were getting on. I have never felt any shame over my trade. On the contrary, it was this trade that helped me actualize the meaning of my life and make a small fortune for myself. I felt quite assured to be able to earn my own living and make a fortune by selling myself. How time flies! It is almost ten years since I came to Australia and more than nine years since I took on this occupation. To some people, it is incredible that I should have transformed from a policewoman of the past to a prostitute of the present. But to me it's only too natural. I'm a lucky woman to have taken on two jobs that are so strikingly different. I don't believe there is any other woman who can have experiences as rich and exciting as I've had.

I don't really think it makes any difference to be a cop or a whore. They are two different concepts and occupations under two different social systems. I am still myself and I haven't changed a bit except that I've become more mature ideologically and more comprehensive in my outlook than I was before. Now I can regard this world from a higher angle. I love my life now. It is like the charming roses out front, so colorful, mysterious, and full of beautiful illusions. I like my present life and profession. I think I may well be one of the happiest women in the world.

I have my own peculiar and unique way of life—I'm no longer a wife or a girlfriend or even a love to any fixed man; I belong to a group of men and my love is shared out among all of them. It is said that love and jealousy are twin sisters and yet I have only love but no jealousy. I love all my patrons, whose ages vary from eighteen to ninety, for late teenagers are young and lovely; middle-aged men are mature and strong while old men are considerate and humorous. It's a universal love without any jealousy because I know much better than any woman that a man who loves you or whom you love is unlikely to make love to only one woman. Sexual desire erupts anywhere and anytime and needs releasing quickly. It has to be and must be released like irresistible torrential waters.

Now that I have become a successful prostitute, I cannot go back to being a qualified wife. Being faced with a single and only cock every day would bore me to death. Always the same cock of the same man cannot satisfy my sexual desire any more. I like the sensual feeling of being fucked by a variety of cocks, cocks of all sizes and lengths. I like the indescribable feeling of being stared at erotically when people are making love to me. I like the wonderful feeling of being courted by a lot of men. The long career of a prostitute has whetted my lust steadily and my desire will never be satiated. I will feel uneasy from head to toe and my muscles will become stiff and tight if my cunt isn't dredged by a couple of men daily after getting up every morning. No, not only my cunt but my mouth and asshole also need dredging daily.

However, all this doesn't necessarily mean I am an indecent woman. It's just my present real life and selling sex is just my daily job. Ten years of working in prostitution already has me accustomed to this way of life. I have gradually taken to rolling with a dozen men or more in succession on my bed every day. But nevertheless, I haven't changed a bit and I remain a good woman who knows right from wrong and loves and hates most unabashedly. I will use more instances in my novel to prove my integrity, honesty and kindness.

I was lost in my thoughts when I was suddenly hugged tightly by someone from behind. I turned back to find it was Peter, one of my regular patrons. He was an Australian-born Greek, who worked in a government office. He told me he was fifty-three but he looked just a little past forty. I winked at him, hinting we were in a public place and there were many pedestrians walking by us. He reluctantly released me and said, "How I miss you! I was dreaming of you all of last night." I stepped back to look him up and down. Peter, measuring five foot seven, wore a black suit, a black tie under a white, collared shirt and shining, black leather shoes. He wore a short cut, and had a pair of sunken, black eyes under thick, black brows and a sexy, big mouth under a high nose. He looked at me affectionately. With a knowing smile lingering on the corner of his mouth, he accompanied me to the front door of my house. I turned the key in the door lock. I had barely shut the door and taken off my coat when he raised my skirt's hem and felt for my private part.

"Bottomless again?" he teased.

"I have to receive nearly twenty clients a day," I answered. "I don't have the time to keep putting on and taking off briefs. I simply leave it naked."

"You have a nice cunt."

"Really? Every woman has. Is there any difference between women's cunts?" I asked.

"Yes. There are cunts and there are *cunts*. Some women have shapely cunts and others don't," he said seriously. "Nonsense!" I retorted.

"If you don't believe me," he said, "You can watch the video in your room and find out."

When we went through the kitchen to the dining room, I threw my coat on the back of the black leather chair. He hastily unbuttoned his coat, loosened his tie and held me in his arms as we headed for the working room.

"Won't go to work today?" I asked.

"Not until ten. You see, my cock's hard and hot, so your house is my first stop." Looking up at the clock on the wall, I saw it was nine o'clock sharp.

"The regular price," I said, "Fifty dollars for half an hour."

"No problem. I've been here hundreds of times. No one knows the price better than me." With this, he produced a fifty-dollar note and tucked it between my bra and breasts. I pulled the note out and put it away in the bottom drawer in the kitchen. When I came back, he had already hung his suit in the wardrobe and placed his shoes under the massage table. He strewed his underwear on the massage table and stood naked on the carpet, his cock stark and stiff, as thick as a flashlight.

I pointed to the huge mirror on the opposite wall and laughed, "Look into the mirror at your cock. How long it is!" He laughed too, "It's getting even longer at the sight of you." I pulled my dress over my shoulders and tossed it away. I stood bare naked on the carpet; my two shapely, white breasts swaying in front of his face seductively. He couldn't resist the temptation any longer. Hastily cupping my breasts, he pressed that hard cock of his into the wet juncture between my thighs.

I pointed to the bathroom and said, "Please take a bath first." "I've just had one this morning and I prefer taking another after fucking."

I tried to struggle myself out of his hold and said, "Just be patient, boy." I took a white towel out of the wardrobe and spread it out on the clean, white bed. Peter calmed down a little and said, "Come on. Turn on the tape recorder and I will tell you the difference between the cunts and *cunts*."

A top pornographic program: *Asian Fever No. 13* was lined up on the sixty-inch, wall mounted television screens.

I picked up the remote control and pressed the "start" button. While upbeat music played in the background, more than a dozen close-up shots of lovemaking flashed across the screen, followed by the first episode: a sturdy Caucasian man led a short, thin Asian girl into a room and laid her down on the bed. He slowly stripped her of her shirt and pants and stooped down to lick the bud of her private part.

With every lick, the little girl groaned, "Oh ---, ah ---, ou."

Pointing to the screen, Peter explained, "This girl's cunt can swallow big cocks for it has a short slit and a circular hole. Generally speaking, the thinner the girl is, the bigger cocks her cunt can hold. Fatter girls' cunts, on the contrary, can only hold smaller cocks."

"Absolutely absurd," I chuckled, "who has told you all this?" "You see, you don't believe what I've told you, but it's true.

One of my friends has a much, much longer cock than me, eight to nine inches long and so thick." With that, he made a gesture showing how long it was. "My friend's girl was particularly thin and she felt especially dissatisfied every time she was fucked. So to satisfy her thoroughly, his friend had to thrust a whole thick ear of maize into her cunt."

Now, on the screen the man's cock was wholly tucked into the little girl's cunt, making the girl cry out loudly and groan heavily.

As his cock had become stark and stiff, Peter pushed me onto the bed, "I can't wait to fuck you," he said impatiently. With this he thrust his hard shaft through to the bottom of my cavity.

"Ouch!" I couldn't help crying out, "How can it be so long today?"

His cock pressed against my cervix so hard that my cunt nearly burst.

"I've fucked you hundreds of times," he winced at me, "And you still can't tolerate my cock?"

"It's not that I can't…" I argued, "But that I've just got up this morning and found myself to be a virgin. Maybe you can come by this evening, when my cunt may be a little looser."

"My cock won't be happy if your cunt is too loose." He arched his body over mine until we were face to face, supporting himself with his hands on either side of my chest and began to bang me to the beat of the music that blared from the television.

I moaned in unison with the girl in the pornographic video as I cried out, "Oh, dear. Oh, slow down. I can't bear the bursting pain."

"Hey," he panted out, "You will soon get used to it." With every piston action of his cock he yelled, "Oh, yes! Oh, yes!" Each yell becoming louder than the one before while he fucked me more and more violently. The house reverberated with a wonderful and harmonious symphony of beast-like yells, the sound of pounding bodies and the background music from the porn video. Gradually, the bursting pain in my cunt was slowly becoming a mix of dull pain and pleasure and I started to enjoy the sensations in my cunt as it began to water and overflow. My loud cries began to turn to hoarse groans from deep in my throat; my head on the pillow turning to the right and turning to the left. As I entered the state of ecstasy, he kept pushing and pulling his big cock in and out of me. The more he fucked me, the more deranged he became. He growled, "You have a nice cunt. You have a sweet cunt. Feel happy?"

"Very happy," I answered.

"You want me to fuck you hard?" he said, more of a demand than a question.

"Yes, fuck me hard! I like this big thing of yours."

He then turned me over with my buttocks facing him and thrust his big cock into my cunt from behind and we were like two dogs mating. He could enter me much deeper from this angle.

"Oh! Oh!" I couldn't help crying noisily.

"That's so fucking good," he exclaimed, and went on exerting himself for a while.

I groaned, "Oh, Yes. Yesss." After I got over the initial pain and subsequent embarrassment, I became used to this position and even began to enjoy myself. I looked into the mirror on my left and found an alluring sensual picture—as I knelt over the bed, my body formed a shapely woman's silhouette; plump buttocks, a slim waist and a pair of white breasts dangling under Peter's supporting arms, swaying with rhythmic exertion from the thrusting of his cock, like two lively sheep hopping about on grassland. Looking into the mirror on my right, I saw the reflection of a pornographic oil painting, similar to one painted by famous Italian artist Botticelli, depicting a sexy woman and a strong man.

This symbolized men's most primitive, basic gesture of sexual intercourse by which human beings reproduce and procreate.

On the television screen, two masculine men and a girl were on a bed. The girl was in the same position as me, with one man's big cock in her mouth and the other man's cock in her cunt, from behind. With a big cock lodged in her mouth, she could only utter some unclear and inarticulate syllables every time she was assaulted from behind. I couldn't stop watering down below and couldn't help but cry, "Ah yes, Ah yes,", as Peter charged me unceasingly and boisterously. In my mind's eye, I saw two or three big cocks fucking me, one after the other and each subsequent cock getting bigger, harder and more exciting than the one before. As I indulged myself in these thoughts, my vaginal muscles contracted at the stimulus of Peter's cock thrusting wantonly inside me when an unpredictable warm thrill rushed into my head and from my head to my heart, through all the length of me, to the bottom of my feet and finally to my innermost cavity, which made me burst out crying, "I'm coming, my dear. Fuck me. Fuck me hard! I'm itching to death. I love you, my dearest." I came, throbbing one, two, three, four, five or six times before I let out several cries, "I love you. I love you. I love you!"

Peter's performance was really wonderful; he continued to pound his abdomen against my buttocks while shouting, "I fuck you. I fuck you. I fuck you!" I trembled like a leaf in a strong gale. He refrained from coming and continued to exert himself until he was satisfied that I had come completely and with a long lingering "Ahhhh--- ---," he pulled out his cock from inside me and spit all of his warm sperm on my hips. I felt so much sticky fluid overflowing between my hips. "He must have had a lot," I thought. Afraid of staining the bed sheets, he held his member with one hand and stretched over to get a tissue from the bedside table with the other. He hurriedly helped me wipe off the white sperm from my hips. I jumped off the bed and drew a clean, white towel from the cabinet and threw it to him, "Go and have a shower!"

With that, I went to the toilet in the waiting room to have a shower. I returned to find he had already lied face down on the towel-covered bed, ready for me to massage his back. Hips bare, I sat astride his back and strenuously massaged his shoulders, his blade bones and then his neck and spine.

Turning his head, he looked at me in the mirror and said, "Hey, you just said you love me. Does that mean you'd like to be my girlfriend?"

I replied with a grimace, "I was made ecstatic by the pleasure I felt when you were fucking me. My head swam and I don't remember what I said. It's over."

"So when it's over, you stop loving me," he said, pretending as if he were a little disappointed.

"I love all my patrons," I said.

He smiled, "I have my own wife."

"And I have my own husbands. But instead of one, I have a thousand husbands and ten thousand lovers," I said.

He pointed to the flickering TV screen on which one man was licking a girl's bud between her cunt's outer lips while another was sucking her nipples. He commented, "Look. This girl's cunt is different from the other girl's. This girl's cunt is shapelier and plumper, not as thin so the slit in her cunt is relatively long and her cunt looks sort of sensuous and is probably very comfortable to fuck because it won't feel too bony. Besides, its outer shape is sexier. Yours is similar to hers, I told you that you have a nice cunt."

With that he looked up at the clock on the wall, "Oh, it's already forty past nine. I must be going now. Or else I will be late for work."

He got up promptly and hastily threw on his shirt, pulled on his socks and trousers and got back into his suit and tie. Scrutinizing himself in the mirror, he said, "Good. Very smart," while I snatched a dress off of a hanger in the wardrobe and hurriedly pulled it over my head. The long, blue, strapless dress fell down to my feet, covering the entire length of my naked body and leaving only my snow-white arms and slender shoulders exposed.

I have more than a dozen sexy dresses of different colors and lengths, all of them easy to pull on or throw off. When I usher in a patron I'll put on one dress and when I see him off I'll change into another so that the patrons always feel a kind of freshness. Swaying my hips in front of him, I led Peter through the dining room to the front door. I opened the door and said bye-bye to him. He bent down to give me a peck on the cheek and said, "Sweet baby, my honey. You are fabulous and fuckable. See you next time." He was walking out on the driveway when a car drove directly toward the house. He waited behind the tall cypress tree until the car was out of sight and then proceeded to his own car, which he had parked beside my garage. With a discerning smile on my face, I shut the door.

I went back to my working room and collected all the used towels into a plastic basket and threw the dirty tissues from the floor into the dustbin in the toilet. I smoothed the sheet on the bed and straightened the pillows, ready for the next client.

The doorbell rang and I went to answer the door, "Morning, Michael."

"Morning, Linda," he replied.

Michael had been one of my regular patrons for seven or eight years now. He had been coming to see me two or three times a week since he was twenty-five or twenty-six years old. He was around six feet tall and had blond hair that fell over his shoulders. His blond eyebrows framed a pair of large, sunken blue eyes, accentuated with matching blond eyelashes, and a pair of pursy lips under a straight, long nose. His oval face and other features gave him a feminine appearance at first sight, especially when he blinked and batted his long eyelashes. He used to be a lanky lad but had put on some weight in the last couple of years.

I closed the door behind me and asked, "Haven't gone to work today?"

"I've been looking for jobs," he answered casually.

He had been looking for jobs for several years now. How could it be that such a handsome young man still couldn't find one? I kept these thoughts to myself and didn't say anything.

I directed him into the working room and he put his backpack on the black massage table and took his wallet out from it. I stopped him and said, "You are out of work so I'll give you a special offer: forty dollars for half an hour."

He happily pulled a fifty-dollar note out between his thin, pale fingers, and handed it to me. I took the money and put it away in the cabinet drawer in the kitchen and took out a ten- dollar note and a bottle of mineral water for him. He accepted the change, drank a little water from the bottle and began to undress.

He wore a tracksuit today so it was easy for him to strip. I took out a towel from the cabinet and hung it on the towel rail in the bathroom. I turned on the sprinkling spout and asked him, "Please take a bath first."

He always took his time bathing, usually five minutes or more. While he was in the bathroom, I took out the washed towels from the washer and tossed them into the dryer before I turned it on and then I threw the used towels into the washer and turned it on as well.

Then I went back to the kitchen, took a bottle of water from the bench and had a sip. I watched the video playing in the dining room, while keeping an ear out for the splashes in the bathroom. Seven or eight minutes passed and the splashes didn't stop. Wondering why it took so long for him to finish his bathing today, I went into the bathroom only to find Michael kneeling under the shower sprinkler washing up his asshole.

"How come you're spending so much time washing yourself up?" I asked.

"I've just finished shitting," he explained, "I have to wash up my asshole."

"Hurry up," I said, "My next customer is coming soon." With that, I went back to the kitchen and watched the TV program over a bottle of mineral water. Another three or four minutes passed before the splashing finally stopped. I knew he had finished bathing and I returned to the working room, ready for work again. I found he was already standing between the bed and the massage table. I stepped in front of him and threw my dress onto the carpet. His two balls, dangling under his cock, were bound by a black rubber band half an inch wide, which was ornamented with dozens of small metal spikes. His balls were bound so tightly that they were completely stretched out and nearly transparent. Each of his nipples was clamped with a metal clip, linked by a silver chain, which dangled from his chest. His bizarre way of dressing indicated that he was an eccentric person in his sexuality.

On the bed he placed a plastic toy cock, an oscillator powered by batteries, and a black leather belt measuring two inches wide and five feet long. All these made up his whole Fantasy Kit. He had me stand before him and I found myself dwarfed in front of him, though I was not very short. He demanded me to pull the chain between his breasts and I obeyed his directions. I pulled and let go of the chain to the rhythm of the music. When his nipples were stretched out, I asked him, "Don't you feel pain?"

He replied, "No. I feel all better." So I pulled the chain about ten more times.

He knelt down beside the bed, turned his buttocks skyward and said, "Lash my hips with the belt!" Following his order, I seized the black leather belt, doubled it up and lashed across his right buttock with a loud "Pa!"

His right hip turned crimson at once but he shouted, "Try your best!" I did and another crimson bruise appeared.

And yet he insisted, "Go on!"

"Your whole hip has turned bloody red. Don't you feel pain?" "No, just a bit, but it's all the more exciting."

This time I exerted all my strength, swung my arm fully and gave him a great thwack, rendering the whole of his right buttock as red as a monkey's.

EROTIC

As if unsatisfied, he kept demanding, "Lash, lash, lash…" I continued to the fast beat of the music from the video when he changed his order, "On my left hip." I set to lash his left hip until it turned crimson, too.

Seeing his buttocks in terrible condition, I threw away the belt and grasped the sex toy from the bed, an electric cock made from some kind of soft plastic. I sheathed a condom on the machine, turned on the power and it began to buzz. I poured some lubricant oil from a bottle, applied it on his asshole and thrust the machine into his asshole with my right hand. The young man leaned forward and all but fell prone on the ground, "Take your time, madam." I began to piston the electric cock in his hole, the pitch of the noise getting higher when pushed in and lower when pulled out. He set about groaning, "Ohhh. Mmm. I like someone fucking my ass with a cock. It feels wonderful and I enjoy it."

I kept laboring to the rhythm of the video music for about seven to eight minutes when he turned over and lay on his back. Sitting on his left, I continued pushing and pulling the electric cock with my left hand and at the same time grasped his penis and swallowed it. He narrowed his eyes and seemed to be enjoying my oral work. "Oh, yes. Oh, deeper, further, deeper. Oh. Deeper, further, deeper!"

"No further or deeper," I forced his penis out of my mouth, "or else you'll hurt my throat."

With that, I began to caress his penis instead, with my right hand while I kept thrusting the electric cock inside his asshole with my left. It was not long before he drawled happily, "Ohhhh. Ohhhh!" and gasped for breath. He threw up his buttocks, and his cock grew harder and harder in my hand until he groaned "Oh. Oh. Oh," and then let out a long howl. I quickened the speed of my hand movements and no sooner did he cry out, "Oh. Oh. Oh, I'm coming!" then he spurted all his sperm through my fingers and spilled it all over his own belly. He heaved a sigh of relief, "I'm really fucking happy."

My right hand continued caressing his cock until he had come completely. Seeing he was satisfied, I quickly pulled out the electric cock, peeled off the condom from it, wiped the sperm off him with a tissue, threw everything into the rubbish bin and went to the bathroom to wash my hands. He followed me to the bathroom. He took his time washing up, as if he were on a leisurely, sight-seeing excursion.

Here's a warning to those women who like to, or have to, rub men's cocks. You must make sure there are no wounds or cuts on your hands before you use them to masturbate your men. We prostitutes, in particular, belong to a high-risk group, as we have sexual contact with various customers daily. If you happen to cut your hands, it will be very dangerous for you to come into contact with your clients' sperm while masturbating them. Your clients may be infected with AIDS, or other venereal or blood diseases and you will be very vulnerable to the viruses. Since my colleagues in the brothel gave me a word of caution with this danger, I have been extremely careful not to cut my hands in any case. If ever I happen to have a cut on my hand, I would rather stop my business than run the risk.

I was making the bed when suddenly, the doorbell rang. I hastily threw on a yellow mini-dress, which barely covered my round hips and left my dainty, white legs exposed. I shut the door to the working room and rushed to answer the door.

After exchanging morning greetings, I asked, somewhat doubtfully, "Lad, have you reached the age of eighteen?"

"I'm already twenty-one years old," he replied promptly, "and I've been here twice."

"Well. That's okay then. Please come in," I said apologetically. I received more than a dozen clients every day and I really couldn't remember whether or not he had ever come before. I ushered him to the waiting room for the ordinary clients. I turned on the porn video for him and said, "Just wait here and give me a couple of minutes to see off another client in the working room."

"That's okay," he replied.

Pointing to the small fridge under the television set, I told him, "You can take whatever drinks you like and they are all free. If you'd like to use the toilet, it's just over there." I closed the door behind me and went back only to find Michael still washing his long hair under the sprinkling nozzle. I urged him, "You'd better quicken up 'cause a new client is already waiting outside."

With an "okay," he got out of the shower cubicle, took a clean towel from the towel rail and slowly rubbed his body from head to toe before languidly strolling out of the bathroom and sitting on the wooden chair by the massage table. Leisurely, he set out to clean his feet by sliding the towel between each of his toes. He began with the first gap between his first and second toes, then the second gap, the third and finally the last one. When he finished working on his left foot, he moved on to his right foot. Much to my embarrassment, I had to stop his personal hygiene practice immediately by asking him to hurry up. I said, "Excuse me, could you be a little quicker; I have a new customer who is waiting outside." While he kept saying "okay, okay," he didn't intend to hurry up at all. It was quite a while before he finished cleaning his feet. He slowly stood up and threw the dirty towel into the plastic waste basket in the bathroom before coming out and sitting right back on the wooden chair again. After he tediously put on his shirt, trousers and jacket, he began to put on his socks and shoes. Sitting back on the wooden chair, he picked up a sock and shook it violently five or six times in the air to get rid of the dust before putting it on his right foot and then repeated the same procedure with the other sock. After that, he picked up a blue sports shoe for his left foot and stretched its opening again and again before putting it on his left foot. He began to lace up the shoe by making a right-handed tie over a left-handed tie to make sure the shoe was securely buckled. Then he slowly repeated the same procedure with the other shoe. After all this, he stood up and went to the mirror to comb his blond hair and slowly pack his electric cock, black belt, two nipple clips and cock ring into his backpack.

Oh, my God. At long, long last. You see, it took him over a quarter of an hour to finish bathing and dressing. No wonder he can't find a job. No boss will tolerate such a slow-paced worker.

I hid these thoughts in my mind and asked, "All finished? Take your time to see whether you've left anything." And indeed he took his time in searching on the bed, under the bed and under the massage table before taking the half-emptied mineral water bottle from the bedside table and leisurely walking out of the working room. I showed him the door and said, "Bye-bye. Have a nice day and I wish you good luck." He paced down the steps with a measured stride.

I hurriedly shut the door and came back to the waiting room. "Sorry to keep you waiting," I said to the lad.

At this, the lad said,"That's all right."I led him to the working room and asked him whether he had had a bath. He answered that he had, so I had him take off all his clothes and piled two pillows near the bed head. He lay on his back on the white sheet I had covered the bed with before. I squatted down between his legs to suck his balls. Young men had strong sexual desire so his cock stiffened in no time at the first licking. I found his shaft stark and stiff and as thick as a club, so I gave him a large-sized condom. After he had put it on, I began to suck his cock. A few minutes later, he said, "Let me fuck you now." He knelt on the bed, and turned my face toward him. As he entered me, he lifted both of my legs onto his shoulders. He kept screaming "Ohh, yes!" as he moved back and forth violently. It took only seven to eight minutes for him to come.

"You have come quick," I said, "So I will only charge you thirty dollars."

I have three to five hundred young patrons whose ages ranged from eighteen to twenty-two. As it generally takes only ten to fifteen minutes for them to come, I only charge them thirty to forty dollars.

Many of my colleagues may ask,"Why are you selling yourself so cheap?" My policy is "Less service, less fee." That's because firstly, these young men come quickly so they take up less of your time; secondly, if you lie idle you earn nothing. Twenty or thirty dollars is better than nothing. Many of my patrons, both young and old, have frequented me for seven or eight years and they are actually my friends, so how can I charge them too much? The business is my own and the main cost is my own body so I can be flexible with the price. I am different from the bosses of brothels in that if they charge too low a price there might not be enough money to share the profits between the bosses and the prostitutes. My price has remained unchanged for many years but I receive fifteen to twenty clients a day so I can still make money on the basis of "Small profits but quick turnover."

Moreover, I know from my vast experience over the years how much sex really means to some men. To them sex is much more important than food. They have to save the money coin by coin until they have enough money to come here. It will sometimes take them two or three months to save fifty dollars in coins. I have mixed feelings but I suppose if I charge them ten dollars more they probably won't have any money left to buy their daily bread when they leave this house.

While the boy lay on the bed, I peeled the condom off his cock and wiped the sperm from his balls. Instead of getting up, the boy continued to lie on the bed and muttered to himself. At first I didn't quite catch what he was saying, but later I made out that his auntie had sent him some texts on his mobile phone. He switched on his phone and showed me a text message containing a video of a beautiful, blonde Australian lady in a red bra and matching panties, swaying her body seductively. Before long she tossed off her bra and revealed her breasts, which were as big as two cantaloupes in contrast with her narrow waist. She continued teasingly swaying her hips for some time before finally taking off her panties. Now a gorgeous and shapely nude was standing in front of me. I couldn't tear my eyes from her beautiful figure, let alone a boy of his age. A nude woman is often compared to a work of art and it is indeed a pertinent metaphor.

"How old is she?" I asked, gasping with curiosity. "Forty-one or two," he answered.

"Incredible." I was surprised, "Judging from her figure, she is at most twenty-one or twenty-two."

"Linda, what should I do?" he asked me eagerly, his eyes fixed on me.

"Don't do anything," I answered, "She is your mom's sister and I think you'd better keep it a secret from your mom."

The lad nodded sensibly and got up for his bath. Before I saw him off he paid me thirty dollars. I looked at the view of his back thoughtfully as he was leaving. This boy seemed to be embarrassed by his auntie's advances. I wondered what embarrassing things in the field of sex haven't happened in this world. It suddenly occurred to me that one of my patrons who was about forty, once told me he liked making love to his girlfriend's mother, saying it was more exciting and enjoyable. Maybe sex itself entices people to explore the unknown and seek out novel stimulation.

I was deep in thought when the doorbell chimed again. I opened the door to find it was the surgeon, a frequenter of mine for eight years. Seeing his sullen look, I said, "Good afternoon, my dear. How come you don't look happy?"

"Divorce again," he muttered to himself as he walked in. "What?" I asked inquisitively.

"Divorce!"

"Well, isn't it quite normal to divorce nowadays? It's a chance for you to remarry," I tried to comfort him.

"I quit marrying," he declared, "or else I'll end up sleeping on the street."

We were on our way to the working room when I asked perplexedly, "But what do you mean by sleeping on the street?"

"I left one house to my first wife and another to my second wife," he grimaced, "I am constantly on the move."

"Well, you are fifty-five this year, what are you working for now?" I asked. He made a sign of a circle with his thumb and forefinger.

"You've been working for a zero?" I guessed.

"No, not for the zero but for the cunt," he smiled.

I also smiled, "So you should be content with this circle. At least you can get a happy release from it."

"It's too expensive to get married," he replied, "No marriage can equal coming here once every few weeks. It's cheaper, cozier and above all I don't get annoyed over trifles."

"And I won't claim any house from you," I added.

At this we both burst out laughing. Every time he came here, he paid fifty dollars for half an hour's massage and I massaged him on his back and then turned him over and gave him oral work. Whenever he comes, he always says, "Very nice. Excellent and I feel much more relaxed now."

Seeing the surgeon off, I looked at the clock and found it was already twenty minutes to one. I went to the kitchen and took out a packet of frozen dumplings from the fridge and a stainless pot from under the kitchen bench. Having filled the pot with water, I placed it on the stove. Then I stopped for a rest. Using a small calculator, I summed up my income: 50+40+30+50. Well, the money from the four patrons this morning added up to no less than 170 dollars. I was watching TV and keeping an ear out for the two mobile phones on the kitchen table when one of them rang loudly.

Picking up the phone, I greeted first, "Hi."

"Hi, please tell me the price," a voice came from the other end.

"Fifty dollars for half an hour's naked massage and ninety for one hour; seventy dollars for half an hour's whole-set service and one twenty for one hour," I answered professionally.

"Could you tell me your address?" he asked. "Of course, it's 331 Creseter Street Garama."

"Okay, I will be there in one hour," the man on the other end said.

Finding the water boiling in the pot, I dumped a dozen or more dumplings into the water and left for the toilet in the next room when I spotted two ceiling lights that had failed. I grabbed a mobile phone and called another frequenter of mine, with whom I had a business relationship for nine years. When he comes to my place, he pays what he should for my service while I pay what I should for his service if I call him for help. And sometimes I will pay him a little more because he is a regular client.

There are workers of nearly all trades among my patrons and I always call them to do the job of, say, installing the air conditioner, repairing the electric lights or fixing the plumbing in the toilets. I pay them all according to their standard rates. So it's very convenient for me to have somebody fix anything if they are out of order in my home.

When my call to the electrician connected, I said, "Hello *Dajiba* (Chinese for *Big Cock*, which he was particularly proud to be called). This is Linda speaking. I have two ceiling lights out of order. Could you come around and have a look?"

"Okay. I'm coming after I knock off," he answered, "I'll ring you before I come."

I put down the phone and found the dumplings had already been cooked. I spooned them into a bowl, made a dish of cucumber and hastily had my lunch over a bottle of iced beer. As I have so many clients every day, I can spare only ten minutes or so for my dinner so I usually eat quickly and sometimes the meal will be interrupted by the arrival of new clients. It is not rare for me to be occupied from morning till two or three o'clock in the afternoon before I can manage to find some time for my dinner. Nevertheless, I feel very happy rather than tired or hungry because, after all, I am earning money. Every evening when I'm counting my earnings, and feel the yellow, green and red banknotes going through my fingertips, I forget all the fatigue of the day. After the washing up, I fetched the dry towels from the drier in the laundry, folded them and stacked them in the cabinet, and then I took out the clean towels from the washer, threw them into the drier and turned it on. Lastly, I collected the used towels and threw them into the washer, waiting for more dirty towels before turning it on.

I was bustling about when the doorbell rang. I hurried to the door and I opened it to find a stranger.

"He must be a new client," I thought to myself and lost no time in greeting him, "Good afternoon, sir."

"Good afternoon, Linda. I am David from Melbourne. I am a peasant working on a farm," he said very politely.

"Welcome. Please come in, David."

The man was quite tall, about six feet and not fat but very sturdy. He had a square face, short black hair, thick eyebrows, a pair of sunken, green eyes and a firm, big mouth under a long, steep nose. He wore a faded, blue denim coat and jeans.

I ushered him into the working room and before I had a chance to speak he exclaimed, "Wow! You have a good set up. Your home's like a five-star hotel."

"I bet you can't find this many mirrors and television sets embedded on the walls of a Presidential suite," I said, not without a note of showing off.

"Very professional, very sensual!" he admired. "It's a professional brothel." I reminded him. At this he burst out into boisterous laughter.

"My house is just a brothel and I am just a professional prostitute. Now, tell me what you want, sir, a full-body massage or a whole-set service?"

With this, I stretched out my hand and began to feel for his cock between his thighs. He didn't dodge but smiled, "I've come just to relax my cock, and I want the service with the highest price."

"Half an hour or one hour?" I asked.

"Of course I want one hour since this is my first time here." "One twenty for one hour."

At this he said, "No problem," and produced two fifty-dollar notes and one twenty-dollar note from his trouser pocket and handed them to me.

I took the money and said, "Thank you. What drinks would you like?"

"What drinks do you have?" he asked.

"Beer, Cola, Pepsi and so on," I answered. "Bring me a beer, please." he requested.

I took out a clean towel from the cabinet and hung it on the towel rail in the bathroom. Having set the shower nozzle's flow to an appropriate temperature, I told him, "You can put your clothes on the massage table and your shoes under it. Then go and have a shower. You needn't worry about your belongings. I'm an honest businesswoman and will never touch anything of my clients' in my home. I've been in this business for eight to nine years and I have thousands of regular clients."

He smiled at my tedious explanation, "Needless to say, I can see that for myself."

While he was taking off his clothes, I went out of the working room into the kitchen, put away the money in the cabinet drawer and came back with two bottles of iced beer. He had finished bathing and began to rub his body dry with the towel. I found his cock, though not very big, about as thick as an ordinary carrot, stiff and hard and a shade of shiny blue. All the pubic hair around his cock and balls had been shaved clean so his bare cock stood out very conspicuously.

I put one beer on the bedside table and handed the other to him. He grabbed the beer, plied open the cap with the towel and drank heavily with his head tossed back, "Ah. What a cool beer. How refreshing it is!"

I had changed the porn video to *Asian Fever No. 9* and it wasn't long before the music with the credit line could be heard and the sixty-inch screen showed a sexy, naked girl standing in front of the camera with a lovely smile spread across her face. The girl strenuously poised her hips to the left; her left leg stretched out and her right bent a little, forming the shape of an "S" with her body. She covered her private part with her left hand and cupped her left breast with her right in an effort to show off her charming and graceful figure.

I pressed the "start" button on the remote control and several close-up shots of cocks pounding cunts flickered across the screen to the fast rhythm of music.

"The screen is so wonderful; it's almost like being at the cinema," David smiled.

"No cinema dares to show you these close-ups," I replied.

"I mean, the pictures on the screen are wonderful," he added.

I covered the bed with a clean towel and piled one pillow on top of another, before taking several sips from the beer bottle on the bedside table. I leaned over to fumble his cock and glanced at the porn video on the screen.

Instead of ravishing me at once like most of my frequenters, he just stood there, quite shy. Showing him the towel covered on the bed, I motioned him to lie down. He obediently lay down on his back, resting his head on the pillows so he could face the sixty-inch TV screen on the west wall.

He couldn't take his eyes off the flickering screen and asked me, "Do you enjoy watching these videos?"

"I'm fed up with them. I've seen them thousands of times," I thought to myself. "The videos are for my clients. Sometimes when my clients can't come, the videos make my job easier by stimulating them."

He then licked his lips, "How gorgeous these girls are. If only I could take one home and fuck her any time I like!"

"You couldn't afford to take these girls home. One of my friends who works for the Taxation Office says it takes seven to ten days to produce such a video and every female actress can get paid up to twenty thousand dollars, while the male actors only get two thousand dollars."

"What a marvelous job, the actors can make love to such gorgeous girls and get paid? I would be willing to do it for nothing!"

"I'm afraid you are daydreaming. Your cock is not big enough. A certain chef who has been my patron for more than eight years always asks the same question when he watches these videos, 'Linda, why on earth are there Asian girls but no Asian men in the videos?' My answer is, 'Asian cocks are not big enough. It's the western, big cocks that they are seeking.'"

David laughed embarrassedly, "Mine is not big enough?"

"Yours is a little bigger than Asian ones but it is nothing compared to some of the big ones I have seen" I said teasingly.

With this, I parted his legs wide and began to lick the skin of his balls, "God that feels good" he groaned.

I kept on licking and he said admiringly, "You are professionally skilled."

"It's been nine years since I took on the job of dealing with cocks," I answered, "Many of my patrons call me the doctor of cock specialty."

We were talking when one of the mobile phones rang. I picked up the phone, "Hello. How are you?"

"Dr. Linda," the man on the phone said, "When can I come to see you?"

"Dr. Linda is engaged right now. You can come in an hour."
"What time exactly?"

Looking up at the clock on the wall, I answered, "Two o'clock."

"All right, see you at two."

I had just put down the mobile phone when the other mobile began to ring, "Occupied?" This was a frequent phrase my regular clients used as they knew I was occupied most of the time. For these sorts of calls, I only needed to arrange the time and didn't need to ask who it is.

As I knew there was an appointment at two o'clock, I answered promptly, "Half past two."

"Okay," the man said. No sooner had I turned off the mobile phone when the one I had put down on the bedside table seconds before rang again, "Hello?" Normally I would answer, "Hello. How are you? How can I help you?" But if I'm very busy, I usually answer more briefly, "Hello. How are you?" Most people ring me to get their cocks serviced, which makes the second part of the answer "How can I help you?" somewhat unnecessary.

This time, I heard a voice on the other end of the phone say, "Can I get into your pants around two o'clock?" He spoke so humorously that I could tell him apart from my other clients at once. As I can receive thirty to forty calls a day, I usually can't recognize clients solely by their voices, but he sounded very familiar to me. I tried to avoid drawing the conversation out any longer as I was conscious of keeping David waiting, "How about three o'clock?"

He at once understood, as if he could read my mind, "Ah, one hour." With an 'okay' I put down the phone.

David smiled teasingly, "Very occupied, aren't you?"

"Sometimes clients will call three times but still can't get an appointment," I explained, "I will be engaged from ten in the morning till four in the afternoon, half an hour for each client. If anyone wants me for an hour, he should make it clear on the phone in advance so that I can specially set aside an extra half an hour for him."

With that I went on licking the skin of his balls, hoping that no more calls would come in.

It was quite a while before he began to groan, "Ah, oh." He swallowed loudly as if he was gulping water to quench a long-felt thirst. I slowly licked along a blue vein behind his balls all the way to the tip of his cock until he gasped for deep breath and turned his "Ah" into a long drawl of "Oh ----." Looking at the video program and mirrors on both walls alternatively, he panted for deep breath, "Fuck. It looks so fucking sensual having my big cock inside your mouth."

"I told you that you haven't seen a real, big cock. I once entertained a twenty-one-year-old Australian boy whose cock was as big as this aerosol can," I said casually, pointing to an air freshener can with yellow and white patterns on the bedside table.

He took in a deep breath, "Can your cunt swallow such a big one?"

"I cautioned him not to thrust his whole cock inside me or else he would have pierced my cunt," I said.

David smiled, "You should have charged him half the price as he could only fuck you half way."

I retorted, "It's his own fault for having such a huge cock. Besides, he had no other place to put his cock apart from my cunt. He told me once that he went to a brothel and all three girls there fled at the sight of his cock.

At last, the boss of the brothel came out to apologize, 'Sorry, sir, but we can't serve you.' 'Why?' 'It's too big. No one dares to serve you, sir.' 'Too big they can't serve me? Then you should refund me.' And the boss did so. The boy finally ended up a patron of mine."

"Really?" David exclaimed.

"It's true," I said, "No kidding. One of my clients said he had five girlfriends but they all broke up with him because his cock was too big and more often than not he caused them to bleed during sex. Finally he had to put a ring pad around the end of his cock to limit the length of it in case he should thrust too deep.

My cunt can handle big cocks because I gradually get used to them."

I began to caress his shaft slowly until it became very hot and stiff. Scarcely had I let go of it when it began to wag like a spring.

I patted his cock with my right hand, "Look, you naughty little one. Why are you behaving like that?"

"Well, it has been suppressed too long and hasn't touched a single cunt for nearly half a year. So let me give you a good fucking right now."

I stood up to find a medium-sized condom from the bedside drawer and tore open its plastic wrapper. Then I picked up the condom's tip in my mouth with its opening facing outward. I put it on his penis and sucked his penis hard while unrolling the rim all the way to the stem of his penis with my hand. Now the condom was perfectly positioned. David couldn't help admiring, "Linda, what an expert you are, even in putting on a condom!"

"You surely would be," I answered, "if you put condoms on a dozen cocks or more a day."

"Who is on top: you, me, or otherwise?" I asked. "You on top," he answered.

"Hey, how lazy of you to let a lady bear the brunt of an exhausting job. I have been working all morning," I jokingly grumbled.

Nonetheless, I felt good atop him as I sank my cunt around his upright cock, with my hands supporting my own weight on both sides of his shoulders. I seductively swayed both my breasts over his face and sucked his long shaft into my cunt.

"Oh, yes," he cried out, "It's so nice being inside you, very warm." "If you feel cold inside it, mine is a dead cunt." He approached to lick my right nipple, which was the most sensitive spot on my body. A thrill swept through me and I couldn't help but groan, "Oh. Oh. Yes." I was mounted on him with his hardness inside me and I moved back and forth to increase the friction between his cock and my cunt.

Flickering across the TV screen was a close-up of a girl mounted on a man, her plump white buttocks moving up and down to the measured tempo of the background music; *The Lass of Ali Mountains*." A long, black cock with two balls was seen jerking convulsively with the rhythm of the up-and-down movement of the girl's hips.

Looking up at the screen, I began to imitate the girl's movements. I sat up, straddled David on the bed and supported my own weight with my hands beside his waist. I moved up and down and sheathed his upright shaft to the beat of the music. I continued to watch the girl's locomotion and followed suit, trying to synchronize with her in every action. As if a conductor were directing us in a chorus, the girl and I were heaving up and down together and shouting to the deafening background music of percussion instruments.

Rotating my nipples with his hands, David narrowed his eyes and groaned, "Oh, yes. Oh, yes." Our groans combined with those of the couple on the screen and formed a precise sexual intercourse march to a 4/4 beat.

This was a hard job for me and within just a few minutes I began to gasp for breath. As I wanted David to come quickly, I continued my feverish thrusting until he too began to gasp for breath. The gasps turned into yells and were followed by a final, long exhausted howl.

"I'm coming. Ohhhh, yes, fucking hellll."

As I sat face to face with him, he nearly knocked me out with his unpleasant smelling breath. I frowned as I continued to heave myself wearily on his cock and felt it jerking rampantly in my cunt for a little while longer. I kept twisting my buttocks against his groin to increase his pleasure.

"Wonderful. I came a lot," he said, thoroughly relieved.

I got off the bed and peeled the condom from his shaft, "You almost filled the condom to the brim today."

Glimpsing at the condom, he said, "A clearance of half a year's stock. So much, isn't it?"

I helped him clean the sperm off between his legs with a tissue and threw it, together with the condom into the dustbin in the kitchen. After washing up my hands, I went back to the bed, turned him over onto his belly and began to massage his back.

Sitting astride his back, I gripped his back muscles and started to rub them.

"Linda," David said, "You've got the best job. You can earn money while you're enjoying yourself all day. If I was a woman, I would also choose to be a prostitute."

"Indeed I think I've got the best job of my life," I said heartily to David.

"You have a cunt that can lay golden eggs," he said. "I see you have furnished your house so magnificently. Your cunt must have earned you a large fortune."

"Mine is not an ordinary cunt. I have insured it for twenty thousand dollars." I said proudly, "When one day it cannot work any longer, my insurance company should pay for that."

"Are you kidding?" he burst into laughter, "You have insured your cunt? It must be the most expensive cunt in Australia, then."

"It's not only the most expensive in Australia but in the world as well. Madonna has insured her breasts and Richard Clement his fingers. Even the footballers insure their feet. My cunt is my ATM so why shouldn't I insure it?" I told him in all seriousness. "How can the insurance company know your cunt cannot be used? Should the manager come and have a try first before he approves your compensation claim?" he asked viciously.

"No, that won't do. If by any chance he comes and gets a free service only to find my cunt is good enough, I would suffer from my own actions. I wouldn't be so foolish!"

"Come on," he turned over onto his back, "Let me have a good look at that valuable cunt of yours."

He parted my legs and tantalized my cunt lips with his right hand, "Nice cunt. I didn't notice you had shaved it."

"I shaved it last night when I was idle, lest any grey hairs grow out." I said jokingly, "Who would come to buy a grey- haired old cunt?"

"No, no. Your cunt looks just like that of a fifteen or sixteen-year-old girl" he said jokingly.

"Now that it has been shaved, it can almost pass for a young one."

"Hey," he heaved a deep sigh, "When you're aroused, your cock takes a fancy to whatever cunt it catches sight of. While I was working on the farm, I hadn't seen a woman for a long time and I even put my cock into a mare that happened to pass by. My sister gave me a good scolding for this scandal."

I know only too well about the torment you will suffer when your sexual desire has not been satiated. "This is just like you eat when you're hungry and drink when you're thirsty. Long-time thirst for sex will drive you mad." I tried to comfort him, "To tell you the truth, when I was once absent from men for two months, I just thrust a beer bottle into my cunt."

His cock erected stark and stiff again, like a flag post.

"I'd like to have you once more." He insisted, "Now that I've come today, my cock should be given a good treat and have its fill." Putting a condom on his penis, I promised him, "Well, just once more? You can have me ten times, so long as your cock can stand upright."

He laid me flat on the bed, "This time let me fuck you. Away from women for half a year, I'm wondering whether my cock still works."

He put his two hands on either side of my waist to support his weight, and parted my thighs wide with his long legs. I effortlessly rested my legs on his shoulders; years of exercising since my early childhood meant that I was still quite flexible and resilient for a woman of my age.

He exerted all his strength and thrust his stiffness deep inside, "Now you can see clearly whether my cock is big or not," he said, with a note of triumph in his voice.

"You really can't imagine what big cocks I have seen before; yours can only be rated as a smaller one," I said to myself. Nevertheless I let out a cry of pain, "ouch!" as he knelt on the bed and spared no effort to pound into me.

There was a fair-skinned, Asian girl on the television screen lying on her side with her knees bent on a yellow and red striped sheet; a masculine, western young man lying behind her. The man lifted up her left leg and nudged his cock into her from behind and moved quickly, making the girl groan pitifully. A close-up shot depicted the brown lips and curls of the girl's cunt, with a big cock moving waywardly inside her. The muscles around the girl's vaginal opening fell into a fit of convulsion. The background music was a Chinese folk-song "Love Song of Kangding." Its strong percussion, mixed with the dual chorus of the merry couple made David even more excited and he noticeably quickened his pace. He cried out happily, "Oh --. Ah --. Ye – s!" The room was instantly filled with an atmosphere of lasciviousness and reverberated with the happy groans and noises of lovemaking. Several minutes later, David had me kneel on the bed and thrust my buttocks skyward. Then he pushed his hardness into me from behind. I resisted his thrusts and cautioned him to slow down.

He turned a deaf ear to me and kept yelling, "I'm fucking you! I'm fucking you!" He moved his cock inside me madly.

The girl in the video was sprawling on a big reef; her buttocks pointed upward, one leg on the beach and the other astride the reef. The man's cock was inside the girl's asshole and moving frantically, stretching the muscles out around it. The girl shouted even more loudly and unscrupulously than before. As the background music changed to a slower beat, David seemed to find his own tempo and thrust rhythmically, looking occasionally at the video and into the mirrors beside us at the grotesque gestures of our mating, "Sexy, very sexy."

Then he announced he'd like to follow the suit of the man in the video, "I want to fuck your asshole."

"Definitely no. My asshole is a restricted area. Once a client thrust his cock, one size smaller than yours, into my asshole and left it in pain for three days. Anyway, you should pay more if you insist on doing so; extra money for extra service. Any prostitute will demand fifty dollars or more for this extra service. I'd be willing to give you a special offer; you can pay me thirty dollars more." I knew only too well he would be most reluctant to do so.

But I had really underestimated his endurance. He held out for another ten minutes. Feeling that he was quickening his breath and his cock's moving frequency, I began contracting my cunt muscles. Then I heard him yell hoarsely, "I won't fuck your ass, if you don't want me to!" He moved his cock to the beat of the music and repeated, "Oh, yes," oh, yes" several times, followed by a succession of "Ah," louder by several decibels. When the last howl echoed across the room, I was ready to remind him not to shout my roof to collapse. But I knew he was about to come so I allowed his cock to throb inside me until he let out a long cry of "Ah," followed by a couple of exclamations "My God, my God." It was quite a while before he calmed down and pulled his soft dick out of my cunt. He had hardly jumped off the bed when I grasped his cock. I said, "Oh, my God! So much sperm again. Oh my! If my neighbors had heard your desperate cries just now, they would have suspected I had cut off that cock of yours." "You are number one," he said, "Now that I've emptied my balls, I can have peace of mind."

"Not only have you praised me as number one," I added, "many of my clients have also said the same."

"I will always remember you." "You are not alone," I answered.

"Linda, now I understand why you have so many fans and so many regular clients," he said seriously.

During David's string of sweet compliments, I had already pulled the condom off his shaft and wiped the sperm off his cock with a tissue "Go have a bath. Now that your cock is emptied, time is up for you. It's time for me to welcome my next client."

HORNY

We were just talking when the bell rang. As David went directly into the bathroom, I grabbed a long piece of dark-blue silk, threw it round my neck and tied the two ends of the material in a bow under the crevice between my two breasts. Parts of my body were exposed where the material failed to cover me, including my white, sensual shoulders. Most of my patrons said it was very sexy, but in fact I had intended to save time. Sometimes I was too busy to toss on a dress or anything else and had to make do with whatever I could find to cover my body.

I closed the door to the working room and hurried to the front door. Before I had time to see who it was, the guy stretched out his hand to probe between my thighs and stammered out his request, "Come on. Let me have a fuck. Just ten, ten minutes, please. My wife is shopping at Woden Shopping Center."

I looked up to find it was one of my frequenters. Every time he came for me, he was always in haste as if he had come to extinguish a fire.

"You stammering fool," I complained, "Co'co'come on but I can't bend over and let you have a hasty fuck at the front door. You are always coming without making an appointment in advance. I have a client at two o'clock and he's coming in no time."

"Do me a favor and let that guy wait a moment. I promise to finish in five minutes," he begged.

I could do nothing but direct him into the waiting room, asking him to wait a couple of minutes.

"Please be qui'qui'quick," he stammered.

I had just shut the door when the doorbell rang loudly. I went to answer and found it was one of my frequenters of five or six years, an Italian man, not so tall but very sturdy. As he had a particularly big cock, I gave him the epithet "Mr. Big Cock." As soon as he stepped in, he extended his hand not to shake hands with me but to feel my private part impatiently.

"Still a virgin now?" he asked.

"A virgin at this time? If you'd like one, please come at six thirty tomorrow morning," I responded.

I settled him in a swivel chair in the west living room and said apologetically, "Would you please wait a minute. I have to finish serving two clients before I can serve you, sir"

Then I ran to the garage to fetch a bottle of wine and a plastic bag and hurried back to working room. David was neatly dressed in a cowboy coat and jeans and looked quite handsome. I handed him the wine and said, "This bottle of wine is for you to drink at home. Here is a plastic bag for it."

"You're very kind," he kissed me on the cheek. Pointing to the back door, I said, "This way, please."

He bent down to kiss me again and took his farewell of me, "Next time I come to Canberra, I shall surely come to see you."

The words in my mind were: "Be sure to find a proper place to put your cock so that you won't have to fuck a mare."

Having shut the back door, I went to the west living room to usher in my Italian client Mr. Big Cock, "Be quick. I'm busy." He followed me, busy all the way lifting up the silk wrapped around my body and fumbling my hips. I led him to the working room and told him, "Be patient and wait another five minutes. I have a client who needs masturbating. It will take no more than five minutes." He kept fumbling between my thighs, "Come back soon."

I went to the waiting room to find the stammering dolt already stripped. His small cock erected stark and stiff at the stimulus of the porn video. I took the smallest condom from the bedside table and sheathed his prick with it while he was busy raising the silk wrapped around me and having me stand at the bed and support myself with both hands on the bedside table. I rotated my hips upward and he nudged his small dick into me and yelled, "Oh, yes. Oh, yes." He yelled for less than a few minutes before he came. I peeled off the condom and he began to dress in a hurry. While I was washing my hands, he tried to force his way out when I patted him on the shoulder, "Please pay the service fee. You're not going to steal your way, are you?"

"Sorry, I almost forgot," he responded, patting his forehead with his hand.

"You always do," I expressed my dissatisfaction.

"Twenty dollars?" he asked, feeling his pocket for money.

"Thirty! Who will be fucked for merely twenty dollars nowadays? Can you find a cheaper service in Canberra?" I got angry.

"I enjoyed less than five minutes. Twenty dollars is not a low pay," he argued.

"Well, just forget it. Pay me twenty dollars," I said at last, "Then what do you want for drinks?"

"No, thanks. I…I must be going—a moment longer and I'll be interrogated by my wife," he said, not without a note of fear in his voice.

Having seen the stammering fool off, I went back to attend to the Italian Mr. Big Cock. He stood there all naked, his stick as hard as a club and as thick as a wine bottle. I was not exaggerating. Every time I caught sight of his cock, I felt my stomach aching at once.

I tossed off the silk on me to a pile on the floor and urged him, "Quick. I'm occupied."

He pushed me on the bed and thrust three fingers of his right hand into my cunt.

"Ouch," I cried out, "Please don't thrust in so many fingers. What sort of cunt can allow in so many fingers?" I protested, brushing his fingers aside with my right hand.

"I hope to thrust a whole hand in it,"he pretended to threaten me.

"Go back to your own wife," I shouted, "You can do whatever you like to your wife, but not to me."

He tried to play his dirty old game again but I brushed his hand aside. I found him the largest condom but it hardly fit him.

"You have to buy the extra large size from the United States," I said, "Has your wife ever complained about your big cock?"

"My wife never allows me to fuck her more than once a month," he answered, "And besides, she has not experienced as many cocks as you have, so she has no idea of the sizes of different cocks without any comparison."

"She can at least have an idea whether yours is too big for her when you fuck her," I said.

When I put the condom on his cock, he pushed me onto the bed, sprawled on me and parted my thighs wide with his legs.

"Take your time. It's too big," I said, a little afraid.

"That's good,"he said, not without pride,"Is there any woman that doesn't like a big cock?"

"But yours is too big," I said, "It's like a mineral water bottle!" Pointing his cock at my cunt, he hesitated a little and then suddenly thrust it inside me so violently that my cunt felt swollen and stuffed at once.

"Ouch," I cried out, "You are murdering me. I pray do it gently."

My cry didn't slow down his pace. Instead, it incited him to act even more enthusiastically. He withdrew his cock a little and thrust it forcefully deeper, "I fuck you!"

"Ouch," I couldn't help crying out, "Take your time, I beg you."

Instead of listening to me, he didn't restrain himself in the least. When his thick length touched my cervix, it didn't stop there and invaded even deeper into me and caused piercing pain to my womb and stomach.

"Be a little tender with me, my dear," I entreated with a trace of weeping, "My cunt hurts and my stomach aches."

"Let me go on fucking you and you'll soon get used to it," he said a little mischievously. "Then you'll enjoy it, dear."

"This guy sounds exactly like Peter" I thought to myself.

He grasped my arms from under my legs. He had such a big cock that I never dared to rest my legs on his shoulders. If I had done so, my womb would have been pierced through by his strong length. Nor did I dare to tilt my hips up; his big cock would have caused my cunt to bleed. With my legs on his arms, he began to piston his big cock slowly but forcibly inside my cunt.

"I love fucking you!" he yelled madly. One pounding after another, each one more relentless than the one before and I was being fucked to tears. But it wasn't long before the acute pain in my cunt gradually turned into a numb pain and thrill. Each of his movements was a strong stimulus to my lustful desire. I actually needed such a big cock, especially during the time before I menstruated. On such occasions, a big cock was a special treat for my cunt. I could guess from this sign that my next menstruation may be drawing near.

Little by little, he aroused my insatiable desire for a big cock. I felt a sensation that was simultaneously painful and piercing and thrilling deep inside me. That sensation forced me to groan, "Oh. Oh, yes." And I began to enjoy his superb cock.

He approached to kiss me. I never kissed my clients because I felt that kisses were intimate and should only happen between loved ones. Though I preferred him to most of my patrons because he could satisfy me more thoroughly and made me come more completely. Whenever I was about to come, I used to shout, "Fuck me harder. Fuck me harder!" During these moments, I would forget all about the exceptionally large size of his cock. Only after I trembled, shuddered and yielded to an unspeakable ecstasy did I feel a piercing pain in my cunt and stomach. Now I was lying flat, quivering and ready to be kissed by him. He seemed very excited and said, "Honey, have you come yet? I like making you come completely and hearing you shout 'Fuck me hard, fuck me hard.'"

"Oh, no," I shook my head, "Not for today. I am too tired and there are still three in the line waiting for their turn. Please come, honey."

He barreled in and out of me frantically and made me cry at the top of my voice, "Ah, yes!" As the tip of his penis pressed against the bottom of my cunt, I let out a cry, "Fuck me. You fuck me!" Maybe this aroused his passion and he began to speed up the pace of his breathing and thrusting movements. He kept yelling. "Oh, yes. Yes." With the last "Yes," his cock filled my cunt possessively and stopped moving. Instead of yelling and shouting like other men, he just collapsed on me motionless, and then his cock jerked violently and caused another heat wave to sweep through my cunt.

After what seemed like a long time, I said to him listlessly, "You've come."

"Let's do it once more," he demanded.

I pushed him off the bed and gripped his cock, saying teasingly, "You always say 'Do it once more.' Look at that dangling thing of yours and say you can do it once more?"

We both laughed and got up. I removed the overflowing condom from him and put it before his nose, "Look how much you've released in it."

"Let's do it once more," he insisted.

"Forget it. Go back and do it with your wife," I refused.

"If my wife should know I had been here with you, she would cut my cock off," he stuck his tongue out.

"If you keep pestering me, I will tell your wife," I said teasingly and urged him to take his shower to make room for the next customer. He reluctantly took the towel I gave him and headed to the bathroom. I made the bed and threw all the dirty towels into the linen basket in the bathroom.

I had barely finished all this when the doorbell rang again. I tossed on a dark-green, lace dress and trotted to answer the door, "Hi, Mr. Twenty-one. Long time no see."

"Yes. I've been working on the Gold Coast for a year and a half. Now that I'm in Canberra, my first leg is your house. How I've missed you. How are you? Are you still very busy?" he chattered in rapid succession.

"The doctor of the cock is always busy," I answered.

"That's because there are too many cases of cock problems," he replied.

He was the boss of a construction company and aged around sixty. He was tall with white hair. Even his brows were white, just like a senior god in the Chinese auspicious painting for the New Year. He had a pair of large, blue eyes and thin lips under a long, pointed nose. We had been acquaintances for six or seven years.

He was a man of humor and wit. Whenever you asked about his age, his answer was unequivocally, "Twenty-one, or to be exact, several months away from twenty-two" hence his epithet, "Mr. Twenty-one."

Truthfully, many of my patrons have frequented me for seven or eight years, and I still don't know their real names, only the features of their faces or cocks. I have neither motive nor necessity to remember their names. It suddenly dawned on me that it was he who had called me earlier and spoke so humorously." I was occupied at the time and could only answer curtly, "three o'clock." To think it was my friend Mr. Twenty-one who I hadn't seen in ages.

He stepped in, bent down to hold me round my waist and kissed me on the forehead, "Are you occupied now?"

"Just wait five minutes in that room,"I pursed my lips, hinting at the waiting room. He held me in one arm and went there, complaining all the way that every time he came he had to wait.

"This means I am very busy. Had I another pair of legs, I would part them for business, too," I said, not without a note of pride in my voice.

"Then you would be able earn double money," he laughed.

Arriving at the waiting room, he fixed his eyes on the TV screen on the west wall, "It seems you have really made a lot of bucks. You've furnished your room with twin TV screens instead of one."

"They also serve you," I explained, "So that you can watch the mating of the couple from any angle."

Watching the porn video on the screens, he was visibly impatient and tucked at the waist of his trousers, "Be quick. Don't keep me waiting for long."

I patted him on the cheek, "Just five minutes, dear. He's bathing now. Nearly done."

I pointed to the swivel chair beside the bed for him to sit on, the fridge for him to help himself to the drinks and said, "The toilet is over there." He nodded knowingly, "Go and busy yourself. I've been here dozens of times."

I shut the door behind me and came back outside to see that Italian Mr. Big Cock was already dressed but didn't have any intention to leave. He whispered, "Let him go home and let us continue."

"Continue? Are you going to pay me double?" I asked.

"You should pay me for what I've done for you," he grinned cheekily.

"You guys always want a free service. There's no free lunch in this world," I answered, urging him to leave, "Be quick." When we were walking to the kitchen, he took his wallet from his trouser pocket and asked, "How much?" He waved a twenty-dollar note at me without any intention to produce more.

"Regular price of thirty dollars. It's a special offer for you," I said.

Then he produced a five-dollar note from his pocket. Getting angry and impatient, I snatched the wallet from him and took out a ten-dollar note together with the twenty dollars he had given.

"Thirty dollars is the lowest price. You can't find a cheaper price in Canberra."

He took back the five-dollar note and tucked the wallet into his trouser pocket and sighed, "It's true I lack money. I should marry you so I can fuck you every day without paying."

"Forget it. Marry me?" I questioned, "How will you dispose of your current wife?"

"I'll divorce her," he said boldly.

"You're simply bragging like President Clinton. It will be your luck if your wife doesn't divorce *you*. Better find an excuse if your cock fails to erect tonight." With this, I shoved him out the door and waved bye-bye to him.

"See you next time," he smiled but I had already shut the door behind him.

Back in the waiting room, Mr. Twenty-one was already lying on the bed, stark naked on his back. He was playing with his small cock while watching the porn video on the wall. I approached him and said, "Stop doing that or you'll come."

"If you wouldn't have come back, I'd have come on my own," he said promptly.

I helped him collect his clothing and shoes and he followed me with his naked buttocks trailing behind him. When got to the working room, I covered the bed with white bed sheets and repositioned the pillows, asking him, "Have you had your shower?"

He lay down on his back and made himself comfortable, "I had one at home."

I slipped out of my dress, pulling it over my head and tossed it in a pile on the floor. I parted his legs and squatted between them. I swallowed his small rod in my mouth and began to suck it.

"Your cock is so hot," I mentioned passively with a sly smile.

"Of course it's hot," he said plausibly, "It has been missing you for a year and a half, and it has protested to me many times and insisted on seeing Dr. Linda for some fun."

"There are so many gorgeous young ladies on the Gold Coast beaches," I asked, "Why must you choose me?"

"Partly because I was too lazy and partly because no one, I think, is better than you. When I felt hot, I used to resort to masturbation."

And he started to groan, "Oh. Yes." And as he groaned he didn't forget to flatter me, "You're the best cock sucker in the world."

I felt his cock throbbing in my mouth and I swallowed it even deeper until it touched my throat. I began to suck it like a baby sucks its mother's nipples. He began to howl, "Oh. Oh. Yes. Yes," and exclaimed "I love that."

Having sucked his cock for a while, I set out to lick along the line behind his penis to the base and then to the slit. He even opened the slit for me to lick with my tongue and cried out, "I'm itching, itching." He slowly took in a deep breath, "Mm......" and then breathed out, "Oh, yes. I feel like a king."

I'd be lying if I said I insisted on every one of my clients wearing a condom during oral sex without any exception. During the first two years of my career, I strictly abided by this rule. But as time went by, I broke the rules for some of my regular clients. I think if a person sticks rigidly to every rule regardless of the specific conditions, he will lose his originality and flexibility. Just as a doctor in his medical field may work wonders to bring a dying patient back to life by making some daring attempts beyond the normal practice. This truth is self-evident in any other walks of life. More often than not, you have to take some risks as the achievements are in proportion to the risks you take. I'm not an unscrupulous worker in my business. My working experience is the warranty of my own safety. It's a life experience gained mainly through seeing, doing and thinking. It is not that I'm denying the importance of any rules. Any organization, profession, or even a governmental department has its own specific rules and practice standards to secure the highest level of its own safety. That's why I regularly go to hospital to have a comprehensive examination, testing blood, sex organs and all other related organs. If one day I am diagnosed as unfit for a sex worker, I will quit my business without hesitation. I should be responsible for all my clients. This is a basic code of my profession.

I caressed his rod for some time before he said,"Put a condom on me. I wish to fuck you now." I found the smallest one in the drawer and put it on him. He stood up to tell me,"Bend over and I'll give you a dog's fuck from behind." I knelt on the edge of the bed with my head against the bed head. He stood on the carpet and thrust his small cock into my cunt from behind.

"Oh. I'm inside you at last!"

"Ouch," I was a little surprised, "Never expected yours to be so hard."

"If only I had a twelve-inch cock to fuck you with," he said.

"If you had such a long one," I laughed, "I would have been pierced through."

"I'll have a plastic surgeon lengthen my cock for me," he said jokingly.

Then he began to slide his small cock inside me and yelled, "Oh, yes. Oh, yes." I did my best to please him by echoing his cries, "Oh, yes. Oh, yes."

On the TV screen now was a black-haired, young man fucking a dark-skinned Thai girl. "The same stuff," I thought. The only difference was that the girl was kneeling in the middle of the bed and the man was kneeling behind her. The close-up shown was a big cock moving back and forth in the girl's cunt. The background music was a three-beat slow Waltz. The music mingled with the boisterous noises from the sexual games on the bed formed a unique lovemaking waltz. Mr. Twenty-one was extremely aroused and turned his head to gaze at the fucking movements of us in the mirrors and simultaneously kept an eye on the porn videos greedily.

"Sexy, sexy, very sexy," he cried as he moved his little cock back and forth like a piston and after a loud "Ah!" followed a proud exclamation, "I'm fucking you!"

Then I exerted my cunt muscles to clamp his penis tightly and immediately felt a hot thrill sweeping through my cunt. He yelled, "My God!"

I waited for him to calm down. When at last he was quiet, I got off the bed to clean all the mess, "Hey. You really came a lot."

"Of course it's proof that my cock is not old for my age," he said complacently.

"Who says you are old? Aren't you twenty-one this year?" I teased.

He giggled, "I hope so."

I wiped off all the liquid stains around his groin and asked him to lie on his face so that I could give him a massage.

After throwing the used condom into the dustbin in the bathroom, I washed my hands and rinsed my mouth. I make it a rule to wash my hands and mouth each time I have served a client to ensure as much hygiene as possible. I'm very strict with this procedure. If ever a client comes three times in an hour, I will repeat the procedure three times.

I said to Mr. Twenty-one, who was lying on the bed, "Just lie for a while. I'm going to piss. I have been too busy to answer the call of nature."

"I've come to watch you piss", he said, startling me. I never expected him to follow me to the toilet.

I was vexed, "What fun is it to watch a woman pissing?"

He squatted in front of me and looked into the toilet bowl curiously, "You don't understand. It's really enjoyable to watch a woman pissing."

"I can't piss with someone watching me like that," I was not used to being watched pissing by a man.

He was about to reach out his hand to fumble my private part when the mobile on the bedside table rang. "Help me fetch the mobile, please."

I took advantage of the time it took him to get the mobile to finish pissing in the bowl. Then he handed the mobile to me and I pressed the "answer" key, "Hello?"

The voice on the other end asked bluntly, "What time is your next available appointment?"

I replied, "Four o'clock."

He said, "I'm coming at four o'clock."

I pressed the flush button when I finished pissing and cleaned my private part with a tissue. Mr. Twenty-one came in and sighed, "Look, I've missed watching you piss."

I said to him, "You'd better lie down on the bed. My next client is coming and it will leave you very little time to enjoy my massage."

"But I've ordered an hour's service," he complained as he climbed onto the massage table.

"I'm not giving you shorter time." I retorted, "I'm still serving you now."

I straddled his back and began to massage him.

"Hey, Linda," he said, "I've just moved to my new house. It is spacious and beautiful."

"You've bought a new house?"

"No. I designed it and built it all by myself."

"You're so smart," I praised him sincerely because he could undertake the work of an architect and a builder at once.

"Of course I am smart, because I am not married," he said jokingly.

I laughed heartily. Indeed in Australia, many men end up sleeping in the street as a result of a divorce.

"A surgeon client said this morning that he divorced twice and was close to becoming a wanderer," I said with a smile.

"It's fairly common these days. Hey, you'll never believe what I saw this morning. I was working on my roof when I spotted my neighbor mating with her large, brown dog through her living-room window."

I patted him on the back, "What nonsense!"

He rolled over onto his back and gestured wildly with his hands, "It's absolutely true. The lady was lying all naked on her back with her legs crossed. At first the large brown dog licked her cunt and it continued licking for quite a long time. It nearly caused me to fall from the roof. Later the large dog climbed on her and began to fuck her, with its hairy tail wagging all the time. And I couldn't bear it so I've come to fuck you."

"I heard my patrons say there were video tapes of women mating with animals like dogs, horses or mules. I haven't seen any of these tapes. I feel quite curious. You're lucky to have witnessed a scene like that."

"Yes, I am," he said.

At that time, his small penis resumed the movements of jerking convulsively. "Look, it's restless again," he said, "Let me fuck you once more. Linda, this time let me do it without the condom, will you?"

"No way. I receive more than a dozen clients a day. If every one of them fucks me without the condom, I would surely die."

"We have been acquainted for so many years," he said very earnestly, "I am clean, you know. I never go to other women except you."

"Still no," I didn't yield a little, "All men say so. They don't like the feeling of wearing a condom. In fact, it's also against the working code to do oral work without the condom. It's a favor to you."

"Then you should use your mouth to serve me this time," he conceded, "Because my cock can't erect very hard for the second time and I will have no feeling if I wear one. It's hard for me to come."

"Okay," I said.

"Can I come into your mouth?"

"Yes, I can wash it out after that," I said. "Or you can just swallow it," he said.

"I can spit it into your mouth and you swallow it if you please," I retorted, "I have to receive so many clients every day and if I eat all their come, I will not have to spend money on food."

"Well, well," he smiled, "You can save lots of money by eating sperm as a substitute food."

I was sitting beside him, supporting myself with my left elbow between his thighs. I took up his cock with my right hand and swallowed it into my mouth; I caressed his balls with my left hand, rolling them around like marbles. He began to groan again, "Ah, yes. Ah, yes."

I knew he was aroused and asked him, "Do you want me to thrust my fingers into your asshole?"

"Yes, yes. I'd like that," he got excited. I took a condom from the drawer and put it on the forefinger of my left hand. I supported my weight with my left elbow between his legs and thrust my forefinger into his asshole. "I'm fucking your asshole!"

"Ouch," he cried out, "Move gently. Mine is still a virgin's asshole. It has never been entered by anyone."

I moved my left forefinger slowly and used my right hand to support the base of his penis as I sucked it in my mouth. It was less than seven or eight minutes before he turned crimson and quickened his breath, "Suck me hard." I knew he was on the verge of coming because my left forefinger could feel his balls bulging gradually until they got as hard as his cock in my mouth. I quickened the pace of my finger movements and my mouth movements as well. He kept yelling, "My God!" "My God!" At that time I felt his cock become harder and harder until at last he came with a long cry of "Ahhhh!" I felt a hot stream ejected into my mouth at once. "Oh," I spat out his cock, "I've taken a mouthful of your sperm!"

"I wanted to squirt my sperm into your cunt," he grumbled, "but you didn't let me."

I helped him wipe the sperm off his cock and balls. Then, I waited until he calmed down before I went to the bathroom to wash my hands, rinse my mouth and brush my teeth.

When I came back, the short hand of the clock was approaching "4" and I urged him to leave.

"Bring me a towel, please," he said.

I took out a clean towel from the cupboard and said to him, "Go and be quick. That small cock of yours should be quiet for at least a couple of days."

Walking to the bathroom, he shouted back, "No. Tomorrow morning it will erect stiff at the mere thought of you."

I seized the opportunity to finish making the bed and changing the towels on the bed when the doorbell rang. I threw a backless, spaghetti-strap dress over my head and it fell down to cover my body, leaving my whole back exposed and my two, round breasts almost bursting out of the low neck-line. I hurried to the front door and stood there agape—it was an Italian client of mine, who was about sixty years old and had known me for nine years. To my surprise, he came to me with a plump Australian girl of a little more than thirty. I knew he was married and his wife was not this girl.

As if he had known the question in my mind, he explained, "This is my girlfriend."

"You know," I said plainly, "I never do threesomes." "Come on," he said, "Leave her alone as a spectator."

"Honestly, I never have any sexual relations with women," I was pleading lack of experience when he said; "I will pay double." After what seemed a brief hesitation, I led them to the waiting room. The girl giggled as she saw his boyfriend pinch my left nipple on the way. The girl seemed a little naïve and I began to take a fancy to her. I told them to wait a moment and then went back to the working room. Mr. Twenty-one had dressed and placed a hundred-dollar note on the massage table. I took it and said to him, "I'll get your ten dollars' change."

"Don't bother. You just keep it," Mr. Twenty-one shook his hand as he was walking out with me.

But I insisted and went directly to the kitchen drawer and took a ten-dollar note for him together with a bottle of wine, "Go home and have a sip. The wine will soften your cock."

He kissed me on the cheek at the doorstep,"I will be working in Canberra for a period and I hope I can visit you frequently."

"Thank you, Mr. Twenty-one" I waved good-bye, "Have a nice day."

I shut the door and went to the waiting room to lead the couple waiting there to the working room. The young man produced two fifty-dollar notes and handed them to me. In response to my question as to what drinks they'd like, he simply answered, "Not for the moment."

I accepted the money and went to the kitchen, thinking to myself: "Nine years ago when I was working in a brothel, a lady there taught me a trick of the trade that when doing threesomes, you should try to keep a distance from the male, lest you should arouse any envy in the female. But anyway, I couldn't lick the girl's cunt today. What interested me most was to suck the male's cock, not the female's cunt because we were of the same sex. God created Adam and Eve. Man should love woman and vice versa. As an ancient Chinese saying goes, 'The opposite sexes attract.' This means that people of the same sex are not supposed to attract each other. Then a good idea struck me that I should make full use of that sex toy— the electric cock. I immediately went to fetch the electric cock from the closet at the end of the corridor after I put the money in the drawer. I stepped into the working room with the toy.

At that time the Australian girl was placing a large backpack on the massage table. I spread a towel over the bed and thought higher pillows might be better for the girl as she was quite plump. I piled three pillows in a stack before I had the girl lie on her back on the white, wooden bed and rest her head on the pillows. Then I began to undress her. I took time to unbutton her black coat and she giggled shyly. I took off her coat and a large- sized bra came into sight. I untied the bra and two white, round fleshy breasts jumped out like lively rabbits. I stood agape at her bright, white bosoms wordlessly. I weighed her breasts, guessing each weighed at least four pounds. Seeing I was interested in her breasts, the girl chuckled and she suddenly shuddered as I touched her nipples. Obviously I triggered her sensitive sex nerves and she started to groan out, "Oh. Oh." I took my time in pulling down her pants to her ankles: huge, white buttocks caught my eye impressively. Thick, blonde pubic hair framed a pair of plump, pink lips, visible between her strong, white legs. From the videos I've seen, Asian girls' lips are usually dark brown in color while Australian girls' are characteristically pink. I have never seen a real cunt of a western girl except in a porn video. Now I have witnessed it in the flesh. Nonetheless, though I appreciate the beauty of such a cunt, I can't oblige myself to lick it!

I showed her the electric oscillator (an artificial cock) and asked her, "Like big cocks? Is this cock bigger or not than his?" I knew the Italian man's cock was not big. He had already undressed and stood at the bedside table. I grasped his cock and asked the girl, "Compare and see which one you like better?"The girl laughed even louder. I took out a large-sized condom from the bedside table and pulled it over the toy cock and came back to stand between her thighs, "I'm using this to fuck you today," I said, threatening with the buzzing machine, "I'll give you a good treat and you're sure to enjoy it."

I applied a lot of lubricating oil to the opening of her cunt, used my fingers to part her lips and thrust the toy slowly into her hole. She shuddered all over and cried out.

I asked, "Too big? Not really, it is far from being the biggest. I've seen a lanky Australian boy whose cock is much bigger than this one. I'm not lying. I did allow him to fuck me. Australian girls' cunts are supposed to be able to allow in bigger cocks, because they have got used to them over many years of evolution. Chinese cocks are not big," I gestured the rough size, "So if Chinese women have large cunts, it's a strange thing."

SEX

I began pushing and pulling the toy cock in her cunt and it made her groan away, "Oh, yes. Oh, yes." She seemed to be enjoying the new toy and I used a finger sheathed with a condom to rotate the tender bud between her lips. Her parted legs began to quiver and continued to part. As the pushing and pulling of the electric cock accelerated, her groans accelerated too. Soon her breathing became hoarse. It was about a quarter of an hour before she jerked violently with an exclamation, "Ah. I'm coming! My God. Fuck me!" I exerted all my strength to thrust the buzzing oscillator deeper into her fat cunt and motioned it steadily and vigorously until she twisted, quivered and collapsed. "Thank you," she said exhaustedly at last.

Seeing she had got over her climax, I withdrew the electric toy from inside her, took off the condom and wiped her private part clean. When I looked back at the Italian man, his tiny cock the size of a small carrot was already erect and stiff. I sheathed his cock with a medium-sized condom and had him stand on the carpet. I knelt in front of him and sucked his cock. He set about yelling his "Ah" and "Yes." The girl knelt behind him and reached between his thighs to fumble her boyfriend's buttocks. The man began to breathe heavily and continued to growl his "Ah" and "Yes." I felt the penis in my hand becoming harder and harder and I decided professionally that he was about to come. But he stood up and said, "Oh no. I want to fuck you!"

"Which one of us do you want to fuck?" I was wondering. "I want to fuck you," he pointed to me.

It was only natural it was me he wanted to fuck. After all, he had paid for my service. As for his girl, he could fuck her any time he pleased and without having to pay any money.

So I stood up and asked him, "Then what position do you prefer?"

"From behind," he said.

"He's going to fuck me but don't be jealous," I assured the girl, "Fucking and *fucking* are different. He fucks me with a condom on just to release his stress while he fucks you skin-to-skin without one to show his love for you." I was dwelling on the difference of fucking when he suddenly thrust his little thing into me from behind. "Ouch," I said, "I didn't expect yours to be so hard seeing as it's not very big."

"I've fucked you so many times," he said, "You still don't know that?"

Then he exerted his cock and began his "Ah" and "Yes" and I echoed "Ah" and "Yes" with him. After a while, I advised him, "You're supposed to save some energy for your own girl."

With that, I got up and stripped off his condom. I had the girl kneel on the bed and part her white buttocks for him to tuck in his cock. I sat leisurely on the bed and caressed the girl's nipples. The girl began to breathe heavily and yelled her "Ah" and "Yes" as if echoing her boyfriend's "Ah" and "Yes." The sonorous male yells and female screams formed a most harmonious chorus. I encouraged them like a cheerleader, "Come on. Fuck her. Fuck her hard."

"Are you satisfied with your boyfriend? Does it feel good?" I asked.

The girl kept on groaning and yelling. On the TV screen, a man lay on his back with a girl astride him, his upright cock inside her cunt. Another man was half squatted on the girl's buttocks, his cock tucked in her asshole. The close-up shot was angled from behind the girl's buttocks. So the two big cocks were clearly seen coming in and out of her cunt and asshole rhythmically to the beat of the soft background music.

The girl must have been greatly affected by the threesome in the video. It was only a few minutes before she let out a satisfied moan. "I'm coming. Fuck me."

The man worked away with his cock and ended up yelling, "I'm coming, too. Fuck you!"

The man dumped all his sperm into the girl's cunt. Both of them quivered for a long time like two fig leaves trembling in the wind. I got off the bed and fetched two towels from the cabinet for each of them to take their bath. I began to make the bed, thinking that while there were no calls coming in, I should call my real estate agency in Sydney to ask what was going on with the selling of my houses.

I went to the kitchen and came back with a bottle of port (Australians like to put port in fridges), a bottle of wine and two Cokes. When they finished dressing, I said to them, "These two bottles are for you to drink at home and the Cokes are for you to drink on the way."

The girl put the wines into her huge backpack, and took the Cokes in her hands. When they were leaving, the girl gave me a hug and said, "Thanks" and the man gave me a kiss on the forehead and said, "See you next time."

They wished to leave unnoticed so I led them through the laundry to the back door and said farewell there.

I hurried back to the living room, grabbed the phone on the desk and dialed the manager of the real estate agency.

"Hello, is that Peter speaking?" I asked, "Is everything okay with the sale of 184, Old Northern Road, Castle Hill?"

"Yes. The deposit has been received," the manager assured me, "And the contracts are to be exchanged on the twenty-second of October."

"No change in the price?" I felt a little relieved, "Is it still six hundred and five thousand dollars?"

"Yes, it is," the manager replied.

"That's good. Thank you. I'll ring you later."

Having hung up, I went to the kitchen to take a bottle of mineral water. I had only taken one or two sips when the doorbell rang and I had to hurry to answer it.

It was a man of medium height, dressed in green and yellow. He was turned toward the direction of the street when I opened the door. I greeted him but he ignored my greeting and kept on looking in that direction.

I stepped over and patted him on the shoulder. Only then did he turn back to look at me. I wondered why that man didn't speak. Was he shy because he was a newcomer?

He made a gesticulation of a tube with the four fingers and the thumb of his left hand and moved his right forefinger back and forth inside the tube. I laughed to myself: he must dumb and came here to seek the pleasure of making love. Seeing he could not speak, I kindly said to him, "The regular price is fifty dollars but I'll give you a special offer of forty, okay?"

He just stared at me blankly, obviously not understanding what I was saying. This time I laughed at myself: "He was most probably deaf too, so how could he hear what I was saying?" I reached out four fingers, meaning forty dollars and he was clever enough to understand it and nodded his tacit agreement.

I led him to the waiting room. He came to the bed and stood on the carpet, wasting no time taking off his clothing. I wondered why he was so anxious but however anxious he was, I kept my practice of paying before service. I reached out four fingers again.

He was just looking on and showed no intention of paying the money. Maybe he was trying to play the fool by feigning ignorance. But business was business and I was no philanthropist. Besides, have you heard of any charity in the sex business? I gave you a special offer the minute I realized you were dumb. What else should I do for you? A free service? If everyone followed suit like you, then what could I pay the electricity and water bills or the chips, Cokes and wines with? I would simply go into bankruptcy.

Thinking of this, I held out the palm of my hand toward his face, meaning, "Please pay first."

Only when he realized that I wouldn't be fooled so easily did he pick up the coat he had strewn on the floor and felt the pocket for money but in vain. He tossed his coat onto the floor and began to search his trousers' pockets and finally found a fifty-dollar note. He rubbed the paper note twice to make sure it was not two notes stuck together. When he assured himself that it was only one single note, he handed it to me reluctantly. I went to the kitchen to find a ten-dollar note for his change, a bottle of wine and a can of Coke. I gave him the change and put the Coke and wine on the bedside table. I showed them to him and indicated they were both for him by pointing to those things first and then pointing to his chest. He laughed like a boy and gave me a thumbs-up to show his appreciation.

I then found his cock was already stark and stiff. I touched his hand and signaled him to take a shower in the bathroom. He declined the towel I handed him and stood there, gesturing his forefinger back and forth into the tube made by his left hand. As it was hard to communicate with him, I had to make do without him taking a shower first. We would be doing it with a condom on in any case.

I took out a condom of the smallest size from the drawer and tossed my dress onto the carpet. I was pointing to the bed and motioned him to lie on it when he suddenly took me in his arms and threw me onto the massage table. The massage table was eleven inches higher than the bed and he stood beside it, parted my legs and thrust his tiny cock into me without a word.

"Hey," I told him, knowing of course he couldn't hear me, "You're really good at playing new games. No one has fucked me in this way."

I was lying where my clients usually did when I massaged their necks. There was a hole in the massage table, so I didn't feel comfortable lying there with my head stuck in the hole. However

I pleaded, he just wouldn't listen and actually he couldn't listen. He kept on nudging in his tiny cock with inarticulate sounds "En… En…." Sometimes he looked up at the porn videos on the TV screens and chuckled, pointing to the videos and then to my cunt. He probably wanted to express his excitement by making a sign of fucking with both his hands.

After a while, he moved me from the massage table to the king-size bed. He had me bend over and entered me from behind, looking from time to time at our mating in the mirrors on both walls and putting out the thumb of his right hand. He sped up the movements of his cock, which made me think he would soon come, so I tightened my belly and exerted my cunt muscles to squeeze his penis in an effort to make him come quickly but in vain. He turned over onto his back again and beckoned me to sit on him.

I complained in my mind: "Of the forty dollars he paid me, I only got a net profit of less than thirty, excluding the wine and Coke. And he wanted to fuck me using the all positions from A to Z?"

He climbed onto my body and resumed the movements of his cock with mumbled sounds "Wu." and "Wa." "Hey, guy," I reminded him, "Be quick. Time is nearly up. I gave you a discounted price and you're trying to make up for lost time?"

It didn't matter what I said, he could hear nothing at all. He just thrust away his cock, like a piston. I could do nothing but remain silent, only wishing he would come as soon as he felt exhausted. Sure enough, he kept moving his tiny thing for more than a dozen minutes before he came suddenly. He made several vain attempts to keep thrusting, then stopped and collapsed on me. He took me into his arms tightly.

He tormented me so much that I was almost out of breath. "Oh, my God," I was relieved, "You came at last. My dumb mate."

It was quite a long time before he dismounted from me and tried awkwardly to peel the condom of his saggy stick. I offered to do it for him and wiped his rod clean. I handed him a clean towel and motioned him to take a shower in the bathroom.

But he ignored my suggestion and without a word he pulled on his trousers. Since he was unwilling, I of course didn't have to force him to do take a shower here. So I went to the bathroom in the waiting room to have a shower and barely had the water wetted my back when the doorbell rang. I hurriedly grabbed a towel to wipe myself dry and threw on a short dress with a yellow, floral pattern. I shut the door to the working room and went to the front door.

I opened the door to find a frequenter of mine for five years. He wore an orange coat, blue jeans and a pair of leather shoes. His coat, jeans and shoes were all covered with a thick layer of dust. You could easily see that he must have been a field worker who came here as soon as he knocked off.

"How come you came again without calling me in advance?" I complained.

"Sorry, but I forgot your number," he said, a little embarrassed. The client was a very taciturn man. He never took the initiative to start a conversation. He responded to every question with only one word or phrase.

"But you can read the *Canberra Daily*. I have advertisements in it every day," I said.

"Very busy, aren't you?" he answered, obviously irrelevantly.

"Yes." I said, "Just wait five minutes."

I led him to the waiting room and took a plastic bag in my hand. When I came back, the dumb guy was already dressed and stood there, a bottle of wine in his left hand and a Coke in his right. I handed him the bag and he put both into it. As we passed the dining table, I pointed to the chips stacked on the table and he understood at once. He went over to choose a packet of chips and put it into his bag. I saw him off at the doorstep. He made a sign of lovemaking to show his intention of visiting my house again.

I nodded smilingly.

I closed the door and came to lead the taciturn man to the working room. As I followed him, I noticed a piece of rectangular mud fell off the sole of his shoes. The clod was the shape of a rectangle because the soles of his shoes had a rectangular design similar to the tread pattern of a truck tire. I frowned at his back, "A literal clodhopper," I said to myself.

After we entered the working room, he promptly handed me two twenty-dollar notes. As a regular client of mine, he had the privilege of this special price. I passed him a towel and motioned him to take a shower first. Just then my mobile rang and I hastily answered only to hear an anxious voice, "When can I see you?"

"At half past five," I answered over the phone while walking to the kitchen.

"There are two of us," the voice added.

"I never do threesomes," I promptly refused, as my head swelled at the mere thought of doing two guys at once.

"Don't worry. We're not asking you for a threesome." He explained, "Just serve us one by one. The second one will be waiting for his turn."

"Have you ever been here before?" I asked. "Yes, we have."

I disconnected the call and put the money into the drawer, took a sip of mineral water from the bottle and went back to the working room. The taciturn man had already lain on his back on the bed. His cock bent a little downward and stiffened. I began to suck his cock while he was lying motionless with his eyes closed. The sucking lasted seven to eight minutes before I asked, "Well, will it do? Do you want a fucking now?"

"Go on sucking," he said. I went on for another five minutes and said, "All right, I'll put a condom on your penis. You can be on top. I've been working all day and feel tired."

I pulled him to kneel between my thighs and guided him to nudge his cock into my cunt. He began to exert his cock slowly and steadily. Just then his mobile on the bedside table rang loudly and he hushed me by putting a dirty finger to his lips. I noticed the dirt under his fingernails. I thought his wife, if he had one, would surely lose any interest to dine with him at the sight of his dirty hands. However, I had no time to comment on his hand hygiene. I grabbed the remote control in haste and pressed the "pause" button to stop the video program. He pressed the mobile to his ear with his right hand, "Hello?"

I could recognize it was a female voice on his mobile phone but I couldn't make out what she was saying.

But I could hear him saying, "I'm very busy working. I'll call you back when I knock off."

I wanted to laugh out loud but I refrained from it. In response to what the woman on the other end was saying, he agreed, "Okay," "Okay," one after another. When at last the conversation ended, he put his mobile back onto the bedside table and said abruptly, "My wife."

I then couldn't help burst out laughing, "You're busy working?

How exhausting the work is. You're working really hard."

I was surprised that even such an honest and taciturn man would be able to tell lies.

"My wife has kept me from touching her for months," he muttered.

"Ninety-five percent of the men coming here have wives or girlfriends. It is not that they don't love their wives or girlfriends less but that they love the stimulus of seeking fresh women more. It's not hypocrisy that you come to me to satisfy your lust and go back home to be considerate to your wife's well-being. Sex is something strange and unpredictable and it is quite different from love. One of my patrons said making love to one woman and only that woman for a long time is unbearable and vice versa. Your wife will also be tired of making love only to you for a dozen or dozens of years. Time will eventually wear down her sexual interest in you, though she by no means stops loving you. The fact that she was telephoning to enquire about your whereabouts proves she does care about you. Having sex is virtually like having meals— you will soon get satisfied and even satiated. If you eat McDonald's or Kentucky's hamburgers at home, you'll sooner or later be fed up with them. But if you occasionally go out and eat at Chinese, Thai or Korean restaurants for a change and then go back to McDonald's or Kentucky's hamburgers, you will be surprised to find much relish again in what you have once lost interest in. In fact, in the field of sex, there is also the problem of *aesthetic fatigue*. You need some refreshment to enliven your sex life, just as you need some seasonings in your cooking. We prostitutes are just serving to the seasonings of men's sexual tastes."

The taciturn man did nothing but giggled, "My wife's call almost frightened my cock into shrinking and sagging. If my wife knew I was here, she would cut off my dick!"

I turned over and said, "That's too bad. If all the men who have wives that come here went home and got their cocks cut off, how could I go on with my business with so many men missing their fucking tools?" I smiled and went on to say, "Let's forget your wife and treat your cock now."

The man lay on his back and I sat beside him, with my left arm supporting my weight between his legs and my right hand moving over his bent cock. His cock erected at once and jerked mischievously. Just then the mobile rang suddenly. He turned instinctively to look at the mobile.

"Don't worry," I comforted him, "It's my call, not yours." "Hello?" I asked.

"When could I see you?"

Looking at the clock on the wall, I figured this man needed at least another half an hour. I quickly calculated the time and said, "At half past six."

"It's too late," he said, "Let's make it tomorrow."

I hung up the mobile and resumed sucking his shaft to make it stiff again. He said to me, "It's your turn to work on top of me." He looked at me and went on, "Once you feel tired, I will relieve you." "I've been working all day," I was unhappy and jumped onto him. I sank myself onto his upright cock and moved my buttocks vertically up and down. Our actual lovemaking was synchronized with the lovemaking of the girl and the man on the TV screen. The white-skinned Asian girl was also sitting on the man's cock. The girl was seen to have her legs parted and her hairy tuft exposed. A thick cock was seen thrusting away inside her cunt madly. I followed suit to the beat of the music and yelled repeatedly "Ah" and "Yes." Just then the doorbell rang unexpectedly and I was greatly annoyed because the timing couldn't have been more inconvenient. The interruption to our intercourse would surely delay this man from coming. I decided to ignore the person who failed to make an appointment in advance and went on with my gymnastics on the taciturn man.

The doorbell kept pestering us and I knew that this time the man below me could never come, because he couldn't concentrate his attention on his sexual organ any longer. I rolled off him, threw on a pinkish, purple dress and rushed to answer the door.

I pulled a long face upon seeing Michael. He was about sixty and of medium build. He had a sturdy physique and was grey-haired with a pair of sunken blue eyes, thick lips and a broad mouth on a square face; a local Australian. He was my loyal fan of nine years and also an old guy I was taking care of. As he was retired and not so well off, I charged him only twenty dollars for each service, including the snacks such as drinks or chips. And he felt much obliged and always limited his stay to fifteen or twenty minutes so as not to take up too much of my time.

Once he brought me five or six pork hooves from his friend's butcher shop and I naturally remitted his fees. Today he had a blue plastic bag with him and they were no doubt the pork hooves again, with which he meant to enjoy a free service this time (I secretly nicknamed him Mr. Hooves, and I shared his story with some of my clients once in a while). As soon as he saw me, he was all smiles and said, "Dear, I've brought you some pork hooves."

I pulled a long face at once, "I've told you a thousand times I can't serve you during the day time. If every other client comes carrying some pork hooves instead of paying cash, what would I pay the electricity and water bills with?"

"I know that but haven't you told me that generally you will be free after five or six o'clock? Besides, I didn't see any car parked in front of your house."

"Many clients never park their cars in front of my house and besides, the absence of a car parked outside doesn't necessarily mean there aren't any men in the house."

I let him in, though I was greatly annoyed, "We were going on heatedly and close to coming when you interrupted by ringing the bell urgently. So I have to start the process from the very beginning. It's a waste of not only time but also of energy. And moreover, the client I'm serving won't be happy."

"I'll take care of it next time," he said shyly.

"Take care. Take care. I've heard it said so many times," I said with resentment. He went to the kitchen and dumped the pork hooves into the sink. But my anger wasn't calmed, "The next client is coming in no time. You should wait for your turn."

"It doesn't matter," he said calmly.

"Maybe you'll have to wait for forty minutes. Maybe one hour," I warned him.

He helped himself to a can of Coke from the fridge and a packet of cashews from the dining table. While walking to the waiting room, he turned back to say "I can wait as long as you want me to."

I slammed the door shut angrily and returned to the working room. I resumed sucking the taciturn man's cock, which was as saggy and fatigued as anything. The man was absentminded. His wife's phone call combined with the disturbance of the doorbell made his cock feeble. I sucked his cock for more than ten minutes but failed, "Hey, big cock. Wake up!" I shouted at his cock. He grumbled in a suppressed and muffled voice,"The doorbell of yours rang so demandingly. I thought my wife had tracked me down here. My cock was taken aback."

"How can your wife know you are here?" I laughed.

"Who knows?" he said with lingering fear, "Maybe she followed me all the way to your house."

"Well," I said, trying to distract his attention, "Stop thinking of your wife and let's get on with lovemaking. Imagine you're fucking a young girl of eighteen. The first thing we have to do is make your cock stiffen again."

After sucking his bent cock for a while and rubbing it with Indian body oil, it finally grew stark and stiff again. "I want to fuck you now," he yelled at me.

"Of course," I said, "Climb on top of me and this position will allow you to more actively control your sensations."

I pulled him up, lay down on my back, parted my legs and raised them at a sixty-five degree angle. He knelt on the bed and threw both my legs over his shoulders, yelling, "It feels really good putting my cock in your cunt."

He went on thrusting his cock, repeatedly groaning "Ah, yes." And I echoed his moans, bellowing "Ah, yes." He looked at the TV screens on the walls and when he saw a western man fucking an Asian girl, the scene made him all the more excited and he sped up the pace of his cock movements. After letting out a long breath and sprawling on me, his stick inside me stopped moving.

"Come?" I asked. "Yes," he nodded.

I heaved a sigh of relief and thought to myself: "It would be a tragedy if his wife's phone call really frightened him into being impotent."

When he calmed down from trembling, I pushed him up, stripped his condom and wiped off the sperm on his cock, "Go and take a shower. My next client is coming soon."

We were talking when the doorbell rang. I shut the door to the working room and went to answer the door. There were two lanky, black boys standing there and I asked them through the security screen door, "It was you who called me just now?"

"We have an appointment at five thirty," the taller lad answered. He had a chubby face, round eyes, a prominent nose and thick lips with a crew cut hairstyle.

"But you didn't say it was an appointment for two men," I argued.

"Let us in and one of us can wait in the waiting room," the taller lad said.

"No. Someone is already waiting in there," I disagreed.

"Have you ever been here?" I asked, knowing the foreign students wouldn't have much money.

"Yes," he answered, "Do you remember giving me a bottle of wine?"

"How can I remember what I have given to somebody or who he is? By the way, how much did you pay me last time?"

"Thirty dollars," he answered briefly.

Hearing this, I felt a little more assured but I still had to be cautious lest anything should happen.

"Well, come in one by one," I said, figuring that a quarter for each and half an hour for both would be adequate. "One of you comes first and the other should be waiting outside in your own car. Tell me, who will be the first I'm going to serve?"

"Let him come in first," the black lad with the crew cut hair said, "He has not been here before. He's my good friend. I hope you can take good care of him."

"No problem," I answered, "I have no discrimination against newcomers."

The black boy who wore many plaits appeared from behind the taller one. I opened the security door to let him in. The boy looked around and admired, "What a nice house!" I closed the door and led him to the west living room. I then seated him in a chair at the desk,"Just wait here for a while. I have a client inside and I have to see him off first."

Seeing the television sets flickering on the north wall, he asked, "Wow, what huge TVs. What size are they?"

"Sixty-five inches. 3D."

His eyes were attracted to the other furnishings in the living room, such as the grand piano, treadmill, and multifunction exercise machine and he couldn't help admiring, "You're surely a rich woman."

"Not rich. Just well off." I said and then asked, "Guy, what drink do you want?"

"Give me a beer," he said. "What brand?" I asked. "Carlton."

"Okay." I knew many boys liked this brand of beer, so I had quite a lot of it in my stock.

I fetched an iced beer from the fridge in the kitchen and handed it to him before hurrying back to the working room. The taciturn man was dressed in his uniform and working shoes. As soon as he saw me, he demanded, "Give me two beers."

"No worries. I won't forget that," I assured him, "Look. Carlton beers. I even remembered what your favorite brand is."

With that, I led him out of the working room and motioned him to leave by the back door. With the kitchen wall as a partition, he and the black boy sitting in the living room wouldn't see each other and their awkward encounter could be avoided. I shut the back door and went back to the living room and led the black boy by the arm to the working room. When he caught sight of the two huge TV sets showing the porn videos on the west and east walls, he said, "I was wondering whether I was in a cinema."

"Can you enjoy such porn videos on a cinema screen?" I asked, "But it's lawful to play porn videos here in my house."

He then looked into the mirrors on the north and south walls for some time and said, "Your room is gorgeous and sensual. It is the equivalent of any five-star hotel rooms."

"And you can't find such large TV screens in a five-star hotel room," I added.

Then I reached out my hands to run over many small braids over his shoulders and asked, "Who has braided these beautiful plaits for you?"

"I have my plaits braided by someone and let them grow all by themselves," he explained.

"I don't believe it," I was wondering, "You have to wash them regularly. How do you do that?"

"I just wash them as everybody does," he said seriously.

I shook my head to show I didn't understand. "Where are you from?" I asked.

"Zimbabwe in the south of Africa," he answered. "Are you here for college?"

"Yes."

Now let's get down to business. I said, "Please pay first, mate. I offer you a special price of thirty dollars. I know you overseas students don't have much money."

He produced a twenty and a ten-dollar note from his trouser pocket and handed it to me promptly, "Here you are."

I gave him a towel, showed him the way to the bathroom and told him to have a shower.

He went to the bathroom and I was putting the money into the drawer when my mobile rang. I always carried two mobiles with me everywhere I went so I wouldn't miss any calls from my clients.

Immediately after I answered, "Hello?" the man on the other end of the phone answered in Chinese, "Dajiba (meaning Big Cock in Chinese)."

I realized at once it was the electrician. I still didn't know his real name. I only remember having called him Dajiba in Chinese and explaining the meaning of these three Chinese characters to him. He learned the characters quickly and now always initiates a phone call with "Dajiba" so I know at once it is the big-cocked electrician. This morning I called to tell him there were two ceiling lights that had gone out of order and he said he would come as soon as he knocked off work.

Dajiba is not only my frequenter of many years but also my full-time serviceman of all the appliances in my house and is on call in almost no time. He has solved lots of urgent problems for me as indeed my business cannot go on without a proper supply of electricity or water.

"Dajiba, you've knocked off?" I asked.

"Yes," he said, "I'll come and examine your lights in the bathroom when you are not busy."

Looking at the clock I said, "Please come at half past six." I figured the two black boys together with old Michael in the waiting room had to take up at least one hour. Having hung up the phone, I pushed open the door to find Michael in the waiting room. I deliberately let my dissatisfaction with him be known and said, "Wait another thirty minutes!" with a sullen look on my face.

He was already lying there on his back without a thread of clothing, looking at the two TV screens alternatively and fiddling with his cock, "Well, well. I'll wait. I'm preheating myself."

I went out with a long face and returned to the working room. The black boy with a lot of plaits stood on the carpet between the bed and the massage table, wrapped in a blanket and wondering where he could make love to me. I went over and pulled the blanket off him, "Why are you covered so tightly. Show me your cock. Is it big or small?"

I was taken aback at an extremely huge cock, black, shiny, as thick as a torch and erected straight like an ack-ack gun with its barrel pointing skyward. I didn't expect such a lanky boy to have such a robust cock. No wonder Negroes are said to have super strong sexual ability. Those who have most sexual scandals are the NBA superstars of the United States. Almost every one of them is a sex maniac with numerous love affairs. They have powerful cocks so they need badly to have a lot of outlets for their surplus of erotic energy.

I took hold of his penis and led him to the bed. He lay obediently on his back on the clean towel I had spread for him. I sat on his left side, with my left elbow supporting my weight between his thighs. I softly rubbed his stick while talking with him, "You have shaved your balls. A good job. Did you do it all by yourself or did you have someone help you?"

"I did it myself," he said shyly, "It looks better."

"It's lucky you didn't cut yourself," I said, "Once I cut my cunt while shaving it and I was so overwhelmed with pain that I jumped to my feet and whirled on the ground."

"Why not try using depilatory cream or fluid?" he suggested.

"Well, the other day a client applied some depilatory cream to my cunt only to burn it for a whole afternoon."

"Well, you have to pay for being beautiful," he commented.

At that time his stick had become stark and stiff and it began to jerk and pulsate. His cock felt stronger and stronger in my grip. I found a large-sized condom and put it on his shaft. I said, "Lad, get up. You're young and strong. You should relieve me of the hard work."

I rolled down to lie on my back and raised my legs to allow him to kneel between my thighs. He squeezed his big cock into my cunt and made it feel at once fully filled and bursting. I couldn't help uttering, "Dajiba!" He didn't seem to understand and asked what I was saying. I answered, "You have a huge jiba."

"Jiba?" he questioned closely, "What do you mean by 'jiba'?" I had meant to say "huge cock" but I said it in Chinese.

"Dajiba." Little wonder he couldn't understand it. This time I said in English, "You have a huge cock."

"You have a nice pussy," we were presenting compliments to each other.

"Is my pussy really nice?"

"Very nice. And you have smooth skin and a sexy figure."

"My prime days are gone. I'm becoming older and fatter," I sighed with emotion.

"No, not fat. You look fairly sexy like that."

"My skin is getting dry. I have to take a dozen baths every day and it has done damage to my skin. Imagine my skin ten years ago; it was really tender, smooth and resilient."

"But your skin remains perfect," he seemed sincerely honest in responding.

He conversed with me but did not waste time exerting his strength to fuck me rhythmically with barbarous yells, "Oh, yes" or "Fucking!" I estimated his age to be twenty-two or twenty-three at most. He was so young and robust. Before I knew it he had bent me at an angle of forty-five degrees, thrown my legs over his shoulders and pressed my knees against his own face. Looking into the two mirrors on both walls, I saw two entangled, nude figures, a black one on top of a white one, forming a striking contrast. A huge black cock was seen clearly coming in and out of a white cunt. He spared no effort to exert his cock with yells "Ai. Ai" for quite a while and then he had me bend over and entered me from behind.

"Oh, yesss. Oh, yesss," these yells were coming from the TV screens in which a man was fucking an Asian girl on a beach. The roars of the waves mingled with the groans of fucking and echoed across the room, which reverberated with a romantic symphony of lovemaking. I felt him quicken the pace of his cock movement inside me, while increasing the frequency of his yells, "Oh, yes." Finally, with a very satisfied groan of "Ah," he cried out, "I am coming. Your room is so sensual. It helps me come quick."

I waited for him to release completely before I jumped off the bed to help him to take off his condom, wiped off the sperm from his cock and had him take his shower.

PUSSY

Just then my mobile rang again. I pressed the "answer" key and greeted the caller. The man on the other end asked abruptly, "Will you tell me what services you can offer?"

"Body massage fifty dollars for half an hour and ninety for one hour; whole-set service seventy dollars for half an hour and one hundred and twenty for one hour," I announced professionally. Having been a prostitute for nearly ten years, I had already had all the business information stored in my brain and I didn't need to search my memory for any of it.

"That's okay," he said, "And what time can I come?" "At nine o'clock."

"Okay, your address, please." "331 Creseter Street, Garama."

"Good. Let's make it nine o'clock tonight." "Okay."

When I put down the phone, the black boy had already dressed. I asked him what drink he would like to have. He said after a short pause, "Beer, please."

"What brand?" "Carlton."

I led him to the fridge in the dining room and gave him two beers of this brand. He asked tentatively, "May I take a packet of chips in addition?"

"Of course you can. Choose as you please."

He picked up a packet of chips and I put the beers and chips into a large plastic bag. I handed it to him and sent him to the door. On the doorstep he kissed me on the cheek, "I love you."

"Thank you."

"See you later," he said, reluctant to leave. I just smiled as an answer.

I closed the door and went to the kitchen for drinks. When the bell rang several minutes later, I knew it must have been the other black boy who was waiting in his car. As soon as he entered, he praised the house, "You have a nice house."

I said, "You should know my house is nice as you have been here."

"Very nice. I like it very much. Do you live alone?" he asked.
"Yes, I live alone."

"Let me live in one of the rooms. I'll come live with you," he suggested.

"No. It's not convenient for you to live here as I have a lot of clients every day. Someone suggested renting my room but I declined."

Looking at the TV sets in the living room he said, "Really high definition. Is it 3D?"

"Yes, it's 3D."

When we entered the working room, he pointed to the TV sets on the walls and asked, "Here are two more large screens. How many TV sets are there in your house?"

"Seven. Six large wall TV sets and one conventional set."

"Wow. You have more TV sets than a Harvey Norman shop does."

"You can say that."

Usually during business hours I turn on all seven TV sets. The TV sets in the waiting room and in the working room broadcast the porn videos and the other four broadcast English language channels. So wherever my clients go, they will feel at home and relaxed. That's one of the reasons why I have attracted many clients.

He handed me thirty dollars and began to undress. I put the money in its proper place and went to the laundry. I threw the washed towels into the drier and threw five used towels into the washer. I started the washer and went back to the working room. I found the boy stripped to his skin as he stood there waiting for me. I asked him, "Why haven't you taken a shower?"

"I have," he said, "Give me a condom."

I was surprised to find this boy's cock was no smaller than the former boy's. As the old saying goes; thinner men usually have bigger cocks while fatter men have smaller ones and thinner women have bigger cunts while fatter women smaller ones.

I took out a large-sized condom and put it on his cock and asked what position he preferred and he said he liked me on top.

It would be more tiring to be on top. As I had been working all day, I begged the boy, "Young man. I'd like you to be on top of me."

As I lay down on my back and stretched my thighs apart, I easily saw in the mirrors on the walls, a black nude and a white nude forming a contrast as striking as day and night.

The black young man was fucking me excitedly and relentlessly. I had not enjoyed sex this much in a long time.

But just a moment later, I was distracted from the ecstasy of lovemaking as I began to calculate how much I had earned that day: $50 + $40 + $30 + $50 +$120 +…. Up to now I had earned 500 dollars! It was a really busy day today and with only two more clients in the evening, the sum would reach 600 dollars.

I saw off the big-eyed black boy and went to the waiting room for old Michael. As I walked in, I found there was still yellow urine left in the toilet bowl, unflushed.

"Why," I said angrily, "You forgot to flush the urine?"

"Sorry," he jumped to his feet and said apologetically, "I almost forgot."

"You don't flush the bowl after you finish pissing at home, do you?" I scolded.

"Yes."

"You must have formed a bad habit of not doing so," I pressed the flush button as I complained. Crestfallen, he held his own clothing, followed me naked to the working room and put his belongings on the massage table. Just then I happened to notice a two-dollar coin lying on the floor and bent over to pick it up, "Who has dropped this two-dollar coin?"

"I must have lost it," said Mr. Hooves promptly.

"How could that be? He just stepped into this room," I thought to myself, secretly despising him for his greediness. I tossed the coin onto the massage table beside the pile of his clothes, "Here you are. You can buy half a pork hoof with it." He put the coin into his trouser pocket without shame and lay down on his back on the bed with his head against the bed head.

"To be frank, Linda," he looked into my eyes, "While I was waiting in that room, I was being tormented by the thought that you're being fucked by so many men. And the thought made me all the more excited. My cock erected hard and stiff in the air. Please marry me, Linda."

"Me, marry you?" I raised one of my brows, "Can you satisfy me with that old cock of yours? I know too well your little thing can hardly last five minutes."

"Hey," he said to me furtively, "We were drinking in a pub last night and a friend of mine betted me that you would marry him and I insisted you should marry me. But I think I'm too old."

"I won't marry either of you. There are not many people who want to marry me but they should stand at the end of a queue of at least one hundred and eighty. Their ages range from twenty-two to eighty and they come from dozens of countries around the world. They are of all races, white, black, yellow, red or brown. They have cocks of all sizes, varying from the biggest to the tiniest, from the thickest to the thinnest. Who am I supposed to marry? Could I marry them all?"

I was indulged in giving my speech when he abruptly requested, "Quick! Suck my cock, please." I had to stop the unfinished speech. I took up his cock and put it into my mouth. I swallowed it as deep as I could until it pressed against my throat and made me feel sick. The oral work didn't last long before the mobile phone rang. I grabbed the mobile and before I had time to say anything a voice came from the other side, "Sweetie, haven't seen you for a long time. Can I come over and see you this evening?"

I recognized him at once from his voice and tone. It was a famous lawyer who had been my lover for eight years.

"Come along at half past six, dear," I said eagerly.

"Ah! For one hour. Dress smart to give me a surprise," he said just as eagerly.

I hung up and went on to suck old Michael. He took out a small bottle of medicine he purchased from a pharmacy and started to breathe it into his nose. I have seen quite a few customers using that before, as it allegedly increases sex drive in men. It emitted a strong, herbal odor. The sucking was interrupted by the buzzing from another mobile. It was a text. I didn't eject his cock from my mouth but I released one hand to grab the buzzing mobile. The text on the screen read, "Tell me how much you charge for half an hour and how much for one hour."

Then I spat out his cock from my mouth and complained, "These guys always send me texts. I am too busy to read them. If I answer each of their texts, how many calls will I miss? Besides, I'm not good at sending texts. I get mixed up with these keys. I can only call and receive calls with my mobile."

"Hurry up," old Michael urged me, "I'm lying here only a few minutes and you have received so many phone calls."

"I haven't finished airing my grievances with you yet," I got angry, "Stop calling me in future unless you've got something important to tell me. Sometimes you call me when a certain man is inside me and his cock is frightened into shrinking back. I thought some other client was calling me only to find you were talking nonsense on the other end. Who cares about the pork hooves you sent me?"

"I was thinking of you," he said.

"I'm neither your wife nor your girlfriend," I said unkindly, "What on earth do I have to do with you then?"

"You have been my girlfriend for nine years," he retorted.

I continued sucking his cock when the mobile rang again. I grabbed the mobile and I sensed at once I was being unfriendly.

"Hello?" I asked.

"May I speak to Linda?" "This is Linda speaking."

The man spoke English with an Asian accent. "Would you please tell me how much you charge?" he asked politely.

"Fifty for half an hour and ninety for one hour." "Is it for a whole-set service?"

I was not in the mood to explain to him the detailed rates in that the whole-set service was seventy dollars for half an hour and one twenty for one hour. That was because I was very busy and also because I knew that those with such accents were most probably overseas students and they usually didn't have much money. So I answered, "Yes."

"How old are you?" he asked immediately.

It suddenly dawned on me that he must have thought I was not a very young prostitute as I charged so low. I told him I was thirty-five years old instead of forty-five.

"I am thirty-five. It doesn't matter, does it?"

I said while sucking Michael's balls with my tongue, "You come to quench your sexual thirst not to find a girlfriend. It makes no difference to me how old you are. In fact, I have some clients who are only eighteen or nineteen."

"Where are you from?" "I'm from Korea."

"You speak in a sort of Chinese accent. Shall we speak Chinese?" he asked.

"Haven't I told you I am Korean and I can't speak Chinese?" I was a little annoyed.

I moved my tongue away from Michael's balls and told him my address and reminded him that it was somewhere behind the Canberra Hospital.

"Please tell me how your address is spelt?"

I had to spell my address word for word for him. And his final answer was, "I'll think about it."

Bullshit. What a talkative fool.

"How old are you really?" Michael asked curiously. "Forty-five," I answered.

"You said you were twenty-eight when I first met you nine years ago. How come you are forty-five now?" he smiled.

"If I say I'm sixty, will you keep seeing me? You certainly will. Which prostitute will offer you service for a few hooves?"

"When I'm eighty and you're sixty-five, I'll still come to fuck you," he went on to say, "Hurry up. My cock can't wait to enter you!"

He rolled over and tucked me under him, poking his cock about between my thighs. "Put on the condom," I demanded.

"What's the relation between us? Surely I can fuck you without that nuisance," he said and taking advantage of my shock and hesitation, he thrust his cock into me and pulled it out at once.

"You really want to fuck me without the condom?" I had a grievance against him.

"So what if I fuck you without one?" he seemed to fear nothing.

"You've gone too far, mate. I'll cut off that thing of yours," I threatened.

"I'm just fucking you, fucking you, fucking you," he said brazenly.

He then playfully moved his cock in and out of my cunt and repeated his old tricks endlessly. I got so impatient that I sat up and gave his belly a push, "Are you finished?"

I turned back to take out a large-sized condom, tore open the sealed bag with my teeth and forced it on his cock. He pushed me down and fucked me deep with a sudden trust, "I fuck you. I love you." I echoed him under his body in order to have him come sooner. My next client was coming soon.

"Wrap your legs around my back," he demanded. I raised my legs and wrapped them around his waist tightly. He began to yell, "Oh! Oh! Oh, yes!" and sped up the frequency of his cock movements. The movements lasted only a dozen more times before he closed his eyes and collapsed on me.

"You are fucking good, you Chinese bastard," he heaved a satisfied sigh.

"*You* are the bastard!" I retorted.

(In English, it's okay to say *bastard* between close friends but it is abuse or even a provocation that will lead to a fight when it is said between unfamiliar acquaintances.)

I pulled Michael up and threw him a towel, "Go and have a shower. My next client is coming in no time. You gave some pork legs for all the services of sucking and fucking. What a deal!"

Having aired all my grievances, I hurried to the bathroom in the waiting room to have a shower. I squatted under the nozzle and used the vaginal washes bought from the chemist to clean the outside and inside of my cunt thoroughly. After washing up, I dried myself with a clean towel. Looking up at the clock hanging on the wall, I found it was almost half past six. I ran back to the working room and put on my favorite rosy, string dress which left my back exposed. I stood before the mirror, turned around and scrutinized myself. I felt at last very satisfied with that appealing lady in the mirror. I then collected all the used towels from the bed and discarded them into the laundry basket in the toilet. At that time the old Michael had finished dressing.

The doorbell rang. I shut the door to the working room and told Michael I would be back in a couple of minutes.

I took a comb from the dining table on my way to the mirror.

I combed my hair hastily before I went to answer the door.

I opened the door and to my expected delight, it was my handsome, immaculately dressed lawyer lover. He was in his forties, neither too tall nor too short; neither too fat nor too thin. He wore a well-cut black suit and a black tie today. His broad shoulders and sturdy physique showed he had frequented the gym. He had grayish blond hair and a square face, protruded forehead and a pair of sunken blue eyes under a pair of blond eyebrows. Under his good-looking Grecian nose was a shapely mouth. His nice appearance and genteel manners characteristic of western gentlemen combined to make him a very handsome and appealing man. He was the kind of man I referred to as a "sharpie": well dressed, cleanly shaven and a smooth talker.

I didn't know his surname or first name nor did I want to ask.

He said to me smilingly, "It looks like you're very busy."

"There is rarely a day when I am not busy." "How long should I wait?" he asked.

"A couple of minutes." "That's all right."

He stepped in and brought with him a refreshing scent of a men's cologne I was very familiar with. He must have spent a lot of time in front of the mirror before he came here. He bent down to kiss my hair, "How I've been missing you. We haven't met for a month, have we?"

"You can say that. You are always so occupied," I said with emotion.

We walked to the waiting room while talking. "Just wait a couple of minutes. Relax and watch the video programs. You may help yourself to any drinks or food in the refrigerator."

I closed the door and went to old Michael. He said, "You're really busy. Does he have a big cock or a small one?"

I pulled a long face and said, "It's none of your business. Hurry up and go." When he passed the dining table, he picked a packet of chips and a handful of cashews, "Give me a can of Coke with no sugar."

I took out two bottles of Coke Zero from the refrigerator and handed them to him, "Look, you haven't paid a penny for eating, drinking, taking my things and fucking me. If every client was like you, my business would surely go bankrupt."

He went to the door, laughing, "We are good friends, aren't we?"

"All clients are my friends. If they were all like you, I would have to live on air with no money earned."

I shut the door behind him and ran to meet my lover, "Sorry to have kept you waiting." Seeing that the lawyer was still standing there watching TV, I asked softly, "Why don't you have something to drink?"

He answered that he had. After I led him to the working room he looked around the room and commented, "I have been away for just a month and the room has taken on a new look."

"To give my clients a feeling of novelty."

He had two fifty-dollar notes in his hand and handed them to me, "Here you are."

"Thank you," I accepted the money and opened a glass door of a cabinet, "Please hang your clothes on the hangers, would you like a shower first?"

"I've just come back from the fitness center and had a shower there."

"I have also had a bath just now. That will save us a lot of trouble."

I paved the bed with clean bed sheets and got the pillows ready. Then I said to him, "Please wait here for two minutes, I'll be back in no time." I turned and went to put the money in the drawer. When I came back, he had just taken off his suit and tie and hung them in the wardrobe. His shirt looked especially white against the flickering reflection made up of all colors in the spectrum from red, orange, yellow, green, blue, indigo to violet. He looked healthy, handsome and robust. His large, dark-blue, smiling eyes were fixed on me. The video was in the "Mute" state and only the erotic pictures could be seen flickering on the screen. Light Chinese music was playing over the stereo. Its graceful melody and leisurely rhythm impressed us with an oriental serenity; creating a warm, romantic atmosphere. He seemed to be affected by the music and said with emotion, "How beautiful. How I adore Chinese music!"

He wrapped his arms around my waist. And I, in turn, wrapped my arms around his neck and pressed my creamy, plump breasts tightly against his chest. We began to dance away to the slow, 4/4 beat, swaying our bodies together. I used to be an avid dancer when I was young and it seemed he was also expert at dancing and could equal me in having a good sense of rhythm. The lyrics of the Chinese melody translated to: "My love is an intangible web; my love is an unbridled wave; why does the thought of you come back always when I am tramping? My heart is the sea in June..."The tune was orchestrated melodiously and sprightly. As I remembered most of the words, I couldn't help humming to the music. When I stopped at the pause of an interlude he bent down to gaze at me, "You have a very nice voice."

I said, "When I was in China, I was not only an enthusiastic dancer but a good singer. Since coming to Australia and becoming a prostitute, I have rarely showed my talents in public."

"Why not sing and dance for me?" he said, "Linda, you're really beautiful. You're one of my small secrets. I enjoy being with you."

"You don't say so," I said somewhat shyly, "I feel obviously older these days."

"No. You look just as young as you did when I met you eight years ago," he said sincerely.

"Really?" I was flattered, "I'm getting fatter. You simply can't stop getting fat after you pass the age of forty. You put on weight even if you only drink water without eating anything else. Look, my hair has turned grey and I have to dye it."

He pointed to his own hair, "I am also grey-haired"

"When blond hair turns grey, the difference is hardly noticeable. So you still look young and robust. As we Chinese put it, you're a gentleman of striking appearance and demeanor."

Just then, I suddenly thought of something and shifted the topic of our conversation, "One thing I'd like to ask you. Remember I told you I bought two houses in Sydney four years ago?"

"I've heard you mention it several times," he answered.

"These two houses cover a land size of 26,000 square feet and I had intended to demolish the existing houses and build four new houses on the land. I would have kept two of the houses and sold the other two. Only recently did I discover that one of the houses is a historic heritage site and is forbidden from being demolished. The other house can be demolished for building two new houses but they can't be sold separately. It turned out to be a different story from what my solicitor told me initially. I asked my solicitor why she failed to share that pertinent information with me in advance and she explained she wasn't able to remember all the cases, as she was dealing with four or five hundred house cases every year."

He smiled, "As a lawyer, how could she not remember her own cases?"

"When I kept demanding an explanation from her, she told me I could sue her and then added that I may as well sue her agency. The insurance company would compensate if anything went wrong. She has nothing to lose, because she had left that agency to set up one of her own. She assured me she would testify on my behalf that it was her fault so the insurance company would compensate me."

"This is a difficult case," he commented, "I'm afraid she won't say so in court. If she insists she has told you anything about it before the sale, do you have any evidence that she is lying?"

"I have no energy to engage in lawsuits." I felt powerless.

"And it's hard to estimate your losses in the sale," he said.

"Well, let's forget that antique (from the time I knew that house was a historic heritage site that couldn't be demolished, I referred to it as an antique). Now no one wants to buy it. As for the other house that can be demolished, its selling price is six hundred and five thousand dollars. I bought it four years ago at a price of five hundred and thirty-five thousand, plus stamp duty of more than twenty thousand dollars, and I have been paying more than three thousand dollars of interest on the home loan every month. Over four years, I've paid the bank more than one hundred thousand dollars for nothing. And what's worse, I have fixed the home loan interest for five years. Now that I know it cannot be demolished for any new buildings, I want to sell the house. And that will mean terminating the contract with the bank and the bank will deduct a penalty of two thousand five hundred dollars. Figured out how much my losses have added up to?"

"What about renting out the houses?"

"Hey," I said, feeling depressed, "They are very old houses and the rent was a mere one thousand dollars a month and something always needed repairing. I was shocked when the tenants presented me with a water bill of one thousand five hundred dollars to pay! It was the astronomically high water bill that made me decide to sell the house. You see, the mention of the house has reminded me of so much trouble."

"You have lost a lot of money this time," he said sympathetically. "I have made a lot of money these last four years," I said, "However I have handed over the hard-earned bucks to the bank on a silver platter. I didn't understand what it was to be 'a slave of the house'. Now I see I have been 'a slave of the house' by submissively working for the bank without any pay for four years."

He was amused, "There's a saying that clever people may be misled by their own cleverness. You are earning money from your business while losing money on your houses."

"And how much more I will lose on these houses will depend on whether I can sell these antique houses," I sighed.

"Now that the problem has arisen," he tried to comfort me, "Let's find a way to solve it."

"I would love to sell these two houses as soon as possible. I get really disgusted at the thought of them. "

"Now, stop talking about the unhappy things," he suggested, "Let me give you a good hug."

Slow waltz in triple time was being played over the stereo. The orchestra presented the distinct rhythm, followed by a percussion of gongs and drums: triple-time beat --- Bong, Cha, Cha; Bong, Cha, Cha. As I had been away from China for a long time, I unforgivably forgot the title of this famous tune but I was quick in shifting slow quadruple-time into slow triple- time step and he followed suit just as quickly. You see, there were no boundaries in art, especially in music. I slowly undid the buttons on his shirt one by one. His blond, hairy bosom looked irresistibly sexy.

"Look," I said, "You look like a monkey."

"So I don't fear the coldness in winter," he smiled, "Do you like hairy men?"

"I have told you so many times I like hairy men." I said, "They are more masculine and look more like real men."

I tossed his shirt onto the massage bed and scrutinized his sturdy, broad shoulders and muscled chest. I appreciated his masculine figure very much: broad shoulders, strong arms, perfectly slim waist and solid hips. I couldn't help but reach out my arms and wrap them around his buttocks while he slowly slid off my rosy, string dress, letting it fall to my ankles and pressed my round, white breasts tightly against his hairy bosom.

"You are just like a glass of red wine. A single sip is enough to make me half intoxicated," he said with a smile.

"You can't drink too much of this wine," I teasingly warned him, "Otherwise you will get as drunk as a lord."

At that time, I couldn't wait to loosen his belt and unzip and free him of his trousers. I tucked my hand into his briefs to fumble his cock, which was as hard as anything. I was only too familiar with his cock and had enjoyed it almost a hundred times for the last nine years.

"You have a nice big cock," I admired sincerely. "It's not big, dear," he patted me on the cheek.

"If yours were small, there would be no cock in the world that could be called big." I wondered, "Hasn't your wife told you what a big cock you have?"

"My wife has never seen any other man's cock," he said seriously.

By then I had already taken off all his clothes and shoes. I came to the bedside table and showed him an aerosol can of air freshener, saying "Compare it with your cock to see whether they are alike in size, and even in thickness."

He laughed and I said, "Well I say your cock is nice. Look, yours is as straight as this aerosol can," comparing his cock with the can, "And besides, the tip of your cock is smoothly pointed. Up to now I have seen at least dozens of thousands of cocks and have never seen a cock as perfect as yours. Among them some are as small as peppers and some are not straight, either bending right or bending left; either cocking skyward or dangling earthward. Yours is really the number one, nice big cock in Australia."

"Am I as nice as my cock?" he asked amusedly.

"As to cocks," I answered earnestly, "I am surely the most qualified judge. The number of cocks I have seen has already exceeded a five-figure number. Some prostitutes may have taken on this occupation earlier than me but they can't have seen more cocks than me because some of them may only serve several clients a day while I am following a price competition on the basis of small profits but quick turnover, so I can serve fifteen to twenty clients a day. What kind of cocks haven't I witnessed? Old or young ones, big or tiny ones, black or white ones, long or short ones, soft or hard ones. Of all the cocks I have seen, yours is the number one, beautiful big cock. Yours is not only nice and big, but also excellent in quality and performance. Some cocks are big enough in size but are lacking hardness. They can hardly last a few minutes before they become saggy and that sort of thing can only spoil the mood. All in all, you are perfect everywhere. If I were not a prostitute, I would marry you. Your wife is really a connoisseur of cocks and fortunate to take possession of yours." I opened my mouth wide and took pains to swallow his cock and began to suck it. The smile froze on his face and he seemed to have fallen into a painful pleasure. We were just engrossed in our foreplay when the doorbell rang loudly. Damn it. Who must come to interrupt us at the most inopportune moment and without making an appointment in advance?

In order to save time, I just grabbed a silk material with a blue, floral design about six feet long and threw it over my body. I drew the two ends of the material and made a bow tie between my breasts. Despite the fact that the make-shift dress failed to cover my shoulders or private part, I hurried to the door. I was about to utter a curse when the electrician knocked into me.

"Darling, you look sexy," he cried, trying to take me into his arms only to find my shaved private part, "Hey. You're just like a teenage virgin."

"I almost forgot you were coming," I brushed aside his hands, "But I have no time to serve you today. I have another big cock to attend to. Your task today is to fix the lights in the bathroom." Then I led him to the bathroom in the waiting room and showed him which ceiling lights were out of order. He went to the garage and fetched an aluminum ladder. He got the ladder steady and climbed up to check the lights.

"I have just changed the bulbs," I raised my head and shouted to him on top of the ladder, "They are both newly bought."

"Then you'll have to pay for the replacement," he said, "I'll go onto the roof to have a look."

"I'll give you a hundred and fifty dollars now. You have to make sure the lights are on tonight."

He got down from the ladder and said, "I have a replacement in my car. We don't need to buy new ones."

"I don't care what you do but you must turn the lights on. Is one fifty enough?"

"Yes. Enough."

"Just go ahead. I have a client to attend to now," I said.

I felt assured of his workmanship since he had been serving me for so many years.

When I went back to the working room, my lawyer friend was lying on the bed, on his back, his eyes fixed on the porn videos on the walls, his ears tuned into the Chinese music and his cock dancing away like a drunkard on a sidewalk. I smiled apologetically and said sorry to him. I immediately tossed the silk material around me onto the floor and sat by his left side on the bed. Propped on my left elbow, I rested my head on his left leg and was now face to face with his big cock. I used my left hand to fumble his balls and my right to grip his cock. My right leg was bent, exposing my cunt, which could be clearly seen from the side mirror.

He reached out his hand to run his fingers along my private part, "What a clean-shaven cunt! It looks like a teenage girl's."

"I have to shave it. The hair is turning grey."

"We grow older with every day," he smiled philosophically. "I just hope I can have as hard a cock as I do now to fuck you with when I turn sixty."

"I'm old now," I said, not without sentiment, "Handsome as you are, you should go to the brothel to find younger and prettier girls."

"I'm really not interested in younger girls," he said very earnestly, "To tell you the truth, I haven't been to any brothel except for your house."

I nodded my agreement. My life experience as a prostitute for years had dissuaded me from the belief that he was a frequenter of any brothel.

"There are two reasons," he went on to explain, "One is that I am indeed too busy. The other is that I have a beautiful wife and two lovely children. The only purpose of my coming here is to seek excitement and relaxation and make me keener on making love to my wife when I go back home."

"Yes, sex exists in your own imagination. Well, if my memory serves me, you have a son and a daughter."

"Yes. An eighteen-year-old son and a fifteen-year-old daughter," he said very proudly.

"You are a lucky man," I said, "Good wife, good son and good daughter. Nothing else is to be desired if you have a happy family life."

"But we are never satisfied with what we already have," he smiled mysteriously, "You see, I often come to see you, don't I? Everybody has his own secret and it's the same with every man and his wife."

"Of course you can't tell your wife everything you do. You would be very foolish if you did. It is not uncommon for a man and wife to keep a secret or two from each other. Perhaps sometimes it is just the small secrets that will lubricate the friction in your life and tint your marriage with a bit of mysterious color."

I supported myself on my left elbow between his legs, my left hand caressing his balls, my right gripping his cock and my mouth opening wide to swallow the tip of his bulging cock. This was the standard posture that I formed during many years of my service so the skin on my left elbow always looked blue. Many clients asked what was wrong with it and some of them guessed the elbow had been bruised because of my carelessness. When I answered jokingly that it was caused by long years of habitual working postures, they all laughed at my witty humor!

I began to suck his big cock and felt it jerking even harder than before. Men in their forties were in the prime of their lives and were most energetic. He took a deep breath and then let out a yell "Oh," followed by a longer howl of "Oh---." I used my tongue to lick the blunt tip of his cock and the small crevice on his cock tip while he thrust his left forefinger into my opening and asked, "Do you enjoy my finger in your cunt?"

"Yes, I do," I answered, "It's very enjoyable."

"How are you feeling now?" he added his middle finger into my cunt.

"Honey, spare me of your extra finger please. I have been busy all day long and so has my cunt. It will be serving that big cock of yours later."

He withdrew his extra finger. A melodious Chinese tune "*A Twig of Plum Blossom*" was playing in the room. Making love to one's lover to such beautiful background music was really an unforgettable experience in life. I couldn't help humming to the tune, though I didn't remember all the words. He narrowed his eyes and seemed immersed in the sexual pleasure as he too hummed along to the exotic background music. When it came to the stanza: "… Love whoever I love without regret; the love is lingering in my heart…" I spat his cock out and began to sing aloud heartily. After singing passionately, I said just as passionately to him, "I love your cock."

"Do you really love my cock?" he asked gently.

"Yes, it's beautiful," I sincerely admired, "It's a work of art. It's simply a perfect copy of the cock of an ancient Grecian statue."

I went on to suck his cock and he kept on groaning with his eyes narrowed,"Oh my. Oh my." for about five minutes before he yelled, "Let me fuck you!"

"What position?"

"You on top of me," he said, "But I'll relieve you when you're tired."

How come every client today chose awoman-on-top position? You all know how to enjoy yourselves and are determined as if by prior consultation to leave me working hard on top of you? Nursing such a grievance in my mind, I mounted him. He poked his cock upright to tantalize the bud and lips of my cunt several times before he exerted all his strength to thrust it into me. My cunt felt at once, filled fully and even bursting painfully and my stomach ached too. I knew his was one of the biggest cocks I had ever seen and it took me several minutes to get over the initial pain of penetration.

We were echoing each other's groans, immersed in erotic pleasure when we heard someone walking on the roof. I hastily explained to him that it was the electrician checking the circuit on the roof. Hearing this, he seemed a little relieved. I prayed that the big-cock electrician would leave soon so that my other big cock wouldn't be disturbed any longer. I knew that having that kind of dick, it was hard to make him come. He was one of those who could only come undisturbed. If the noise on the roof went on and distracted him from the sexual intercourse, he wouldn't be able to come at all. But the noise of the heavy steps on the roof grew even louder. In order to distract his attention, I began sitting up and down on his cock to the beat of the music and shouted one, two, three and four. He threw up his hips to meet me and it was seven or eight minutes before he said, "Well, let me relieve you. Look, you are gasping for breath."

"Never mind. Actually I'm exercising. My family doctor told me that sexual intercourse is the equivalent of walking four miles. Since I serve so many clients every day you can easily guess how many miles of walking my daily work entails. That's why I'm getting stronger and stronger."

"You've got the best job," he smiled, "Making money, getting exercise and enjoying yourself, three in one."

"I think I've got the best job of my life," I confessed.

At that time, I felt totally worn out and rested my head against his hairy, barrel-like chest, "Well, let me have a break. I've had too much exercise and I'm really exhausted."

He gently wrapped his arms around my waist and said, "Now have a break, baby. Have a break." He bent down to kiss my right nipple. No sooner had his tongue tip touched my nipple than a piercing, pulse inched through my body all the way to the length to my toes. I was immersed in a feeling of thrilling relaxation. I narrowed my eyes and moaned heavily, then let out a long howl of "Ohhh..." With his big cock squeezed by my cunt, I twisted my buttocks in all possible directions to give him more pleasure, making him yell at the top of his lungs, "Oh, yes! Oh, yes!" My female lecherous gasp and his male carnal roar combined to form a wonderful duet of sexual intercourse. We were on top of the world and reaching our climaxes almost simultaneously.

"Just have a break, baby," he said, "Let me relieve you."

I dismounted from his belly and was about to lie on my back beside him when I thought of something, "Wait a minute, honey. Now that there's no noise coming from the roof, I'll see if the electrician has finished his work."

I closed the door and went to the bathroom barefoot and bare-hipped, to have an inspection. How wonderful. The big- cock electrician was fabulous. The ceiling lights were shining brilliantly there. I went to the back door and found that the electrician had left. I shut the back door and went to the front door to see it closed too. I hurried back to the working room, "Honey, no one will disturb us. I closed all the doors and now we can enjoy ourselves as we please. Now come on, gentleman. Mount me and fuck me until you've had your fill!"

CUNT

I left the door to the working room open, as we now had the whole house to ourselves. When he saw me come back bare-hipped, he took hold of me and threw me onto the bed, "You hot chick. Now I can shout out loudly: I want to fuck you! I want to fuck you!"

"You snake!" I said.

He came at me like a fierce wolf, "Let me treat you today with my big cock. I'd like you to have your fill of it."

With this, he probed his stick into my wet opening. I dodged and said, "Just wait a minute." I sat up and began to measure his cock's length by gripping it with my hands. Two grips and more.

"Look how big your cock is," I smiled, "It should be an XXX size."

"It's not small indeed," he said, kneeling on the bed. "Your dad's cock must be a big one."

"But I have never seen my dad's cock."

"Generally speaking, the gene of big cocks is heritable. Big-Cock Grandpa should have a big-cock dad. Their male offspring most probably have big cocks. By the way, your son must have a big cock too, does he?"

We were playing jokes on each other when he asked me, "Do you like bigger cocks or smaller ones?"

"Haven't I told you I prefer bigger ones? Everyone does, men and women alike. I have several clients who have smaller cocks.

They often pester me with silly questions such as how they can have their cocks lengthened and I advise them to find a good cosmetic surgeon to enlarge and lengthen their cocks."

We burst out laughing. He pushed me down on the bed and yelled, "Let my big cock fuck your big cunt."

"Hey, hey," I tried to correct his statement, "Everybody likes big cocks but no one likes big cunts."

"But I do" he said, "Because small cunts can't swallow my big cock."

"My cunt has been widened by repeatedly filling up with cocks. When I first began my career in the brothel, I ran away immediately at the sight of any big cock. And this made our boss very angry…"

We were both laughing when his mobile phone buzzed. He put his forefinger to his lips, gesturing me to be quiet. I stopped laughing as he picked up the phone.

"Hello Darling, I just got off work and I am now at the gym. I will stay here for an hour and a half. I will bring you a bunch of roses when I come back." I couldn't hear what the person said on the other line, but it was clear it was a woman. He kept repeating "yes" and "okay," and finally he said, "Darling, I love you" and switched off his mobile. He then held me in his arms and said the same thing. I thought he was still thinking about the woman on the phone, so I asked him, "Was that you wife?"

He nodded.

"Who, between us do you love more?" "I love both of you equally." He replied. "Aren't you clever?" I jested.

"Enough talk, let me fuck you."

As I lay under him, I spread my legs apart and wrapped them around the narrowest part of his waist. He suddenly thrust his cock all the way in until he filled me to the hilt. I couldn't help crying out, "Ouch. You're hurting me! Take your time!"

"Sorry, I was too rude," he apologized. "I was almost pierced through," I said.

"Hold out a little longer and you'll feel looser and more comfortable."

How similar he sounded to the two big cocks before him, I thought. He knelt on the bed and used his powerful legs to thrust his peerless cock inside me, causing my thighs to be dampened with lust fluid. The lust water continued soaking my thighs to the rhythm of his pistoning cock. He was less and less scrupulous and cried out, "Oh--- Ah--- Aye--- Yes!" Each cry became louder and longer than the one before and reflected his innermost, carnal pleasure. I echoed him. Each of his relentless thrusts reached as far as the opening of my womb and made me thrill and shudder with ecstasy.

At that time I already regarded him as my husband, my sweetheart, my lover, my honey or my dearest one. If he had asked me, "Do you love me?" I would have answered without hesitation, "Yes, I love you. I love your big cock. I love your body. I love every part of you!"

I savored every impact of his cock. It was so energetic, so relentless, so satisfying and so enjoyable. I was experiencing a sense of pleasure that made me thrill and shudder. I was driven by him to the brink of collapsing from carnal ecstasy.

Before I became a prostitute, I had married twice and had several lovers, but it was not my past husbands and lovers but my clients who had given me the highest level of sexual satisfaction. There were a lot of masters at lovemaking among my clients but only a few of them, say at most a little over a dozen, who could make love in perfect unison with me to reach the sublime of carnal enjoyment. After years of practice, we could now match perfectly in mating and knew each other's favorite positions or most sensitive parts as well as the timing of each stage of lovemaking.

So we fucked away to the beat of the music, from fast quadruple time to slow triple time and vice versa. While he pushed and pulled his cock deliberately slowly, his fingers ran gently over my nipples. He knew only too well they were the most sensitive spots on my body and he could make me come more quickly just by caressing them. My nipples erected and hardened at once and a hot thrill ran through the length of my spine to my heart and down through my legs to the soles of my feet.

This ecstasy of sex reminded me of one of my lovers— Zhang Haiyang, an out-and-out playboy, who had relations with countless girls in China. Memories of him flashed through my mind: he was making love to a girl of eighteen. With every movement, he would ask, "Do I fuck you happy?" The girl was savoring every fucking movement and answered, "Happy. Very happy."

The close-up scenes of Zhang's lovemaking sessions kept flashing before my eyes. His cock was steadily grinding inside the girl's cunt, making her cunt lips flap in and out with a lot of bubbling water. I was imagining that I was the girl under him and a hot thrill ran down my spine. My head suddenly became blank and I yelled out, "I am coming! Fuck me hard! My darling." As if encouraged by my yelling, he sped up the pace of his cock movements inside me, his belly pounding against mine. I groaned painfully for a while before I said, "Fuck me harder, darling."

One, two, three, four, I reached my climax four times in succession. This time I came completely as if my brain had been sluiced thoroughly by water. The big-cock lawyer's continual yells "Oh. Oh." nearly joined to form a long continuous howl "Oh ---," followed by a soul-stirring "Ah ---." He ejaculated all the sperm as white as yogurt on my belly.

He breathed heavily for a while before he said to me with a smile, "Hard work isn't it?"

"This is the best way to exercise," I said, "Like I told you before, I have just walked four miles according to my doctor. And moreover, what we were doing was high-quality sexual activity."

"Do you tell every client this?" he asked, not without malice. "Yes," I said, "I do intend for them to come here more frequently. It's much better to come here than to go to the fitness center, which is both exhausting and tedious." "You're really good at doing business."

"You can't do your business well without promotion." I smiled, patting him on the cheek, "How can I be frequented by so many regular clients if I only sell flesh without proper hospitality?"

He couldn't help laughing, "What a smart businesswoman you are!"

I got up to fetch him a towel and told him, "Go and take a shower. Then I'll give you a massage on your back. It has taken me sometime to attend the electrician so let me make up for the time wasted. I'll give you an extra fifteen minutes' service."

Then I went to the bathroom in the waiting room to have a shower. I squatted under the nozzle and cleaned my private part thoroughly from outside to inside.

Honestly, I'd be lying if I said I fucked every client with a condom on. I do have a couple of frequenters who I make love to without condoms. After years of acquaintance, some of my clients have also become my lovers. They don't go to just any brothel. Instead, they only come to me for a change when they grow tired of their wives or girlfriends. Our relationships are built on trust. I exercise sound judgment in deciding on a short list of those who can have direct contact with my cunt without that thin layer of rubber.

This lawyer has been my patron for over eight years and only in the past six months has he been able to make love to me without that scumbag. After years of observation, I am certain that he is not a frequenter of any brothels apart from my house. As for him, and a few other patrons, I can offer services in a more loose and unrestrained atmosphere and they can gain more sensual pleasure from me than from their wives or girlfriends.

When I finished bathing and went back to the working room, the big-cock lawyer had lain face down on the bed. I sat astride his back, gripped his shoulders and massaged them with my forefingers and thumbs. He breathed out a satisfied groan, "I must say you have a strong pair of hands."

"I'm jumping and hopping from the bed to the floor and from the floor to the bed all day. It is virtually a special kind of exercise. And surprisingly, the frequent sexual activity is beneficial to my health. For six or seven years, I haven't got any flu or discomforts such as headaches or stomachaches. My cunt, which used to suffer from inflammation, has now been eliminated of any diseases and passed all the medical examinations in the hospital. I guess exercising my cunt muscles every time I fuck may account for all this. The more I exercise my cunt the healthier and stronger it becomes."

"Your cunt has seen the world," he said teasingly.

"I have seen more cocks than eight generations of women in my family added up."

"Linda, could you tell me honestly,"he asked me, in sad earnest, "How many clients do you make love to without condoms?"

"A good question," I answered, "If I said I only make love to you without a condom, I'd be lying. I must admit there have been several others over the last ten years."

"I'm jealous knowing you fuck others without condoms," he said.

"Well, I'm jealous that you sleep with your wife at home." We both laughed.

After I finished massaging the lawyer, I went to fetch a bottle of wine while he was dressing. I said to him, "A bottle of wine for you to drink at home."

He declined by waving his hands, "No thanks. So as to avoid my old girl questioning where it came from."

I saw him off at the doorstep and right before he left, I grabbed his shoulder from behind and whispered to him "You really should double check if you have left your cock at my place, your wife wouldn't be very happy if she found out that you have left something behind."

"Don't you worry about that, my little elf," he kissed me on the forehead. "I will see you next time."

"Have a good night." I said.

I looked at the clock to find it was nearly eight o'clock. No wonder it was so dark and it was high time I found something to stuff my stomach with.

I took a pack of beef steaks out of the fridge, turned on the stove and let the steaks sizzle on the non-stick pan. I then grabbed a bottle of low-alcoholic beer and a bag of salad from the fridge as well. I drank the beer over the salad and occasionally threw one or two red peppers into my mouth. I am addicted to hot and spicy food. Around the time of my menstruation, I can swallow up a bowl of rice without anything else except the peppers. I savor every mouthful I eat, especially after I have come completely. It was a coincidence this evening that I not only had I just come but it also happened to be a couple of days before my menstruation. So I needed something particularly hot to whet my appetite. The beef steaks were now ready. I put the steaks on the plate, cut them into pieces and forked one piece into my mouth."Wonderful!" I said, "But not hot enough." Well, peppers were not hot enough and I searched the fridge for garlic. When I found some garlic, I peeled a few cloves and ate them raw. I crunched the raw garlic cloves, loudly. As if that was not enough to reduce me to tears, I added a raw, Chinese onion and finally, a piece of raw ginger into my mouth also. The combination of the hottest peppers, green onions, garlic, and ginger tasted extraordinarily hot. The taste of burning heat excited the taste buds of my tongue and made everything taste more delicious. I savored the beer over the steaks. I had just gulped down the last of the beer. The icy fluid flowed through my throat to my stomach and I felt comfortable and intoxicated. How delicious. How wonderful! I took another bottle of beer and went on to drink more.

When you reach the stage of half drunkenness, how could you remember the doctor's warning not to drink alcohol? The warning had already been thrown out the window. I was chewing the steak with the garlic and two red peppers when the mobile rang. I hurriedly swallowed down the food in my mouth.

"Hello?"

"How are you? Are you busy?" A voice on the other end came through the receiver and I recognized at once it was the sixty-two-year-old Brazilian man, a frequenter of mine for six years.

"No, not really," I said, "Come along."

"I'm coming in two minutes," he said promptly.

I supposed he must have been roaming around my house to see whether I had any clients with me and called in when he found no sign of any. I hastily had several sips of beer and tucked the half-emptied bottle back into the fridge.

Then the doorbell rang and the first sentence I heard was, "Old boy." Every time he came he said so. He used to be a little fatter. But recently he listened to his doctor's advice and went on a diet. The result of his efforts was apparent.

"You are a little too thin," I said.

"To be thin is better than to be fat," he put emphasis on "to be thin" as he raised two ten-dollar notes, two five-dollar notes and some coins in his hand. Every time he came, he invariably brought some coins with the notes, which added up to either thirty-five dollars or forty dollars. As he said he had no money and was out of work now, I charged him only thirty-five dollars for each service. This time I saw he was holding five two-dollar coins in his palm. I took thirty-four dollars and returned the other three two-dollar coins to him.

I led him to the working room and as he claimed he had taken a shower before coming, I piled one pillow on top of another and had him lie down on his back, "Would you like to listen to the light music or the background music of the videos?"

He answered that either would do.

I knew he liked dancing so I played light Chinese music for him. The screens only showed pictures without any sound. I got down on my knees and looked at his cock. His was neither big nor thick. It was just like a brownish-black-colored carrot. Grizzled hair about an inch long, sprawled from the area around his cock all the way to the navel of his belly.

I grasped the cock between his thighs and sucked it into my mouth. It was easy for me to swallow his cock to the hilt.

"You're the best sucker in Canberra," he said happily.

"Some have said I am the best sucker in Australia. My clients come from Perth, Brisbane, Melbourne, Sydney or Adelaide, from all over the country, or even all over the world. They generally acknowledge me as the number-one sucker in the world."

"Indeed," he said as his long fingers ran down his own belly, "You are the most professional, most expert sucker."

Then I began to suck his cock the way a baby suckles his mother's nipples. He cried "Oh ---" "Ah ---" and yelled, "I love that!" I changed course to lick the under part of his blunt tip and this caused him to shout even louder, "Wow ---" followed by a long howl of "Oh ---" and repeated exclamation, "Beautiful. Too beautiful."

He asked me, "Do you like my cock?"

"I like any cock," I spat out his cock, "whether they are big ones or small ones, black ones or white ones. Cocks are my ATM."

"Is my cock nice?" he asked, "Is it a large-size one or a small-size one? Or a medium-size one?"

"Yours is a medium-size one," I was telling him the truth. But I dared not say that his cock was not beautiful or anything like that. Every man believed his cock was the best just as every woman believed she was the most beautiful. That's because ordinary men actually had no opportunities to witness the cocks of other men. But as for me, things were different. For nearly ten years, I have witnessed so many cocks, big or small, old or young, black or white, simply an exhibition of cocks galore. I have grasped and weighed and sucked more than a dozen cocks a day. How many beautiful cocks can be found among a sea of cocks?

He smiled and said to me, "I want to marry you."

"How many times have you told me you want to marry me?" "Three or four times?" I was not the least bit surprised, "And haven't I told you I don't want to be married? I would be sick to death of facing one and only cock all day long. You don't think there aren't any men willing to marry me because I am a prostitute, do you? Your offer of marriage isn't exactly some act of charity. To tell you the truth, there are at least one or two hundred men on a long list who have proposed marriage to me and their ages range from twenty-two to eighty."

He smiled again, "I have never married in my life." "Then you have no children?"

"I have two sons. They are now grown-ups."

"I'm afraid I will never marry again." I sighed, "I like my present lifestyle. I can fiddle with a variety of cocks at will and appreciate the beauty of them the way I appreciate works of art. Cocks can make me intoxicated and immersed in endless pleasure. So I don't want to get married."

I went on to suck his tiny cock and made him yell, "Ah, yes!" again. But it was not long before he began to grunt,"Hey, Linda. What's in your mouth that has made my cock so hot?"

"How come your cock feels hot now? I had some peppers quite a while ago, and besides, I rinsed my mouth just before you came," I smiled.

"No, no," he argued, "You have to rinse your mouth again. My cock can't endure anymore." When I helped him pull his little thing out, it had turned crimson red.

He jumped to his feet and paced around the room. Playing with his little cock in one hand, he aired his grievances, "Ouch, my poor cock. It is almost burnt to death."

"My mouth has been numbed by the hot peppers,"I chuckled, "I've lost all my senses in my mouth."

"Lost all your senses in your mouth?" he protested, "but my cock is burning as if it were on fire. Ouch, I can't bear the pain anymore."

He paced about on the floor in anguish, not knowing what to do. I came up to comfort him, "Stop pacing, it won't do you any good. Why don't you try cooling your cock with cold water?"

He hurried into the bathroom to try my suggested therapy while I ran to the sink to gargle hard and brush my teeth with toothpaste.

When I finished rinsing my mouth and came back to the bed, the old boy from Brazil was already flat on his back. I squatted between his thighs and began to suck his penis. He sighed,"Now your mouth feels cooler."

"It's a special service called the *pleasure between ice and fire*," I said casually.

"Yes," he agreed, "My cock was undergoing coldness and hotness alternatively. It can really give you a kick."

"You're lucky," I said, "Some of my other clients have asked me for this special service, but I simply refused. The other day, I sucked a client soon after I ate some peppers. He later commented that his cock enjoyed the feeling of hotness and that it had greatly whetted his sexual desire."

"Well," the Brazilian old boy said,"I can make do with a mild hotness in your mouth, but don't try serving me immediately after you've had some hot peppers. They are so hot that my cock will be cooked on the spot."

It was about a quarter before I said, "Let's make love, shall we?" I found a medium-sized condom and asked him, "You're on top of me? Or would you like me from behind?"

As his cock was not hard enough for me to sit on him, I didn't ask him if he wanted me on top, so as not to hurt his pride as a man.

"I'll be on top," he answered.

I tucked a pillow under my buttocks, which was his favorite position, so that he could thrust his tiny cock deeper. He used his right hand to help his tiny cock erect by pinching the root of his cock and supporting it. He sprawled on me and I raised my legs to let him in. I echoed his yells, "Oh, yes. Fuck me," my arms wrapped around his neck and my legs around his waist. He pounded away his cock and kept yelling, "Eh –."

His impotent cock was hovering inside my cunt for a while before he complained, "I'm afraid your cunt is a little too loose. My cock has no feeling in it. I guess you need vaginal tightening surgery to suture part of it."

"If so," I retorted, "you'll be satisfied but what about my big-cocked clients?"

"I don't care," he answered, "It's all well if I'm well."

"How selfish of you," I said, "You're just thinking of yourself. How about I pinch my cunt with my fingers to adapt to that little thing of yours?" We both dissolved into a roar of laughter.

"I like to fuck you while watching your pretty face," he said, ogling me, "Look into my eyes, Linda. You're so pretty."

"I'm older now." I evaded his eyes and heaved a sigh, "So many of my patrons vied with each other to praise my beauty. But these last two years, I feel my beauty is beginning to fade away. Almost every part of my body is quickly aging and I'm afraid my cunt is among them."

"No, you are not old," he said earnestly. "I can't find any wrinkles on your face. Your cunt is nice except that it's a little too loose."

"Yes, I have no wrinkles in my eye corners," I tried to explain, "But that's because I have never had babies. As to your complaint that my cunt is a little too loose, I have no other comment. But didn't I pinch my cunt to make it feel tight for you?"

"But how come I can't feel your cunt?" he was wondering. "An old cunt can't be young again," I sighed.

"How old are you?" "Guess."

"Thirty-eight? Or forty?"

"Wrong guess," I said, "I'm now nearly fifty."

"You, nearly fifty?" he laughed, "Incredible. Some women are still very sexy in their fifties while some girls fail to be sexy in their teenage years. I hope I can be strong enough to fuck you in my seventies."

"I will go on with this business as long as there are customers who are willing to patronize me," I said, with a longing look in my eyes,"Until one day, some customers begin to complain about the old woman. Who cares about that old cunt of hers? And one by one, the customers will walk away. Then I will stop business. When no one comes, with whom do I do business with?"

He burst into laughter, "Live and fuck. It may be your motto."

"Why not?" I argued, "Unless no client who comes is willing to pay me. As far as I know, there is a prostitute named Cooper in the United States. She is now ninety-six and still in service; the oldest prostitute in Taiwan is already eighty, old enough to be my grandmother. She began to receive clients at the age of sixty. Despite the fact that she was caught soliciting clients by the police and was forbidden to do it again, she stayed in service well into her old age. I'm nearly fifty now and my goal is to continue my business for another thirty years before I retire."

"Now I needn't be afraid I will have no cunt to fuck." He said childishly, "It's less expensive to come to you than to live with a girlfriend. Besides, I often quarrel with my girlfriends. Over the years I have tried living with a couple of girlfriends but invariably end up separating. Within only a couple of months, we would start quarrelling with each other."

"Many of my clients have said so too. It's less expensive to come to me. But anyway, I think couples that live together should tolerate and understand each other. Everyone has flaws and makes mistakes."

We were chatting and chatting without noticing that his cock was quite obviously shrinking and sagging. Seeing that our intercourse couldn't be continued, I said, "Come on. Let's stop the chatter and refresh your cock."

He pulled out his shrunken cock from my cunt and managed to nudge it back into my cunt with the help of his hand and continued, "I can fuck you."

Just then, the doorbell rang. Having no more appointments at this hour, I knew it must be some rash guy who tried to take advantage of every possible gap in time to cut in the waiting line. He was too careless not to notice the car parked in my car spot near the garage. I had to pull his cock out of my hole, "Sorry, but you have to wait two minutes."

I grabbed a black spaghetti-strap dress, threw it over my head and went to the door barefoot. I opened the door, "Hey. Did you come here yesterday? How come you've come today again? And without an appointment. I am busy now."

"Sorry," he apologized, "I came back to the hotel when I knocked off. After a shower and dinner, I still felt uncomfortable with my cock. So I can't help coming here to see you."

This was a new client about forty. A muscleman; not tall but strong. It was obvious at first sight that he was a sturdy and masculine man. He was a worker on a construction site. His home was in Sydney. Apart from his big cock and occupation, I knew very little about him. I didn't know nor had I the necessity to know his name, his age, his address, his telephone number or his marital status. We are prostitutes, not doctors and do not require our clients to register their personal details when they enter our houses. That will frighten them away. They will be wondering why a prostitute should know so much about them and whether she will inform their wives or families.

Our business is just a trading of money for sex, nothing else. I led him to the waiting room, "Please wait here for about a quarter. Maybe you can watch the TV for a while." I closed the door and went back to the working room. The Brazilian old boy was lying on his back listlessly. As his tiny penis was soft and shriveled, the slack of the condom dangled to one side. I snatched off his condom and said, "That guy must call at the most inopportune hour."

I put his cock back into my mouth to suck and mumbled my complaints at the same time. Soon his cock began to erect and jerk and after another five minutes, it was stark and stiff. "Let's dress the cock quick while it remains hard, lest it slacks again."

Barely had I said that when his cock was dressed with a medium-sized condom. "What position this time?" I asked him. "Bend over and let me fuck you as a·dog does," he answered.

"You may as well fuck a bitch," I said.

"I like to fuck you while looking into the mirror at your round breasts. You have two nice breasts and your nipples are not black."

"Many of my clients say I have nice breasts and one of them pointed out that women who haven't borne children have pink nipples instead of black ones. I haven't seen the nipples of women after birth, so I can't prove whether it's true or not."

I referred him to the videos, "Look. That girl has black nipples so she must have given birth to children according to that theory."

I then knelt in front of the mirror, supporting myself with both my hands on the bed. He stood behind me and nudged his tiny cock into my cunt, "Aye. Aye. I fuck you!" With this, he gathered all his last strength to piston his cock inside me and asked, "Can you feel my cock?"

"It is too small," I sniggered in my mind but said openly, "Yes, I do."

With every movement of his cock, my two plump, white breasts swayed and bumped against each other and it was a perfect pornographic painting. We both looked into the mirror at our moving figures and smiled, "How beautiful. How sensual."

Then he bent over to wrap both his hands around my waist and fumbled up toward my nipples, "You see. Your nipples have hardened and that means you're hot."

"I cannot be hot today as I have been fucked so many times. But I'd still like you to fuck me. I like the feeling of cocks inside me."

"You like being fucked by me?" he seemed to not believe me. His hands kept on caressing my nipples and I felt a hot thrill run from my breasts, through my spine and down to my feet. But I thought his cock was not big enough or hard enough to make me come. You just couldn't count on such a tiny thing. Besides, I had come twice today and a third orgasm was hard to achieve. And more importantly, I had little time left to waste on the Brazilian old boy. I had to finish with him as soon as possible as I had another big cock waiting for me in the other room.

So I tautened my belly, squeezed his cock rhythmically with my cunt muscles and further stimulated him with erotic groans, "Ah, yes." He also quickened his movements and it was not long before he roared, "I fuck you!" and flopped on me. I kept my hips lifted up for him until he came completely and then jumped off the bed, "Well. Good boy. You came quickly."

"I know you are busy," he said pleasingly, "So I came quickly to make room for your next client."

"Thank you," I said.

I tidied up all the dirty things and asked him,"Will you have a shower?"

"I'll go home and have one to save you time."

I thanked him again. While he was dressing, I threw on a violet-colored dress and went to the kitchen to fetch six bottles of sugar-free Coke (as he had told me he had high blood sugar), put them into a plastic bag and handed them to him,"Take them home and drink."

Having seen him off, I hurried back to the waiting room only to find the client from Sydney had already undressed and lay on his back, fiddling away with his cock.

"How are things going over here?" I asked, "You're getting impatient, aren't you?"

"Yes. If you hadn't have appeared just now," he said," I'm afraid my cock would have come by my own hand. It's very, very hot."

Picking up his shoes and having him carry his own clothes; I led him to the working room. When we entered, he tucked a fifty-dollar note under my bra. I put the money under my mobile on the bedside table. Then I paved the bed with a clean white towel and had him lie down.

He lay on his back on the towel and I settled between his thighs and began to lick the inside of his thighs, gradually making him groan, "Ah, yes." I slowly shifted and continued to lick up the length of his thighs, making him tremble, "Yes, that feels good."

Now I was licking his balls. He had shaved his balls and the area around his cock and the skin of his balls felt like walnut skin. He set out to yell, "Ah ---, Ah ---. You are the best in the world!"

At that time I had swallowed his cock and kept it in my mouth. Though his was not as thick as the lawyer's, it was almost eight inches long and a little thinner than the air-freshener aerosol can. It was straight and shapely. Very nice. I sucked one third of his cock but that didn't satisfy him.

"Can you do deep throat?" he asked tentatively.

"No I can't." I refused bluntly,. "If your cock tip touches the uvula deep in my throat, I will feel sick and vomit. I have once seen a video in which a girl tried her best to gulp a cock as long as thirteen inches down her throat. She began to vomit at first and ended up with snot in her nose, tears in her eyes and white foam all around the corners of her mouth. I hate that. It is torture."

"But you are still the best," he said, "Your oral work is the best that I have ever enjoyed."

I kept his cock in my mouth and ran my tongue over the blunt tip of his cock this way and that way until he burst out yelling, "My God! Oh, fucking yes! Oh, terrific…" I kept on sucking his cock for some time before he paused and said, "Stop. I want to fuck you. One more minute of sucking and my cock will come. But I'd like to come in your cunt."

I found a large-sized condom and put it on his cock. "What position?"

"Sideward."

He turned onto his left side, facing the mirror on the wall, rotated my hips toward his cock and raised my right leg skyward. He exerted his strength to thrust into my cunt from behind and exclaimed, "I'm fucking you!"

A plump white leg and a hairy, strong thick leg were seen in the mirror twisted together and swayed back and forth with the thrusting movements of his cock. His cock was pummeling away vigorously in my cunt. As his stick was extraordinarily long, he put a great length of it in slowly and then suddenly thrust it to the hilt. The couple in the mirror was enjoying their carnal pleasures.

Every time he thrust his dick into my pussy, he would pound his hairy tuft against my shaven tuft very loudly and I couldn't help groaning out, "Aye. Aye. You're fucking me to death with that big cock of yours."

"Are you complaining that my cock is not long enough?" he asked and exerted even more strength to thrust deeper and deeper. I had to clench my teeth and endure his relentless assaults. I echoed his "Ah, yes. Ah, yes" to induce him to come soon. My white breasts were swaying before my bosom with every thrust of his cock. He looked into the mirror in front of us and then looked back into the mirror on the cabinet.

An erotic scene of his cock moving madly in my cunt could be seen clearly in the mirror and he said, "Very exciting. Very sensual."

As he watched he sped up the frequency of his movements and the pace of his breathing until he let out a long howl, followed by a desperate yell, "I fuck you!" And before long he had thrust his cock to the hilt, to the bottom of my cunt. His body trembled with mine, "Ohhhhh---, Oh---. Oh---." From his bitter groans I knew he had come completely.

COCK

I waited for a while before I helped him take off the condom and wipe clean the residual sperm around his private part. I had him lie face down and massaged his back, shoulders, spine and hipbones with my left and right elbows alternatively. He noticed from the side mirrors that I had a particular sitting posture and turned back to ask me, "How can you sit with your legs crossed like that? If I were to sit in this way, my legs would cramp."

"I practiced doing the splits in my childhood and served as a policewoman for more than ten years in China. My legs are extremely flexible because of years of exercise. I have no trouble sitting motionlessly with my legs crossed like that for half an hour."

"You're really an interesting woman," he said.

I looked up at the clock to find it was five to nine and said, "Take a shower, honey. My next client is coming in no time." I handed him a towel and sent him to the bathroom while I stayed to make the bed.

Hearing the doorbell ring, I tossed a dress over my head, put on a pair of slippers and took the money on the bedside together with my two mobile phones in both hands. (I need the mobile phones because my clients will contact me at any time. I used to only use one mobile. But when some clients took off with my mobile, I was cut off from communicating with the outside world. So I now need two mobiles. If one mobile goes missing, I can use the spare one. Since I lost my original mobile, I have been content with using cheaper mobile phones. No thief will bother stealing mobiles that are worth less than thirty dollars.) I headed to the kitchen, hid the money in the drawer and went to answer the door. As I knew it was a newcomer who had made an appointment, I dressed up and ran my fingers through my hair to make it look tidier.

Scarcely had I opened the front door when I heard compliments pouring in, "Wow. You're so gorgeous. You're so beautiful. You look exactly as the advertisement says. Wonderful!"

I was wondering who that fellow might be who was overwhelming me with so many lavish praises and whether I was really as beautiful as that fellow praised. When my clients praised my beauty years ago, I would think I deserved it but now I was no longer young and I was a woman who was approaching her fifties. If I were in my early forties, I would acknowledge my clients' compliments deservedly, but now I was not so confident when they praised my beauty, because I knew I was not young any longer.

"Thank you for your compliments," I said and ushered him into the house. He was a gentleman in his fifties. He was slim and stood around six feet tall. A pair of sunken brown eyes, a pointed nose and a round mouth sat under his grey short cut. Judging from his grey but neatly trimmed beard, I thought he must have been a man of taste.

He bent down to kiss me on the cheek, "Nice to meet you."

"Nice to meet you, too."

Then he fixed his covetous eyes on me while speaking to me, "You're really pretty."

I thanked him again and led him to the waiting room, "I'm sorry to keep you waiting for a couple of minutes. I have to see off a customer before I can serve you. Would you mind watching the TV for a while? And please help yourself to any drinks in the fridge."

I closed the doors of the waiting room and went to the fridge in the kitchen to pick up a bottle of beer for the customer from Sydney. I pushed open the door to the working room to find him already dressed. I handed him the plastic bag and said, "Take it home and have a drink. You may choose a packet of chips on the dining table for your midnight snack."

He chose one packet from the dining table and I saw him off at the door. He said, "I will come tomorrow."

"Thank you," I said, thinking to myself, "If you come tomorrow, you will have come to me three days in succession."

I shut the door and went back to attend to my new client. He followed me to the working room. He looked around and the first things that attracted his eyes were the huge screens and shining mirrors on the walls. He couldn't help admiring, "What a good setup!"

"Where are you from, sir?" I asked.

"I'm from Brisbane and I've come to Canberra on business."

"You are great to have your own business. Nowadays it is hard to run a business profitably."

"Yes, but hard as it is," he said, "business has to be done by someone."

After the small chat about business, I got down to my own business, "Well, would you like a half hour's massage or a one hour's massage?"

"No. I want sex," he said bluntly.

"Well, since you are a newcomer, I'll give you a special offer; fifty dollars for half an hour or ninety for one hour. Normally for sex, the price should be seventy dollars for half an hour and one hundred and twenty for one hour."

He was obviously happy with the price and said, "Thank you. Thank you."

He took out a wallet from the back pocket of his trousers and produced a fifty-dollar note. As he did this, his eyes ran up and down my face and were then fixed on me, making me feel uneasy. After I accepted the money and thanked him, he went on to flatter me, "You are very gorgeous."

I went to the kitchen and put the money into the drawer and came back with a Coke and a bottle of mineral water in my hands. I showed him the drinks and asked, "Which do you prefer, sir?"

Seeing the two drinks in my hands, he smiled, "Either will do." He took the Coke and water, put them on the bedside table and kept flattering me, "You are an angel. You are gorgeous." His shower of compliments simply made me embarrassed. I said to him, "Please take a shower first, sir."

I took a large, white towel from the cabinet, hung it on the towel rail in the bathroom and turned on the shower nozzle, "Please wait a minute. It will take several minutes for the water to get hot, because the hot water tank is some distance away, outside in the courtyard."

When I came back, he had taken off all his clothes and put them on the massage table. He still didn't shift his gaze away from my face. I ran my fingers over his cocky stick and said, "Look, it's getting impatient."

"I must have it cleaned for your sake," he said in a pleasing manner. While he was showering, I went to the laundry to take the clean, dried towels out of the drier, before throwing in more damp, washed towels and turning it on. I started a new cycle on the washing machine with five used towels whirling around in it. I took the clean towels back to the working room, folded them up and stored them in the glass-door cabinet. The bearded client had finished showering and came out of the bathroom, his cocky stick pointing skyward and his beard covered with little glistening drops of water. I helped him dry his beard with a towel and turning him 180 degrees, I helped to wipe his back dry. Then I pointed to the large towel I had spread on the bed before and motioned him to lie down on it.

I had piled two pillows on the bed and had him lie on them. Spreading his legs apart, I settled between them and bent down to lick his balls with my tongue tip. Soon his ball skin became tautened and he began to groan loudly, "Ugh---. Ugh---. You are the best."

Covered with thick, grizzly hair, his ball skin was very rough and thorny. So as to avoid hurting my tender tongue tip, I licked his cock along the blue vein on the back and slowly ran my tongue upward to its blunt tip. He could no longer help crying out, "Ah---, ah---." At last I took his cock in mouth and he said, "My God. My God. You are the best sucker in the world."

I was not surprised when my old patrons ranked me as the number one, yet I wondered why my new clients also called me number one. It seemed that I was really an expert at sucking cocks and it was widely acknowledged. I often laughed up my sleeve: Only excellent doctors, lawyers or artists are said to rank number one in their own fields respectively; who has ever heard of a prostitute being ranked as number one in the art of cock sucking? Has it become a special study or craft that can be compared to the specialties of doctors or lawyers?

I sucked his cock in my mouth and made him wild with joy by licking his cock tip and the crevice in it. He groaned loudly and moved in fits and starts, disclosing his innermost, unspeakable ecstasy. It was not long before he began to gasp like a running dog and finally he burst into a loud yell, "My God!" No sooner had he yelled out than I felt a hot stream being ejaculated into my mouth. I was caught unprepared so I hastily sucked his cock for a few seconds before I spat his cock out of my mouth, "You've left me a mouthful of your sperm!"

Seeing sperm dripping from his cock tip, I took two tissues to wipe his dangling cock. Then I went to the bathroom to brush my teeth, rinse my mouth and wash my hands as well. When I came back, I wiped his cock dry with the tissues and said, "Come on. Let me massage your back."

I motioned him to lay face down on the bed and he obeyed my direction but his eyes were still reluctant to leave my face as he turned his body. He kept flattering me, "You are so beautiful. You are so perfect." I was wondering whether I was worth the profusion of praises. After all, I was no longer a young girl in the prime of her life but a woman approaching her early fifties. But anyway, I enjoyed the endless praises as it was a woman's universal weakness --- vanity. And I felt I was lucky to still look relatively young for my age.

I had just mounted his back and gripped his shoulder muscles, ready to massage him when the doorbell rang. I jumped off the bed, threw a green, floral-patterned dress over my head and said to the bearded man on the bed, "I'm sorry to keep you waiting, sir. Just wait a couple of minutes." With that I hurried barefoot to answer the door. On my way to the front door, one of my mobiles rang inopportunely, "May I make an appointment now?"

"Have you ever been here?"

"No, I haven't," the voice over the phone said, "It's the first time for me. A friend of mine has given me the telephone number."

This was the business I was running, a business that depended mainly on the circulation of reputation. Credit and reputation were much more important than anything else.

I thought I could finish the job in the working room in another fifteen minutes and the client at the door was allowed only half an hour. I looked up at the clock on the wall and it was nine fifteen, so I answered, "You can come at ten o'clock."

"Your address, please."

"331 Creseter Street, Garama, not far from the rear gate of Canberra Hospital," I answered briefly.

I was then near the door and when I opened it, I found a medium-built man of about sixty. He was a Chinese man, neither too fat nor too slim. There were dozens of Chinese men among my clients and the youngest one of them was a little over twenty. They came from all walks of life in Australia. Every time I received a Chinese client, I claimed to be a Korean and talked with them in some simple Korean sentences like "*Anianhamiyu*" or "*Kongbanhanyu*" I had picked up elsewhere. Actually, some Chinese customers could make out my Chinese accent but they felt it embarrassing to make further enquiries and I naturally left the supposition unproved.

The client standing in front of me was from Hong Kong. He was the owner of three restaurants in Canberra downtown. He came to Australia with his parents when he was a boy. But he was now a frequenter of mine for nine years. Seeing I was talking with someone, he didn't interrupt me. I opened the door while talking on the phone and nodded my consent to let him in. I repeated my address on the phone and the caller answered, "I'll be there in forty-five minutes." Then I hung up the mobile.

He was now in the house. "Sorry," I said. "Are you busy now?" he smiled.

"Yes. I'm afraid you'll have to wait fifteen minutes," I said apologetically.

"Rarely are you unoccupied," he said, still smiling.

While we were talking, we were already in the waiting room.

I said to him, "You're my old patron so please feel at home."

I closed the door and went back to attend to the bearded man in the working room, "Sorry to have kept you waiting."

He was lying on his back now and I asked him, "Can you come a second time?"

"You are so pretty," he said heartily, "I can surely come a second time."

I thought that not everyone could necessarily come a second time, so I said, "Some men can within a short time but other men absolutely can't. And this has little to do with the age. I have a client from Melbourne who is sixty-five years old and he is able to come twice within half an hour. It is very easy for him to come. Several minutes on his cock and he will come in no time. And another dozen minutes of massaging plus a hand job and he will come again! I have another client, an Indian overseas student, who is nineteen years old. Oh, damn it. It is extremely hard for him to come. I will work strenuously for thirty to forty minutes on him but he just can't ejaculate. It's really a sweaty job, a tormenting job."

Gazing at me, the bearded man on my bed said, "When I was young, I could come seven or eight times a day."

"It's commonly believed young people come easily. But on the contrary, I have several young clients who are notoriously difficult to come. They are just my headaches. I always feel guilty for not having served them well."

I knuckled my temple and said, "Sex depends on your imagination but not wholly on your age."

I was then sitting at his left side and supporting myself on my left elbow between his thighs. I settled on his left thigh and began to perform a hand job on his cock. After groaning "Oh--- Ah---Yeah---" he kept on yelling, "I'll come for you." But however hard I tried, his cock remained inactive and he just wouldn't ejaculate. I had to settle between his legs and began to suck his cock. His cock felt slippery and infirm in my mouth and failed to harden again. Despite his effort to cooperate with me by sweating away, he just wouldn't come. Looking at the clock, I found it was already nine thirty and said, "Dear, if you fail to come, just leave it for next time. Time is now up and I have another client waiting for me."

"Never mind," he said tolerantly, "You have done your best. If I were ten years younger, I would have come already. That's the evidence I'm getting old, isn't it?"

"You are not old," I tried to comfort him, "Once a client showed me his driver license which said he was born on May 13, 1920. He had been driving his car for three hours from Batemans Bay to see me. Another client claimed to be ninety-five years old but I hadn't checked his license so I couldn't prove whether he had told me the truth or not. Anyway, both of them are old enough to be my grandfather."

Hearing my story, he laughed, "I hope I can drive my car to see you when I turn ninety."

"Then I would be eighty at least," I laughed, too, "I would be called Granny Masseuse instead of Miss. Masseuse. When some client asks me for a service, I will take out my false teeth and ask, 'Do you want a toothless service or one with teeth? If you want a toothless one, the service fee will be doubled.'"

He was greatly amused and burst out laughing and his long beard shivered with the laughter. I gave him a towel and had him take a shower.

While he was showering, I took the mineral water from the kitchen table and gulped half of it down, thinking I was so busy that I could hardly find any time to have supper or even drink water. If only I could have a dinner that could last me a whole week. And I could still make just as much money. I was indulging my whims and fancies when the doorbell rang again. I went to find it was another regular client, wearing his work uniform, who hadn't made an appointment in advance. I scolded him, "You have come without dialing first again, haven't you?"

"I've just knocked off," he answered, "So I've come to see whether you're busy or not."

I sighed that here came another guy who would find any opportunity to jump the queue. "You have to wait here at least fifteen to twenty minutes," I said, as I knew the Chinese man queuing in the waiting room would come quickly enough for me to save dozens of minutes and I knew equally well that I had an appointment at ten o'clock. So I had to finish the Chinese man and the guy standing in front of me now in half an hour.

He understood he had to wait but he said he was willing to do so.

I led him to the west living room and seated him in the swivel chair, "Please wait here for a while as I have another two clients to serve and I have to see off one via the back door first."

I took a can of Coke from the fridge and handed it to him. As he was my regular client, I knew what his favorite drink was. I went to fetch a bottle of wine from the garage and sent it to the bearded man, "A bottle of wine for you to drink at home."

He had dressed and accepted the wine gladly, "This is the best service I have ever received."

I helped him pack the wine together with a Coke and a mineral water into the plastic bag. He said, "It's as if I were at the checkout in a supermarket."

I led him through the dining room to the back door. When we were passing the dining table, I asked him, "Do you like chips?"

Glancing at the plastic bag in hand he asked me in wonder, "You have given me too many gifts. Are you intending to go on with your business?"

"Never mind," I said hospitably, "Help yourself to whatever you like on the table. I will content myself with a net profit of forty dollars from each client."

He took a packet of corn flakes from the table and said, "It's very generous of you."

We went through the laundry door and parted at the back door. He kissed me affectionately on the forehead, "Next time I come to Canberra, I am sure to visit you again."

"Good night," I took my farewell of him.

I closed the laundry door before I came back to the waiting room. And no sooner had the door opened than the Chinese man flew over to take me into his arms as if we were long-parted lovers. He buried his head in my bosom and sniffed greedily. Then he took a deep breath before he said, "Oh, how wonderful your breasts smell. I've really been missing you. It's at least two weeks since we last met."

"Let's go to that room," I led him by the hand.

Before we went to the working room, I had changed the Chinese music to the background music of the porn video. He was a frequenter of mine for nine years and he took me for a Korean all that time, and always asked me whether I had ever gone to see my parents in Korea.

I paved the bed with a white towel, repositioned the pillows and asked him if he wanted a shower first.

He told me he had just had one when he knocked off. So I said to him, "Just lie down and have a rest. I have to go and greet a client outside."

I closed the door and hurried to the west living room. I pushed the client on the swivel chair into the waiting room, "Please wait here for another quarter and help yourself to any drink you like in the fridge."

Then I hurried back to the working room to find the Chinese restaurateur lying on his back on my bed, his legs parted wide.

I was familiar with his cock as I had fiddled with it hundreds of times. It was neither too thick nor too thin and was just as erect and stiff as it was when I first saw it nine years before. But the last two years his cock was obviously slackening and lacked the required hardness. More often than not, it surrendered before it became hard. He often told me jokingly, "Linda, I'm getting old."

"So am I," I admitted, "These last two years, my age has begun to show. I'm getting slower to react."

"I hope I can fuck you for another ten years," he said.

"I hope I can run my business for ten or twenty more years," I said, "And so long as clients keep coming, I won't stop working."

I was then settled between his thighs and kept his cock in my mouth. As I sucked it, it stiffened and jerked. He kept yelling "Ah--- Oh---" for about five minutes before he suddenly declared, "Let me fuck you. I'd like to fuck you."

I tucked a pillow under my buttocks and threw my legs over his shoulders ready for him to get in me. He stood up on the floor and tried to thrust his little thing into my cunt. More often than not, he would try quite a few times before he succeeded. However, he performed well enough today to find the right opening and succeeded in entering it. I prayed for a quick ejaculation for I had another client waiting in the waiting room. At that time, I was not in the mood to enjoy the carnal pleasures of sex but was occupied by the sole thought of how to make these two clients come quick and leave quicker. There was a long line of clients waiting to fuck me. Yet as the saying goes, more haste, less speed. If I urged him to come quickly, it would surely distract his attention and most probably delay his ejaculation further.

With every movement of his cock, he began to groan his "Ah--- Ugh--- Ah---good fuck." I felt his little thing come to harden in my cunt, though its hardness still couldn't compare with that of the western big cocks. So it was very easy to deal with this cock. You should only echo him with "Oh--- Ah---" for several minutes and you could make him come. He ejected all his sperm on my belly. After that, he said to me, "Just go ahead with your own business. I'll go and have a shower."

He was really a reasonable and considerate customer of mine. He had produced two fifty-dollar notes and put them on the bedside table. Though he knew I would by no means accept so much money, he produced as much every time to show his generosity as a wealthy boss.

"I can only accept forty dollars," I declined his generous offer, "As you came quickly, I'll give you ten dollars' change."

"You can keep it, Linda,"he said as he made for the bathroom, "It really doesn't matter to me."

But I insisted on putting the second fifty-dollar note by his clothes on the massage table and added the ten dollars' change beside it.

Then I took a towel to the waiting room and said to the client, "Just one more minute, as I have to take a quick shower first." I quickly finished my shower and started to dry my body with a clean towel. Pushing the bathroom door open, I asked the man,""Do you need a shower?" And he answered promptly, "Yes, I need one as I came here immediately after I knocked off."

"Then have your shower here in this room," I said, "So as to save time."

Putting the used towel on the tiled floor, I took a clean, white towel to the man in the waiting room. He was already under the shower nozzle. I hung the towel on the glass door of the showering cubicle and closed the door to the waiting room. When I came back, the Chinese boss was dressed and his hair was combed, shiny and neat. He was looking into the mirror at himself, "Look at me. Not different from when I came?"

I smiled an understanding smile, "You look much younger and more energetic than when you came. You look like a boy of only twenty-one."

"I wish I were a boy of twenty-one. But I'm not. I'm getting old. When I was young, I was always followed by a group of girls."

"Honestly," I said, "Looking at you from the back, you look like a boy of twenty-one."

He laughed heartily, "From the back, I might attract some girls but from the front, I could frighten old women into fleeing."

"Not so hopeless," I said, "Your figure still looks young and you are still handsome enough to attract girls or young ladies."

We were talking and laughing until we arrived at the door. He said at the doorstep, "See you later."

"See you," I waved farewell and closed the door behind me.

Seeing off the Chinese restaurateur, I went back to the waiting room. The client in uniform had had his shower and had a large white towel wrapped around his lower part. Holding his clothes for him, I accompanied him to the working room and put his clothes on the massage table. While I was making the bed, he produced a twenty-dollar note and a ten-dollar note from his coat and handed them to me, "Only a head job."

I thanked him for his money, put the notes into the drawer in the kitchen and hurried back to the working room. I knew very well my next client would come at ten o'clock by appointment and there was only ten minutes left. If we were not lucky, we would end up leaving the job unfinished and get halfway through only to be interrupted by the doorbell. So I had to hurry, running all the way to do these jobs in succession.

When the client got ready, I prostrated myself to suck his tiny cock. This client had blond hair and a pair of blue eyes in sunken sockets. He was strong and sturdy, but strangely enough he had a tiny cock. It is assumed that western men have bigger cocks but this is not the case with every western man. I used to be ignorant of this and only after I became a prostitute and witnessed thousands of cocks did I come to know that some western men had even smaller cocks than Chinese men. This client's cock was no bigger than that of the Chinese man who had just left. It was barely the size of a small carrot. This client was also younger, about forty years old, so his tiny cock was easy to harden by sucking. He began to cry boisterously, "Ah---. Oh-

--," and "Fuck you" and started to exert his little cock by holding my head steady and thrust it deep into my throat. His hands held my head more and more tightly and this was beyond the limit I could bear. I stopped it by brushing his right hand aside, "Stop doing it. I don't like it!"

He withdrew his hand, apologized and flopped down on the bed again.

I was about to resume the sucking when I heard the doorbell ring. I tossed a pink dress over my head and put on my slippers. I closed the door to the working room and opened the front door. I found two Australian boys in their late twenties standing in front of me. They were both stout and sturdy. One wore long, blond hair and the other wore a blond short cut. I had encountered some young men making trouble and I remembered calling the police station. In fact, I called the police station more than once.

I didn't open the security door and talked to them across the security mesh, "Why are you coming in a pair? I can't serve two men at the same time."

"Can you serve us one by one," one of them asked, "and let the other one watch TV in the room?"

I knew if I allowed the two boys to come at once, I could absolutely not serve one in the working room and let the other wait in another room. The two boys would encourage each other and start causing trouble. So If I had to serve two young men, I would allow one of them in first and let the other wait outside the house.

The long-haired lad asked the price and I answered fifty dollars for each one.

"There are two of us," he said, "Give us a discount. How about forty dollars for each of us?"

"I'll give you a special offer of forty-five dollars each."
"Okay," they agreed, almost in unison.

They began to play rock-paper-scissors to decide who would be the first to make love to me. After playing several rounds, it had been decided the long-haired boy would be first. I led him to the waiting room, "Watch the video for a while and drink anything you can find in the fridge. The toilet is over there." Looking in the direction I pointed to, the boy nodded his understanding.

"Wait for five minutes." With that, I closed the door and went back to the working room. The tiny-cocked man was leaning against the pillows and fiddling away with his little thing. I went over to settle between his legs and began to suck his stick. He yelled for more than five minutes before he came. I offered him a shower but he said he would rather go home to take one. I parted with him at the back door and pointed him to go westward. If he went eastward, he would be confronted by the boy waiting outside at the front door. Generally I won't have my clients meeting each other. Some of my clients point out that Canberra is a small city and you'll most probably encounter your boss or your neighbors at my place as bad luck would have it. After all, sex is the last private secret of any individual. I should respect my clients' privacy.

Seeing off the man in uniform, I led the long-haired lad to the working room. The lad cried out the minute he came into the room, "Wow! How gorgeous! How sensual!"

When he saw the porn video being played on the sixty-inch TV sets on opposite walls he commented on the size of the TV, "The TV sets in this room are much larger than those in the other room."

"These two are sixty inches while those are fifty inches."

He went over to feel along the sliding glass door of the cabinet with his finger tip and said, "Good cleaning job. Immaculately clean and beautiful."

"You said it. It's my daily routine to clean all the furniture after I finish my work."

He went over to feel the mirrors on the south wall, "Wow. The whole wall is tiled with mirrors. It must have cost a lot of money?"

"The mirrors on the opposite walls of this room and the sliding glass doors to the two cabinets in the waiting room altogether cost me three thousand dollars."

"That is so expensive, Linda!" He exclaimed, "I have been to nearly two dozen brothels in Australia but I've found none as gorgeously and tastefully furnished as your place. You have a good setup."

"When I began to work for my boss nine years ago," I said, "there was only a bed and a toilet in the room with some ornamental paintings on the wall. But I don't know what the interior design and furnishings of brothels are nowadays."

He added, "There are TV sets in some rooms in brothels but they are not as large. Nor are the rooms equipped with twin TV sets that are playing the same videos."

"I have run a restaurant in China." I said, "I furnished my house by copying the layout and interior design of the multifunctional hall in that restaurant. And they look very much the same."

Just then a question jumped to my mind; how a boy of his age had been to so many brothels so I asked him, "How old are you?"

"I am twenty-eight," and as if he had known the question on my mind he went on to answer, "My work is to run errands all over the country."

With that he produced a fifty-dollar note and handed it to me. I took the money and said, "Wait a minute. I'll give you change for five dollars. Do you need a shower?"

"I don't mind one." He said, "I've been walking all day long."

I took a towel from the cabinet, passed it to him and asked him what drink he wanted.

"VB beer."

I went to the kitchen to fetch five dollars' change from the drawer and two cans of beer from the fridge. I put them all on the kitchen bench and went to the toilet to answer the urgent call of nature.

Oh my! Having had a good shitting and a good pissing, I felt so relieved. It was incredible that I had been too busy to have gone to the toilet. After all this, I cleaned my anus and had a shower in the bathroom. Having dried my body, I went back to the working room naked, with two cans of beer in one hand and a five dollars' change in the other.

The long-haired lad was standing beside the bed with his lower part wrapped with a large towel. I handed him the beer can together with the change of five dollars. He thanked me politely and opened the can to have a sip of beer, "Very nice." I put another can of beer on the bedside table and stretched out my hand to feel his hair. His hair seemed to have been washed but not dried yet. It was dripping wet. I hastily took a towel from the cabinet, folded it in half and spread it on the piled pillows. If the pillow was drenched with dripping water, it would be very uncomfortable for my next client to lie down on it. I paved the bed with a long towel and had him lie on his back. I sprawled between his legs and sucked his big cock. I was already very worn out and had to muster my last strength. I took a deep breath in and then began to blow at his shaven ball skin.

I tried to relax myself by letting out a long, drawling puff of air only to make him amused. "What are you doing?" he asked.

"I'm blowing your balls to lift their spirits."

Look at me. What was I saying? I was so tired that I began to talk nonsense. Soon my relentless licking began to make him groan, "Oh yes. Ah, yes." Then I put his cock into my mouth. Damn it, cock in my mouth again! My tongue tip was beginning to hurt. Suddenly a song I heard ten years ago in China occurred to me: "Mom is going to remarry as it is going to rain. What do you say I should do?" I almost forgot the words.

The exotic tune and words I was humming made the long-haired lad laugh. He asked, "And what the fuck are you doing now?"

"I'm singing praises for your cock." I said.

"My cock? Even I can't understand what you're singing. Can my cock?"

It didn't matter whether you could understand it or not, I thought. I was just trying to relax myself. COCK, cock, nearly two dozen cocks a day almost drove me mad and I was now fed up with the mere mention of them.

Not satisfied with my sucking, he offered to fuck me.

I found him a large-sized condom and said, "On top of me, young man. I have been completely exhausted by all these damn cocks."

I pulled him up by his arm without listening to his protests. I lay on my back on the bed and threw my legs over his shoulders. He knelt between my thighs and exerted all his strength to thrust his cock into my cunt to the hilt. "Ouch!" I cried out, "Take your time, lad. Your big cock is hurting me."

He was so rash a young man. He fucked me incessantly and mercilessly until I gasped for breath.

He sighed hoarsely as he thrust his cock violently inside me, "I'm fucking you. Your pussy is very nice." You must be enjoying yourself but my cunt is hurting, I thought to myself. I'd like you to fuck quick and come quick so that I could finish my job quick.

The lad was fucking me away and more and more licentiously. I had to echo him with lustful groans: "Oh, yes. Oh, yes." He went on for another ten minutes and he was on the brink of coming. He gasped and bent my legs and my body to a forty- five-degree angle, my knees almost touching my breasts.

I tell you, my legs were extremely flexible due to my early childhood training. This training had benefited me so much now. Besides, I never stopped exercising when I served as a policewoman. And last but not least, since I came to Australia ten years ago, I had been rolling over and doing all kinds of acrobatic movements on the bed nearly every day so I could deal with any young men and suffer any torments without being hurt too much.

I prayed that so long as I could be exempted from riding his cock I could reconcile myself to lying down and bearing his fucking as it was the best form of rest I could get then.

At last, he came and I finished another job. He hastened to move his cock several times and flopped on me, gasping for air.

"Lad," I said, "Tired out? Fucking is one of the three most exhausting jobs. A Chinese saying goes that fucking is the most exhausting among the most strength-consuming jobs across the countryside: making bricks, collecting wheat and fucking." No one but the Chinese can understand this saying. So I explained to him in simple language why fucking is so exhausting, "You are doing an extraordinarily hard job. As my doctor puts it, 'Lovemaking once is equivalent to four miles of walking.'"

He was prompt in responding, "You receive more than a dozen clients a day; how many miles of walking is that?"

"I can't figure out how many miles a day I actually walk," I answered, "But I am getting stronger and stronger and I never get the flu, headaches or any other discomforts."

"Look," he said, licking his lips, "How good it is that you can enjoy yourself, exercise and earn money all at once. If I were a woman, I would be a prostitute, too."

"Boy," I patted him on the shoulder, "I'm busy today. Hurry up and have a shower now. If you can urge your mate to be quick, I will charge him only forty dollars."

The lad nodded sensibly and turned to go to the bathroom for his shower.

I hastened to make the beds and went to the laundry to fetch dried towels from the drier. I was busy spreading the towels on the bed when the mobile rang, "Linda, my darling. May I come to see you tonight at midnight?"

"Okay."

I had just put down the mobile when the other mobile rang, "Please tell me the price."

"For a nude massage, fifty dollars for half an hour and ninety for one hour."

"All right, do you do whole-set service?"

"The price for a whole-set service is normally seventy dollars for half an hour and one and twenty for one hour. But I have a special offer for my regular clients: Sixty for half an hour and one hundred for one hour. I have a sex worker's license, so it's lawful for me to work at home."

"Oh, you have a license? I have no license. My driver's license has just been suspended by the police," he replied. I giggled and he joined in giggling until we burst out laughing. After a while, I stopped and asked him, "Have you ever been here before?"

He said honestly that he had not. Then I said, "You can also get the special offer at night. Sixty for half an hour and one hundred for one hour." Actually it was a common practice in business to attract prospective clients.

He thanked me and went on to ask, "Do you do BDSM?" (Bondage, Discipline & Sadomasochism)

"Yes, no problem."

BDSM clients often like to be hung up and whipped with a belt or a strap in order to whet their sexual desire. It is essentially a sexual fantasy.

"Can I kiss your body and lick your pussy?"

"Yes,"I said, wondering why the client had so many questions. "Can I fuck your asshole?" he asked at last.

I hate being asked this question. I tried that once but my asshole hurt for a long time afterward. From then on I refused to do that service, however much money clients were willing to pay.

"Sorry," I answered abruptly, "I won't have my asshole fucked by anyone. I won't be tortured for money. I will feel pain without any pleasure on my part. Besides, if the cock I encounter happens to be a big one, my asshole will be torn up and I will have to find a surgeon to repair it later. I don't want to be a penny-wise and pound-foolish woman by earning dozens of dollars and paying ten times as much later for the operation fee. You may as well go to another girl for this service."

Having voiced my grievance, I hung up the phone. The long-haired boy had dressed and I gave him a bottle of beer from the fridge and he chose a packet of chips from the dining table. I saw him off at the door.

Soon the doorbell rang and in came the short-haired lad. I ushered him into the working room and collected forty dollars from him. It took me only twenty minutes to send him away and he contented himself with his share of beer and chips when he left.

I looked at the clock on the wall and it was already eleven o'clock, near midnight. I hastened to the kitchen and dumped all the money in the drawer to the floor. I sat on the floor and began to count. Wow. Today's income added up to 885 dollars! Another client and the sum would reach 900 dollars. Excluding the cost of 200 to 300 dollars for wines, chips, chocolates, drinks and so on, I would still get a net profit of 600 to 700 dollars.

Though I felt my age was beginning to show and I could no longer work twenty-four hours on end as I did six years ago, when my income invariably exceeded 1,000 dollars each day, I was content with making a daily earning of such a sum as today, for a woman approaching her fifties. My hands full of money, I flopped on the floor and smiled to myself, forgetting all the hardship and weariness of the day. My knack for earning money, if you ask me, comes down to: First, I have inherited the fine tradition of the Chinese of being earnest and diligent in work and airing no complaints about adversity. Second, I have displayed the revolutionary spirit of defying any hardship, danger or pain to my cunt. Third, I believe in the business practice of making money by toiling myself to the last drop of sweat and on the basis of small profit but quick turnover. I do everything with all my might without sparing any effort or caring for my health. And last but not least, I can look at every situation from my clients' angle and take care of their every possible need. I am considerate of my clients and my service is very comprehensive. After years of positive interactions, I have formed relationships with my clients that resemble those between friends or lovers. Now I boast a network of thousands of clients and I never lack clients. Sometimes a client or two may underpay me by ten or twenty dollars but I don't care about that. Ten or twenty dollars may buy them a lunch or a supper. When I meet with some old men or disabled men, often I even serve them free of charge.

Icounted the money and stood up to put it away in the safe and went back to the kitchen. I heated the leftovers in the microwave and finished it all. After having my late supper, I went to the working room and played some English songs over the stereo. I scrubbed the bathroom while listening to the music. The dreamy tunes of "One Way Ticket" and "Never on Sunday," with their bouncy and forceful rhythm, reverberated in the spacious room. And it made me feel as if I were walking on a blooming field in the spring breeze. With an old towel, I cleaned the mirrors on the walls and danced bare-buttocked to the beat of disco music as I worked. Accompanied by the music, I had cleaned the entire working room and bathrooms in no time. Jumping and hopping all the while, I toted all the bed sheets, pillow cases and towels to the laundry and refilled the mini fridge with beers and drinks. Finally, I finished cleaning all the other rooms.

I went to the kitchen, picked up a bottle of mineral water and no sooner had I opened the cap than the doorbell rang. I had to put down the water bottle and hastened to answer the door. It was twelve o'clock sharp. As all my clients knew I was busy, ninety-nine percent of them were very punctual in their arrival. My next client was called Jim. He was of medium build and a little fat with a protruding belly which matched his figure. At a guess, I would say he was around fifty. He was wearing a cap today. I was wondering why so many men in Canberra wore caps four seasons, all-year round. Under his cap, Jim had a chubby face with a pair of sunken blue eyes framed with a pair of gold-rimmed glasses; a sensual, pointed nose, and an ample mouth with a smile always lingering on it. Today he wore tracksuit pants and a beige canvas jacket, both looking considerably worn. It seemed he was destitute as I had never seen him wearing any new clothes for the past nine years.

Scarcely had he entered the house when he untied his tracksuit pants. To my surprise, he produced his cock and showed it to me. What surprised me more was that he shook his cock with one hand and waved a twenty-dollar note with the other. I snatched the money from his hand and said, "Give me the money before you play with your cock."

He shook his cock and made his pants rustle. Suddenly the rustling reminded me of what I had heard over a certain phone call where the caller didn't display their caller ID. The moment I picked up the phone, there was no answer except the strange noise of rustling from the other end. At first I responded with curses. It must have been some wicked man whose cock wanted attention but who lacked the required money. That man called to harass me and enjoy himself at the same time by masturbating upon hearing my voice. So every time I heard such a rustling noise on the other end of the phone, I hung up at once because I was too busy to argue with him. I just ignored him even though I knew who the caller was.

I had just thrown Jim's twenty-dollar note into the drawer when he lifted the hem of my dress and thrust his saggy little thing between my buttocks. I pushed him away, "Quit doing that. You can't fuck a girl if your cock isn't stiff enough. Go to the inside room. The kitchen is not the place for you to fiddle with your cock. If you don't stop fiddling, I will cut off your little thing to save you the money on coming here, for good."

You could play whatever joke you please on a familiar frequenter without annoying him.

"I would begrudge losing my cock," he grinned. "Every man has only one cock. So it's my priority to protect it."

"Have you seen any man who has more than one cock? Just one cock has cost you a lot of money. Can you afford to have two?"

We walked into the working room, talking and jesting. I pulled my dress over my head and tossed it onto the floor. I stood in the nude, watching the old gentleman take his time undressing. He took off his cap and put it on the massage table. Then he took a small comb from his canvas jacket pocket and began to comb what little grey hair he had left on his head. He blew at his comb and carefully combed a few hairs on the back of his head. Looking at his shining, oily bald head, I felt at once uncomfortable with my own hair. I stood bare- buttocked in front of the mirror and looked into it. I ran my fingers through my hair, praying that it wasn't getting thin on top. If that should happen, it would be a small catastrophe. He didn't seem to be much older than me. If I should become bald like him, I surely couldn't continue my business by claiming I was only thirty-eight rather than sixty-eight. Women tended to look older than men of the same age just because they got bald earlier.

I remember when I was working in the brothel; there was a lady who was in her fifties. She only had a few hairs on her head so she had to be wigged to serve her clients. When the wig was knocked off by a voracious guy, she would make a scene and become very embarrassed.

While Jim was carefully combing his hair, I was nervously massaging my scalp. It was some time before he put his comb back into his pocket, took off his canvas jacket and his torn, white singlet, untied his white sports shoes, took off, one by one, his red socks, one of which had a hole causing his toe to stick out; tucked his socks into his shoes respectively, pushed his shoes under the bed and at last took off his tracksuit pants and put them on the massage table with his other clothing. There was nothing left on him except his black briefs. He gripped the narrow strap of his briefs with his right hand and tightened it firmly upward to expose his round buttocks. He supported himself on the massage table with his left hand and protruded his buttocks toward the mirror. He swayed and twisted his hips in all directions to the beat of the Chinese music.

"Come on," he gave the signal to start, "Slap my hips." I went over and gave him a good slap on his right hip. "Slap harder!"

"Thwack!" I gave him another slap. "Slap even harder!"

I swung my hand to give him a harder one. "Change your hand," he said.

"My left hand is for your left hip," I answered.

I swung again with my right hand to give him a harder slap.

A very loud "Thwack!" indeed.

"Ouch," I said as my hand turned crimson at once. "My right hand is hurting. I have to relieve it with the left one."

This time I swung my left hand around before I whacked his left hip with it. I hit away at his hip until it turned crimson. Then he turned back and pulled out his saggy stick from under his briefs and rubbed it against my shaven cunt as his cock remained slack until he came at last.

I have seen a few men like Jim whose cocks are not hard enough even though they are not very old. It's hard to imagine how they can interact sexually with their wives or girlfriends, if they have any. A man can be satisfied when his sperm is ejaculated. But how can a woman be satisfied if no cock is tucked into her cunt and she always feels empty inside? A woman can try being licked but the satisfaction gained by licking is greatly different from that gained by fucking. That's why I say only a couple of men can satiate my sexual desire. I have a dozen or more frequenters who can satisfy me. Some of them boast big cocks, some are good at fucking and others can serve me by licking my cunt and the pleasure I receive from every individual client is unique.

DICK

He kept rubbing his cock on my cunt but in vain. "Stop," I got impatient. "It's useless doing that. Let me help you. Take off your briefs first." With that I snatched off his last strip of clothing. He pulled me into his arms and held me tightly, his cock still prodding against my tuft. I was not afraid of his cock as he could by no means thrust it into me. Wrapping my hands around his hips, I flopped onto the bed and pulled him on my naked body. I had him sit astride me and place his tiny stick between my breasts. Then I used both my hands to push my breasts from both sides toward the middle to form a groove, which held his cock tightly. Now he was free to slide his cock in the groove. This was often referred to as Spanish Breast Fucking.

He slid his cock in and out of the groove between my breasts for about five minutes before he came. I got up to wipe the sperm off his body and had him take his shower. As I knew he always took his time to bathe, his shower usually lasting seven or eight minutes; I put on a blue mini-dress and went to the kitchen. I retrieved a plastic bag full of walnuts from under the kitchen bench. I cracked the shells and enjoyed the kernels.

I made a rule to eat a couple of walnuts every day. Old people said walnuts benefitted the growth of hair. The last few years I have worried about my hair thinning out so I've been eating walnut kernels every day though I wasn't sure whether this folk prescription was effective or not. Each time I saw Jim, I ate more. I cracked them open, one by one and had eaten seven or eight walnuts before I knew it. I was about to crack open another walnut when Jim slowly paced out of the working room, with his cap on his head. It suddenly dawned on me that the reason many men in Canberra wore caps was probably because they were bald. On second thought, I had seen many young men in their thirties who shaved their heads cleanly but wore nothing on their heads. They looked just like the famous Chinese comedian Ge You. A bald star.

Well, there was no point looking into the cause of why men in Canberra wore caps. Jim wearing that cap didn't stop me from enjoying my walnuts. So I cracked another walnut and it might have been my tenth one. He looked at me in surprise, "What are you eating? You're making a noise as loud as a mouse gnawing at something. Aren't you afraid you might break your teeth?"

Looking at his bald head I retorted, "I'd rather have a broken tooth than have a bald head." He smiled too.

As I knew he was fond of chocolates, I took eight chocolates from the dining table and put them into a plastic bag. "Here you are."

"Thank you very much," he said.

"Go elsewhere next time," I said. "You've paid me twenty dollars but the chocolates I've given you are worth five dollars.

I've earned only fifteen dollars from you. Where else can you find a cheaper service?"

I saw him off at the door and came back for my walnuts. Thinking that no more clients were coming for the time being, I went on to appease my hunger with walnuts since I hadn't had much food throughout the entire day. Soon I had finished another twenty walnuts together with a bottle of mineral water.

Another strange idea struck me that if I ate too many walnuts, too much oil would prevent the new hair from growing out. If that were the case, it would be too bad. It was a golden rule to never go to extremes. I put away the bag of walnuts and scooped the shells into the dustbin.

The doorbell rang at nearly one o'clock. It might have been a certain nocturnal animal at the door. I went to answer the door with a long face and mumbled, "Why did you press the doorbell without giving me a call first? Don't you think it's too late an hour to come here? It must be your cock that keeps you awake."

The unexpected guest was a lanky black boy, not very tall. Naked waist down with his pants in his hand, he abruptly came over and pressed his rigid cock against my tuft. I was only wearing a dress with no underwear on underneath. So I cautioned myself to keep a distance away from his cock. It was really too hard and too long.

Brushing away his cocky stick I said, "Quit doing that, lad. Don't thrust it blindly without a condom on. Among all the boys I've served, no one is like you. Who fishes out their cock before they've even entered the house? Don't you fear other people will laugh at your nakedness? I'm afraid you're drunk."

"No. I haven't drunk much." He argued, besides, who will laugh at my nakedness since it is late at night?"

"Come over and let me perform an alcohol test on you," I said, moving my nose near his face, "Oh, don't be stubborn in denying you're not drunk. The strong alcoholic smell emanating from your mouth nearly raised my roof."

The black boy looked at most to be in his early twenties but had been my enthusiast for three years. The first time he saw me, he proposed to marry me.

"A boy of eighteen marrying a woman of forty-six?" I remembered saying then, "Do you think it's a children's game of playing house?"

From then on, every time he met me he always pestered me to be my boyfriend until at last I became fed up with his proposition. I just turned a deaf ear to what he said.

He strutted into the room in front of me. I knew too well that the purpose of making me his girlfriend was to get free services from me. So every time he frequented me, it was my initiative to mention the service fee. He was unwilling to pay unless I asked him to.

He continued to stand there, playing the fool. I had to say, "Please pay first. I've offered you so cheap a price. Are you still grudging the mere twenty-five dollars for a service?"

I also knew he was an overseas student here and not well off. But he badly needed an outlet for his strong sexual desire. So if I was not occupied, I would give him a fifty percent discount. I could help the lad solve his urgent problem and at the same time I could also make some money, however little it was. Anyway, a cunt lying idle could earn no money at all.

To my surprise, he reluctantly produced a fifty-dollar note from his trouser pocket and handed it to me. It was not his habitual practice. He usually gave me small notes of twenty, ten or even five dollars added up. He would hand me a pile of small notes and demanded, "Give me the change!"

"Do I have a record of not giving you enough change?" I felt insulted, "I charge any other client fifty dollars for one service but I charge you only twenty-five just because you're a foreign student. The half-price discount rate is a special offer for you. You should thank me for not charging you double for your extra long cock." When I first met him, I was impressed by his extra long cock. Hence his epithet "Mr. Long Cock."

The black boy, not as tall as me nor as strong, had an extraordinarily long cock of thirteen inches. It was neither a joke nor an exaggeration. Once I took an air freshener aerosol can and compared it to his cock. After careful measurement, the result of the comparison was that his cock was an inch longer than the can but not as thick. An old saying goes that, a woman doesn't fear a short and thick cock but a long and thin one. His cock simply gave me an awesome impression as if it could pierce through my cunt if it were to be thrust into it. So my legs shivered subconsciously at the mere sight of his cock.

"Do you want a drink?" I went on to ask. "No," he answered abruptly.

I wondered what the matter with the black boy was tonight. Every time he had paid his twenty-five dollars, he would invariable ask for two or three beers to make up for the cost. Why did he act so differently? I went to the kitchen to get twenty- five dollars and came back to hand it to him for his change. He had undressed. His small figure, black and shining, with too long a cocky shaft sticking skyward, looked awkward and out of proportion.

He put the change into his pocket and hastened to poke my tuft with his cock. I took off my dress by pulling it over my head and pushed his stick away, "Be patient and put on the condom first."

While I was walking toward the bedside table, he kept pestering me by poking his long stick against the groove of my hip. I turned around and gave him a smack on his cock, "Look.

What are you doing? You're just thrusting it aimlessly, sometimes here and sometimes there."

I chose a medium-sized condom and put it on his cock only to find it was thick enough in diameter but too short in length. You couldn't use a large sized one on him either, because it would be too loose for his long, thin cock and would likely come off in my cunt while he fucked me. If that were to happen, there would be serious consequences. So I had to make do with a medium- sized condom and of course it couldn't cover the entire length of his cock. Looking up at him, I asked, "How come you have so long a cock?"

"Mine can't be counted as a long cock," he answered. "There are other boys in our country who have longer cocks than me."

"Are you from Papua New Guinea?"

"No. Papua New Guinea seems to be in southern Africa. Maybe … Not right, either. Papua New Guinea may be in Oceania, near Australia. I'm from South Africa." I couldn't hear distinctly what he was muttering. I only remembered during our first meeting he had told me he came from Papua New Guinea. But his mention of southern Africa suddenly reminded me of one thing relating to Africa. All African boys had long cocks. It was no wonder a boy from Sudan in eastern Africa had a cock similar in thickness but a little longer than his.

Whenever I encounter such long cocks, I usually let these boys on top of me. I lie on my back on the bed and say, "Come on, young mate. Go ahead and do the harder job. I have been working all day long."

Seeing that I had spread my legs apart, he came at me like a hungry wolf, thrusting his long thing to the hilt and hurting the opening of my womb.

"Hey," I cried, "Take it easy! I say you must have drunk too much today. You are too rash!"

Without a word, he got down to his job of fucking by moving his cock violently. His every movement seemed to touch my stomach and I yelled, "Ouch. Ouch. Take your time. You rash guy."

Even when he was sober, he used his long cock to fuck me rashly. Now that he was drunk, he fucked me even more savagely. Feeling pain in my abdomen, I pushed him away. "Hey. You have paid me only twenty-five dollars so you can't fuck me for half an hour."

I just wanted him to come sooner. I would lose my life if his brutal fucking was to last for another half an hour. When I found he was trying to raise my legs over his shoulders, I got into a panic. "No! No! Your cock is too long and you would pierce my cunt in this position."

"Then bend over," he suggested, "and let me fuck you from behind?"

"Absolutely not. You would make my cunt bleed. As for you, I can make do with only one position of you being on top of me. The other day, I received a twenty-one-year-old Australian lad who had a cock not only long but also thick. I only allowed half of his length into my cunt instead of allowing him to penetrate me fully."

"You should have charged him half the price," he smiled, "Since you had allowed only half of his cock into your cunt."

"Actually I charged him the full price of fifty dollars so you should feel obliged to me for the special offer with fifty percent off."I continued,"You must speed up, mate. Don't occupy my time by fucking me endlessly since you are unwilling to pay more."

"If you were my girlfriend,"he said,"I would not pay a penny."

"Stop daydreaming, guy" I said, "To find a girlfriend you'd better go to your classmates and choose one among them, not me."

"I did," he looked helpless, "But she didn't like my long cock and soon fired me. Today I went to an Australian girl's house to drink with her. Then we went to the bedroom. But no sooner had my cock entered her cunt and moved only a few times than she jumped to her feet and showed me the door. After all, it's not my fault to have a long thing. It is just because I find your cunt can hold my long thing that I'd like you to be my girlfriend."

"Forget it," I said, "Leave me alone. I've told you a thousand times I can't be your girlfriend. This is my business and business is business. The time you can fuck me depends on how much you pay. You have had me for more than twenty minutes, which is already an extension of five minutes on your fifteen. You should thank me for this special favor."

"The time we spend discussing the length of my cock shouldn't be included," he said shamelessly, "We might as well start counting the time anew."

"No starting anew," I argued, "I can deduct the time by ten minutes. Now there is only five minutes to go and you have to hurry. If you don't, I'll get angry."

Once he held me tightly and kept fucking me endlessly, despite my pleadings that he was hurting me. I slapped him heavily on the face. When he heard I would get angry with him, he knew I meant what I said. So he quickened his pace. He wrapped his arms around my waist and held me so tightly that I had to lay flat and parted my legs. I could make do with this position as his cock thrust in me slantingly instead of directly. I knew he was going to come from his effort to accelerate his movements. I told myself to hold on for another couple of minutes and then everything would be over. And I must forget my stomachache for the time being.

He began to groan until he let out a long, loud howl of "Oh… oh…" Oh my goodness! I had to hold my breath when he exhaled a pungent gush of alcohol breath toward me as he climaxed. He sprawled flat on me and I waited for him to come completely and withdrew his cock from my cunt.

"You are thin yet you have a long stick. You are young yet you ejaculated so much. See how much you have ejaculated?" I complained as I showed him the condom filled with white fluid.

"How many seeds for babies are there in it?" He was wondering.

"Go back to find a fertile plot to sow your seeds," I teased him. "Hurry up and take your shower. My next client is coming soon." In fact, I had no client by appointment. I just intended for him to leave soon, lest he kept on pestering me. He sat idly on the bed as if he hadn't heard me at all. I dragged him up, "Go and take your shower. Don't be a dog in the manger. You are a student and you can't afford to sit here as you should pay me fifty dollars if you intend on sitting on this bed for half an hour."

Hearing this, he got up reluctantly and made for the bathroom, where I had hung a clean towel for him. I knew he would, like Jim, take his time showering and it took him at least ten minutes. So while he was taking his shower, I went to the kitchen for some water. I might have had too many walnuts and my throat felt dry and sticky. I had just had two sips of mineral water when my mobile rang. I switched on the mobile and said hello before a voice came from the other end, "Hi, Linda. Are you busy now?"

"No, not really," I said. "Why. Do you want to patronize me?" "I'd like to hug you."

He sounded as if his tongue tip was stiff. He must have drunk a lot. So I said, "Are you drunk? If so and you cannot drive here, you can come tomorrow."

"No. I'm not drunk."

Just as the black boy argued he hadn't drunk too much even if he walked with swaying legs, no one would admit he had drunk too much even if he actually had done so. It was universally true with drunkards in every country in the world.

"Okay," I said, "As you please. Come anytime." "Well, I'll come in twenty minutes."

I took up the water bottle and emptied half of it to quench my thirst and relieve the itch in my throat. Then I carried all the dried clean towels from the laundry to the working room. When I was passing the bathroom, the black boy was washing his head. I went in to plead with him to be quick, "Hurry, my lord. As you'll be charged fifty dollars for taking up space on my bed for half an hour and another fifty dollars for taking up space under my nozzle."

Looking up at me, he remained silent and kept on washing here and there slowly. I went back to fold the clean towels. When I finished the work and he was still in the bathroom, I went in again to urge him, "Have you finished showering yet?"

He was just idling away his time by scratching here and there and drying himself from head to toe. I snatched the towel from his hands and pushed him into the room, "Go and put on your clothes."

He was obliged to shift to the massage table and put on his clothes one by one. Having dressed, he asked for some cream.

"You are a boy and what's the use of the cream?" I asked, "There's Nivea Body Cream on the bedside table." He screwed open the cap and applied some cream on his face and then went on to apply it on his hair. I slapped him softly on the face, "Is this cream for your hair? Hurry up. It's late at night and who will appreciate your face in the dark?"

I had such a hard time getting rid of the guy only to hear him say "See you later," at the doorstep.

"Go to hell!" I cursed in my mind. I wished I wouldn't see him ever again. He only paid me twenty-five dollars for almost an hour of my time. If it had happened in the daytime, I would have kicked him out. But I was still polite to him, "When you come next time, don't drink so much. Too much wine will get you into trouble."

Truthfully, I was not serving those older boys or young men for the sake of money. I only charged them a mere twenty or thirty dollars each time. Imagine a lad around twenty with an insatiable lust standing at the door of your house, waving a twenty-dollar note in his hand, persistently ringing the doorbell to be allowed in. If you didn't allow him in, he would find any excuse to cause trouble by kicking down your door or breaking your windows, disturbing your neighbors or damaging the trees and flowers in your garden. To add insult to injury, sometimes he would run off with the cover of your doorbell and a new replacement would cost you twenty to thirty bucks. I would have paid too dear a price for not letting him in. When I'm not too busy, I may as well let him in and spend ten minutes or so doing something to satiate his lust. Besides saving me from the aforementioned troubles, I could also make some money off him, however little it might be. After all, they were only boys around twenty who were not mature enough to behave themselves and it was by no means a good solution to call the police every time such trouble arose.

I saw him staggering away and shut the door behind me. It was barely two minutes before the doorbell rang again. This man really came at an opportune time.

I went to the door to find a man about forty-five years old with a very short cut. He had a pointed shapely nose, a pair of concaved blue eyes and thick, pouty lips. He was also one of my regular clients of more than three years. I found his eyes looked blank as he entered.

"What's matter with you? Are you drunk?"

"A, a little too much," he stammered, as if his tongue were tied. "A little too much is just too much."

He staggered to the working room, and I followed closely behind him. "Go and have a shower" I directed.

"I have just had one at home," he said, staring blankly at me. "Then just lie down."

I tucked the pillow under his neck and began to undress him, "It seems it will be hard for you to come tonight. Remember once you also had drunk too much and I had a really hard time squeezing all the sperm out of your balls after a good hour."

"That time I had drunk more than today," he said. "I guess you haven't drunk less today."

I heard no response from him and turned to find him lying on his back on the bed. I took off my dress and sprawled between his legs, with my temple and ears resting on his navel, my hands feeling his chest and my breasts pressed against his cock. I assumed this position to relieve myself of fatigue and relax for a while.

He was sober enough to understand the situation, "Tired out? How many cocks have you served today?"

I answered while fumbling his chest, "About twenty altogether. Big, little, black, white and even drunken cocks have worn me out and my neck has stiffened. Do me a favor and massage me."

He reclined his head on the pillows and clamped his forefingers into the hollows of my collarbones. I raised my head and swayed it in both directions as he was massaging me. The vertebrae in my neck cracked audibly.

"Damn it. I've got occupational disease from nearly ten years of cock sucking. My neck stiffens and so do my shoulders." I grunted as I turned and twisted my neck as he massaged it.

He exerted his strength to grip my collarbone, which made me very comfortable and relaxed. I kept praising his skills, "Wonderful. Mm. Very good." Hearing I was praising him, he sat astride my back and began to massage me diligently. He massaged my neck and my shoulders. I suddenly felt refreshed. His skilled and forceful massage had relieved me of a whole day's fatigue.

Then it suddenly dawned on him, for he asked, "Who of us should pay for the service?"

"Well, I'll pay you but I won't attend to your cock," I said.

"So let's play labor exchange," he smilingly suggested, "I'll massage you for twenty minutes and you should deduct this twenty minutes from your service time."

"That's a deal."

Thus, he massaged me for fifteen minutes more and I then went on to suck his cock. He usually came quickly but today, as he was drunk, his cock turned hard and soft alternatively. I became worried that he would fail to come, however hard I tried. If I was to keep futilely sucking his cock all night long, it would be a real nightmare for me.

He rested his head on the pillow and narrowed his eyes, his legs and belly tautened. Many of my clients appreciated having their balls caressed but he, on the contrary, never allowed me to touch his. So I had to grip his thighs and sucked his tiny cock neither too slowly nor too fast; neither too tightly nor too loosely and it was hard to manage the right balance, especially for an oral job. Though my mouth ached, I held out because I knew if I stopped halfway and shifted to another position he would be frightened back and I would have to start again from the very beginning. It would make me even more exhausted. So I persevered for about half an hour before I felt he was quickening his breath and his tiny cock began to convulse in my mouth. I persisted until he let out a long, heavy groan. He came at last!

I quickly withdrew my mouth to let his white sperm drip down along his saggy cock. I got up and commented, "Quite a lot of stuff out of a not so big cock." He just lay on the bed and grinned in silence.

I went to the bathroom to clean my mouth and hands and went back to wipe the residual sperm off his cock. He asked me, "Linda, can I stay here for the night?"

"Darling," I said, "I never put up a client for the night. You see, I have to get up at seven o'clock every morning and if I am not granted a quiet, restful sleep alone for several hours, how can I go on with my business the next day? After years of preconditioning, I have formed the habit of sleeping alone and I won't be able to sleep if I have someone lying beside me."

"I understand," he smiled.

I stood up and got the bathroom ready for him to have his shower. But I paused and added, "It's strange that while most women go to work in the daytime and go to bed with men at night, I go to bed with men in the daytime and go to sleep alone at night."

"Hence your title of Dr. Linda. You have distinguished yourself from other women."

"Yes," I agreed, "Many clients now refer to me as the Doctor of Cock Specialty."

While he was showering, I tidied the bed.

"Linda, you're a diligent woman," he praised as he came out of the bathroom, "You have a very admirable attitude toward your work."

I charged him forty dollars and sent him off with six beers, "Satisfied this time, aren't you?"

"See you next time," he took farewell of me at the doorstep.

Having seen him off, I thought it was high time I called it day. No clients were supposed to come at this hour of the night. I looked up at the clock and found it was already two o'clock in the early morning. I decided to get down to writing. It was interesting to jot down all the amusing incidents that occurred during the day. A thousand people would have a thousand different sex stories. Since all I see and hear about are cocks, cunts, buttocks and assholes and all I do are fucking jobs, oral jobs and asshole jobs, none of this would strike me as odd. Though I am bored with these things, they would probably sound weird to ordinary people. I feel I must record all the details of my experiences, which are beyond the imagination of most people, into a true account of the life of a prostitute.

I was writing attentively when the doorbell rang again. I got up to open the door and through the locked security screen door, I saw some boys standing outside.

"What are you doing here, boys? You are under eighteen and it's against the law for you to come here. Do you know that?"

There were four of them, all around the age of eighteen. The fatter boy pointed to the shorter boy and said, "Today is my brother's eighteenth birthday. How much would you charge if he entered alone?"

"Fifty dollars for half an hour." "Can it be a little cheaper?"

"I can charge thirty dollars if it doesn't last long." "Twenty dollars," he kept on bargaining.

"No."

He turned back to ask the shorter boy, "Michael, what about thirty dollars?"

The shorter boy looked at me and said, "You are a beautiful woman."

I said thanks and sent the boys away. When I shut the door, I couldn't help shaking my head and laughing to myself. I was now notoriously famous. I was well known to nearly everybody, old or young. In this small city of Canberra, there were more people who knew me than those who knew the Australian Prime Minister. These boys rang my doorbell days before for the sole pleasure of having a look at me. They knew they hadn't reached the age of eighteen but they all had primitive sexual curiosity and impulses as this was the nature of men.

I was writing away with my unfinished account of the day's events when my mobile rang loudly in the small hours of the deep night. I should remember to switch off my phones at this hour. I picked up the mobile, "Hello?"

"Linda, can I come see you at this time?"

"Don't you think it's too late an hour to come to see me?" "Do you still remember the man in the wheelchair?" he asked,

"That's me. I'm Peter."

I could only remember I had three or four clients who were in wheelchairs but I couldn't remember their names, let alone know who was who. In Australia, it was very common to find one's name duplicated by thousands of others. But on hearing the caller was a wheelchair-bound man, I answered promptly, "Go ahead and come. I'm waiting for you."

"I'm coming in half an hour or forty minutes at the most," he said.

I understood such people were slow in moving so I waited patiently and continued with my writing. I wondered whether this Peter was the young man who suffered from high-level paraplegia due to a serious collision of his motorbike dashing against a roaring locomotive when he was twenty-one. I had seen him three or four times and I knew he was a man of fortitude but I hadn't seen him for several years.

It was around three fifteen at dawn when I heard someone parking their car outside. I went to open the full-length glass door, which usually remained locked. I opened it today because my house wasn't wheelchair accessible through the front door on account of the steps outside.

I went out to find him unloading his wheelchair from the driver's seat. I went over to help him unfold the wheelchair. Glancing at me, he said, "Linda, How are you? Thank you."

I clapped my hands together and said, "Surely it's you. I was wondering whether it was you or not." It was none other than Peter, the lad with high-level paraplegia.

He moved slowly out of the car. I moved the chair, using the hand bars at the back, as near to him as I could. He supported himself on the wheelchair seat with one hand and inched his hips toward the seat. He then withdrew his right leg with difficulty from the car and settled it slowly on the pedal of the wheelchair, before repeating the same procedure with his left leg. Finally, I pulled the wheelchair away from the car and shut the car door. He locked the car with an electronic key.

I pushed his wheelchair to my room. I had some difficulty in doing so on a slight slope. He exerted himself in turning the wheels with his hands and we joined our efforts to maneuver the chair to the threshold. I pushed down on both bars with my weight and raised the front guide wheels on the threshold. Then he turned the wheels hard and I pushed the wheelchair in coordination with him. Before we finished counting one, two, three, we were inside the threshold. I went back to close the security door first and then the glass door inside.

Looking at his face, I asked him, "Lad, how come you've become so old by growing a beard and developing a potbelly? It's a mere three or four years since I last saw you."

"Five or six years," Peter said with emotion.

"Yes?" I said with emotion, too, "You came soon after I moved to this house. I remember you were a handsome young lad then but now you've turned into a man. Even your voice has turned hoarse."

"I'm now thirty years old," Peter said.

"I remember when we first met; you were only twenty-two or at most twenty-three. How time flies! Everyone is getting old," I said not without sentiment. The elapse of time was likely to make one sentimental.

He motioned me to hand him the bag that hung on the back of the wheelchair and took a fifty-dollar note from it, "Fifty dollars as before?"

"Yes," I said, "The price has remained unchanged for the past seven or eight years." I accepted the money and asked, "What drink do you want?"

"Beer."

I took a bottle of beer from the fridge and handed it to him, "Here you are. When you leave, I'll give you another six bottles."

I put away the money and pushed him to the working room. He looked around at the furnishings in the room and said, "A lot of changes have taken place. I remember when I came last time, the TV set was over there in the corner, and it was much smaller than the two on the walls now."

"I started from scratch then."

With that, I finished spreading the sheets and pillows. I moved the wheelchair as close to the bed as possible. He supported his weight by pushing his hands on the armrests of the wheelchair and shifted his hips inch by inch to the edge of the bed. During this process, I stood aside looking on as I couldn't figure out where I could lend a hand. When he moved himself to the middle of the bed, I pushed the wheelchair aside and helped him take off his trousers by pulling the trouser legs off one by one and then put the trousers on the massage table. When I helped him tear off the adhesive strap of his adult diaper, his tiny cock appeared shyly and timidly.

I took a small towel from the cabinet, moistened it with warm water and then wrung it out so it was just damp. I came back to help him clean his cock with the moistened towel. After that, I told him, "Take off your coat and try to feel at home."

I helped him take off his coat and let him lie down. Actually he was half lying with his upper body somewhat raised as I tucked three pillows under his back. I remembered he had said if he lied flat he had difficulty in breathing. He often slept with his torso bent upward. This position was of course very exhausting and painful.

I had a good memory for these kinds of things. If my clients told me to take notice of something, I would remember their directions and requirements clearly the next time they came. Now, to Peter, I was just like an elderly sister taking care of her brother or like a nurse taking care of her patient, doing everything softly so as not to hurt him. He looked at me with gratitude, "Thanks very much, Linda."

I smiled affectionately, "That's all right."

Sitting at his side and supporting myself with my left elbow, I began to suck his tiny cock. I continued sucking for about seven or eight minutes before I asked him, "Do you have any feeling?"

"Yes, I do," he said.

I remembered he had had no feeling in his own cock several years ago. It erected hard but he had no feeling at all and of course no sperm could be ejaculated.

"Do you think you can ejaculate this time?" I asked again. "Yes, I can."

It seemed he was in a much better state of mind than he was several years before. He had grown much more mature and experienced. I again got down to sucking his cock, which was becoming harder and harder in my mouth. But he said, "No, not this way. You have to suck harder. Harder!"

Only then did I realize he needed a particularly strong stimulus to make him come. So I tried to jerk him off with my right hand but in vain. He was so choked by excitement that his face turned crimson. He rubbed his cock desperately and had me pull his ball skin hard. I at first didn't dare to apply great strength to it. But by his renewed pleadings, I went to the length of stretching his ball skin so thin that it became nearly transparent. Only by very strong stimulus could he experience some vague sense of sex due to the poor sensitivity of the stump of his lower limb. At that time he was gasping for breath. Under the joint efforts of his rubbing and my stretching, he let out a cry of "Ah---" and then he couldn't help yelling happily, "I have come at last!"

Looking down, I found only a few drops of water around the tiny crevice in his cock tip. He couldn't come as an ordinary man by ejaculating a lot of sperm. However, I thought it was not bad for him. It was beyond the imagination of ordinary people how hard it was for a disabled young man to regain a feeling of sexual desire. No wonder he cried happily, "I have come at last!"

I helped him clean his cock and massaged his legs and feet. But I was afraid that the second service had no effect on him. I heaved a sigh and massaged his shoulders. When time was up, I helped him put the adult diaper on by sticking the adhesive strap back to where it was. Then I helped him sit into the wheelchair and pushed him to the dining table. I took a six-pack of beer from the fridge and let him choose a packet of chips and several chocolates from the table. I picked up some more chocolates for good measure before I packed all these into a plastic bag and sent him to his car. I watched him back his car out of my parking space and merge into the traffic safely before I came back and shut the door.

I couldn't help comparing myself to Peter in my mind. How fortunate I was to have my sound hands, feet and legs and be able to do whatever I wanted to do. What on earth had I to complain about? Many others couldn't earn money simply due to their limited capital, qualifications or attributes, such as a nice appearance or a shapely figure. Thinking of this, I couldn't feel more content with my own lot. Glancing at the clock, it was already four o'clock at dawn and it was high time I went to bed.

I took a bath, put on my pajamas, switched off my mobile phones and plugged them into the chargers. Having checked whether all the doors and windows were locked, I turned off all the lights except one in the bathroom. The last thing was to disconnect the doorbell. I went to bed and it was only a few minutes before I fell sound asleep.

September 26, 2010

I was too tired.

I was sound and fast asleep when a loud pounding at the door woke me up. At first, I thought I may have been dreaming but as I opened my eyes between sleep and wake, I found it was only six thirty in the early morning. The pounding at the door was coming from the front door. It suddenly dawned on me that someone was really battering my security door! Who was the guy that was so agitated by his libido that he had to batter my door so early? I decided to ignore him and pretended not to hear the noise. But he kept on pounding at the door endlessly. I figured it might have woken up all the neighbors nearby so I had to get up to see who it was.

I opened the door and flew into a rage at once upon seeing who it was, "You again! I've told you so many times that I won't begin work until nine o'clock. You're always battering at my door in the early morning."

I shouted at him angrily across the security door and shut the door before him with a loud "Bang!" Then I went back to bed to resume my sleep.

He had interrupted my sleep more than once. In order to prevent some clients from coming in the night, I always disconnected the doorbell before I went to bed. When some clients came to ring the doorbell only to find it was mute, they would know at once what it meant and would be sensible enough to leave. That guy, unlike those sensible fellow guys, had learned how to knock at my door loudly!

I had not lain down for a few seconds before he began to smite on the door again. I sensed he didn't intend to leave.

Afraid of disturbing the neighbors nearby, I had to get up and open the door, "You aren't leaving, are you?"

"Please. Please," he was already sort of weeping, "I promise this is the last time." He waved a fifty and a twenty-dollar note in his hand, "I will pay you more."

Moved by his pitiful words, I changed my mind, "It's the last time, I tell you. You mustn't do this again. You should know it's only been two hours since I went to sleep at four o'clock in the early morning and I can't go back to sleep when I finish serving you."

He looked shamefaced and said, "I won't. I won't of course."

I took the fifty-dollar note from his hand. How could I overcharge a young boy like him?

He was a handsome lad of twenty-something and had already been my young habitué for more than two years. He had a nice, slim figure and stood about five foot five, with black hair, large eyes, a sharp nose and a pretty mouth.

I was wondering why he didn't mind an old lady like me, with age and weariness written on my face. Sometimes I resented looking at my own image, especially when I got up between half sleep and half wake and when I had neither washed nor combed.

After he went to the working room, I put away the money and took a towel for him to take a shower with. When he finished showering, I had paved the bed with white towels and switched on the video programs on the TV sets. He lay back against the pillow and searched back and forth between the porn programs with a remote control in his hand. I settled myself between his legs to suck his cock. His cock was well proportioned, neither too big nor too small and neither too thick nor too thin. It was about six or seven inches in length and a little thinner than an aerosol can of air freshener.

Nice-looking as it was, his cock was one of those that were very hard to make come. Every time I served him, I couldn't help fancying, "His must be a powerful cock to make love to women with. He must be an expert at fucking if he is earnest in it." But I had never made love to him as most young boys hated using condoms because the layer of rubber would surely numb their sexual sensitivity. They preferred oral jobs and I confined the clients who had the privilege of receiving my service without condoms to a very few frequenters of many years and I had to make sure they were not taking drugs. I made it a rule to thoroughly cleanse my mouth and hands after every oral service.

It took me almost twenty minutes to make him ejaculate today and he was sensible enough to be prompt in taking a shower and getting dressed. I was such a person whose bark was worse than her bite. After all, he was a boy and I gave him ten dollars in change before he left.

"See you later," he said.

I smiled and patted him on the shoulder, "Never come so early next time, baby."

I activated the doorbell and switched on my two mobiles lest I overslept. Actually I was very punctual in my business hours. I invariably got up at nine or ten o'clock whether or not I had clients in the morning.

Putting the mobiles on the bedside table, I went to bed and nestled myself into the warm quilt. I was half sleeping when I was woken up by the doorbell. Looking at the clock on the wall, it was only eight fifteen. Just my luck! It was another early bird. I got up with reluctance and opened the door. It was a frequenter of mine for over six years, a taxi driver in his fifties with long hair and a big cock. I couldn't have a grievance against a senior even if he came a little earlier. I opened the door and offered my morning greetings and then I said, "You came so early. Actually I don't open for business until nine o'clock."

"I was driving along here," he explained, "So I thought I'd drop in on the way."

"Doing the early shift from four o'clock?" I asked. "I'm off shift today."

"Then why did you get up so early?"

"I always get up at six sharp every morning, no matter when I go to sleep the previous night," he said. "I don't think one needs so much sleep. You can have a never-ending sleep after your final death."

He always spoke in a low and muffled voice. As he was speaking, he produced twenty-five dollars from his wallet and tossed it onto the kitchen bench. I had never charged him more as each time he only came for ten to fifteen minutes' oral service. He walked into the working room without being led by me as if he were walking around at home. When I put away the money and went back into the room, he had already stripped and stood on the floor, butt naked. He reclined his head on the pillows I had prepared for him.

"I've had a shower at home," he said without being asked, "So my cock is very clean."

I was squatting between his legs when I heard him say, "Do you know I'm going to be operated on next week so I've come today to see how much I can come."

I was startled at his utterance and asked, "What operation?"
"Operation for prostate cancer."

I was momentarily speechless. I hesitated for a few seconds before I told him what I summed up from my clients' experiences, "You come back to see Doctor Cock after your operation. I have seen a lot of these cases so I know a cock after an operation for prostate cancer can hardly come, and not much. The cock can have the feeling of ejaculation but no sperm will come out from the crevice of your cock tip."

"I hope my cock will still remain as big and hard after the operation."

"Maybe," I went on to say, "Maybe your cock won't be as big as it is now and moreover, it might not be able to erect at all."

Then I was holding his cock in my mouth and sucking it hard. "Ah. Ah," he groaned, "You are number one. So beautiful."

"Linda," he asked abruptly, "Did you become a prostitute because you were born into a poor family?"

I spat his cock out of my mouth and looked up at him, "I remember you asked me the same question before and I have told you that my family was not well off but we were by no means poor. Do you suppose I was a country girl coming from the outback of China, who could only live from hand to mouth so she had to flee to Australia to become a prostitute? To tell you the truth, I came from Beijing, the capital of China. My father is an engineer and my mother, a teacher. Do you think I have not seen the world? I served as a policewoman for ten years, owned my own business and was once the boss of a large restaurant. I graduated from a famous University of Prostitution in Beijing."

"Oh, I see," he said, "No wonder you're so professional in sucking cocks. It turns out you had graduated from the University of Prostitution."

"It's really naïve of you to take everything I say so seriously," I laughed, "I was joking when I mentioned the University of Prostitution. Actually, I meant to say I was a graduate of a famous university in Beijing. Prostitution is outlawed in China."

"Why is it outlawed in China?" he asked indignantly. "Without prostitutes, how can men's cocks be satisfied when their sexual desire surges high?"

"Don't ask me," I said, "Ask the Chinese government for its reason to ban prostitution in China."

"And the reason I chose this occupation," I went on to say, "is that I love this occupation itself and the pleasure I get from it. I became a prostitute out of my own free will and I was by no means compelled by any circumstances to do all this. Now do you still think all I can do is suck big cocks?"

Fiddling about with his cock, I added, "I can sing, dance and play the piano. I can also write novels. I'm planning to write about you in my novel."

"No, no," he laughed heartily, "Please don't write me into your novel. If my wife were to know all about it she would surely wring my balls off me alive."

"But you can still keep your cock in case your balls are wrung off alive."

"Without my balls, my cock would then be of no use at all. It would be like the ears of a deaf person -- a useless ornament on your face."

As we were laughing and jesting, I found he gradually became merrier and merrier. I went on to say, "Because I have served in the police force, I can do one more thing that other ordinary prostitutes cannot do. I can do Chinese Kung Fu--- Chinese martial arts. If one day I'm bullied or even cornered by you, I will surely give you a good kick. Though I am approaching my fifties, I'm wondering whether you can withstand a hard kick from me or not."

This time it was he who was startled, "Wait. Wait. Linda. How old did you say you are? Approaching your fifties? No. I remember you told me you were thirty-seven or thirty-eight years old."

"That's a lie," I said, "Anyway, I don't care if you know how old I am. Many of my patrons have guessed my real age and yet they are still coming to me, aren't they? Who doesn't grow old? Only devils don't grow old. Aging is the law of nature and no one can be an exception. Just forget it."

He was still somewhat in doubt, "From whatever angle you don't look like a lady approaching her fifties."

I sat up to show him my hair, "Look. My hair has turned grey. Of course it is not apparent because it has been dyed black. Or…" I pointed to my eyes and went on to say, "After the age of forty-five, a woman's eyes become swollen as if she were always sleepy, unlike the eyes of young ladies in their twenties. Luckily for me, the swell of my eyes doesn't seem as apparent. Some women even have eye bags."

"Are you kidding?"

"Why should I be?" I said in all seriousness, "Even if I am now in my sixties, you are sure to come to me as usual, aren't you? Can you find a prostitute in Canberra who is willing to do an oral job for a mere twenty-five dollars?"

He smiled childishly, "Aren't we old friends?"

I swallowed his cock into my mouth and he began to groan loudly. "Ah--, Ah--." I sucked it for several minutes before he came. Then I handed him a clean towel and motioned him to take a shower. While I was making the bed, he got dressed and asked, "Hey, Linda. You say you're approaching your fifties yet you still look so beautiful. When you were younger you must have been much prettier than you are now. I guess you must have been fucked by your superiors when you were serving in the police force in China."

"No," I smiled, "But my colleague did. Yet that was the affair between two individuals and no one was supposed to have the right to interfere in it. What I resented most was that I had been sexually exploited by the landlord of the restaurant. It was really a harrowing experience. After I quit the police force, I went to a suburb of Beijing, in the *Huairou District*, to run a restaurant. I was young and pretty then but I had to be fucked by the landlord, an influential official, for six or seven years for nothing. You know, I'm selling sex now at a rate of fifty dollars for half an hour or ninety dollars for an hour. I was much younger and prettier then than I am now. Even at my current rate, how much money do you think I have lost over those six or seven years? That bully was then a member of a certain committee and an influential official. I knew he was abusing his power but I had to suffer in silence and swallow the anger and humiliation."

"You should go back to claim your compensation for your suffering," he said with indignation, "If he refuses, you can sue him in court."

"Yes," I agreed, "Next time I go back to China, I will square accounts with him. If he doesn't compensate me for my losses, I will lodge a complaint to his superiors. But I'm afraid he is already retired."

"In that case," he suggested, "You can deduct the sum from his pension."

By that time, he was already dressed and I sent him to the door. He kept on thanking me, "Thank you, my dear, my young lady."

It was nearly nine o'clock when I sent him away. It suddenly occurred to me that I should go to the bank to pay my mortgage. While I expected no clients by telephone appointment, I took the due money from the safe and put it into my purse; carrying it in one hand and my mobiles in the other. I locked the door, checked the two front doors, went to the back door to make sure it was locked also and went through the backyard. A lady in the neighborhood was watering her garden. When she caught sight of me, she friendlily greeted me, "Morning, Linda."

I responded merrily, "Morning. It's a fine day today, isn't it?" "Yes, isn't it? How fine it is today! Going out?"

"Yes. Doing some shopping."

With that, I went southward along the street. On my side of the street, there were rows of houses with a variety of designs and styles. All kinds of flowers were in their full bloom on the lawns in front of each house. Spring was present and everything was so beautiful. I thought while walking: I was lucky to have such good neighbors. The lady of the old couple was near seventy, about the age of my mother, plump and kind-faced while the gentleman was a little more than seventy, neither too fat nor too thin, and warm-hearted and enthusiastic.

In a business like mine, occasional disturbance from clients in my neighborhood was unavoidable but my neighbors never complained about it. As I was running a prostitution business, I had to get along well with my neighbors. If they would frequently lodge complaints or grievances to the local council, I would have a hard time.

But on my part, I was very friendly to my neighbors. For example, our two houses shared one water meter and since I moved into this house seven years ago, I have never had my neighbors pay any fraction of the water bills. When Christmas Day came, I would always send some wines and drinks to them as gifts. Whenever small jobs arose around my house, I would ask the old gentleman to lend me a hand and I paid him more than the regular rates. I felt happy in doing so. Sometimes when I was away on holidays, the couple would help take care of my house. We always remained on friendly terms with each other.

I was deep in thought when I met a lady who led two little black poodles. The poodles were running in front, followed by their mistress. I stood aside to let them pass. The lady, running breathlessly after the dogs, didn't forget to greet me, "Morning. Linda."

"Morning," I responded smilingly.

I waited for them to pass and went on walking, thinking to myself: What good neighbors. All the people in the neighborhood knew I was a prostitute but none of them looked down upon me. Whoever saw me greeted me politely. In this beautiful country of Australia, I had realized what was meant by equality, freedom and serenity. I came to love my second motherland. I love the people and surroundings here, I love the landscape and climate here and I love everything here.

I was indulging my reverie when I felt someone following me and approaching quickly. I turned to find a gentleman walking up behind me. I stood aside to let him go first. He thanked me politely and went on his way.

I responded just as politely.

After years of preconditioning, I had formed a habit of avoiding being followed by anyone lest something unexpected should happen beyond my control. A Chinese saying goes: "Harbor no ill intention against others, but never relax vigilance against evildoers." (*Love your neighbors, yet don't pull down your hedge.*) By nature, I never intend to hurt others but I'm always vigilant against any potential attackers. There are goodies and baddies in every country and dangers may lurk anywhere and come upon you before you can even sense them. Wherever you go and whatever you do, you should keep your eyes open and always remain alert. So I usually wear pants instead of skirts when I go out. I wear closed shoes and always walk with my heels touching the ground first. By doing so, I not only exercise my ligaments but also look more vigorous and more deterrent to any potential criminals. I carry self defense weapons in my handbag. My principle is that I will not attack anyone unless I am attacked. If some malicious guys should attempt to assault me, I would surely win in a cut-throat fight with them.

Additionally, I prefer walking on the right side of the street lest an oncoming vehicle suddenly deviates from its normal course, in which case I can escape in time. When I walk near high-rise buildings, I avoid walking too close to them as you can never know what will fall from the top. All in all, I'm always on full alert when I go out.

Today there were few pedestrians and little traffic in the street. In Canberra, it was very quiet and you might go three to five hundred yards before you could meet a passerby. I was walking at a leisurely pace. The vista of verdurous lawns, dew drops on the grass leaves glistering in the morning sun, and pink, creamy peach flowers blooming on the distant slope was really a feast for the eyes. Listening to the birds chirping and chattering in the trees, I walked down the street and turned at the first traffic light. Then I suddenly spotted hundreds of snow-white cockatoos playing and jesting on a stretch of lawn. The little white creatures had round heads crowned with lush, yellow-green crests. They naturally looked noble and untarnished as if they were from the Garden of Eden. No wonder all Australians liked them so much. Now they were stalking around and pecking something in the grass fields. What a beautiful and peaceful scene!

I was wondering why all the cockatoos of this large flock were females. And where were the males? Looking up, I found hundreds of silver male cockatoos lined up on the power line like valiant soldiers waiting to be paraded by their commander. Perhaps disturbed by my appearance, many males flew off the power line and landed onto the ground, chasing the females about. Some of them flew away in pairs and others jested, flirted and mated on the lawn as if no one were nearby. I felt greatly amused: it was animal instinct.

Then one of the mobiles rang. "Hello?" I answered.

"Hi Linda. I'm the engineer from Papua New Guinea. Can I come see you this morning?"

I was on my way to Woden Shopping Center and was planning to go the bank and supermarket. Now that the business call came in, I may as well go back and earn the money though I was half way to my destination. I said, "Yes, you can. When are you coming?"

"I'm coming in twenty minutes."

"Okay," I was already on my way back home.

I recognized his voice at once. He was not a Papua New Guinean but a local Australian. He was sixty-three years old this year and he worked for an Australian mining company as an engineer. Working in a mine in Papua New Guinea for several months on end, he found it difficult to meet women. So every time he came to me, he insisted on taking some nude photos of me. I agreed on the condition that he couldn't take any picture of my face.

In the past, I never allowed my clients to take nude photos of me even if they offered to pay more money. But I made an exception for him because he was one of my patrons for over five years and besides, I understood what the solitary life in a deserted mine meant for a single man. I myself lived in Papua New Guinea for several years. This reminded me of my former husband Ian Thomas Philip, from whom I had just finished registering my divorce.

Ten years ago, my second husband also served as an engineer for an Australian mining company. The worksite was also in Papua New Guinea. It was the first time I had entered with him into a foreign land—Papua New Guinea. I had left fond memories there of a sweet and happy life shared by my husband and I. Now, ten years later, we were separated but I had been greatly obliged to my former husband up till now because if it were not for him, I could by no means come to Australia and settle here in this beautiful country. I remembered that on the morning of September 2nd, when we finished all the divorce procedures in a lawyer's agency in Sydney, he sent me to the bus stop. We parted in the drizzling rain and I looked at him through tearful eyes, "Darling, I'm not a competent wife. Wait for me. I'll pay you all that I owe you."

When he tried to wipe the tears from my eyes with his hairy hand, I was almost heartbroken. What troubled my conscience most was I had been hiding the fact up till the day we divorced that I was working in a brothel in Canberra. Whenever he came from abroad on leave, I would fly from Canberra to Sydney to meet him, telling him and his family that I was serving as a pianist and singer in a night club in Sydney. At that time, I vowed that I must write an excellent novel for my dearest Ian Thomas Philip. He was now working in South Africa. One month elapsed and I didn't even know how he was getting along there. How I wished he could live a happy life in a foreign country. Tears came up to my eyes at the mere thought of this. It seemed I could neither remarry nor have my own children for the rest of my life. If I remarried, I would owe another man. I married twice and I owed two men too much. My heart was overwhelmed by sad memories.

I shed my tears while contemplating. Marriage is like a fathomless cave. Those who haven't entered it yet are trying their best to rush in while those who have are trying their best to struggle out. And still others who have managed to come out are falling in it accidentally and are trying to come out again. People keep coming in and out and finally end up feeling totally exhausted. In the end some choose to stay outside rather than go in while others choose to stay inside rather than come out, not caring whether it was good or bad inside.

It seemed I had to stay outside.

I kept wiping off the tears that were rolling down my cheeks while walking home and it was lucky I wasn't noticed because there were hardly any passersby in the street.

Before I knew it, I had arrived at my own house. I saw the engineer's purple car was already parked in my parking space. I dried my tears and forced a smile, "If you came a little earlier, you wouldn't have found me at home. I was on my way to the supermarket and I turned back as soon as I received your call."

He came out of his car and patted me on the back, "Why.

You're weeping? Anything wrong with you?"

"No," I said, trying to conceal my sorrow, "Some sand grains got into my eyes."

I turned the key in the keyhole and opened the security door. I told him to hold the security door for me and opened the inner wooden door.

"Please come in,"I ushered him through the door. I turned on the lights in the kitchen and hung the handbag in the cupboard in the kitchen. I then led him to the working room and switched on the TV sets and stereo, as well as the lights in the room. He began to undress. He was of medium build, muscular with a big cock. He said he went jogging every day so he kept fit and looked very healthy.

I handed him a towel and sent him to the bathroom. I went to my own bedroom to take off my coat, trousers and shoes. I went back to the working room bare-hipped. He had showered and dried himself. He was searching for something in his coat pocket. I knew he was looking for his camera. Surely enough, he took out a camera the size of his palm and started photographing my breasts with clicks and flashes. I dodged to avoid my face from being photographed. I kept pleading while dodging, "Stop shooting me. It's your fifth time. You should be content with the dozens of photos you've already taken of me. You can't make it a rule to take photos of me every time you come."

He turned a deaf ear to my pleading and went on clicking away his shutter. Seeing I couldn't avoid being shot, I found I could only distract him from taking photos by pushing him down on the pillows and sucking his cock. He took several photos more before saying, "Suck my cock."

I sat beside him and no sooner had I kept his stick in my mouth than he clicked his camera several times. The glare of the flashlight enraged me and I brushed away his camera, "Enough! How many pictures have you taken?"

I had a bottom line in my mind: You could shoot me grasping your cock with my hand but you can't shoot me sucking your cock with my mouth. Seeing I was taking it seriously, he got up at once and muttered while putting on his trousers, "Linda, I've been coming here to see you for the past few years and I thought you were a well-bred lady. But now you are arguing with me."

Seeing his hands tremble as he put on his trousers, I knew he was not feigning anger. But I was angry, too, "How many times have I told you not to shoot my face? But you do it anyway. Besides, you can't take pictures of my face every time you come. None of my other clients are even allowed to take pictures of me, even if they are willing to pay extra fees. You ought to thank me for giving you the privilege of taking my picture."

While I was reasoning with him, he had already dressed and got ready to leave. I stood in his way, "No, you can't leave unless you have paid."

"No service no pay," was his angry reply.

"In any case, you should pay me for the nude photographs." "I'm going," he pretended to leave.

"If you leave, I'll call the police," I threatened.

"If you don't call the police, I will," he said, somewhat timidly.

Neither of us would budge an inch. The little old man's face turned red with anger and I was gasping angrily, too. We were in a stalemate for a couple of minutes before he took the first step to give in, "Then you do the oral job for me and I'll pay you fifty dollars."

With that, he began to take off his clothes with his trembling hands. I was afraid of angering him too much and to relieve the tension, I patted him jokingly on the hip, "I never thought you were so stubborn, like a mule."

The old man was not amused at all, so I knew he was much angrier than I thought. But he managed to climb onto the bed and lay on his back. I helped tuck another pillow under his head, "Cheer up, old chap. You're not tall yet you have a big cock for your height."

The old man refrained from laughing. I picked up his cock with one hand and struck up a conversation, "Are you married?"

"Yes."

"Have children?"

"Yes, a son and a daughter. Both are grown-ups."

"Wanted to call the police?" I said, poking a finger at his face, "If the police should come, they would phone your wife and then your son and daughter, informing them you were visiting a prostitute. You'll be bringing shame on yourself."

Hearing this, he smiled grudgingly. I went to suck his cock, "Look. The cock of yours has been frightened into shrinking and sagging. Let me give it a wet kiss."

I tucked his cock into my mouth and began sucking it. The old man started to groan deeply and hoarsely, "Eh---. Eh---." I found the old man was in high spirits again so I sucked his cock even harder and ran my tongue tip from time to time along his cock tip. The old man seemed to have forgotten his unpleasant conflict with me and was carried away by unspeakable ecstasy.

As he yelled, "Oh, yes! Oh, yes!" I shifted my tongue tip along the length of his cock and then along the blue vein at the back of the cock to his balls and back to his cock tip.

When my tongue tip reached his balls, the old man shivered all over for a while before he came at last and drawled a long groan of "Eh-------."

White sperm flowed from his cock tip along the length of his cock and to his balls. I jested at him, "You're really in your green old age. Old man, young cock. Look, you have come much more than young guys do."

This time he laughed heartily, "Thank you for making me angry."

"I made you angry and you came more than usual." I replied, "So let me make you angry again next time."

With that, I had him turn around so I could massage his spine, "When will you go back to Papua New Guinea?"

"Next month."

"How many months are you going to stay there?" "Four to five months."

"Does it rain frequently there?"

The old man raised his head and asked me in surprise, "How do you know that?"

"I lived there for ten years," I answered with great familiarity, "The houses there are all made of wood and it's a quake-prone land (an area where earthquakes frequently occurred)."

"Yes. Yes," he kept nodding.

"Is your mining site open-cut or underground?" "Open-cut."

"It's safer to stay in an open-cut site."

With our casual, friendly chatter, we let bygones be bygones. Like an old couple after a routine quarrel, we decided to forgive and forget. Finally he paid me fifty dollars and I gave him an extra bottle of wine as a favor. He promised me at the doorstep, "I will try my best to come see you before I leave Canberra."

Having sent away the stubborn mule, I found it was nearly ten o'clock and I felt somewhat hungry. I planned to cook a packet of instant noodles with two eggs. I had just put the noodles into the pot when the mobile rang. I answered, "Hello?"

"Hello. Boss. Are you occupied?"

I recognized at once by his voice that it was James, a Greek old man of sixty-three. We had been good friends for the last ten years. Nine years ago when I left the brothel, I was homeless. It was he who rented me a two bedroom unit to start my own business. From then on I always called him my "Boss" whenever I met him and the first thing he would say as a password over the telephone was "Boss." He also knew I was always busy so the sentence that followed was invariably "Are you occupied?"

"Not really, please come."

He said he would come in five minutes and hung up the phone.

Expecting he would come in five minutes, I took up the chopsticks and hurriedly gulped several mouthfuls of noodles, gulped down half a cup of milk and after a short gasp, swallowed an egg. Barely had I swallowed the mixture of noodles and egg when the doorbell chimed. It was really prompt of the old guy. With the egg halfway down my throat, I went to open the door. The old guy was wearing a gorgeous, yellow linen T-shirt and a pair of silver linen trousers; the T-shirt tucked into his trousers under a potbelly. He wore a pair of black, shining leather shoes on his feet. He was strongly built though not very tall. He had a big round head with scarcely any hair on it apart from a circle of grey hair on the back of his head. He had a pear-shaped face, a pair of sunken eyes, a sharp, haughty nose, a pair of thick lips and a curved mouth with whiskers above it. Altogether, he looked like a kind and amiable gentleman.

I opened the door and stretched out my hands to fumble his beer belly, "Come on. Turn this way and come in sideways," I said jokingly, as he was so fat he could barely squeeze through the doorway, "You're dressed very neatly today. Why haven't you gone to work?"

"Who goes to work on Sundays?" he asked.

I suddenly realized that I had been working seven days on end and forgot it was Sunday! "Hey," I exclaimed,"This morning I was going to the bank and I was called back half way by a client. Lucky I didn't go."

"You must have lost your head over making money. You toil yourself from morning till night to earn sweat money. Can't you spare yourself a day off ?"

"A day off?" I asked, him as well as myself, "For what do I need a day off ?"

"You can spend the day taking a walk on the beach and enjoy watching the waves roll in from the sea."

"But you can't find a cock on the beach. I'm not interested in a beach without naked cocks."

"What else are you interested in except cocks?" he was truly curious.

"I count on cocks to make money."

"Linda," he was greatly amused, "You are now an expert on cocks. The length of cocks you suck every day can easily add up to ten feet. And all the cocks you have seen up to now can make a bridge long enough to run across the vast ocean between Australia and China and then make a U-turn back to Australia."

"If you say so," I replied, "why are men's cocks always acting on impulse?"

We were jesting and laughing when we arrived at the working room. He told me, "When I got up this morning, I had planned to drive to see a friend of mine but my cock protested, 'No, I have to see Dr. Linda first.' So I made a U-turn and came here."

He unbelted and raised the waist of his trousers, "Look, I have lost fifteen pounds. I weighed two hundred and forty-three pounds in the past; I'm now only two hundred and twenty-eight pounds." Then he showed me his belt, "The original hole was here," he pointed to the next one, "Now it's here. Three holes inside the original one."

I patted his protrusive potbelly and said, "You are always talking about weight loss but I can't see any sign of it."

"It will take some time to really show. You needn't doubt it, madam," he soothed himself.

Then he had stripped and stepped on the scale without a stitch on. He couldn't see the marking on the scale screen because of his bulging belly and had to ask me for help, "Linda, come see what my weight is."

Glancing at the scale reading, I informed him that he was 231 pounds.

He protested at once, "Oh no, I don't think your scale is accurate."

I responded jokingly, "You can go home to find a more accurate scale if you're not satisfied with mine."

I paved the bed with clean towels and repositioned the pillows. He climbed onto the bed with difficulty and I asked him, "Have you taken a shower?"

"I immersed myself in the bathtub from early morning and stayed in the bubble water for half an hour. I have cleaned my cock and asshole thoroughly and you can check by smelling them."

He reclined on the pillows and stuck his big buttocks out for me to smell. I patted him gently on the buttocks and said, "Smell? I will serve you not only by smelling but by licking. But, mind you, this service is supposed to incur an extra charge."

"But we are good friends," he smiled pleasingly.

FUCK

I pushed him down onto the bed with my hands on his buttocks, "Lie down, please. I imagine it's very tiring to keep sticking out your buttocks. You can stick them out later when necessary."

I powdered his back with talcum powder and spread it evenly. Then I ran a finger over his back gently and he twisted his fat back, "Ha. Ha. That tickles!"

I was amused to see him wriggle his fat body funnily. To further stimulate him, I slid my finger tip slowly from his back to his waist. This sent him arching and twisting his fat body more violently and he laughed chokingly, "Quit doing that. I can't bear it. I'm being tickled to death."

Now I got down to massage his shoulders and backside. It was not long before he stuck out his buttocks and asked, "Lick my asshole, please."

To ordinary people, it is a humiliating job to lick another person's asshole. But I regard it as one of the items on my service list. Of course I don't like this item. I hate licking a person's asshole and I usually avoid undertaking this item of service unless specifically requested by my customers. Only when I am with some of my regular patrons of years, who feel freer and more unrestrained with me than with their own wives or girlfriends, do I consent to their requests for that service.

I spread his big buttocks apart and stuck out my tongue tip to lick his asshole.

He wagged his big buttocks and said, "Oh. Oh, Linda. You're number one!"

I licked his asshole again and again until he yelled, "Oh, yes! Oh, yes!"

After a while, he made a rather unreasonable request, "Linda, would you please side your tongue into my asshole?"

I thought to myself, it was true you had cleaned the outer part of your asshole but what about the inside of it. No, I definitely wouldn't do it in case I should taste your shit inside. I ignored his demand and continued to lick the outside of his asshole. Several minutes later, he changed his request, "Lick my balls, please."

I shifted my tongue tip onto his balls and he began to groan, "Eh---, eh---," followed by repeated yeses. He went on to ask me, "Suck my cock." I fulfilled his wish and sucked his cock into my mouth. His next demand was, "Swallow the whole of my cock into your mouth." I tried my best to suck his tiny cock deep into my throat but in vain because his protrusive big buttocks were in the way. I ordered him, "Turn around and lie on your back."

He turned over his body clumsily and I sprawled between his thighs, but his towering belly prevented me from seeing his face. Brushing away the hair around his groin, I pulled his cock hard and said jestingly, "A little cock among a lot of hair."

He smiled,"Tomorrow I'm going to have my doctor transplant my cock hair onto the top of my head. So when you suck my cock in future, my hair will stand on its ends at once on my head."

He was a jocular fellow and his optimism and humor had kept him in very high spirits. Whenever we were together, we laughed at and played jokes on each other.

He was bald headed. Some remnant grey hair grew scarcely around the back of his head near his neck. I made fun of these grey hairs, "If your pubic hair was transplanted onto your head, you would look more like a curly poodle."

"A poodle with naturally curly hair and I wouldn't even need a perm in future."

I sucked his cock while jestingly talking with him and he kept on demanding,"Deeper. Further, deeper. Oh, even further, deeper."

He modulated his yelling, "Oh, yes!" while arching his hips; his potbelly rising and falling like a frog's belly. He belonged to a group of men who became very boisterous in groaning, yelling and gasping during sex. I quickened my pace of swallowing his cock in and out of my mouth while using my tongue tip to tantalize the sensitive glans of his penis. His cock gradually grew harder and harder in my mouth until the skin of his balls tautened tightly like a walnut shell. He started to gasp heavily, "Oh--- Oh---" followed by a deafening, prolonged yell, "Oh-------Fu------ck!" And with that yell he shook and shuddered greatly. Oh my! I imagined this deafening yell would have frightened the passersby to death.

Looking at him, I found his cock, balls and every part of his groin covered with a thick layer of white sperm. He heaved a deep sigh, "Fucking hell! I have never felt more relaxed than I do now."

"Look, how much you've come?"

"It's true that my cock is not very big but I have two big balls. They count most," he said proudly.

I wiped off the white fluid around his cock and cleaned it with wet towels. Then I sat beside him and massaged his legs while making small talk with him.

"You are worthy of the title of 'Cock Specialist'," he then struck upon a whimsical idea and suggested, "You should set up an 'Oral Sex College' teaching girls how to suck cocks and as soon as they have learned the required skills, issue them proper diplomas."

"Meanwhile, you can establish a 'Sex College' teaching men how to fuck cunts" I quipped.

"No. No," he said, "I'm an amateur in this knowledge. And my little cock will be of little use there."

We were exchanging banter with each other when a bright idea suddenly struck me.

I'd like to challenge all the governments around the world as to why none of them have ever established a college that teaches thousands of years' worth of knowledge about sexual intercourse. Sexual intercourse could be established as a new subject or branch of learning, as sexuality accounts for an unbelievably large percentage of our daily lives. An adequate knowledge of sexual intercourse and a consequently harmonious sex life among couples could contribute markedly to both familial and societal stability.

Based on my ten years of life experience as a prostitute, I estimate that at least seventy to eighty percent of men and women around the world lack rudimentary knowledge about sexual intercourse. As sexuality is man's most covert and private behavior, it's natural that it is never discussed publicly in any forums or seminars. Not everyone views sex as an entertainment or a communication between the sexes. Many have sex furtively. Men only aim to ejaculate their sperm and women get through it cursorily before they pull on their underwear in haste. I have personally heard a lot of women complain that they have never experienced an orgasm in over thirty years of their married lives. Even women who have given birth to a dozen or so children have never enjoyed a single orgasm. These poor women! They have missed out on the most enjoyable part of their lives. Many of my clients have come to vent their grievances that their wives had eloped with other men. They could list a variety of causes for their wives' betrayal but couldn't admit that the ultimate reason was that they were unable to satisfy their wives. They had never given their wives or girlfriends any sexual pleasure. In most cases when a woman elopes with a man, a likely explanation is that she is running away from a man who doesn't know how to satisfy her sexually to another man who can offer her more sexual enjoyment. These men lack the most rudimentary knowledge about sexual intercourse. They don't understand the essence of sexuality, believing that the sole purpose of sex is to make men ejaculate or make women pregnant. It is also the same with many women. I have often heard my clients say, "Since I got married more than thirty years ago, my wife has never attempted to suck my cock." Those women have no idea about the necessity to give their men enjoyment through oral sex. Most of them find it dirty or even nauseating to lick their men's cocks or assholes, (similarly, most men also refuse to perform oral sex on their partners) and that's why so many married men are thronging to my house. Naturally that isn't a problem for me as it is good for business, but if these men were to find other women outside their marriages who knew much more about sexual intercourse than their wives did, things would be different. They would become lovers, which would surely lead to the breakdown of their families. So, in my opinion, both men and women should learn more about sexual intercourse and it will help stabilize families and marital relationships.

So I'd like to put forward this formal proposal that the countries which have already legalized prostitution should establish colleges that can impart knowledge of sexual intercourse to ordinary people and teach them how to make love effectively. It will surely contribute to the stabilization of society.

I'd also like to make a suggestion that the countries which continue to outlaw prostitution should amend their laws as soon as possible. Sexuality reflects the most basic and most instinctual desire of humans. If these desires cannot be satisfied, people will be carried away by madness, craziness or insanity. I remember when I served in the police force in China, a colleague of mine once told me a story about a widow who lived unwed for a long time. When she saw a cock mating with a hen, she suddenly lost herself in a fit of bitterness and self-pity. She chased the two poor birds about wildly and beat them away with a stick.

On the other hand, the lonely men aflame with unfulfilled sexual desire probably account for most cases of rape, molestation or abnormal sexual behavior. To think of the poor men who are unable to find wives or girlfriends their whole lives, or the dutiful men who are deprived of the possibility of enjoying sex because their wives lie ill in bed all year round but still refuse to divorce their spouses and especially those disabled men who deserve special care by the governments of all countries. How to vent their burning sexual desire and how to appease their unbearable sexual hunger remains an unsolved social problem. How can we sound off about humanizing laws and regulations if we ignore the necessity to protect humans' most basic and instinctual desires? The legalization of prostitution in western countries such as Australia and the U.S. I think, manifestly embodies the humanization of laws. However, in countries where prostitution is still outlawed, it is even more necessary to set up colleges to impart knowledge of sexual intercourse to people, which can surely stabilize families and societies by decreasing divorce rates. Most people assume that human sexual behavior is inherent, instinctive or self-taught, but harsh reality has proven this assumption to be wrong. In fact, more than seventy percent of people on this planet are sex-blind: they don't know what real sexual intercourse is at all.

I sincerely hope that people can learn something about sexual intercourse through reading my novel.

I know quite well that even in countries like Australia or the United States where prostitution is legal, at least sixty percent of people will label prostitution as a menial calling, never mind the countries where prostitution is outlawed and prostitutes are looked upon as despicable whores.

Seeing I was in deep thought, James asked me, "What are you thinking about, Linda?"

"I was thinking about my book," I said, "I was thinking to include your suggestion in my book that a university should be set up to teach the art of lovemaking."

"Have you heard of Xaviera Hollander, an American prostitute who wrote the book, *The Happy Hooker* forty years ago?" James asked again.

"Her book caused quite a sensation around the world," he added.

"I've heard many of my clients mention that book," I was touched, "Have you read it?"

"Yes, of course," he said and went on to tell me the story of Mrs. Xaviera Hollander and the publication of her novel. I was almost moved to tears. I shared the same occupation and experiences as the book's author. Those who have never worked in this profession could never understand how enjoyable it can be. I like this calling as I do my life. My motto is: Never too late to serve. Both Xaviera and I love our chosen careers and enjoy our lives working as prostitutes.

Prostitution is perhaps the most primitive job in human history. I think there must have been a lot of other prostitutes throughout history like Xaviera Hollander and I who loved and enjoyed the life of prostitution, but the people and values of certain time periods didn't allow them to speak out openly about their vocations. Many Chinese people are familiar with a play *Sunrise*, written by the famous playwright Cao Yu, which vividly depicts the life of prostitutes living in China's old society (before 1949). In his play, Mr. Cao Yu described prostitutes as oppressed and exploited people living on the bottom rung of the social ladder. I beg to differ from him on this opinion. As Mr. Cao could not have personally experienced life as a prostitute himself, he could only observe the lives of prostitutes from his own angle. He took for granted that those wretched girls were sold to brothels by their family members because of poverty. This was certainly the case with a lot of girls back then but there were also several prostitutes who, after years of this lifestyle, came to love and enjoy their professions. However, the people and values of that time period kept them from speaking out the truth about their own feelings. They had to keep low profiles.

When I was a policewoman in China, we often patrolled streets lined with discotheques or karaoke bars. I used to look down on those girls who provided sexual services and there must have been contempt in my eyes when I inspected and questioned them, as I just couldn't imagine the kind of lives they were leading. I had thought they must be living in disgrace and were ashamed of their own behavior. Ironically, when I came to Australia I became a prostitute myself. Initially a novice in my calling, I had much difficulty in adapting to a completely new lifestyle. After ten years of preconditioning, I have developed a sense of pride in my job as the '*number-one prostitute*' in Australia. I'm no longer the girl who shed tears in shame as she took off her dress before her clients.

Times are different and the social environment has also changed. I can now speak out my innermost thoughts and feelings and can understand why Mrs. Xaviera Hollander loves her calling of prostitution so much and pursues her career so persistently. To me, she is a superwoman and a heroine. I admire her courage and daring so heartily that I look to her as my role model. She's really a worthy member of the elite in our calling. If I had lived in the United States forty-five years ago, I couldn't have been as accomplished as her because prostitution was illegal then. I just lacked the courage, daring and drive that Mrs. Xaviera Hollander possessed. Forty-five years ago in 1970, more than ninety-eight percent of American people couldn't accept prostitution as a lawful occupation. When Xaviera first took on this calling, many men came to sleep with her and gave her watches, necklaces or rings as gifts, instead of paying her in cash. It was later that her clients began to pay her in cash. Her job gave her much pleasure in having sex with a lot of men and she came to like her calling. As prostitution was not legal then, the police had sealed her house door four times and put her in prison twice.

Once a cunning reporter asked her a caustic question, "Why do you want so many men to fuck you?"

"It's my job and I love it," she answered smilingly, "I love my men and I get paid money for having sex. I really enjoy it." Some other journalists reported her story in the newspapers, referring to her as "a dirty prostitute." Many people talked abusively in her face whenever they met her, "You are a dirty woman. Go to hell you bad woman!" But nevertheless, Mrs. Xaviera Hollander continued her pursuit dauntlessly and persistently.

In 1971 when her autobiographical novel was published, the American government prohibited its citizens from reading it and burned all her books. But she was not discouraged and kept on working as a prostitute and writing about her profession. More than five years passed and her book began to be known to the public and was later translated into a dozen or more languages. It was not long before her book was filmed by Hollywood studios and adapted into operas by Broadway troupes. Mrs. Xaviera Hollander succeeded at last. She has become the leader of the calling of prostitution and has proved to the world that there are excellent women of high wisdom, quality, morality, daring and ability among prostitutes. If she could serve as president, she would be able to administer her country very well because of her great courage, wisdom and fortitude.

I would be dwarfed in comparison to her in writing. I'm in a more favorable environment than she was and it is much easier for me to write on behalf of prostitutes, not only because prostitution is lawful today in Australia but also because I don't have to write under unbelievably high pressures from the government, media or people of all walks of life.

I heard James say Mrs. Xaviera Hollander is now over seventy years old. After finishing fifteen books on prostitution, she has settled in the Netherlands (she is not American and went to the when she was twenty-five).

I should follow the forerunner of modern prostitution, Mrs. Hollander in pursuing my career. I will love my job and enjoy my life as a prostitute and write books on behalf of prostitutes for the rest of my life. I feel it is my duty and responsibility to justify the trade and reflect the credit we rightly deserve.

I know full well that I alone cannot change the world, nor can I change the ideas of most people in it, but I can, at least after the publication of the English version of this book, correct most people's ideas about prostitutes. I'm planning to send a copy of my book to each president or premier of all the countries in the world, free of charge of course. I'd like to make it known to all that we prostitutes, just like the doctors, nurses or lawyers of the world, are working honestly as true professionals, so our work should be respected by others. I know there are a lot of people who don't approve of what I am saying, but I believe there will be a day, be it thirty, fifty or a hundred years from now, when people will think that it's as natural for a man to go to a brothel as it is for a patient to go to a hospital, and it's as proper to visit a prostitute as it is to visit a doctor.

In my book, people will find lots of true stories about how I cared, like a professional doctor or a considerate nurse, for those lonely old men who had lost their partners in their old age and how I sated the sexual desires of those who suffered from sexual hunger. Also in my book, I suggest those countries that have legalized prostitution should set up special colleges to spread knowledge of sexual intercourse and those countries that continue to outlaw prostitution should amend their laws so as to pave the way for the legalization of prostitution. Because human sexuality itself is not only a culture that deserves studying and researching, but it is also a social problem that demands serious consideration of the governments of all countries. I estimate that at least one to two percent of the male population of the world is suffering from sexual hunger just as famine victims are suffering from starvation. As I have described in my book, a Mr. David from Melbourne, driven by his insatiate lust, went so far as to fuck a mare. This sounds ridiculous to most people, but not to me. I know that was because Mr. David suffered from sexual hunger for so long that he had to find an object, be it a woman or a female animal, to vent his sexual frustration. I have collected so many similar cases, including one in which a client of mine fucked a bitch, that I couldn't include all of them in one book. I have witnessed a lot of men shivering nervously because of long separation from females when they came to visit me. Their hands would tremble as they handed me money and they would find it embarrassingly hard to undress themselves. When the time came that they were on my body, they would be at a loss as to how to guide their cocks into my cunt. Many of them had scarcely found the opening to my private part when they prematurely ejaculated their sperm on the bedding. Those who have wives or girlfriends could never imagine how it feels for a man who can't find a woman and suffers pangs of sexual hunger. It is not impossible for some men to exist who have never had any sexual contact with a woman all their lives. During the ten years I have been a prostitute, I meet with a lot of them and I always feel sorry for those wretched guys. On the other hand, there are also some women who have never experienced orgasm all their lives even if they have been married and given birth to children. It's really deplorable for a person to live a life without enjoying any orgasms or sexual ecstasy before he or she returns to heaven.

Another thing I'd like to mention here again. I sincerely suggest that the Chinese Government amend its laws so as to legalize prostitution in China. At the mere mention of this suggestion, my eyes begin to moisten and soon become filled with hot tears. I'm tormented by complex feelings surrounding this topic. This is an issue that has weighed on my mind for a long time. I must make clear my good intentions first, lest the Chinese Government misunderstands me. This suggestion to the Chinese Government is based on my bird's-eye view and life experience as a prostitute for ten years. I can honestly declare I absolutely have no ill intention against socialism and the Communist Party's leadership in China. I was born in China and spent nearly forty years – the former half of my life – living there. I love my motherland and the Chinese Communist Party. I even filed an application for Party membership but it hadn't been approved before I left the country. I served as warder in a prison in Beijing and I worked so hard there that I was chosen as an advanced policewoman through public appraisal in the Prison Bureau. Though I'm now serving as a prostitute well known in Australia, quite different from a police officer, I remain a woman of good personality, fine quality, high morals and rigid principles as well as a woman who can tell right from wrong, advocates justice and abides by laws. From my experience as a prostitute, I know for sure there are a lot of men in Australia who are suffering from sexual hunger and I can reasonably assume there are still more men in China who are suffering from the same hunger, because there are no lawful prostitutes there who can help alleviate the worsening situation. This is a grave social problem that exists in almost every country in the world and it should command more attention from all the governments the world over. As China is a country with great influence on other parts of the world, any amendment to its current laws will surely affect every other country in the world.

I know as China is a highly populous country, its government fears that once prostitution is legalized in China, the situation will get out of control when a considerable portion of people will indulge their sexuality and won't be able to extricate themselves. But I don't think this will be an issue, as the government can keep the porn industry under control by managing it systematically. As a matter of fact, lawful prostitution had existed for more than a thousand years in the history of China before The People's Republic was established in 1949. After which, prostitution was outlawed by Chairman Mao Zedong, who, ironically, owned dozens of women throughout his life. I don't mean to speak ill of Mao as he was a great leader and the forerunner of the Chinese Revolution; my idol since my early age. But, to err is human. A saint may make a mistake sometimes, as he himself put it, "Everybody makes a mistake and it doesn't matter unless he refuses to correct it…" What I mean is that each legislation, however perfect it may seem, has its flaws and even if it has none, new flaws will come up as time goes on. The legalization of prostitution in China doesn't mean the change of the Chinese socialist regime. It's only my personal suggestion and it's up to the Chinese Government whether to adopt it or not, but I'm convinced that the solution of the problem of sexual hunger would be really helpful to the stabilization of society, as some men can never find a suitable sexual partner all their lives. It's also a social problem faced by almost every country in the world.

It's true I haven't had as much difficulty in publishing this erotic autobiographical novel as Mrs. Xaviera Hollander did forty years ago, but I didn't do it entirely without burden either. Most of my family members still live in China and prostitution is outlawed as dirty whoring there. You can imagine what burden they would have to carry, and how they would be able to face their relatives, friends or colleagues. My mother, who is over seventy now, has grown up in the Party's education and Chinese traditional ideas, so she can never be ready to accept the fact that her beloved daughter is working as a prostitute in Australia. She will feel sad, bitter and heartbroken when she comes to know the truth. She will be an old lady in great torment for a long time, say several years or even a dozen years or so… I may as well leave it alone until she knows it, when I will explain to her that my calling in Australia is by no means a degrading one as most Chinese will assume, and one day she will understand me. After all, she is a well-bred and well-educated lady. Perhaps there is another possibility that she will never understand or forgive me. In that case, I will feel guilty for the remainder of my life.

Why I'm pushing along for the publication of this erotic autobiographical novel is that I'd like to make it known to all that we prostitutes are just trying to sell our own bodies to make money and our honest work does no harm to anybody. When a famous American prostitute was interviewed by a reporter, she asked, "What's wrong with me if I make money using my body while a lawyer does so using his brain?" I'd also like to tell all the people reading my book that prostitution is an indispensible calling in every society and we prostitutes are playing an irreplaceably important role in stabilizing social order by serving those who have special sexual needs.

Through years of serving people as a prostitute, I have come to love this calling of prostitution. Today, I will not feel inferior to others just because I am a prostitute. Instead, I take pride in becoming a well-known prostitute in Australia and I think it is my honor, my pride and my achievement to be one. My excellent service has won me a reputation as the *number-one prostitute* and has won me many patrons as well. So, I am no less superior to President Obama in social status. In this world, there should be no difference between noble jobs and menial jobs, or between elites and manual laborers but a difference between men and women. I'm committed to my beloved career of prostitution and I will write more books on behalf of prostitutes. I vow to succeed and I'm sure to succeed.

Seeing I was still lost in my thoughts, James quickly changed the subject, "Otherwise, Linda, let's open a large brothel jointly." "I have no interest! It will take up too much of your energy and painstaking attention. I had owned and run a restaurant in

China just as you do. It was fucking boring to manage a staff of forty-something people. Anyway I will no longer undertake any management of people. Chiefly because I have had enough."

James was a very smart businessman. He and two other partners opened a large restaurant in Westfield, which covered an area of 22,000 square feet. Every time he came to see me, he carried thousands of dollars' worth of cash in his coat pocket and wore brand-name clothes and shoes costing hundreds of dollars each. But he was stingy toward me in particular. He only ever paid me thirty dollars for each service.

But on the other hand, I did owe much to him. He had lent me a hand during a critical moment in my life. We had a tacit agreement that he should only pay thirty dollars every time he came to see me.

He had made this suggestion more than once. He regarded me as an expert at this business and wanted very much for me to co-open a large brothel with him.

I analyzed the feasibility of the business in detail: "It was commonly believed that the boss of a brothel could surely earn big money but this was not necessarily the case. Take the brothel I worked for nine years ago as an example; the boss had a hard time either when he had clients but no available prostitutes or when he had available prostitutes but no clients. And the boss couldn't set a flexible price like I do now. If the boss charged the client thirty dollars, how could he share it with the prostitute? What prostitute would be willing to suck a big cock for a mere ten dollars? So you must set a bottom price and you couldn't set too low a bottom price in the face of fierce competition from other brothels. If you charge too low, no prostitutes will work for you. If you set too high a percentage's share for the prostitutes, you will surely lose money. Because you would have to pay the rent of the house, the bills for water and electricity and the boarding for the prostitutes, you couldn't earn a single penny excluding all the costs and would most probably lose money. Moreover, if you had more prostitutes and more clients, it would mean more trouble. Should any accidents happen to you, you would bear all the consequences. I heard a client of mine say two months ago, a brothel run by a Korean set on fire and the boss was badly burnt."

"There are more cases like that," I went on to say, "The other day, I heard another client say he had seen a report in a newspaper that a Chinese Australian opened a brothel in Melbourne. Maybe she couldn't hire enough prostitutes, so she bought some from Thailand and made them work for her in the brothel. To control those girls more effectively, the lady of the brothel tried to restrict their personal freedom by making them work without proper work visas. Someone informed the police of this and the police acted on the report and sent her to court. Finally, the judge gave her a sentence of six years' imprisonment. She was trying to make more money only to be thrown into prison. It really isn't worth it!"

James nodded thoughtfully, "Well, no trade is easy indeed. The staff members in my restaurant cause trouble now and then and I have to reprimand them one after another."

I couldn't agree more with what he said, "I know only too well about such things from my own personal experiences and life lessons. Actually I am also a boss now, a boss of myself and a boss of a lot of cocks. I'm in charge of thousands of cocks. In this sense, I may be considered a big boss."

James burst into laughter on hearing what I had just said. We were jesting when a phone call came in, "Hi, Linda. Can I come see you?"

I recognized at once by his accent it was a Pakistani overseas student. I answered, "Yes, please come on over."

James winked at me, "Your big cock is coming." "He has a little cock," I said.

"Would you double charge him if he had a big cock?" "A unified price for all cocks, big as well as little ones."

After a brief pause, James said, "Linda, may I ask you a question?"

"Yes?" I was wondering what he meant.

"Suppose there's a wealthy man offering you a considerable sum of money on the condition that you quit your present trade and marry him," James asked, "Would you accept his offer?"

"No," I answered, "I wouldn't. It's not a happy life living on the handout money of a man. However much money he would give me, it only proves his ability, not mine. In that case, when I'm lying on my deathbed, I won't be able to look back on how much I've earned all my life. I'd like to go on making money the way I'm doing now, so that when I die, I will be able to make an evaluation of my life and figure out how much money I've earned collectively and self-sufficiently throughout my life."

"It seems you will go your own way till the end of your life," James smiled mirthlessly.

We were smiling and talking as I saw off the old man. I went back to the kitchen and took up the bowl of unfinished instant noodles. I had just had two mouthfuls when the doorbell rang again. I had to put down the bowl to answer the door. The man on my doorstep stood less than five foot five. He was not too fat but carried a potbelly. On his long face, I observed a narrow nose, sunken eyes; one of them a little slanted and a small pursed mouth. He had a short moustache and was missing his left front tooth. He wore an old blue T-shirt and a pair of jeans on his protruding hips. He pattered into the house in a pair of worn leather shoes and couldn't wait to put his hand under my dress.

I brushed his hand aside, "What are you doing?" and went on to ask, "Haven't you gone to work today?"

"Today is Sunday and I needn't go to school," he said word-for-word.

Somehow since the day I met him, I had had the impression that he was a bit slow in responding so I had to question him again, "When I first met you eight years ago, you said you were studying in school. Haven't you graduated yet?"

"Not yet," he was honest in answering.

I thought: Though that guy was about my age, he probably wouldn't graduate until he parted with all his front teeth. I asked him, "What drink do you want?"

"Beer."

I took a beer from the fridge and handed it to him. He pulled off the tab of the beer can and drank while walking to the working room. Putting down the emptied can on the bedside table, he came at me again.

"Wait. Wait. Take your time to undress," I tried to calm him down.

He giggled and began to undress slowly. He took off his clothes one by one and threw them onto the massage table. He tossed his worn shoes together. As I was walking to the bed, I tumbled over one of his shoes accidentally and in a fit of temper, I kicked them to the corner under the massage table. He continued giggling and came at me for my breasts. I had let my dress fall to the carpet and said, "Be careful with my breasts. Do you think you're playing with a basketball?"

Then he kissed me on the face madly. I wriggled myself free and pleaded, "Don't kiss me on the face. You're pricking me with your moustache."

I lay on my back on the bed and he came upon me giggling.

He sprawled on me and kissed away at my lips.

"Quit kissing," I protested, "And away with your moustache!"

He then moved forward a bit, parted his legs and knelt astride my face. His ball skin was right over my lips and I began to lick it. His buttocks kept rubbing my face back and forth and with every rub, he let out a groan of "Ah---." Soon he endeavored to tuck his carrot-like cock, bent somewhat upward, into my mouth.

"Let me suck your cock in a better position," I begged, "Your cock is not straight. If you thrust it into my mouth, I'm afraid it will be cut by my teeth."

He giggled and got off my face. He knelt on the bed while I sat up and kept his cock in my mouth. No sooner did I begin my sucking than he yelled, "Ah---! Ah---!" I urged him, "Be quick. You have only paid twenty dollars. Let's shift to fucking!"

I found him a small-sized condom and put it on his cock, ready to fuck. As I knew he was a poor overseas student, I had been charging him only twenty dollars each time for the last eight years and he was sensible enough to finish as quickly as possible when he saw that I was busy. But he would sometimes hang on me for a longer time. Today he was trying to make me suck his cock for a little longer, "Suck me another five minutes, will you."

"No, I won't," I said firmly, "My next client is coming in no time."

He reluctantly got down from the bed and stood on the carpet. As soon as I sat on the edge of the bed and spread my legs apart, he charged into me with a yell at the top of his lungs. He moved his tiny cock in and out deliberately slowly, back and forth, back and forth until he collapsed with a loud cry on my body. After a while I pushed him away, laughing at his potbelly, "Your belly rather than your knowledge has progressed rapidly, hasn't it?"

He swayed his hips as he entered the bathroom. I hung a clean towel on the towel rail for him and he began to shower. It was a real cleaning ritual for him. He stood under the shower nozzle and washed his head, his face and his hips thoroughly. I knew from past experience it would take him at least seven to eight minutes to finish bathing. So I hurriedly threw all the dirty towels into the washer of the laundry and returned to the kitchen to finish my unfinished meal. Then my mobile rang, "Linda, are you busy now?"

It was a call without a caller ID displayed and I didn't recognize who it was but I knew for sure it was a frequenter so I answered briefly, "Not really. Please come."

"Let's meet in ten minutes." "Okay!"

Putting down the mobile, I went back to the kitchen to do my washing up and when I finished all the cleaning chores in the kitchen, the overseas student from Pakistan came out of the working room, still in his worn shoes. He clipped a twenty- dollar note between his two fingers and handed it to me across the kitchen bench, "Thank you for your service."

"What else do you want to drink?" I reached out to accept the money.

"Beer," he said.

I went back to the fridge to take out a can of beer for him, "Anything else?"

"No, thanks."

Sometimes he would choose a packet of chips. In that case, I would have earned at most fifteen dollars from him. I knew very well that those overseas students had a hard time here because I had undergone a similar life when I had to tighten my belt with everything and besides, he usually didn't take up too much of my time. I left the kitchen to show him the door. I asked him, "Where do you plan to spend your holiday?"

"To Sydney," he answered inarticulately, pointing to his backpack.

"You should focus on your studying instead of playing. How come you always say you're going to Sydney every time I ask you?"

He chuckled as he made for the doorstep saying word-for-word like a robot, "See you next time."

"Don't drive too fast. See you."

I shut the door behind him. Figuring my next client would come in no time, I hurried back to the bathroom and got everything ready just in time before the doorbell rang. I ran to the front door and recognized at once it was a client of mine for more than five years, my favorite sexual partner "Hard Thing." He was an expert who knew best how to quench my carnal desire.

"Damn it. Why it's you?" I was pleasantly surprised as I couldn't recognize his voice over the phone. I even hit him gently on the shoulder flirtatiously.

He was of medium height but stoutly built like a young man in his prime. You needn't undress him to see that he was a muscular man without any redundant flesh on his belly. He had a notoriously hard cock, twice as hard as average young men's cocks. He held a black motorbike helmet under his right arm. He was a motorbike fanatic despite being fifty and something of age. His chubby face held a pair of shrewd blue eyes, a nice pretty nose and a curved mouth that looked very amiable and lovely.

He grinned as he entered the house, "While I was on my way here, my cock became squirmy and restless inside my trousers."

Looking down at the part between his thighs, I found his hard thing had already made a tent of his trousers. I smiled and fumbled it, "It is still hard and rigid."

"If you please," he bragged, "it can fuck you for three hours without getting saggy."

"Three hours? Oh my," I feigned shock, "Your cock can manage it but my cunt couldn't bear it. I'm planning to keep my cunt as a golden-egg laying goose. If you wear it out, what can I make my living with in future?"

We were walking to the working room, jesting with each other when something suddenly occurred to me. I turned back, "The beer! I almost forgot it." I knew his drinking habit well so I fetched two bottles of VB beer from the fridge for him and put them on the nightstand. When I came back to the working room, he had put his helmet on the bedside table and started to undress. He said, "I'll have a shower first."

I took a towel from the cabinet for him. Seeing his cock jerking rigidly, I felt my face burn and at the same time I had a tickle in my cunt like something hot was swelling inside it. I was fond of his cock because it had given me a lot of pleasure and happiness and it had brought me to the sublime of sexual ecstasy. His was one of my most favorite cocks.

Soon he finished his bathing and came out of the bathroom. He took up a bottle of beer and knocked off the cap. He gulped down half of the bottle in one breath. He put the half-emptied bottle on the bedside table and said, "Let me drink some beer to warm up my cock before I give it full play. You may as well give it a good sucking first."

With that, he lay down on his back on the clean white towels I had spread out for him. I tucked two pillows under his hips and he arched to get ready for my service. I prostrated myself between his parted thighs and kept his burning cock as hard as an iron bar in my mouth. I was startled by his yells, "Oh, that feels so good! I've been missing it for days! I simply couldn't contain myself from the desire."

I started to suck his cock slowly and it jerked violently, becoming harder and harder. "So amazing!" It was only a few minutes before his cock erected upright and shook away like a spring coil in the air. He stopped me and said, "I may as well get up and fuck you."

With that, he got to his feet and stood on the floor. I sat on the edge of the bed and spread my legs apart. My cunt opening confronted his thick cock. He needed no aiming and thrust his rigid stick right into my hole. He seemed to be intoxicated, "Ah, that feels so good. I'm happy to be inside you again. I love watching my cock moving in and out of your cunt."

His undisguised tantalization further whetted my sexual appetite. My lust fluid flooded through my already damped tuft. He was not in a hurry to move his cock further into my cunt. Being overflowed with lust fluid, my cunt squelched shamelessly with every movement of his relentless cock. I began to scream and yell as I was taken away by the unspeakable ecstasy. I groaned heartily, "EH---." "Ah---." "Oh, yes." He echoed with repeated "Oh, yes. I love fucking you." All these groans in bed, combined with the mating noises of the couple on the screen made me totally confused as to whether I was in reality or virtual reality. I felt as if I was soaring through the skies.

I felt a shivering swell surge from the soles of my feet and I began to run my finger gently over the swollen red bud between my cunt lips. My finger was covered at once with a sort of sticky fluid flowing out from my cunt. I felt a piercing thrill surge through my entire body and flow from my bud, through my spine, my legs, and down to the soles of my feet. Now he deliberately slowed down the pace of his movements inside me as he knew I hated fast movements at the last stage of coming. I narrowed my eyes and tried to concentrate my attention to the pistoning cock in my cunt. I cried in my mind, "Darling, fuck me harder. I love this cock of yours."

I was deep in my carnal reverie when I felt as if a hot flow of electricity was generated from the bud of my cunt and ran throughout my body and back to my cunt. I couldn't help cry out, "Darling, fuck me even harder," while he continued to exert his strong cock mercilessly. I yelled repeatedly, "Darling, fuck me harder!"

CUMMING

I came four or five times and I couldn't stop trembling violently. He kept moving inside me for a while until I came completely. He asked me, "Now are you satisfied?"

Gazing at him affectionately, I said with emotion, "Bad guy. Only you can quench my desire."

"Would you like to come once more?"

"Coming with you once can make me satiated for three days. I have to save some strength for the next client," I explained, "Go ahead and come yourself."

"You're eager for the next course even though you have an unfinished course in front of you," he quoted a Chinese saying jestingly. "You're just an insatiably greedy woman."

"As long as there are cocks coming to see me, I will have money to make. I can't count on you alone. Your cock has only contributed fifty dollars, which can't even cover my mortgage for a single day."

"Watch how I settle with you."

With that, he got down to thrusting his cock inside me. I was frightened into panic, "Ouch. Ouch." I prayed he would take his time and do it more tenderly. His cock, though not too long, was very thick and when his cock filled me, I almost burst inside. But he just ignored my pleadings and began his final charge. I frowned to bear all this. Soon he breathed heavily and with three yeses, followed by a desperate yell of "Fucking Hell!" he collapsed. He pulled out his cock, covered the tip with his hands and spilled all his sperm on my abdomen. He cried, "Ah! I feel fucking relaxed now."

I handed him a clean towel, motioning him to take a shower and I myself went to the bathroom in the waiting room. I came back to find him sipping his beer on the bed and said to him, "Please lie face down on the bed so I can massage your back."

"No, thanks. Let's have a chat," he went on to ask, "How long is it since you moved to this house, Linda?"

"Almost seven years, I suppose."

"So I have known you for more than five years," he stated. "Yes. If I date back to the times of Narrabundah, some clients have been with me for more than ten years."

He took another sip and said, "Linda, I have no sexual relations with anyone except you and my wife. I never go to brothels. I like you because you're a very nice lady. I've been visiting you and I've never regarded you as a prostitute but a good friend of mine."

I knew he was sincere in saying so, "Yes. Many of my clients also say so."

"It's deplorable that some people don't understand this. They always feel they are superior to others," he said not without emotion, "I think in this world there should be no difference between all people besides gender, regardless of whether they are high or low in their social status. All men are created equal whether you are a farmer of the land, or a manager of a company or an official in the government."

"I can't agree more now," I said. "But years ago when I first took on this profession, I felt inferior to anyone else and confined myself to the house. Even when I went to shop in the supermarket, I kept a low profile in case I met some of my acquaintances."

"Men come to you to relax themselves," he explained, "It is not that they don't love their own wives but that the dull routine of a long period of marriage has sapped their original lust."

"Sexuality is really strange in itself," I commented, "Though your wives or girlfriends remain attractive enough, you find no novelty in them and you simply get more excited when you catch a casual glimpse of a woman, maybe much less attractive than your wives or girlfriends."

"Yes," he nodded his agreement, "Now that most people live under great pressure from both life and work, it's natural to find someone from the opposite sex to have a small chat with about anything simply to relieve your repression. Take me for an example; I'd like to chat with you instead of with my colleagues or my wife. By doing so, I can escape the pressure and satisfy my sexual desire all at once."

"I think sexual satisfaction may be the best outlet for pressure," I said, "I know this from personal experience. Sometimes when I feel tired from work or annoyed about something, I make love to one of my old patrons madly and the carnal satisfaction he gives me eases me so thoroughly, both physically and mentally that I wonder whether I should pay him instead of being paid."

"So," he grinned, "you're supposed to pay me today, are you?"

I realized at once I had made a mistake and grimaced by sticking out my tongue. Just then the mobile phone on the bedside table buzzed and I picked it up, "Hello?"

A voice on the other end asked, "Hi, may I have an appointment for two hours?"

"What time?"

"I'll come in twenty minutes," the man said.

The hard cock in the room stood up and said, "Go ahead with your business and I'll leave."

He began to dress and at last he had put on his black motorcycle jacket and helmet. He took out a fifty-dollar note from his pocket and handed it to me, "I was joking when I demanded you pay me. How can I fuck you without paying you?"

I took the money from him and said, "Tut-tut! You've only paid me fifty dollars. Where else can you find such a cheap service? Oh yes, you have drunk three beers plus a bottle of wine you'll take from me. Maybe I'll only earn less than forty dollars."

He patted me on the cheek, "Hey, hey. After all, we're an old couple of so many years."

We walked out of the working room, jesting with each other. I retrieved a bottle of wine for him from the garage, "Don't forget me when you're enjoying the wine with your wife this evening."

He took the bottle from my hand and said smilingly, "I won't forget you even when I'm sleeping with my wife."

I patted him gently on the shoulder and sent him off via the back door.

I figured there would be about ten minutes left before the next client arrived and I took advantage of this gap to refill the fridge with beers and other beverages. I quickly finished this task and began to do the washing up. Through the window blinds, I caught sight of a figure coming toward my front door and ringing the doorbell. When I opened the door I said to myself that this was unlikely to be an appointment of two hours.

The man was a little over twenty with a fat build, a huge head, yellow hair, big eyes, a straight nose and thick lips. When he saw me, he said, "I came to you last week. Could I pay for today's service next Tuesday?"

"No" I refused promptly, "I don't know you and I have been doing business in cash even with my old patrons of many years. Besides, I haven't heard of anyone owing money to a prostitute."

But he kept pleading, "Please. Please!"

I waved my hand dismissively, "Go, go, go and hurry up. My next client is coming."

He reluctantly turned and left. I was about to close the door when I saw a stately, European blonde lady coming toward my house. She was about five foot eight and her blonde hair fell over her shoulders. She wore a blouse with blue flowers on a white background, a red mini skirt and a pair of red shoes with a matching handbag on her arm. I had thought the lady was intending to ask for directions. Only when "she" came nearer to my front door and greeted me, "Hi Linda, the appointment of two hours!" did I recognize "she" was a client who had come to me twice before. "She" was a local Australian man of about sixty. Every time he came, he liked to dress as a lady.

"I didn't recognize your voice over the phone," I said, "Please come in."

I ushered him in and went on to ask, "What do you drink?" "Just a bottle of mineral water, please," he stalked directly to the working room.

I took a bottle of mineral water from the kitchen fridge and followed him to the working room. When he entered the working room, the fucking scenes from the porn program *"Orient Fever 11"* immediately excited him. Pointing to the screen and shouting, "Look at that!" he began to dance and sway his hips to the rhythm of the music. I had to say the old guy had quite a good sense of rhythm and every time he came he would showcase some novel performance. Not only did he sway and twist his own body but he also looked from time to time into the mirrors on opposite walls at his own reflection. While dancing away he took money out of his red handbag. To please the old guy, I also swayed my hips, keeping pace with his movements. As he swayed to the right and then to the left, I followed suit. I saw in the mirrors, two ladies dancing devotedly to the music, a black-haired Asian lady and a blonde-haired European "lady."

He waved four, fifty-dollar notes in the air and I took the notes one by one from his hand, "The money is mine. Thank you, sir. I will give you a special offer -- a hundred and sixty dollars for two hours." I made a full circle in the air with the notes in my hand before I made a 360-degree turn out of the working room. I took forty dollars' change from the kitchen drawer and gave it to him. He put the change into his handbag and put the bag on the massage table. I began to unbutton his lady dress. On the TV screen at that time were two men and a girl jesting and playing on the lakeside with the background music of slow, four- beat tunes. The clean, smooth melody sounded like a murmuring stream winding itself down a hill.

We slowed down our swaying with the ebbing rhythm of the music. I undid his buttons, one by one until a bright, red bra came into sight. I helped him undress his blouse and tossed it away into the air. I helped him unfasten his bra, rubbed his cheeks with it and threw it onto the massage table. He smiled and ran his fingers through his long hair and then twisted his torso. I helped him take off his miniskirt and briefs. His long flaccid penis knocked against the inside of his thighs with each swaying movement. I reached out to feel his balls and then went on to grasp his cock. He stopped me, "Take your time. It's too easy for me to come and I obviously don't want to end the game too soon."

I snatched off his blond wig and exposed his shiny bald head with a circle of grizzled hair above his neck. I swung his wig two circles in the air before it flew across the room and landed onto the massage table. Then I had him lay face down on the bed and

I sprawled onto his back. I ran my creamy, ample breasts across his body for quite a while to the beat of the music and then I sat astride him to massage his back. When I slowly arrived at his buttocks, he lifted them up and requested, "Please thrust your hand into my asshole."

I knew his asshole was a big one. The first time he asked me to thrust my hand into his asshole, I was startled, thinking if I followed his instruction and tucked in a fist, his asshole would burst. Now I knew from experience that his asshole had no difficulty in allowing in a whole hand, so I agreed, "No problem. But let me put on a pair of rubber gloves first."

"Please do it without the rubber gloves," he pleaded. "I cleaned the inside of my asshole thoroughly before I came."

"I can't, sir," I said, "If I thrust in my hand without the gloves, it will stink to the sky when I finish the job and how can I serve my next client with that hand?"

Finally, I insisted on putting on the rubber gloves and lubricated his asshole with ample oil. I tried inserting two fingers of my right hand, then three fingers, four fingers, five fingers and at last, my whole hand into his hole. I slowly turned my right hand inside his asshole just as someone turned a key in a keyhole. I turned my "key" this way and then that way and I thrust it forth and then back until I felt something dry and hard in the depth of his asshole. It must have been his dried shit. I congratulated myself on putting on the gloves, or else I couldn't have imagined what would happen to my hand. He kept encouraging me to thrust my hand further and further and I was really afraid I might poke a hole in the intestinal wall of his stomach. I kept on moving my hand in his asshole very carefully for about half an hour until he changed the rules of the game. He had me lie underneath him and nibble his nipples, first the left one and then the right one. With each nibble he kept encouraging me, "Use your strength! Do your utmost!" I was really afraid of biting off his nipples. Upon his renewed pleadings, I kept on nibbling hard until I found much to my horror, that his nipples were cut and bleeding. I stopped the game resolutely in spite of his insistence that I exert all my strength. But he seemed to savor the strong excitement of the process and was very happy. I spent another half an hour lying between his legs sucking his cock while pinching his two nipples with my hands.

His nipples then became very hard and stiff. Like many men whose most sexually sensitive spot was precisely their nipples, he at last reached his climax by having his nipples stimulated relentlessly. He breathed heavily, lying on his back. After I rinsed my mouth and cleaned my hands, I offered to clean his dick and his balls, which were covered in semen. Then I offered to massage him. But he declined and said, "No, thanks. Leave me alone to lie for a couple of minutes and I'll take my shower."

Looking at the clock, I found the whole service lasted only one hour and forty-five minutes so I said, "As you ended the service a quarter ahead of time, I will refund you ten dollars." (And on an already very low-price basis.)

"But you can keep it," he said.

I insisted on refunding him ten dollars and at last he said, "Well, if you insist. I have never seen a lady doing business in such a fair way."

"Many of my clients have made similar comments," I said, "I never cheat my clients on time. I remember the practice in the brothel I worked for nine years ago. If you had paid the money for an hour but enjoyed only ten minutes' service before leaving for any reason, the boss there would never refund you any money."

"You're running your business so differently from others and that's why you have so many frequenters."

"Actually many of my clients insist on leaving me tips," I said, "But I never accept them. I only say, 'If you're satisfied with my service, return to my place again.'"

We were discussing managerial principles and tactics when the doorbell rang. I had him take his shower and I went to answer the door only to find it was the guy who had come earlier to buy service on credit. I asked him, "You said you had no money and wanted to fuck me on credit. How come you have the money now?"

"I've just borrowed some money from my friend," he said in embarrassment.

I reconciled myself with the amount of forty dollars in my mind and thought that forty in cash was much better than any amount on credit. I led him to the waiting room and told him to wait five minutes. After that I went to the kitchen to drink some water. While drinking I listened out for the sound of running water in the bathroom. If the water stopped, the client would start to dress and after a while I supposed he would be ready. I lost no time to fetch the clean towels from the drier and filled the washing machine with some used towels before I met my departing client. The "lady" was dressed neatly with "her" red handbag. When "she" came out of the working room into the dining room, her bright red, high-heeled boots knocked on the floor with crisp sounds. I saw "her" off at the doorstep and "she" turned round to say, "Have a nice day, madam."

I went back to the waiting room to usher the young man into the working room and had him take his shower. When he finished bathing and came out of the bathroom, he just stood beside the bed with a big towel wrapped around his waist. I told him, "Take off your towel as no one can fuck with a towel wrapped around him."

As he took off the towel, the sight of his body suddenly made me feel disgusted. A bright red area the size of a small dish was visible around his navel, with some dried scuffs dotted on it, apparently infected with a certain skin disease. Maybe it was psoriasis or "thrush," as ordinary people might call it. I had seen one of my clients who suffered from such a skin disease. They said the disease was hard to treat and impossible to cure. I had consulted some of my patrons that were doctors as to whether this disease was contagious. Though their answers were unanimously "no" and it was a blood disease, I felt quite uneasy to contact such a client.

"Lad," I said not without fear, "It is not that I'm unwilling to serve you, but that if I am infected with your disease, my skin will become infected and no client will come to me."

With that, I ran to my bedroom to find two medical plasters from the bedside table and returned to apply these plasters right on his affected part around his navel. I quickened my pace and he thrust hard into me with his humongous dick and came within a couple of minutes.

Then I spent less than five minutes messaging his back but he turned around to ask for another fucking. I sheathed his penis with a medium-sized condom but this time he wanted me to bend over against the bed and he forced his penis into my cunt from behind. The young man exerted all his strength to piston his cock into me and pounded against my buttocks very loudly. My body bent forward with every pounding.

"Hey, lad," I shouted back, "What's the use in you exerting all your strength? Anyway, you can't lengthen your cock enough to fill my cunt." Turning a deaf ear to me, he kept on pounding me and with every pounding he cried, "I'm sorry." And after numerous cries of "I'm sorry," he still didn't come.

"Young man," I began to feel impatient, "Stop saying 'I'm sorry,' leave your 'I'm sorry' for next time."

But instead of coming, he settled his penis in my hole without any intention to withdraw it.

"Say, time is up. It's time you left." "I haven't come," he argued.

"Who promised you could come twice in half an hour?" I asked.

"I've paid you forty dollars," he was not amenable to any reason, "So I'm entitled to come twice. Twenty dollars for once."

"Where does your price list come from? If you go to a brothel with forty dollars, it's a wonder that the boss won't show you the door and blacklist you."

But he persisted and refused to withdraw his cock from my cunt. I had no choice but to push him away, jump off the bed and snatch his condom, "Go, go, go. Go and take your shower," I cried somewhat desperately, "Oh, yes. Leave me my plasters behind you!"

I tore the plasters off his belly and threw them into the dustbin. I ignored his murmuring complaints, closed the door to the working room and rushed to the bathroom in the waiting room. I scrubbed hard every part of my body, lest I was infected. I was washing away under the nozzle when the doorbell rang again. I thought that it must be another rash guy who came to my door without an appointment.

I hurriedly threw on a dress and went to the door. It was a fortyish newcomer. He was tall and stout, with tanned skin. He wore blue denim overalls. I told him to sit in the waiting room for five minutes and I went back to the working room. The silly fat boy had already dressed but still couldn't tear himself away from my house.

I took him by the arm, "Hurry up and leave. Do you think you can pay only forty dollars and fuck me all afternoon?" Finally I managed to push him out my front door. His last words were,"I will lodge a complaint to the Fair Trading Department."

"Go ahead," I encouraged him, "But you should lodge the complaint to the Prostitute Association instead of the government saying you are entitled to come twice for the forty dollars you paid. Oh, yes. It is Sunday today and no one will serve you. You'd better go tomorrow during business hours."

I shut the door and came back to the waiting room. I ushered the new client to the working room. While making the beds, I was casually chatting with my client, "Today's Sunday. You didn't go to work?"

"No."

"Do you live in Canberra?" "Yes."

"Do you live far from here?" "Not really."

So I had to get down to business, "Do you need half an hour's or an hour's service?"

"Let's begin with half an hour," he said as he took three twenty-dollar notes from his coat pocket and handed them to me, "It was my doctor who recommended that I see you."

"Have you brought your doctor's referral letter with you?" I smiled, "Which doctor recommended you to come to me? I have several clients who are doctors."

He referred to the doctor's name but I had no impression of him at all and neither did I try to search for it in my memory because there was no need for me to remember the names of my clients. So I said to him, "Those doctors are qualified to solve the problems of their patients' headaches, loin aches or buttocks pains but they are at a loss as to how to solve the problem of their own cocks. They had to come to see me – Dr. Cock Linda for a cure to their cock problems."

My new client laughed at what I had said. At my question as to whether he had taken a shower, he answered, "Yes, I have taken my shower at home."

"Then take off all your clothes and put them on the massage table," I told him and he did as I ordered.

"Now lie on the bed."

I took the money to the kitchen and put it away in the drawer before clutching a ten-dollar note and a plastic bag from the second drawer. Then I went to the garage for a bottle of red wine and put it, together with the change, beside the pile of his clothes on the massage table.

He lay face down with his fat buttocks pointing upward. I patted him on his hips and said, "Why are you showing me your fat buttocks if you'd like me to solve the problem of your cock? Please turn over."

He shyly turned over. I took off my dress and settled between his legs, "Well, the thing is not very big, is it?"

"Not only is it not big but it is not hard either," he was a little frustrated.

"How long has it been since you last had an erection?" I asked professionally as if I were a real specialist in andrology.

"More than half a year," he answered.

"Well, more than half a year. Good. No problem. If it were longer there would be no cure. Last month a frequenter of mine brought a friend of his to me, claiming he was forty-two years old and still a virgin. At first I refused to believe it until I caught sight of his penis. His penis was literally like a dead caterpillar and didn't react to any stimulus. No matter how hard I tried to awaken it sexually, be it by caressing or sucking, it just lay dormant. I asked him whether he had ever been with a woman or masturbated. He answered no. He had neither played with his cock nor touched any woman. I spared no effort to arouse his dormant cock but in vain. The forty sweaty minutes I had spent arousing his cock was a sheer waste of time. I said, 'Sorry, I have done my best and you'd better find a more competent doctor than me'."

With that, I had already held his limp penis in my mouth and I hadn't sucked it for a minute when I began to cough.

"I don't have the flu," I was in a hurry to explain, "I just have a lump in my throat. Maybe an allergy to cocks. I just can't help coughing at the sight of cocks."

"I've been in this trade for nearly ten years," I went on to say, "So I have to suck a lot of cocks every day and I have to rinse my mouth after each oral job. As a result, I have developed a chronic *pharyngolaryngitis* (sore throat). Every time I hold a cock in my mouth, I get a dry throat and sometimes begin to cough. It's my old trouble."

"Haven't you seen a doctor?" he asked.

"No use," I said, "My doctor has prescribed me a dozen or more medicines but they have all proven to be ineffective. Besides, I can't reveal my identity to my doctor by saying it's an occupational disease that is caused by sucking too many cocks a day."

"You can suck the cock of your doctor," he grinned wickedly, "He's sure to cure you of your cough."

"But my doctor is a lady," I said.

"Oh, no wonder your doctor can't cure your cough."

"Well, all is well if you don't have the flu," he smiled, "If my cock is infected with the flu, it would be a disaster. My wife will trace the cause of why my cock performs so poorly with her."

"Nonsense," I smiled, too, "Who has heard of a cock being infected with the flu? I have no flu and neither have I any problem with my blood and sex organ. You may feel assured as I have them tested regularly."

With that, I began to run my tongue tip slowly around his cock tip and cock opening. Meanwhile, I grabbed the base of his cock and vibrated it in a narrow range without touching his cock tip, in an effort to further whet his sexual desire. He couldn't help groaning and screaming out "Oh!""Ah!""Eh""Yes!" in succession and from time to time yelling, "You're number one! You're the best doctor in the world!"

I smiled, "I am Dr. Cock."

"Oh, Dr. Cock. Worthy Specialist in cocks."

I ran again my tongue tip across the tautened skin of his balls and his little cock immediately erected like a carrot, stiff and stark. I was amused, "Who said something is wrong with your cock. Look, it works quite well."

He looked a little perplexed, "It's a mystery why my cock won't erect when I am with my wife."

"Oh, it's a common fault of many men, not just you alone. The dull routine of everyday life with your wife will undermine your desire for her gradually. So you may as well come to me for a change and then you can erect at will before your wife."

He laughed too. I spent another twenty minutes helping him achieve his climax. Then he collected his sperm in a little plastic container, one used in hospitals for urine tests, and screwed the lid of the container tight, saying he would send it to Canberra Hospital for a sperm test.

I massaged his back for the rest of the time. When I finished, I let him go to the bathroom for a shower and I went to the other bathroom to gargle and wash up. After that, I put on a long, strapless dress and waited for him to get dressed. I presented him with a bottle of red wine in a plastic bag, "This wine is the magic medicine Doctor Linda has prescribed for you. Take it with your wife this evening and you will find your cock is harder than ever."

Finally he paid me fifty dollars for an additional half an hour's service and before he parted with me at the door he said, "I will come next week."

I shut the door and went back to the working room. To my surprise, I found the ten-dollar note I had given the client as change tucked between the wall and the massage table. I picked it up and rushed to the front door. I had scarcely got there when I found the client's car had already backed out of my parking space and was turning into the street. I waved the ten-dollar note in my hand and shouted to him, "Hey, your money!" Stopping his car and rolling down the window, he stuck his head out and said, "Hey, that's your tip." I ran over and returned the money to him, "I never accept tips. If you're satisfied with my service, you may keep the ten dollars and visit me again next time."

"That's very kind of you," he said, "See you next time."

I was much amused that he was saying what I was supposed to be saying when we parted.

No sooner had I seen off this client than my mobile phone rang again, "I'm coming in twenty minutes."

"No problem."

I had barely disconnected the call when my other mobile rang, "May I have an appointment for an hour?"

Looking at the clock on the wall, it was already one thirty in the afternoon. I figured that if a client was coming in twenty minutes, the earliest appointment I could offer would be after two o'clock. So I answered, "Two fifteen, this afternoon."

The voice on the phone said, "This is Philip."

I thought about these common Australian names: Philip, Thomas and John. Too many namesakes made me confused.

And I didn't know which Philip was this Philip. All I could do was arrange the clients' appointments in succession without any overlap in time. I was lost in my thoughts when another phone call came in, "Please tell me your price."

"Fifty dollars for half an hour and ninety for an hour," I answered promptly.

I hadn't expected the voice on the other end to suddenly shift to Chinese, "Do you speak Mandarin?"

"No!" I said in English without hesitation.

Hardly had I uttered this word when I realized I had actually revealed my nationality.

The man on the other side continued to speak Chinese, "Hi. How old are you? Can I come over to have a chat with you?"

I kept pretending I didn't understand Chinese, "Could you please speak in English?"

The man had to speak English, "If I am very handsome, can I come serve you by massaging you?"

I understood at once that it must be a young Chinese boy who had just come to Australia and wanted to find a woman to marry or live with in order to solve the problem of his citizenship status. This was not the first case I had encountered. The other day, a twenty-two-year-old Indian boy insisted on marrying me and I said to him, "I am forty-nine while you're just twenty-two. Why on earth would you want to marry me?"

"So I can stay in Australia," he answered.

I knew that young Chinese man had a similar agenda, so I told him, "Sorry, mate. I can't do you this favor. It would be most appropriate if you wanted to find a place to satisfy your sexual desire here but it'd be wrong if you wanted to find a girlfriend to stay with. I am too old for you. You should search among your classmates or colleagues for your Mrs. Right."

The man hung up the telephone without saying anything more. I had just put down the mobile on the kitchen bench when the doorbell suddenly rang. I had supposed the client might have come earlier than his scheduled appointment. But when I opened the door, in came a Chinese boy of about twenty-seven or twenty-eight with a small build, small eyes, small nose and mouth. He carried a paper bag with him and was awkwardly astride the threshold, as if hesitating about whether he had arrived at the right place and thinking how an Australian prostitute could live in such a fine house. At the same time I also thought, "Do you suppose you are still in China, where the street walkers are chased into fleeing in all directions by the policemen. Prostitution is a lawful occupation in Australia and mine is a legal business." Actually a lot of new clients were taken aback at the splendor of the furnishings in my house and wondered whether they had arrived at the wrong address. They didn't expect that I was a well-known prostitute and had good managerial skills in running a business. So not many other prostitutes' operational surroundings were comparable to mine.

I guessed the guy in front of me must have been the person who called me in a strong Asian accent yesterday. Needless to say, another seeker of a lady patron! It was absurd. I was a well-known prostitute and had experienced many handsome men. Even if I was not a well-known prostitute and was over fifty years of age, I could by no means degenerate myself into becoming the girlfriend of such a guy.

I said abruptly, "Either come in or go out. Don't stand in the way."

He ignored my presence as he stormed directly into my house.

"Where are you from, sir?" I asked.

Instead of answering my question, he asked me a question, "Where are you from?"

With that, he went further inside with no sign of stopping. I followed him and shouted, "If you're looking for young ladies here, you'll be disappointed." At that, he turned round abruptly and with an "I'm sorry" he rushed out as rashly as he came in. It suddenly occurred to me that yesterday he told me he was a Chinese man over the phone. My judgment was soon proven: Such a mean, crude man claims to be handsome! Forget it. Even if you paid me, I wouldn't like you to massage me. "Humph!" I snorted in contempt.

Barely had I seen off this Chinese young man when the doorbell rang. I opened the door to find it was a very handsome Australian lad, who was about thirty, neither too fat nor too thin and about six foot tall. He had a short blond cut, a square face, a broad forehead, sunken blue eyes, a high nose, white teeth and a proportional mouth. It suddenly dawned on me that he *was* the client who was saying, "I'm coming in twenty minutes," when calling in to make his appointment. As I had to receive dozens of calls every day, it was not uncommon I would be confused and fail to tell who was who sometimes. Some clients just dropped in by pressing my doorbell and some other new clients didn't even know they had to make appointments first before coming. I had just mistaken the young Chinese boy for the person who had made the appointment by saying, "I'm coming in twenty minutes." It was not until the Australian lad came in that I realized that young Chinese boy hadn't made an appointment at all; he just dropped in by pressing the doorbell.

This Australian lad was my young frequenter of nine years. Three years before, we even had a small fight because he tried to pay only ten dollars for my service and I refused. But a couple of months later, with a fifty-dollar note in his hand, he was standing at my front door apologizing to me for his rudeness. We reconciled with each other and became friends again from then on. Now he pushed a bicycle, wearing a dark-blue sports shirt with a helmet on his head and a dark-blue backpack on his back. I pushed the security door open to let him and his bike in. He placed his bike against the treadmill in the west living room. As he took off his helmet, he wiped away the sweat from his head. I handed him a clean towel, "It's Sunday today. Didn't go to work, did you?"

"I'm still attending school," he answered casually.

I was laughing up my sleeve that here came another old student. I knew he had been in school for at least eight or nine years. But this old student was definitely different from the old Pakistani student who came here this morning. This old student was pursuing further study while the Pakistani old student was sure to be too dull to finish school. However, I was always willing to offer a special price to anyone at the mention of being a student. I handed him a bottle of mineral water I took from the kitchen fridge and sent him to take his shower. I knew it would take him seven or eight minutes to finish showering so I went to take an apple from the fridge and washed it. I was waiting over my apple when my mobile beeped. It read, "I saw your advertisement on the internet and I'd like to know your price." I told him via a text message, my price as well as my address and gave him an appointment for three o'clock.

Several of my clients had told me that they knew me from the advertisement on the internet. It was said that a client from Sydney, having visited me once, had written this advertisement and put it on the internet. I myself hadn't gone on the internet and hadn't known up to now who the kind volunteer was that had done me this favor.

I was enjoying my apple, while listening out for the splashing sounds in the bathroom. I suddenly felt an urgency to urinate and went to the bathroom in the waiting room to answer the call of nature. The urgency for pissing soon turned into an urgency for shitting. So I was sitting on the toilet endeavoring to relieve my internal pressure while chewing the apple. The overseas student came in stark naked, with a fifty-dollar note in one of his hands and a short little cock in the other,"I've been searching the world for you, only to find you enjoying food and relieving your bowels at the same time."

"Are you airing your grievances?" I got angry, "I think it's me that has the right to do so. You're making me too busy to have the time to piss and shit." With that, I stood up and pressed the button to flush the toilet, with the unfinished apple held between my teeth. After I washed my buttocks, I took out the apple from between my teeth and sighed, "I'm so busy I wish I could have another pair of hands and legs." Then I took the money he handed me and said, "You're still attending school so I will offer you a special price of forty." I put away the money in the kitchen drawer and gave him the change of ten dollars. He was very happy and thanked me.

When we went back to the working room, I tossed my dress onto the carpet and laid him on his back on the bed. Then I settled between his legs and grasped his familiar cock, "You remind me of my boyfriend from ten years ago, who was from Holland and much like you, very handsome. He is supposed to be fifty years old now. If I hadn't come to Australia ten years ago, I would have followed him to Holland."

"Really?" he grinned.

I thought the young man was good enough from any angle except for his small cock. My Holland boyfriend had a real thing between his legs. Something more than twelve inches in length.

After I sucked his cock, he raised his legs and had me lick his asshole. I never charge my frequenters extra fees for those extra services such as asshole licking as they were my close friends and lovers. To some extent, they feel more at home with me than with their wives or girlfriends. I cleaned his asshole with lubricating oil again to make sure it didn't smell though he had already cleaned it thoroughly. I lay on my side by his left leg, my left elbow on the bed and my head in my left hand, so my mouth was right in his asshole. While licking his asshole with my tongue tip, I applied baby oil to my right hand and cupped the root of his cock with my right thumb and index finger. I moved my right hand back and forth around his cock and from time to time I licked his balls. He was so excited that he raised his legs high with his own hands and yelled, "Oh, my god! That feels so good! You're the best master of oral work in the world!"

It took me less than ten minutes to help him come in a long groan. I told him to lay face down and began to massage his back. I asked him, "How many more years will you study at school?"

"Three years."

"By the way, what's your major at school?" I asked curiously.

At my question he gave me some very professional jargon, which I didn't understand but I knew he was studying for a doctoral degree. I said, "Learn more while you're young, for learning is rewarding. When I was young, I used to immerse myself in piles of books. I think this reading has been very beneficial to my future development, especially to my career as a prostitute. I'm now writing books about prostitutes."

"Learning is a hard thing."

"No pain, no gain. Take my writing for example, I have been writing for nine years and I write my book into the early hours of every day. Even though I have been working so hard, I estimate it will take me at least ten years to finish this book."

"You're a woman dedicated to a cause, Linda," he praised me.

"I am not one of those who live on the handouts of men. Whatever work I've taken on, I always rely on my own efforts and earn my own bread."

At that time the doorbell rang and he was very sensible in saying, "Go ahead with you business. I'll go to the bathroom."

"A student is not well off," I said, "I'll refund you ten dollars." I then went to the front door.

"Oh, my dear," the man before me was all smiles. "Haven't seen you for a long time. I have been abroad these days. As soon as I came back, I wanted to be with you again."

The man stood five foot nine, very healthy and muscular. I could sense his big cock through his clothes as if they were transparent. I knew it very well. He had a square face and black hair. A pair of big shining eyes sat under his protruded forehead and a broad mouth under a pointed nose. He wore a leisure tracksuit as he didn't need to go to work that day.

Six years before when he showed me his employee card and told me he was a policeman, I felt a sense of intimacy with him. As he had regarded me as his buddy and fellow, I couldn't wait to tell him my secret that I was also a policewoman and showed him the photos that proved my former identity. From a policewoman to a prostitute, what a sharp contrast in professions! We both laughed and we shared the same view that prostitution was not a lowly, menial job everybody frowned at.

"In China," I said, "if a policeman is found buying sex, he will be disciplined at the police station and will most probably be dismissed from his position in disgrace."

"Policemen?" he said bitterly, "They are also flesh and blood and they naturally have their own desires. Besides, prostitution is lawful in Australia. What's wrong with visiting a prostitute in my spare time?"

I led him to the waiting room and had him wait for five minutes. He waved his hand and politely said, "Never mind. Go ahead with your work. I have a lot of free time today." I went back to the working room and refunded the old student ten dollars. Before he left I gave him a box of cashews so that he could eat them if he felt hungry while riding his bike.

SEXY

After I saw off the student, I ushered the policeman to the working room. Every time he came he would put down one hundred dollars on the bedside table without even the vaguest hint on my part. I handed him a towel for him to take a shower. I went to the kitchen to get ten dollars' change and a bottle of mineral water and then went to the garage to fetch two bottles of wine. As a general rule, I gave every client a bottle of wine as a farewell gift, but I gave the policeman two because I felt an affinity with his occupation.

When I came back to the working room, he had already finished showering. I put the drinks on the bedside table before I pulled out the massage table and covered it with white towels. I ordered him to lay face down on the massage bed. I began my massage on his neck and back, "You have your own wife, but you often visit me."

"But we have a long-distance marriage," he sighed, "She is a policewoman and more often than not, she works in one country and I work in another. The separation will last several months or even half a year. What do you think we should do to satisfy our sexual needs? Now my wife is working in Papua New Guinea. Maybe she is wallowing with a man on her bed."

With that we both laughed. And I went on to ask him, "What country did you say you have just returned from?"

"Fiji."

"It's very hot there, isn't it?"

"It's an island and has a maritime climate. So it's not too hot there."

"Most inhabitants there are black people?"

"There are many Chinese people doing business there." "I remember you said you have been to many countries."

"Yes. I've been to the United States, Papua New Guinea, Indonesia, China…"

"What's your impression of them?"

"Hey, once in Los Angeles, we went out by taxi and the black driver wanted to steal our things. When we told him we were policemen, what do you think he did? He simply drew out a gun. We had to flee to the hotel to call the police."

"You Australian policemen have no authority in the United States."

"The things in America are of course out of our orbit. The American policemen have authority only over their own state and cannot interfere with the affairs in the other states."

"I hear many of my clients say that in some cities in the United States, it is not safe to walk in the streets. I have never been to the United States. If I have a chance, I'd like to go there to see that part of the world."

"If I was to take my family for travel, I'd choose to go to China. There are so many security guards and it's very safe everywhere. Moreover, it's convenient to travel in China. You can, for example, take the high-speed trains. The surroundings inside are so clean and so quiet as if you are traveling on a plane."

I was very happy to hear him sing praises of China. After all, I myself was Chinese and I felt proud of my homeland.

"These years, China's economy has developed so rapidly that many people say China will be the largest economy in another twenty years. By the way, is it extraordinarily difficult to find girls when you're traveling in China?" I hardly opened my mouth without talking shop.

"Not necessarily so," he said. "It all depends on which cities you're traveling in. At that time I was working in Beijing and lived in a hotel run by the government. When I went to bed, some prostitutes knocked on the door of my room."

"Did you enjoy yourself with any of them?" I asked with interest.

"No. If I was caught sleeping with a whore by the Chinese policemen and then they informed the Australian police, I would surely get into trouble."

"The Chinese government has outlawed all prostitutes but prostitutes are everywhere to be seen. It is said that in some cities in Southern China, such as Canton or Shenzhen, men are queuing in front of the massage houses as if they would go in to do some shopping. And there are more ironic things to come. A customer of mine told me that almost eighty percent of sex toys sold in the sex shops all over the world, such as the electric oscillators and simulated cocks or pussies, are all made in China."

"Yes, Chinese are born businessmen."

"In my opinion," I commented, "Sex is something we cannot do without and every one of us needs it. If people's sexual desire cannot be satisfied one way or the other, they are more likely to get ill, to be driven mad or to get out of control. If prostitution is lawful, people can go to brothels and pay to satisfy their sexual lust and thus spare the women around them; if there are no prostitutes, they will most probably assault any females they happen to meet. What are the harms of prostitution? Prostitution is playing an indispensable role in stabilizing society and families."

"That's why so many rape cases happen," he expressed his assent.

"As a matter of fact, it's better to legalize prostitution as here in Australia and at the same time regulate prostitution by making prostitutes pay proper taxes and undergo regular medical examinations. And it's irreproachable for people like you and government officials to come here to be massaged and relaxed for a while after work."

"Yes," he agreed, "We're living under great pressure, from work as well as from life."

"Who do you think is not living under any pressure?" I asked, Whether you are rich or poor, work for others or work for yourself, everybody is living under pressure. As long as you live, you can never escape from it."

"You have to live under pressure until you die, when you will be free of any trouble," he sighed.

"It's the only way and last destination for everybody. No one can escape from it." I sounded like a priest.

"It seems you should enjoy life as well as work at the same time."

"A person's lifespan is only several decades long."

By then, I had finished massaging his back and legs and began to caress his cock and eggs. When I ran my fingertip around his asshole, he couldn't help groaning heartily, "Oh, yes. Ah, yes!" I lay sideways on his lap, my left elbow supporting me between his legs. I used my left hand to rub his ball skin and touch his asshole and my right hand, lubricated with baby oil, to masturbate his big cock. His cock, though big, just wouldn't erect very hard. This kind of cock was rated as slack and soggy, the most difficult kind of cock, in my opinion, to deal with. It was hard but not hard enough to be stiff and stark; it was soft but not so soft that it was unable to erect. Even the limpest cocks were easier to cure: A sucking and some rubbing, and it would surely come. It took me almost twenty minutes to make him come. It was a really hard job!

I thought to myself that maybe the policeman suffered such great work pressure and his head was occupied with so much trouble that his cock couldn't erect hard enough. Several years ago, I received several policemen, who had similar problems with their cocks. The guns they were using were hard enough but their cocks weren't. Alas, each trade has its own troubles. It's impossible to achieve climax, or come, if one is laden with troubles and weighed down by anxiety. Once I was serving a client but however hard I tried for forty minutes I simply couldn't help him come. Finally he explained he was indulging in thoughts about how to crack his own hard nuts. I said no wonder he couldn't come and complained it was just a waste of time if he was distracted like that. He laughed in embarrassment.

Having seen off the cop and cleaned the room, I ushered in my next client. He was a young man of about thirty and said he was from Egypt. He saw the classified advertisement on the internet and then came by the address listed on it. No sooner had he been led into the working room than he began bargaining with me, "May I pay you twenty dollars?"

"Twenty dollars? Go to other places for a try. Who in Canberra will serve you for a mere twenty dollars? I charge fifty for half an hour but I can give you a special offer of forty. This is special only because you're a new client."

"Or I'll pay thirty?"

"Forget it, guy. I have never seen a young man who is so interested in bargaining. Forty is the final price or else you can leave." Finally he reluctantly produced two twenty-dollar notes from his pocket. I put away the money and went back to the working room only to find he had finished his showering and was lying on the bed. He ordered me about in a dominant way, "Suck my cock," or "Caress my balls," or "Lick my asshole." I tried my best to suppress my seething anger in obeying his whimsical orders. There were always people who demanded the best service and the highest level of sexual enjoyment for the least possible pay. If that had happened in the past, I would have been greatly irritated. Luckily, I'd been in this trade for many years and had seen various kinds of people, especially men, in the world so all my edges had been worn down and I became sophisticated. I always refrained from disputing with my clients and tried my best to satisfy their different demands, whether they were young or old. Finally he wanted to fuck me and I demanded he put on a condom.

"Can I do without that thing?" he asked.

"I receive a dozen or two clients a day," I reasoned with him. "If every one of them fucks me without that thing, what will become of my cunt in the end?"

"You see," he said, "the man on the screen is fucking without one."

"That's because the director intended the porn film to stimulate the viewers' lust more strongly," I explained, "Besides, the actress and her partner had undergone a thorough medical examination before they entered the studio to act out the fucking scene. As for you and me, we have never seen each other before and don't know each other. How can we fuck without a condom?"

At last, he put on his condom reluctantly. As soon as I finished the job, he dressed quickly and came with me to the dining room. Seeing so many snacks and nibbles displayed on the dining table, he couldn't wait to get his hands on some cashews here and some almonds there and demanded two beers of me. "Don't take the food with your hands, lest they are polluted and no other clients will eat them. If you'd like something, tell me and I will pack it for you."

He said frankly he wanted cashews and I packed a circular plastic container with them, thinking it would cost five dollars, and put it into a plastic bag. He took a bottle of beer in one hand and waved a second beer in the other hand.

"Hey, put the beers into the bag to spare your hands," I shouted at him but it seemed he simply couldn't tear himself away from my house and even had a suggestion for me, "Linda, let's make a deal. I introduce a boyfriend to you and you can earn twenty thousand Australian dollars by marrying him."

It was odd, I think, that two men in one day should come to make a deal with me on citizenship status. I was wondering whether he had solved his own problem of citizenship. One of my female friends told me that arranging a sham marriage for the purpose of acquiring Australian status (permanent residency or citizenship) cost sixty thousand dollars. It might be the most lucrative business in Australia currently. But as for me, I wouldn't do any illicit business even if you offered me two hundred thousand or two million dollars, let alone twenty thousand!

"Forget it," I said, "Make haste and leave. Do you think I will discard my profitable business to mix with you guys in causing trouble to the government? I'm busy now. Other clients are coming." As I nudged him, he reluctantly started to move his feet, not forgetting to pick up a packet of chips from the dining table at his convenience. I shook my head resignedly in seeing him off. These types of men always tried to gain extra advantages wherever they went.

When I came back to tidy up the working room, I heard the doorbell ring loudly. I hurried to the door to open it. It was a short, bald man in a greenish-yellow uniform. He was a frequenter of mine for more than four years. Usually he came to me once every other month or so. So I had quite an impression of him.

While sucking and massaging him once, I heard him say he was a gardener. "There are some herbal plants in my front garden," I said to him, "Can you change them into woody plants so my roses can look more beautiful against them."

"Yeah," he said, "But let me have a look first before I leave."

After the service, he paid me fifty dollars and I handed him a six-pack of beer. Then I showed him to my front garden and he told me, after a brief inspection, what herbal flowers should be substituted. Finally I told him, "You just give me a quote then. I don't mind spending a little more money if you can make my garden look more beautiful." He promised to contact me as soon as he got his quote ready.

After he left, I came back to walk around my front garden and backyard as well. When I found some scraps of paper and empty cans littered in the street, I went over to pick them up and threw them into the garbage bin in my backyard. I was stretching my back when I spotted a yellow-top bin (for recyclable garbage) and a green-top bin (for green organic garbage) left by the curb in front of house number 129, where my neighbor the doctor lived. I supposed because the doctor or his secretary were very busy, they must have forgotten to pull the garbage bins back to their house. So I went over to pull the bins, one in each hand, to their courtyard and at the same time collected the paper bits and twigs strewn on the doctor's driveway. Just then my mobile phone rang.

"Are you free, Linda?" I recognized at once it was the short Indian and said, "Just come by."

"Okay. I'll come in five minutes."

It seemed that he was already nearby. I continued to collect the rubbish around my house and even that on the lawns across the street. I raised my head only to find a short bald man less than five foot two stalking toward my house with a protruded belly and wearing a pair of slippers. I hurriedly dumped the rubbish into the bins and went to open my front door. He came nearer to the door, "Are you working on your garden?"

"I've been busy all day. I like to take advantage of the interval between clients to take in some fresh air."

Scarcely had we entered and closed the front door before he stretched out his hands to feel my bosom, "I love you and miss you very much." I laughed up my sleeve that I had so many lovers. I was also tired of hearing such compliments. I patted him on the hand, "Don't be too anxious."

He extended his hand to fumble my buttocks. "You're really like a monkey," I said, "You can't keep your paws to yourself the moment you come in."

"Really," he said, "I really love you very much. Spare me a night to sleep with you."

"No," I refused resolutely, "If I should put you up for a night here and you were to keep me awake all night, I would be unable to get up in time the next morning to get to work."

"Just for one night," he begged.

"Not even half a night," I said resolutely.

Then he tiptoed to kiss me. He cupped my face with his hands and drew my lips to his.

I twisted my head to avoid his mouth,"I never kiss my clients. I only kiss cocks."

"Just a light kiss. I like you. I love you."

I dodged though I didn't intend to offend him. Because I knew sometimes a mouth might smell worse than a clean cock and moreover, I only kissed ones I loved. For nine years since I became a prostitute, I had actually only kissed two men because I accidentally fell in love with them in succession. Now I was unable to fall in love with any man because whenever I met a would-be lover, I'd be inclined to imagine him being a man with all other men's merits, who of course never existed in reality!

Besides, I myself had my own demerits and shortcomings and it was no wonder some men would frown at me. Love was between two people and never originated from one side. It didn't necessarily happen between just any couple and it was a product of instinct and sixth sense. But at least now I didn't experience such a feeling. No matter how young or handsome the man, my heart refused to be moved and without the moving of the heart there would be no love.

We fought our way to the working room and he kept tiptoeing to rub his lips against mine, thrusting his tongue into my mouth and wetting my lips. I tried to divert his attention from his upper part to his lower part by stripping him and then began to suck his dick and he started to moan loudly, "Oh, yes." "Ah, yes."

"Oh, Linda. You're sucking my cock," he spoke in a mixed language of English and Chinese, using Chinese every time he mentioned the words "cock" or "cunt."

After sucking his cock for a while and fitting a medium- sized condom on his cock, I sat on the bed and spread my legs. He thrust his mediocre shaft into my cunt and murmured, "My cock is in Linda's cunt." He kept on babbling something like "cock in cunt" in Indian. But I didn't understand what he was saying as a whole. With every movement of his cock, he uttered a word, either in English or in Indian, or a mixed language of English and Chinese. Some stimulating words I guessed were about sexual organs like "cock" or "cunt." I turned a deaf ear to his four-letter words; if only they would make him excited and ejaculate sooner, and the sooner the better. Sure enough, it was only seven or eight minutes before he came. He was characteristic of his silent ejaculation and sometimes I didn't even know if he had come. He was always babbling something so only when he stopped wriggling on my body could I ascertain he had come.

He was sprawled upon my belly for quite a while before I shuffled him down the bed and peeled his condom off. When I told him to take his shower, he demanded, "I'd like you to massage me."

"You have always underpaid me," I complained, "You reduced the service fee from fifty dollars to forty-five dollars, then from forty-five to forty and now you only pay me thirty dollars a service. How can you have the nerve to ask for a massage?"

"But I am your frequenter of more than five years," he snorted.

"My frequenters of more than eight years always pay me the full price," I retorted.

Seeing there was no room for further negotiation, he hung his head in shame and had to go have his shower. After showering and dressing, we went together to the east living room. He bent down over the dining table to take cashews with his hand.

"Stop taking cashews with your hand," I said, "I will pack you some." With that, I packed him a box of cashews and handed him two bottles of Cola. Only then did he reluctantly produce thirty dollars from his pocket and hand it to me.

When I saw him off at the door, it was beginning to drizzle. Since it was less likely that any new clients would come, I thought I'd better take advantage of this gap to cook something for myself. I hadn't even had my lunch since I had some instant noodles in the morning. It was already five thirty. I went back to the kitchen and was about to place the chopping board on the kitchen bench when the phone rang, "When can I come to see you?"

On hearing his voice, I knew at once it was my "Old Sticker" for more than six years and answered, "You can come right now."

"I'll be with you in ten minutes."

I figured I couldn't make a meal and have it within so short a time so I went to the toilet to have a piss and collected the dried towels from the laundry and tidied them up into piles in the working room. Just then the doorbell rang and I went to open the door.

"I love you," he said abruptly before I opened my mouth. He was a short, bald man of a little over fifty and often wore a baseball cap. He was a good man but a little lazy. Whenever you asked him whether he had found a job yet, he would answer he had not, but in fact he was not seeking one seriously.

"You see," I teased him, "Old tricks again. I have told you it is the one hundredth time you have said those three words."

"Maybe the several hundredth time."

"It's okay you know it." I said. "Haven't I made it clear to you that you love me but I don't love you?"

"Why don't you love me?"

"Simply because you have a tiny cock and more importantly, it is not straight."

"If we get married," he compromised, "You can go on seeking and enjoying your big cocks as usual since you like them."

"So what will be the difference then?"

"Then I don't have to pay for you to suck my cock."

"While so many clients are on a long waiting list to pay me to suck their cocks, why should I suck yours free of charge?"

"Because I love you."

"But I don't love you. Anyway, you can't force a person to love you," it dawned on me that all that he had said boiled down to one main idea –to get my service for free.

He went on to say,"If we get married, you can earn the money for me to spend and I can also share your house."

"Unless I have gone mad," I laughed heartily.

"Anyway, you have made so much money you can't spend it all and you have so large a house you can't occupy every room at once."

"But I will spend all the money before I die and I like to sleep in this room today and in that room tomorrow, as I please."

We exchanged words jestingly all the way to the working room. I looked at the man and heaved a sigh, wondering why a man like him, who was a little over fifty, would always daydream of reaping what he had not sown rather than earning honest money by his own sweat. If apple pies did fall from the sky, they were not meant for the lazy people. He produced thirty dollars from his pocket and handed it to me, "If you insist I pay you thirty dollars now, I will have no money left for my supper this evening."

"Look at the thirty dollars you paid me. Ten dollars will go to the six bottles of beer I'll give you as gifts when you leave. Four or five dollars will go to the box of cashews I'm packing for you now. Your long shower will cost me more than a dollar plus another dollar for the electricity for TV programs. All told, my net profit is less than fifteen dollars. You could never find a cheaper service than mine throughout Australia."

At my detailed cost analysis, he lowered his head in shame. He said embarrassedly, "I know these years you've been taking care of me. After all, I am a poor man."

"If only my fellow prostitutes knew my price list, they would surely laugh at me with contempt. Selling too cheap."

"Why should you care about other people's contempt? It's trifling as long as you can earn bucks."

I nodded my agreement and thought, "Whatever others comment, it's all okay if I can still make money excluding all costs. My wealth has been accumulated little by little."

I handed him a clean towel for his shower and went to the kitchen to put away my money. Then I poured myself a cup of milk and took an apple from the fridge; washed it and had a big bite of it to alleviate my hunger.

Just then the doorbell rang again. I thought it must be another man who came without an appointment. I opened the door to find a short old man wearing a pair of thick prescription glasses. He was balding on top with a few grizzled hairs drenched in the rain. He raised with great difficulty a leg and stepped over the threshold. I went over to help and asked, "Have you made an appointment, sir?"

"Yes. I made one over the phone this afternoon."

Only then did I recall that an old man had made an appointment for five thirty. But I didn't know it was the old gentleman in front of me. I said, "Sorry, but if I remember correctly you don't live in Canberra, do you?"

"No," he said, "I drove three hours to come here. I live in a village north of Canberra."

I ushered him in and had him wait for about ten minutes in the waiting room. Then I hurried back to the working room and the lazy man was already on the bed. I nestled in between his legs and started to suck his cock when his mobile buzzed. He glanced at his mobile screen and put a finger to his lips, signaling me to keep quiet. I immediately set the TV to "mute" mode. He answered the mobile and I could make out a lady's voice on the other end. I withdrew to the kitchen to finish my leftover apple. I didn't return to the working room until he ended his phone conversation.

I lay on him and began to perform my oral work with his pants on. I hadn't resumed my oral work for a couple of minutes when his mobile rang again. He picked it up and said, "I am shopping at Woden and I will be back in another ten minutes or so." I didn't hear the rest of the conversation before he disconnected the call. I settled between his legs and grasped his tiny thing. It wasn't long before his mobile rang again. And this time the screams on the other end became somewhat hysterical.

He said again and again, "Yes. Yes. Yes. Okay. Okay. Okay. I'll be back in no time." With that, he lay back on the bed but his little thing could no longer stiffen. I felt his cock, like a boneless worm in my mouth, with no reaction at all for at least ten minutes. His cock seemed to be asleep when his mobile rang again. He jumped to his feet and nodded into the mobile, "Yes. Yes. Yes." I laughed up my sleeve, "You're clearly scared to death of your wife (or girlfriend). And you are dreaming of marrying me?"

I lost all interest in eavesdropping and simply went to the kitchen to resume the enjoyment of my half-eaten apple. I waited until there was no sound emanating from the working room. But when I returned I found him already dressed. I asked, "Are you leaving?"

"Until next time. Something urgent has come up and I must be going now."

"It's not my fault you couldn't come," I smiled, "and I will not refund your money."

"Leave it for the next time," he said.

He knew well I would charge him less when he came next time. He had had two similar experiences when he was occupied with other things and simply couldn't come however hard I sweated myself on him. The next time he came I was to charge him twenty dollars, including free beers and this amounted to a free service. He carried six bottles of beer in a plastic bag I had taken out from the fridge and trotted away.

I hurried back to the waiting room to attend to the old man who had come from afar.

"Sorry to have kept you waiting, sir," I said.

"Never mind," he said and tucked a fifty-dollar note into my hand. I showed him the working room, "Please come in," I asked, "What drink do you want?"

He said he wanted no drink and went directly to the working room. I put away the money in the kitchen and went back. The old gentleman was undressing with trembling hands. While undressing he said, "I've already taken a shower at home."

"All right," I said, "Since you have bathed, let me prepare the bed for you."

While I was unfolding the sheets, I had a small chat with him. "It's some time since I last saw you."

"I've been travelling in the United States for nine months," he said.

"How is it over there?" I asked, "Must be very interesting. I hear the things in America are much cheaper than here in Australia."

"Yes."

"Is there any difference between the United States and Australia?"

"No great difference in lifestyles and customs."

I signaled the old man to lie down. Finding there was something wrong with one of his legs and he had much difficulty in climbing onto the bed, I helped him raise his leg first, then took a pillow from the cabinet and piled it atop the two pillows already placed there so that his head would be raised higher and he might feel a little more comfortable. When I settled down between his legs and took up his cock, I knew I had a hard nut to crack. The old gentleman had come to me four or five times before and during his first visit I spent forty minutes working on him but in vain. I wished for better luck today. I held his cock in my mouth and began to suck it. The old man remained silent and kept his eyes closed. Having sucked his cock for a while, I felt his body tremble discernibly.

"If you feel uncomfortable anywhere," I said, "Please let me know."

"Very good," the old man said, "But I'm afraid I still can't come. It's been too long. The last time was nine months ago when you helped me come."

"It's no good for your health not having sex for over half a year."

"My wife died," the old man said with emotion. I knew the old man was living alone in a small village of a few hundred people, where there was not a single prostitute.

I held his tiny cock in my mouth and began to suck it softly but forcefully as a baby suckled its mother's nipples. By and by, his cock became stiff but slacked again quickly. I ran my tongue along his cock tip and opening but his cock only jerked once or twice before becoming placid again. Seeing it was no use sucking his cock, I tried masturbating it with my right hand after I applied baby oil to it. I exerted all my strength and kept on rubbing and rubbing. To my disappointment, twenty minutes passed and there was not the slightest sign that he would ejaculate. His cock remained in a state of being neither too soft nor too hard. He said apologetically, "So much for it. Let's try next time."

"If you could quit thinking about anything else except the sex and fucking, we will do better," I tried to comfort him, "Come on. Let's try again."

Once more I began masturbating him. Another twenty minutes elapsed and he still didn't come. He just kept on saying, "Next time. Next time." Glancing at the clock, I saw that one hour's time was up. I had to accept my failure, and told him to take his shower.

I didn't know why I was particularly sad when I couldn't help a client come. I put on my dress and packed a large box of cashews for the old man as I knew he didn't drink. When I saw the old man drooping down and limping out of the working room with noticeable difficulty, I reached out to help him and handed him the box of cashews. When he went down the steps, he lowered one of his legs first and then the other one. "See you later," he said to me.

I saw him limping off in the drizzle toward his car, then opening the car door and climbing in. I felt very sorry for him. He drove three hours to see me in order to solve the problem of his cock but I let him down and let him leave disappointedly. I was an incompetent Doctor of Cock! I was to blame and so was the lazy man. I had found it a rule that if I couldn't serve a client well enough, I couldn't serve the following one well either. I kept reproaching myself and was not in the mood for eating.

Generally, I could help every client come but occasionally I would encounter a case in which I found I was at my wits' end. Whenever that happened, I would accuse myself of incompetence.

I came into the working room crestfallen. After tidying and cleaning the room, I went to the bathroom. Scarcely had I drenched my hair with shampoo when the mobile rang, "How much? Address?" I told the man my address and he answered he would come in twenty minutes.

I quickly finished bathing and wiped myself dry. I tossed on a violet-colored dress and combed my hair so as to let it dry sooner. I would always try to find time to dress up before new clients arrived. I would comb my hair neatly, put some powder on my face and dress as sexy as possible. As for my frequenters, things were different. Whether I applied make up or not all depended on whether I had any time or not. It didn't matter if I made do without any makeup. My old frequenters were not very particular about my appearance.

It was not long before the doorbell rang. I went to open the door. There on my doorstep stood a tall and stout man about thirty years old. He had a moustache on his plump face; thick brows and big eyes. He seemed somewhat hesitant. I could read his mind and knew the reason. It must be because of my age. I knew it was a critical moment to test my skills of persuasion. I had to persuade the wavering prospective client to enter.

"Good evening handsome lad! Many young men have been here today. My clients have included five or six young men aged from eighteen to twenty," implying that he was not the youngest. He stepped in and I closed the door. I asked, "What drink do you want? Beer, Cola, Pepsi, lemonade, strawberry juice, orange juice or just mineral water?" I had a variety of drinks and I quickly enumerated their names. He simply said, "Water please."

I took a mineral water from the fridge and handed it to him, "Cool enough! It is getting warmer so it's exhilarating to have a cool drink, isn't it?" At that time, the most important thing was to keep the conversation smooth and continuous and avoid awkward silence so as to let your clients feel your enthusiasm without losing your demeanor at the same time.

The young man accepted the water and said, "Thank you."

I beckoned him to the working room and he stepped in. I followed by his side. He hesitated at my bedroom when passing it. It was not unusual, as many clients before him had taken it to be my working room. Nevertheless, I still preferred to keep my bedroom door open with the wall-mounted TV showing programs. As I had mentioned before, during my working hours all seven TV sets in my house were on so that my clients could enjoy porn programs wherever they went.

I nudged his back signaling him to walk on. When at last he arrived at the working room, he was lost in silent wonder at the luxurious furnishings around him: The two huge, sixty- inch TV screens on opposite walls were showing porn programs with soft background music. The cream-colored bed covered with white sheets and diagonally placed pillows stood beside the professional massage table by the wall. He couldn't help praising, "Gorgeous!"

"Yes," I answered, "A twenty-one-year-old Hong Kong lad once said to me, 'Linda, I've been to more than two dozen brothels but found none as professional as yours; clean, elegant and impressive.'"

I went on to say, "I have a sex worker's license and can lawfully work at my own house. My clients include doctors, policemen, soldiers, university students, engineers and government officials at various levels." Through such briefings I dispelled any misgivings and ensured that my clients could enjoy themselves with ease. I usually initiated a new client with the following opening remarks, "I'm Linda. I have thousands of clients and many of them refer to me as Doctor Cock."

With that I quickly got down to business, "Would you like a massage for half an hour or one hour?"

"Half an hour."

"Fifty dollars for half an hour."

He took out a fifty-dollar note from his wallet and gave it to me. Only then had this deal been secured. I handed him a clean towel for his shower and I went to put away the money in the kitchen drawer. When I came back, he was standing there with a large towel wrapped around his waist. I went over, unwrapped the towel at my leisure and patted him on the hip casually.

"Shall I lie down," he asked, "on my back or stomach?"

"You may as well lie down on your back, young man," I said, "I will help you come first and then massage you. And you can probably have a second climax. But I can't say for sure, because some men can come twice but many only once."

"It all depends on your head," I went on to explain.

He laughed and lay down on his back. I sprawled between his thighs and held and fondled his cock. Judging by the size of his cock, I guessed his parents must have come from a Middle Eastern or West Asian country.

I asked him, "Want my oral work with the condom or without?"

"Without," he said without any hesitation.

I knew at once he had been a frequenter of massage parlors. After I inspected his cock and found nothing abnormal with it, I held it in my mouth and began to treat it with my traditional ways: first, nibbling it as a baby would its mother's nipples; second, licking his cock tip, cock opening and ball skin; third, holding his cock in my mouth and rubbing it and last, running my tongue tip along his cock and the vein under it.

His cock erected stiff and stark and he demanded, "Let's do the 69 position and let me lick your cunt."

SIXTY NINE

In the 69 position, the man lies on his back while the woman lies on top of the man in reverse, so her cunt is on his face while she simultaneously sucks his cock. The number 69 symbolizes the mutual pleasure that can be experienced in this sexual position.

"You'd like to lick my cunt?" I asked, "Well, let me wash it up as I just had a piss."

I went to the toilet and squatted under the sprinkler, washing up my cunt thoroughly inside and out. Having dried it with a clean towel, I came back to ride his face with my cunt right over his mouth while swallowing his cock into my mouth, "Ouch!" I cried out in pain, "Your moustache!" He licked my cunt so clumsily that his moustache pricked my tender cunt lips. I raised my buttocks suddenly. After he apologized, I sat back over his mouth but he still couldn't find the precise location of my clitoris and just gobbled away at my private part like a greedy cat licking up its dish bowl. With a loud "Ouch" I decided to call it quits. "Well. Well. It's probably better if I just suck your penis."

I rolled off his body, wondering how a man of over thirty should be so ill-informed about how to lick a woman's cunt properly! How could my cleanly shaven and tender cunt stand the pricking of such a thick moustache? I crawled back between his thighs to suck his cock for a short time before he whimsically asked, "Can you suck my nipples?"

"No problem," I answered, "There are men who like their nipples sucked, but not many."

I had seen too many men boasting about how many porn videos they had watched and how many porn books they had read, but in fact, they simply hadn't learned how to send a woman into ecstasy by licking her pussy. They would squat between your thighs and lick your cunt away blindly, pricking your tender clitoris with their moustache. You were just tortured instead of being pleasured by such a man.

All men should learn something from reading my book. Don't just pick out some sensuous excerpts to read and masturbate over. In this way, you will have learned nothing from my book. Instead, you should closely study the techniques I am about to teach you to please your wife or girlfriend by licking her pussy skillfully and artfully.

You should part the woman's cunt lips with your fingers and run your tongue tip around her clitoris or the crevice in it, not too hard and not too soft. If you do it too hard, the woman will feel pain and if you do it too soft, she will not feel aroused enough. Only by licking her clitoris or crevice moderately and evenly can she feel ecstatically and achingly aroused. She will become mad, insane or even wild with the untold pleasure you give her if you keep licking her pussy continuously in such a way. Generally, licking a woman's cunt opening, anal opening or the part between them is less exciting than having her clitoris licked. Sometimes, her pleasure can be doubled if you poke one or two fingers into her cunt and piston them while you're licking her clitoris. In most cases, the woman's sexual desire will be further whetted and she will quickly reach her climax. You should attack the main target – her clitoris, and concentrate on licking it until lust water spouts out of her cunt opening. Don't lick her clitoris one moment, her cunt opening the next and her clitoris again. If you do this when the woman is about to reach her climax, you will put her in an awkward situation by interrupting her orgasm. At the crucial moment, you should continue licking her clitoris and clitoris opening until she reaches her bliss, until she spurts water from inside her cunt and until she cries out, "I love you!" Only by licking your woman in this way can she have an orgasm and love you to the greatest possible extent.

In the ten years in my trade, I had fallen in love with only two clients solely because of their excellent abilities in fucking or licking. It doesn't matter if you have a little cock so long as you are adept at licking. You can also make your woman happy, mad or wild. If you don't boast a big, hard cock and at the same time you have no idea how to lick, what else will make your woman take a fancy to you? It's a little wonder she will leave you for another man.

You shouldn't seek only your own pleasure when making love to your woman, but instead you should try to understand how she is feeling. If you just thrust a little cock into your partner's cunt and come within a mere five minutes without caring about her feelings, your partner will lose interest in making love to you. She may not tell you explicitly but she is sure to find a man who can give her more sexual pleasure than you. The reason some women will seek out affairs, elope with other men or divorce their husbands is because their men can't give them the sexual pleasure they deserve. Before I became a prostitute, I married twice and had several lovers. All my past husbands and lovers failed to satisfy me and make me come. I found it difficult to bring up the matter and had to resort to masturbating in the toilet. I managed to reach my climax by playing with my clitoris with my own hands and spouting out lust water, though the orgasms were much less satisfying than those I got through being licked or fucked by men.

Remember to learn how to please your women by licking their pussies. As to how to please your women by fucking their pussies, I have told you enough in my stories about my lawyer client or Mr. Hard Cock. Engaging in flirtation, dirty talk and foreplay with your women will help enhance arousal. A man who can neither fuck nor lick can never make the woman he loves come to love him madly.

The above techniques are summed up by a prostitute of ten years. And only a prostitute of ten years who is writing her book can be so outspoken. If I were an ordinary housewife, I wouldn't tell men such things without reservation and neither would I scold a green-hand licker like that, "Hey, hey. Don't you know how to lick a lady's pussy? What on earth are you licking at?" To a client like the one in front of me now, I won't say anything about it. What I can most likely do is suspend his licking license, (red p plater of course).

After all, sexuality constitutes perhaps the innermost secret behaviors of human beings. Almost everyone, be it a man or a woman, will be shy about telling his or her partner after sex, "Why, mate. You just haven't satisfied me this time." However, if you want your partner to enjoy sex, you should take the initiative in asking, "Do you like it when I do this?" or "Are you happy with me doing that?" If he or she is still shy to say anything, you should observe how your partner is groaning ecstatically, crying lustily or twisting a certain part of their body to understand whether he or she is enjoying what you're doing.

To be frank, in the ten years in this trade, I still hesitate to speak out to a client if he has made me uncomfortable, "I'm unhappy with you doing this," let alone the respectable ladies out there. I believe that more than ninety percent of women will be too shy to tell her sexual partner that she has failed to achieve her orgasm.

More often than not, when serving my clients, a certain one of them would have succeeded in arousing my sexual desire, and just as I was about to reach my climax, he would come suddenly and his cock would become limp at once, leaving me in such an embarrassing state that I had to wait until the client left and masturbate myself by pistoning away an electric cock in my thirsty cunt. Sometimes, to totally relax myself physically and psychologically, I had to add my fingers to help satiate my desire by making my lust water spurt out like a fountain.

Any person, be it a man or a woman, will find it unbearable if he or she is interrupted halfway by an improper action when he or she is about to come.

I remember when I was serving in the police force in China; a colleague of mine lent me a "porn" book, a diary written by an army prostitute, in which she wrote: when our soldiers were taken captives, the enemies tried to extort confessions from them through cruel torture, but our soldiers would rather die than give in. The enemies had no alternative but to resort to other dirty tricks. They tied their captives one by one and ordered the Army prostitutes to suck the cock of one of them until it became hard. When the cock was about to ejaculate, the prostitute was ordered to stop sucking it right away. Then the same process was repeated again and again until the captive could no longer bear the impulse to spurt out his sperm while being prevented to do so. Most captives ended up throwing in the towel with this novel torture and yielded to the enemies' demands. You can imagine how cruel it would be if a man is made to stop just as he is about to come. And the same is true for women. It would be inhumane to leave a woman alone when she is about to reach her climax. She couldn't bear the burning hot desire for long. You don't need many of such instances of humiliation and frustration to drive her to seek other men who can quickly appease her insatiable desire.

Today I have explained to you in detail how a man can satisfy his woman by licking, which I would have difficulty telling my clients in their presence, lest they protest they have paid to be served by me instead of serving me. But if you, my dear reader, still haven't learned something from this book, you're a fool that has failed me.

As to how a lady can satisfy her man by sucking his cock, I've well and truly illustrated those techniques in my stories in which I have served my clients with oral jobs. They are easy to learn for any female reader of this book.

I hope my readers, both men and women, can learn some workable tips in fuckology, which will prove especially useful in enlivening the sex lives of couples.

I reclined myself at his left side and sucked his right nipple with my mouth and pinched his left with my right hand. At the same time I masturbated his cock with my left hand. So I applied triple stimulation to him by coordinating my mouth and both hands. He began to yell, "Yes. Yes. Fuck me hard!" He uttered a long desperate "Oh ------" and groaned, "I'm coming!" I didn't pause until his tensed body relaxed entirely. I was surprised to find his whole chest covered with white sperm, "Oh my, lad. You're so strong! You ejaculated so much!"

"I haven't had sex for such a long time," he sighed.

It took me quite a lot of tissues to wipe the come off his chest. "You're worthy of the epithet Doctor Cock," he said happily.

"Many clients address me as Doctor Linda when they phone me," I said not without pride.

"Well, I feel fantastic," he continued his praises, "You're surely number one."

"Number one is not bad. I'm content to be called that."

While chatting with him, I turned him over and massaged his back and then I struck up another topic, "Were you born in Australia?"

"Yes."

"How old are you?" "Thirty-two."

"Where are your parents from? You look Indian or Pakistani in appearance."

"I don't know where they are from."

That was strange, I thought. Maybe he didn't like this question or maybe he simply didn't know the answer to it. But few people in the world should be ignorant of where their parents were from. I asked again, "What? You really don't know where your parents were from?"

"My foster parents are from England but I really don't know where my biological parents were from. I was an orphan abandoned by them at the orphanage."

Only then did I realize the truth. I said, "It seems to me you look Middle Eastern."

"Maybe," he said plaintively, "And maybe I could find them, but I don't need them."

We were chatting when my mobile rang again. Hearing he was a new client, I told him the price and arranged for him to come in twenty minutes. Then I came back to attend to the present client. I turned him over again on his back and rubbed and squeezed his cock with my right hand which was lubricated with baby oil.

Several minutes later, he rolled off the bed and stood on the floor. He had me put a pillow at one corner of the bed and told me to rest my head on the pillow with my face turned to the ceiling. He stood near my ears, pressing his ball skin against my lips and his cock against my chest. I grabbed his cock and put it between my plump breasts. Then I began to suck his balls in my mouth and rubbed his cock with my breasts. In his desperate groaning and moaning, I felt his balls become harder and harder in my mouth and his cock hotter and hotter in my breast groove. I knew he was about to come, so I quickened my pace in masturbating him with my hands. Soon he was beginning to breathe heavily and I could feel his hot breath run across my belly. Suddenly I heard a desperate yell, "Oh, my God! I'm coming!" My hands were at once covered with a thick layer of clammy fluid and I guessed he must have spurted a lot of sperm. However, I didn't stop my hand and mouth work until he got his breath back and his cock dangled down. I stood up to find my chest covered with a layer of yogurt-like sperm.

"Good boy," I praised him, "You're strong. You managed a second time after all!"

He was overjoyed, "I thought I couldn't come any more, but you're really the expert in this field."

"I've been doing this job for nine years, to be exact, nearly ten years. I deal with cocks every day and I know them only too well. I am more familiar with cocks than with the air around me. There are certain skills involved in masturbation. You can't handle the cock too loosely or too tightly. When you're moving your hand along the cock, you should exert your strength as evenly as you can. You must use your wrist to lead your hand's movement. And different clients have different preferences.

Some prefer quick tempo while others slow tempo. Some prefer ample oil while others less. When the cock is on the verge of coming, you can surely anticipate it through the sense of your hand so don't change the direction or the tempo of your hand movements in this nick of time, otherwise you will hold your client back from coming. In that case, you will lose your time and energy by having to do it again from the very start. When he is about to come, you should continue moving your hand along his cock while it is jerking in spasm so that your client can enjoy the exciting sexual pleasure of ejaculating his sperm."

"Whoa, you can write a doctoral thesis on the cock," he said in admiration though jestingly.

"I'm writing one," I said, "And it will be published next year if everything goes well."

I gave him a bottle of wine and asked him what snacks or nibbles he preferred.

"No," he answered, "I am very fussy."

I had heard many of my clients say this word but I didn't know what it really meant. Having explained it for a long time, he managed to make me understand that this word just meant "being particular about food." I couldn't help laughing to myself: You say you are particular about food and yet you are still so fat? I had him take his shower and got myself ready to receive my next client.

I was lucky to have a brief gap of five minutes between this client and the next one. My next client was above average in height and neither too fat nor too thin. He wore a suit and tie and had thick eyebrows, big eyes, a high nose and blond hair. Judging by his appearance and clothes, I guessed he must have been a government official or a senior clerk in a certain company. He asked for a massage for an hour. When asked whether he would like a beer, he politely declined so I charged him eighty-five dollars with a deduction of five dollars from the regular price. When he finished bathing and lay on the bed, I struck up small chat with him. I asked his age and he answered fifty-three.

"Fifty-three? Incredible!" I said, "You don't look that age. You look only a little over forty." Though the client knew I was only flattering him, he was still very happy.

"By the way," I asked him casually, "Do you live in Canberra?" "No," he answered, "I live in Darwin (the northernmost coastal city of Australia, near the equator). I've come here to attend a meeting."

"A client of mine from Darwin said it was particularly hot there," I said, "and there were only two seasons: dry season and wet season. By the way, do you prefer hot weather or cold?"

"I prefer cold weather," he answered, "You can put on more if you feel cold, but if you feel hot, can you go window shopping in your birthday suit?"

"Yes, but I like Canberra with its four distinctive seasons. Spring in particular. It's neither too cold nor too hot."

"I've heard the waters in Darwin are swarming with crocodiles, some of them as long as sixteen to twenty feet and some even longer than this room," I said as fear registered on my face. "They say the crocodiles will come ashore and lie on the marshes motionless, looking like a log from a distance. If you lose your vigilance and come near, they will pounce on you in a fraction of a second. You wouldn't have any chance to escape its terrible jaws. My client said there were invariably several cases of crocodiles killing people there every year."

"Yes," he added, "It was reported in the paper a few days ago that a man went fishing by the river never to return. He had told his wife he was just going to see if there were any fish or lobsters in his net but he failed to come home that night. The next morning, his wife found his fishing boat and mobile phone left by the bank but her husband vanished as if he had evaporated—he must have been killed by a crocodile."

"I heard another client of mine tell me three of his friends went fishing by a river one day,"I went on to say,"When they were taking a rest in the woods beside the river at noon, a crocodile crawled onto the shore, assaulted one of them and carried him away between its jagged teeth. The other two tried to chase the beast and rescue their companion from its jaw but in vain. It was really very shocking!"

"The crocodile won't kill you on the scene," he provided more frightening details for good measure, "It will drag you into the river to drown you and soak your body in the water for three days to soften the meat before devouring it."

"You're no match for a crocodile," I said, "It's so terribly powerful."

"Yes," he said, "An adult crocodile weighs over a ton. You'll be helpless if you're in its claws."

"One of my clients from Adelaide once told me that their shores were swarming with sharks and a boy of about sixteen fell overboard to be swallowed by a shark! It must be extremely horrifying to witness a man swallowed alive in your presence."

"Some time ago it was reported in the newspaper that a man fishing for abalones at the bottom of the ocean was swallowed by a huge shark, leaving only his head and arms outside the shark's oversized mouth. With great presence of mind, the man stabbed the knife in his hand right into the shark's eye. The shark was startled and spat him out. He was hurried to the hospital to be examined by the doctor. Incredibly, he had only several minor injuries."

"It was really lucky of that man," I commented, "By the way, which is fiercer, a shark or a crocodile?"

"Shark," he answered.

"Either, I think," I said, "That's why I don't like to go to seashores or riversides to swim."

Having had an interesting talk, I asked him a routine question as a usual practice to any client, "Would you like me to work with the condom on or without?"

"Without."

Alas, another guy who didn't want a condom on!

Actually through my own practice and investigation among my clients, I know very well how my fellow prostitutes are dealing with this problem. As our clients are people who have seen the world, they fly from one country to another all over the world and frequent whatever brothels they encounter. They know the rules. However, my fellow prostitutes are not as frank as I am in revealing the secrets of the trade. Generally, ninety-five percent of clients want oral work without condoms on while only one percent of clients want to make love without condoms on. As for me, so long as I haven't found anything wrong with the cock, I will do the oral work without the condom on. I wash my mouth thoroughly after each client, though. But when it comes to lovemaking without condoms on, I am very strict and limit them to a very short list of my old patrons and frequenters. I take every possible precaution to protect my cunt—my biggest asset.

I remember nine years ago when I first took on this profession, a prostitute who came from Manchuria, China told me, "If you do every job with that bag on, you will go nowhere." There is something so subtle that can only be apprehended but not expressed. It all depends on the individual prostitute's understanding or her instinct. Once you have experienced more cases, you'll know how to deal with each case. As for my cunt, I'd like to say it has become all the more cleaner and healthier by being used frequently. It's easy to understand that I exercise my sex organ as I exercise the other organs or limbs of my body. I exercise my cunt every day and I pay special attention to its sexual hygiene, so I have not had the slightest gynecological ailment in all the years since I became a prostitute. By contrast, I used to experience vaginitis or cervicitis more often than not before I became a prostitute.

When I sucked him without a bag on, he said, "You're the best sucker. I have been married for many years but my wife has never sucked my cock."

I smiled, "Sex itself is a mystery. If you have stayed with your partner for long enough, you will lose sexual appeal to each other. Many of my clients have complained that their wives are unwilling to suck their cocks. I think that's because of the lack of cooperation between the two parties. Sexual appetite toward each other should be whetted more often. As for me, it's a different matter. I suck cocks and lick balls because it's my job. I look at these things purely as my occupational duty and I never feel shy or ashamed about them. If I'm married to a man and keep sucking his and only his cock every day, I'm sure to feel fed up with it."

While chatting leisurely with him, I massaged his chest and thighs and then I knelt between his legs to perform oral work and he spilled out much more sperm. He said, "I haven't enjoyed sex this much for such long a time."

Then I massaged his back and finally I helped him masturbate for a third time. It was not easy for a man of fifty-three to come three times in succession within a short time.

Now he looked very relaxed and happy, "My cock has been emptied today and I will have a sound sleep tonight, just as a baby does."

"Yes. You will always fall sound asleep as soon as you have released your sexual anxiety."

During the whole hour I served this client, I was turning a question over in my mind as to why the old gentleman from the countryside wasn't able to come. It dawned on me that it was because he had suspended sex for nine months that his cock passage was blocked. The gentleman's parting brought me back to reality. When he left he said, "I'm sure to be your frequenter in future. So long as I work in Canberra, I will come see you." Then we parted as we exchanged "Good night."

It occurred to me as I shut the door that I needed something to fill my stomach. I was about to open the fridge when a call came in and I recognized from his voice that he was the big cock from Wollongong.

"Is Doctor Linda available now?"

He had been my old patron for more than three years. I answered, "Go ahead. I've just finished a job."

"Well, I'll come in five minutes."

Regular clients called me simply and briefly. Usually several words would do it. I took out two oranges from the fridge and poured myself a mug of milk to alleviate my hunger. I suddenly remembered I hadn't eaten my walnuts today so I took some from the pantry and began to crack them. It sounded incredible that I, as a lady of near fifty, had perfect teeth and could go so far as to set her teeth on a hard walnut. Sometimes my clients would be startled, "Linda, do you want to part with your teeth?"

I was cracking my nut when the doorbell rang and I hurried to open the door. He was a funny-looking man of about fifty. He was rather thin with a little round head, blue eyes, a little pointed nose and a bald head. As he entered, I gave him a pinch on his nose, "Big Cock, come again? What drink do you want this time?

"Just a bottle of water," he said as he walked in. He took the mineral water I handed him, opened the cap and had a sip. As the walnut shells on the kitchen desk aroused his attention, he asked, "You like walnuts, Linda?"

I stood beside him and ran my fingers through his hair and said,

"Walnuts are beneficial to your hair."

"Really?" he wondered, "Then let me have one or two. And new hair will grow on my head tomorrow, won't it?" He handed me a fifty-dollar note and I put it in the drawer. "How can it grow so soon," I said, "Do you suppose the nut is a panacea or a wonder remedy?"

He took up the kernels I had cracked and threw them into his mouth. Seeing that he seemed to enjoy them, I cracked three or four more walnuts for him. He was grateful, "Linda, you have really good teeth."

"I used to have better teeth when I was young," I said, "Now I'm getting old."

"Old? How old you are now?" "How old do you suppose I am?" "Thirty-eight?"

I shook my head. "Forty?"

I shook my head again, "I'm forty-eight, nearing fifty." "You really don't look your age."

"Don't look my age? My age has obviously started to show these two years."

I found he actually liked walnuts very much and said, "I'll pack you some walnuts when you leave."

We walked chatting merrily into the working room. I gave him a towel and he took off his clothes and tossed them onto the massage table. He walked, with his hips bare and his cock dangling between his legs, into the bathroom. Shortly after I repositioned the pillows on the bed, he stalked out of the bathroom with his stiff straight cock erected upward. He had a long and thick cock, thick at the root and round at the tip. The size of his cock seemed a little out of proportion to his thin body. This immediately reminded me of the adage, "Thin men have big cocks while fat men have little ones; thin women have big cunts while fat women have little ones."

I grasped his big cock in my hand and asked him,"Does your wife dislike your big cock?"

"She doesn't like sex either," he said, "I just came from a Wollongong brothel. I was there last night."

"You went to your local brothel?" I was a bit astonished, "Weren't you afraid your wife would cut off your stick if she found out?"

"My wife knows I go there," he answered, "But she doesn't care as long as I don't find a girlfriend outside the marriage."

When we were chatting, he was already lying on his back on the towels covering the bed. I settled between his thin legs, opening my mouth wide and endeavored to gulp his big cock into my mouth, "What a big cock you have. I just can't hold it in my mouth."

"Do you know you're the three hundred and thirty-eighth woman I have ever fucked?"

I was shocked, "How can you remember it so clearly?"

"Every time I fuck a woman," he explained, "I draw a line on my notebook so I remember it clearly. And you know my favorite women are you and a forty-four-year-old lady in a Wollongong brothel. For a while I almost fell in love with her. I had even intended to divorce my wife and marry her."

"If you lived with her for long enough," I said, "You'd find her glamour will soon fade away and life will become staler with each day. A policeman client of mine once said, 'Have sex with a person and always the same person and you will be bored to death someday.' I reckon it's not just the policeman alone, but almost every man."

"But you can't imagine how entranced I was when I was with her," he licked his lips, "She ran her tongue tip along my thighs, balls, asshole, toes and every possible part of my body."

"Are you hinting that I should lick your asshole?" I said, "I can also do that and more. I've been in this trade for so long that I don't care if I'm sucking cocks or licking assholes. I regard them as my career duty and if anyone pays the extra money I will offer him any extra service he wants. As for you, my old patron, I will suck your asshole free of charge. I'm willing to do it for my old lovers and I don't think it's too great a favor. But actually I can't bring myself to suck toes. I hate doing it. I have only sucked the toes of one client, and only twice. I just couldn't very well refuse his demand, as he was a patron of mine for over nine years. I did it against my will. But I have no problem with sucking assholes, as thoroughly washed assholes are as clean as mouths."

I turned him over and had him kneel on the bed with his hips raised upward. I rinsed his asshole carefully with lubricating oil and then I sat behind him, grasped his buttocks and began to run my tongue along his asshole. I found his asshole muscles tightened and his legs tensed so I patted his hip, "Be relaxed, guy. Are you ashamed of being with me? You just think of me as your old love at the Wollongong brothel."

"Come on," he turned around and said "Go ahead and suck my cock. I can't stand the itch any longer."

"You men's cocks are itching all the time," I teased, "If they aren't, how can women like us make a living?"

I opened my mouth wide to swallow his cock into my mouth and said, "Among all my clients, you have the biggest cock."

"Apart from its size, what about its shape?"

I narrowed my eyes, recalling all the nice cocks I had ever seen. There were so many of them and they all looked like real works of art, even nicer than those electric cocks bought from sex shops.

"Your cock is big," I said. "But as for its shape, it can only be rated as second class."

"I am content with being second class," he smiled widely, "That's because you have appreciated too many cocks. You're actually a connoisseur and an appraiser of men's cocks."

I was sucking his cock in my mouth when he groaned, "Oh, no! My cock is itching like mad. Let me fuck you!"

I hurried to the bedside table to search for a large-sized condom and sheathed his cock with it. As his cock was as thick as a glass at the root, I couldn't push the condom down to the end. So I tried to widen the opening of the condom with two of my fingers but I still couldn't do it. Perhaps as I pushed too hard or accidently cut his cock skin, he cried out, "Ouch. My cock!"

"Oh my," I said, "Isn't your cock a little too big? Even the largest size condom doesn't fit it. I'm afraid you have to go to the United States to buy extra-large condoms. It's said there are a large number of extra big cocks there."

With that, I continued the hard task of pushing down the condom to the base of his cock but in vain, "You have to do it yourself. I'm at my wits' end."

He managed to do it by widening the opening of the condom with his fingers. I lay on my back, with my legs spread apart and raised high, and said, "Come on." Facing me, he then knelt on the bed between my thighs and with a "thwack" he thrust his big cock into the depth of my cunt. I couldn't help crying, "Ouch! You're piercing my cunt with your big cock!"

"Haven't you adapted your cunt to my cock by now? I've put it in you so many times."

"The problem is that your cock seems to become a little bigger each time you come. You stop growing but your cock doesn't."

"But it will surely stop growing," he said, "When I am over seventy years old."

"That won't necessarily be the case," I said, "I have a client who is Italian. He is eighty years old but his cock is as hard as a twenty-year-old lad's."

He knelt there, exerting himself in pushing and pulling his big cock. My cunt felt like it was going to burst as his enormous penis swelled painfully inside me. I knew it took me at least two or three minutes to get used to such a big cock before I could enjoy it. I clenched my teeth, "Mate, I'd rather you sprawled on me and did the fucking. You're striking at me so forcefully that my stomach aches."

He then sprawled on me and exerted his hips upward. I saw in the mirror, one white nude body piled on top of another; his body heaving against mine, his huge cock pistoning my cunt sensuously and relentlessly. He caught me looking into the mirror and he looked into it too. He exclaimed, "How sexy!"

"Look into the mirror;"I called attention to his cock,"It looks especially big in the mirror. Though my cunt has been widened by many cocks over the years, it still can't hold your big cock. Do you find your cock is at least one size bigger than the ones of the two porn actors on the screen?"

On the screen, an Asian girl was seen kneeling on the bed and sucking a cock while holding another in her hand. In the next close- up, we were confronted with a large cunt. The cunt was cleanly shaven, with a tuft of black hair half an inch wide and half an inch long right under the girl's navel. He smiled, "Look; that girl's pubic hair looks just like the moustache under my nose, doesn't it?"

Only then did I realize he was freshly shaven, leaving only a thin strip of moustache unshaven on his face. This made him look all the more funny. I smiled, too, "The hair on your head has moved to the place under your nose."

"How distinctive I look!" he grinned, "Besides the unique look, I boast an extra big cock. I may as well become an actor working for a porn producer so I can make money and make love at the same time."

"In shooting a porn film, your cock, in my opinion, cannot last long enough though it is big."

"I'm getting old," he sighed, "When I was young, it could erect indefinitely. It could easily last thirty or even forty minutes on end."

He was pistoning his cock faster and faster. Knowing he was on the verge of coming, I held my breath and then yelled, "Oh, yes! Oh, yes!" while clamping his cock tightly with my cunt muscles. His breathing became heavier and heavier until he finally cried out, "Fucking you. Oh my!" followed by my yelling, "Fucking!"

He closed his eyes painfully and thrust his cock into the bottom of my cunt. He trembled and twisted, gasping for breath. I patted him on the hips, "Now has your cock stopped itching?"

He took in a few more breaths, "Yeah, but it will itch again in a couple of hours."

"Come back if it still itches," I teased him.

"Then I'll be doing nothing but driving back and forth all night."

Just then the doorbell rang and I shouted, "Oh. There's another insensible guy coming!" I was insincere in saying so, though. Actually I was happy there was another guy coming to give me money, and hoped it would be at least fifty dollars.

I pushed the big cock away and told him, "Put away your condom yourself and throw it into the dustbin but not into the toilet bowl."

I snatched up a length of silk with a yellow and red floral design, wrapped it around my waist and made a bow with two corners of the material across my breasts. I hurried barefoot to the front door. I opened the door to find it was the construction worker from Sydney. Another thin man with a big cock.

It was really weird that all the cocks I encountered tonight were huge ones and it seemed my poor cunt couldn't avoid the fate of being pierced. I said to the worker, "Well, you've been coming here for three days on end."

"I didn't want to come here," he smiled, "But my cock didn't agree. It kept on stirring and prevented me from going to sleep." With that he stretched out his hand and fumbled my private part through the thin layer of silk, "My cock can't make do without it."

I brushed his hand away, "Quit and be patient." I took him by the hand and we hurried to the waiting room, "Wait here for five minutes."

"Be quick," he pulled at the crotch of his trousers, "I can't wait to …" I promised, "Yes," and threw the door shut behind me. When I hurried back to the working room, the little head with the big cock had dressed. He said, "Go on with your work. I'm leaving."

"You're not leaving," I said jestingly, "aren't you going to stay the night here? I will charge you at least three hundred dollars for one night."

"I would have to go hungry for a week," he said just as jestingly, "If I paid you three hundred dollars."

"Hurry up and leave," I landed a soft knock on his shoulder, "Another big cock is here. He's in the waiting room."

"Bigger than mine?" he raised his brow, "You'd better take your time."

"It's none of your business," I said, "My cunt only likes big cocks."

We walked laughing and jesting out of the working room. I took a bottle of wine from the garage and a bag of walnuts from the kitchen cabinet. I packed them into a plastic bag and handed it to him, "Go home and drink. Alcohol will stop your cock from itching."

He took the bag from my hand and pecked me with a kiss on the forehead at the door, "See you later."

"See you later. Have a good night."

I came back to the waiting room and led the construction worker to the working room. As soon as we got there, he handed me fifty dollars and told me he had had a bath in the hotel. I covered the bed with white towels and straightened the pillows for him and he couldn't wait to strip. I put away my money in the kitchen and came back, untying the silk material while walking. When I got to the working room, I let go of it and it fell to my ankles. I knelt between his thighs and snatched up his cock at once, "It seems that your cock can never part with Doctor Linda."

"It cannot go a single day without you," he smiled. "Then what will you do if you go back to Sydney?"

Just then his mobile phone began to ring. He signaled for silence by putting a finger to his lips and picked up the phone from the bedside table, "Hi, dear. I've just knocked off and was dining outside." He was reclining with his legs crossed. I was holding his cock in my mouth, wondering who was dining. Maybe his cock was. In response to the female voice on the other end of the phone, he answered, "Don't worry. I will take care of myself." He went on to mumble something and finally said, "Good evening, dear. I love you." Then he switched off the phone.

"You're really good at cheating on your wife," I laughed at him.

"It's unknown who is cheating who," a sneer flitted across his face, "Maybe she is now making love with someone on her bed.

We are six of one and half a dozen of the other. Out of sight, out of mind…"

I finished serving the construction worker and sent him to the bathroom. I was about to take a breather when the rooms were suddenly plunged into darkness. I thought the power failure must have been caused by an overload trip. I could hear the construction worker yelling from the bathroom, "What's the matter? What's the matter? It's pitch dark here!"

"Maybe the main switch has tripped," I said, "Let me find a torch and fix it."

With that, I groped my way to the dining room and fumbled the table for the flashlight. Soon I got hold of it and found my way in the torch light back to the working room. The construction worker had already come out of the bathroom. He asked as he dried himself, "May I help?"

"Perhaps," I said, "You'd better put on your clothes first." He followed my advice and I also put on my dress and a blue overcoat.

I flashed the torch to guide him to the porch. On opening the front door, we found the ground was littered with pieces of paper. We opened the security door to further examine what had happened there. To my disgust, I found two piles of shit on the red doormat! It suddenly dawned on me that it must have been the mischief caused by those young villains.

"Those sons of bitches!" I cursed.

"Who could be so evil to have done this in front of someone's front door?" The construction worker was also indignant.

"I've always been harassed by some teenagers," I shrugged helplessly, "As the proverb goes: Child is the father of the man. These uncouth teenagers are sure to grow into criminals who are capable of anything."

I cursed as I went out. In the torch light, I found the outer walls, meter box and even the padlock all smeared with nauseating nasty shit. When I unlocked the meter box, I found it badly damaged. The thick lid was severely twisted. Someone must have tried to pry the box open but in vain. So, with the box still locked, a little rogue must have put his hand in through a rift they had made and turned off all the switches in it. I was wondering why all the rooms experienced a blackout tonight. Every time a trip occurred, there were always one or two rooms that were not affected by the power failure. They had turned off all the switches this time. No wonder.

After unlocking the padlock and opening the damaged lid of the meter box, I closed the circuit by pushing on all the switches one by one. Suddenly light flooded every room, including the ceiling lights in the corridor.

The construction worker broke out into curses when he found his white van's doors and windows had also been stained with filthy yellowish shit, "Damn those uneducated villains!"

Just then, we heard some rustling in the bushes across the street. Grabbing a club from his van, the construction worker rushed toward the brushes across the street.

"Let's call it quits," I shouted after him, trying to stop him, "They're running faster than foxes and you can't catch them."

In fact, I was worried he alone would be no match for a gang of young lads. However, no sooner had the construction worker reached the bushes than some black shadows fled out of sight.

I had to accept such a rotten deal and clean up all the mess. I went to the backyard to fetch the reel of pipes and the hose and connected them to the tap to wash up the construction worker's stained van. I sluiced the front and rear windshields and all the doors and windows of the van before I washed the red doormat and threw it on the brick post box for the sun to dry it. Then I collected all the filthy paper pieces stained with shit and threw them into the dustbin in the backyard. Finally I took out two used towels and dried up his van for him.

ARSE SERVICE

I had not cleaned up all the mess before the construction worker returned from playing cops chasing robbers. He gasped breathlessly, "Damn it! The little rogues took to their heels. If they didn't, I was sure to break their legs!"

"Lucky you didn't," I said, "If you did, you were asking for trouble."

"Can you tolerate those little rogues?" he asked, "Why don't you call the police?"

"It's no use" I said, "Soiling my doorstep or turning off the switches in my meter box are just minor offences to cause mischief. The police won't put them into prison for it."

"In my opinion," he said, "If you won't call the police, you can ask some friends to help you catch them and teach them a lesson by breaking one of their hands or legs. They will remember the lesson for the rest of their lives and dare not to play the same tricks on you."

"I couldn't agree more," I said, "A customer of mine once said he and his partner were running a food grocery and the shop was frequented by burglars at night. They called the local police many times but to no avail. Finally they had to invite some friends to help them. They lay in ambush in the shop waiting for the burglars. One night when the bad guys came to steal things, they rushed out and caught two of them. They stripped the guys, tied them to the trees and gave them a good beating. From then on no theft happened in their shop."

"They deserved it," he said, "Due punishment should be meted out to those little rogues!" Looking at his cleaned van, he smiled and thanked me, "It's very kind of you to clean my van for me."

"That's all right," I said, "It's my duty to keep my customer's car clean. It's because you came to patronize me that the little rogues smeared your van with shit. Those bad villains need a good whipping!"

With that, I ushered the construction worker back into the house. I took six cans of Coke out from the kitchen fridge and he chose a packet of popcorn from the stacks on the dining table. I packed them all into a big plastic bag and saw him off on the doorstep.

Then I put all the things back to where they belonged. Only then did I find it was high time I came back for my own meal. I had just put the stainless pot on the magnetic stove when the doorbell rang. I opened the door to find two men standing before me. I always felt frightened at seeing two men at once, "I don't do double."

One of them, a little fatter than the other, explained, "I have been here before and I won't come in today. I've brought a friend of mine here this time." With that he shoved a long-haired man to the front, "This is my friend, from Sydney." The man was not more than thirty and seemed a little drunk. I ushered him in and shut the door, "Has your friend told you what the fee was here?"

I didn't remember how much I had charged each individual client, as I always charged them according to the circumstances. Sometimes I charged a young man only thirty or forty dollars because he had a slender purse. If a boy a little older than eighteen searched all his pockets and could find no more than twenty dollars, I would serve him on the condition that I was not too busy at the time.

But he said, "Fifty dollars."

I rejoiced that I could earn another fifty. I led him to the waiting room and informed him, "Please pay fifty dollars first." I usually had my new clients pay cash upfront lest they said they couldn't pay when the service was finished. You couldn't cut off their cocks and keep it as a mortgage, could you? He took out a fat wallet from his trouser pocket and handed me a fifty-dollar note. As I went over to take the money I smelt a strong stench of alcohol and I asked him, "Have you had a lot of liquor?"

"Not much. Only five or six bottles." "Five or six bottles? Not much?"

I handed him a towel and had him take a shower. I went to the kitchen and hid the money. Then I grasped a pear and began to bite at it. I had been so busy that I had no time to make myself a meal and had only eaten whatever I could lay my hands on. While eating the pear, I went to the laundry to inspect the towels and they were not dried yet. I inspected the stock of drinks in the fridge and found half of the stock had been consumed. I rushed to fill the fridge with more drinks. When I finished eating the pear and threw the kernel into the dustbin, I hurried back to the working room. The new client was standing beside the bed, with a large towel wrapped around his waist. I loosened the towel and a very big cock was seen dangling between his thighs. Another big cock!

It seemed that all big cocks were having a get-together tonight. I felt sorry for my cunt. Having served some big cocks, it was already worn out and had to muster up its residual strength to deal with a new big cock. It seemed as if big cocks liked to get together. No wonder nine years ago while working in a brothel, my boss asserted that this trade was a mysterious one because sometimes all big cocks came together coincidentally in one morning and all little cocks in one afternoon, and at other times all old men came together coincidentally in one morning and all young men in one afternoon. There must be something supernatural behind all this.

I took one towel from the cabinet to cover the pillow with and another to cover the bed sheet. I had him lie on them and settled myself between his legs. First I licked the inside of his thighs and then moved my hand along his cock. He was lying on his back and made all kinds of weird sounds, "Oh, yes. Oh wow. You're the best." He then bent his legs and exposed his asshole to me, "Suck my asshole, please."

"Extra fee applies for extra service," I said. "How much is the extra fee?"

"Twenty dollars."

"Could you charge less?" he was bargaining with me, "What about ten?"

"Well," I agreed, "Ten dollars, for the sake of your friend."

I went to the bedside table for lubricating oil. I squeezed a little from the plastic bottle and applied it on his asshole, "It's all right to suck your asshole but I must check if your hole has been washed clean." Then I wiped his asshole with a tissue and said, "Well, it's rather clean."

After I had wiped his asshole clean, I reclined by his left side on the bed with my head right below his asshole. I supported myself with my left elbow and my head rested in my left hand; licking his asshole with my tongue tip. At the same time I masturbated his cock with my right hand and I felt his big cock becoming harder and stiffer in my hand. He uttered some strange groans from his throat and yelled in a trembling voice, "Oh my. Little wonder people call you number one. You are indeed worthy of this name." But his next demand made me angry, "Stick your tongue into my asshole."

I had intended to ignore this demand and continued my job as if I had not heard it. Stick my tongue into your hole?

What if I stuck my tongue in there and it was stained with some shit? Finding I had not followed his command, he exposed the inside of his asshole by spreading his buttocks apart and pressed my head into his asshole with his legs. I turned away and took a tissue to wipe his hole again and went on licking it. But he persisted in pressing my head into his hole over and over. At first I suffered it all silently, thinking it was his first time here and it was not good to offend him, only to find he showed no sign of stopping it and kept pressing my head into his asshole all the harder until I got angry and swung my arm and struck his hip with a loud "thwack".

"I'm a prostitute, but I'm a human as well," I said, "You should respect me. You can't treat me like a dog! Yes, you paid me to lick your asshole and it's my job. But it doesn't allow you to act unreasonably and force me to lick the inside of your asshole. Can you go so far as to force me to lick your intestines? I tell you, whoever can't show due respect to others cannot be respected by others."

He was startled back to sobriety, "Sorry," he apologized, "I'm sorry. I have drunk a lot."

"But you said minutes ago you that hadn't drunk much."

Seeing he was apologizing repeatedly, I stopped my reproaches and to ease up the tense atmosphere, I even said jestingly, "Look, you've drunk so much wine that your eyes have turned green." At my unintentional joke, he just smiled, "Green is the true color of my eyes."

I jumped to my feet and went over to scrutinize his eyes, "No wonder I found your eyes were somewhat different from blue eyes. When I arrived in Australia, I heard people say the eyes of some Australians and Europeans are green. I have seen green eyes for the first time today."

The small chat over the color of his eyes easily smoothed away the displeasure between us. I said to him, "Kneel on the bed and let me lick your hole. My reputation will be ruined if you pay the extra fee but can't get the extra service accordingly."

He knelt obediently on the bed and I sat behind him, with my left hand caressing his eggs and my right hand, applied with baby oil, moving back and forth along his cock. He yelled, "Oh" "Yes" followed by a long groan, "Fuck me with your tongue." So I licked his asshole inch by inch and never stopped my hand's movement along his cock. Soon his body began to tremble and twist and it was no more than five minutes before he collapsed, "I've come. Don't stop licking. Fucking hell. Oh my."

I didn't stop my licking nor did I stop my right hand's movement. After he had reached his climax, I raised my head and heaved a sigh, "Oh, you guy. Aren't you relaxed now? Aren't you sobered up from drunkenness?"

He fell flat on the bed, "I have enjoyed the best oral work today."

I got up and rushed to the toilet to wash my hands, rinse my mouth and brush my teeth. He lay on the bed yelling, "Your phone!" I hurried in to pick up the mobile from the bedside table and had just said "hello" before he spoke back, "I am the Iraqi, the one who often introduces clients to you, remember?"

I recalled I had such a construction worker, who often brought clients to me but we hadn't contacted each other for a long time.

"Of course I remember," I answered. "How many clients will you bring here tonight?"

"Four," he replied. "What time?"

"In twenty minutes." "Okay!"

I told the present client on the bed, "Turn over and I'll give you ten minutes' massage. But be quick. My new clients are coming soon." After the massage, I asked him what drink he would like and his answer was, "Beer."

"Now pay me the ten dollars for the extra service. Then go have your shower and I will fetch you the beers." He took a ten-dollar note from his wallet and handed it to me. I put on my dress and went to take six beers from the fridge. I put the beers on the massage table and ran to the laundry. I took the dried towels from the drier, folded them up and put them away in the cabinet. After that I collected a full basket of dirty towels from the toilet and threw them all into the washing machine. When I finished all the chores and went back to the working room, the long-haired man was already dressed but still seemed half drunk and half sober. He held his beers tightly in his arms. I thought to myself that he was indeed an incurable drunkard who never forgot his alcohol at any moment, no matter what might happen around him.

I gave him a gentle push and said, "Go. Let me see you off. Go home and have an early sleep. Don't drink anymore."

He staggered on his way and I sent him safely out of the house. I hurried back to finish piling all the towels in the cabinet. I looked round and thought I should change the bed sheets but I had some difficulty in pulling up the mattress as it was thick and heavy. Because an ordinary mattress could last me no more than one year, I had a very solid mattress specially made for me and of course it cost me much more money.

I pulled the heavy mattress away with great difficulty only to find a thick black wallet lying on the ground. It must have been left by that drunkard. It was not unusual for a client to leave his belongings such as a mobile phone, a wallet or a pair of sunglasses at my house. If I could find their phone number, I would ring the owner of the lost property and wait for them to collect it. But the drunkard had made no appointment and he was brought here by his friend so I had no information about him, such as his phone number or his address. I thought I'd better keep it for him and wait for him to claim it. I didn't even open the wallet to see what was in it but just threw it into a drawer in the kitchen. I was making the bed when the doorbell rang. I hurried to the front door and pulled it open. I found two men instead of one standing in front of me. What a striking contrast between the two men! One was as corpulent as the other was bony. There were another two men stepping out of a car and making their way to my house.

I asked in a loud voice, "How many of you are there? I suppose a squad of soldiers have come."

"Isn't it good I've brought you so many clients?" the thinner person at the door said, "You can make more money. By the way, are you going to give me a free treat since I've brought you so many clients?"

"There are so many gentlemen standing in the queue waiting to give me money. Why should I give you a free treat?" I recognized at once by his voice he was the short bald Iraqi with little eyes, a pointed nose and thin lips.

"Or else give me a half price offer?"

"Half price? Well, I will allow half of your cock in and leave the other half out of my cunt. Will you accept this term?"

As I ushered them in, we talked jestingly and boisterously. I let in the four men. They took the liberty of enjoying cashews or almonds from the table and someone shouted out for beers. I took enough beers from the fridge to go around and said, "All of you to the waiting room. Don't make too much noise in here."

At this, one of them picked up a box of cashews, another, a box of almonds and a third, a large bag of chips. All of us arrived at the waiting room and I asked, "Who will be the first to come?"

A thin man came over and I told the remaining three, "Be quiet, gentlemen. The neighbors across my backyard have gone to sleep already." I shut the door and led the thin man to the working room. "Fifty dollars for half an hour," the first thing for me to do was to give him a quote for the service.

He took a fifty-dollar note from his wallet and I had him take a shower. After I put away the money in the kitchen and went back to the working room, I found the thin man standing near the bed with a towel wrapped around his waist. I pulled off his towel, "Now little cocks are getting together." He giggled, "Isn't my cock big?"

"I can ascertain in a second where a man is from at a mere glance of his cock without looking at his face. Asian men's cocks are usually small with a few exceptions; among them are the Chinese, Indonesians, Japanese, Koreans, Thai, Vietnamese and Burmese. Their cocks are smaller while men from India, Pakistan, Iraq and Lebanon have bigger cocks, though much smaller than those of men from Australia, European countries, the United States or Africa."

"Then is my cock rated as small or big?"

"Big among the Asians but much smaller compared to those of Western men or black men."

"So I'm supposed to fuck Asian women's cunts," he said. "If I am to fuck Australian or European women's cunts, I would find them too loose for me."

"It's true. I have a twenty-two-year-old client. He is an overseas student from Pakistan. He said he had tasted more than a dozen Australian or European girls but had little satisfaction when entering them. Because their cunts were too large and loose for his tiny cock and he could even tuck his whole hand into them. I was teasing him that everything of him was small so his hand might do the job."

With that, both of us burst out laughing. It took me twenty-five minutes to help him out. I gave him a bottle of wine and had him rest in the waiting room.

Next, in came a man of medium height but stout, with a big head, grey hair, large and bulging eyes, a bulbous nose, thick lips and a fat face. He followed me to the working room. He told me he was called John and I told him to pay fifty dollars first and then take his shower. I put the money in the drawer and came back to cover the bed with clean towels. Thinking he was rather fat, I got three pillows instead of two for him so that he could lie down more conveniently with his protruding belly. When I got everything ready, he came out of the bathroom with his pendulous cock below his potbelly. I said to him, "Lie down on the bed."

He lay on his back and I sat between his legs, resting my head on his belly at the navel, "Very comfortable. Your belly is like a soft pillow." I felt really tired out and wanted very much to take a couple of minutes' rest in this way. He patted his own belly and smiled, "I don't like it but feel helpless about it. I take a fancy to eating. I eat whatever I like and drink a lot of beer. My doctor has warned me against drinking, but I just can't tear myself away from it."

"Neither can I," I said, "I like beer so much that I manage to refrain from drinking it for a month and sometimes two or three months before I take it on again. I've started to drink less these days but I don't know when I could really quit drinking beer."

"It's really hard to quit drinking," he couldn't agree more, "However, my doctor doesn't ask me to quit drinking. You may as well change your doctor."

"I don't think a new doctor would allow me to drink,"I smiled, "I'm now a patient with a fatty liver and I have been warned if I go on drinking, my fatty liver will become an alcoholic liver.

Then it will do me no good. So a new doctor will surely not allow me to drink, either."

"But I don't care so much," he said, "I will drink as before."

"I live not far from your house," he went on to say, "I will be your frequenter in future. You have very good surroundings. In America, prostitutes walk about in the streets, solicit clients, bargain with them and then go to the hotel together. You really have much better surroundings than some five-star hotels."

I said with pride, "My motto is: First-class surroundings plus first-class service for a third-class price."

"You may as well raise your price."

"No. I have a self-knowledge I am not worth a higher price. It is not that I'm getting old now but that I have set a fixed reasonable price since the very start, when I took on this trade nine years ago."

"And it's a clever tactic in business as well."

"Yes. I have a lower price but a bigger flow of clients so I can still make money."

"All is well if you can make money."

"By the way, have you ever been to the United States?"

"Actually I am an American citizen and have lived there for thirty-two years. My wife, son and daughter all live in that country."

"Is the United States a nice place to live in?"

"Some places are not safe. I run a Pizza Hut there and I have had three experiences in which black people pointed their guns at my forehead and robbed me. I myself have two guns but you can never predict exactly when someone will point a gun at you."

"It sounds terrible indeed," I said.

"So when I arrived in Australia, I felt things were totally different. It's very safe here. I'm now applying for Australian citizenship."

"It is said that Australia is the fittest place in the world to live," I went on to say, "Is it easier for an American to apply for Australian citizenship?"

"Yes, it's much easier."

"So is it easier for an Australian to apply for American citizenship?" I asked.

"What for?" he asked.

"I'd like to have American citizenship. When I finish writing my book, I plan to present a lecture with famous American prostitutes, and I will not have to have a visa to go there."

"Australian citizens don't need a visa to go to the United States."

"Even if I don't need a visa to go there, I still want to apply to be an American citizen."

"What for this time?" he was perplexed.

"If the Chinese government outlaws prostitutes and wants to put me into prison," I said, "It would be easier for President Bush and Prime Minister Howard to combine their efforts to rescue me then."

He burst out into laughter.

"I hear that in America, well-known prostitutes drive Rolls-Royces to attend their lectures."

"As a matter of fact, there are not very many prostitutes in the United States who are both wealthy and well known. No matter what you're doing, do it well and it's not easy to be known to all."

"My dream is to not only be the first prostitute in Australia but also the first prostitute in the world. We have a first lady, first miss, first player, first driver, but no one has claimed to be the first prostitute. But I am willing to be one. Anyway, to be first in a trade is always worth trying. We Chinese have a saying that you can stand out in whatever trade you are in. I am standing out in this trade and claim to be the first prostitute."

My facetious words made him burst into laughter again.

I rested my head on his belly and had fun when my head moved up and down as his soft belly expanded out and contracted in. I took a rest for a couple of minutes and felt quite relaxed. I slid my head from his belly to his private part until my mouth touched his cock. I held it in my mouth and started to suck it. It was not long before his little penis hardened and erected. I kept on sucking harder and harder. I swallowed his cock deep into my throat and ran my tongue over his cock tip. He enjoyed it very much and couldn't help groaning out, "Oh……" Suddenly, I felt a warm stream in my mouth and I pulled it out to find a trickle of white sperm dripping along his little cock and I grabbed some tissues in a hurry to wipe it off. I then went to wash my hands and mouth and came back to massage him. Two or three minutes later he began to snore loudly. Look, such was a typically healthy man who could eat his fill and sleep like a log any time he pleased. I waited for about a quarter before I woke him up, "Is it enjoyable to have a sound sleep immediately after you come?"

"Yes, I'm sure to sleep like a baby tonight,"he said contentedly.

I resumed sucking his cock and this time the process lasted only a couple of minutes before he came for a second time.

"Too hot," he said, hanging his head in shame, "I haven't had sex for two months."

"Doctors say it's harmful to your health being cut away from sex for a long time."

"So I'll come to you twice a week." "How old are you?"

"Sixty."

"Then once a week or once every two weeks will be suitable for you at your age."

As I had another client to attend to, I hastened him to take his towel for his shower. When I went to the waiting room, the bald Iraqi with little eyes told me that the fat man and the thin man, who had enjoyed the service, were going out to smoke cigarettes. I guessed the fat man would go home and opened the door for them. The bald Iraqi with little eyes mumbled from behind, "I'm also a man and need some comforting. I will envy them if I can't enjoy what they have enjoyed."

"You can come in as soon as your friend finishes bathing and dressing."

Just then the fat man John, who had just enjoyed his slumberous bliss staggered out of the working room. When asked what drink he wanted, he responded predictably, "Beer."

"Beer? Think of that beer belly of yours!" I smiled.

"Beer! I'll regret it on my deathbed if I quit beer,"he smiled too.

I gave him a six-pack of Tooheys New. He snapped the top off one of the bottles and raised his head to drink the beer with several gulps. I patted him on the shoulder, "Hi, guy. Drink the beer with your two mates outside. This mate of yours would like to have some fun in here."

He left smilingly and winked at the bald little-eyed man, "Enjoy yourself."

I shut the door and led him to the working room. He handed me fifty dollars and stripped instantly. When he took off his shoes, a terrible smell emanating from his feet assaulted my nostrils, "Oh, my. What a smell! I could smell that a mile away."

"I know," he was very embarrassed, "I'm sorry."

"Sorry?" I was disgusted at the smell, "Away with it or I'll go faint."

I threw him a towel and told him, "Go and give your stinky feet a good wash!"

I shoved him into the bathroom. Then while holding my breath, I picked up his smelly shoes, threw them into the backyard and came back to heave a long breath. Oh, shit! I had never smelt such a terrible stench from the feet of any of my clients. I gasped for breath.

The smell was almost unbearable! I muttered as I walked to the working room. The bald, little-eyed man was already on the bed and I asked him, "Have you washed your feet clean?"

"Yes. Clean."

"Clean? Why do I still smell it? No, we should use some air freshener spray." With that, I sprayed the aerosol freshener into the room and the bathroom. And for good measure, I pointed the aerosol at his left foot and pushed away at the button.

"Hey, what are you doing?" he cried as he pulled away his foot. I went on to spray some on his right foot. He began to yell, "Oh! It's too cold!"

"You feel too cold? Well, who can bear the stench from your feet?"

I patted him on the hip and said, "Well, you can stretch out your legs now." I put the can back on the bedside table and settled between his legs. I picked up his cock and began my oral work. After repeated and prolonged groans followed by a chain of yeses, he came at last. I helped him wipe off his come. "If my girlfriend knew this," he said, fear lingering on his face, "she would likely cut my penis off."

"This tiny cock of yours is not worth cutting," I was making fun of him, "Anyway, a pair of scissors should do it."

"You are being crueler than she would be," he laughed, "to use the scissors."

"What's the difference between cutting off and scissoring off ?" I asked. "It would achieve the same result – getting rid of this cock of yours."

"If your scissors happened to be blunt," he said, covering his private part subconsciously as if someone really intended to cut off his cock, "How could I stand the intense pain?"

I turned him over to massage his back and continued our aimless chatter, "I remember you told me last time that your girlfriend is very rich, is that true?"

"Yes," he answered, "Fortune was on her side. She won ten million dollars from the lottery and bought ten houses with the sum of money."

"Then she will give you one or two houses, won't she?"

"Far from it," he said resentfully, "She has become more temperamental since she won the lottery. I have to nod and bow before her. She hasn't given me any houses but instead she often has me repair the houses for her."

"I think repairing houses for her is perhaps your best fate," I sneered at him.

Looking up at the clock on the wall, he cried out, "Oh, I must be going now. My girlfriend will call for me any moment."

He got shakily to his feet and threw on his clothes in a hurry. Seeing him searching every corner for his shoes, I went to get his smelly shoes from outside, "Look at the shabby shoes of a man with a wealthy girlfriend!"

"The shoes are good enough," he laughed, "It's my feet that smell terrible."

"I know."

I came to the kitchen and took six Cokes from the fridge. He took the Cokes from me and picked a packet of chips and several chocolates from the dining table and left. At the doorstep, he said to me, "When your house needs repairing or painting, call for me."

"Good. Thank you."

"Bye-bye!" I smilingly closed the door behind me.

Having seen off these men, I came back to find it was eleven o'clock at night by the clock on the wall. Now it was high time I indulged myself with a solid meal. I took out some chicken chops I bought from the supermarket, put the pan over the magnetic stove, ignited the fire, turned on the range hood and poured some oil into the pan. Then I added onion slices and began to fry the chicken chops. Soon the kitchen was filled with an enticing, wonderful aroma. I took a white Cola (with no sugar) from the fridge, as I was trying to follow my doctor's order to refrain from drinking alcohol. After all, my age was beginning to show and I was diagnosed with a medium level of fatty liver. I'm inviting Death if I go on with my hobby of alcohol. Anyway, life belongs to us only once. So I had to make do with Cola tonight. When the chicken was cooked, I cut the chops with a knife and devoured them all like a wolf. I had a life-long habit of eating quickly without chewing food properly and hardly any food shreds would get stuck between my teeth. But alas, now I was really getting old. For the last half a year, I got something stuck between my teeth every time I finished my meat. What a queer thing it was. I used to have even and regular teeth when I was young and no such thing could have possibly happened. I took out my dental floss and went to the mirror to clean my teeth one by one with it. This reminded me of a time ten years before, when I first met my Australian husband Ian Thomas Philip, who was thirteen years my senior. He used to depend on floss to clean his teeth. I always wondered why the old guy had such bad teeth when I never needed such a thing as a dental floss for my even and regular teeth. But as time quickly elapsed, I found I couldn't do without it for almost every meal. Though my teeth remained even and flawless, they were no longer as sparkling white as before.

I could clearly remember when I first took on this trade; many of my clients praised me, "What pearly and neat teeth you have!"

I no longer hear of such praises. Life is but a span. Life is but a dream.

Youth is so fragile and is fading at an accelerating pace. A woman in her prime will undergo a small change in her beauty every five years and a bigger change every ten years until she reaches the age of forty; from then on she is on an irrevocable decline. After the age of fifty, she will go from bad to worse year by year or even month by month. I suddenly became sentimental at the thought of this cruel process women had to endure. What worried me most was that I was certainly aging with every day until one day I would become an old goat. My patrons would flee at the mere sight of me and I will be driven out of this trade. I would dreadfully deplore the loss of my youth and cry desperately for a wonderful remedy for rejuvenation. Remaining young forever is human's greatest dream but aging and dying is the inevitable law of nature. No wonder the Empress Wu Zhetian of Tang Dynasty proclaimed in her last years, "I'm willing to exchange my Kingdom of Tang for my youth!" But she could not and neither could I. What little I could do was let nature take its course and take advantage of the rest of my life to do something—say, write a masterpiece about sexual intercourse— something I could hand down to the next generation...

Just then the doorbell rang. I tossed away the used dental floss and went to answer the door to find two twenty-year-old Indian students of medium height standing before me. For almost half a month, there had been three or four Indian students come by every evening to visit me. They got my information by word of mouth. They were all introduced by friends because I charged very reasonably. Thirty dollars for quick service of fifteen to twenty minutes and forty to fifty for half an hour. Relatively lower prices plus free entertainment attracted many young Indian customers to me.

I told them across the security door, "I never do double." But they said, "We'll come one by one."

"I charge fifty for half an hour," I said.

"But my friend told me thirty dollars for half an hour."

Seeing that it was another one introduced by his friend, I couldn't charge him a higher price, so I agreed, "Thirty dollars? Okay, but it'll be a quick service and you can only come in one by one. One of you has to wait outside in your own car."

"It's rather cold staying in the car," they pleaded, "Let us come in together."

Judging by their appearance, they didn't look like bad guys so I allowed them in together. I led both of them to the waiting room and asked, "Who will be first?"

"I will," the fatter little man said.

So I told the thinner young man, "You can wait here. Watch the TV program and enjoy any drink from the fridge. By the way, the toilet is over there." With that I closed the door to the waiting room and led the fat guy to the working room. I asked him to take a shower first. He took thirty dollars from his trouser pocket and handed me the money, which he must have got ready in advance.

"Go and take your shower," I said. "I won't," he said resolutely.

"Hey. I have recently found you Indian boys don't like bathing. Go and take a bath. If you don't, how can I suck your cock?" I took a towel and hung it on the rail in the bathroom for him and he began to take off his clothes. While doing so, he told me, "Bring me a bottle of beer."

"You can't until we finish the transaction," I said, "You already smell strongly of alcohol."

"Just one more bottle," he kept on pestering me.

I had to fetch him one from the fridge and put away the money in the drawer. When I came back with the beer, he was lying on the bed. He snatched the beer from my hand, opened it and drank it with several gulps. I sat by his left side, facing him and patted him on the belly, "What a big belly you have. You shouldn't drink any more. How old are you?"

He went on gulping down some more beer before answering me, "Twenty-three."

"You are just twenty-three and have a big belly like that," I said, "It is sure to develop into a potbelly when you reach forty."

He simply turned a deaf ear to me and went on drinking.

I took up his pepper-shaped cock, which was wrapped in foreskin. I've found most Indian boys have such cocks (wrapped in a layer of movable skin called foreskin). Such cocks were my headaches because it was especially hard to wash the inside of them and they smelt strongly of urine. Whenever I encountered such cocks, I peeled them open by telescoping the foreskin down and made sure the inside had been cleaned properly. As soon as I pushed down his foreskin, he cried out in pain.

"What are you crying for?" I said, "Look at the urinary calculus between the foreskin and your stick. Go back and give it a thorough wash. How it stinks now! Your parents should have taken you to hospital and had the foreskin cut off when you were still a child. Then you won't feel pain when you have sex once you get married."

He refused in silence but I forced him to his feet and obliged him to take another shower. I followed him to the bathroom, telescoped his foreskin down his cock and cleansed it inside out under the showerhead. I helped him wipe his cock dry and climb onto the bed.

"Linda," he said "This is the first time I have ever had sex with a woman. I'm a virgin boy."

"You don't look like it." "But it's true."

"Since you're a virgin boy," I said, "I'm going to suck your cock with the condom on."

"No. I don't want you to suck my cock with that bag on."

I scrutinized his cock and felt sure there was nothing unusual about it, so I held it in my mouth. He was carried away by the ecstasy and began to groan, "Oh, yes. Ah, yes," "Wow." After a while, he said, "Please lick my egg skin." I ran my tongue along his tautened egg skin but I didn't expect his sudden proposal, "Linda, I love you. I want to marry you."

"You love me?" I said calmly, "You're only twenty-three while I'm near fifty. Isn't it a farce that you want to marry me? I have told many young men your age that you've come to the right place to satisfy your sexual desire but the wrong place to find a girlfriend. You should search among your classmates or colleagues for girlfriends or wives. You're not in an advantageous position if you try to find your girlfriends among the women of our trade. What fine men have we not witnessed?

In my mind, I despised such a little man. Old as I was, I looked down on him, let alone the younger prostitutes. You have no money, nor good looks, nor talent. How could I take a fancy to you? Another sentence lurked in my mind, "Love me? Is your cock competent?"

At first, whenever I heard some tiny-cocked man say they loved me and wanted to marry me, I invariably got very angry. It was an absurd suggestion to marry me when their cocks were below average in performance. But later, as more men proposed to marry me, I began to laugh up my sleeve. While I could see and compare more than two dozen cocks a day, ordinary men had little chance of seeing or comparing themselves to other men's cocks. All men considered their own cocks to be the best.

The little fat man with the bulging belly said, "If I could lengthen my cock, would you marry me?"

At this, I was annoyed and amused at the same time, "If you could, I wouldn't. Answer me a question frankly first. Why on earth would you want to marry me?"

"If I marry you," he answered brazenly, "I will become an Australian citizen."

"Well, many kiss a baby for the nurse's sake. You have an ulterior motive. You want to make use of me. To be frank, I won't do you this favor. I can't cope with all the cunning questions asked by the immigration agency clerks. It's foolish of me to discard my lucrative business and get mixed up with you in cheating the government and inviting trouble into my life."

"Several days ago," I went on to say, "An old customer of mine, who is already sixty-three, told me he had married a girl of thirty-one from a brothel. After the wedding, her two sons managed to immigrate to Australia and then she filed for a divorce in court. And what was worse for the poor old guy, she got half of his property for her alimony. Do you want to rob me of half of my property by following suit?" He remained silent.

"I've advised many of my clients," I went on to say, "If you want to marry an Asian girl, you should never choose one among the prostitutes, who have seen too many men. You can never take the lead in your marriage even if you get married. Whenever you offend her over any trivialities, she will elope with any other man immediately. Take me for an example, once a prostitute, always a prostitute. I can be a good prostitute but I will never be a good wife. Attending to a single man would bore me to death. So if you're looking for a wife, please find one in some Asian countries such as Thailand, China or Vietnam. You can find a clerk, a teacher or even a worker and bring her to Australia for marriage. But take note; please don't let her be involved in any sex industry. If you do, she will soon change. As she contacts more and more men, she is sure to leave you and elope with other men."

He then had me suck his cock and pressed my head against it with his hand. I brushed his hand away and said, "Stop doing that!" And after a while he said, "Let me fuck you."

I found him a small-sized condom and said, "You lie on me. You should exercise more to prevent your belly from growing too fat."

With that I lay on my back on the bed, spreading my legs apart for him to thrust his little cock into my cunt.

"Do you like my cock?"

I hesitated to say that I had no feeling at all with his tiny cock moving in vain in my cunt so I could only say, "I have seen too many cocks so what I love most are big cocks." He toiled away puffing and blowing on me, moving his little cock in me. I just perfunctorily dealt with such boys; nothing could be said of enjoying any sexual pleasure. I thought of helping him come as soon as possible only to find him tormenting me for a quarter without any sign of coming. I complained, "You're not like a virgin boy. You're like a Don Juan who has played with dozens of women."

From time to time he kissed randomly at my face, mouth or nose and wetted my face with saliva smelling of alcohol. I brushed his head aside, "Stop kissing my face. I don't like that."

Still his cock refused to come so I said, "It's because you have drunk too much. You'd better let me squeeze your cock instead."

I shoved him off my body, had him lie on his back and snatched the condom off his cock. He exposed his asshole by spreading his buttocks apart, "Lick my asshole!"

"Mind you, extra fees apply," I said.

As a matter of fact, if he were an old client of mine, I would serve him without any extra fees. I just didn't want to spoil the young man by allowing him to enjoy more service without paying more money. He stood there with his buttocks spread apart, "Linda, I love you. You lick my asshole!" He was being a rascal so I held down his legs, swung my right hand and smacked his abdomen with a loud "thwack." Though I knew I wouldn't hurt him by striking this part of his body, he was startled by the sudden attack and began to behave himself. By then he had become much more sober and allowed me to masturbate his cock. I took great trouble to help him come. He had drunk too much and it was very hard to make him come. After reaching his climax, he asked for more beer instead of getting dressed.

"Go wait for your friend," I said, "The fridge there is filled with beers." I sent him to the waiting room and led the lanky lad to the working room. I had him pay his thirty dollars and asked him to take a shower. When I came back, he was lying on the bed. I was about to pick up his cock when the doorbell rang. I went to open the door and it was another Indian lad, but taller and more handsome than the previous two. I ushered him to the west living room and settled him in the swivel chair. Although they all came from India, I wouldn't have them encountering each other if they hadn't come together. The door to the waiting room was designed so that it couldn't be opened from inside so that if a client should get drunk and wanted to rush out, it would be impossible for him to encounter another client who happened to step out of the working room. If the client in the waiting room wanted to leave, he could inform me by knocking on the wall so that I could go release him and avoid him running into the client coming out of the working room. I told the newcomer to wait for two minutes and then went to the waiting room. When I pushed the door open, I found the little fat lad holding a beer bottle in one hand, almost empty and another full bottle of beer in the other. There were two more beer bottles on the bed. I was both annoyed and amused, "Lad, are you thinking my service was not worth the thirty dollars you paid and trying to make up for it by drinking up all the beer stock in my fridge? Look at your belly. It is swelling like a balloon. In a minute, you'll be searching everywhere for the toilet." With that I took a bottle from the bed and put it back in the fridge and handed him the other bottle, "Well, three beers is enough or you'll be unable to find your way home."

I helped him to tuck a beer into his trouser pocket, "Lad, drink it outside in your own car. I have another new client who will be waiting here."

"Okay," he got to his feet and staggered to the door, with a half-emptied beer bottle in his hand. Having seen off the little fat lad, I hurried to the west living room and pulled the newly arrived Indian boy out of his swivel chair and led him to the waiting room, "You'll have to wait here for another fifteen minutes as I have another client in the working room being served but he'll be finished soon."

I ran back to the working room and squatted between the thighs of the thinner Indian boy. Picking up his cock, I found it was another uncircumcised one typical of Indian boys. The foreskin was wrapped tightly around his cock with only a pointed tip exposed, like a big green pepper the length of about six inches. I tried to slide his foreskin down to see whether it was clean, but it was wrapped too tightly around his cock. I had to content myself by smelling it. Well, it didn't smell too bad. It seemed his cock had been cleaned quite thoroughly. So I held his cock in my mouth and began to suck it. Soon he was breathing noisily through his teeth.

It was not long before he suggested, "Let's get down to fucking!" I found him a medium-sized condom and slipped it onto his cock. He had me stand on the floor and support myself with my hands on the bedside table, with my plump buttocks parted wide and pointing upward. Standing behind me, he thrust his pointed pepper-like cock into my cunt. Unlike a normal cock which had a ring at the tip to give the woman more pleasure as it rubbed against the sides of her cunt, such a foreskin-wrapped cock had a mushroom-shaped tip that lacked this function.

The boy was young and strong and his cock was as hard as iron. He could be heard pistoning his cock inside me noisily and yelling, "Oh, yes. Fuck!" Even the noise of the bedside table knocking against the bed head came into chorus. It was about ten minutes before he cried out loudly, "I fuck you!" He came at last but he continued pressing his belly against my buttocks and shivering for a long time before he calmed down. When he pulled his cock out of my cunt, I turned to look at the dangling condom full of white sperm, "Boy, you really have a large stock."

"That's because I haven't touched a girl for half a year," he confessed. I helped peel the condom from his cock and threw it into the dustbin.

FUCKABLE

As it seemed he didn't feel like a shower, I thought it might make things simpler. I waited a while for him to get dressed and sent him to the front door. No sooner had the door closed than the doorbell rang. I opened the door and it was the little fat man, "You again, guy. Want more beers?"

He smiled but kept silent. He just raised something black in his hand. I went over to find it was the remote control to the DVD player in the waiting room. I patted him softly on the head, "You bad boy." Actually he was not a bad boy like those who stole anything they could lay their hands on whenever they felt aggrieved. I was somewhat touched and came back with two more beers for him. He came over, tiptoed and kissed me on the cheek, "I love you, Linda."

"Boy, you're too young to know the real meaning of love." Having shut the door, I went to the waiting room and led the

Indian boy to the working room. Only then did I get a chance to have a close look at him: very thick black hair fell to his shoulders and he had a comely face, a high forehead, a pair of watery eyes, a straight nose and thick sexy lips. His dark skin looked very healthy. He was a really handsome young Indian man who reminded me of the hero in a famous Indian film "Awara," which was very popular in China years ago. The boy in front of me was perfect except for his height --- no more than five foot seven.

"I have been here before, maybe last year," he said shyly, "I am a medical student at Canberra Hospital."

"It's a very promising occupation to be a doctor in Australia. I often go see my private doctor. Every day her patients form a long queue. She can receive as many as fifty patients a day, much busier than me." I went on ask him, "How much did I charge you last time?"

"Thirty dollars," he answered.

I knew the score and said, "Well, thirty dollars but only for fifteen to thirty minutes not half an hour, as I am particularly busy now."

"Linda," he said, "I've just parted with my girlfriend and I am sad. She is Indonesian and we loved each other. We had prepared to get married but her parents didn't agree. We had to separate. What do you think I should do?"

"Since you love each other" I said, "You should defy all obstacles to be united."

"It's difficult," he lamented, "And the language barrier between us. She has gone her own way." He then turned to me, "Linda, I like you. I love you."

I was wondering why one courter was followed by another and I said with a deep sigh, "Lad, you're too young and I'm nearly fifty. You're supposed to come here to resolve your sexual urges. I'm not fit to be your love. There's a great age gap between us and besides, we have different views on a lot of things. You should find one among your peers of a similar age."

In spite of my dissuasion, he pressed himself to embrace me and endeavored to kiss me. I could understand his feelings as I had had similar feelings when I was young. A lovelorn young man desperately needed another lady to fill the vacancy left by his love. But, I was certainly not the right one for him. In order to make him understand sooner that ours was merely a relation of business, I told him, "Lad, I have made it a rule never to kiss my clients and be quick. Please pay me the thirty dollars."

He produced a fifty-dollar note from his pocket and asked, "Do you have the change?"

"Yes. Just a minute. I'll get the change for you."

With that I walked away with the money and asked him what he'd like to drink.

"No, thanks," he said, still at a loss. "All right. Let's drink later."

I went to fetch a twenty-dollar note from the kitchen drawer and handed it to him, "Do you need a bath?"

"I've just had one. You can feel my hair."

I ran my fingers through his thick long hair and said, "Oh, yes, it is still damp!"

I laid a towel on the piles of pillows and covered the bed with another towel, "Take off all your clothes and put them on the massage table." He followed the instructions instantly and fell flat on his back on the bed. I climbed into the triangular place between his legs and took up his medium-sized cock. He asked, "Linda. Is my cock big or small? My girlfriend liked it very much."

It was because your girlfriend hadn't the chance to see any nice big cocks I thought, but couldn't speak out too frankly. So I said ambiguously, "I like big cocks."

With that, I took up the aerosol can of air freshener from the bedside table and aligned it with his cock, "I have seen a twenty-one-year-old Australian boy's cock as big as this and as straight as it is nice."

"If I found a doctor to extend my cock to this length," he said, "Could you love and marry me?"

I laughed, "It's not a matter of your cock's length. Love is so complicated a state of mind that you are too young to understand it. I myself can't explain it to you in a word or two. You'll come to know it as you grow older."

Then he said, "Linda my baby, please suck my cock." "Without a bag on?"

"My lad," I smiled, "You're calling me a baby? I'm nearly fifty and it is I who should be calling you a baby."

I looked at the cock in my hand, small but hard with no foreskin. Its skin was glossy and there seemed nothing wrong with it so I held it in my mouth. He began to yell out of strong excitement, "Oh! Ah! Yah! Eh…" until at last he could no longer bear it and said, "Linda, let me fuck you."

I found him a medium-sized condom and sheathed his cock with it, "Mate, you lie on me and do as much exercise as you can. Doctors say fucking is as good a form of exercise as jogging. Fucking as exercise can do a lot of good for your health." So I lay on my back and spread apart my thighs to allow his cock to enter my cunt. I wrapped my legs around his waist and he moved his cock in me slowly but rhythmically. I groaned as he groaned, "Linda, You've got a nice pussy. I love your pussy."

I echoed him, "Oh, yes. Oh, yes." Making perfunctory love with such young guys brought me no pleasure, let alone sexual ecstasy. Besides, I had toiled myself for a whole day so what I wanted most was to help him come and nothing more. I was thinking when he asked me, "Can you feel my cock?"

How could I say I had no feeling at all? So I said, "Yes, I feel it."

"Do you like it? Do you love it?" He became very excited, "Let me kiss you!" and he tried to do it. But I threw a wet blanket on him by saying, "Lad, I kiss only cocks, never lips."

"Just one kiss," he pressed his lips against mine and stuck his tongue into my mouth. I had to give him a perfunctory kiss but didn't allow his tongue into my mouth. At last he cried out, "Ah… I'm coming! I love you, Linda!"

I waited until his surge waned down and then I had him take his shower. I told him a new client was coming soon. I did so deliberately to let him know there would be no possible love between us and the relation between us could only be that of a sex worker and her client. He said, "I'm not in the mood for a shower. Let me go home." I asked him what drink he wanted and his answer was, "Lemonade."

I went to the kitchen to fetch him four cans of lemonade and a packet of chips. I put all the things into a plastic bag and handed it to him. At the doorstep he gave me a kiss on the cheek, "I love you."

Having seen him off, I realized I needed a good rest. I went to the kitchen and did the washing up. Now I could entertain myself by counting the money earned. 790 dollars in total. I had surpassed my intended target once more. I had set myself a moderate target of earning an average of 600 dollars a day. Thus I could get a net income of 400 dollars after excluding the cost of 200 dollars for expenses. Every evening as I counted the colorful notes I had earned that day, I would forget all the tiredness and humiliation I had undergone. I was deriving great satisfaction from counting the money and putting it away in the safe when it suddenly occurred to me that I hadn't phoned my mom in two days. So I went to the living room to get the calling card and dialed Mom's number in Beijing, China. Looking at the clock, it was five to midnight in Australia, or five to ten in the evening in Beijing (a time difference of two hours because of the Daylight Saving Time system). After the phone rang three times, Mom answered it and I greeted her merrily, "Good evening, Mom."

"What's up?" Mom was wondering, "Why are you so happy?" "Why not?" I laughed, "I've made big money."

Up till now, I hadn't told any of my relatives what I was doing in Australia. I just told them I was running a small company in Canberra.

Mum said thousands of miles away, "It's good you can earn money. The company must be going well."

"My clients line up in a long queue every day," You could never guess what they are queuing for, I thought. They were queuing to fuck me.

"For any trade, as long as the clients are queuing, it proves you are doing very well in your business," She went on, "Nowadays in China only a few businesses can be profitable. You should work harder to make more money."

"When you cease to worry about money, you're sure to be in good spirits." I said buoyantly, "Do you remember the Huaifu Restaurant I once ran in Huairou, Beijing? Oh my, I worked day and night and didn't earn a penny. Instead, I owed so much to others. It almost worried me to death."

"Yes. The Huaifu Restaurant was really a money trap."

"If I hadn't come to Australia," I said, the fear lingering in my mind, "I would have been overwhelmed by the debt. Maybe I would have committed suicide by jumping from the third-floor window of the restaurant."

Mom probably couldn't bear to listen to me indulging in my past misery so she changed the subject,"The other day your sister and I discussed He Chen's (my twenty-one-year-old nephew) cost of studying in England for five years. We estimated the sum at one million renminbi. If you are making big money, you should help your sister. If you're planning to publish a book, do it quickly to earn cash."

I suddenly got very angry, "Forget it. Don't mention it anymore. When I came home last time, didn't I agree to offer two hundred thousand to cover his first year's fees? As to the remaining tuition, it would depend on my next year's capacity to earn money. The more the better, of course. And besides, as he is a twenty-one-year-old adult, can't he pay his own way? Look at the overseas students here in Australia. They are even younger than him and most of them work part-time jobs to support themselves."

"Anyway, you should cover half of it," Mom argued. My fury began to rise. It had been less than a month since I returned from China and my contribution should jump from two hundred thousand to five hundred thousand. What do you think I am doing? Running a bank? I was so angry that I shouted, "No, he is not my own son! I would if only he was kind to me but he isn't. Every time I sent him on some errand, he showed great reluctance. I can't imagine he would take care of me when I grow old and poor in my senior years."

"After all, you are his aunt," Mom kept pestering me on the other end of the line.

I flew into a rage, "To be frank, it's none of my business! Do what you want. I don't care."

With that, I hung up the phone abruptly and flopped into a chair, breathing heavily. I reminisced with bitterness through the vista of the last ten years since I had been abroad. It was as if I were their cash cow or ATM. Whenever they needed money, they counted on me to supply them with endless Australian dollars. Mom wanted to buy a house, my sister took a fancy to a car, my nephew would like to go abroad to study the latest branch of science. On every occasion, I had to open up my wallet without exception. Take the case of He Chen; I had promised to finance two hundred thousand dollars of his studies but the sum suddenly soared to five hundred thousand, and within a month! Was this money something I owed you? You want me to publish the book as soon as possible? No, you just want me to make more money for you to squander. Aren't you afraid the publication of my book will bring you disgrace instead of cash? Were you thinking I was writing lyrical prose about my Australian travels? (Of course, they only knew I was writing a book but had no idea what I was writing about.) I only had myself to blame for all this so I punished myself by slapping my face. Every time I phoned Mum, I invariably began with the sentence, "I've made big money." If you have been making big money, who do you suppose they will ask for financial assistance? My family members must have thought I had enough money to burn and could supply them with it endlessly. The more I thought about it, the angrier I got. I picked up the mobile on the writing desk and threw it onto the ground when it rang loudly. The mobile, though cheap, was solid enough!

I picked it up from the carpet and answered in a huff, "Hello?"

"Baby, can I come to see you?"

"Coming fart!" I blurted out, in a mixed language of English and Chinese.

"What?" he obviously didn't understand and I was quick in responding, "Oh, I mean you can come along."

Now I could make out who the caller was. He was my patron of over six years. He was my best sex partner and the best pussy licker who could satiate my sexual desire.

"I will come in twenty minutes," he said. I got to my feet at once and went to the bathroom to scrub my body clean. I changed into a very sexy dress with a green floral design. Knowing he was fond of music, I found a porn DVD "Oriental Fever" bought in Sydney and inserted it into the DVD player. This video program showed Lesbian sexuality from start to finish with western orchestral background music. In its preview, two girls were seen kissing and tantalizing each other's plump breasts followed by the title: BARELYLEGAL 100% ALL GIRLS. The music sounded kind of like traditional light music.

After I had got everything ready, I already forgot the irritating economic dispute with Mom. I jumped to my feet at the chime of the doorbell and hurried to open the door. "Hello, my dear. Good evening."

"Good evening, my sweetie," he responded.

The man was less than five foot two in height and around my age. He had a round body, a round head, round blue eyes, a pointed nose, thick lips, a short haircut and a shining forehead. All this made him look round like a ball. It seemed you could send him rolling along at once with a gentle push. I ushered him in and stood in front of him. He was half a head shorter than me. I noticed he wore a pair of very eye-catching, pointed shiny black leather shoes. I had never seen such a pair of long-pointed shoes. They seemed too exaggeratedly long against his height. He wore a black suit today and smelt strongly of cologne. It seemed he had intended to meticulously dress up.

Suppose we turned up together in the street, we were simply like a modern version of Snow White and one of her dwarfs. He was definitely no match for me to walk hand in hand along the street with, but he was matchless in his performance in bed. He could easily bring me to the sublime of sexual ecstasy, even though he was short in height and his cock was small in size.

He wrapped one of his hands around my waist and whispered into my ear, "My beautiful girl." I thought "beautiful aunt" might be more accurate, though I was no older than him. We entered the working room together, my arm wrapped around his shoulder. I opened the door of the glass cabinet and hung his suit in it. He produced a fifty, a twenty and a ten-dollar note from his pocket and handed me the eighty dollars, "Baby, this money is yours." I had given him a special price with ten percent off because he could bring me to bliss by licking my pussy until it watered torrentially. I laughed up my sleeve. He paid me money to make me come.

I thanked him for the money. He said, "That's all right." Where could I find such a good thing? I asked him, "What drink do you want?" He said, "A bottle of water."

"Okay," I answered, humming a familiar tune, "I'm going to be another man's bride tomorrow so let me love you for the last time…" After putting away the money in the drawer, I took a bottle of mineral water from the fridge and walked back to the working room, humming all the while. By that time, I had cast aside all the unpleasantness of the financial quarrel with mom or the publication of my book.

Stop thinking of that, I thought. I was going to enjoy myself whether he was tall or short, thin or fat. The glittering lights, light music and all the laughing girls on the screen provided a wonderful background for us to take liberties with our own bodies and give rein to our lust. I wriggled out of my dress, tossed it away and hopped onto the bed. He stripped quickly and lunged at me on the bed, "Baby oh my, let's have a good kissing. Haven't seen you for a month. How I've been missing you!"

He pressed his round fat body against my back and began to snort his nose through my hair, "What fragrance!"

Then he moved his mouth slowly to the back of my ear. I felt his warm breath caress my lobe, which made my whole body tingle. I chuckled, trying to wriggle myself free, "Stop. I can't bear the tickling in my ear."

"Come on, let me kiss you."

"But not my ears," I said, hinting, "I can't bear the tickle there. I'm afraid of being kissed on my ears. My sensitive part is not there but on my pussy."

"Don't be impatient," he assured me, "I'm beginning with your ears first and then your back, your asshole, your toes, your bosom and finally your pussy."

"Quit kissing my ears," I pleaded, "You're just making me uncomfortable."

Disregarding my pleadings and strong reaction to his ticklish kisses, he kissed away persistently until I almost choked with laughter.

"Please let me get up," I said, trying to guide his interest to my desired part. "I'll show you some newly bought DVDs. All about girls licking cunts. Techniques well worth learning."

I fetched for the remote control on the bedside table. The first thing we heard was the girls yelling madly "Fuck me! Fuck me! Look at my pussy!" followed by a song that sounded like lots of girls chuckling.

I was amused, "What fun it is to listen to this song."

"No fun in the world compares to you," he retorted, "You're the real fun while the girls in the video can only be looked at but cannot be enjoyed."

"I will collapse in no time if you go on playing with my body like that."

He pressed himself against me again, skin on skin, "Come on. Let me give you a good kiss. I haven't had my fill in kissing you yet." Now his lips turned away from my ears and went slowly down my neck to my shoulders. I enjoyed it very much. My ears ceased tickling and I began to gradually be myself. I felt greatly relaxed and the fatigue of the day was fading away bit by bit. I moaned and said coquettishly like a spoiled little girl, "Oh, darling. How I am enjoying this."

"Enjoy yourself," he said, "Let's go on with our kissing."

Then he ran his lips slowly down my back and covered every inch of it. After that he kissed from my left buttock to my thighs and finally to my asshole, which was a forbidden place for me. I couldn't bear other people touching my asshole even softly, let alone kissing or licking it. I said, "I can lick yours but please spare mine."

"Just once," he pestered.

"Not even once," I was resolute, "I don't like it."

"I'm expert at licking assholes," he said persuasively, "You're sure to like it."

"However expert you are," I said, "the problem is that I'll be disgusted by it instead of enjoying it."

"Well," he conceded, "Let me kiss your buttocks instead."

He shifted his lips from the valley to the right hill of my buttocks, "You have nice buttocks."

"My god, I have nice buttocks? I thought they were too bulky. Your comment might have been correct seven years ago. But it makes no difference to me. After all, it's you not me who is kissing them."

He ran his mouth deliberately slowly from the inside of my right thigh to the bend of my knee, then along my shank, and finally to my right foot. He held the toes of my right foot in his mouth.

"Oh, I would be overwhelmed by your special favor. But I like pacing the carpet barefoot, so my feet would be too dirty for you."

"But I don't repel them."

"I won't have you doing it even if you don't repel them. I will feel guilty."

"How about you wash your feet clean before I suck them?"

"I won't have you kissing my feet even if they have been washed clean," I said sincerely, "As a matter of fact, I don't like my feet or my asshole being kissed by anyone. It will make me feel disgusted instead of pleased. You may as well spare yourself the time."

He ran his tongue along my left thigh to my left calf and slowly shifted from my neck to my bosom. At the same time he began to caress my nipples. As he was doing so, unspeakable ecstasy thrilled through them. I knew he was whetting my sexual desire. When he held my right nipple and started to nibble it, I couldn't help moaning heavily, "Oh, my dearest."

He ran his tongue tip along my nipples bit by bit, making my nipples erect hard and stiff. He raised his face and said, "Your nipples have hardened. You must be aroused!" "Oh, yes," I responded. At my response, he nibbled away my nipples until I was paralyzed with indescribable pleasure. I nearly melted as he licked me. In my groaning, he shoved his head downward to my navel and then to my shaven cunt, "You have a teenage girl's cunt, so tender and glossy."

"Tender and glossy?" I smiled to myself, "If I hadn't shaved my cunt, it would have bristled your tender tongue with hard grizzly hair." He licked my cunt for quite a while before he adeptly spread my pussy lips apart with his fingers and landed his tongue tip directly on my clitoris – the female's most sensitive part. I instantly felt a hot wave surge inside my cunt. Oh, my gosh. What a relentlessly thrilling sensation! It ran from my clitoris to my heart and then through my legs to the soles of my feet until every part of my body was swimming in ecstasy. I began to gasp for breath, "Ennn… Oh, yes. Aooo…" My legs stretched rigid and tense and my body arched upward. I imagined I was the Empress Wu Zhetian (the most lustful empress in China's history) and he was my most obedient minister serving my insatiable lust, heart and soul. I prayed in my mind, "Spare no effort to lick me well. Oh, yes. A little deeper and still deeper! On the right place! I will promote you and give you more wealth…" I still imagined him saying most obediently, "Your Majesty, it's my first duty to serve you well. I promise to lick you until you're satiated whatever my wife will feel."

I kept imagining: I was the Empress Wu! And suddenly without my awareness, I cried out, "I am coming!" I thrust my middle finger and forefinger into my own cunt and yelled,"I love you! (For the time being.)"

My body jerked and quivered as I repeated, "I love you. (He knew we were provisional lovers. A moment later I would be a prostitute again and he a client.) I throbbed once, twice, thrice… until I calmed down after coming four or five times.

"Thank you," I said to him.

"Shall I lick off the liquid you have produced" he suggested and, brushing aside my hand, was about to stick his tongue into my cunt when I stopped him, "No, thanks. After coming, the clitoris becomes too delicate and sensitive to be licked again."

Actually most women, after their orgasm, would much prefer to keep cocks in their cunts rather than being licked or caressed.

So I said the feelings were different when a woman was made to come by a cock or by lips. However, the man between my thighs was now my favorite licker and every time he came, I would deem myself to be Empress Wu or Empress Chixi (the most lustful empress second only to Empress Wu in China's history). His wonderful licking could really remove all my fatigue of the day.

After a brief rest of a couple of minutes, I offered to serve him, "Come on. Let me suck your cock. Lie down, please." I had him lie down on his back and held his cock in my mouth. He was heard heaving heavy breaths through his teeth, and then cried out, "Oh, yes! Fuck!" I knew he liked his balls to be held in my mouth and I slowly shifted from his cock to his balls. It was lucky his balls were not too big, like two pigeon eggs, and I could nest both of them in my mouth. Just then I heard him let out a loud sigh from deep within his throat, "Fuck my balls!" I began to swallow his balls into my mouth and spit them out; swallow them and spit them out again. He couldn't help moaning repeatedly, "Oh, yes. Oh, my god…"

"No!" he jumped to his feet, "I have to fuck you."

I sat up with him at the bedside and then flopped onto my back. I spread my thighs wide for him to thrust his little cock into my cunt. "Hey," I protested, "You're trying to play a new game by fucking with no condom on?"

"It's more satisfying skin against skin."

For old sake's sake, I allowed him to have his own way, "But please don't ejaculate in me."

He was beyond himself, yelling away like a mad man, "Ah, yes! Oh, yes!" He didn't piston his cock for five minutes before he suddenly stopped his movement inside my cunt. I felt at once that he must have come, "Hey, guy. What on earth are you doing? Are you intending to inseminate me with your child?"

With that, I broke away from him and jumped to my feet. While I disengaged from him, he held his cock in his hand and stood there agape with surprise, "Ah… Ah…Ah…" I rushed to the bathroom and washed the inside of my vagina under the nozzle, worrying I had been inseminated by him. If so, I would have big trouble. I had been refusing so many handsome young men to inseminate me up to now. But I was relieved to think that I was near my fifties and might not be fertile any longer. Besides, I may have already run out of all the eggs I would produce. However, I still took precautions for possible conception by washing my cunt thoroughly, inside and out, until I felt sure there was nothing left inside my vagina. Then I took the towel from the hanger and wiped my body dry with it. When I went to the working room, the short man had already finished bathing and dressing. He stood there waiting for me. He served me more than I did him. I enjoyed forty-five minutes while he only fifteen minutes of the hour he had paid for. I put on my dress and said, "I'm much obliged to you for having brought me to my climax. So I'll send you away with a box of chocolates as a gift." I went to kitchen to fetch a box of chocolates for him, "What else do you want for your drink?"

"No, thanks. That's very generous of you."

I laughed up my sleeve. I enjoyed most of the hour you paid for and I'm regarded as generous? The clicks of his black, shining, pointed leather shoes against the floor brought me back to reality. I opened the door for him and he tiptoed to kiss me on the cheek, "See you next time, little baby."

"Little baby"? I thought "old baby" might be more accurate. Though I have told him I'm thirty-eight. "Good night, dear," I waved good-bye to him.

He stepped out the door and strolled to the car he had parked in my driveway.

I shut the door and felt extremely relieved and refreshed. All the fatigue of the day vanished like smoke as I realized the amount of my earnings reached almost 900 dollars. Though it was one o'clock in the early morning, I did not feel the least bit tired. Maybe money was the best exhilarant. I went to turn on the tap and fill the bathtub before coming back to scrub the floor of the working room. Then I washed the dirtied rag under the tap with detergent powder and came back to the working room. I switched on the stereo and turned up the volume. As my windows were all double glazed and soundproof, no sound could be heard from inside my house. I hummed to the rhythm of "One Way Ticket." The strong, 4/4 beats of the song excited me. The whole house reverberated with the beautiful music. I went to the bathroom, turned off the tap, wrung the rag dry and began to scrub the corridor with the damp rag. As I worked my way along the corridor, I moved the rag to the beat of the music: ta ta ta ta. The rag invariably reached either the right or the left side of the wall at every fourth beat. My rag followed the rhythm of the music, like magic: one, two, three, four and before long I was dripping with sweat. My dress was dampened with sweat and stuck to my hips. It made me feel uncomfortable so I wriggled out of it and tossed it onto the carpet. Now I was mopping the floor with nothing on. Seeing the rag getting dirty again, I threw it into the bathtub and washed it before finishing the mopping with it. Twenty minutes passed and the floor became shiningly clean.

Just then my mobile rang, "How much do you charge?" "Fifty dollars for half an hour and ninety for one hour." "Can you give me a gold shower?"

"No problem."

"Can you piss into my mouth?" "Come along."

"Will you charge extra fees?" he didn't feel quite sure of the price.

"I will piss into your mouth and not vice versa. How can I charge you extra fees?" I assured him, "Just come along."

"Thank you."

Another fancy client, I sighed. I put away the cleaning rag and washed my sweaty body clean in the bathroom, thinking I should drink more water or else I wouldn't have much urine to piss into his mouth. I hurried to the kitchen and took a large bottle of mineral water from the bench, opened the cap and emptied half of the bottle. Soon I felt my belly bursting with water. I was about to gulp the rest of the water in the bottle when the doorbell rang. Hey, the guy was rather quick in action. I ran to the working room and snatched the blue silk material and wrapped my body with it, leaving half my white bosom exposed. I opened the door and said, "Good evening, sir. Come in, please."

In came a fat and tall lad. I wondered how such a young lad should become a sexual deviant and enjoy other people pissing into his mouth. Did he think urine was a delicious drink? But I asked him politely in spite of the unspoken criticism in my mind, "Is it the first time you've been here?"

"Yes."

I led him to the working room, "Fifty dollars for half an hour, lad."

I knew from my experience that I might as well offer the young man the price for half an hour as most probably couldn't afford the price for one hour. And he said, "My friend told me the price was forty dollars."

"Well, forty dollars is all right," I answered.

He produced two twenty-dollar notes from his trouser pocket and handed the money to me. I asked him what drink he would like and he shook his head. "Then I will let you take some drinks with you when you leave," I said.

I put away the money in the kitchen drawer and came back to the working room, worrying I could no longer control the urge to piss if the young man didn't allow me to piss into his mouth. I said, "Take off your clothes and enter the bathroom so I can piss it into your mouth." The lad stared at me in bewilderment, "Why do you want to piss into my mouth?"

It suddenly dawned on me that I must have confused him with that sexual deviant, "Did you call to make an appointment just now?"

"No," he said, "I didn't call you. I'm a drop-in client." "Sorry," I said, "But I thought you were the man who called just now. Do you need a bath?"

"I've just had one."

"Then just lie down on the bed," I could no longer resist nature's call, "Excuse me, but I have to go to the toilet first."

He lay on his back on the bed, watching a porn program of two girls licking each other's cunts with a funny chattering song as the background music. I sat on the toilet and pissed very loudly. I had a torrential piss indeed. If this piss should be poured into anyone's mouth, he would be drunk with urine. I turned on the tap in the washing basin and washed my hands and my cunt as well. I dried them up with a dry towel, went to the bed and squatted between his thighs. I didn't hold the fat man's cock for fifteen minutes before I helped him come and then I massaged his back for about five minutes, "Now you can take a bath. By the way, what do you want to drink?"

"Ordinary Coke," he said.

He took the towel I handed him and went into the bathroom. I went back to the kitchen and packed six beers into a plastic bag for him. I put the Coke and the beers onto the kitchen bench and waited for the fat guy to come out. I asked him, "Are six beers enough for you? If not, I can bring you two more."

"More than enough," he said, "It's so kind of you."

I sent him out the front door and wished him "Goodnight". When I came back, I was surprised to find the door to the working room closed. I opened it only to find the Blu-ray image flickering blankly on the two TV screens on opposite walls. The damn son of bitch had stolen my DVD disk. The DVD disk cost thirty dollars plus six beers that were worth five dollars. I was losing money. His shower cost electricity. All in all, I did this job for nothing. Damn it! It was indeed a losing deal. I tidied the bathroom in the working room and carried the used towels to the laundry to be washed in the washing machine.

The doorbell rang again and I opened the door to find a fair and clean boy, with a tuft of blond hair bristled like a proud cock's comb along the top of his head and the sides of his head shaved clean – a hairstyle that Beckham wore in the Korea-Japan World Cup. I asked him, "You don't have an appointment, do you?"

"No," he said, "My friend recommended you to me. I come from Sydney."

"Have you reached the age of eighteen? If not, you are not allowed in." I warned him.

"I'm already twenty-one," he said, showing me his driver's license.

I let him in and asked him if he'd like a drink. He said he would like none for the moment.

"Then let's talk about it when you leave," I said, thinking I would take precautions next time I hand out drinks and never let them take advantage of my trust again. These young guys couldn't reconcile themselves to the special prices I offered them. They just stole anything at their convenience. Thinking of this, I charged resolutely, "Fifty dollars for half an hour." He didn't bargain as expected but took out a fifty note from his wallet. After sending him to take his shower, I went to the kitchen and put away the money.

He lay on the bed, appreciating his surroundings, "Linda, you have a gorgeous interior decor. You must make a lot of money."

"Yeah, you earn money to spend it," I said, "What I have earned has mostly gone on the furnishings."

"How much can you earn in a week?" he asked innocently.

"It's a secret of mine," I just smiled.

"I can also make a lot of money," he said proudly, "I can earn two or three thousand a week."

"What do you do," I was surprised, "to earn so much?"

"Drug trafficking," he answered as naturally as if he was selling computers or teaching mathematics.

"Oh, my gosh!" I was shocked, "I pray you never come again. If the police track you to my house and suspect me to be your client, my business is bound to be ruined."

"No police are on my trail. I am always on alert."

"It's no use being on alert. Are you on drugs?" What worried me most was having clients who were addicted to drugs.

"No, I'm not on drugs myself. I just sell them."

"Since you're not on them," my fear shifted to curiosity, "Why are you selling drugs?"

"To make big money."

"If I were you, I would quit; however lucrative this business is. I absolutely abstain from any illegal business. If the Australian government should outlaw prostitution today, I wouldn't postpone closing my business tomorrow," I went on to say, "Have you heard of the case a couple of years ago? A twenty- year-old Australian boy, whose mum was Vietnamese, was taken into custody by

Singapore Customs for trafficking drugs. After staying in prison for three years, he was sentenced to death by the Singapore court and despite the Australian government's repeated pleadings, he was ultimately hanged."

"No," the boy's face turned a little pale, "I haven't."

"It's worthwhile to watch the news," I preached and threatened, "Don't set your heart on drug trafficking. In case you're caught by the police, you will go to prison, not to mention hell."

The boy rolled his eyes, "I have been doing it for years without being caught by the police."

I sighed, thinking to myself, "It will be too late if you're caught. You will cry over spilt milk then."

With that I quickened my pace in making his cock come. When I saw him off at the door, I warned him never to come back. While I was caught off guard, he spat in my face.

"Hey, bastard," I got furious, "I was giving you the advice for your own good. Never come here anymore. I'm scared."

The lad left without looking back. My heart kept pounding with fear.

Glancing at the wall clock, it was two thirty in the early morning. It was high time I switched off my mobile and went to bed. I had to get up early to go to the bank. I was about to switch off the mobile when it began to chime. A low voice came from the other end, "Linda, may I come by?" Now that I had already answered the call, I couldn't very well refuse him. He said he would come in five minutes.

I inferred the client couldn't have lived far away from my house. I couldn't make out who he was, though his voice sounded familiar. It was not strange, as I attended so many clients a day that I could hardly tell Tom from Dick or Harry. It wasn't important, as it would come to light immediately when the client showed up.

I soon went to answer the door and found it was my Chinese client of three or four years. A tall, thin man with a flat, square face and big eyes – a typical oriental man. I asked him, "Have you just knocked off?"

"Worked overtime in the office." "Worked so late?"

"Hadn't intended to go home."

We walked in, talking casually. I offered him drinks but he declined.

Once in the working room, I handed him a towel for his shower. Shortly after I got the sheets and pillows ready, he finished showering and tossed his used towel onto the massage table. He threw himself onto the towel-covered bed and said with timidity incongruous with his age, "I can at last have a brief rest. What a tiring day!"

"What kind of work has tired you so much?" I asked.

"It's really tiring to work for others. Look, how you're getting along. You're your own boss and earning more money. If I were a woman, I would follow your lead."

"It's also tiring to work for yourself. I spend seventeen to eighteen hours a day working and I see nothing except cocks all day long."

"The more cocks you see," he smiled, "The more money you earn."

I knelt on the bed between his thighs and picked up his soft brown cock. His cock and balls were circled with long black hair so they were too bristly for my tongue. I swallowed his cock into my mouth, which had never erected in its real sense since I knew him. Honestly, it didn't even harden when he was ejaculating. Sometimes when he was asked to put on a condom, he would try many times before he was able to thrust his flaccid cock into my cunt, and what was more, his cock didn't last longer than a couple of minutes. Today, sure enough, I didn't hold his cock in my mouth for five minutes before he came so I had to turn him over to massage his back. I massaged him for half an hour and said, "Now, go and take your shower."

"Linda," he said, "I'd like to spend the night here."

It was not his first time that he had put forward such a suggestion and I knew he was testing my reaction.

"Good," I said, "But I'm afraid it is too expensive for you. It will cost you three hundred dollars for a night."

He was perplexed, "What time is it. Don't tell me you're going to work all night long."

"I never put up a client here in my house even if I am not working. I can't go to sleep while someone is lying on my bed and if I can't go to sleep how can I continue to work tomorrow?"

At that he got to his feet reluctantly and went to take his shower. Did you think I would take a fancy to your good looks? To your cock that always let me down? Even if your cock could erect hard enough, its size was far from satisfactory. What nice big cocks hadn't I seen before? My ideal boyfriend should not only be good looking but also have a nice big cock. And the cock should have not only size but also hardness. It should have not only hardness but also endurance. By these criterions, yours should be put at the end of a very long list.

As he went to the bathroom to take his shower, I followed him in there to wash my hands. He pointed to the dustbin overflowed with used tissues and condoms and smiled, "Linda, you're indeed busy and prosperous. The overflowing dustbin marks your success."

"As the dustbin is not big enough, I'm planning to replace it with a big crate," I also smiled.

"Wow," he was amazed, "That means you can serve two hundred customers a day!"

"If I had two pussies," I said, "I could surely serve two hundred a day."

After bathing, he took his time to get dressed. Just then my mobile rang, "Linda, may I come?"

"Yes," I hung up and turned to him, "Look, the next client is coming. Unless I switch off my mobile, I'm afraid I will have to stay up for the whole night."

"Won't you go to bed after attending to that client?"

"Yes. I must switch off the mobile at any rate or I will be occupied by cocks around the clock."

I followed him out of the working room. He looked at me but showed no indication of paying me so I had to say, "Since you haven't drunk any beers or other drinks, I'll give you a discount of five dollars. So just pay me forty-five dollars." He slowly took a twenty note, two ten notes and a five note from his wallet and handed them to me one by one. I said thank you and he said that's all right. I thought in any case I had to charge my clients a proper fee for my services. If every client became my lover and could enjoy me free of charge, how could I make a living? I gave him a bottle of mineral water and saw him off. I looked up at the wall clock and it read 3:00 a.m. In any case, I had to switch off my mobile!

Hardly had my finger touched the "off " key when it rang loudly in the still of the early morning. Shit, another cock! But I had to answer it, "Hello?"

"Dr. Linda, my cock needs an emergency treatment badly." "Is the cock cold or feverish?"

"Feverish. It must be a bad cold. A very high fever." "Then come along."

I went to the working room and changed into a doctor's white gown with my two ample breasts nearly bursting out of the specially cut low neck. The ready white gown I bought from the market was purposely shortened by several inches so the cleft of my hips were exposed. I searched the drawer for my stethoscope and hung it around my neck. When I got everything ready, the doorbell rang. I hurried to open the front door and stepped out to open the security door.

He was a thirty-four-year-old taxi driver; a patient of mine for more than nine years. He was as heavy as 440 pounds, with a fat, round face, a body resembling a huge ball and a potbelly hanging almost to his knees. His two thin legs, which didn't seem to belong to the rest of his body, could hardly support all his weight. I stood beside him and could hear him breathing heavily. His cock must have had a very serious fever today as he breathed three times faster than usual. So I said, "Why didn't we come to see the doctor since we have such a high fever?"

"My cock has a fever twenty-four hours of every day and I had expected to grit my teeth and hang on but I deteriorated so much that I couldn't go to sleep. So I have to come to you, Dr. Linda."

"Can we step forward? Try it."

"Let me have a try," he raised his leg with difficulty and tried to step over the threshold. I followed him and stooped to fumble his private part. If someone happened to be behind me, he would invariably focus his torchlight on my buttocks, "Why is Dr. Linda diagnosing his patient at the doorway?

"Oh my," I cried out, "Your private part is wet. Pissing your pants or just coming?"

(I had several clients who couldn't ejaculate their sperm unless I dressed up as a doctor and frightened them into entering a state of sexual illusion or fancy. The man I was attending was just one of those serious cases of a syndrome called impotent-unless-frightened-by-a-doctor.)

I felt his crotch and he instantly halted his leg and groaned out, "Dr. Linda, my cock falters at your touch and I can't move my leg."

I patted his fat buttocks with a smack, "You should go in first. You can't take off your trousers and have me diagnose your cock here, can you?"

He was panting heavily and had much difficulty with stepping over the threshold. I had just shut the door before his trousers fell to his ankles. He could hardly wait to be laid on the operating table!

"Hurry up," he cried impatiently, "Kiss my cock. My darling, I'm missing you."

"How can I kiss it while it is dripping wet? Have you wet your pants? You may as well take your shower first."

"I haven't wet my pants," he defended himself against my accusation; "I've just had my shower and pulled on my trousers before I dried myself. So my crotch is wet."

I peeped into his trousers and sure enough, he had nothing on and his crotch was drenched with water, "Well, I can't suck your cock right here. Please come in."

Holding the waist of his trousers with one hand, he reached out the other to fumble my escaping breasts, "You have shapely breasts."

"Not only you but almost all my clients admire my breasts. They are my best assets and I count on them to make big money."

He nosed his way through my breasts and tried to nibble my nipples. I hit him smack in the face with my stethoscope, "Too impatient to wait? Go to the working room." But he still managed to have a bite at my nipple. He staggered with difficulty to the working room. I said, "Strip and get on the bed."

As he let go of his trousers, they fell to his ankles again. He slid off the heel of his left shoe using his right foot and then removed his right shoe in the same way with his left foot. Having panted for a while, he stepped out of the left leg of his trousers and then the right. I kicked his trousers together with his shoes into the space under the massage table, "Take off your coat, too."

He struggled to wriggle himself out of his fat shirt, before handing it to me. I threw it on to the massage table. I looked at his corpulent potbelly. I was all too familiar with this belly as I had touched it more than a hundred times. It was so huge that it hid his cock and balls from being seen by anyone who stood before him. You could only see them by sitting on the floor and lifting his belly with your hands.

He managed to climb onto the bed and I prepared three pillows especially for him so he could lie down more comfortably. If he had his head rested on lower pillows, he would have much difficulty inhaling enough air to breathe. He reclined on the bed, his huge belly hanging off the bedside like a loose bag. I nudged his belly inward a little, "Are you ready?"

He moved his ass inward slightly and I took the stethoscope from around my neck and pressed it against his belly, making a pretence of listening to it professionally, "What trouble are we having?"

He felt my two tender breasts with his hands. I had purposely unbuttoned my white gown so that my breasts could work their way out of the low neck line. He said pesteringly, "Mm… I want to drink your milk." With that, he aimed his mouth for my nipples. I had to cry, "Take your time. Don't hurt my nipples."

He held my nipples in his mouth. They were my sensitive spot and a sense of unspeakable rapture thrilled from my nipples to my cunt. But I definitely knew he was by no means the right man to satiate my lust. As he was not handsome and more importantly, he had too tiny a cock. I wouldn't have any feeling making love to him. I treated him wholly as a patient. The thrilling feeling he gave me pleased me greatly but it was not strong enough to arouse my inner desire.

For us prostitutes, we don't need to arouse our sexual desire in attending to our clients. Sexuality is a very complicated process. Some men will depend on a fantasy to come. You have to make him come within a limited time since he pays you for half an hour's or one hour's service. If you can't, you must admit it as a failure. Of course, every profession has its failure rate. My failure rate for the past few years has been about 0.05 percent. That is, I have only one failure out of every two thousand cases. So I am referred to as "Number One" and I myself am very proud of my superb capacity and professionalism. He took hold of my right breast, appreciating, caressing and kissing it, "What nice breasts. As nice as those of a teenage girl."

"That's because I haven't given birth to any baby, have I?"

"How happy I would be if I could sleep with your plump breasts in my arms every day."

"But you can't afford it," I teased him, "It would cost you one hundred and eighty dollars if you should sleep with them in your arms for just two hours."

He then shifted his mouth from my right breast to my left one, which was not as sensitive as the right one. I had asked some of my clients and they said they also had one nipple that was more sensitive than the other. As my left nipple was less sensitive, he couldn't arouse me by licking it. He paused embarrassedly when he found his licking and kissing was in vain. I found ten minutes had passed and I knew he came for half an hour's service every time. I had to get through the whole job within the remaining twenty minutes.

"Let's do a check up of your cock and balls," I said, getting to my feet and walking to the bedside. I pried his legs apart and knelt between them. His cock was nowhere to be found as it had shrunk into his balls and I had to pull it out with my fingers. However, by stimulating his balls, his desire would become aroused and his cock would gradually stick out from them. Holding his balls with my stethoscope, I ran my finger over them and their skin became tautened, "Are you itching?"

"Oh, my god. Very nice and I miss that."

I was lapping his ball skin with my tongue and my hand crept to his asshole. He began to gasp for breath, "You're beautiful. You're my baby. I love that!"

His little cock could be seen sticking out from his balls slowly but steadily. I felt it and it was hardened. He pleaded, "Suck my cock, please."

I held his cock in my mouth and it felt extremely hot. I started to suck his cock as a baby does its mum's nipple. He squealed like a pig and kept screaming before he uttered, "Fuck me hard, Linda."

I jumped to my feet, snatched off my stethoscope and rushed to the bedside table to find the smallest condom for him. Sitting astride him with my white gown on and pushing his dangling potbelly upward a bit, I suddenly sank myself on his cock. I sat up and down on him with his little thing held inside my cunt, "I fuck you. I fuck you! How does it feel?" I did the up-and-down movement rhythmically and more and more violently until he screamed, "Ah, yes! I'm coming!" I slumped on him, exerting my cunt muscles to pinch at his poor cock relentlessly. I felt his cock jerking inside me several times before it slackened. I rolled off his body, carefully withdrew his condom and showed the bag filled with his white sperm to him, "Look, how much you've come? No wonder you came for an emergency treatment. Now you are satisfied?"

"Yes," he grinned, "Now I can go home for a good sleep. Thank you, Dr. Linda."

"You don't have to thank me. Get up and pay me." I reminded him, "And do you need a shower?"

"No, thanks," he said, "I will have one at home."

I preferred he didn't. I was really exhausted and I needed badly to sleep.

The big fat man struggled to get up when he said, "Linda, I have something to tell you."

"What is it? I'm listening."

"When I was about to knock off," he told me with great relish, "a lady got in my taxi. She had just finished her job in a restaurant. She looked to be in her early forties, very sexy and very coquettish but she later told she was sixty-four."

I was spurred at once by this as I worried I was withering of age with every day and on the verge of quitting my trade. Upon hearing a lady many years my senior was still in business, I got very excited as if I had been given a shot in the arm, "What did she say?"

"I asked her what her price was and she answered a hundred and fifty dollars for one hour. I went on to ask how much she could earn a day and she said around seven hundred dollars a day. I was impressed a lady of sixty-four could earn seven hundred a day! It would take me two or three days to earn as much."

"Oh," I smiled to myself, "Surely she can't tell her clients her real age when she serves them. If she did, she would only get five instead of a hundred and fifty dollars for an hour. She has to halve her age and say she is only thirty-two." He couldn't help laughing a lot at what I said.

I went on to tell him another anecdote, "Nine years ago when I was working in a brothel, a very gorgeous, forty-year-old lady from Shanghai was sent out to answer a call one night (a jargon in brothels meaning going to the client's home to serve him). Her boss had her tell the client she was only nineteen because the client fancied young girls. The lady retorted, 'My son is eighteen while I am nineteen?' Everybody around burst into laughter at once."

"It's not bad being a prostitute," the big fat man grinned wickedly, "You don't have to fear unemployment, at least."

"A woman, as long as she looks young and sexy, can always attract customers and make money. The government has not set an upper age limit for prostitution. In the United States, a prostitute in her eighties is still at work. I have told some of my clients I will stay in my trade until I cannot move or get up."

Helpless laughter contorted the fat man's face, "In my opinion, everybody is actually selling himself. The only difference lies in the way he or she does it. Someone sells his brains; another one sells his labor. We taxi drivers are selling our labor and time, aren't we?"

"Yeah," I added, "We prostitutes are selling our bodies and brains as well. Whatever you do, you must beat your brains to earn money. A famous American prostitute once said, 'A lawyer makes money with his brain while we prostitutes with our bodies. So what's wrong with us doing this business?' I will go further as to say, we prostitutes need to be better equipped than lawyers. The lawyers need only their brains but we need both our brains and bodies."

I took his trousers and shoes from under the massage table and threw them to him. Having dressed, he took a wallet from his pocket and found a fifty-dollar note for me, "Here you are."

"Thank you," I said, "And what do you want for your drink?"
"Red wine"

"Want any chips?" "Yes."

"You can find some on the table," I said, thinking it would only make him put on more weight.

"Anything else to drink?"

"Another bottle of mineral water, please."

Oh, yes. It was well worth the fifty dollars he had just paid. Yet I went to the garage for a bottle of red wine, went to the fridge for a bottle of mineral water and put both into a plastic bag. He swayed his way out of the working room and picked up a packet of chips from the dining table. I saw him off at the door and he turned and asked me, not without spite, "Linda, shops and markets close in the evening every day. When do you close your legs every day?"

"I won't as long as customers come to see me," I smiled.

"It seems you can never close your legs as customers will not stop visiting you."

"Yes," I said proudly, "I'll never be short of customers around the clock unless I switch off my mobile phone. Next time when I go on a holiday, I'll post a notice on my front door which reads: Gentlemen, my pussy needs a holiday so I'm going to keep my legs closed for two weeks, Linda."The fat man doubled over with laughter and could hardly move a step, "If I were a woman, I would be a prostitute. You can earn money just by opening your legs. What fun it is to make money and enjoy yourself all at once!"

After he stopped laughing, he walked down the steps with great difficulty. I saw him staggering slowly toward his car in the dim street light, saying silently to him: "If you were a prostitute, I'm afraid you would have much difficulty in opening your legs."

I switched off both of my mobiles and turned off all the lights and TV sets in the house. Just then the doorbell rang insistently. I went to answer the door with my pajamas on. In front of me stood a thirty-year-old bony Australian man with blond hair, a small face, small eyes, a snub nose and buckteeth. He measured no taller than five foot six.

"Sorry for being late, Linda," he said, sweat dripping from his forehead.

I opened the door and said, "Another two minutes and I would have turned off the doorbell."

He rushed headlong into the house, wiping off the sweat from his forehead, "I have called you twice. In the first call, I asked if you could give me a golden shower."

"Hey." I said, "It was you who asked me to piss into your mouth?"

"Yes," he went on to say, "In the second call, I asked you whether I could come in. Actually at that time I was stopped by the police for an alcohol test. What I meant then was that I was late and asked whether I could still come. You said yes. I was delayed by the police for quite a long time as I did have some liquor."

GOLDEN SHOWER

It suddenly dawned on me that at that time I was reckoning with that Chinese client only to be interrupted by the fat taxi driver so I totally forgot that call. The thin man took a fifty-dollar note from his trouser pocket and handed it to me. I turned on the light in the kitchen and put away the money in the drawer. He asked me eagerly, "Have you drunk much water?"

I had attended to this little man a couple of times. He always liked me to piss on his cock. When his cock was under the hot torrential shower of urine, he alone could easily masturbate himself into coming. I said, "A moment ago I mistook another client for you. He was wondering why I told him I would piss into his mouth."

"Somehow, after emptying half a bottle of whisky, my throat feels dry and especially thirsty for urine."

"I had drunk a lot of water," I said apologetically, "I couldn't hold all of it but emptied most of it so I'm afraid there is little urine left in my bladder."

"Never mind," he comforted me, "Do your best and I'll be content with what little is left of it."

"Last minute preparations are better than no preparations at all." With that, I took the water bottle from the kitchen bench and emptied it with several gulps. After we went together to the working room, he had undressed and tossed all his clothes onto the massage table.

"Please turn on the porn video on the screen," he became impatient, "I like watching girls pissing into men's mouths."

"Wait a minute," I said, "Let me change to a new disk for you." I turned on the TV set and the DVD player and fed a new DVD into the slot. Then I pressed the "start" button on the remote control. After several ordinary fucking scenes, an Asian girl flashed across the screen lying on her back on a pale-blue settee. A Caucasian man could be seen kneeling on the ground with nothing on. He parted the girl's cunt lips with his fingers and ran his tongue tip along her clitoris. The girl cried out before a trickle of golden liquid spurted out of her pussy into the man's mouth. The girl apologized to the man,"Sorry, but I did not do it on purpose. It was because you have made me so turned on with your licking." Wiping some residual urine off his mouth corner, the man went on to lick the girl's clitoris until another trickle of yellow urine spurted out.

The blond-haired client was in high spirits, "What fun it is to watch the girl pissing into that man's mouth! Come on. Piss your urine into my mouth. Quick!" I took a white towel from the cabinet and accompanied him to the bathroom. I spread the white towel under the nozzle and had him lie on it. I parted my legs and stood astride him. He said, "Please squat over my head."

"Do you really mean me to piss into your mouth?" I double checked at the last minute, "But it's embarrassing for me."

"Of course I mean it," he said, "I'll get very excited."

I had to part my legs and stood astride his head, my thighs near his ears. He opened his mouth wide and encouraged me, "Come on. Piss now!"

I could piss on some of my clients quite naturally before, but how could I have the heart to piss into a man's mouth? I tried several times contracting my bladder but I just couldn't piss a drop out. He was waiting and yelling impatiently, "Come on, Linda!"

I closed my eyes and poured torrents of urine into his mouth. He gulped down most of it. I opened my eyes to find his face was flooded with filthy yellow urine. I distributed in a hurry the rest of the urine onto his cock. He wrapped his hand around his cock and began to move it along it. It only was a couple of minutes before he shouted,"I'm coming!" I pulled him to his feet,"Quick! Be quick to take your bath."

I turned on the shower nozzle and sluiced him with a torrent of clean water. I also washed my private part at my convenience. Then I washed his back with soap and his hairy chest. He enjoyed the shower and said, "I'm so happy showering with a woman."

"Are you married?" I asked.

"No," he answered, "but I have a girlfriend." "Isn't your girlfriend home today?"

"She has gone to Sydney to see her mother."

"So you have taken advantage of the opportunity to come here?"

"It's the same with men or women," he smiled, "illicit intercourse is perhaps the most entertaining."

I scrubbed his body thoroughly with soap and then had him stand under the nozzle and washed his cock with warm water. Finally I spent six or seven minutes helping him achieve his climax once more. Glancing at the clock, I figured that half an hour's time was up so I turned off the nozzle and helped him dry his body. After he got dressed I saw him off at the doorstep. Looking at his back, I couldn't help wondering why a young man like him should have the fantasy of drinking women's urine. I must say that nothing is too weird in the world of sexuality.

September 27, 2010

When I woke up the next morning, it was eight thirty. Older people slept less. Four or five hours were enough to make them feel refreshed. It suddenly occurred to me that when I lived with my former husband Ian Thomas Philip, I was often perplexed to find he would stay up until midnight either smoking or watching TV. I wondered why he should trifle away the precious night hours instead of having a sound sleep. Now that I have reached that age, I understand better.

I got up and went to the kitchen. I took out the stainless cooking pot and filled it with some water before putting it on the electromagnetic stove. Then I put a packet of instant noodles and two eggs into the boiling water. Several minutes later, I served the noodles and eggs on a plate with some green bean sprouts as a topping. It was just to my taste and I enjoyed it very much. With the delicious breakfast came another busy working day.

I switched on my mobile and planned to go to the bank to pay the interest on the house loan. I got dressed and took out the money from the safe. I picked up the handbag and was about to leave when the mobile rang, "Linda, I'm coming." I could make out at once without any further information that he was the Australian-born Indian, Tony. He was the owner of a business company and drove a brand new black Benz. Wealthy but very grudging, he insisted on paying sixty dollars for an hour's service for which he was supposed to pay ninety. I could do nothing about it as we had been friends for years. He was probably only one or two years my senior. When asked my age, I told him I was forty and he was in half doubt. I didn't mind whether he believed it or not, but I just wouldn't tell him my real age. The fact that I was of similar age to him would spoil his interest in me. I remembered the first time I met him, I told him I was twenty- eight. At that time, not only Tony but almost all my clients believed it as I indeed looked younger than my age. Many years passed and all my frequenters, old patrons, old friends became many years older. I was of course no exception and I didn't mind telling them my real age as they wouldn't leave me just because of my age. Sometimes I said I was forty-five and sometimes forty- eight. In fact, I didn't even know my own age exactly.

I had to put down the phone and cancelled my initial plan to go to the bank. I changed into a long dress, with my back fully exposed and my breasts half exposed. A string loop of the sexy gown hung around my slender neck. I had not seen him for quite a long time and decided to give him a surprise. The doorbell rang and this time it was the back doorbell. He invariably came to me by the back door. Every time he came, he parked his car on my lawn with the car hood close to my wall and found something to cover the plate. It was a standard practice for some of my clients to conceal their number plates. Once, a client happened to park his car in my parking space. Later, when asked, "What were you doing at 331?" by a friend of his, he explained to him, "I was helping Linda repair her gate." On hearing that, I doubled over with laughter as I asked him, "Why didn't you say I was repairing your cock?" As a matter of fact, everybody sometimes needed an excuse or two, especially for their wives or girlfriends.

Apart for some deviation; generally speaking, ninety-five percent of my clients were civilized gentlemen. If they wanted to park their cars in front of my house, they would park them on the concrete parking space. However, some uncouth guys must park their cars on the lawn behind the spacious parking lot, leaving two ugly ruts on my manicured lawn. I felt particularly unhappy when I found few clients that had parked their heavy pickups on my lawn. My heart ached for my lawn but I wouldn't offend them by scolding them too severely. I remember once I told a pickup driver not to park on my lawn in future, but next time he came, he again parked his pickup on my green lawn. He had forgotten my advice. He was simply selfish.

Some people never formed good habits during their childhood and always behaved rudely wherever they went. Suppose he had a beautiful lawn that was precious to him, I think he would never park his car on it. I think wherever and whenever we go, we should always think of others…

I hurried to the back door and opened it. Tony measured a little taller than five foot six. His curly hair used to be black but had since turned grizzled. He preferred not to dye it, saying it was his natural beauty. He had full confidence he was a handsome man though his waist was apparently thicker than before. He wore a loose tracksuit today and a strong smell of cologne permeated my nostrils as he strode over the threshold.

"Wow," I cried, "Wonderful scent! Didn't go to office today?"

"No," he answered proudly, "I am my own boss and I can set my own flexible working hours."

"I'm also my own boss but I have to work seventeen to eighteen hours a day."

"You're a demon for work and making money."

"Who hates money? The more money the better. No one complains about having too much money."

When he came in, he patted his belly, "I've lost eleven pounds." How come he began to resemble James, who preached the benefits of getting slim every day but his belly remained the same. But I echoed, "Yes, it's hard to get slim. My doctor asked me to lose another twenty-two pounds but I only lost seven pounds by going on a strict diet for three months. When I eat a little more food, I've already put on eight pounds."

"But you don't have a potbelly."

"But I'm much fatter than before. I can't fit into most of my old clothes."

With that we arrived at the working room. He stood in front of the cabinet mirror and twisted his body this way and then that way, "Hey. Do you think my belly has become a bit smaller than the last time?"

"No. On the contrary, it looks a bit larger than the last time." He took off his clothes and threw them onto the massage table.

He looked into the mirror and murmured to himself he had lost eleven pounds…eleven pounds…

I nudged his belly and said, "Step on the scale and simple arithmetic will tell you whether you have lost any weight or not."

Having tossed away his trousers and underwear, he went bare-hipped to the bathroom scale and stepped on it, "No, your scale is not accurate. I weighed one hundred and eighty pounds at home but one hundred and eighty-seven pounds on your scale here."

"If my scale is not accurate," I smiled, "Just go back home to weigh yourself there."

I thought he was not the least bit different from my "boss" James who also had the nerve to say my scale was not accurate. I took a towel from the cabinet and handed it to him, "Now give your big cock a good wash and your asshole, too."

"Wait a moment," he said, "I've held back some water in my bladder. I'd better weigh myself again after I have pissed." With that, he lifted the lid of the toilet seat and began to pass his urine noisily. After peeing, he muttered to himself as he shuddered to shake the residual urine off his cock, "Now let's see what my weight is. Look, it's one hundred and eighty-two pounds, isn't it?" "You've passed five pounds of urine in one stroke," I laughed.

While he was showering in the bathroom, I went to the kitchen to fetch a bottle of mineral water for him. He soon came out with his big cock dangling between his thighs. I found few cocks of this size among the Indians. He took the mineral water I handed him, had a small sip and put it down on the bedside table. He then lay on his back on the bed, "Come on. Come suck my cock. It erected hard and stiff this morning."

"Hard and stiff this morning," I teased him, "but soft and listless now."

"Take it easy," he said, "Hold it in your mouth and it will get as hard as anything."

I slid off my dress and tossed it onto the carpet. I slumped at his left side, took up his cock and pushed the skin down his shaft, "Oh my. What a smell! You should have given the inside of your cock a good wash. I am almost overcome by the stink of your cock."

He ignored my protest and seemed to mutter to himself, "I may have had too much fish."

"Nonsense," I retorted, "If you have had too much fish, it may smell fishy. But it smells of urine. Get up and wash it again!"

"I won't," he just took it lying down; "You help me wash it." I had to do it by applying a lot of lubricating oil on his cock and scrubbing it with tissues. Strangely enough, some clients' cocks still smelled after being washed with soap but the smell disappeared thoroughly when washed with lubricating oil. Even baby oil or pure water didn't have the same effect as lubricating oil. After I washed and dried his cock, I held it again in my mouth, "Why your cock tastes salty. Is it that you've had too much salt?"

"I don't know. Actually I haven't."

"Some clients' sperm tastes salty, some sweet and others' bitter, like medicine."

"So does my sperm taste salty or sweet?"

"Why," I said, "You haven't ejaculated your sperm yet today. I suppose it may be related to what food you've had today."

I sucked his cock for some time before he raised his legs and said, "Suck my asshole."

"Have you washed your asshole clean?" "Yes, I have."

"You always say you have washed everything clean. But look at your cock. You claimed you had washed it clean, but how it smelt!" I poured some lubricating oil on the tissues, used them to wipe his asshole and asked him to look at the stains on the tissues, "If you say you have washed it clean, then what's this?" Glancing at it briefly, he kept silent and spread his buttocks for me to wipe his asshole as if he were a baby being taken care of by his mother.

Truthfully, he was more at home having sex with me than with his wife. He told me many times he loved his wife very much and he did everything to take good care of his sick wife. I believed he was a responsible man who loved his family.

After I had wiped his asshole clean, I sat down and reclined by his left side, with my left hand supporting my head and my face right up against his asshole, balls and cock. As I ran my tongue across his asshole, its muscles instantly contracted inward and then jerked several times before he groaned, "Oh!" and then let out a loud fart.

The fart, smelling strongly of onion, assaulted my nostrils instantly and sent me fleeing at once, "Look at what you're doing! You're polluting the air with your stinky wind."

"I'm sorry," he said embarrassedly, "I did have some onion this morning."

I hurried to the bathroom to wash my face and rinse my mouth and went back to resume my oral work, "Mind you. You mustn't fart again! If you do, I'll leave you alone. You don't mean to suffocate me with your stinky farts, do you?"

He spread his buttocks apart and exposed the pink tender flesh inside his asshole for me to lick with my tongue tip. Soon he could not help moaning loudly as if in great agony until finally he yelled out, "Oh, my god!" Applying baby oil to his big cock, I used my right hand to masturbate his cock and at the same time smacked his asshole with my lips. All this sent him to the bliss of carnal pleasure and he was beyond himself uttering any possible moans and groans.

I felt his cock swelling steadily in my hand and he accelerated the frequency of his moans and groans until at last he yelled out, "I'm coming!" I didn't pause and went on licking his asshole relentlessly. He couldn't help but jerk and quiver like a fig leaf in the wind. I suddenly felt a strange sensation on my right palm. When I took to my feet to inspect what had happened, I found not only my right hand but also his cock, belly and hairy chest, all covered with a warm, thick slippery layer of liquid. Wow, what a scene of sperm!

"You really have a huge stock."

"In fact, I haven't ejaculated for more than a week."

Before I came to Australia, I experienced sex with a dozen or more Chinese men but I hadn't witnessed such a scene of overflowing sperm. I reckon the amount of sperm a man ejaculates isn't directly related to the size of his cock. Some men have little cocks but ejaculate a lot. Neither is it related to the size of men's balls; some men with balls as big as baseballs ejaculate less. And neither is it to do with the age of men. Some people assume that young men ejaculate more than old men. But more often than not, some younger lads ejaculate much less than older men do in their sixties or even seventies. However, as to each individual man, his amount of ejaculate is of course related to his age. When he is young, he ejaculates relatively more but as his age increases, the amount he ejaculates decreases.

I helped Tony wipe the sea of sperm off his body and massaged him. Then I turned him over as I would a turtle. Now he lay face down on the bed ready for me to massage his back. I sat astride his bottom and applied baby oil onto my hands before I massaged him slowly from his shoulders downward. As my fingers ran along his shoulders and waist, skin furfures kept peeling off his back. I couldn't help complaining, "You look very decent but you've never once washed your cock or asshole clean. You haven't even deigned to scrub and wash your own back clean when you take a bath!"

"But I can't reach my own back," he argued, "and you didn't help me with that."

"You can do it easily," I said as I showed him how to do it, "just by taking the ends of a towel and sliding it across your back. You're being lazy."

"Where else other than here can I enjoy being lazy?" he replied frankly.

I said nothing and got down to massaging his back, thighs, chest and arms. It was not long before I finished my work. Seeing no clients' calls had come in, I asked a favor of Tony, "Hey, would you please take me to Woden Shopping Mall? I have to go to the bank. Let me fetch you two bottles of red wine as a token of my gratitude."

"No problem. With pleasure."

We both got dressed. I grabbed my handbag and locked the door before we left. When I got into his car, I sat in the passenger seat on the left-hand side (as all vehicles in Australia keep to the left side of the road) and fastened the seatbelt, "Your car always looks brand new and immaculate."

"Sure it is," he said, "I often wash my car."

"You wash your car well," I said teasingly, "but you don't wash your asshole well. It often remains stinky until I wash it well."

"That's because you are not my wife," he said just as teasingly, "Otherwise there would be no problem with my cock hygiene."

Joking and teasing, we drove along the road toward Woden Mall. "Hey," I asked, "Can you explain why I am so dull as to be computer illiterate nowadays? I invariably lose track when I'm writing on the screen. As soon as I sit in front of the computer, I lose any inspiration. When I was in China, I had an e-mail address and knew a little bit about computers. However, when I came to Australia, I became so busy tackling various cocks, big or small, that I refused to learn the computer. I even get a headache at the mere sight of it."

"The fact that you're computer illiterate doesn't mean you're dull," he smiled, "The English writer J. K Rowling handwrote her Harry Potter novels. There's a black writer from South Africa who can't use a computer, either. Even in China, I suppose there are a lot of writers who can't write on computers."

I heaved a sigh of relief as if a stone were lifted from my mind. Being computer illiterate didn't mean you were foolish or dull or left abandoned by the modern age.

"You know I am writing my autobiography," I said, "I was a policewoman in China for ten years and have been a prostitute in

Australia for as many years. If I am to write my life up to now into a book, it's sure to be a wonderful story; an instant success. The queue of people wishing to buy this bestseller is sure to be very long."

"Ha, ha," he laughed, "A policewoman turned prostitute."

We were chatting and jesting when my mobile rang. I thought the call must have come from a new client. I had just said hello when I recognized it was a lady. I was about to say I wouldn't serve any women when she said, "Is that Linda speaking?"

"Yes," I replied, "This is Linda."

"I'm from Canberra Hospital. It's time for you to have a medical examination."

I knew the government stipulated that we should have free medical examinations regularly and I answered, "No problem. I'll try to make arrangements to go the hospital in the next few days."

"Make sure you are there in the morning," she told me. "Okay. I will," I assured her.

We arrived at Woden Mall and I asked Tony to park his car in front of Dick Smith, a well-known electronics chain in Australia. The original antenna that came with my newly-bought sixty-five inch 3D TV set was a little small and I wanted to buy a larger one. I was entering the store when the sensor beeped and a red light flashed. I instinctively hugged my handbag tightly and eyed the clerk near the checkout, indicating I had no opportunity to steal anything from the store. The clerk smiled and motioned me to move in. I knew the rape alarm in my handbag was the culprit and I should figure out how to silence it. I went to the aisle for TV antennas and picked up the largest and therefore most expensive one. Then I took it to the checkout counter and paid for it. I was about to leave when the store alarm beeped again. So I hugged my handbag again. Enough! You damned little gizmo (the rape alarm). Yet the clerk waved his permission to let me go.

You could say I was occupied every day, busying myself receiving clients' calls and serving them. Time is money and half an hour idled away meant fifty dollars less earned. So I was on the run to save time.

I hurried through the north gate of the mall, overtaking every person I caught up with, and went upstairs to the second floor and kept hurrying on. Seeing I was in such a hurry, all the other passersby tried to make way for me. I thanked them and excused my way onto the escalator on the second floor. St George Bank happened to be near the escalator and I trotted to the glass door of the bank. I was about to push open the glass door when I saw a gorgeous couple come out; a tall handsome, blond young man in his late twenties and an equally beautiful Australian girl. Wow, was that, my young "old" client of seven years or more? Though I could not recall his name, I knew so well every hair on his body. When his eyes met mine, he bit his lower lip while I pretended not to know him. I had an unspoken agreement with my clients. No matter how intimate we were in my house, we wouldn't greet each other if we met in public places. Otherwise it would cause my clients a lot of trouble. Luckily the girl didn't seem to sense anything at all. I gazed at the girl with admiration. What a beautiful girl she was, young and fashionable. When she stood beside her lover, everybody couldn't help but acclaim them as the perfect match.

I went up to the machine to pick a queuing ticket and sat down to wait in a chair. I was lucky there were only a few people waiting in the line so my number, thirteen, was soon called to counter seven. Wow, thirteen was my lucky number. Though a lot of other people didn't like the number thirteen, it was the number I have loved since my childhood and the odd numbers five and seven were also among my most favorite numbers. The clerk behind the counter greeted me smilingly, "Good morning, Linda."

"Good morning," I responded.

"Depositing or transmitting money?" she asked.

They all knew my bank balance and most probably knew my profession. But I wouldn't tell them voluntarily unless asked. Anyway, I didn't care. But years ago when I first took on this profession, I used to stay under the radar lest I should meet with some of my acquaintances. Now that I had been in this business for ten years, I really didn't care about any comments or gossip.

Mine is a legal business and I never violate any law or cause any social disturbance. I have earned my money penny by penny through honest labor. I'm proud that every penny of my wealth is gained by the sweat of my brow and not by theft or robbery.

"Oh," I was back in reality, "I'd like to pay this sum into my account. This is the money I owe the bank."

"Why do you owe money to the bank?" the clerk raised her brows.

"The damned loan is an interest trap for me." I said with resentment, "I've been toiling all day for the bank."

The clerk didn't quite understand what I said but counted away the money I handed to her. "Three thousand two hundred dollars in all," she said.

"Yes, that's it," I confirmed the sum and handed her my card. The clerk swiped the card on her computer and the computer fed out a receipt.

"Linda, this is your receipt. Have a nice day." "Thank you. You have a nice day too."

I put away the receipt in my purse and tucked it into my handbag. Well, the handbag became lighter with no banknotes in it. I carried the TV antenna and scurried out of the bank. I was lucky I was not in a shopping mall in China; otherwise I would have to push my way through a throng of people. I was walking briskly and overtaking any passersby in my direction. Suddenly I caught sight of an old couple who snuggled up to each other, talking and laughing. The old man raised his head and nodded at me. I was startled, thinking: "Pray don't nod at me sir, lest your wife should discover something from the exchange of our eyes." I didn't dare look him in the eye. What I feared was not myself but that I should ruin a happy family. Luckily the old lady didn't seem to notice anything unusual, thinking the old gentleman was always so kind to everybody else. I remembered the old gentleman had a little cock and didn't last long. And he had a cardiac pacemaker implanted in his chest. Well, forget it. I had so many clients in the small city of Canberra that I simply couldn't avoid bumping into them.

Brushing the thought aside, I made my way headlong to the south gate of the mall. I was walking hurriedly when I met a black man and his wife, who were both a bit plump and in their fifties. The black man turned out to be my old client for over nine years. He had said he came from Fiji and had been in Australia for more than thirty years. He had a big black cock about the diameter of a mug. He winked at me and I leered back as they walked toward me. When we approached close, I pretended to have lost my balance and threw myself at him. He held me in his arms and said, "Be careful, madam." I struggled out of his arms and said apologetically, "Sorry, but I almost slipped on the ground." His wife gazed at her husband suspiciously, "What's up? Who is this?"

"The floor is too slippery in the mall," her husband attempted to conceal the truth from his wife, "That lady almost fell and I was helping her get to her feet." His wife shot daggers at me with her eyes as she slipped her arm into her husband's and they continued on their way.

To the left of the gate was the renowned supermarket chain, Coles and to the right; the equally prominent Woolworths. Where to do my shopping today? Well, first to Coles for beers. I went up to the rows of trolleys, complaining about the capacity of the trolleys: "Why don't they design a double-decker trolley for bigger loads?" I tried to pull a trolley out from one of the rows but it wouldn't budge; as if the trolleys had been welded together. I was about to try another row when a gentleman came to my aid and pulled one out for me.

"Thank you," I said smilingly

"With pleasure," he smiled back.

It seemed I was clumsy in my attempts. Maybe I was pulling the trolley in the wrong direction or not pulling it hard enough. I pushed the trolley into the supermarket and fortunately my handbag didn't trigger the security sensor this time. I hung the TV antenna on a small hook in the front of the trolley and walked to the drink aisle.

Wow, a special price for beers today! Seventy dollars for two boxes and ninety-nine for three. You didn't need to be a mathematician to know you could save two dollars a box if you bought three boxes. Moving my handbag to my front, I bent down to lift a box of beers and dumped it into the trolley. I pushed the box to the edge to make room for another eight boxes. I should stack them in an orderly fashion otherwise I won't be able to fit nine boxes into the trolley. I loaded the trolley with the second box, the third box…

"Linda, Let me give you a hand." I looked up to see a mustached little man; tall and thin. He wore a blue uniform with a name tag on his chest. He was the manager of the supermarket. He bent down to lift a box and put it into my trolley.

"Thank you," I said, "But I can manage. I'm younger than you so leave it to me." (Actually I just looked younger since he was a little older than me.) Despite my protest, he continued loading my trolley ardently and it wasn't long before the nine boxes of beer were stacked into a neat pile. I wiped off the perspiration from my brow and said, "Thank you. Mr. Manager."

"You're welcome," the little old man responded. He was really a kind gentleman, who had helped me carry things or load trolleys many times. I was wondering how to express my gratitude when he asked me, "Shall I have someone help you push the trolley?" I declined his offer instantly, "No, no. I can manage it myself."

I pushed my trolley to the grocery aisle. It was so heavy that I had to trudge my way; pushing it with great difficulty. Soon I found the trolley became uncontrollable and it deviated sometimes to the left and sometimes to the right. I tried to get it back on the right path but in vain, "Damn it. This trolley is hard to handle."

I was murmuring to myself when I found all the passersby looking at me amusedly. Maybe my trolley was overloaded. When I arrived at the fresh food aisle, I picked up whatever I could find; cucumbers, eggplants, tomatoes, cabbages, carrots, peppers and so on. The trolley was jammed with boxes of beer and there was little space left for the vegetables. I packed the plastic bags with vegetables and tucked these bags into every possible recess in the trolley. Then I added fruit to the load, apples, bananas, oranges and kiwi fruits. Well, what was the name of that fruit? I had never seen it. It was round and red and its skin was like that of a pineapple. Hey, whatever its name, as long as it was new to me, I'd buy some to have a taste. Oh, there was another fruit I had never tasted so I'll take some of that, too. Oh, yes, here was the durian. Its smell would repel anyone but no one could resist the temptation of its delicious taste. Besides, durian was said to be an aphrodisiac, that is, it could make men's cocks erect harder and last longer. Could this kind of fruit have a similar effect on women and whet their sexual appetite, too? I took a durian and felt it. Its surface bristled with many thorns. I picked up the yellow net that held the durian but found nowhere to put it in the trolley. I had to hang it on the handle bar of the trolley and leave it dangling in the air.

I took out the shopping list and read through it. I still had a lot of things to buy, such as eggs, fish, meat and washing powder but there was no space for them. Yet there was one thing that was indispensable to me – milk. In any case I had to bring home two bottles of it.

The loaded trolley seemed too heavy and I had to exert all my strength to push it forward. I staggered my way and bent down to exert my legs so hard that the tops of my shoes could hardly hold my feet. The trolley squeaked under the heavy burden. I cautioned myself not to be hasty lest some items might fall off the overloaded trolley. I had to slow it down and managed to push it to the dairy aisle. I grabbed two bottles of milk and held them, together with the trolley handlebar in my hands. Then I made my way to the checkout counter. The high pile of goods in my trolley blocked my view so I had to peer around it occasionally to make sure I wasn't knocking into other customers.

All the other customers around were looking at me curiously: the lady piled so many items in a trolley as if she knew for sure she was the one millionth lucky customer who could take home a full trolley of goods free of charge. But despite others' speculations, I had to take so much food home, as I had many clients to feed. Fortunately, there were scarcely any customers standing in the queue today. Seeing there was only one customer before me, I stopped my trolley and put the milk bottles on the ground. I hurried to the personal care and hygiene aisle for a box of tissues but when I got back, I found, to my dismay, my trolley had been pushed aside and only my milk bottles remained in their original place. A lady was taking various items out of her trolley and putting them onto the counter. Oh, my gosh. You must be pretty impatient to jump the queue, lady. It's not the way Australians behave. Why are you so impatient? You didn't have so many men waiting for you at home. I had no choice but to pull the trolley back in line and stand behind her. I was also to blame as I shouldn't have walked away, though briefly. The lady in front of me turned and nodded at me apologetically. So I nodded back and reconciled myself to being behind her. Soon it was my turn to check out and I dumped the two bottles of milk on the conveyor belt first to make sure no one could jump the line again. I moved a box of tissues and then all the bags of vegetables and fruit onto the belt. The cashier behind the counter smiled to me, "Going to have a party, lady? So much food!"

"Yeah," I smiled back, "They're all for the party." With that, I put all the items onto the belt one by one but the cashier couldn't keep up with my speed. Seeing him measuring the items one by one, I took advantage of the time gap to run to the snacks aisle, took four packets of chips in my left hand and another four in my right and ran back to dump them onto the conveyor belt. I ran back and forth like that three times before the cashier asked me, "Shall I find you another trolley?"

"No, thanks. I can manage," I said, thinking if you found me another trolley, who would push it? And went on to say, "Mate, will you please check these beer boxes first?"

"No problem. How many boxes are there?" "Nine. All are discounted."

"Yeah," the cashier smiled, "They are discounted."

The cashier took up the electric infrared scanner and ran it through the barcode on the beer box with a beep. I guessed the following process must be the computer instantaneously calculating the total price of all the beers by multiplying the price by nine. I pushed the trolley through the checkout passage only to find all the checked items strewn on the table and piled up into a huge heap with tissue boxes stacked on top of the beer boxes. How could I carry that mountain of goods home? I was unable to see the people in front of my trolley and vice versa. I tried my best to load my trolley with what I could and hung what I couldn't on the handlebar. I piled the rest of the bags full of fruit and vegetables on top of the heap precariously, leaving the last three on the ground. I didn't care too much. I'll pay the money first. Glancing at the screen in front of me, I found the total sum was 670 dollars. Okay. No problem. I took out a credit card from my wallet for the cashier to swipe (I had five gold credit cards. The banks vied with one another in lending me money just because I paid back on time and enjoyed a good reputation among them).

After checking out, the cashier handed me a receipt the length of a foot and a plastic bag with two bottles of milk in it. Shifting my handbag to my back, I took the milk in my left hand and the three bags from the ground in my right. I exerted all my strength to push the trolley, clenching my teeth and straining my feet. The heavy trolley began to move slowly but there was worse to come. Things kept falling from the overloaded trolley. First, it was the bag of apples. It fell on the ground and a passing gentleman picked it up for me. I thanked him and relocated it on the tissue box and patted it down to secure it. And I had to toil on with the trolley, chanting work songs to cheer myself up. I had much difficulty in getting the trolley started and I hadn't moved a few steps before a heavy bag fell over onto the ground. A gentleman came over to help and I had to put the bags I was carrying in my hand onto the ground to take my lost property from him. I thanked him and went to put it back into the trolley on top of the tissue boxes. I tucked it to make it more secure in its position, praying it wouldn't fall again. Then I picked up the bags from the ground and began to push the trolley. I didn't even notice another bag fall overboard as I approached the south gate. A lady happened to find it and picked it up for me. This time I took it, together with the other three bags in my right hand. I trudged my way toward the south gate.

Out of the south gate, I arrived at a slope. As I made a further effort, the trolley skidded to the left and a packet of chips fell over the rail of the trolley onto the ground. A girl picked it up and handed it to me, "Your packet." I said, "Thank you. You can keep it." The girl's mum was standing beside her and told her daughter, "Give it back to that lady, honey." "Just a packet of chips," I said, "please let her have it"

The lady helped push my trolley up to the taxi rank. The first taxi sped up to leave at the sight of my overloaded trolley for fear that I had too much luggage for his car. Stupid driver! He didn't know I always gave the driver a generous tip. The drivers in the know vied with each other for the chance to drive me home. I was walking to the second taxi when the driver in the third waved to me, beckoning me into his car. I pointed at the taxi before him, meaning if this car refused to take me, then it would be your chance. I pulled open the door of the second car, "Ready to go now?"

The driver was a fat old man. He sat on the driver's seat without moving and looked up at the trolley behind me. I said instantly, "I will give you an extra fee. It usually takes only eleven or twelve dollars to get to my home but I'll give you thirty instead." The old driver cracked a broad smile at once, "Okay, Okay, Okay." He hurriedly got out of his car and opened the trunk for me. I rejoiced to find it was a station wagon with more storage space than an ordinary taxi. I quickly picked up some plastic bags from the ground, opened the door and threw them onto the back seats, "I'm putting them on the seats to save space." The old fat man smiled, "Seems a pickup will be more fitting for you."

"Every time I do a lot of shopping, many taxi drivers scramble to take me for more tips," I said in case he refused me. But he came to help me with the trolley, "You've bought a lot of things indeed. How many kids do you have?"

"About one hundred." The old fat man's smile froze. He was greatly perplexed.

"It's true," I said in all earnest, "One hundred old and young kids."

He knew I was kidding and at that time we had moved the trolley to the boot of the taxi. The driver of the third taxi stuck out his head and asked, "Hey, John. You've got a good job today. What's the offer?"

I put up three fingers, meaning thirty dollars. The old driver helped me move the things from my trolley into his trunk. Bags and bags were piled so high in the boot of his car that I was afraid the driver could hardly see anything from his rear-view mirror. The old man burdened himself with a beer box and I went over to help him. One by one we had stacked all nine boxes into a pile in the car. The old man gasped for breath and I felt sorry for him. After all, he was rather old (maybe not as old as me but he looked older than his age due to his corpulence). The loading work was done and we got into the car. When I fastened my seat belt, I took out my purse and handed him thirty dollars. He took the money and said, "Thank you very much."

With that, he started the car and it jolted to the road. I felt the car was weighed down by the load. Turning on his indicator, the old man turned the steering wheel slowly and pulled out of the taxi rank. The car took to the road, drove 500 yards, turned left and right and finally ran along the main road to the traffic lights. Seeing the light was yellow, the old man was about to run through the intersection but then the light suddenly turned red. He jammed hard on the brakes and the car came to a grinding halt. A great noise of crashing glass was heard from the trunk and I regretted buying so many beers today. The old driver was startled at the loud crash and looked at me. I said, "Never mind. It's all on me if any bottle has broken. You needn't worry."

Actually he could see nothing as the tissue boxes blocked his view, "You've bought so many tissues. Have you got a bad cold?"

"Yes," I answered, "A bad cold. Tears and snot all day. There's no end to it."

When the light turned green, he went on driving. Another set of traffic lights and a left-hand turn and we were on Creseter Street. The Canberra Hospital was on the left and my house on the right. He was now driving as I directed. Seeing no traffic, he made a right-hand turn and drove up to my driveway. "Drive slowly otherwise your chassis will scrape the humped surface of my driveway." He pulled up his car slowly into my parking space right in front of my garage. He asked, "Why did you attach an additional reinforced gate to your garage?"

"Years ago several drunkards recklessly headed their car into my garage. I was afraid they would damage my newly fitted roller door so I attached a gate reinforced with thick steel bars to the garage. Even that was not strong enough. A year ago in the early hours of morning, they played the old trick again. Look at the big dents in the two steel bars."

I got out of the taxi and showed him the dents in the gate.

He asked, "Won't you open your garage door?"

I pointed to the right and told him, "Let's unload the things from the car and pile them here before I open the French door and move them into the garage from there." The old driver opened his trunk and I shouldered two beer boxes and carried them to the French door. He followed me with one beer box, "You're strong, young lady. You're stronger than me."

I laughed up my sleeve at being called "young lady." I thought strong as I was; he was most probably younger than me by at least a couple of years. I said, "I always carry two beer boxes at a time." We worked this way and in the end he had carried three boxes and I six. Finally we carried all the items from the back seats to the French door. I took a five-dollar note from my purse and handed it to him, "This is the tip. Thank you for helping me carry so many things. And by the way, do you like chips?"

He took the money and answered, "Yes." I gave him a packet of chips, thinking if you went on eating such junk food as chips, you would soon become as fat as the other driver who could only become aroused by the sight of a doctor; then you would have to come visit me – Dr. Cock.

"Thank you. Have a nice day," I said.

The old fat man drove his taxi away. I shifted the handbag to my chest and fumbled for the key to the front door. I was about to open the door when the mobile buzzed, "I want to fuck you!"

I had long been used to this kind of remark since I took up the profession, so I said, "Just come along."

"I'll come in ten minutes," the voice on the other end informed me. I had better move all these items into the house as soon as possible. I opened the front door, went to the French door, rolled up the blinds, opened it from inside, and then opened the black security door. I picked up the bags piled on the ground and threw them in. Soon all the plastic bags were heaped beside the dining table. I carried in the tissue boxes and then beer boxes one by one and stacked all the boxes into a neat pile on the other side of the dining table. Finally I brought in the TV antenna and placed it in front of the 3D TV set in the west living room. The floor was scattered with a mass of plastic bags, leaving no more space for me to get a foot in. I was busy stuffing the fridge with fruits, vegetables and milk when the doorbell rang. I flattened the crumpled plastic bags littered on the floor in haste and put them away in the second drawer of the cabinet for future use.

I went to open the door, "Good morning!" I looked up. Who was this? An elderly man of eighty-seven who wanted to fuck me! Shit. Even if you were offered a ready pussy, what could you do with it with your limp cock?

"Good morning, Angeles" I greeted him.

The old guy was tall and stout, neither too fat nor too bony. Most people who saw him might think he was only sixty-eight, but in fact he was eighty-seven. He was quite healthy but had some erectile trouble – some difficulty in making his cock hard enough for fucking. I ushered him in.

"Have you had your breakfast?" he asked.

"Yes. I have," I answered loud enough so that an elderly man with his hearing aid could hear clearly.

"What did you have for your breakfast?" "Cocks."

"You cannot do without them even for a minute," he burst into loud laugher.

"Don't you have pussies on your mind all day long?"

"I'm getting old," he sighed, "I'm now just covetous of pussies.

I'm yearning for lust yet unable to succumb to it."

"But just yearning itself is worth yearning for," I comforted the old man.

He smiled and bent down to kiss me on the cheek, "But yearning is not enough anyway. We should have some real fun."

"Real fun?" I raised my brow, "Can you fuck me?"

"You remember I managed to fuck you last year?" he argued, "I could until I had the prostate operation."

"It should be classed a faulty surgical treatment," I advised like a lawyer, "You're entitled to lodge a complaint…"

"Well," he touched his private part and changed the subject, "My doctor says making love frequently makes you live longer."

"Then," I retorted, "I can live five hundred years because I make love every day."

"You can surely live a thousand years and never die," Angeles said.

"It's tiring to live five hundred years, after all," I said, "I'll be content with two hundred and fifty years."

"Quick," he cried eagerly, "I can't wait to fuck you!"

He wrapped his arm around my waist and I gripped his shoulder. When we got to the working room, he took out a rectangular black wallet from his pocket and searched it for a fifty note folded many times. He unfolded the note with trembling hands and tucked it into my shorts. (I wore a pair of black shorts with an elastic waist at the time).

"Here's your money," he said, "I kept it for a long time. My wife never allows me to have a secret purse."

I smiled and took the money from my shorts, "Even if you tuck the money into my cunt, it can't help make your cock hard."

"My age is showing," he chuckled, "It's in need of replacement."

"So it is," I said, "by the way do you need a shower now?"

I took a clean towel and hung it on the hanger in the bathroom. With the money in my hand, I went over to unbutton his coat and then his trousers. I helped him take off his thin sweater and the rest of his clothes sleeve by sleeve and tossed them onto the massage table, "It's getting warmer. Why are you dressing so warm?"

"Old people are afraid of cold," he explained.

He took off his coat and unzipped his trousers. The trousers instantly fell to his ankles and I knelt to unlace his shoes one by one and put them away under the massage table. I then pulled off the legs of his trousers one by one and folded them on the massage table. His last piece of clothing was a pair of grey briefs. I pulled them off to find they were smeared with yellow shit. I was annoyed, "Look at your dirty asshole. Go and give it a good wash!"

I patted him softly on the hip and stripped the briefs off his legs. He was trying to tear my shirt open and stretch out his hand to fumble my breasts, "You have a bra on today?"

"Yes," I answered, "It's not strange because I went out shopping this morning. Well, go shower before you touch me."

I pulled his hand off me and patted his hips. He had no choice but to stagger slowly toward the bathroom. I went to put away my purse and money in the kitchen drawer. I suddenly caught sight of the wallet left by the Sydney drunkard, wondering why he hadn't come back for it. I might as well have someone contact the RTA – the Road Traffic Authority for his personal information. I hurried back to my bedroom and stripped. Then I went to the bathroom to wash myself clean and wiped myself dry with a clean towel. When I was back at the working room, I found Angeles with one of his legs on the toilet seat, rubbing between his toes with a dry towel. I went over to help and wiped the drops off his back, "Well, we are ready to go to bed."

OPEN LEGS

He reached out his large dry hand to touch my right breast, "Let me suck it first." With that he held my nipple in his mouth and suddenly bit it. I cried out, "Ouch. Stop biting it!" He raised his head, "Maybe I'm sucking it too hard."

"You didn't even realize you were biting my nipple," I said, and later realized it was because his false teeth had no sensitivity at all, to say nothing of a sense of propriety. So I urged him to get onto the bed.

He took me by the hand, "Let me feel your nice cunt first." With that he poked a trembling finger and dug it into my cunt, "How nice. It's wet. You're aroused."

"It's wet because I have just had a bath." "Can I lick it?"

"No, I don't want you to do that."

"Just once," he was pestering and pressed me against the bed. I had to lie on my back and stretched my legs apart. He knelt down and spread my cunt lips open, "Very nice." He then ran his tongue along my clitoris and then my orifice. He smacked my clitoris and orifice alternatively and greatly aroused my desire especially since I was close to my menstruation and more sensitive around that time. His skillful licking almost melted me and he said, "I am so eager to fuck you."

"If you had met me ten years earlier, you would have been capable of fucking me." I said, "Now you have to be content with being a spectator."

Looking at the wall clock, I found half of the time had passed so I said. "You may as well lie down and let me suck your poor thing."

"I'd rather you licked my cock while I stand rather than lie down."

I knelt on the carpet and held his limp cock in my mouth. I sucked it hard. He groaned continually and begged me, "Please feel my balls." I sucked his cock and synchronously felt his balls. He pulled my head toward him and his buttocks began to rock back and forth as if he were fucking my cunt instead of my mouth, "I'm fucking your mouth! I'm fucking your mouth!" He began to groan and moan with increasing frequency. I found his balls became tauter and tauter in my hand and his cock harder and harder until he let out two prolonged howls, "Ah -- -- --" followed by a loud yell, "I'm coming!" Despite his proclamation, I kept licking his balls and sucking his cock until he achieved his climax. After a moment, he realized something and said, "I haven't come at all."

"I know you haven't," I said, "You just had the feeling of coming but in fact you didn't. Many clients who have had a prostate operation have a similar experience."

I stood up and went to the bathroom to wash my mouth and hands. I washed my cunt as well and dried it. I came back to say to him, "Let me give you a massage."

"No, thanks," he declined my offer, "I must be going to fetch my wife at Woden Mall."

It occurred to me that I saw him this morning at Woden Shopping Mall. He walked past me with an old lady by his side, and winked at me. Well, it seems he took advantage of the short time his wife was shopping to visit me.

I found a clean towel and soaked it with warm water in the bathroom sink. I came back and washed his cock and balls with the warm towel, "Well, put on your clothes."

He pulled on his briefs and I helped him put his trousers on, one leg at a time. Then I pulled up his zipper and buckled his belt. When he was ready, I sent him to the front door. I took his elbow in my hand and said, "Take care."

"See you later, Linda," he said with a broad smile as he descended the doorsteps.

I couldn't help thinking what a happy life he was living. He was expecting to visit me later! Nowadays many young people seemed frustrated and listless all day. They should follow the good example of this old gentleman in their attitude toward life.

When I came back, I toiled away in moving all the beer boxes into the garage. I had just moved three boxes when the doorbell rang. I went to answer the door. The client was a corpulent Greek man with a potbelly. He had a big head with a receding hairline, a wry nose, a broad mouth and a pair of big eyes. He was in his seventies; an old patron of mine for nearly ten years. Today he came with the aid of a four-wheeled walker. I approached him and took his arm, "Long time no see."

"I was in the hospital," he explained, "I had an operation on this knee. An old man is like an old car in disrepair for years. Almost all the parts on me need either fixing or replacing." With that, he lifted his right leg over the threshold. I held him by the elbow, "Take your time. Don't be in a hurry."

"Thank you, Linda," he said.

I supported him as we entered the house. He said as we were walking, "Haven't seen you for so long a time. I really missed you. I couldn't move after the operation. It was my wife who nursed me and waited on me in the hospital for more than a month."

I accompanied him to the working room. He put a fifty- dollar note on the massage table. I asked him, "You surely can't take a bath yourself, can you?"

"My wife just washed me before I went out," he said.

After I had got all the pillows and towels ready, I began to take off his clothes and then tidied them into a neat pile on the massage table. The last thing I did was take off his large, loose white briefs. They were very clean so I believed he had had a good wash before he came here. I helped him onto the bed, moving his right leg onto the bed and then the left one. As he had a big potbelly, I prepared three pillows for him so he could recline comfortably on the bed. We had known each other for nearly ten years, I was familiar with every detail of his body. He had big balls and a short but thick cock. If he came at all, he only ejaculated one or two drops of sperm. In most cases, he needed the strongest stimulus to be able to come. Every time he came, I sat astride his waist with my face directed toward his cock and my cunt toward his face. It was the so-called 69 position. As today his head was reclining higher than usual, I had to stand with my buttocks toward his face. I bent down in a downward- facing dog position to hold his cock in my mouth while he played with my cunt from behind. I began to swallow his cock into my mouth and blow it out. It was not long before he started to breathe heavily. Soon he began to moan, "Oh – Oh-- --" just as a weeping baby until at last he exhaled a long breath through his nostrils, indicating he had come.

I withdrew his cock from my mouth. There was hardly any liquid around the opening in the cock. I attributed it to his age. I got off the bed and washed his cock, as well as his balls and the inside of his thighs with a warm towel. Then I applied some baby oil to his knees and began to massage them amidst small talk, "Life is but a short span! We are all getting old. All my patrons are getting old together with me. Boys have become men and men old men. Yesterday I saw a client of mine, the boss of a Chinese restaurant, bending like a lobster while walking."

"Exactly," he said sentimentally, "Look at my legs. They were perfect just a couple of years ago."

"I also feel there's something wrong with my legs," I echoed, "Either a pain in the soles of my feet or some discomfort in my knees when I get up every morning. It's said every adult has a noticeable change every five years and an even greater change every ten years."

We were chatting when a call came in, "Baby, When can I come?"

"In ten minutes."

I hung up and continued the small talk about the brief span of life with the Greek old man.

"Life is but a dream," I concluded, "Little wonder the Japanese like using the metaphor of sakura to represent the short life of humans. In next to no time you're approaching the end of your life." Glancing at the wall clock, I found there was little time left for the old man so I helped him get dressed. Just then the doorbell rang. I shut the door to the working room and went to open the front door.

No sooner had I opened the front door than a voice came in, "Dear, this is for you." I was happily surprised to see a bouquet of crimson roses and a big heart-shaped balloon appear before me. I accepted the bouquet, "Thank you, Mr. Smith."

He was a farm owner about sixty years of age, who owned a large plantation and a large meadow. As my old patron, he always brought me some gifts, such as fruit, vegetables or flowers, whenever he came to visit me. We walked shoulder to shoulder to the kitchen bench and I planted the roses in a vase. He asked me, "Do you like them?"

"Roses are my favorite; gorgeous, fragrant and elegant," I answered, "Though, in an unguarded moment, you're bound to be stung by its thorns."

"You're just like a rose," he smiled, "that enjoys stinging others."

"It all depends," I smiled too, "I never sting good guys."

I led him to the waiting room. After I saw off the Greek old man, I ushered Mr. Smith to my working room. As he looked round the room, he commented, "You really have more TV sets than an appliance shop."

"The other day, a young client also made a similar comment. I like watching TV. Beautiful figures are coming and going. You can see them wherever you go. When I'm not attending to any clients, the figures on the screen keep me company and prevent me from feeling lonely."

"You always need someone to keep you company?" he laughed.

"Yes, I do until I die," I cracked a joke.

"Then I'll keep you company," he volunteered promptly.

"A good idea," I said, influenced by the jesting atmosphere, "Then we will have our own Garden of Eden, where we, old or young, can seek our individual pleasure."

"I've just come back from a graveyard not far from here," he said with great emotion, "One of my friends died of myocardial infarction at the age of fifty-eight. His wife was all tears over his death. When the priest asked her whether her own coffin was to be buried beside her husband's or stacked on top of it; she answered tearfully, 'For thirty years since we married, he lay on top of me. Now, I'd like a change.'"

"When I die," I said, "I'd like to be in between, with eight thousand on me and ten thousand under me."

"Do you fear death?" I asked.

"Everybody does," he replied, "who doesn't fear leaving this beautiful world, never to return?"

"I don't fear death," I said, "but I fear the dying pains on the death bed. Several days ago, a client told me that his friend was bedridden with cancer in Canberra Hospital. He could not eat or drink unassisted and was only lying there waiting for his last day."

"And what appalled everyone was," I added, "the night he died, some doctors hurried in to give him resuscitation and the last words he heard were, 'You're going to die tonight.' Can you imagine what the poor dying patient must have felt then?"

"Maybe the doctors did it with best intentions," Smith smiled, "They wished for the patient to be able to leave some last words to his family members."

"If I could choose my way of dying," I said, "I think the best way is to go to sleep tonight and not wake up tomorrow morning."

I suddenly asked Mr. Smith,"Do you believe in the existence of a soul after death? You know, my old landlord was Greek, a Christian. He said the soul would hover over his own body when he died. I say it's nonsense. How many millions of years have passed in history and how many people have died during this period? If everybody had a soul after death that hovered away, where do they dwell? The earth is sure to be overcrowded with these souls."

"I believe in souls in the afterlife," Smith asserted his conviction.

"By no means do I believe in them," I said as resolutely.

When I was in between Smith's legs giving him blow job, he said, "I really wish I could bring you home to teach my wife how to give such a fantastic blow job."

I replied, "I will never follow you home. What should I say if she asked how we met?"

He laughed upon hearing my reply and said, "That was just a joke! My wife would castrate me if I really brought you home." I replied, "I heard from one of my customers that ten years ago; there was a woman who had castrated her husband with a knife and had the dick thrown outside because he had extramarital affairs."

Smith laughed even harder, "There was indeed such an incident and the husband had his dick mended back and went on to film a movie about sex education."

I replied, "I've asked the doctors about that and they said that if the dick was castrated for a short period of time, there is a possibility it would remain functional if it was mended. But if the time was too long, there will be no use for the dick because it would be dead." We both laughed. Half an hour passed and I finished serving Mr. Smith and saw him off at the door.

Business was brisk in the morning but strangely enough, the clients I served were all old men without exception and what was worse, all had little cocks as if it had been prearranged in advance. In contrast to this, the clients I served last night were all big cocks. I was musing about this when the doorbell rang. I went to open the door and found a bony old man in his late seventies, wearing a bright red coat, a snow-white shirt, a white bonnet and a blue scarf dancing in the wind around his neck. With several pink roses in his hand, he gasped for air, whooping like an asthmatic patient, "Linda, this is for you."

I accepted the roses, "Thank you very much. But how come you didn't call in advance?"

"I did," he replied, "but you didn't answer. So I've come to see what's wrong with you."

I put the roses in a vase on the kitchen bench and smiled, "There's nothing wrong with me. Look at me to make sure."

"I was worrying about you."

He had been one of my clients for nearly ten years. I remembered years ago he proposed to marry me on the false assumption that I loved him as he did me. He was heartbroken and reduced to tears when I declined his proposition. I told him I loved all my clients alike and he was just one of them. He cried sadly like a child and no one could appease him. I was also heartbroken at his tearful exhibition. From then on, he visited me every two or three weeks and every time he came, he would dress himself with elaborate care and brought my favorite roses with him. So he was among my premium clients I attended to with particular care. I only charged him twenty dollars for each service and that amounted to a free service if he was to take ten dollars' worth of red wine plus beers and chips when he left.

I had been serving as a prostitute in Canberra for years and unlike those moonlighting prostitutes working among different brothels, I came to form a strong attachment to some of my clients. There was a mixed feeling of love and affection, like the plain feeling between an old couple, rather than the ardent love between young lovers. It was a love in its broader sense, a nonexclusive love or a universal love. We were concerned for and took care of each other like family members. Our friendship existed in a big family. All of us lived in concentric circles with me at the center. We didn't pry into each other's private lives. We just enjoyed all possible pleasures imaginable. We formed a big family, in which I was the patriarch, or rather matriarch, and there were grandpas, dads, uncles, sons and even grandsons. I was also like an empress with my favorite ministers visiting her majesty every day while I granted them all my special favor.

I stopped indulging in reveries and led the old man to the working room. When he stripped, his ribs were conspicuously protruding from his chest. I stood behind his skinny body and began to clean his asshole with a toilet tissue. "Oh, my old lover," I said, showing him the yellow stain on the tissue, "You haven't washed your hips, have you?"

He said breathlessly, "Maybe my car was too bumpy when I was driving."

"Bumpy as your car was," I said, "it couldn't jolt the shit out of you. As you're getting old, your asshole is naturally getting loose, though."

With that, I took more clean tissues and wiped his asshole several times until it was thoroughly clean. During the whole process, he just stood motionless, like a baby, gasping for breath. When I left to wash my hands, he said from behind me, "Suck my cock."

I knelt on the carpet and held his carrot-sized cock in my mouth. His cock was really tiny, limp and crooked as well. Soon he demanded, "Let me fuck you. Last time you gave me good sex." I obediently lied on my back and spread apart my thighs, ready for him to fuck me. These older men's cocks were like trifling toys for my cunt because their cocks, being very limp, could last only a couple of minutes and came quickly. But I was happy as long as I could please them in this way and they felt satisfied sexually. The old man, now kneeling on the bed, raised both my legs on his thin shoulders and supported himself with both of his arms. He exerted all his strength to tuck his tiny cock into my cunt but in vain. I had to help him by holding his cock and rubbing it against the outside of my cunt. I saw the old man's bony hips swaying violently and heard him huffing and puffing. Soon the frequency of his panting accelerated before he jerked suddenly and blew out several long breaths followed by a cough. I knew he had come.

I waited for a while for him to put down my legs. "Thank you, Linda," he said.

I jumped to my feet and drew some tissues for the old man. He held his cock with one brown, withered hand and cleaned it with the other. He never washed his cock after "making love". He knew I was healthy so he most probably didn't wash it at home either. Maybe when he woke up at night, he would pull at it and indulge in my residual scent. But as for me, I could never allow such an unhealthy habit. I didn't belong to him alone so I must keep my cunt clean by all means. If any unsheathed cock touched the flesh of my cunt, I would certainly go to the bathroom to clean my cunt thoroughly as it was my most valuable asset in this trade. I was about to go the bathroom when the old man bent down to kiss me on the lips, "I love you."

I patted his cheeks and said, "So do I."

I went to the bathroom, turned on the nozzle and squatted down to wash my cunt. Just then the doorbell rang. After drying my body, I snatched up a yellow silken scarf, wrapped it around my waist with two corners of it tied between my taut breasts and rushed to the front door. It was a tall thin man wearing a pair of sunglasses. I didn't recognize him straight away. He rushed in under my arm and cupped my breast in his hand at his convenience. Only when he took off his sunglasses did I recognize him. He was Chinese, about forty-five, with little eyes and a pockmarked face. He had visited me several times. I did not know who told him my address and he never called in advance to tell me when he would come. He paid no more than twenty dollars but it took only a dozen or more minutes for him to come.

If I was not occupied it would be a convenient arrangement but if I had other clients I would rather not serve him.

He knew the way well, as if he were at home and walked toward the working room. I said, "Please stay in the waiting room for a while. I'm attending to a client now and I will serve you after he leaves."

I sent him to the waiting room and returned to give my "old lover" two beers, a bottle of red wine and a bag of chips. On the doorstep he told me, "I often mention you to my mom."

"What?" I was a little surprised, "Your mom knows you're visiting a prostitute?"

"Isn't it a natural thing," he argued, "since I have neither a wife nor a girlfriend?"

"Then what did your mom say about it?" my surprise changed to curiosity.

"I told my mom you were a good woman and she said she would come visit you someday."

"Pray don't let your mom come here," I pleaded, "That will embarrass me greatly. I'm not your mom's daughter-in-law. What should I say when we meet?"

"I will tell her you're my wife," he said as we both laughed.

Seeing my "old lover" stepping down happy and satisfied with the gifts I had given him, I was slowly filled with an indescribable softness. It was my greatest pleasure to do anything I could to warm the hearts of these lonely old men.

After I saw him off, I led the Chinese guy into my working room. He tucked a twenty note into my hand and I put it away on the bedside table under the mobile phone.

"Have a shower first, "I told him. "I won't until after fucking."

He lay on his back on the bed and I applied lubricating oil to his cock (an average-sized cock among Chinese men). He spread his legs apart and I knelt between his thighs. I held his cock in my mouth and began to suck it.

He was happy and praised me, "You're the best sucker and the best sex worker in Canberra."

I thought you were polite enough not to call me a prostitute. Just then, I smelled a terrible odor. I was annoyed to find he hadn't cleaned his asshole, just as my "old lover" hadn't either.

"Oh, my gosh," I complained, "How could you leave your asshole dirty after shitting?"

"I'm sorry," he said. I gave his asshole a good wipe and scrub until I was sure there was no remaining stink. I washed my hands and came back to resume my work of sucking his cock. His cock remained limp and I guessed it was related to his age. Soon he started groaning and moaning, "Oh, yes. Oh, yes." Suddenly he shouted, "I want to fuck you!" I thought, "Where on earth can you find a place to fuck for a mere twenty dollars?" I may as well make him come as soon as possible in case a new client comes soon. So I found him a small condom and lay down on my back on the bed. He got up, raised my legs on his shoulders and thrust his cock into my cunt, "Hey, hey, hey. I'm fucking you," and he went on to ask me, "Can you feel my cock inside you?" I answered bluntly, "It's too little."

He didn't mind my sneering because he couldn't imagine what shapely and powerful cocks I had witnessed. He thought his cock was the best in the world as every man does, whatever his nationality. As a matter of fact, the world of cocks was so large that their cocks were nothing compared with the big ones.

It took only a couple of minutes for him to come. Seeing he had come, I set about getting tissues and helping him remove his condom but he just wouldn't let me remove it and insisted on going to the toilet himself.

"But you can't throw the used condom into the toilet bowl," I warned him, "It will clog the sewer pipes." He grasped his condom instead of throwing it into the dustbin. I was angered by his stupidity, "Throw it into the dustbin!"

Seeing I got angry, he reluctantly tossed it into the dustbin. I handed him a towel and had him take a shower. After I fetched the dried towels from the laundry and got ready to fold them in the working room, I heard a loud torrential sound from the bathroom. I knew he had flushed it down the toilet. I peeked into the dustbin, and there was no used condom. My guess was proven at last.

It was really disgusting that men behaved like that. It was beyond reproach, though, that some men used tissues to carry their own sperm home. I disliked such men as the Chinese who behaved so selfishly. If you didn't want to leave your sperm in the dustbin, you could do otherwise but shouldn't flush it down the toilet. You shouldn't do anything at the expense of others. It was awfully selfish of them! And I wondered on what grounds they should be doing this. What was the use of keeping the sperm at room temperature? It was medically proven that sperm, once exposed to the air, could last a very short time and besides, it was not something worth keeping.

What exasperated me more was his uncivil behavior. After he had got dressed, he went to put on his shoes. He put one of his feet on the edge of the bed just for the convenience of tying his shoelaces.

"Hey!" I shouted at him, "Why did you put your foot on the bed? You're dirtying the bedding. There's a chair over there and you can go tie your shoelaces there."

"My shoes are not dirty," he argued.

"Not dirty?" I got indignant, "Do you behave this way in your own home?" It was apparent he was a selfish man who didn't care for other people at all.

After sending away the vile Chinese man, I went to the kitchen to find something to fill my stomach. I opened the drawer and incidentally came across the wallet the drunkard had left behind. I must find a way to inform him. It seemed he had drunk a lot last night as he hadn't yet contacted me for his wallet. I was thinking about this when a call came in, "Are you free now?"

"Yes, I'm free. Are you coming right now?" "I'll be there in ten minutes."

I began to toil away with moving the remainder of beers to the garage and stuffing fruit and vegetables into the fridge. While I was doing this, I came across some unusual fruit buried in the back of the fridge; red, ripe and very inviting. I cut one in half and had a taste. It was very soft and sweet; the right thing for old ladies but not for a lady like me, who still boasted perfect teeth. I tossed it aside and picked up an apple. It was crisp to my taste. Just then the doorbell rang. I left the unfinished apple on the bench, gulped down what little was in my mouth and went to answer the door.

We exchanged greetings at the door. He was a tall and thin man of about fifty, one of my clients for the past two or three years. He had a short blond cut, a prominent nose, blue eyes and a tanned face. He had never revealed his identity but I guessed he was either a government official or a clerk in a company. We were on familiar terms with each other. The relationship between us was a business one in nature. As soon as he came in I said to him, "Would you do me a favor, sir?" I turned to take out the drunkard's wallet, "This is a wallet left here by a gentleman last night. Could you call the RTA for his contact details so that we can call him to come collect his wallet?"

"No problem," he grinned. Then we went to the desk in the west living room. He looked up his number in the directory and placed a call to the drunkard. I clutched the receiver, "You left your wallet under my bed last night. Will you come collect it?"

"I have been looking for it everywhere," he said, "but I never expected it would be at your house. Thank you very much, Linda. I will have my friend fetch it in a moment." Hanging up the phone, I went with the gentleman to the working room. He gave me a fifty-dollar note in exchange for a clean towel and went to take a shower. I took a bottle of red wine and put it on the massage table. When he was finished showering, he dried himself on the towel and came out of the bathroom. In the soft music of the porn program, I knelt between his thighs and sucked his cock. I asked him, "Would you like me to lick your asshole?"

"Yes, I'd love that."

"Then show me your buttocks."

He turned his buttocks toward me and to my dismay, I found his asshole bristled with thick hairs. I had to brush them aside before I bent down to lick his asshole. My relentless licking made him so excited that he didn't even know how to groan, "Ah, yes." "Oh, yes." "Yah…" "Wow…" After that he turned around and knelt on the middle of the bed with me. I stretched out my left leg and bent my right to suck his cock. He looked into the mirror on the left, "It's so sensual seeing my big cock sliding in and out of your mouth." I looked askance at a typical handsome blond man, with a hairy chest and strong muscles tangled with a snow-white, voluptuously curved, black-haired oriental woman. A straight, thick cock was sliding in and out of my mouth. I couldn't help wondering at the creator of man and woman. What a sensual scene of intercourse! His breath became more and more heavy, "Oh, my God! Wonderful."

He gazed at my protruding snow-white tender buttocks and said, "Wait. Wait. Keep this position. Don't move." With that, he got off the bed, aimed his cock at my cunt and got ready to thrust it in. However, I stopped him, "You must wear a condom before you can fuck me."

"Let me rub my cock against your pussy first," he said and ran his cock back and forth between my asshole and my cunt opening, making me itch all over. After a while he said he wanted to fuck me.

I sheathed his cock with a large-sized condom and knelt on the edge of the bed with my toes downward and my buttocks pointed upward. He stood behind me on the floor. He parted my pussy lips with his fingers and peeped askew into my cunt, as if looking for something. I wondered whether he was looking for the opening to thrust his thick cock into. Mind you, there were only two openings there so be sure not to confuse them. The upper hole might be a more expensive place to fuck. Take care!

"May I fuck your asshole?" he said, the upper one clearly being his intended target.

With my buttocks pointed skyward and looking askance at his cock, I replied, "Yes, you may but you have to pay thirty dollars more for the extra service."

"But I haven't brought enough money with me," he laughed.

"Then you'll have to be content with the lower opening," I laughed too, "As a matter of fact, if I have to, I can hold your cock in my asshole. But some clients' cocks are as thick as that can of air freshener," I said, pointing to the aerosol can on the bedside table, "I can't bear a thing as thick as that. I won't do the service even for three thousand dollars, let alone thirty dollars. My asshole would burst."

At that he laughed all the more heartily, "By the way, have you insured your asshole?"

"No," I answered, "Because it is used less frequently."

All of a sudden, he thrust his cock right into my cunt, making me lean forward, "Wow. That cock of yours might not be large in size but it is vigorous in strength," I said.

He looked sideways into the mirror on the right wall and I looked in the same direction. What a perfect pornographic painting! I arched my round, sensual, creamy buttocks upward while my buxom breasts dangled seductively; a masculine, virile Western man stood behind me and pulled his cock in and out of my cunt. His cock was seen becoming longer and longer until it was the size of a huge carrot. The vivid portrait of fucking made my cunt itch and water and I suddenly felt a burning hot, strong urge for him to fuck me deeper still. He seemed to be able to read my mind and did it as he yelled madly, "I'm fucking that young pussy of yours!"

I was enjoying his barbaric assault, and didn't mind being called a "young pussy" as opposed to an "old cunt." I cried out demandingly, "Fuck me harder!" He seemed to enjoy pulling out his cock deliberately slowly and then thrusting it suddenly back into my cunt. We looked in the same direction, like two viewers enjoying a porn film, and watched attentively as the two figures made love in the mirror. I was indulging in the carnal pleasure when I felt his last pounding reach the opening of my womb. I suddenly felt an acute pain mixed with an unbearable itch inside me, "Ah, you're fucking me to death!"

He kept pistoning his cock in my cunt as he chanted his work song, "I'm fucking you. I'm fucking you. I'm fucking you." I shouted unscrupulously, "Fuck me to death. Fuck me to death!" I felt my "young pussy" swollen with lust and bursting from his huge cock. A thrill of ecstasy ran through my body from my head, shoulders, knees and toes. My cunt watered with lust and flooded as he kept toiling in me with the squelching sound of lust water as background music.

The wonderfully wet sound caused by lovemaking coupled with the sensual cries of the couple fucking in the porn video excited us even more. Sex might be the most enjoyable and pleasant entertainment in the world. Yet some people never appreciate or enjoy it all their lives. They have sex furtively and with a guilty conscience. How people differ in their attitudes toward sex!

Of course no two people in the world are the same. Otherwise the world would be intolerably monotonous. Well, let me enjoy myself, think what one may. I used my left hand to support my weight and my right to tantalize my clitoris. It was not long before an acute, relentless itch radiated from my tender bud to every part of my body, overwhelming me with indescribable sexual bliss. I imagined an eighteen-year-old lad exerting all his robust strength to fuck me and yelling, "I'm fucking you! I'm fucking you!" And I yelled in my mind, "You're fucking me to death! You're fucking me to death!" In my sexual fantasy high, I couldn't help but cry out, "I'm coming!" I remained on my high for a while, "Darling, fuck me hard. Fuck me hard. I love you." Then with a shudder, I trembled and quivered violently, while he pounded his belly against mine, "Fuck you. Fuck you. Fuck you!"

Suddenly I cried out,"Ouch! How dare you fuck my asshole? You'll be charged an extra fee for it."

"Sorry," he said, "Wrong place." He withdrew his cock from my asshole and tucked it into my cunt. His frenzied clamor was followed by a painful squeal. He thrust his cock straight in the depth of my cunt and I could feel it jerking palpably inside me. He gasped for air, "Well, I'm discharged and I'm now sure what I am to speak about in this afternoon's meeting. I was muddleheaded all morning."

I withdrew his cock from my cunt, "Yeah, many clients say they make it a rule to refresh their brains before attending important meetings."

"I feel my brain is refreshed at once the second I come."

"I have a similar feeling," I couldn't agree more, "as soon as I have come, my brain becomes clearer and cleverer, and is keener for diction when writing." I was about to get up when he stopped me, "Wait. Wait." With that, he slowly reeled out a white thread from my asshole.

"What is it?" he wondered.

I had a look at it and smiled, "Oh that. It's a green bean sprout I ate for breakfast. You tucked your cock into the wrong place and fucked my asshole. So you found one."

"Sorry," he said, "but look at the screen. The man is fucking the girl's asshole. I couldn't help it and accidentally slid into your asshole." At that time, the porn video was showing a Caucasian man penetrating a girl's asshole while another girl knelt beside him and licked his balls. A moment later, the man pulled out his cock from the first girl's asshole and thrust it into the second girl's mouth. The second girl sucked his cock and smacked her lips, "Very tasty!"

"Of course it's tasty," I couldn't help laughing out loud, "As it's just been pulled out from an asshole."

The girl sucked the western man's cock for a while before he let out a chain of frantic yells, "Ah, Ah, Ah… Yes, Yes, Yes…" With the yells, a profusion of white sperm was squirted right into the girl's mouth. The other girl, who he had fucked before, now opened her mouth to receive the sperm that the first girl spat from her own mouth.

"Two dirty girls," he giggled.

"They might think it exciting and sexy to do so," I said.

We both laughed. Then he got up and went to take a shower while I was doing my tidying up. He got dressed and wrapped the bottle of red wine with a plastic bag. I sent him to the door and he kissed me on the cheek, "Thank you very much."

It was certainly a good bargain that he had paid me to satisfy me sexually. So I said, "You're welcome."

No sooner had I pulled open the front door than I slammed it shut behind me, "You'll have to go out via the back door. A client is coming toward the front door."

With that, I led him to the laundry and showed him out the back door. I hurried back to open the front door and said, "Oh my sugar daddy, why didn't you call in advance before you came?" An old gentleman with a white helmet on and his clothes soaked in sweat stood on the doorstep, wiping beads of sweat off his forehead and gasping for breath. Apparently, he was tired out, "I've been jogging for the sake of my health and I was passing by so I dropped in to visit you."

I stretched out to hold him by the elbow, "Is that cock of yours beginning to itch?" I couldn't believe he was strong enough to jog by himself but I didn't say it. Seeing him crossing the threshold with difficulty, I said, "Take your time, Papa."

"No problem. I can manage."

He did manage to step over the threshold. After breathing heavily for a minute, he whispered in my ear, "To tell you the truth, I've just had a pill of Viagra. Its effect on my cock is beginning to show. It is becoming stiff. The medicine really works."

"Whether it works or not is to be seen later," I said, poking a finger on his forehead.

He went in, gasping for breath, "My doctor said the Viagra pills were very effective. She said the nurses in the nursing home often fed Viagra pills to senior men who couldn't move and had to lie in bed all day long. The nurses did so to make their cocks erect hard lest they fell from the bed."

"Papa," I almost choked with laughter, "You can't take your doctor's joke too seriously. She was just pulling your leg."

"No joke," he said in all earnestness, "Wait and see how I will fuck you so hard, you will cry for help. I even feel uncomfortable now to have my cock erect so hard."

He was obsessed with the intention of fucking me but had never succeeded in entering me even once. I took an iced mineral water for him from the fridge. When we arrived at the working room, Papa took off his white helmet and put it on the massage table, leaving his grizzle-haired head exposed. He was a little over seventy, one of my loyal fans. He spoke humorously, all his speech punctuated by two words – cock and cunt, though his own cock always let him down. He then took out a wallet from his bag and handed me 120 dollars, "As usual, an hour and a half." That was my special price for the senior clients, forty dollars for half an hour. I accepted the money and handed him the mineral water, "Sugar daddy, drink some water first."

"Don't you feel hot?" I went on to say, "Jogging plus Viagra is too much for an old man like you. You'd better take your time."

"No problem," he said, patting his own belly, "There's nothing wrong with my health. I'm just getting a little older. If I were ten years younger, I would have fucked you for two or three hours on end."

"Daddy, if I were ten years younger," I couldn't accept what he said, "It would have been little wonder if my strong cunt reduced your little cock into falling head over heels for me. You may as well take your shower now." At that time, he had taken off all his clothes and put them on the massage table. He staggered to the bathroom bare-hipped, murmuring to himself, "Let's wait and see how I'll conquer you."

"Let's wait and see how I'll be conquered by you," I said, smiling to myself.

I put away the money in the kitchen drawer. Knowing it would take some time for the old man to finish his bathing, I began to bite at the half-eaten apple while doing the washing up and tidying the kitchen utensils. I kept an ear out for the splashing sounds in the bathroom. When the splashing stopped, I knew the old man must have finished his bathing. I dried my hands with some tissues and went back to the working room. I found the old man standing in the bathroom with one leg on the toilet seat. I went over to stop him, "Daddy, quit doing that, otherwise you might hurt your balls."

"It's still wet between my thighs," he said.

I helped him dry his back, "All right. Go to the bed."

"Wait a minute. Let me see if my cock has gone stiff. The doctor said it worked," he said, stirring his cock.

"I'm more effective than any Viagra," I got impatient, "Hurry up and lie on the bed. Let me give your cock a course of treatment and it will get stiff and hard."

I had made the bed and stacked two pillows in a pile for him. He climbed onto the bed bare-hipped. He first landed his right shoulder, then rested his head on the pillows; lay down on his right side and finally shifted himself into position to lie on his back by throwing his left shoulder backward, "Suck my cock first." I parted his legs and sprawled between his thighs, "Let's begin with your balls and then your cock. One by one."

As I slowly ran my tongue across the skin of his balls, the old man whooped, "Wow-- --" followed by a long whistle, "Sh-- --" and then grinned in a grimace, "Ah, I have been missing it for days!"

I continued my oral work while he was gasping and yelling, "Yes. Yes!" I felt his white cock turning from hard to soft and from soft to hard alternately in my mouth. Maybe the Viagra he had taken ceased to have any effect? Or maybe it hadn't yet taken effect? Just then the mobile buzzed and startled the "daddy." Damn it. The call couldn't have come at a worse time. I said "Hello" over the phone and heard a man on the other end say in a strong Asian accent, "May I make an appointment?" Judging by his accent, he must be from either China or another Asian country like India, Vietnam or Indonesia. These past two days, there had been quite a few Asians calling to ask for price. I looked up at the clock and found the "daddy" needed another hour so I told the Asian caller, "Two thirty." He went on to ask, "Address, please?" I told him my address quickly. I put down the mobile and said to daddy, "Sorry, let's start again."

I sucked his cock for less than eight minutes before the daddy said, "Well, the drug is beginning to work." I was ready to witness the wonders of modern medical science only to find his cock remained almost unchanged, no harder than before. The drug belied its name. It had very little effect, if any. The drug might have had a psychological effect on the brain rather than a physical one on the cock. However, I pulled him up and said, "Get up and lie on top of me so it's more comfortable for you to exert yourself and what's more, it can make your cock even harder."

I got up and lay on my back on the bed. He came upon me and tucked his cock aimlessly into my cunt. I had to guide it with my right hand to the right path and he kept shouting on me, "I'm fucking you! I'm fucking you! I want to impregnate you so you'll have to marry me."

I remained cool and unmoved. I wouldn't marry any man no matter who he was. My task was to please you. I would be happy only if you could feel happy for the present.

I tried to tuck his cock in but it soon slipped out. I tucked it in again but it slipped out again. I vainly repeated the process numerous times and it exhausted me and made me sweat profusely. He was also reduced to gasping for breath, and murmuring repeatedly, "I'm fucking you. I'm fucking you." With every "I fuck you," he moved his hips upward once. I held his cock in my hand helplessly. I could neither tuck it into my cunt nor make it come. I may as well resort to my tried and trusted method. I had him stand up and applied some lubricating oil to my labia, "Come on, and try to enter me again."

I lay back down and he got on top of me again. I pressed his hips against mine and guided his cock with my right hand into my cunt and this time we managed it. He cried happily, "I've entered you at last."

I said just as happily, "Yes, you have." "Are you happy I'm fucking you?" "Yes, I am."

I thought the most important thing was to make them happy and it didn't matter at all whether I was happy or not. We tormented each other for a dozen minutes and I felt his cock hardening steadily in my hand. To whet his desire and speed him on to reach his climax as soon as possible, I echoed his cries, an "Ah, yes" here, an "Oh, yes" there, a "Wow" or just "Fuck me hard." I held his cock in my hand neither too tightly nor too loosely and stimulated it to a turn. Hearing his breathing quicken, I knew he was on the verge of coming so I pretended to be enjoying the sex also and narrowed my eyes, "Fuck me hard!" And he yelled, "I'll fuck you to death!"

I felt a warm and viscous liquid spurting into my palm. He was coming! The daddy's should be ranked among the most difficult cocks to make come. I let him lie on my prone naked body for a while before I pushed him off. My bosom and belly were covered in sweat as if sluiced in water. Now I had a clearer picture of my doctor's assertion that making love once amounts to walking four miles. Daddy's exertions would surely extend his lifespan by at least ten years. Look what happiness and benefits I had brought to "daddy" and those older friends of mine.

This inevitably reminded me of my own daddy. Why on earth was my own daddy not offered such excellent services and entertaining recreation to become healthy? My daddy was struck down with cerebral thrombosis at an early age and was rushed to Huairou Hospital in a suburb of Beijing. He hadn't received better treatment for lack of money. He died shortly after I went abroad and I missed the last chance to see him off on his deathbed. Later my sister told me that after the oxygen supply was cut off, daddy still lingered for eighteen hours in the hope of seeing me for the last time before he died. I could never think of this without tears welling up in my eyes and the wealthier I got the more I missed my daddy. It was my lifelong regret. If only I had had enough money then to save my daddy.

"What's the matter? Am I hurting you?" the surprised voice of the present "daddy" brought me back to reality.

"I'm missing my own daddy," I said with great sadness. "If you are," he said, "You can fly back to see him."

"My daddy has gone to too remote a place," I sighed and got up to fetch some tissues, ready to wipe the sperm off the inside of my right thigh. The "daddy" couldn't tear his eyes off my cunt, "What if I have made you pregnant?"

"If so," I said resolutely, "I'll have my own way to deal with the situation."

"If so," he asked eagerly, "Could you bear it for me?"

"You're daydreaming," I said, his suggestion being absurd, "If I am to bear your child, what about all the other clients? Forget it and go take your shower. Then I will give you a massage."

When he went to the bathroom, I picked up my mobile and took it to another bathroom. I had just turned on the tap and begun to wash my private part when the mobile buzzed, "What's your price?"

"Fifty dollars for half an hour's nude massage and ninety for one hour; seventy for half an hour's whole-set service and one hundred and twenty for one hour."

"For what time can I have an appointment?" "Three o'clock."

After disconnecting the call, I went on bathing. I had not squatted down when the mobile buzzed again. I washed my cunt perfunctorily and turned off the nozzle hastily before I stepped out of the bathroom.

"Hello?"

"Hi, sexy. Haven't seen you for days. When can I come?" The voice on the other end of the line was so familiar to me, but I just couldn't recall his name for the moment. Judging by the fact that he was calling me "sexy," he must have been an old client.

"At half past three."

He hesitated for a moment and I realized he must feel it was too late. So I said, "Or you can come at three fifteen." The three o'clock appointment was made by a new client and typically a new client would cancel at the last minute. So I sometimes left each of them only fifteen minutes. The man on the other end of the line agreed, "Fine."

I dried myself with the towel and went back to the working room. The "Papa" was already sprawled on the bed and I massaged him from the top of his head to the soles of his feet, kneading him with my knuckles inch by inch and knuckle by knuckle. Papa fell asleep soundly. He had enjoyed himself very much indeed. I looked up to find it was approaching two thirty and high time I woke him up, "Hey, Papa It's time to go home. It's too expensive to sleep on this bed. You'll have to pay me extra money."

It was two twenty sharp so I said, "As you're leaving ten minutes earlier, I'll refund you twenty dollars. Take it and buy yourself something you like for supper."

I went to the kitchen to pack a box with cashews and grabbed a mineral water. Then I went back to the working room with these gifts and the twenty dollars' change for him, "Here's your refund and some snacks for you to enjoy this evening."

"Thanks," the "Papa" said.

I put the bottle of mineral water, the box of cashews together with the half-emptied water on the bedside table into a plastic bag. The daddy; dressed up decently, with his white helmet on, stalked out of the working room and I sent him out the door. I took his elbow down the doorsteps, "Mind your step."

"See you later, Linda."

I ran back to tidy the working room. Just then the mobile buzzed, "Is your address 331 Creseter Street, Garama?"

"Yes."

"I am already at your door." "Then please come in."

The man spoke with a strong Asian accent. Judging by his voice, he was not old.

LIMP DICK

I went out of the working room to the dining room and through the blinds of the French door; I saw a bean-green car parked on my driveway. The man stayed in the car and didn't come out. When at last he exited the car, he stood at the front door without touching the doorbell. I went to open the front door and then the security door, "Will you please come in?"

The young man hesitated and I knew well he doubted my age. I didn't dare to answer, when asked, that I was only twenty- eight as I used to. I answered thirty-eight instead. I was not sure what age I had told the young man over the phone. He obviously didn't believe I was that age, and must have thought I was forty- eight at least.

He looked me up and down, hesitating whether he should come in. I realized it was that critical moment, where I had to persuade a wavering client to stay, "Come in please. I have seen many young guys like you. Though I'm a little older than you, I can offer you a first-class, quality service. I have as many as five hundred lads as my frequent clients."

I hinted that he was not my youngest client. When he came in, I asked, "What do you want to drink; beer, Pepsi, Coke or just water?" I wanted to express friendship and hospitality.

"No, thanks."

"How long have you been here in Australia?"

"Do you live in Canberra?" I tried to make him comfortable with me as soon as possible by chatting casually.

"Yes."

"How long?" "Two years."

I understood at once he was holding either a student visa or a work visa.

"I've told many overseas students that this is the right place to solve their sex problems but the wrong place to find their girlfriends. You should find a girlfriend among your classmates or colleagues instead of any brothel."

What I said made the young man flush and I went on to say, "And what's more, the girls working in brothels have experienced so many men, who are handsome or wealthy or both. They usually will not place any value on you. If a girl happens to become your girlfriend for some time, you can't keep her for long as you can't supply her with what she wants most. You won't be able to prevent her from leaving you in the end."

I led the lad to the working room and I supposed when he saw the furnishings in there he would give up the prospect of finding a girlfriend in me. I knew very well many overseas students were trying to find a lady patron in order to solve the problem of their status. Many overseas students, including the Chinese one last night, proposed to marry me but it was a vain effort. No prostitute would develop a crush on these poor students. The lad's face turned from red to pale.

"Where are you from?" I asked. "Korea."

I knew I was in for trouble now. I had been pretending to be a Korean when I received Asian clients. I had thought he was Chinese when he entered the house. I looked him up and down and found he was really Korean; tall and thin, with a small head, face, nose and eyes, "Are you really Korean?"

"Yes."

"How do you greet a person in Korean?" "Annyeonghaseyo."

"How do you say, 'Have you had dinner?'?"

"Bab meog eot ni."

Now a fake Korean encountered a real Korean. "Since you're Korean," I confessed, "I'll tell you the truth. I'm Chinese; from Beijing, China. But I always claim to be Korean when I receive Chinese clients. Did I tell you I was Korean over the telephone because I couldn't recognize whether you were Chinese or Korean then?"

He smiled knowingly and I asked, "Would you like an hour's service or half an hour?"

"Half an hour."

I guessed he had probably intended to stay for an hour and then changed his mind to take the half hour service when he saw me. He had got himself into a situation where he knew there was no possibility of finding a lady patron but had been reluctantly persuaded into coming in and now found it improper to take to his heels at once. Anyway, the price of fifty dollars for half an hour was not expensive.

"Fifty dollars for half an hour." He gave me fifty dollars and I had him take a shower first.

"I have had one."

"Then take off all your clothes and put them on the massage table."

The young man looked worried and didn't say a word unless spoken to. I put away the money in the kitchen and took a mineral water from the fridge. I asked him, "Do you want to drink some water?"

The young man shook his head so I had to put the water on the bedside table. He stripped, except for his briefs and stood at the side of the bed embarrassedly. I went over to help him take off his last strip of clothing, "Why do you still have your briefs on. Show me your cock."

The young man's face turned as crimson as a lobster and, hearing what I said, turned from red to pale. He was at a loss as to what to do. I told him to get on the bed and lie down. He followed my instructions and did so but crossed his legs tightly, leaving a small brown cock exposed. It was a typical Asian man's cock but among the smallest Asian ones, no longer than a double-A battery. I tried to spread his legs, "Why do cross your legs so tightly? Relax and show me your little cock."

I stirred the tiny cock dangling between his thighs, "Hey, my little guy. Wake up. We're home!"

He couldn't contain a snort of laughter and I began to lick the skin of his smooth balls. Unlike the balls or assholes of Australian, European and African boys, which were bristled with a lot of hair, the balls or assholes of Asian boys were rather smooth and hairless. It was interesting that Australian and European boys had yellow, brown, red or grizzled hair (when old) while African boys had curly black hair.

I held his cock in my mouth and began to suck it. His tiny cock jerked and turned now hard, now soft. I knew what had caused his poor performance – his failure to concentrate his attention on sex. He was distracted by his own trouble. I wouldn't have him going on this way. I had to find a way to make him relaxed.

So I asked him, "How old are you?" "Thirty-one."

I thought as much. He had deemed it a romantic meeting between a thirty-one-year-old lad and a thirty-five-year-old young lady. Though the lady was a bit older, it didn't matter much. But as he came to see the real person, he found the error in estimating my age was beyond his tolerance. Though he had effectively fallen into a trap and was cheated into lying on my bed, it was a loss of a mere fifty dollars anyway. So he was lying there absentminded, not caring about the performance of his own cock. Seeing his impotence, I sat at his left side and made my last effort to suck his cock, supporting myself with my left elbow between his thighs and my face in his private part.

I said, "The other day an Indian lad came and found I was too old. He pestered me to tell him how to go to the Fyshwick brothel," and I went on to say, "Mate, don't waste too much time on that. If you'd like to solve your sexual problems, go to a brothel but if you want to find a girlfriend there, you'll be totally disappointed. Whoever is in this trade won't elope with ordinary folk like you. If you won't take my advice, you'll end up wasting so much time and money for nothing and what's worse, you'll neglect your studies. You may as well devote all this energy to improving yourself."

The lad gazed at me nonchalantly and I wondered whether he was listening to my preaching. He gave me an impression that he must have encountered some tremendous trouble or was weighed down by some huge worries. I had to go on, "That Indian boy wouldn't listen to me and went on pestering me to tell him the phone number of the brothel. I said I didn't know but he could find it in the newspapers. But he insisted on going there so I had to show him the door."

The lad wasn't listening to me and merely stared at the ceiling blankly. I said to myself that although I was an expert in comforting cocks, I couldn't find a cure to every mental problem. I may as well make him come as soon as possible to relieve him of his stress. Despite my efforts to please him by sucking his cock, he simply said, "Let me fuck you."

I found him a small-sized condom and pulled him up, "You lie on top of me." With that, I just lay down on the bed and parted my legs.

My purpose was to have him concentrate on sex by lying on me and fucking me. But I was wrong. Scarcely had his cock touched my cunt when it hopelessly turned limp. He said, "I'm tired."

I knew it was not because of his tiredness but because of his absentmindedness. I knelt down to caress his cock and soon the cock seemed somewhat hardened. I pulled him up, "Come on. Try once more to fuck me."

In less than a couple of minutes, his cock became dead limp. I felt desperate as he was not in the mood to fuck me. However hard I tried, I simply couldn't make him come. I got ready to try sucking his cock again but he was not enthusiastic at all. He said, "I quit. I'm tired out and I want to go home to have a sleep." I was at my wits' end. You could lead a horse to water but you couldn't make him drink. I gave up and let him take his shower.

I felt extremely frustrated every time I failed to make a client come. I said, "Sorry for not having satisfied you. I'll refund you ten dollars."

"You don't need to," he said expressionlessly.

But I was determined to refund him ten dollars. After he went to the bathroom, I went to the kitchen to fetch ten dollars. When I came back, he had dressed. I insisted on refunding him but he declined. I at last managed to stuff the money into his pocket. I offered him the mineral water but he declined to accept it. I saw him off at the door. Watching him leave, I couldn't help feeling sorry for the lad. Well, every individual had his own problems, whether rich or poor. Life was not easy for anybody!

With a weary sigh I closed the door. I was heading for the laundry when the doorbell rang. I turned back, wondering whether the lad might have left something behind him. When I opened the door, a tanned Caucasian man about sixty years of age stood on the steps. He had a thin, angular face with a big nose and unruly, grizzled hair. He looked me up and down before he said, "Sorry, but I have to leave." Apparently he was not interested in me at all. My age again, I thought. It was no use touting for such a client again. It would be a sheer waste of time. I had been in this trade for many years and I kept my dropout rate under 0.05 percent; a remarkable achievement a lot of young prostitutes would admire. I shut the door and walked back into the house, thinking resentfully that you should look into the mirror to see how old and ugly you were before you rejected me for my age. I had many regulars in their late teens and I didn't care a bit whether you would come or not. Such an isolated dropout case would have no effect on my business reputation. I went grumbling to the laundry and took the dried towels to the working room, folded them up and put the dirty used towels into the washing machine. When I heard the doorbell, I felt relieved that I had left only fifteen minutes for the new client so I didn't waste time waiting in between the two clients. I went to answer the door, "Oh, my god. I haven't seen you for ages. Why haven't you visited me for such a long time?"

The tall, handsome man was an Australian-born Indian; probably a couple of years younger than me. But he naturally assumed he was my senior as I had told him I was forty. He looked very much like the hero in an Indian film "Awara", from many years ago. He patronized my business every two or three weeks when he worked in the Taxation Office in Canberra. He had a very beautiful wife and two lovely daughters and he often told me he loved his wife very much. However, he also admitted he sometimes needed some novel sexual adventure for a change and then went back to be a loving husband.

When he came in, he towered over me, almost a head taller than me though I was not short; measuring five feet four inches tall. He kissed me on the forehead, "How I missed you. I am not working in Canberra now. I was transferred to Sydney."

"You're still so young and handsome," I said, wrapping my hand around his waist.

"You're also still beautiful."

"Oh, no," I said, "I'm getting old. Just now a client fled from me."

"You're kidding," he smiled, "Who could flee from such a beauty?"

"Believe it or not," I said, "Another ten years and you'll surely flee from me."

"I will surely visit you in another twenty years if I ever get the chance. Do you have any plans to quit and retire?"

"I'll work for another thirty years."

"Why not?" he smiled, "Work while you can work and earn what you can earn. Linda, you have found yourself a good job, one that is better than any other job. Look at me. I work for the government and have to retire at the age of sixty-five. But you're different. You can tell your clients you're only thirty-eight when you reach the age of sixty or even seventy. You can still go on with your business. Who will demand to check your birth certificate before fucking you?"

"Yes," I sighed, "Now that I have come to love my job, I will go on working until one fine morning when I open the door and a client will stand aghast at me, wondering whether he has met an old witch before he takes to his heels at once. He will say, "Oh, my. Too old to be a prostitute," then the clients will become few and far between until my house is totally deserted. Only then will I quit."

Both of us burst out laughing. When we arrived at the working room, he looked around and said, "Wow, great changes have taken place in a year. All the furnishings have been upgraded!"

"I'm getting older so I have to make up for it by improving my business environment. Actually it is another way to attract potential clients. Sometimes a client will be dissatisfied with me but will reconcile himself with the gorgeous surroundings."

"You're really a remarkable business talent."

"I am a remarkable fucking talent," I said happily, "I can write a one-million-word-long thesis on fuckology."

We burst into roars of laughter again. He said, "Let me tell you a story about an old prostitute. Two years ago, a police friend of mine stopped at three o'clock in the early morning. A gorgeous lady got out of the car. My friend checked her driver's license. Her age on the license was eighty-two. He questioned where she was going and what do you think she replied? She said she was a call girl on her way to her client's house."

"Well, if she can why can't I," I smiled, "By then I'll have become a Goddess of Cock who has appreciated thousands upon thousands of cocks."

"If you have experienced about two dozen cocks a day," he said, doing his arithmetic interestedly, "the amount of the cocks you've seen in a year will add up to four or five thousand. I'm afraid I couldn't have the chance to see as many cunts."

"So I'm happier than any other woman in the world," I laughed heartily.

I handed him a clean towel and he gave me seventy dollars, "You haven't raised the price, have you?"

"No. Instead of raising my price I've reduced it. Do you have a ten-dollar note?"

He took out a ten-dollar note and exchanged it for a twenty-dollar note with me. He said admiringly, "You really have a unique way of doing business."

"I once heard an entrepreneur say," I said not without a note of pride in my voice, "that if everyone does the same thing in the same way, we will get the same result and only by doing them in a unique way can we get satisfactory results."

"That's very smart of you, Linda."

When asked what drink he would like, he answered, "Fanta." I returned to the kitchen and put away the money. I came back with a can of Fanta in my hand for him. I was on my way to the working room when the mobile buzzed, "May I have an appointment for two hours?"

Glancing at the clock, I found it was nearly four o'clock and I hadn't even had my lunch. I'd better put off the two-hour appointment until eight o'clock. So I replied, "At eight o'clock."

"Okay, see you at eight o'clock."

Barely had I hung up the mobile when the doorbell rang. I hurried to the front door to find a gentleman of sixty or so, whom I seemed to have seen somewhere. He said smilingly, "You still work here?"

"Where do you suppose I should work? This is my house."

He kept his smile on his face, "Do you remember me? I visited you last year. I live in Brisbane. I've come to Canberra to see my daughter."

"Excuse me for my bad memory. But usually I can remember most of my clients after I have met them in person."

"Today I have specially come to see you but I can't stay for long. I will visit you someday when I am free."

With that, he kissed me on the back of my right hand, "Honey, you still look so gorgeous."

I laughed up my sleeve, "Am I gorgeous? My beauty is fading fast and it won't be long before you flee at the sight of me. I waved my hand, "Have a nice afternoon."

I closed the door and headed for the working room. I was half way there when the doorbell rang. I had to run to attend to the Indian man first, who had just finished bathing and was now lying on the bed. I put the can of Fanta on the bedside table, "Enjoy your drink. I'll be back in a moment," before I went to open the door and recognized at once it was the fat drunkard from last night, "Are you here for the wallet?"

With that I ran back to the kitchen and dashed toward the door after I took the wallet from the drawer.

I said, still gasping, "Here it is. Won't you open it to see if anything in it is missing? Actually I didn't even open it to see the contents. Your phone number on the license card was identified by another person."

He smiled friendlily, "There's no need to check it. Thank you, Linda."

"I charge every one of you fifty dollars for half an hour and ninety dollars for one hour. It's my business. But I won't be interested in the other content in your wallet, even if it is a thousand dollars or more. There are often customers who have left their belongings, such as watches, mobiles or wallets, at my house but I will always keep those items safe for them" The fat man expressed his gratitude to me.

I then went back to the working room and said apologetically to the Indian man, "I'm sorry to have kept you waiting."

"That's all right." He asked, "Is it a common thing to wait for you?"

"Yes, because I have too many 'patients'."

"That's mainly because there are too many men with cock problems."

I then let go of my dress and it fell to my ankles. I knelt between his thighs and grasped his cock, "It hasn't changed much since last year."

"Can there be any change with cocks?"

"Of course. These years many clients' cocks have shortened a lot. A German's cock used to be very big but it shortened by an inch and moreover its tip became twisted. The doctors said there was no cure for such cases."

"Really?" he asked perplexedly.

"When I worked for Philip's brothel, an eighty-year-old man told me, 'Linda, my cock was thick and long when I was young.' But I didn't believe him at that time, thinking he was boasting. To what extent can a cock's size and length change? Yet it turned out the German's cock really did shorten by an inch. Only then did I believe a man's cock might shrink when he grows old."

"I don't want to see my cock shorten," he smiled.

"It's too early to predict. Let's wait and see what happens in ten or twenty years' time."

"Even then I don't want to see that."

"That's something you can't control," I said, "By the way, why didn't your wife come along with you today?"

"If she did, could I come visit you? Actually since I was transferred to Sydney, I have been to Canberra twice but each time my wife accompanied me here so I couldn't come to your house."

"Today we can indulge ourselves in any pleasure."

"You're so busy and I don't even have any time to have a chat with you, let alone indulge ourselves in pleasure."

"Now let's have a good chat."

"Linda," he looked into my eyes, "How much can you earn in a day?"

"Well, not much," I said,"How much do you think I can earn from these cocks?"

"Linda, I'm not talking to you as a tax collector."

"If you were a tax collector," I said, becoming a bit vigilant, "I would pay you tax on one cock and leave the other two for myself. Besides, can you stay at my home and count how many cocks I have served in a day?"

"We can," he smiled "but we won't."

"Last time the owner of a Chinese restaurant refused to pay the due tax so the officials of the Taxation Office stayed in his restaurant and watched how many customers came in a day. It was too much, I think."

He was amused by what I had said, "But you have to pay a certain amount of tax. It won't do if you don't."

"I did," I said, "but I earned less than I paid. I not only pay your Taxation Office but also pay the bank."

"Everybody deposits money into the bank. How come you pay money to the bank?"

"Do you remember I talked to you about the two houses I had bought four years ago in Sydney?"

"Yes, I do," he said, "and I remember you said you would reconstruct four new houses on the original plot and sell me one of them so that we could be next-door neighbors."

"New houses?" I said with resentment, "Forget it. I had bought a heritage building. Not only can you not demolish it but also, you have to pay the government for failing to preserve the historic building if you should damage it. I asked the solicitor who acted as my agent in purchasing the houses. What did you think she said? She said she didn't remember that. It was really heartless of her. When she was first commissioned, I gave her a tip of six hundred dollars. When the sale of the first house was completed, I paid her eight hundred dollars as a regular fee and credited an additional two hundred dollars as a bonus to her account. Five months later when we were ready to buy the second house, I made it clear to her that this shabby house was to be demolished. She agreed and offered to negotiate with the real estate agent about the price and told me that she had succeeded in cutting down the price by five thousand dollars. I was so glad that I paid her eight hundred dollars as her regular fee and another four hundred dollars as her bonus. After I paid her all that money in fees and bonuses, she had me face the fact that I bought a heritage house which couldn't be demolished. What made me more indignant was that she claimed I could go to court to sue her. She said she wouldn't care because she and her agency were insured so she wouldn't lose any money. I was really unfortunate to meet such a bad solicitor. For four years, I have paid the bank a large sum of interest for the house loan. No one would purchase such a heritage house even at its original price."

He said, "You can consult a lawyer."

"I have consulted a lawyer and he said it was a complicated problem," I said, crestfallen,"I'm considering selling it in a couple of years and recovering as much as possible. But I'm afraid I can't sell it within ten years."

"Why are others earning money from property while you're losing money?"

"Indeed. But it was my fault that I couldn't speak English and I put too much trust in a solicitor without any professional ethics. If only I could have consulted the relevant government branches. I was ignorant of house transactions back then."

I had a long conversation with the gentleman from the Taxation Office about various subjects. Soon after I saw him off, the old Brazilian came. I asked him, "You came the day before yesterday. How come you're here again?"

"I can't help missing you."

When I was in China, some men were laughed at for squandering all the money they earned over a lifetime to have sex. As a matter of fact, there are such people in all countries, who eat sparingly and spend frugally but never begrudge spending to go whoring. Take this is old boy from Brazil for example; though I only charged him thirty-five dollars each time, the little sum added up to a large amount as he frequented me often. He was sixty-three years old and didn't own a house. He lived in a rented unit. He proposed to marry me many times and only when he discovered there was no hope did he give up. I sneered at his idea of marrying me for the purpose of sharing half of my property. I would rather give him the heritage building to save me the trouble of paying the installments. But I still dared not to disgrace him in public. In my opinion, such a man, like the Italian Prime Minister, Berlusconi, was addicted to girls and cunts. It was all well and good that human beings liked sex by nature but it would make no sense to spend all your time in bed having sex. Look at me. It is my work; it is my duty to roll around with men in bed. I should be thankful to God that I chose it as my career. Holding the thirty dollars the Brazilian gave me, I jumped with joy, "What a happy life I live!"

The Brazilian old boy was perplexed, "What has made you so happy?"

"You can't find a job that is better than mine. I can make money by enjoying myself."

"I wish I also had a pussy." "You'd be a monster if you did."

We were chatting jestingly when the mobile rang, "What's the price?"

"For fucking or massaging?"

Most readers may think this conversation is fabricated. How can two strangers talk like that over the phone? But actually these are men calling prostitutes for a price. Nothing will sound strange in such conversations. Take the following one as an example:

He said,"Of course I want to fuck your pussy. Can I fuck you without a condom and spurt all my sperm into your cunt?"

I replied, "I have to serve several customers a day and if every man wants to come in me, my pussy would become a pond of jizz. If you want to ejaculate, then you ejaculate into the condom."

"What can you do? What about a fantasy?" "What do you mean by a fantasy?"

"You shit in my asshole and then lick it clean. A job an ordinary prostitute can't do."

"Sorry, but I can't do that, either. I might be 'number one' prostitute, but I can't do everything. You'd better find yourself a super prostitute elsewhere," I put down the mobile.

Just then, the mobile buzzed and I picked it up, "Hello."

"Are you a sex worker?" asked a man, who seemed civilized enough not to address me directly as a prostitute.

"Yeah," I tried to sound as civilized as he did, "what can I do for you?"

"How much is it for a big cock to fuck a little cunt?" he asked.

Wherever fucking cunts was concerned, even a most civilized gentleman would show his true colors without any exception.

"A single price for big or little cocks,"I answered professionally, "Seventy for half an hour and one twenty for one hour."

"How old are you?" he went on to ask.

"Thirty-five," I answered after a brief pause. "Are you a busty girl?"

"Yes, of course," this time I answered without any hesitation, but I wondered whether I was a busty granny instead of a busty girl.

"Do you wear long hair or short hair?"

"Long black hair," I was glad I had just dyed my hair recently. "Are you fat or slim? Will you tell me your height?"

"Medium height, about six foot four, and neither too fat nor too thin."

"Your weight?"

"A hundred and sixty-five pounds."

"Mm, you're a very sexy girl. What about your bust measurement?"

"Thirty-one."

"Waist?" "Twenty-nine." "Hips?"

"Thirty-two and my trousers are twenty-eight long." "Is your cunt shaven or not?"

"Cleanly shaven."

"Could you send me a color photo?"

"Sorry, but I can't," I was thinking I couldn't even send a text to my clients, let alone a photo. And if I could send you a color photo of me, you would be frightened away.

The man on the other end of the line kept silent for a long time… I sighed and put down the mobile before I turned to the Brazilian old boy, "I was wondering why he should ask so many questions for the mere purpose of finding a prostitute to solve his sex problem. It was as if he were a king searching for a queen or a Chinese emperor searching for a concubine."

"He seemed to have too many questions," when the Brazilian old boy was answering, the mobile buzzed again, "Hello. Is that Miss. Linda speaking?"

"Yes," I answered, "What can I do for you, mate?"

"I have seen your advertisement on the internet," he said, "Maybe we can cut a deal."

"What deal?"

"I pay you five hundred dollars," he explained the details of his suggestion, "and you allow me to take pictures of you fucking your clients. I will upload these pictures to the internet."

"But I never allow my pictures to be taken while I'm fucking my clients," I said, "Even if I agree, my clients will not. If pictures of them having sex with a prostitute are uploaded to the internet, their wives or girlfriends would cut off their cocks in a frenzy. You may as well go elsewhere and make a deal with other ladies who are willing to do so."

I put down the mobile and told the Brazilian old boy, "That guy was offering me money for pictures of me fucking my clients and he was planning to upload them onto the internet. Are you willing to have the scenes of our fucking photographed and uploaded to the internet?"

"Absolutely not," the Brazilian old boy got into a panic, "If my son or daughter-in-law should see them on the internet, I would die of shame."

"I couldn't agree more," I said, "I'm afraid no client of mine will be willing to have their picture taken having sex with a prostitute and uploaded to the internet."

"Stop," the Brazilian old boy seemed to find something and began to complain,"None of your bullshit! What the hell is going on here? I've been lying on your bed without being attended to for a long time, and during this time you received three calls! My cock can't wait any longer."

"I remember receiving more calls during one service," I tried to appease him by citing worse cases, "Once a client of mine was lying on bed only to be interrupted by ten telephone calls in a short period of half an hour. The client ended up failing to come. I had to give him fifteen minutes' extra service…" I had scarcely finished my sentence when another mobile buzzed. I pressed the "answer" key and said, "Hello."

"Are you a massage girl?" A man said, "I'm playing with my cock. Could please talk dirty to help me come?"

"Sorry," I said, "but I'm too busy to serve you now."

After I hung up the receiver, I turned to the old boy and said, "That guy's masturbating. He wanted me to talk dirty to him."

"He can talk to those girls who are specialized in talking dirty over the phone," the old boy said, "It costs only a dollar ninety per minute."

"You're right," I said, "He can't pay me for the service over the phone."

"There seems no end to your talk on the mobile," he said, "Please switch it off."

"Okay," I agreed, throwing my mobile aside, "Let's start sucking right now." With that, I squatted between his legs and held his cock in my mouth.

I looked up at the Brazilian, thinking he had only paid me thirty-five dollars and had already taken up so much of my time. There was still a lucrative client with a two-hour long appointment waiting after him so I had to make him come as soon as possible. I sucked his cock for some time and urged him to get to his feet, "Hurry up. Hurry up and fuck me. The next client is coming."

With that I bent over and got ready for him to fuck me. He stood behind me, trying to tuck his cock into my cunt and complaining, "You're always thinking of money, money. What else do you think about?"

"What else can I think about except money?" I retorted, "I just know without money I can go nowhere. If I pay loan interest one day late, the bank will fine me a hundred dollars immediately."

The Brazilian was puzzled how fucking was suddenly related to a home loan. As for me, I felt annoyed at the mere thought of the two damned houses.

After sending the Brazilian away, I took a roasted duck from the fridge I had bought from a Chinese restaurant and heated it in the microwave oven. Then I prepared a bag of vegetable salad I had bought from the supermarket. I hastily appeased my hunger with a can of sugar-free Coke. Then I did all the washing up.

Looking at the wall clock, it was five to eight in the evening. I changed into a full-length, blue dress and dressed myself with elaborate care for the newly-arriving client.

It was eight o'clock sharp and the doorbell rang on time. I opened the door with a greeting, "Good evening, sir." He was tall with long, blond hair falling over his shoulders. He had a pair of azure eyes, a large, square mouth and an extraordinarily big nose under a protruding forehead; a metal ring about half an inch wide piercing through his right nostril and another ring ornamenting his right brow. He wore a loose, blue tracksuit with a blue backpack on his back. I ushered him in and he bent down to kiss me on the cheek, "Good evening, Linda."

"Good evening, is it your first time?" "Yes."

"Do you know me from the advertisements in the paper?" "No. I saw your advertisement on the internet."

"These days," I said, looking up at him, "many new clients say that they found me on the internet. It is said a client from Sydney who had visited me put my information on the internet. The information is so detailed that even the position of my piano is clearly stated."

"Yes, exactly," the long-haired client said.

As we walked to the working room, I asked him, "What would you like to drink?"

"Nothing, thanks. I just had some water at home."

When we arrived at the working room, I asked, "You have made an appointment for two hours?"

FANTASY

"Yes."

"One hundred and twenty dollars for one hour and two forty for two hours. I'll give you a special offer. One eighty for two hours; at a rate of ninety an hour. Is that okay?"

He took a wallet from his backpack and pulled out four, fifty-dollar notes. I went to put the money away in the kitchen and retrieved the twenty dollars' change, together with a bottle of mineral water for the client. When I came back to the working room, I was horrified to find the client taking out of his backpack; a coil of thick ropes, a knife, a pair of scissors and a vice. I was greatly puzzled whether he had come to fuck me or otherwise? And what was the use of the knife, scissors or vice? Was he going to use the scissors to pry my cunt open or cut his cock off?

Looking in terror at these tools, I said, "You've come to solve the problem of your cock, haven't you? Why did you bring so many tools with you? Any of these tools will be too hard for a cunt."

"Don't worry," he smiled, "This is my sexual fantasy. I have been addicted to this fantasy since my puberty."

With that, he uncoiled the thick rope, had me take the end of it, and cut it where it extended a little longer than three feet. We repeated the same procedure four times until we got four pieces of thick rope of the same length. I lined the ropes on the massage bed. Then he slowly stripped and I helped him place his clothes on the massage table.

When at last he stripped off his last piece of clothing – a pair of black briefs, I found his cock dangling long, like a dead fish. To my astonishment, the blue vein along the front of the cock was also pierced through with three metal rings, about an inch wide. I found the purple skin of his balls at the base of his cock was quite loose. To my knowledge as a sex worker, loose ball skin was most probably caused by too much masturbation. His dark cock was bristled with yellow hair. I had him lie down on the bed, but he said, "Let me lie on the floor."

"Why must you lie on the floor?" I asked curiously. "This is my fantasy," he said.

"I spread a large white towel on the floor for him, "Do you need a pillow?"

"No, thanks."

With that he took up the vice and pinched his own cock. Then he lay down on the floor, closed his eyes and began to murmur something as if saying his prayers. I was greatly amused. It was the first time I had ever seen a client having sex like that. I sat beside him, helping him caress his cock. He kept on murmuring something that I couldn't understand at all. My urgent task was to make his cock harden soon and thrust it into my cunt to satisfy my own lust. Somehow I always had an insatiable desire for all cocks. But, to my dismay, my client's cock remained limp like a dormant snake.

"Linda," he said helplessly, "my cock just can't erect." "Why?"

"My cock hasn't erected since I took up this sexual fantasy when I was eighteen years old."

"Do you have a girlfriend?" I asked him. "No."

"How old are you?"

"Forty-three," he answered.

"Forty-three means you are in the prime of your life. You can marry, as a Chinese saying goes, a girl three years your senior and you will soon get rich."

"Why would I marry a girl three years my senior? Nonsense! I have neither a girlfriend nor a fiancée. I'm a bachelor."

"What's the harm in being a bachelor? Look at me. I'm a spinster who will never marry again and I'm childless as well. I'm not lonely as I have the company of a variety of cocks from different countries around the world."

"You don't feel lonely but I do," he said, "I live all by myself so if I'm alone, all day. I play with my cock, making it come and come without stopping. Until at last my cock can no longer come."

I laughed up my sleeve, "It turns out his cock won't erect because of his compulsive masturbation and not for any physical reason. His self abuse has spoiled his own cock and made him impotent for all."

We tormented each other for more than an hour and he simply showed no sign of coming soon. Sweat was pouring down his cheeks and his hair was also soaked. Even the towels on the ground were dampened with sweat. At last he asked me, "Do have a large plastic bag?"

"Yes," I answered, "For what purpose?" "You put me into the bag."

I recalled I had a large plastic bag which had been used to pack a newly-bought mattress and I hadn't yet had time to throw it away. I rushed to the garage to get it and came back with it. I told him to stand in the bag and pulled the bag up until his head was inside it. He said, "Fetch me the four ropes on the massage table. Use one to tie my feet and another to tie one of my arms to the bed frame. Use the third one to tie the vice pinching my cock and the fourth to tie around my neck. Then tighten the rope around my neck and pull the rope tied to the vice…"

Here I'd like to warn you if you're also a sex worker working at home. When your client suggests a fantasy and wants to tie your hands or feet or to put a collar around your neck, *do not* obey his order. You will get into great danger in case the client has some sinister designs against you. Things are different if you work in a brothel, where your boss and your colleagues will come to your rescue immediately if you cry for help. If you're working alone at home, it's no use crying or screaming as no one will hear you. Recently, a client of mine told me that in Sydney or Canberra, a forty-year-old Australian prostitute was strangled with a dog collar around her neck by someone. When the suspect was caught by the police, he argued that it was an accident when he was playing fantasy with the prostitute… I mean once you're tied hand and foot or collared by someone, it's no use at all struggling for your life, however strong you are.

I followed his directions and tied him up. His left arm was tied to the frame of the massage bed and his right arm led his right hand back and forth to caress his cock. At the same time, I stood up to pull the ropes. I didn't dare exert all my strength lest I should strangle him and I would be caught by the police as a murderer. But he kept urging me to pull harder. Though he gasped heavily for breath, he kept pressing me, "Pull the rope around my neck, hard."

"No, I won't or you'll be hanged."

"It's nice to be hanged so I can see God." "Who is God?" I asked.

"God is our almighty Lord," he said, "I want to see Him. There are too many bad guys in this world. I'd like Him to punish them."

I heard the client begin to talk deliriously about the Almighty God punishing bad guys. I cautioned myself not to pull the rope any harder lest I should really strangle him. The inside of the huge plastic bag was then covered with white vapor coming from his mouth. I found him fiddling with his cock and murmuring something. I was worried that he showed no sign of coming. Every time I failed to make a client of mine come, I would feel sorry both for him and for myself as well. If he still didn't come, I would have a sleepless night tonight. Then he told me to untie the rope around his neck. The other three were still tied tightly.

"I want to drink," he said.

I took the half-empty bottle on the bedside table and poured some water into his mouth. He drank it with several gulps before he said, "Enough."

After I put the mineral water back on the bedside table, he told me to take up the knife from the massage table and cut into his hairy chest. I was terrified. You're abetting me to be a murderer. Seeing I was hesitating, he said, "I'm not asking you to kill me. I just want you to stimulate me by cutting hard into my flesh with the knife. Then I will have the feeling that I'm going to see God. When I cry, 'I'm coming,' I will come."

I took up the knife on the massage table and ran the knife across his chest with a trembling hand but just didn't dare to cut into his flesh.

"Come on. Cut me hard," he encouraged me, "Cut a cross in my chest."

I just couldn't bring myself to cut into his flesh. Just then his right arm struggled out of the binding and used the knife to cut a cross in his own chest. The blood began to ooze from the cuts and he sped up his hand movements along his cock. Finally he began to yell loudly, "Oh, yes. I'm coming! My God!"

He raised his legs several times and then lowered them until he calmed down at last. Oh my. His fantasy had brought him to paradise to see God. It was said that only after one died could he get to see God. In the mind of the Chinese, heaven was God. I sat on the carpet, not knowing what to do and gave my fancy a full scope. I was relieved to find him slowly come to. He was sweating all over and I helped him untie all the ropes, "Sir, I just can't bear your fantasy anymore. Next time I'd like you to find another girl to do that. I will surely get into great trouble if one day I kill you accidentally." This fantasy addict reminded me of another fantasy addict's perverse performance, who never came unless his hips were burnt with a red-hot iron. This was just one of the freaks in the world of fantasy addicts.

He sat up and ran his fingers through his blond hair, "You will never be able to kill me. If my body is to be killed at all, my soul is immortal…"

I didn't believe in souls after life so I said, "Forget it. I won't argue with you about the existence of souls. You'd better take a shower and go home."

He stood up and went to the bathroom for his shower. I began to tidy the towels on the ground. I collected all the ropes, knife, scissors and vice on the massage table and packed them into his blue backpack. When he had finished dressing, I saw him off at the door. I looked up at the wall clock and found it was already half past ten in the evening. I began my cleaning and cleared all the rubbish away.

As I liked music very much, I always played music at the highest volume on the stereo even when I was doing the cleaning in the working room. The stereo was playing English songs; the one playing now was Smoke Rings by K.D. Lang. I swept the broom in dancing steps, to the beat of the beautiful melody, humming along with the tune from the stereo. Singing and dancing, I wiped the walls of the room and the mirrors on the cabinets until they were gleaming and clean. Then I collected all the towels and sent them to the laundry for washing.

Just then the doorbell rang. I hurried to open the door and found a young man in his early twenties standing there. He was tall with black hair and facial contours similar to a Chinese man but he had a higher nose, with sunken eyes and brown irises. In fact his parents were New Zealanders. He often came to see me. I remembered the first time he came to me, he was only nineteen years old. His eyes were not big but they could surely make you tremble. Every time he narrowed his eyes and ogled at me, I would feel a thrill run down my spine. Actually when I was young, I had two lovers and I didn't feel as excited when they stared at me.

When he entered the house, he fixed his leering eyes on me, "Linda, I haven't seen you for a year. I've just come out of prison."

"How come you were thrown into prison at so young an age?"

"Because I hurt someone badly in a gang fight."

"Young guys are unreasonable," I sighed, "For what reason did you fight them?"

"But I never fight women as I love them."

He came near to kiss my cheeks and lips, "And I love you, too." "Hey. Stop saying 'love'. You seem to forget how old I am."

He used to frequent me and say he loved me. He even proposed to marry me but I refused his proposal. I said it was quite impossible as his mother might be younger than me.

He said the same thing again today as soon as he entered. Brushing his head aside, I said, "Young man, you're too young to know what love is. You may as well find a girlfriend among your peers. There is too big a gap between our ages."

He just wouldn't listen and pulled me hard into his arms, "I prefer older and more mature ladies. My mom was a prostitute. You're just as beautiful as she was."

"You're too young, baby," I said, "You don't really understand many things in life." I led him to the working room. He sat at the edge of the bed but was reluctant to produce the money, "Linda, I came out of prison days ago and haven't found any work. So let me fuck you free of charge, just once?"

"What prostitute would let you fuck for nothing?" I said sneeringly, "You can search Canberra or the world and find no such prostitute."

"I'm messing with you," he smiled.

He fumbled his pocket for a while before he produced some money; two tens and two fives. I put away the money in the kitchen and came back to the working room. He stared at me, his eyes becoming hazy with lust, making me very uneasy. I wasted no time in pushing him down on the bed and began to suck his long cock. I was scared to hear him say, "I love you." For the ten years since I took on this trade, I've lost the ability or intention to experience the true feeling of loving a man. Sometimes I would feel like taking a man in my arms and kissing him lovingly. But a moment later I would be at a loss. Sometimes when a certain man fucked me to orgasm, I would cry out, "I love you!" But after that I would forget him completely. Love and sex were two different things.

The boy lay on the bed, his eyes narrowed, "Linda, suck my cock hard. It itches as if it were on fire."

I sucked hard on his cock and ran my tongue along his long shaft. At last he said, "Linda, fuck my ass!"

With that, he produced a rubber rod about eleven inches long from his pocket, made of eight red rubber balls connected with each other from the smallest to the largest. A rubber ring about one and a half inches wide hung under the largest ball. "What's that?" I wondered.

"This is a fantasy toy I bought from the sex shop," he answered, "It resembles a cock. You can tuck into my asshole and then slide it through my asshole by its pulling the rubber ring."

"I never imagined a fake cock could be made like that I said, "It looks just like my favorite food from my childhood – candied haws on a stick."

"It's most exhilarating to be fucked by a chain of balls sliding in your asshole," he beamed with expectations, "especially when the balls are making some grinding sounds inside you."

"Seems it doesn't fit a condom."

"There's no need for that," he said, "It's my personal item and it's for my use only."

While he lay on the bed on his back, I spread his knees apart and applied a lot of lubricating oil on his asshole before I thrust the "balls on a stick" into his asshole. First the smallest ball. The muscles around his asshole began to contract and with a loud puff, he let out a fart. Then the second and third balls. The fourth ball was quite large and with it he let out another fart. I felt some resistance in pushing in the eighth or the largest ball, so I asked him, "Are you all right?"

"No problem," he said, "Go on!" I went on sliding the ball rod until at last I managed to thrust all eight balls into his asshole. In the whole process he had let out several, stinky farts.

"Linda," he urged, "come on, fuck my ass!"

I had to squat between his thighs, sliding away the fake cock in his asshole and sucking away his real cock in my mouth. Soon he began to groan, "Ah, yes. Ah, yes." Ten minutes later, he tried to change roles, "Linda, let me fuck you!"

I found him a large condom and put it on his cock. He stood up, with the rubber ring at the end of the fake cock dangling outside his asshole. As the fake cock was actually a chain of balls on a stick, it stuck in his asshole without slipping out (unlike the electric cock, which was likely to slip out if a client was fucking me with one in his asshole). He asked me to kneel on the bed and bend over. He came over to thrust his long cock into my cunt, "I fuck you. I love you."

"You can fuck me," I said, "but you can't love me. I have so many lovers. Can I love each and every one of them?"

He pistoned his cock noisily as he pounded his belly against my buttocks violently. Ten minutes or more later, he cried out, "I've come!" I peeled the condom off his cock and pulled the rubber-ball rod out of his asshole before he went to take a shower. I went to another bathroom to wash the stained rubber rod with a brush in the sink and then placed it beside his pile of clothes. When he left, he took two bottles of beer, a large packet of chips and some chocolates with him. All this might account for fifty percent of the thirty dollars he had paid me. What did you think I could do with such a boy?

When I saw off the black-haired boy, it was already eleven o'clock in the evening. I sat down to tot up the day's income. I was glad to find the total income was 670, well above the desired target of 600 dollars. After putting away all the money into the safe, I settled myself in front of the TV set and began to search for my favorite programs. I had hardly warmed the sofa under my backside before the doorbell rang again.

I hurried to answer the door and saw it was an old client of mine for seven or more years. The other day I saw him making a speech on the TV. It was said he was working for the government but I didn't know what particular work he was doing and I didn't ask him for more information because I knew it was no use doing so.

He was in his forties and about five foot ten; neither too thin nor too fat. He looked very stout with thick black hair, a handsome square face, a pair of bright eyes, a straight high nose and a grinning mouth. Today he wore a dark-blue suit and looked very smart. He usually came without any appointment. He just asked me whether I was busy and if I answered yes, he would leave at once.

"You've arrived at the right time," I said when I saw him; "It is only five minutes since I finished serving the last client."

"To arrive early is not as good as to arrive at an opportune time," he was very happy.

"Yes, you've arrived at an opportune time," I said and warmly ushered him into the working room. He took out a fifty-dollar note from his suit pocket and put it on the massage bed. I handed him a towel for him to take a shower. I put away the money and came back with an iced can of VB beer. He had finished bathing and lay down on the massage table. I put the iced beer on the bedside table and asked him, "Just knocked off?"

"I knocked off long ago," he said, "Dined together with some friends. I was just driving by here and dropped in."

"The other day," I said, "I met a young man working for the government and he said that the working hours for Australian government offices are only seven hours and twenty minutes."

"That's true," he said.

"But the working hours for the Chinese government offices are eight hours," I asked, "How come our working hours have odd minutes?"

He explained in detail the formula by which the working hours were calculated but I was left only with a vague notion.

"It was said that the Canberra Congress has passed a new act legalizing gay and lesbian marriage. Is that true?"

"Yes, that's also true." He answered, "But I don't quite know the concrete articles. That's not the thing we are in charge of."

We were chatting while I was massaging his back. Then I turned him over and began to massage his hands, shoulders and head. Finally I began to masturbate him by rubbing and squeezing his cock. While I was doing so, he liked me to put a condom on two fingers of my left hand and tuck them into his asshole to stimulate his sexual desire. He was very quick in coming. I needed only a couple of minutes and he was quiet when he came. He never yelled but thanked me repeatedly. I wiped the sperm off his cock and washed my hands carefully. I then massaged his soles. Ten minutes later, I set out to make him come for a second time by adopting a brand new technique – *hand-mouth aligned method.* I sprawled between his thighs to apply sufficient lubricating oil to his asshole, and pulling a condom on the forefinger and middle finger of my left hand, thrust the two fingers into his asshole. Meanwhile, I held both of his balls in my mouth and sucked them. Then I oiled my right hand and used it to rub his cock in a downward direction (reverse hand masturbation). Thus, my hands were aligned with my mouth. Hence the *hand-mouth aligned method.*

Some clients, when served with oral jobs or masturbation, liked me to thrust one or two of my fingers into their assholes to massage their prostate glands. If a man is lying on his back, your finger can dig upward to find his prostate gland (and if he is on his belly, your finger can dig downward to find the gland). When his cock is about to come, your finger will feel his balls hardening and bulging. At that time, you should be careful not to massage his prostate gland too hard or too gently. If you massage it too hard, his glands and balls will feel pain, but if too gently, you will fail to whet his sexual desire. Meanwhile, you can suck his cock with a moderate pace and grip. Your mouth in coordination with your hands will soon make the man come.

By adopting my new hand-mouth aligned method, I succeeded in making him come in less than five minutes. He was very strong so he could come again within half an hour, which few young men could do now. He got to his feet and went to the bathroom with his towel. He said while heading for the bathroom, "Now that the pressure of a week's hard work has been relieved, I can have a sound sleep tonight."

"Actually," I quickly rejoined," it's not a bad thing for you government officials to have a relaxing hour after work here or in some brothel. Sexual satisfaction is perhaps the best outlet for work pressure."

"Exactly," he echoed, "But there're still many others who regard sex as something very private and avoid discussing it or conceal their true desire."

"As for me," I said, "I now regard sex as something very common, like drinks when you're thirsty or food when you're hungry. Nothing very special."

While I waited for him to shower and get dressed, I packed a plastic bag with beer and a red wine and handed it to him before he said "good evening" and left.

When I came back, I sat on the sofa to watch an English teaching program, "Follow Me." It was not ten minutes before the phone on the desk rang. I picked up the receiver and said hello.

"What hello?" it was a female voice, "Mom's absolutely mad with you!"

It was my sister. I couldn't make head or tail of it, "How come Mom's absolutely mad with me?"

"Yesterday when you hung up the phone, Mom refused to sleep or eat and sat on the bed looking blankly all day. We were waiting for you to call back again but you didn't. Mom's blood pressure has risen to 200mmHg and no drug is effective in lowering it."

"Is that so serious?" I said, "Mom urged me to publish my book as soon as possible so that I could finance your son to study in Holland. I was pressed so hard that I got angry and hung up the phone. I'm not in very easy circumstances so don't press me too hard."

"Who is pressing you hard?" my sister said,"You do what you can to finance He Chen. We will cover the gap in the funds. We can sell our house as a last resort."

"Who wants you to sell the house," I responded quickly, "There is no need for that. Besides, the one million Yuan is to cover He Chen's tuition and fees for five years, not for one year. So give me a year, when my book is sure to have been published."

The tense atmosphere suddenly relaxed. We were sisters after all.

"My book is promising," I said, "It seems I can leave something to this world."

"God has eyes," my sister said,"He can see you have no child."

How could she know I had had twelve abortions? I held back bitter tears and gossiped with her about some other things.

At last my sister said, "Hurry up and call our Mom. She is waiting at home!"

I ended the conversation with my sister and got through to Mom, "M-u-mmy!" I shouted.

"You're not intending to drive me mad?" Mom said on the phone.

"Who's intending to do so?" I asked.

"So it's me that is intending to do so," Mom said in a fit of pique.

"After all, we're mom and daughter," I said, in a reconciliatory tone, "So there's no point in making each other angry." I went on to ask, "Has He Chen called back?"

"Yes, he has," Mom said, "I told him on the phone I had a quarrel with your aunt in Australia."

"What did he say?" I asked anxiously.

"He said, 'It's your business if you have a quarrel between yourselves. In any case, she's my aunt. Whether she's willing to help me now or not, I will take care of her in the future regardless.'"

"What I meant," I said, "was to teach him to be independent by working some part-time job. It will benefit him in the long run."

At last I told Mom, "Don't worry. I will publish my book very soon. It is very promising. Another woman author of J.K. Rowling's stature will come from Australia."

"If you can't be the second," Mom said, "You can be content with being the third."

"No," I said proudly, "I don't want to be the second. I'd like to surpass her."

I at last appeased Mom's anger by quarrelling jokingly.

I had no sooner disconnected Mom's call than the mobile rang, "Is that Miss. Linda speaking?"

"Yes, sir," I answered as politely, "What can I do for you?"

"What services do you offer?" he asked, "And what's the price, please?"

"For nude massage, it's fifty dollars for half an hour and ninety for an hour; for a whole-set service it's seventy for half an hour and one twenty for an hour."

"Can I make an appointment for a whole-set service for one hour?"

"Yes."

"What time?"

"Twelve o'clock at midnight," I said and hung up the mobile.

I settled down to watch TV programs for a while. It suddenly occurred to me that he was a new client so I had to dress up. I took out my favorite rose-colored dress from the wardrobe and put it on. Looking into the mirror, I found my white shoulders were all exposed and my plump breasts half exposed. I turned round to see myself from the back. My bare back looked smooth and glossy and the hem of the dress hardly covered my buttocks. Any man who caught sight of my back would surely thaw before me. All was gorgeous except for one thing – my face, which showed my age however hard I powdered it. Leave it as it was. Those with bad eyes might think I was only in my early thirties. Only after I confessed to him I was forty-eight would he believe it was my real age.

I wish the new client could be near-sighted, I thought when the doorbell rang. Talk of the devil and he would surely appear.

"Coming," I said as I went to open the door. It was a tall man with red curly hair, a high forehead, sunken eyes with a straight, high nose and a square mouth. He looked to be a man of fortitude and confidence. Judging from his sharp appearance, I guessed he might be either a government official or an executive of a large company. He was in his forties and looked extremely smart in his grey suit, white shirt and a plaid tie.

He scrutinized me for a while at the door and said, "You're a charming lady."

He had a discriminating eye and I was sure that the transaction had been secured. I went over and said, "Welcome, sir. I'm Linda. I promise to offer you a first-class service, with everything included."

As he approached me, I also scrutinized him. Wow, what a handsome gentleman and half a head taller than me. He kissed me on the forehead, "No wonder you're so popular on the internet."

I smiled at him, "Oh, you didn't find me through the ads in the paper?" It turned out that I should owe all my popularity to Information Technology. Thanks to the client from Sydney who had posted my advert, I had become a celebrity on the internet.

Pointing to the piano near the French door of the west living room, the man said, "Just as it said on the internet, a brown grand piano standing there."

"Is my photo on the net?" I was wondering, "If the Sydney man comes back next time, I would like him to upload my photos from twenty years ago onto that net so that I will be more popular."

I noticed he was staring at me. To distract his attention from my face, I posed another question, "Where are you from, sir?"

"From Europe."

"There are so many countries in Europe. Which country, to be specific?"

"I'm from France."

"Oh, from France," I asked, "For what reason are you here, business or travel?"

"Neither," he answered briefly, "I've come to attend a meeting." Pleased with my judgment, I guessed his occupation, "You must be a government official and have come to have a meeting with our Premier and his ministers."

He smiled and made no comment. I went on to say, "Two years ago, I attended to a client from England. He pointed at a golden badge clipped to his coat and said he was working for the Queen. He also came to have a meeting and boasted he could call Premier Howard to come here.

'You are kidding,' I said.

'No, no kidding,' he said in earnest, 'I told Mr. Howard that your service was number one in Australia. I hope he will visit you and you can charge him three hundred dollars for an hour. I will call President Bush and recommend your service to him. When he comes, you can charge him 600 dollars, because he earns more than Mr. Howard.' But up to now, none of them have ever showed up."

He was greatly amused by my story and burst into laughter, "Now who else would you like me to call to come?"

I enumerated all the leading politicians in the world, "Bush, Clinton, Obama, Blair, Berlusconi, Sarkozy and the German Chancellor Merkel. Oh no. Merkel is a female."

Chapter Two
Soul's Incarnation and Goddess' Birth

Day One: March 14, 2011

It was between 4:00 and 6:00 pm on March 13, 2011 when I was writing about my French guest.

Toward six o'clock, something incredible happened when I penned the names of several presidents and premiers in my writing. (I have been writing my own accounts for more than nine years every day except when I feel too tired. I have accumulated thirty notebooks of my diary, amounting to several million words but no similar things like that have ever happened.) When I was writing the names of Bush or Clinton, I felt my heart oozing out like running water. It was a totally new feeling, quite different from the inspiration in writing that was often mentioned. My heart was oozing out from the very bottom while my soul was soaring out from somewhere in the depth of my body. That feeling didn't originate by any means from my heart or my brain. My out-oozing heart and out-soaring soul were flowing through separate paths via my right arm through my right hand to the paper under my pen. It suddenly occurred to me that I was going to produce a masterpiece; something unusual and unique whatever it was dealing with. Otherwise how could you explain why my soul should encounter those presidents and premiers? (I used to be a person fostered in an atheist country and had never believed in the existence of any soul.) I had no faith in any religion and never worshipped in any church.

Four years ago, I had a discussion with my landlord James about the existence of the soul. He was a pious Christian and believed in the soul. He said when you died, only your body decayed but your soul soared away. I remember sneering at him, "It's said that humans have existed for thousands of years. If everyone has a soul and when he dies his soul remains, how can you locate so many souls? I'm afraid the world would be overcrowded with all those souls. In my mind, when a person dies he leaves nothing except a dead body just like a dog or a cat. After his death, he ceases to feel anything and doesn't care whether his body is stewed or boiled for food. As for me, I don't think it improper for my body to be used as manure for the garden after I die."

However, I now have a thorough apprehension of the existence of the soul and I can say for sure it is my personal experience instead of an illusion. I can prove, without any shred of doubt, that people are ensouled. At least before they die, people indeed have souls and their souls can be separated from their bodies. I'm now feeling that my soul has been connected with the souls of those presidents and premiers.

I don't know what will happen to my soul and body, respectively - when I die. Maybe my soul will die together with my body. Maybe my soul will be separated from my body and become another entity. I really don't know what will happen until I die. But even if I know the answer at the moment I die, I won't have the time to write it down. God, I'm afraid, won't give me the chance to do so. You simply cannot illustrate such a unique experience as mine as easily as you say, "Hey, come here. I'll show you a beautiful vase." I'm trying to illustrate it in my own language as clearly as I can. I can predict the book I'm writing is going to be a unique masterpiece because my personal life experiences and thoughts are quite different from those of common people as well as those of presidents, queens or first ladies.

Why are there so many men accompanying me every day in my life? This lifestyle has lasted for nearly ten years and I hope it can last forever. Maybe it is God's will to have me tell the world that people do have souls. And I also realize clearly that every person has been created by God to serve a specific purpose to the world. It is not that you can be a president or a billionaire or a gang leader of the mafia simply because you want to but that they are all prearrangements of almighty God.

My heart began to thump wildly in my chest. It suddenly dawned on me that God had made it clear what I was meant for. I went on writing a dozen lines or so when the doorbell rang. I steadied my nerves before I went to open the door. It was an old man with a big head, big ears and big eyes. He was seventy-seven years old then and my patron for more than seven years. I didn't even greet him but ushered him in indifferently.

I led him to the working room but I was not in the mood for work at that time. My brain was still occupied by the process of my soul leaving my body. Had I told this to my friend Lisa (my best friend, who I made the acquaintance of at the airport when I went to China last year), she would have been startled. My mind was a mess when I absentmindedly accepted thirty dollars the old man handed me and put it away in the kitchen. I was wondering how to explain all this to my friends and family. I walked with the old man to the working room like a sleepwalker, thinking all the way about the strange feelings I had just experienced. In the working room, I still couldn't concentrate on my job. I forced myself to hug the old man for a while, found him a medium-sized condom and put it on his cock. I sat on the edge of the bed with my legs apart for him to fuck me and it was less than three minutes before he came. I peeled off the condom from his cock and had him take his shower. I was still indulged in pondering over the incredible things that happened to me just now.

Soon the old man was standing by the bathroom door, rubbing his body with a towel across his back, pulling at each corner of the towel. He said, "I have called you so many times but the line was always engaged and I couldn't get through to either of your mobiles."

I was startled at hearing this and the blood suddenly rushed to my head, "What? You said you couldn't connect to me? My two mobiles were right at hand and no one seemed to be calling at that time."

It suddenly occurred to me that last night, a grey-haired old little man had also come to complain that he couldn't connect to me. I was then busy with writing. I used to receive quite a few calls while writing. Was it God's will to prevent me from being disturbed because the things I was writing recently were extremely important?

To reassure myself, I asked him once again, "What time did you say you couldn't get through to me?"

"Right before I came. Both of your mobiles were engaged." "Thank you for telling me that," I felt excited.

"I've lost my old girl," he said, his eyes becoming bloodshot, "My wife has died."

The tears rolled down his cheeks and my eyes were brimmed with tears, too.

"I'm sorry to hear that," I said, "Just a minute. I'll give back your money."

"For what?" he was somewhat perplexed.

"For nothing," I said, "I just want to give back your money."

I felt God looking at me and saying, "You're doing the right thing."

I ran to the kitchen for the money he had paid me and ran back to the working room. The old man just refused to take the money but I persisted. After a fuss, I finally tucked the money into his coat pocket. There were often times when I refunded money to my clients. If the clients declined to take the money, I would tuck the money into their trouser pockets or coat pockets. Some clients would dodge my refund by covering their pockets with their hands but I always managed to make them accept the money, and then to stop them changing their minds, I would push them along until they had left my house. Today I felt it was also God's will. I pushed the old man out of the toilet with both of my hands.

I took a bottle of mineral water from the kitchen fridge and a packet of chips from the dining table and then pushed the old man to the back door and saw him off there. The old man shed a lot of tears and said, "Linda, I will come back to see you in a few days."

At that time, I was still in a frenetic state of mind. It was most likely people in such situations would badly need a listener but my best friend, Lisa was living in Sydney. Whether or not to tell her about the bizarre things that happened to me? If I told her about it, it would make her worry whether I had gone mad writing. If I didn't, I felt I couldn't contain the excitement inside myself any longer. I was in a dilemma whether to tell her or not but finally I yielded to the temptation to contact her, "Lisa, have you heard of anyone whose heart and soul have both drifted away when writing?"

"Yes," Lisa promptly answered, "And it's when a great masterpiece will appear. There were many such accounts in history when great writers or great artists produced their great masterpieces." Bullshit, I thought, as a writer myself, I knew these accounts only too well.

"But I felt my heart oozing out and my soul soaring out of me when I was writing the names of presidents."

"Linda," she heaved a sigh, "I haven't heard of any experience like yours, neither have I read of such cases. Be sure to control your state of mind, otherwise you may become schizophrenic." Sure enough, my best friend deemed my mind to be deranged.

"But my mind isn't deranged," I argued.

"Well, which presidents were you writing about?" she asked. "I was writing about President Bush, President Clinton, Prime Minister Blair, the Italian Premier, the French President and the German Chancellor. The German Chancellor is a lady." "Maybe you daydream about them visiting you so often in your mind that your imagination is running away with you," Lisa was playing psychiatrist at the other end of the line.

Oh, yes? I hesitated and before I could say anything, she began to advise me, "Linda, be sure to take enough rest. Don't burn the candle at both ends by working and writing at once. You'd better not exceed the limit of five thousand words a day in your writing."

Actually no one had ever asked me to write like crazy. I was only impelled by an inner urge to write. My brain was stocked with such a large repertoire of anecdotes and jokes that it would surely burst if its content wasn't released in time. An old English gentleman came to encourage me this afternoon, "Linda, write as much as you can and keep the manuscript in your safe. It is your main asset. For some writers, their mental resources were quickly exhausted and they could never write anything again. The potential productivity varies from writer to writer. Some can write several millions of words all their lives while some others dozens of millions of words." I said to the old man, "I can write dozens of thousands of words a day but I am occupied by serving these cocks of yours."

Just then the doorbell rang and I had no time to explain to Lisa, "I'll have to hang up. My client has arrived." Actually it was a rash client who hadn't made any appointment in advance.

I disconnected the call and opened the door. A man younger than me was standing before me. He was tall and thin, with long black hair, brown skin, a long face, a high pointed nose and thick lips. He was somewhat afflicted with a stammer. He was from the Middle East and might have lived in Australia for a dozen years or more. He was now living in Sydney and would come to see me every time he came to Canberra on business. His friend recommended me to him.

I led him in as I reprimanded him, "You didn't call me in advance again, did you?"

"I, I ha -- haven't got your phone number."

He stammered out his "haven't"and trailed it lingeringly with difficulty, blinking his eyes rapidly as he spoke. I stood beside him and was surprised to find I was half a head shorter than him. At that time my soul was wandering outside of my body so my state of mind was unstable. I led him into the working room and charged him the service fee. Every time he came, he didn't pay willingly unless you told him to.

"Pay first."

He searched his wallet for quite a while before he produced a fifty-dollar note, "I have come so many times and ha -- haven't had even once the privilege of a free service," he stammered out his grievance.

"Tut, tut. Even my oldest client of over nine years hasn't. No money, no honey."

After I handed him a towel and had him take his shower, I put away the money in the drawer in the kitchen and went back to the working room. I endeavored to calm myself down but could hardly hold back my tears. Regardless, I had to go on with my business. No sooner had he thrust his cock into my cunt than the doorbell rang. My next client came by appointment. He reluctantly withdrew from me and stammered, "Te --- tell him to come in an hour."

I hurried to open the door, cursing back, "Shit! How can you have the cheek to blame a client for coming at the appointed time? Besides, you can't expect to pay half an hour's fee for an hour's service, can you?"

I opened the door to find it was an Indonesian client, who had been to my place three days before. He looked like a southerner from China, with dark-brown skin, black hair, black eyes, a little nose, trim teeth and thick lips. He looked old for his age and though I looked younger than him, I guessed he was around my age. He stood a little taller than me. Judging by his stocky build and kind face, I figured he must have been a good-tempered, amiable person.

Last time he stayed for an hour, but however hard I tried, I still couldn't make him come. My vain efforts lasted forty- five minutes and he explained it was just because he was not familiar with me yet. In the remaining fifteen minutes, he made me totally satisfied by licking my bud (my clitoris). It was a role reversal with that Dwarf Wu. (In that case, I spent forty- five minutes making him come while he spent fifteen minutes making me come. So I think Dwarf Wu's money was well worth it.) When the Indonesian man left, he paid me ninety dollars but I thought my service was not worth that much so I insisted on refunding him twenty dollars. I deemed seventy dollars was more than enough. I took a bottle of white wine from the fridge for him as a gift and yet I still felt guilty for a long time after he left. I felt I owed him something.

Today he came once more and I got excited at the sight of him. I took him by the hand and led him to the waiting room. I tried my best to hold back the tears. Having had him wait, I went back to the working room, bent over and got ready for the Middle-Eastern man to enter my cunt from behind. At that time I was not in the mood to enjoy or savor the pleasure of lovemaking. My brain was still swimming in a swirl of souls. After the Middle-Eastern man came, I massaged him for a dozen minutes or so and sent him away by promising to give him several cans of beer. Strangely enough, he was particularly intuitive not to accept the gifts that time, or ask for this or that as he usually did. He said politely, "You may as well leave them for other clients."

Despite his protests, I packed him six cans of beer and saw him off. As soon as I turned back, I burst out crying. Tears kept rolling down my cheeks but I had to wipe them off my face because business must continue. I led the Indonesian man into the working room. He couldn't wait to say he had had a shower and we threw ourselves onto the bed together. I lay on his left side and buried my face in his chest. Yet to my dismay, the tears couldn't help welling out of my eyes. He obviously noticed my perverse behavior and was somewhat annoyed. Actually I was then preoccupied by a question: How come I had been intended by God to be a president but finally ended up becoming a prostitute? I was reduced by this great grievance to uncontrolled weeping. The Indonesian man was perplexed and wondered whether I was unhappy to be with him, "If you're unhappy, I can leave."

I stopped crying at once, "Please don't leave. I'm unhappy just because the old gentleman before you said he had lost his wife. I'm feeling sorry for him. You see, I'm a soft-hearted sympathetic woman." But as a matter of fact, I was lamenting my own fate of missing the chance to be a president instead of caring for that old gentleman.

I braced myself up and crawled between his legs. I took up his little cock, held it in my mouth and began to suck it. He acted cooperatively so it was less than a quarter of an hour before he came. Then he kindly refused my offer to massage his back and went to the bathroom to wash up and get dressed. I charged him fifty dollars and gave him a bottle of red wine as a gift.

I was seeing off the Indonesian man when the gap-filler Brazilian old boy came. No sooner had he walked across the threshold than he tucked a fifty-dollar note between my white breasts under the neck of my short, tight, blue-and-white striped dress. He might have found a job recently. He looked at the golden note between my soft breasts and said with a smile, "Look, how beautiful you are." Fortunately, I had become more emotionally stable by then. Maybe my repressed emotions had been released through crying as I became much more relaxed. My face lit up when I saw the money and I whirled around on the floor in excitement. The Brazilian old boy kept saying, "Beautiful, beautiful. Very beautiful." I put the money away in the kitchen drawer and gave fifteen dollars' change to the Brazilian old boy.

We went to the working room and there I perfunctorily finished my oral work on him. After that, I lay on my back on the bed and tucked a pillow under my buttocks with my legs spread apart for him to lick my cunt. While he was working away between my thighs, I was beyond myself with my soaring soul. It turned out that people did have souls and it feels really pleasing and placid to see your own soul swimming in your body. While he was struggling to tuck his limp cock into my cunt, the Brazilian old boy complained, "Your bulging belly is preventing me from getting to your pussy."

"What?" I got furious, "Complaining about my belly? You can't get to my pussy because you have a little cock."

The old Brazilian boy was just a thoughtless and outspoken person whose bark was worse than his bite. He was ready to make whatever comments that came to his mind without considering others' feelings. Take me for example. I was becoming fatter so I was very sensitive about any mention of my weight, but every time he came to visit me, he was always complaining about either the looseness of my cunt or the size of my belly. Though I knew he didn't really mean any ill intent, no one would be pleased by such remarks.

No wonder the old Brazilian boy was always out of a job. How could he please his employer with his bitter words and the way he spoke them? Even if he wanted to flatter his employer, what he said would invariably sound offensive and lead to him being sacked.

There are quite a few people in the world who don't know the art of communicating. Though they usually bear no malice toward others, they actually hurt everyone with their indiscriminate, thoughtless, albeit good-willed remarks.

Seeing off the Brazilian old boy, I felt tired out, both physically and mentally as if this day's work had exhausted all my strength and vigor. The only thing I wanted to do then was lie down on the bed to have a rest. I had no intention of eating anything. I lay on the bed in my own bedroom, pondering over all the weird things that had happened to me that day.

Last night, I stayed up until three o'clock in the early morning writing my story. I got up at nine thirty this morning and six hours of sleep was normally more than sufficient for me. I sometimes wrote late until six o'clock the next morning, then slept for three hours on the bed and got up at nine completely refreshed. But oddly enough, I awoke this morning feeling extremely feeble, as if I had got seriously ill and had a heavy weight on my mind. I felt sick but could not vomit. At the same time, I had no appetite to eat or drink. The only thing I wished to do was to write. A great urge to write suddenly swept through my body and made me sweat profusely. Even when serving clients, my hair was drenched in sweat. I served them in succession and had no time to sit down to write even a single word. The morning passed by and I had served, in a state of numbness, seven or eight clients altogether. I had nothing but a few sips of water. The Brazilian old boy was complaining about my round belly, but I found I had become noticeably thinner within a single day. I used to be quite plump before. It was not until four in the afternoon that no more clients came in and I suddenly felt extremely relaxed. I exhaled greatly in relief: I could continue to write my story at last. I was writing about the red-haired official working for the French government and mentioned the names of some presidents when the weirdest thing happened…

Having finished the paragraph, I felt much more comfortable as if a great weight had lifted from my mind. Then the old man whose wife died came without a phone appointment…

Lying on the bed, I was lost in contemplation at how my soul should rendezvous with those presidents and premiers and why I failed to be a president since God intended me to be one. At last I couldn't help laughing at myself. It dawned on me that God had not appointed me as a president; he just ranked me as the same level of a president. He sent me to be a prostitute so as to let me chronicle a profession looked down upon for generations. I am the number-one prostitute in the world today. I am to be the queen of queens among prostitutes and I am to be in charge of all cocks, big or small, all over the world…

Day Two: March 16, 2011

It was really a heart-stirring moment. I was greatly shocked and shivering with cold. I was massaging a sixty-five-year- old fat man after finishing oral work when a vision came to me: "I am Goddess incarnate. I am superior to anyone in the world. I will serve as the re-maker of humankind." To be honest, I was trembling all over with fear the minute I wrote this line. A sudden fear gripped me that that weird feeling would strike me once more. If that were the case, I was afraid I would lose control over myself. These three oracular sentences slowly sank in my mind, making me burn and burst. I felt as if an imminent destructive catastrophe would happen to this world. I felt the house as well as myself shaking violently. I was so panicked that I hastened the old man to get up and hurriedly sent him away via the back door before I phoned Lisa. I was then shivering with cold like a malaria patient.

When her mobile phone was connected at last, Lisa said she was giving lessons in her classroom but I insisted, "No, I'd like to talk to you right now."

It seemed that she left her classroom with her mobile phone. I told her, "Lisa, what has become of me? It seems I was not writing my book. How come I should write down lines such as I was Goddess incarnate? …" I was interrupted abruptly before I finished my sentence, "Linda, stop writing at once. You know in history many great writers and artists, say Van Gogh the famous painter, suffered from mild to severe schizophrenia. Are you familiar with the Chinese writer Lu Yao, the author of the novel "Life"? He died from overwork in writing. Don't burn the candle at both ends. I have read your work and I appreciated it very much. You really have a gift at writing. It must have been the genes passed on to you by your parents who worked hard.

So why are you in such a hurry to finish a great task in one stroke? You can go on to write for many more years. Now lock all the manuscripts in your safe and come to Sydney for a period of relaxation. By doing so, you can divert your attention from writing for the time being and try to refresh your mind. Be sure to stop writing and lock away all the written things and hide the key out of your reach, otherwise you will easily slide back to the old habit of writing too soon."

What she had said enlightened me immediately and calmed me down a lot. I had to admit that my mind might have entered a delusional state on account of writing overtime. In order to improve my gloomy mood, I may as well give up writing for the time being. I might go to the supermarket for a change so I took up my handbag and purse, locked up the door and headed for Woden Shopping Mall. However, I lost my usual merriment and was somehow crestfallen and in low spirits on my way to the shopping mall.

I was by nature an open-minded and cheerful woman rather than a sorrowful and melancholy woman. But today I was burdened with great worries and I couldn't help weeping over the fates of people, young or old, coming or going in the mall. They looked so good and kind and I loved them all, no matter what colors their skins were or what their nationalities were. I was preoccupied with a thought that I was Goddess incarnate that looked down from the high sky at ordinary people. Poor people! A great catastrophe was imminent and you were all ignorant of its coming. I could foresee its coming but was not sure about the exact time. I became so frightened. I was afraid that by the time I told you all about it, it would be too late.

When I was in Coles supermarket, I was not in the mood to do any shopping. I aimlessly took dozens of bags of chips for my teenage clients. I went up to the checkout counter and got ready to hand over the card to be swiped. The sight of the young clerk made me weep again. The young clerk looked at me perplexedly as I wiped away the tears from my cheeks, and asked if he could help me. I forced a smile and shook my head.

I then came to the Japanese fast-food counter and tears again rolled down my face when I saw the young salesgirl behind the counter. The girl raised her eyes indifferently. I bought three boxes of vegetables and stuffed pancakes. I had bought this Japanese-style food several times, the names of which I still hadn't remembered until now. I went on to buy five boxes of shredded kelp and twenty boxes of sweet and sour ginger. (The boxes were very small, in typical Japanese delicate packages.) I hadn't fed myself well for a couple of days on end and I had never felt so weak in the ten years since I became a prostitute. I used to be as strong as a cow before this incident. When I called a taxi to carry the boxes of beer home, I would unload two boxes of forty-eight cans at a time and the taxi drivers would praise me in admiration, "Young lady, you're as strong as you're young." As a matter of fact, I might be quite older than most of them.

But this time I was really not in the mood to buy any beers for my clients. I pushed the trolley to the front gate of Woden Mall and called for a taxi. The taxi driver helped me transfer the goods from the trolley into the car and started the taxi to go to my house.

We arrived at home at around 12:00 pm, March 16, 2011. I gave the driver fifteen dollars together with a blue packet of chips and sent him about his business. After I carried all the items to the French door, I unlocked the front door and entered the house. I then opened the glass door and the security door before I carried all the shopping into the house.

I closed the door behind me yet still couldn't set my mind to rest. I was wondering whether there was indeed a Jesus two thousand years ago, and more important, whether there was to appear a Goddess two thousand years later. But I was not Goddess, was I? Yes, I was Goddess incarnate. Goddess's soul was infused with me. I was absolutely not an ordinary woman. I WAS Goddess reincarnated.

At that time, I was so emotionally unstable that I began to burst out crying: "Oh my God! Why are you delegating this formidable task to me? It's too much for me. Who should I turn to for help and advice? Who can understand me now?" I kept wailing until I gasped convulsively as if I were bereft of my parents at once. I had an ominous presentiment that we could no longer continue living on this Earth and it was my bounden duty to carry you to a very remote place. I wept sadly for half an hour. My neighbors must have been wondering how merry Linda, who was all smiles every day, should be crying so sadly without end. Linda must have been quarrelling or fighting with her client. They must have been hesitating whether they should intervene between the quarrelling parties as the dispute was between a prostitute and her client instead of between a man and his wife. Hey, stop imagination, I told myself. I'd better phone Lisa first and confide in her about what was on my mind. I suppressed my sadness and wiped off my tears, "Lisa, I'm telling you I am not an ordinary mortal. I am Goddess incarnate."

"Linda," Lisa said over the phone, "Don't frighten me. What you said is making me have goosebumps all over. What on earth are you saying? Who has been infused with you?"

"Goddess. Goddess's soul," I said most earnestly, "Listen, Lisa, 'I am Goddess incarnate; I am greater than anyone in the world; I am the re-maker of humankind.' Does it sound like my usual wording and intonation? Do I have the guts and confidence to say so? Goddess's soul must have infused with me."

"You know," I went on to say, "It reminds me of another thing. Mrs. Huang, my typist from Guangdong, China once complained to me that when typing my manuscript, she found I often misused characters in Chinese proverbs, sometimes all four characters were incorrectly written. If I were not Goddess incarnate, how could I use such proverbs I had never come across so accurately? I hadn't learned their meanings in school nor had I learned how to use them." But the more I said the more confusing it sounded to Lisa.

"Linda," she seemed at her wits' end on how to advise me, "Even if you're a Saint instead of a mortal, you should be modest. The great statesman as Chairman Mao always regarded himself as an average member of the public."

"If anything happens to me," I said, "be sure to inform the Australian government of my work." Would Lisa think of my words as my last will and testament? Sure enough, she became alert and said, "Linda, take care of yourself. Don't take it too hard whatever difficulty you meet with."

I thought she must have been worried about my situation and she was taking precautions against my possible follies. As a matter of fact, I was worrying about the mission God had delegated me. What if I was retrieved by Him because I failed to finish His mission? Putting down the receiver, I felt I was the very Goddess with a halo radiating over my head. Even when I was lying under my customer, I couldn't help playing with some strange ideas like "How dare you fuck a Goddess?" or "You are sure to be punished for your lust!"

I suddenly felt exhausted and a little dizzy. My friend told me, "You shouldn't write more than five thousand words a day otherwise you will be tired out and what's worse, you are likely to be immersed in your own story until you finally can't get out. You may be driven mad by it." However, my intuition told me I was not going mad. If I could be spared the hard labor of serving so many cocks a day, I could turn out 10,000 words or so. But these days whatever I wrote, I felt extremely worn out; my energy draining away and my soul wearing out. I felt desperately tired both physically and mentally, as if my entire skeleton had fallen apart.

I obviously knew I was no Goddess nor was I a saint. I was but an ordinary mortal with ordinary flesh and blood. Was it true that there was indeed a God in the world? In the past I didn't believe in any god and I would always get into arguments with anyone who mentioned the existence of God. Yet from the very afternoon of March 14, 2011 when my soul and heart experienced a real separation from my body and something tangibly flowed through the veins in my arms, I began to believe 200 percent that people did have souls, at least while they were alive and that souls didn't always combine with bodies but they could, very occasionally, be separated from bodies.

Human beings are different from animals in that they have souls. Souls are by no means illusions or a product of the subconscious but are concrete streams of consciousness you can conceive distinctively. I always questioned whether there were certain extraordinary people who were different from ordinary people and could sense a different third dimension or even a fourth dimension that others couldn't? Or rather, they could sense the World of *Xuanmiao (mystery)*, a philosophical term sometimes referred to in Chinese Culture?

If I record all these things and write them down, will any of my readers laugh at me as a mad woman? Actually I have been asking myself, "Is there anything wrong with your brain?" In case there is, it is predestined and no one can do anything about it. Forget it and go on writing, following your own feelings. In case I have gone mad and died, I must get ready to be picked up and sent to the morgue the next day. Anyway, I came into the world in my birthday suit and I will bring nothing with me when I am retrieved by God.

What worries me most is if there is indeed a God and He has chosen me to be the messenger to inform humans of a grave warning concerning their life and death but I fail this mission, I will be the chief culprit for all humankind. I shuddered at the mere thought of the aftermath and felt chilled to the marrow.

I didn't want to eat anything these days and looked wan and listless. But I had never had such feelings before when I was writing. I had been dedicated to writing for more than nine years and had written down many things. Maybe God was moved by my passionate devotion to writing and knew I was a woman of perseverance and fortitude so He chose me for the mission to send a message to people on Earth. It turned out that God worried that he had chosen some writers who could not hold on to the end and didn't know the true purpose of what they were writing about.

From my girlhood, I was a thoughtful girl and a diligent student, who always ranked first in my class from year one to year twelve. I even taught myself some parts of the courses that my teacher hadn't yet touched. By reading the examples in the text books in subjects of Chinese and Mathematics, I finished all the exercises by myself correctly, without making a single mistake. As I stood up in academic performance, I was promoted from year three directly to year five so I spent one year less than other pupils finishing six years of primary school. In my middle and high school years, I was always ranked first in academic achievements in the class. Though I had not been specially trained for literature, I knew I was gifted in writing and had a ready and facile pen. But how my arduous writing should lead to these weird things was beyond my ken. I found I was not writing my autobiography anymore. Instead, I was releasing some unforeseeable prediction; some ominous and very urgent warning that must be delivered within the shortest possible time.

Every day I had an insatiable and uncontrollable desire to write and a holy sense of mission impelled me to hurry before it was too late. But I was also aware that if God would like me to complete the mission, he was sure to allow me sufficient time to find someone who could understand me. If I were to preach my mission to ordinary folks they would deem I must have gone mad because my preaching was beyond their full understanding. I had to meditate over the significance of my mission and why it should have fallen to me.

I was trying to straighten my confused thinking. I didn't intend to have gone mad neither did I intend to have gone idiotic. If it was a stage of mania a devoted writer had to experience; a normal abnormality, I could very well take it as it was and take a rest by halting the writing for a while, getting away for some relaxation or going back to China to see my Mom…

I couldn't help but burst out wailing and I was crying very hard as if I were heartbroken. I strongly felt my heart constrict. What had become of me? I was so excited that the words I was now writing became almost illegible. I tried my best to control my emotions and go on writing…

My writing hand began to shake and go numb and I kept asking myself, "Are you really ill, or insane?"

If I was really insane, how come I didn't overcharge or undercharge my clients; how come I didn't beg my neighbors for food and how come I kept my business as usual? Obviously I was not insane. Only my recent behaviors deviated a little from normal or at most my emotions seemed to go beyond control.

I was frightened out of my wits by the weird feeling I had at ten fifteen this morning and now I was really scared. I could hardly control my emotions. If not for a close friend I could confide in, I would have broken down! Fortunately, I got through to Lisa in time and her soothing words finally calmed me down.

Later, I pressed my hand on my heart and asked myself, "Have you gone too far in your writing?" The answer was negative. "I am Goddess incarnate; I am greater than anyone in the world; I am the re-maker of humankind." These three sentences were not the product of my illusion but a solid truth coming naturally to my mind. As the meaning of them sank in, I was greatly shocked and couldn't help shuddering with cold. I had to call Lisa for help, for I couldn't extricate myself from the obsession of the statement.

I was still terribly frightened at the mere thought of that shocking moment.

I was too exhausted to stay awake. But I just couldn't go to sleep lying on the bed. My brain was filled with rotating pictures of rows of houses collapsing, huge trees being uprooted, mountains of mud avalanching, black filthy torrents gushing from the Earth's crust crevices… I was startled out of my prophetic imagination and jumped to my feet. I had to write it out. I was obliged to write it out. I must write it out immediately! It was imperative for my readers to see what would become of their world before it was too late. Gripped by this fear, I sat by the desk to resume my writing. The grotesque and horrible pictures in my mind reminded me at once of the great earthquake, tsunami and radioactive leakage that happened recently along the Japanese eastern coast…

I didn't have the habit of watching news reports and besides, my book had come to its home stretch so I had less time to watch the news regularly. I just caught some casual glimpses of news programs when I was near the TV set. So I began to wonder whether the prophetic imagination of the catastrophe in my mind might be visual persistence caused by the continuous disaster reports on the TV.

It reminded me of my two customers yesterday. An Australian guy who was a few years my junior came around at ten in the evening. He had a slender, five-foot-ten physique and a head of curly black hair with an oval-shaped face. His forehead was high and he had big eyes. His nose bridge was tall and he had a nicely-shaped mouth. He looked dashing in a green, army uniform. He is the boss of a private company and has a couple of guys working under him. He had been my old customer for nine years. I remembered when I felt terribly lonely five or six years ago after I had broken up with one of my clients, I asked him, "Can you be my boyfriend? You are allowed to come to my place and I will not charge you a single cent. If you have the time, we could even go to the movies or have dinners." He replied, "I still keep in contact with my ex-wife whom I have divorced not long ago. I'm afraid that I would hurt you should we get together during this period of time." I could see that he was a man of responsibility. I had never brought this matter up since but he remained one of my favorites.

We reached my working room while we chatted. He asked me, "How much is it for one and a half hours?"

I replied, "I will give you a special price of a hundred and twenty dollars."

He took out two fifty-dollar notes and one twenty-dollar note from his wallet and passed them to me. I chatted with him while I took the towels out from the wardrobe. When we talked about the Japanese tsunami, I asked him,"Have you heard of the speculation that the world is going to end in 2012?"

"Yes," he answered, "Many people are talking about it. It's known to almost everybody across the world."

"You see," he cleared his throat and went on to say, "There are only too many people on this planet. Every possible place on the earth is populated. Yet we can't modulate our population by means of wars as we did in ancient times. God has to do it in His own way."

"These days,"I said,"I am haunted by an ominous premonition of doom." My English was not good enough to discuss the subject further and express my real feelings fluently.

At this point in time, he had stripped off all his clothes and walked into the bathroom with a towel in his hand. As I was about to put the money in the kitchen drawer, I realized that I was holding one fifty-dollar and one twenty-dollar note instead of two fifty-dollar notes. It was odd because I saw him giving me two fifty notes, where did the other fifty-dollar note go? I pondered really hard on that and had searched every inch of the carpeted room. Questions like "Did I drop the money when I handed him the towel?" or "Did he only give me one fifty-dollar note instead of two?" kept lingering in my mind. I mumbled as I searched again but to my dismay, I could not locate the lost note. I stood outside the bathroom and asked, "Honey, did you give me the right amount just now? How is it that I only have one fifty-dollar note?" I looked at the two notes closely and double checked them. As he lathered himself, he replied, "I must have paid you less. I will give you another fifty dollars when I finish showering." After washing himself, he walked out of the bathroom, wiping his body with a towel. He walked toward the bed and took out his wallet from his shirt. He passed me a fifty-dollar note and I said apologetically, "I'm sorry." He replied, "Don't worry; perhaps I'm the one who is supposed to be sorry because I gave you less."

I put away the money into the kitchen drawer and took a bottle of mineral water from the fridge before I came back to the working room. He had already lain on the towel-covered bed. I placed the mineral water on the bedside table for him. He had a slender physique and even though he didn't have a buff body like an athlete, his muscles were lean and he had a round and perky ass that was very sexy. I rode his ass to give him a back massage and after a few minutes, he arched his ass upward. I proceeded to lick his asshole. He had waxed his asshole before visiting me and the surrounding skin of his asshole was not pigmented. His asshole was clean and round, and looked very sexy to me.

Sitting at the end of the bed, I pulled his two buttocks apart and started to lick his asshole deep inside. I was not afraid to lick inside his asshole because I knew that he had washed his asshole clean each time. I licked his asshole deeper and deeper and he groaned, "Ahhh, yeah, ohhhh, yessss." Each moan and groan he made was heartfelt and to be sure he was really comfortable, I asked him, "Honey, is it good for you when I lick your asshole?" He replied, "Of course! It's extremely good! Other than my wife, I've only had a few other lovers, Linda. None of them have ever satisfied me the way you do, and they don't ever lick my asshole." I said, "Women don't necessarily lick any man's asshole. I lick your asshole because I have a special affection for you. I feel like giving my old lover a good ass lick."

I had licked his asshole for a long time and he let out many heartfelt moans and groans. I had him turn over and lay on his back while I lied in between his legs, picked up his dick and started to suck on it. His dick was also very sexy and it was the perfect size; like an aerosol can of air freshener. The shaft was long and straight while its head was round and smooth. I sucked on his dick like a child sucks its mother's nipple for milk and I licked the head of his cock from time to time with my tongue tip.

I continued licking the division between both his balls under his shaft. I used all the methods for blowjobs; suck, lick, sweep, and blow. He was under my mercy. His dick belonged to those dicks that took a long time to ejaculate and the whole process went on for about twenty minutes before the end of his cock turned really red. I looked at his cock and said, "Oh, poor thing. It's so red." He smiled "Stop licking my cock. It will drop off if you lick it any longer. Come on, let me fuck you!"

I took out a large-sized condom from the bedside cabinet for him. I pulled him up and said, "Don't be lazy! Come and do some work!" After which, I lay on my back and he climbed on top of me. He used his legs to separate both my thighs and forcefully thrust his cock into me. I felt a sudden surge of pain down there and I involuntary shouted, "Slow down, honey!" I knew that I needed time to get used to such big cock.

He heard me cry painfully and said, "Am I too rough with you?" I said, "Your cock is too big!" He wrapped both of his hands around my waist and hugged me before he penetrated deeper into my cunt with rhythmic moves. "Let me fuck you, Linda. Fuck, your vagina is really tight. My cock feels really warm in you. Fuck! Do you feel good with me inside you?" Shaking my head and narrowing my eyes, I groaned seductively, "Oh--- I'm coming. Fuck me harder, Honey." He continued to penetrate deeper into me and I could hear his tummy pounding against my belly. Ten minutes or so later, his breathing got faster and faster and the rhythm of his thrusts got faster, too. He let out a few moans and yelled, "Fuck Linda Fuck!"

At this point in time, the thrusting suddenly stopped and I could feel his cock jerking five or six times inside me. He lay on me and said breathlessly, "That is the ultimate release! I feel so relaxed right now that I can't even feel my limbs." He rolled off me and lay on his back. I got up and used a tissue to remove the condom from him and said, "You have ejaculated so much! It's almost reached the brim of the condom!" He replied, "I haven't had sex for two weeks!" I threw the used condom into the bin and used a tissue to wipe the sperm residue off his cock. I cleaned my hands and went back to massage both of his legs. I asked him, "Do you believe in God?" He replied, "Yes I do, what about you?" I said, "I had never believed in the existence of God until something weird happened recently. But I still have my doubts about God." Just then the doorbell rang and I got out of bed with only a skirt on to answer the door.

I opened the door and in walked an Australian guy around fifty. He was a blue-eyed blond, with a small head and a small face; a sharp nose with thick lips. He was also one of my old customers for almost a decade. He was a drunkard and you could rarely find him sober and walk steadily when he was here. It was nothing unusual this time and he could not walk in a straight line when he came in. I couldn't help complaining, "Why are you always coming without making an appointment?" Instead of answering my question, he approached me and raised his own question, "Are you busy now?"

"When did you notice I was not busy?" I retorted while directing him into the waiting room. He paced into the waiting room impatiently and roared, "You make him leave earlier! Don't keep me waiting for too long!"

"You always arrive at the perfect time," I said scornfully.

I went back to the working room and told the good-looking Australian guy lying on the bed, "It has been an hour since you arrived. I will refund you thirty dollars because I have another customer waiting in the next room." He replied, "Sure!" and he got up for a shower. I picked up the bottle of mineral water from the bedside cabinet and walked to the dining room to grab six bottles of low-alcohol Cascade beer and placed them all into a bag. The good-looking Australian guy had already walked out of the working room, properly dressed by that time. Then I passed the bag of beers to him. He took a packet of chips from the table and I sent him to the door. He smiled and said, "May you be prosperous!" before he left. I replied, "May your businesses thrive!" before I closed the door.

I walked into the waiting room and saw the drunkard sitting on the swivel chair. He had pulled his pants below his knees and held his cock in his hand as he commanded, "Come on and lick my cock quick!" He took me by my arms and pushed my head down to his cock. I resisted and said, "You've got to pay me first before I can start serving you." He retorted, "You have to lick my cock first before I can pay you!" I flung his hands away and said, "No, you've got to pay me first." Then he had to give in and took out two fifty-dollar notes before he handed them to me and said, "This will do right? So come on and lick my cock now." I replied to him, "Go to the room over there and clean your cock first before asking me to do a blowjob on you! I will go and get you your ten dollars' change." I turned and headed to the kitchen drawer to get his change while he carried his pants and walked toward the working room.

After I went back to the working room with the ten dollars' change, the drunkard had placed a fifty-dollar note beside his wallet on the bedside table and said, "I found a fifty-dollar note between the sound box and the chair." It suddenly dawned on me that I had dropped the note while talking attentively with the good-looking Australian. I was so elated that I ran toward the drunkard and planted a kiss on his cheek. I said to him, "You are such an honest person! I love you!" Even though he was always drunk and we did quarrel a lot over alcohol, I was very moved when I found he behaved with such nobleness. It seemed that an alcohol addict was not necessarily a person without integrity. "Hey! Quick, help me check who called me tonight?" I was a technology idiot. I not only didn't know how to work a computer, but I couldn't use a cell phone either. I couldn't even find a missed call sometimes. He took my phone and pressed a few buttons and the numbers showed up. I saw the number ending with a '9' immediately and dialed the number. The call connected and I said, "This is Linda speaking. I am truly sorry, you haven't paid me less. A customer accidentally found the missing fifty-dollar note just now. I was too engrossed in chatting with you and dropped it behind the sound box. Please come back and get your fifty-dollar note."The good-looking Australian replied, "I'm reaching home now. Please keep that for next time." I apologized repeatedly and he just said, "It's okay!"

After I ended the call, I couldn't help wondering what would have happened if the drunkard had pocketed the fifty dollars for himself. Should the good-looking Australian realize that he was indeed short of the fifty-dollar note when he reached home, what would he think of me? (I tend to believe that everyone should know approximately how much money they had in their wallet, at least most people do.)

Looking at the honest drunkard before me and thinking of the big-hearted, good-looking Australian, I realized that I loved my customers all the more! All these years had passed and all my customers had become good friends who were worthy of my trust. And we were brothers and a sister beyond any tricks or calculations…

I had licked the drunkard's cock for an hour and we talked about such topics as God, the tsunami in Japan, mishaps that would happen on Earth and the world's destruction in 2012…

Westerners might not understand me due to the language barrier, but a normal Chinese person would think that I am mad if I were to let them know all of my thoughts and emotions. Yet I am more sober, and saner than many other people.

If there was indeed a God, this was His Providence. If I were mad, I could be sent to an insane asylum and be left there alone. From my girlhood I was a dauntless person in nature and never afraid of death. It's imperative for me to inform the Australian government of the impending danger. I must find the best translator in Australia to put my writing into English as soon as possible. I didn't want to review my written material lest a seemingly minor revision should lead to a possible distortion. My writing was holy providence instead of my personal opinion.

I was lost in writing when I was brought back to reality with a start by the doorbell. The client was a lanky man and had a horse face, little eyes, a little nose and a little mouth; his blond hair was tied with a rubber band into a ponytail. He wore a dark-blue denim uniform. He had been a client of mine for nine years; the boss of a construction company. Recently, he had undergone an operation on his prostate and his cock couldn't erect any longer. While I was sucking his cock, I felt a warm, salty stream in my mouth. I spat out his cock and found a trickle of urine dripping from the opening of his cock tip. Another consequence of the prostate operation – not only could his cock no longer erect, but he could not control his urine either. I rushed to the bathroom to gargle my mouth and came back to clean his cock with a small towel… Because I was haunted by visions of God, souls or Goddess, I served him for a mere ten minutes or so before I sent him away.

I was still shuddering at the visions from last night: the avalanching mud, gushing filthy water, collapsing houses, fallen trees strewn on the ground… I had written my "will" and intended it for the Australian government. I was writing "My writing was the holy providence instead of my personal opinion," when I was awakened by a call from my former landlord James, "Hello, boss. Are you busy?"

A new client came before I was retrieved by God, I thought. Well, even Goddess had to earn a living. No one would know I was Goddess and offer me a free lunch. I calmed down and said, "Come along."

It was less than five minutes before the doorbell rang, "Dingdong, dingdong." The doorbell sounded different today, more pleasing to the ear than before. I went to answer the door.

James, my former landlord, was wearing an expensive looking, light-grey T-shirt, a pair of dark-grey linen trousers and a pair of black Italian leather shoes. His grizzled moustache and shining round eyes showed he was a somewhat shrewd and humorous man.

"You're not busy, are you?" he asked, "I have rarely seen you at leisure like this."

"I'm busy writing my will," I said in all earnest.

"Will?" he was astonished, "What do you mean by will, since you have no children? How much do you intend to leave me?"

"You still want more money even though you already have so much?" I sneered at him, "It's so greedy of you. I am writing the will for the whole of humankind."

"Are you going to go west?" he asked jokingly.

"It's not up to me," I said, "I am to die if my mission fails. Oh yes, if anything does happen to me, be sure, for the sake of our friendship of so many years, to send my writings to the Australian government. I deem God will send another woman to resume the unfinished mission."

James seemed to be confused by what I had said. He came over to see what I was writing but to his disappointment the Chinese characters were all Greek to him. "It's beyond my knowledge," he admitted.

"Go find a translator, a top translator in Australia," I said seriously.

He felt my forehead with the back of his hand, "Are you delirious? I can't understand a single word you're saying."

"Delirious?" I argued, "No, I'm shivering with the highest fever. The Earth is to explode in no time. See how many people died in that great earthquake and tsunami in Japan? If the Earth does explode this time, what death toll will it take? Half the whole population on earth? I am the messenger God sent to warn you of the impending catastrophe and to inform you of His advice that we human beings should be transported to another planet as soon as possible."

James looked at me in great wonder, not knowing what I was saying as if I were an alien from another star, "What's the matter with you today, Linda?"

"Nothing," I said in sad earnest, "The disaster is imminent. Measures must be taken to prevent the Sword of Damocles from falling down. You told me about the existence of God but I wouldn't believe it. Now I'm firmly convinced of the existence of not only God but also the soul."

"How come you're convinced now?" he was wondering. "I'm possessed by the soul, by the soul of Goddess."

James stood in awe, "What do you mean by possessed?
What's your premonition?"

"This Earth is to explode," I said, "What death toll will it take? God sent me to save you human beings."

He seemed half convinced, "You say you're Goddess?"

"I'm by no means a mortal," I declared, "You see, I've had no attachment to any children all my life but what I care about is all the people in this world, male or female, young or old. I hope they all live happily and I'd like to bring all of them to another star."

James was a pious believer of Christianity all his life but he was confused by me then. I went on to say, "I remember you saying once that you met somebody one night in the street. He was possessed by a three-hundred-year-old soul. But I am Christ from two thousand years ago, reincarnated."

James was taken aback and staggered back a few steps. I grasped him by the hand, "Don't leave. I am not joking. I'm indeed the Christ incarnate."

James was really terribly frightened and his forehead was dripping with big drops of sweat. Maybe he was wondering whether he could witness not only a person possessed by a soul 300 years ago but also Christ incarnated in the daylight. He was almost reduced to kneeling down before me, the "Goddess." I stopped him from getting to his knees, "You needn't kneel before me until I am proven to be Goddess."

Urbane and worldly as James was, he was bewildered. He said tentatively, "It seems my cock can no longer enjoy your, Goddess's service."

"Well," I said, "I'd like you to lick my cunt when I am proven to be Goddess."

When I led James to the working room, he stood there dumbfounded. Would it be too audacious to let the holy Goddess suck his mortal cock? His cock failed to erect however hard I tried to suck it. I was tired out, "Hey, what's on your mind? That cock of yours, how come it has become a stale sausage?"

"Oh," he explained, "I feel quite differently when a Goddess is sucking my cock. When I meet God one day, He is sure to punish me by licking your asshole."

I gave him a pat on the hip, "I haven't been proven to be a Goddess, have I? You just regard me as Doctor Cock Linda."

I tried to ease his nervousness by concealing my true identity but in fact, I still considered myself as the sanctified Goddess.

It didn't matter whether I licked cocks or assholes of men of all ages. What was most important for me was to save all the people on the Earth. I had some difficulty in making James come and his fingers shook when he was putting on his trousers. He might be wondering whether he could have the privilege to see Linda Goddess next time.

Seeing James off, I found I couldn't control my emotions anymore so I quickly dialed my best friend, "Lisa, you have to come. The sooner the better. It's very urgent indeed. Drive your car, oh no, come by plane. No, no, a spaceship should be faster, take one if any."

This barrage of imperative sentences had rendered Lisa speechless, "What's happening? You sound so worried."

"We must have a good discussion," I said, "I have to inform the Australian Government now. I have a foreboding that a destructive disaster will happen to the Earth. I am not writing a book. Instead, I am writing the writing on the wall, God's will or God's Providence."

Lisa knew well I was raving mad in writing my book and she heaved a sigh, "Linda, urgent as it is, I can't get to your place until tomorrow."

I was restless and said the first thing that came to my mind, "If you don't come now, I will call the police station."

I was burning with worry over the fate of human beings all over the world. Driven by my sense of responsibility and holiness, I got ready to go through fire and water for the sake of saving them all. Actually I had great difficulty in controlling my emotions when Lisa said, "Well, I have just dismissed my class. Anyway, you should allow me some time to do some packing before I come to your place."

Just then the doorbell rang and I said to Lisa, "A new client is coming. I'll get back to you as soon as I finish serving this client."

Yes, I was Goddess. But Goddess also had to make a living. I was not so foolish as to throw away the money I could earn as easy as winking in half an hour. So I ushered the new client into the working room and settled down between his legs to suck his cock. I served my client but my brain was occupied with the concerns of Goddess. Just then, the living room phone rang and I picked up the receiver, "Linda, what on earth have you written? Can you fax it to me?"

It suddenly dawned on me that I could take advantage of such an advanced communication machine instead of having Lisa come in person by spaceship. I must have been too excited to think of this. However, I was not prepared to admit my folly so I answered, "Well, I'll fax it to you in a moment."

"What exactly do you feel?"

"I can predict a destructive disaster will strike the world," I said worriedly, "Look at the great earthquake that happened in Japan."

"Oh, my sister. How can it be so dangerous? Besides, if there is any sign of an imminent world-wide catastrophe, there are so many presidents and scientists who are constantly on alert. You must have gone into a trance on account of overworking yourself writing."

As if awakening from a dream, I calmed down all at once. It seemed I could see everything much more clearly than before and the porn video on the screen became more distinct. Since my soul had drifted away from my body when I was writing a couple of days ago, my brain had been in a mess and I couldn't see clearly as if I were in a misty night.

But I was not ready to recognize my overreaction. I faltered, "I will fax what I have written to you in a while."

I settled down to have an afterthought, "Are these all products of delusion or illusion originating from my overwork in writing?" After I finished this hour's service and sent off the client, I was still lost in deep thought as to why I could write about things that were beyond my own understanding. I just couldn't get a logical answer to this question. Mm, no, it's a sealed book. I thought I had to call Lisa for further discussion. She read widely and was well informed. Maybe she could help me in making the decision.

"Lisa," I asked over the phone, "Have you ever heard of anyone who has written a book on astronomy while he himself doesn't understand a bit of what he has written?"

"Yes," she answered over the phone, like a walking encyclopedia, "Most of these cases happened in remote areas to minorities. Some of them have little schooling and some were even illiterate. Yet they can produce great works, works they themselves don't understand at all. Even scholars cannot make sense of them."

I couldn't help admiring this friend of mine. She was such a learned lady, read so extensively and knew almost everything. I should congratulate myself on having such an intelligent and understanding friend. It was last year when I went to China to visit my mother that I made her acquaintance. Her husband saw her off at Sydney Airport. They were hugging and cuddling, unable to tear themselves from each other in the lobby. I knew they must have been a loving couple. As my ex-husband was also Australian, I naturally felt I had something in common with her. When we had a chance, we quickly fell into a free and easy conversation. It turned out that her parent's home was in a city not far from Beijing. A few minutes passed and we became good friends and exchanged each other's telephone numbers. Now we were bosom friends that could confide in and consult each other. To think two women could become the closest of bosom friends in an alien country!

"Anyway, I will fax the writing to you," I said, "See what I have written."

"There is no need to," she said, "You just read several lines to me and I can guess roughly what you've written."

I picked up my manuscript and was about to read when the doorbell rang. I said at once, "Wait a minute and I'll read it to you later." I knew only too well that making money was my first priority over any Goddess or sealed book. How could I have a decent life without making enough money? I ushered the client into the working room and made love to him at will on my bed, still thinking about the contents of my sealed book in my mind. "Sealed book." "Sealed book." Finally it dawned on me after two hours' meditation that the so-called "sealed book" was nothing other than the writing of a peak statement when a writer concentrates all his or her energy devotedly for a long time on his literal creation. The "peak stage" was like the point of a nail that could pierce anything. That was to say my writing was just the sublimation of my inspiration when I entered the peak stage of writing.

Goddess, God's will, soul incarnate, number-one prostitute or prostitute baron were all delusions, which were all beyond my own understanding. I was convinced no writer could achieve the feeling of being a soul incarnate without reaching the sublimation of their inspiration.

The word "soul," before I found it, just meant a concept to me. I looked it up in the dictionary and the definition was "an imaginary spiritual phenomenon that exists in superstition."This definition was far from being correct. Soul is not by any means "an imaginary thing in superstition." It is something real you can feel and quite different from any delusion or illusion. When people write in total contemplation, their souls might soar outside their bodies. If you haven't had such an experience, it just means you haven't reached that level. That is why few great writers in history could leave us a legacy of great classics while many others could only produce mediocre essays or poems.

The existence of the word "soul" itself meant someone had found it. Ordinary people didn't believe in it because they hadn't encountered it all their lives. I guessed many great men such as Chairman Mao Zedong must have had the experience of feeling the soul since he had written so many great works. I wondered whether he had had any records of such an experience. Maybe he had the experience but hadn't recorded it. Maybe he kept it a secret in his inner mind, thinking the soul was exclusive to him alone.

It has been many years since he passed away and I have no chance to ask him about his own experience. However, I believe that everybody has his own soul and that there was no saint, divinity or superman in the world. We were all mortals with flesh and blood except that some people were more perceptive. As I mentioned before, everybody is endowed with a different and specific capability or talent since they are all created by God. I myself have some doubts about all the above statements and they only serve as a reference for those who are interested in them. These statements reflect what I was feeling at the time and after I calmed down, I of course became suspicious of the existence of God. In my mind, I would prefer the theory of evolution; that men have evolved from apes, since I had never seen in person what God was like. If someday I died and encountered God, I would soon come back to report to you all whether he was like Saint Claus. For now, let's suppose God did exist because I refer to him later in my writing.

I also wondered how many other great authors, composers or painters had found their souls and I was eager to have a discussion with them about their experiences. Restricted by my own narrow horizon, I didn't know whether there were any records in historical archives about the existence of souls nor had I the honor to be among the great authors. I was just an ordinary writer sitting all day at home, trying to prove to people that everybody had his own soul. I also knew well I was endeavoring in the field of writing and would improve my writing technique further in time.

I hoped that among so many great writers and artists, there must have been some who shared similar feelings with me; the feelings with which the master painter Picasso could create his wonderful images, Van Gogh his exquisite scenes and Rembrandt his lifelike nude figures. What those master artists did was express with colors and lines; the world, their inner minds and their souls. Similarly, I would like to express with my pen to my readers, my real feelings when I reach the sublime in writing. I was convinced there must have been other writers that shared the same experiences as me. The question was whether they had chronicled their real feelings with their pens. This unique feeling made me imagine I was among the greatest writers. A writing career could be compared to mountaineering. Every athlete vied with one another to reach the summit. Some were exhausted and quit the competition halfway but I felt I still had the strength and energy to make a last dash and had the potential to reach the peak.

I made up my mind that so long as I didn't break down or go mad, I would try my best to dash to the final destination. I was sure I could. I would record these unique feelings in my last dash and share them with my readers.

My book may serve as a multi-purpose book for a great variety of readers. I hope everyone can find something they might need in my book. Casual readers can enjoy a variety of anecdotes and jokes about sex while serious-minded readers can find a lot of strange phenomena, mental or physical, for their reference.

Since my prophetic vision I had undergone great changes physically. I'd like to leave this to the medical scientists for their research project. In the couple of days right before my soul's drifting, I sweated profusely and the slightest step would make me break out in a cold sweat. I did my best to save as much energy as I could in serving my clients. I had clients on top of me and was fucked passively and yet I felt extremely hot and was drenched in sweat as if I had been pulled out from water.

Since the time my soul drifted away, I had lost five or six pounds almost in no time and my waist had become visibly slimmer. The excess fat under my belly soon disappeared and my belly became so plain and glossy that my clients said I was at least five years younger than before. I looked into the mirror at myself: my face beamed with a healthy glow. I became more energetic and had a good appetite. I was happier and spoke more resonantly that I couldn't tell it was my own voice. And strangely enough, I stopped sweating. I was remolded thoroughly and became a brand new woman. I guessed that with every soul drifting and incarnation to Goddess, not only does a person's writing talent improve greatly but also his body would be purified and sublimed. I felt now I had a broader scope in writing and a stronger desire to write. Every day so many fresh inspirations welled out of my brain that I didn't know when I could put down my pen for a rest. Good dialogue and interesting episodes seemed inexhaustible. Lisa was very much worried about my mental health. She said if I kept burning the candle at both ends my health would be greatly undermined. But I felt I was vigorous enough to turn out ten to twenty thousand words a day if I could be freed from my daily chore. I thought I would have a headache if I sat idle without writing something. On the contrary, if I kept on writing, I felt much more relaxed as if a great weight had been lifted from my mind.

I suppose the phenomenon of the soul drifting out of a body may be recurring in my future writing but I won't be afraid of it anymore because I know it has a real existence in your feelings and represents something spiritual. I have found the soul that has evoked much controversy for centuries. Not everyone believes in the soul. I myself didn't believe in its existence or that of God.

This time I really felt and sensed its existence. It does exist inside everyone's body, though it's something invisible and intangible in another dimension. I'm sure most people don't find their souls in their lifetimes.

Let me take an instance to illustrate it. We Chinese like to climb watchtowers when we travel to the Great Wall near the city of Beijing. The view from the first watchtower is of course different from that of the fifth one. You have a broader view and can see much more from the fifth than from the first. When I'm on the fifth tower and tell a person on the first that I have seen the soul but the one on the first argues he can't see anything and asks repeatedly, "What on earth have you seen?"

"I have seen the soul," I say.

"How come I can't see anything?" he asks doubtfully. "You can't unless you climb the fifth tower."

"But I can't climb it," he will say, "Could you please take a photo of the soul?"

"But you can't take a photo of a soul," I shrug my shoulders to show I can do nothing to help.

I try to convince him of the existence of the soul but he argues that seeing is believing. However hard I try, he just won't believe it. I believe because I have found the soul but he hasn't. This is why the issue of the soul's existence has been a controversy for centuries. Another example: you can never know the feeling of spacewalking if you have never been to space. If you're an astronaut, you will naturally know what it is like to walk in space. Take me for example, I always say I'm happy being a prostitute and as happy as a queen. No ordinary woman can imagine it because they don't have such an experience. It's safe to say I'm the happiest woman in the world. I enjoy my sex life to the accompaniment of background music every day. I can change my sex partners by a dozen a day. I am even happier than the Empress Wu. Her sex partners (male concubines) were all Chinese natives while mine are the products of a variety of ethnic groups. I have found the fun an ordinary woman can't imagine having!

Those who enjoy reading my porn anecdotes may probably be tired of this tedious and dry theoretic theology. Let's strike another chord.

Day Three: March 18, 2011

It was about 3:00 pm on March 18, 2011. I was serving an eighty-one-year-old, short Austrian old man. He said he was the hierarch of a big family of four generations with fifteen grandchildren and great grandchildren, the youngest of them being only one year old. He had round eyes, a small nose, and an oval mouth on an asymmetric face. I guessed he must have had a set of false teeth when he held my nipple between his teeth and didn't stop until I cried out in pain. He was my old lover for nearly ten years. It was more than seven years since he first came to know that my most sensitive spot was my right nipple. Now he was lying by my left side, sucking my right nipple and thrusting a finger into my cunt while I lay flat on my back and fumbled my bud with my right middle finger, imagining myself to be a queen or an empress making love to one of my favorites or being licked by them. A few minutes later, I changed my role into a young man in my imagination and he was fucking a girl stealthily in a covert place. The girl had one of her legs raised high to be fucked by her lover from behind. The cock was working away…

He was my veritable "old lover" because not all my customers could make me come every time. Besides, I had insufficient time for my own entertainment. I had to earn money. Even an empress or prostitute baron couldn't live on air alone. When I grow old, the Australian government will not automatically offer me a pension. I had to earn my own old-age insurance. I had several clients whose duty was to satisfy my sexual desire. Whenever I felt tired or worn out, they had to try their best, by any means, to make me come and I would be refreshed and become a new woman.

The eccentric old man had asked as soon as he entered the house, "Hi, how are you getting along with your book?"

"Very well, thank you," I answered, "I think I've got the most valuable things. My book includes my writing experience, anecdotes about sexual intercourse, ukiyo-e of life (mainly about men), common sense, humor and small jokes. I will show that I have seen and experienced the world without any reservations. My book is not a mere display of literary genre or writing techniques and it cannot be compared to the masterpieces of the great writers. My book is just a plain book. It's none other than a collection of my life experiences, my autobiography, and my vulgar pornographic jokes. Everything and every feeling in it, is fully and truthfully depicted. This is a true account of my real life and I have written it out in a frank and detailed way. Some writers can't and others won't write out their own accounts of their lives, so, let me do it."

Not wishing to listen to my tedious explanation further, my old lover said, "So I can't wait to read your book. I hope I can have the pleasure of perusing your masterpiece in my lifetime. When are you publishing your book?"

"Soon." "How soon?"

"As soon as you would like it," I answered, "I'll try to get it done by this September or October."

"I'm wondering whether I can live to that day."

"I'm sure you can. Hold on until after it is published," I said jokingly, "In case you can't hold out until its publication, don't worry. I will bring you a copy of it when I go to heaven myself to meet you."

We had walked to the working room, talking and laughing and when we got there, we stripped off all our clothes and lay naked side by side on the bed. As he climbed astride me and tried to kiss my mouth, I swerved to avoid his tongue's intrusion but in vain. He would say some honeyed words when he was aroused but I still couldn't do so against my will. The relationship between us was just that of a business one. If there was any love between us, it was love in its broad sense, some sort of affectionate care. I was hoping to add some more enjoyment to his later years because it was said he and his wife had divorced just after their golden wedding anniversary. I always wondered why so many couples, young, old or middle-aged, vied with one another to get divorced. Nowadays, it was a long marriage if it could last five years, let alone seven years when the itch happened. I heard a client say the divorce rate in Melbourne reached as high as sixty percent. This figure could not be verified yet. However whether it was true or not, the divorce rate had hit an all-time high. I myself had been married twice and divorced as many times. I made up my mind to never again go to the registry office, either to get married or divorced. I was content with my life now being the number-one prostitute with so many men at my feet. It was great fun to get down to writing my own book after I had seen off all my clients.

My old lover was holding my right nipple in his mouth. But today, however hard he tried to please me by sucking my right nipple, I felt indifferent to it. I just couldn't tear myself away from the writing of my book. New ideas and new stories kept popping into my head and I couldn't stop myself from thinking of them. I was bursting with these ideas and stories and I had a very urgent desire to write all of them out. But at the same time, I was afraid I would be worn out from overworking myself. I was struggling with my mind and at last I had confessed to him, "Dear, I'm afraid I'm too tired to come today."

He stared at me in surprise, "Have you taken up with another man, a younger one with a bigger cock?"

"No," I explained, "I'm worn out from a lack of sound sleep last night."

"I will be jealous," he threatened, "if you've taken up with a new boyfriend."

He had thought he was the only man who could thoroughly satisfy me in making me come but actually it was not the case. I usually had several men on call at any given time, each of whom could serve in his specific way to slake my sexual lust. As mentioned before, no other woman could ever know how happy I was. The feeling of coming through being fucked or licked by a man was quite different from fumbling a man and masturbating yourself at the same time. Each one of my men had his specific use and I would decide which man should bring me to bliss case by case, depending on my emotional needs, or the situation. Of course I enjoyed all this on the condition that it didn't affect my business.

So today I had to serve that man first and earn money from him. Though making money was always my priority, it was all relative. The elderly or widowers, I would serve free of charge. The young men, I could charge as little as twenty or thirty dollars each time because they didn't earn much money for the time being. And those I loved; I paid them instead of getting paid.

As chance had it, after the Austrian old man came a man I loved, my big cock. He stood nearly six foot ten with a butch haircut. On his chiseled face sat a pair of sunken, shining eyes, a long, thin, pointed nose and a square mouth. He always became shy at the mere sight of me. I had known him for more than three years. He was a clerk in a company and an amateur athlete of boxing and martial arts. His sinewy arms, flat abdomen and strong thighs made him look like a perfect muscular sportsman. Why he always became shy at the mere sight of me was that I all but fell in love with him. I had fallen in love with my clients only twice in my nine-year career but each time I suffered a double blow by vainly investing my emotions as well as my money and ended up being hurt and heartbroken. So I was now unmoved by any man, however handsome he was and however big his cock was. I didn't want that envy nerve of mine to be touched again. Though I rolled with a lot of men on bed every day, I would fly into a rage of jealousy on hearing the man I loved was sleeping with another woman. If I did fall in love with a man, I would love him heart and soul and devote all I had to him, even my life. I was a devoted, one-track minded woman in love so I now dared not kindle my love rashly. I refused any mixed relations with any man. As a matter of fact, with so many men at my feet giving me money, it was only too natural for me to distribute my love equally among all of them.

Yet now I somehow felt my heart strings were struck by affection and I felt like loving him. My friend Lisa often warned me not to burn the candle at both ends by only working and writing. She suggested I change my way of life once in a while to stay mentally healthy; diversify my recreations by, say, taking a casual walk or having a candid talk with my bosom friends. It wouldn't take too much of my time, but it might be beneficial for my writing. So I decided to indulge myself for a while.

I was in good mood today as the man offered to massage me. I lay face down on the bed and enjoyed his skillful massage of my back. As I needed to take a lot of baths every day, my skin had become dry and itchy. So when he applied the baby oil evenly along my body and began to massage me with his elbow inch by inch from top to toe, I enjoyed it a lot and felt somewhat moved, even a little embarrassed – he was paying to serve me. He seemed to be able to read my mind, "You don't need to be embarrassed. You must be tired out by working all day long." Several minutes passed and he had me turn over. I caught sight of the knot-like muscles on his arms and they at once reminded me of the statues of ancient Greek or Roman sculptors. I couldn't help admiring that a masculine man's body should look so spectacular in reality! I looked down at the cock between his muscled thighs, erect, stark and stiff. I opened my arms and murmured softly, "Hug me."

As he threw his manly body upon me, my heart began to pound violently in my chest. It was a long time since I had such a feeling. I had appreciated so many men on the bed that I was indeed at a loss as to which one was my real favorite. I was afraid of being involved in such a swirl of love affairs as I was too vulnerable to devoted emotion. I refused to fall in love with a man unless I could love him ardently and wholeheartedly. He was staring at me lovingly but I swerved to avoid eye contact, wrapping my hand around his neck while he wrapped his around mine. He pressed his lips against mine and I against his. When his tongue intruded into my mouth, my heart throbbed and my legs naturally spread apart. It had been a long time since we started making love without a condom because we had built up a trust between us. As he deliberately slowly thrust his long, thick, straight penis into my cunt, I felt an unspeakable sensation; my insides itching and contracting. He asked me in a low voice, "Linda, do you want me to fuck you?"

"Yes," I murmured, "I'm so happy. Fuck me hard, won't you?" But he kept moving deliberately slowly, allowing me enough time to savor the exquisite sensation of lovemaking. He knew well I didn't like quick, cursory movements. He thrust his cock deliberately slowly but resolutely and forcefully until it reached the opening of my womb. His wonderful fucking techniques rejuvenated me and made me feel at least ten years younger. My gate of love seemed to be opening slowly but steadily with a creak. I was afraid of this gate being opened but I expected it to open wide at the same time. My dreary life needed moistening and warming, especially when I was writing at night. I was so crazy about writing that I would be driven mad unless a real love stopped me. I would rather risk falling in love again than being driven mad like that. I was longing for a sweet love, be it a blessing or a curse.

I narrowed my eyes and began to moan, "Oh yes. Fuck me, darling." He turned his lips to my right nipple; the button to arouse me and bring me under his control. I felt a warm thrill running through my nipple to my heart and I couldn't help cry softly, "I love you!"

"Me too," he responded, "You are so beautiful!" With that he patted me on the bosom, "This part in particular."

He took my hand and directed it to touch my own clitoris. His mouth was now shifting to my right nipple and his left hand caressed my left nipple. Though my left nipple was not as sensitive as my right one, it was still reacting promptly to the tantalizing stimulus, as though a feeble electric current was running from it to my heart. I suddenly felt a strong thrill running all through me, from my heart to my chest, my belly, and my legs to the soles of my feet. I closed my eyes and indulged in my imagination: A Prince Charming was fucking a "Goddess" until at last I couldn't help yelling out, "Ah... ..." I was coming!

"I am coming, dear," I said with a shudder, "Fuck me hard. I love you!"

"I love you!" I shuddered again and repeated "I love you!" thrice in succession.

The triple exclamations of "I love you!" were quite different from those I shouted when other clients satisfied me. They seemed to have flowed from my heart naturally. I knew I was about to press the button to switch on my love. He moved his cock quickly and violently to quench the lustful itch in my cunt. Then he waited until I had completely calmed down and lay down on his back on the bed, "Now it's your turn to fuck me. Come on."

I sat astride his thighs and directed his hardened cock into my cunt, my plump white breasts dangling over his face and his back arching to meet me. He bucked up and down under me violently, "I'm fucking you. I'm fucking you!" It was three to five minutes before he yelled, "Ah --. I have come!" With that, he withdrew his placid cock quickly, "Lest I make you pregnant."

I laughed up my sleeve as it was absurd for a woman of my age to get pregnant. "Maybe in the next life," I giggled.

His flat belly was covered with a clammy mess of white sperm. "Oh, so much!" he exclaimed with pride.

"Big cock, big sperm," I said. (As would be dwelt on later in my thesis "On Cocks"; the quantity of sperm actually had nothing to do with cock size.)

Then I gave a soft peck on his lips, "Maybe I have fallen in love with you this time. Wait for my decision when my book is published."

"I'll wait for your decision," he said, his blue eyes looking into mine with a moving glitter.

"If you're free next week," I went on to say, "Let's dine out, my treat." (I always paid the man I loved and not vice versa, which was under constant attack from my girlfriends for selling myself so cheap.)

"Okay," he agreed, "Let's make a reservation and I will pick you up that evening."

While he went to take his shower, I went to my own bathroom. I squatted under the sprinkler and washed my private part, thinking, "How come his cock performed so satisfactorily? It was only because his cock couldn't satisfy me that I hesitated when he proposed to marry me. I had seen many men who appeared very masculine and boasted big-sized cocks but failed to perform well in bed. They usually took up boxing, wrestling, martial arts or football as their careers. Maybe their much exercised limbs had drained all their vigor and strength from their cocks. Of course not all sporting men's cocks experienced poor performance but those men were more likely to have such problems. As to the present man, did he secretly exercise his cock or did he develop new techniques at home these days? Anyway, his performance in bed today was perfect. I may as well try him out several more times. Ah yes, one more thing. By no means could I tell him my real age. I remembered having told him I was forty-three instead of fifty-three. There was no exception that a prostitute would be willing to disclose her real age to her clients.

Having been made to come satisfactorily by him, I was thoroughly released from the great pressure due to overwork on my writing and felt totally refreshed. I gave my Prince Charming two bottles of red wine and a farewell kiss on the cheek when he left, "See you next week."

I closed the door and came back to the west living room. Seated on the sofa, I clicked the remote control randomly to see if any of my favorite programs were on. I was tired of watching the news about the Japanese earthquake for fear that I would become Goddess again after seeing human catastrophes. But whatever programs I tuned in, the screen invariably showed the miserable scenes of various kinds of disasters. The Chinese satellite channel reminded me that I should give my Mom a call. So I dialed the phone number of my mother in Beijing. On hearing a "Hello," I called out, "Hi, Mom!"

A roar of laughter came through the phone, "Who's your mom? You must be so confused by writing to not recognize your own sister's voice."

It was my sister. I had actually recognized her voice but I was just making fun of her. These days whenever I phoned home, I would always boast of my book as a unique, wonderful and unprecedented book. When asked to read some passages to them, I hesitated about whether to read them any. When asked to mail some pages of the masterpiece, I demurred and fobbed them off with the excuse that I had to keep it a secret for the moment. My family members were all confused, assuming there must be something wrong with my brain. I then said,"Hey, sister. A new literary star is rising in Australia's horizon and I will rank with the great artist Picasso. Picasso was a great painter and I am a great writer."

"Look," my sister became impatient; "Here you go again. By the way, who's Picasso?"

"Well," I said, "You haven't seen him but I have several times. We often discuss my work."

"What you're saying is beyond my ken," my sister was greatly confused, "Can you tell me some other things?"

"Of course I can," I answered, "have you had your meal?"

"What time is it? Is it lunch or supper that you're asking about?" she was somewhat annoyed; "I have just had my lunch but not supper yet."

"Any interesting news about China?" I asked.

"Yes. Haven't you got on the internet for news?"

"Got on the internet?" I asked, "I don't know how to. The Apple computer I bought in China last time is still on my desk on display. And I haven't even touched it yet." I gestured at the computer beside me, "I've paid two hundred dollars to rent an email address and eighty dollars to access the internet. Yet I haven't even had a glimpse at it."

"That's a waste of money," she was right about that.

I thought I had wasted much more money on other occasions, which I would tell her about later.

"Well, since you haven't checked the news,"my sister said,"let me tell you some. A panic about buying iodized salt, even salted pickled vegetables broke out in many places in China. What do you think people are saying online? There is a couplet on the net, which says that *the Japanese eat iodized salt as an antidote for radioactive harm while the Chinese buy iodized salt and anticipate radioactive harm.*"

I was greatly amused and rocked with laughter so violently that I almost fell off my swivel chair. No sooner had my laughter stopped than my sister said, "The horizontal scroll is: *Salt is out of stock.*"

I burst out laughing loudly when I heard my sister say, "Listen. There's more to come. A joke online goes that when the nuclear radioactive fallout caused by the Japanese earthquake began to spread, the heads of all countries began to worry. The Chinese President prayed, 'Let the wind blow to the north.' The U.S. President prayed, 'To the east.' The Russian President prayed, 'To the north-west.' And the Japanese Prime Minister said, 'As you please.'"

I was then doubled up with laughter and wondered why my laughter today was more resonant than before and whether it had something to do with my incarnation a few days before. Having fun with my sister over the phone relieved me of most of the depression caused by overwork on my book.

Disconnecting the call, I went back to the kitchen, thinking whether the online joke was true or not, there was no point in the world leaders quarrelling amongst themselves. We were all brethren. We were either relatives or neighbors. No point in wishing the wind to blow in a specific direction. It was better the wind carrying radioactive dust blew into space.

I was about to pick up a mug to drink when the phone rang again. I thought it must have been my sister who had forgotten to say something and ran back for the receiver, "Mom." I was intending to make fun of her again but I heard a male voice on the phone, "Linda, we have a buyer."

"What buyer," I was slow to react.

"That heritage building of yours," the man said, "Someone has expressed an intention of buying."

Only then did I recognize it was Peter, my real-estate agent. "What's his offer?"

"Four hundred and eighty-five thousand."

I was speechless. I bought it for 505,000 and I was now selling it for 485,000? What a losing transaction!

"Few buyers dare to buy that house of yours," the agent patiently explained, "It can neither be demolished nor can it be renovated. And besides, it may collapse at any time. If it does, the government will fine you. Guess who offered to buy your house? It is the same buyer who bought your first house, number

184. He is an architect and he knows how to renovate such a house. There have been nearly sixty prospective buyers who have inspected that old house of yours and none of them dare to buy it."

I remained silent for a while before I made up my mind finally, "Sell it so long as someone wants to buy it. I thought it would take me ten years or even much longer to sell it. Maybe I might become a caretaker of heritage houses for the Australian government. I can neither demolish nor renovate the house and am ready to be fined if it collapses as if the government were the house owner. Sell it. Sell it without delay! It's a good thing I can get rid of it within a year. Sell it immediately."

"So shall I prepare the contract?" Michael said.

"Okay," I replied, "Go ahead with the contract and send it to me. I will sign it."

I put down the receiver and sat down in the sofa, figuring my losses in mind, I have lost at least 200,000 in the past four years. The down payment was 70,000. The loan insurance was 7,000 plus 2,700 of loan interest every month. All these in the past four years added up to 130,000, not including the annual 10,000 for house and land taxes. Even if the house was rented out for 240 per week and I can get a deduction of nearly 1,000 a month, I should throw in extra money every month. And this does not include the annual water bill of 1,700 to 2,500 together with the stamp duty of 18,000. I have paid all these as a contribution to the revenue of the Australian government. You can search the world in vain for such a generous fool as me. Only the prostitute baron can afford to do so!"

I lost more than 180,000 dollars on the sale of my first house last October and more than 200,000 this time (The two houses were next door to each other; number 182 and 184 on Old Northern Road, Castle Hill in Sydney.) It seemed I had to work another four years for nothing! I should attribute the blame for all this to the two ladies in Sydney; my loan agent, Miss. Sunny (Chinese epithet Lady Disappointing) and my solicitor, Ms. Ice (Chinese epithet Lady Nitwit). I gave Miss. Sunny a bonus of 2,500 dollars and Ms. Ice 600 next to her normal service fee and the two ladies collaborated to help me purchase these two houses. I had made it clear from the very start that my purpose in buying these two houses was to demolish them and rebuild four houses for investment. I bought them just because they covered a large area of 26,000 square feet.

Once the contract was in effect, the real-estate agent Peter told me that one of the two houses could not be demolished by law and as for the other, even if it was demolished and new houses were built on its original site, the ownership of it couldn't be split. I went to confront Miss. Sunny with this information but she confessed "I had no idea the house had these kind of issues." I turned around to ask Lawyer Ice why she didn't tell me about the situation earlier. She just replied, "Oh, sorry. I forgot about that. I have hundreds of property sales' contracts to handle every year; how could I remember every detail of each particular case?"

I didn't know my solicitor before the transaction. She was introduced to me by Miss. Sunny. Though it seemed too late then, I had to sell the two houses anyway, however much I would lose. (The stories about these two ladies will be dwelt on later.)

Now let's come back to the original topic – my soul. A question kept recurring in my mind; why would my soul drift, together with my heart, inside me along my right arm and right hand out of my body as my pen ran the names of some presidents? It was something like a spark of inspiration that flared accidentally when one had concentrated too intensely for too long a time. It was something invisible and intangible. When the soul swam inside you, you could distinctively feel it. It wouldn't go separately but it always went with the heart. The way your soul drifted was different from the way your heart flowed from your body. I could feel them travelling slowly along two different veins out of my body.

People say you will surely succeed if you do something with heart but I must say you will surely succeed if you do something with both heart and soul. Many people fail to mention the soul because they cannot find their own souls or even doubt whether there is a soul at all.

As is said in the literary circle, a certain book has a soul. That means this book must have been written with heart and soul. Since my soul was incarnated, I thought I had been writing with heart and soul. I was writing naturally and coherently without using my brain as if my pen were guiding my thoughts and not vice versa. My brain seemed to be filled with a rich vocabulary and endless anecdotes and episodes. New ideas and bold concepts kept springing up in my mind. As my friend Lisa put it: "Art is a creation and sublimation. In practicing writing, you will be constantly improving and surpassing yourself." Her encouragement convinced me that I was not marking time in my writing but instead I was progressing steadily step by step. Maybe sometime on one fine morning, I would have surpassed myself by a great leap in my literary capability.

I remember one day I was under a delusion when I was writing. I hurriedly called Lisa, "My soul must be incarnated, because I can write out proverbs I have never learned or heard of. I must be a certain god incarnate."

Of course I was not a god incarnate. It must have been because I kept writing for years and with the development of my literary capability, it was quite natural that many new words should well up in my mind. I didn't believe there was any god incarnate in the world. The soul was something spiritual that existed in your body. Was it a fact or was it just something like the thinking process or result in your mind? Would the soul decay with the body after the body died? Or would it transform into something transcendental? Would it drift out of the body and fly away? Or would it, as some religious doctrines had it, leave the body and soar to heaven the minute the body died? I couldn't say for sure for the moment but it was doubtless that the soul, as something spiritual, dwelt in our bodies when we were alive.

Now let's get down to explaining what illusion is. I believe illusion happens when you concentrate on an artistic creation too much for too long a time. Science fiction movies must have been created by their authors under a kind of illusion. It's well known that in his late years, Chairman Mao began to deem himself as a god in his writing. It's quite natural when an author goes into a trance during his writing, he will most probably be oblivious of his identity and deem himself as secondary only to God. This is when the illusion arises.

When I proclaimed arrogantly, "I am Goddess incarnated; I am greater than anyone in the world; I am the re-maker of humankind," I was in my delirium and my head was muddled. I was under the delusion when saying, "I'm superior to any president. I'm the king of kings. I'm the prostitute baron and unprecedented super prostitute." As a matter of fact, how could I be superior to any president? I was even smaller than a toe of them. It was too arrogant of me to say, "I am Goddess incarnate. I am the re-maker of humankind." It was just wild talk under a paranoid delusion. Furthermore, what was the use for a prostitute like me to worry about the future of humanity while there were so many statesmen and scientists watching on? It all sounded ridiculous and absurd to me now. Yet it also showed my great fraternity, my devotion to the safety of human beings and my dauntless spirit in the face of any catastrophe. I was not a president but I had the qualities of a president, such as fortitude and tolerance rarely seen before in a woman. If I had been born a thousand years before, I would surely be Empress Wu. Not that I could reign over a huge empire as she did but my talent in writing could well be comparable to her talent in administration. By "talent in writing," I'm not referring to ordinary literary talent but a boldness of vision expressed in my writing and thinking.

I knew well my writing left much to be desired but I seemed to see Chairman Mao waving to me and Picasso waiting for me. This was by no means my wild talk under delusion but a deliberate statement in sober earnest. Because I was a woman of action with great audaciousness, determination and perseverance, I wouldn't admit failure easily before I reached my goal. I knew I had the potential to catch up with or even surpass those great writers in creating masterpieces. I was like a soaring eagle spreading my wings and flying higher and higher until I was over Mount Everest. I waved to the people at the foot of the mountain, "Hey, I've found something new!"

Nowadays I was writing my book in a state of trance. Even when I was rolling around with my clients in bed and making love to the background music, I was always obsessed with my work, adjusting its structure or creating new plots. I was infatuated by writing and thinking, and was almost lost to the outside world.

Actually I had no particular goal in life. I was seeking neither fame nor social status. I preferred an independent and solitary life without caring too much about other people's opinions. I didn't want to make more money, either. I was quite content with a certain amount of money, just enough to allow me to live decently. My best friend Lisa knew very well the destination of every penny I earned these years. She described me as a squanderer who distributed my hard-earned money casually. In my mind, money was an external thing that could come and go. God would surely reprimand me if I said to Him, "I've brought you one hundred million dollars," after I died and went to see Him in heaven.

Now that I turned prostitute baron because of a turn of fortune, I should do my best to serve those men who were lonely or old or those who were suffering from sexual thirst or sexual pervasiveness. For men who have wives or girlfriends, it was hard to imagine what it was like lying in cold beds and spending endless nights reviving their fond memories of their prime days. What little I could do was give them as much warmth and comfort as possible so that they could peacefully leave this world with a smile and romantic satisfaction instead of a cold memory of this desolate world.

For years, I was keenly aware of the untold loneliness and solitude of those old men. The only pleasure they could find was to come hug me every one or two weeks. That might be their best enjoyment spiritually and physically. Some seniors in their eighties or nineties couldn't come at all yet if they could hug me for half an hour they would be in higher spirits and had a sounder sleep when they went back home.

Women outside this profession were not able to enjoy the contentment and pleasure derived from bestowing love and care on disadvantaged groups of men. Neither did I care about others' insulting gossip that I was a cheap bitch. Money was no longer my main priority in my business. As mentioned before, I often offer my service free of charge and I would continue to do this in future whenever necessary. I now regarded my business as a divine mission and a solemn duty. Since God appointed me as the number-one prostitute and had me accomplish this book, I was obliged to complete His mission by writing all this down arduously, truly and completely without skipping over any details.

Never before was there a prostitute like me who could expose her life so thoroughly and so comprehensively to the light of day. I was different from other prostitutes elsewhere in that I had seen almost every variety of cock, of men from different countries and different races. Rare prostitutes in the world have seen more cocks than me. There were cocks galore indeed. They were different in size and shape, some shapely and others grotesque; some like flashlights, bananas, sickles or even birds!

Most people may refuse to believe the soul in my writing, in which case I say I have seen the soul but you haven't. It's easier to prove the diversity of cocks than to prove the existence of souls because I can take photos of cocks but I can't of souls. It's no exaggeration to say that for billions of men in the world, every cock is unique and a thousand men may have a thousand kinds of cocks. No cock in the world is identical as no leaf is identical under the sun. Someone says no woman's cunt is identical but I admit I haven't studied it yet for lack of sufficient samples. I guess it's true with the cunts by analogy. I have studied cocks so thoroughly that I will dwell on them later in my thesis on cocks and give detailed explanations for the relations between their sizes and their performances.

Now I have another subject for further study. My previous subject was why my body as well as my writing ability had changed so greatly since my soul was incarnated. My new focus is whether there is a relation between the huge progress in my writing ability and the consequent increased frequency of my making love to men. My sexual desire is much stronger than any ordinary woman. I usually need more than a dozen men to satisfy my lust and I have to come two or three times a week to be completely satiated. My clients are my friends and some are my confidants who I usually make love to without condoms. In most cases, we can reach our climaxes almost simultaneously. At that precise moment, our brains and sex organs will be on the brink of touch and go. To make me enjoy it all the more, their cocks will stay in my cunt a little longer and afterward, their sperm will be spilled on my belly. There will always be a residual amount of their sperm in my cunt before they ejaculate, even if I get up immediately and wash the inside of my cunt in the bathroom. When I am on my sexual high, my brain cells together with those of my cunt are alert so I interpret that a man's literal inspiration seeps through his sperm into my body via my spine all the way to my brain.

There has not been one writer among my male clients, yet every one of them might have an element of literary talent in them. By making love to each of them, I felt I had been collecting and accumulating the essence of each of them and absorbing each rich element they possessed into my brain. I could not say for sure whether this had affected my brain but every time I come with a man, I feel extremely sober and newly alert as if every pore of my body has been thoroughly cleansed. When I got down to my writing, I found the most pertinent, forceful words seemed already at hand. I had a feeling that I was not writing by myself but writing collectively by pooling the wisdom of all the men I had made love to.

I'm a keen observer of people and things. I am genuinely interested in watching everyone I meet and learning by heart the details of what they say and do, even the particular looks in their eyes. For years, my clients have brought with them a plethora of anecdotes and jokes every day. These raw materials have been refined and enriched in my brain, becoming even funnier and circulate in no time among my clients. Though I was bright when young, I was not good at making or telling jokes, innocent or dirty. Yet, recently I turned into an expert joke writer and teller. Some plain episodes that didn't seem funny at first, after being processed in my brain, become classic facetiae and make audiences fall about laughing at hearing them. Not only my talent for making jokes but also my capacity of writing has progressed steadily over the years. I could easily convert some plain episodes into funny dramatic stories that would make my clients double with laughter. I had an uncontrollable urge or an irresistible impulse to write at any time.

I'd like to write on and on until all the interesting episodes, anecdotes and stories have been dumped out of my brain. I knew too many mysteries people all over the world didn't and couldn't know. It was my bounden duty to write them all out. I didn't want to strain myself too much otherwise I could easily turn out ten or twenty thousand words a day.

Now that I have found the soul, delusion and a period of insanity, I wouldn't take them for granted when these phenomena recurred again. I would stabilize my emotions and adjust my mood in due course. I might become the most prolific writer in the world and I could keep on writing until I turned out millions of words. I had the confidence though I was not absolutely sure until the prospect came true.

I am a woman with a strong will, an agile mind, a good memory and strong self control. I always marched dauntlessly in achieving my goals. I would exert myself to the uttermost and was willing to make any sacrifice for doing anything I thought was worth doing.

I had a personal belief that there were not too many people in this world who had found, conceived of, or experienced their own souls. I was even more convinced of this belief when I went back to China in the fall of 2010. My niece had bought me a Chinese dictionary and as I looked up the definition of "soul" in it, I found to my dismay that the answer read as follows: Soul – something spiritual that superstitious people refer to as being able to leave one's body and act of itself.

That meant up to now in 2011, the Chinese dictionaries still dogmatically defined a soul as a product of superstition. In China's profuse historical chronicles, there had been no accurate and detailed record of the existence of the soul. China was among the earliest countries that had their own written classics, but it had a vague definition on souls. Being an intangible image, the word "soul" remained inexplicable in Chinese literature.

Yet souls were far from being a product of superstition. They were something spiritual that did exist within our bodies. They could be separated from our bodies and act independently. Their existence and movement in our bodies could be sensed distinctly. The fact that a word existed for "soul" in the Chinese vocabulary meant there must have been some people in Chinese history that had found them but failed to record them in time and explain them clearly. Their descendants could find no trace in the archives so they had to regard souls as the product of superstition.

I even guessed that Chairman Mao must have found the existence of his soul as it was characteristic of him as a living divinity but he deliberately concealed it from all of his subjects. So did Picasso but he couldn't depict it in words so he had to depict it in his paintings. That was why some of his paintings looked so grotesque and were still beyond our understanding. I was not boasting when I was saying Mao as well as Picasso beckoned to me in the field of literary writing. I could not only catch up with them but also surpass them. I reiterate here that I am neither Goddess nor saint. I am only a little more sensitive, intelligent and intuitive than others. We know there are geniuses in the world whose IQ's are many times higher than those of average people. I myself might be one of them in the field of writing. I was neither foolish nor insane nor was I telling nonsense in my delirium. I was a normal woman with normal flesh and blood. I was eating with a good appetite like a wolf and slept soundly like a log. When I was quarrelling with my client this morning, I could cry, "Damn it!" So, as you can see, I was not insane, indeed. The more I thought about it the more convinced I became that my writing was only too important to humankind. Though I was not a re-maker of humans, I could offer humans something that hadn't been written about in literary history. In my writing, I was now flying at a very high altitude and was soaring still higher. I could reach the Moon and even deep space. No one could catch up with me there.

Perhaps I might be the first to record what it was like to sense the soul and I hope whoever has also sensed his or her soul can share or discuss with us their valuable experience.

Day Four: March 23, 2011

Driven by an uncontrollable impulse to write, I had to get down to writing at once. So I served two clients perfunctorily and sent them away. Then I took up the pen and wielded it madly on paper. After a dreamless sound sleep for six hours, I was perfectly sober. That was because last night a client satisfied me thoroughly and released all the pressure brought about by my mania for writing. That thirty-five-year-old Australian man, after a flesh-to-flesh caress for a while, thrust one finger into my cunt and bent another to tantalize my clitoris. It took him only fifteen minutes or so to bring me to the peak of bliss. When I sent away my last client, I wrote late into the deep night. I went to bed at two thirty in the early morning and didn't wake up until a certain client's phone call woke me up at nine fifteen. I had a sound sleep and woke up oblivious of all the worldly trivialities of the day.

There was a client of mine who worked for the government. He had made it a rule to come to me to refresh his brain whenever he had a meeting in the afternoon. He said that by ejaculating all his sperm he became completely refreshed and quickly regained his ability to think clearly and thus would invariably impress all present with his clarity of speaking at the meeting. I had the same feeling as him. After I had come, my brain became clear and much wiser than before. And besides, I had a better appetite and slept a sounder sleep.

A better appetite and a sounder sleep was the common feeling of all those who had enjoyed an ecstatic sexual life. According to the theory of Chinese traditional medicine, a happy sex life could prolong a person's lifespan, to which I couldn't agree more. It seemed there would be no problem if I lived for one hundred years or more with many men from various countries serving me as Goddess.

It was at 11:20 on March 23, 2011 when the doorbell rang. I knew it was my Papa coming because he had called in advance. I opened the door to find he was wearing a cream-colored bowler with sweat pouring down his face. His grizzled moustache as well as his grizzled eyebrows was drenched in sweat, as well as his T-shirt, which clung to his back. He limped to the working room by dragging his right leg, which he couldn't bend. The crotch between the legs of his dark-grey trousers seemed damp too. With a large, blue, canvas satchel slung across his shoulder, he said as he was walking, "It's hot. It's sweltering hot today."

"I haven't gone out yet," I said, "So I didn't know it was so hot outside. It is too hot for autumn, I think."

"It's weird it's so hot," he complained.

When he arrived at the working room, he rummaged through his satchel for his wallet and took two fifty notes and a twenty note from it. Handing me the notes, he said, "Here's the money."

"Papa needn't be in a hurry," I soothed him; "You may as well pay me later."

I handed him a towel and had him take his shower. When he finished bathing, he went back to the working room and stood on the carpet, savoring the porn videos playing on the wall TV sets. The video was showing a promiscuous party. On an oblong table covered with a purple blanket stood four, naked Western girls, surrounded by four, naked, tall Western men. A girl was sucking a big cock, the second was making love with a man, the third had a big cock in her asshole and the fourth girl's clitoris was being licked by a man. That was the first time I had ever seen a girl's outer lips as long as the fourth girl's. Her lips were so long that they were hanging out like a dog's tongue. The man was seen using his hands to pull at her lips and his tongue tip to lick her clitoris. The whole room reverberated with an uproar of indecent cries from the TV set. The girls kept groaning sensually, "Ah, yes…" and the men kept roaring unscrupulously, "Oh! Fuck!" Papa was quite pleased by the obscene scenes and cries, "Dirty movies, dirty girls; same songs, different singers."

Every time he came, papa used to be greeted with the *Asian Fever* porn videos on the TV sets. He was accustomed to the

Asian girls' lustful cries but today when he unexpectedly saw the Western girls fucking and heard them groaning, the novel stimulus made him extremely excited. Papa staggered toward me and whispered against my hair, "I've had Viagra again today and my cock is now stark hard. When I ravish you in a second, I will fuck you to death. You will be very satisfied. I'd like you to cry and groan like those girls, and better and louder than them, while I'm fucking you. I promise to make you satisfied today." I laughed in my heart, "Stark hard? When ever have you made me satisfied?"

I helped Papa lie down on the white bedding I had paved in advance. Then I spread his legs and rested my head on his huge white abdomen. Nestled comfortably on his soft belly, with one of my ears against his navel, I was deep in thought, wondering why the definition in the Chinese dictionary still classified the word "soul" as a concept of superstition. In fact, it was not by any means. It did dwell in a person's body. Could anyone in the world prove its existence? It was impossible. Maybe people speaking languages other than Chinese might have found the soul's existence…

I wavered in my thinking. Papa noticed my distracted state of mind and asked me what I was thinking about. I answered I was intoxicated in the light music. Actually I was lost in meditation. Since last September when I planned to string together like beads, all the characters and episodes I had accumulated in more than nine years, I had been found in a trance more often than not while fucking my clients. I would be amused by the characters I had created and mysteriously burst into laughter suddenly. The clients would find it hard to guess why I laughed abruptly for no reason. I had to cover it up by saying, "Your cock looks ridiculous." This would make my clients look down between their thighs, wondering whether anything was really wrong with their cocks.

I settled by Papa's left side, nodding my head to the music and leaving the largest part of my mind obsessed with the writing of my book. And incidentally I tried to stretch my neck. For the last ten years, I had been sucking one or two dozen cocks a day and my neck started to become strained three years ago. Stretching my neck would temporarily relieve the pain, but not cure it. Papa noticed my neck's rhythmic movement and asked, "Why are you so happy today?"

"I'm supposed to feel happy seeing your cock, aren't I?"

And he felt happy and came over to press his lips against mine, his moustache pricking my tender lips. A stinky smell from his mouth began to assault my nostrils. I said, "I may as well suck your cock."

I settled myself between his thighs and held his mediocre white cock in my mouth. His cock should only be ranked as medium sized among Western men. But it was not five minutes before he stopped me and said, "Let me fuck you. I took a Viagra pill before I came."

"But I can't see any improvement in your cock's hardness," I snickered and with that I quickly lay down on my back on the bed, applying some lubricating oil to my orifice. Then he got on top of me. I grabbed his cock with my right hand and tried to tuck it into my cunt. I tried many times but in vain. I was at my wits' end and had to resort to my old trick. I drew his cock near my inner right thigh and wrapped it with my right hand. I used my fingers and palm to simulate my cunt and held his impotent cock rhythmically. He exerted all his strength to fuck my hand. I wondered whether he was feigning ignorance or he really didn't know the truth. His cock was working away in my hand and he kept yelling, "I fuck you!" "I fuck you little mischief!" and "I must be tender today, lest I fuck you to tears as I did last time…"

Ignoring his playacting, I groaned my own, "Ah yes. Oh yes," with the sole purpose of pleasing him. As he thrust forward, I farted. He said proudly, "Look. I've fucked you to fart."

I patted him on his huge belly with my left hand, chuckling to myself that it was far from the truth. I had been busy all morning serving clients and writing my book and I had scarcely any time for my breakfast. So I had to make do with some cold milk and it fermented in my stomach. The fermented milk turned into gas in my intestines and when he accidentally pressed my stomach, the gas naturally escaped as a fart.

Twenty minutes or so passed and I felt Papa's cock turning harder and harder in my hand and his breath becoming heavier and heavier. I knew well I couldn't disturb him at this moment so I narrowed my eyes and pretended to have been intoxicated in his fucking. I kept yelling, "Oh! Oh…!" until I felt a hot stream oozing through my fingers and I knew Papa had come.

He sprawled on me motionless and I waited until he came to. I rolled out of bed and pretended to wipe my cunt and then the inside of my thigh. For fear Papa would check my cunt, I told him "I'll take a shower and come back to massage you."

He was gasping on the bed, "Now I can have a good sleep when I go home."

"Now you can live at least five years longer," I shouted back. "I hope I can come fuck you again at ninety."

"I hope I can have the strength to open the door for you when you turn ninety."

When I came back after bathing, Papa was already lying on the bed. I poured out some baby oil onto my palm and began to massage his back. It was less than a quarter of an hour before I heard him snoring gently – Papa had fallen asleep.

Just then my mobile phone buzzed and I took it up immediately, "Are you busy now?"

Seeing Papa was nearly done, I answered, "Not really. Come along, please."

It was my Uncle, an eighty-year-old short, stout Greek old man with a potbelly. He was an old patron of nine years and every time we met we greeted each other like old lovers after a long separation. He liked to narrow his big, round, blue eyes and pout his lips to kiss me, saying with vinous breath, "I love you, my little baby." But every time I swerved to avoid being kissed

–I didn't enjoy kissing my clients. I could kiss their cocks but not their mouths unless it was a man I really loved.

It was less than ten minutes before the doorbell rang and I had to say sorry to Papa, "You can go to the bathroom now and I will refund you twenty dollars for the time you are short." Papa left obediently to have his shower. I went to answer the door. My Uncle was a head shorter than me and his potbelly was very conspicuous. When he entered, his belly came long before his head. He was wearing a light-blue shirt today with the neckline open and a blue tie dangling loosely. His thin-haired round head was incompatible with his fat round potbelly. His dark-blue trousers were too loose for his legs but comfortable enough for his waist with the last hole in his belt on the middle of his potbelly. He was old but he still ran a grocery shop. It was said he had a large extended family with four generations living together.

Since we met when I was working with Philip, he had been my patron and had been coming to visit me every one or two weeks. He said when he first came to Canberra by boat in 1949, it was a small town with only 20,000 people and the main mode of transport was by boat. Now Canberra had developed into a medium-sized modern city with a population of nearly 400,000. The urban streets were lined with various European style buildings – shops, offices, an airport, bus stops, and railway stations. The city enjoyed excellent services of communication and transportation. The Canberra Airport was under construction for extension and in a year or so; a new large international airport would be put into service. By then I would be able to fly to China from Canberra and wouldn't need to travel via Sydney…

In the past ten years, many of my old friends, patrons and fans told me a lot of things about Australian history. The knowledge of this country made me familiar with its past and present. I was beginning to take this city and country as my second homeland and I enjoyed every day of living here. I was born in China but I would probably spend my remaining years here in Australia. I should live up to my parents' expectations.

My Uncle staggered toward me, "Are you busy?" "You have to wait two or three minutes."

"Never mind," he said, "I have plenty of time today."

He staggered into the waiting room by himself and I called out to him from behind, "Help yourself to any drink you like from the fridge."

I shut the door and pushed open another to the working room. Papa was already neatly dressed. I returned twenty dollars to him and took a large bag of cashews from under the cabinet. He said, "Thank you. It's generous of you." I took two bottles of mineral water from the fridge for him to drink on his way home. It was a forty-five minute walk from his home to mine and the round trip might take him one and a half hours. The long walk would be good exercise for him and together with an hour's enjoyable sexual activity, would most likely be beneficial to his health.

"See you later, Linda," he said.

"Have a nice trip home, Papa," I said, helping him walk down the steps.

When I closed the door and went back to the waiting room, Senior Uncle was sitting in a chair watching the porn video, holding a Pepsi in one hand and caressing his wriggling cock under his pants with the other, "It's quite unruly today."

Seeing I was approaching, he jumped to his feet to wrap his hands around my neck and smacked me on the lips.

"Oh Uncle, let's go over there," I was trying to avoid his kisses. Senior Uncle waddled toward the working room and I followed him. When there, he threw a fifty-dollar note on the massage table and stood beside it waiting for me to undress him. I undressed him every time he came to visit me. I pulled off his tie from around his neck but accidentally ruffled some of his grizzled hairs. While I was straightening his hair, he tried to kiss me again,"I love you." He narrowed his eyes as if carried away by his own affection and snouted his lips in search of mine.

"I can't undress you if you keep behaving like that," I wriggled away and as I went on to unfasten his buttons one by one, he couldn't wait to kiss me here and there, on the cheek, on the lips or on the neck, tickling my face and wetting it with his saliva.

"Wait a minute," I giggled, "You must be patient. You are tickling me all over."

"How I wish my cock could be hard enough to fuck your itching cunt," he said, smacking his own lips, "I would give you a good fucking!"

"Since the day I knew you," I smiled, "You have never succeeded in putting your cock into my cunt. But I'm sure you could if I had come to Australia ten years earlier."

"No," he said, not ready to take his humiliation lying down, "If my cock can't fuck you, my fingers can!" With that he pushed me down on the bed despite my protests and got on top of me. I was lying on the edge of the bed, with my thighs open and my legs high on his shoulders. Stark naked himself, he gripped my right knee with one hand and thrust two fingers into my cunt. I cursed under my breath, "Damn it. You're making me sick to death! Why are you applying your saliva to your fingers instead of lubricating oil, which is the right thing for my pussy? Do you know there are a lot of bacteria and viruses in your saliva, especially after you have had meals? Before doing each oral job, I will gargle with mouth wash. I will brush my teeth and then gargle to ensure adequate hygiene. Well, I will have a good gargle after you leave." However, I was just complaining inwardly.

He moved his fingers quickly and forcefully inside me. As he fingered me more and more violently and there seemed to be no end to it, I began to be fearful about the possible consequences.

"Take your time, my dear Uncle," I besought him, "You think you're dredging a sewer?" He had to withdraw his two fingers from my cunt and put them under his nostrils, "Mm, it smells wonderful." Then he put them into his mouth, "Mm, it tastes wonderful, too."

"Oh, Uncle. You have lived eighty years and still haven't learned how to make a woman happy by caressing her pussy," I thought to myself, "Your wife has also idled away her life. As the saying goes, live and learn or rather fuck and learn. Most people suppose they know well enough how to enjoy their sexuality but they actually don't. The Uncle's wife must have been deprived of all the happiness and pleasure a woman can savor all her life."

As a client put it: "My wife is a bitch. She makes love with other men." Why didn't he try to feel what his wife was feeling when he fucked her for only five minutes and then flopped into his dreamland, leaving his wife unsatisfied in an awkward situation. If I were his wife, I would sooner have eloped with any other more potent man.

However, few women were privileged to enjoy the same level of sexual pleasure as me. I had a dozen men to serve my lust every day and less masculine men had no nerve to propose to me. So I had to reconcile with being a prostitute baron.

My dear male readers, you should study my book hard and learn some useful techniques to please your wives and girlfriends in bed. Even if you want to go to brothels for pleasure, you should also be armed with rich knowledge of sexuality to satisfy your partners. Lovemaking is supposed to be a double-edged sword - either blade should be sharp enough to cut into flesh. It is supposed to be satisfying for both sexes. Otherwise, one party will surely lose interest in sex.

Suddenly, the doorbell rang and I went to the front door. Another Uncle came again. He was a legendary stingy miser. It was ten years since I first met him and every time he came, he brought only twenty dollars with him. And most annoying of all, once he said he had no money with him after the service. I got very angry, "You're not welcome in my home. You're the last man I'd like to see." It was at least half a year before he returned but every time he came, he still had only twenty dollars in his hand and no more.

This Junior Uncle was a bus driver. He was tall and stout with a big head, big eyes, thick lips, a big vegetable nose plus a big cock. Every part of him was a size bigger than those of ordinary folks. He was most loathsome in that he was very stingy and always bad-mouthing whoever he met. He paid only twenty dollars for each service, and when he left, he never forgot to take a bottle of red wine and a can of Coke with him. If all the other costs were subtracted, it was bordering on fucking me free of charge every time.

And what was more, every time he finished, he would wash himself carefully under the shower. For every five minutes he spent fucking he would spend ten minutes bathing. After deduction of costs, I could earn a net profit of a mere ten dollars. You could search the world in vain for so cheap a charge from a prostitute. Only a prostitute baron as me could stay in business on such a low rate. I had to face the reality with resignation. After all, he was a bus driver with a low income. But not all low- income bus drivers behaved as meanly. I had another bus-driver client who was nearly the same age as this Uncle, in his sixties. Every time I advised him my rate was fifty for half an hour, he insisted on paying me sixty. We even had small quarrels over the ten dollars. Finally he gave in and let me tuck the ten dollars into his trouser pocket.

Well, it was no use talking about that. Forget it. Little was better than nothing. Ten dollars was also money earned, though little. Now I was ushering the XXXL Uncle in. He asked me in a low voice, "You are busy, aren't you?"

"Don't you see I'm desperately busy?" I asked gruffly, "Please stop creating chaos."

He grabbed my hand and guided it into his trousers, "Can you feel how hot my cock is. It's like a hotdog fresh from a sizzling pan."

"Just wait a minute," I drew back my hand, "Be patient."

Actually when he entered, I already noticed the tent his cock had made between his thighs. Honestly, being in this business so many years, it was not uncommon to see such tents, large or small. Sometimes when a new client was bargaining with me about the price on the doorstep, I would look down accidentally to find such a tent appear as if a gun had been concealed under his pants.

I handed him a towel and beckoned him to take a shower, "Please take your shower first."

When I closed the door to the waiting room and came back to the working room, the Senior Uncle said to me, "I'd like you to lick my asshole today as I've washed it thoroughly and it is very clean. You can have a look at it to be sure."

With that, he bent over and lifted his buttocks skyward with both his hands supporting his weight on the bed edge. He waited for me to inspect it and I said,"I have to sit on the ground to check your asshole if you're standing by the bed edge like that. You should climb onto the bed and then I can sit on the bed to inspect whether your asshole is clean or not."

The Senior Uncle had some difficulty in climbing onto the bed with his protruding belly and lie with his face on the pillow. He knelt on the bed; his buttocks raised high and his head against the cream-colored headboard. I drew out two pieces of tissue from the box on the bedside table, wiped his asshole and showed the stained tissue to him, "Look, what's this? You said you had washed it clean? You should have cleaned the inside of the hole by digging your finger in and cleaning it. How can I lick such a stained, filthy asshole?"

The Senior Uncle was speechless in front of the irrefutable evidence – the residue of yellow shit on the tissue. I had to apply lubricating oil around his hole and clean it with a tissue. The muscles around his asshole convulsed as I cleaned them. I had much trouble in wiping them clean. I sat behind his big white hips, spread his buttocks open and tucked my tongue into his asshole. He kept saying, "Deeper, deeper, further deeper!"

With that, he pressed his head against the bed head and spread his buttocks wider with his hands, exposing the tender insides of his asshole. A troublemaker indeed, I thought, "Shut up. My tongue can't go any deeper; shall I use a stick instead?"

"Do you like my asshole, honey?" asked the Senior Uncle, "Go deeper and deeper still."

I was licking his asshole and kept an ear to the splashing of water in the waiting room toilet. As the splashing stopped, I said to the Uncle, "Just wait a minute. I'll be back right away."

"Go ahead," he flopped onto the bed, "I'll wait for you."

I arrived at the waiting room to find the Junior Uncle lay naked on the bed, his big cock erected skyward like a flashlight. I sat between his thighs and heard him say, "Suck my cock."

I opened my mouth wide and held his big cock in it. He said, "Deeper. Further deeper."

"An inch deeper and my throat will be clogged," I retorted. Soon he went on to say,"Suck my balls."I did as he instructed.

Two or three minutes later he said, "Lick my cock," followed by "Suck my balls." I shifted my mouth between his cock and eggs like a shuttle. My patience was really exhausted, "You're asking for so much for only twenty dollars. Ah, yes. Less than twenty dollars. I can only earn less than ten dollars from you excluding the wine and Coke you'll take when you leave."

He poked me on the forehead and said, "We're old friends, aren't we?"

"If every client claims to be entitled to pay a much discounted price as twenty dollars by being my friend," I asked, "How can I pay all the electricity and water bills?"

He seemed to be tongue-tied for a moment but went on to say, "Come on. Come on. Quit talking like that. Let me fuck you!"

I found him a large condom and put it on his cock. I bent over against the bed with my buttocks lifted up, "Quick. Someone's waiting in the other room." He wasted no time in fucking me from behind, "I'm fucking you. I'm fucking you! Your cunt is so hot inside."

He hadn't repeated "I'm fucking you" three times before he came quickly. I stood up and peeled off the condom from his cock, "Go and wash yourself." He said, "Then hand me another clean towel."

"Haven't I just given you one?"

Look, what a troublemaker he was. I shut the door and went to fetch another towel for him. When the Senior Uncle saw me come back, he lifted his pale buttocks high again.

"You don't need to lift up your buttocks just now," I advised him, "It will tire you out to do so too early." The Senior Uncle reclined back on the bed.

I went to the waiting room to hang up a towel for Junior Uncle and carried the dry, clean towels from the laundry back to the working room. I was folding the towels and having a small chat with Senior Uncle, "So, why didn't you go to work today?"

"I did," he said, "but in the middle of work I saw some young ladies doing their shopping in my shop. My cock stirred incredibly and became erect. I took advantage of the interval when there were fewer customers and went out to see you."

"Did you close your shop?"

"No. There are two employees serving the customers."

I thought to myself that it was so absurd that his employees were working for him while the employer was enjoying the pleasure of cock sucking and asshole licking. I waited for the splashing in the waiting room toilet to die down and figured the Junior Uncle had finished dressing and then closed the door to the working room. When I got there, the Junior Uncle was stepping out of the waiting room. He had me a twenty-dollar note said, "Here's your money." He didn't forget to kiss me on the lips with a smack. I took the money and sneered at him in mind, "Here's my money. Twenty dollars. He must be grudgingly paying it to me. Judging by my standard, you can't find a cheaper prostitute in Canberra, not to say in the world."

Handing him the wine and Coke, I asked, "Well, go back to resume your work?"

"Yes, and in a hurry or else I'll be late."

Seeing him off on the doorstep, I cautioned him, "Be sure to drive slowly."

"See you next time," he said as he left.

I went back to resume serving the Senior Uncle by sucking his asshole, thinking I should finish writing about the Papa, Senior Uncle and Junior Uncle and return to the very beginning of this book. When I was writing about the red-haired French client, the weirdest thing happened when I felt my soul was incarnated. When it came to the writing experience, one episode was followed by another continuously so the structure was stretched. I was afraid I had drifted too far from the topic to go back. I was worried about how to end this part of the writing and compile all of it into a well-organized book. I was in deep thought when the doorbell rang. I was surprised because I had no appointment at this time. It must have been some rash guy who came without an appointment.

I was cursing to myself as I headed for the front door. The doorbell kept on ringing "Dingdong. Dingdong." I guessed someone must have pressed the bell button too hard so it couldn't bounce back. If it couldn't, the doorbell would keep on ringing.

I hurried to open the door and then the security door. I tried to get the bell button back in place.

"Why didn't you give me a call before you came?" I got somewhat angry, "And you don't need to press the doorbell more than once. Look, you have damaged it and made it continue ringing."

He was short with a round fat belly. He had a big head with thin blond hair hanging over his shoulders. On his diamond-shaped face sat a pair of sunken eyes typical of Western people and a conspicuous red brandy nose, making him look somewhat shifty. He was also a client of mine for three years or more. But he didn't come often, sometimes every one or two months and other times every three or four months.

Seeing I was not happy, he kept apologizing. I glanced aside to find he was carrying a black canvas bag. "It's some meat I've brought you," he explained.

Thinking I had never asked him to bring me any meat, I said abruptly, "I don't want any meat. I have just bought three hundred dollars' worth of meat and fish from a Chinese butcher's shop yesterday. I'm not short of anything."

He opened the bag and showed me the contents, "Look, all fresh meat. I can sell it to you for half price."

I looked suspiciously into his bag, wondering why he could sell it to me for half price. Maybe the meat was stale? He dumped the meat onto my kitchen bench and I found the meat was unexpectedly fresh. It was all T-bone lamb. I had bought this sort of meat before and I knew it was the best part of a lamb. It was priced high in the supermarket. I stole a look at the meat. A dozen or more lamb chops were packed in a black plastic box sealed with cling film and priced at twenty-eight dollars a box. I suspected they were stolen goods but dared not ask. Seeing I was still hesitating, he said, "How about it? Two hundred and forty dollars for the lot but you can pay me just one twenty."

He took out the boxes one by one and there were seven of them. "But I cannot consume so much."

"But, I need money," he said.

As I heard he needed money and he was my old friend, I consented. I had enough cash to buy them and I could store them for future consumption. And besides, I could send Lisa several boxes as gifts when she came to Canberra in a few days. I took 120 dollars from the drawer and handed him the money. When he left, he asked for two bottles of beer.

I took three cans of beer from the fridge and asked him, "Do you want more?"

"No, thanks," he said, "More than enough."

After seeing off the long-haired fat man, I felt greatly amused. I had planned to end the loosely strung episodes today and return to the story of the red-headed French official from last September but it turned out that God was sending me more interesting material. Since my soul was incarnated and "Goddess was born," I had been accumulating more and more amusing anecdotes and humorous stories. God must be telling me: Hey, you prostitute baron. Don't forget when you're writing this large collection of jokes, there were many people in the world who liked stealing.

It reminded me of a boy aged thirty-five, who one day told me that he had stolen two bottles of wine from the supermarket, each of them worth a thousand dollars.

I was surprised, "Oh my. Have you been spotted by the police? If they track you down here, I will be suspected to be the person who helps dispose of the stolen goods."

"I have been stealing for more than thirty years," he said with a note of pride in his voice, "and have never been caught by the police, not even once."

"Anything you do or say may be used against you as evidence," I said jestingly, imitating a policewoman giving the Miranda warning to a suspect, "But I didn't catch you stealing so I needn't call the police."

Of course all this was my suspicion because I didn't catch the long-haired guy stealing indeed. I saw the Woolworths trademark on the packages and I was sure he didn't buy them at the marked price. No fool in the world would sell at 120 dollars what he had bought for 240. Another piece of evidence: The fact that he said he needed money meant he had none and then with what could he buy those quality lamb chops? I had a strong suspicion that these things were of questionable origin.

I remember an opulent lorry driver once told me they often stole things while delivering goods to supermarkets. He said, "Don't take things from one and the same box. You are less likely to be found if you steal some from this box and some from the other one."

Anyway I had paid the money for the lamb chops no matter how he got them. As for me, I hadn't taken anything from anybody nor had I overcharged anybody a penny all my life except when I was working ten years ago in a brothel. I planned to leave to start my own business with a fellow prostitute and I stole several condoms and a bottle of lubricating oil from the boss before we left. I had had a guilty conscience up until now. I did the minor theft only because I was afraid I couldn't find a place to buy the condoms and lubricating oil as we were in Australia for only several months. If I could meet the Chinese boss of that brothel now, I would pay him back the amount of 1,000 condoms and 100 bottles of lubricating oil. Furthermore, I would award him a premium for leading me on the road to the success of my business.

My ex-boss reiterated to me then, "Prostitution is as legal a profession in Australia as medicine or law is in China. No one can look down upon you..."

To think about the things that happened these days. Everything was so amusing. This God was really apt to provide me with endless materials. I used to be an atheist who didn't believe in God. From the time my soul was incarnated and Goddess was born, I've started to believe there might be a God and wondered whether it could be God's arrangement that Jesus was born 2,000 years before and a Goddess 2,000 years later. I was deviating from the subject again. Actually I never meant to deify myself. I was a common woman, not an immortal; yet all these weird things have been happening to me.

Take this morning for example; a tall and stout new client came and frowned and gasped at the very sight of me as he thought I was obviously older than the age I had told him over the phone. Did I look thirty-five? I was flattered if you said I looked forty-five. It was weird he didn't desert me after my persuasions but instead, he happily received my service. After an oral job, I straddled his hips to give his back a massage. He objected to me using my hands to massage him, but instead he had me sweep my long hair along his back, saying the caress of my hair was much more enjoyable than fucking itself. Half an hour later when he finished, he got dressed and said to me, "That's really the best sexual experience I have ever had." On the doorstep, he promised he would come visit me again.

Such unusual things had been happening for days. All my clients behaved very well. Even those who were in their late teenage years didn't come to make trouble after drinking. It was not a coincidence that all these unusual things happened at once within a short period. It must have been the thoughtful arrangement of God – He meant to make sure I could write this masterpiece of "The Number One Prostitute" in an undisturbed environment. Oh, God. My God! Since you have chosen me to complete this great masterpiece, why don't you grace me with your presence? Just show up even at night in my dreams, so I could offer others a description to confirm their belief in your existence?

I went back to the working room to lick my Senior Uncle's asshole. It was not long before the doorbell rang. I walked to the door unwillingly, nagging to myself, "Who's intruding on my business? Didn't you assume I'd be licking someone's cock? Uncle must have been interrupted in his enjoyment. How can he enjoy himself if the doorbell keeps ringing now and then?"When I arrived at the front door, I pulled a long face upon seeing Old Michael standing on the doorstep with a pink plastic lunchbox in his hand.

"Linda," he said, "I've brought you stewed pork hooves."

"You should have called me in advance," I grumbled discontentedly, "By the way, you have to wait for half an hour."

He slipped in and put the lunchbox on the kitchen bench, "No problem. I can wait longer than half an hour. I have enough time."

"I have cooked it for you," pointing to the lunchbox, he went on to say, "Eat it while it's warm."

"But I have no time for it," I kept a straight face, "I am kept so busy serving these cocks of yours that I have hardly any time to eat or drink with you guys constantly coming and going like this."

I took Old Michael to the waiting room and he sat there watching the porn video and enjoying cashews and drinks. I was afraid by the time it came to his turn half an hour later, few cashews would be left in the box.

I went back to the working room and yawned at the Senior Uncle. Just like me, he had also lost interest in the old game and hated being made to get up and lie down over and over with all the inconvenience of his great belly.

"This time," I said, "Lie straight and stretch your legs apart." I had him lie on his back and tucked three pillows under his neck for fear that he should feel uncomfortable with his head positioned too low. I was about to crawl in between his thighs when a bad smell of old man assaulted my nostrils. I coughed and retreated to the bathroom. I took out a plastic bowl and filled it with some warm water and brought it to the Senior Uncle. Having dripped some Dettol disinfectant liquid into the bowl, I began to rinse the old man's cock and balls. His cock was also one wrapped in foreskin, and a thick layer of white dirt was incrusted underneath it. I used my hands to wash his cock in the warm solution and Senior Uncle was enjoying it so that he groaned like a young baby, "Ennn, so warm, so comfortable. I feel as if I was putting my cock in your cunt." Having cleaned his cock and balls, I set about cleaning the insides of his thighs. Oh, my. He said he had had a shower? There was a residue of baby powder between the wrinkles of his thighs that I had applied last time! It took me quite some time to rinse his cock, balls and his inner thighs before I dried the lower part of his body with a clean towel.

Then I crawled into the space between his thighs and held his chili-pepper-like cock in my mouth. He pressed my head down and said, "Mm. Deeper further. All the way. Well done, baby."

I didn't think it a great problem to tackle his cock because even with his entire cock in my mouth, it still didn't touch my throat. If it were the Junior Uncle's cock, things would be quite different. His big cock had barely entered my mouth when it pressed my throat to such an extent that I almost choked. The Senior Uncle was saying, "Fuck my asshole!"

I put a condom on my left forefinger and thrust it into his asshole. He moaned before he cried out, "Ouch. Take your time. Take your time!"

"Do you remember how you were fucking me?" I smiled mischievously to myself, giving him a harder push.

Holding his cock in my mouth, I ran my right hand over the skin of his balls. He shouted anything you could imagine, "@#$%^&*!" before he yelled, "Fuck me. Fuck me!" I moved my left forefinger back and forth in his asshole like a small piston.

It was not long before he began to groan, "I'm coming. Don't pull your mouth away and drink my sperm!" I wasted no time in spitting the white clammy liquid out of my mouth.

"I told you not to spit it out," he was somewhat annoyed, "Drink it all and it will do you good!"

"If I drink the sperm of every client," I retorted, "I will need no food to keep my body and soul together." With that, I went over to wipe the stain off his cock and balls. Then I went to the bathroom to rinse my mouth. I fetched two towels from the cabinet, moistened them with warm water and handed one of them to the Senior Uncle for him to wash his hands and used the other to clean his cock and balls. After that, I threw the two dirty towels into the laundry basket. When I was cleaning his cock and balls, I found the flesh around his leg joints was crimson, just like a baby's hips that had been soaked in a wet diaper for too long. I went over to have a closer look and found some blood oozing from his skin. I guessed it was caused by the chafing of his inner thighs from walking because he was too corpulent. I took up the baby powder bottle from the bedside table and told him, "Uncle, let me apply some baby powder to your leg joint or you will feel more pain when you sweat."

"Thank you," he said. I spread his thighs open and applied a lot of baby powder there. When I was applying the powder, the Senior Uncle couldn't help crying out, "Ouch! Be careful. It hurts!"

"Your leg joint is bleeding," I said, "It's normal for it to hurt."

When I finished my medical practice, I helped him take to his feet and get dressed. I even helped him put his shoes and socks on before I sent him off.

Sending off Senior Uncle, I went to receive Mr. Hooves, Old Michael in the waiting room. He held my head and raved, "I love you. I'll fuck you. When I heard your customer's loud howl from the working room, I knew he was enjoying you very much and I felt excited and thrilled. My cock erected at once and jumped like a fish that had just been pulled out of water. I didn't expect he would let out such a loud cry of ecstasy."

"Can you imagine what noises men utter at the verge of ejaculating their sperm?" I said, "Some grunt like pigs; some bray like donkeys; some howl like wolves; some wail like ghosts. Some make noises between cries and laughter. Others cover their cocks and remain silent; still others hold their cocks and scat wildly.

"Let me have the fun of crying in pleasure like the man before me," Mr. Hooves said, as he came over to kiss my lips. I had to dodge his bothersome attempts. In a brief struggle, he pushed me onto the bed and stripped off my dress. I could hardly put a large condom on his big cock when he thrust it into my cunt. He yelled, "I'll fuck you hard! I'll fuck you to death!"

However, it was not long before he surrendered, "I'm getting fucking old. How come I've become tired out so soon? Come on. Sit on my cock!" With that, he lay down on his back and had me sit on his cock. I straddled him face to face in a squatting position and guided his cock into my cunt. I began to glide up and down on his cock loudly. Soon I was breathing heavily when he ordered, "Turn around and face your plump buttocks toward me. And then sit on my cock, it will be more sensual."I obediently followed his instructions. While striding him facing his feet, I guided his cock into my cunt and began to lower and lift my torso alternatively. Having been engaged in serving my clients for a whole morning, I was almost exhausted, so I had to prop my hands on the bed to support my own weight. Cramping his cock with my cunt muscles, I twisted my buttocks in all possible directions to gain maximum pleasure for both sides. It was only five minutes before he said, "Wait, wait! Keep this position and don't move." At that time, I was just sitting on his cock with my face toward his feet. He got up from under my buttocks, grabbed my buttock cheeks and inserted his big cock into my cunt from between them. Then he began to yell at the top of his voice any conceivable groans and moans, "@#$%^&*+~!" until he let out a desperate howl, "Oh, fuck me dead!" After he came at long last, I said, "Look, the rotten hooves of yours are well worth it, aren't they?" He said nothing but hurried to the bathroom to wash up his mouth, cock, and asshole. His apparent indifference made me understand that his love only existed momentarily when he was coming and as soon as he came, I became a stranger to him as before. I found he resembled me in that we could both separate love from sex. After the lovemaking, he was still himself and I was still myself, separate and distinct.

Old Michael dressed quickly and muttered, "The cashews you gave me just now have become stale and are not fit to eat."

I took out a half-finished packet of cashews from the kitchen cabinet and threw it to him, "Here you are. They were bought yesterday. Fourteen dollars a packet. There's a lot left in the packet."

"Give me a can of Cola," he said.

I took a can of Diet Coke from the fridge and handed it to him.

"Plus a bag of chips," his greed knew no limit, "Then give me a plastic bag."

When he left, he was all smiles, "Thank you Linda. See you later."

Farewell, Mr. Hooves, Old Michael. I secretly wish you would stop frequenting me and stop stuffing my refrigerator with pork hooves. For quite a long time, I cooked pork hooves every day and the stock lasted me nearly six weeks.

Sending him off, I felt like settling down for a rest. Holding the bowl with three cooked hooves in it in one hand and a glass of fat-free milk in the other, I went to the west living room and put the food and drink on the writing desk. I took up the remote control and settled on the sofa to watch my 3D TV. All the English channels were showing news reports about the Japanese earthquake and tsunami. I was afraid the miserable scenes would rekindle my old memories and cause me to become Goddess incarnate again. I quickly switched to the Chinese channels but to my astonishment, I couldn't find any Chinese programs at all. All the channels were blank. There must have been something wrong with the satellite dish on the roof. Three years ago, a Chinese man named Paul from Tianjin helped me install a black dish that was nearly seven feet wide on my roof. He had been on call whenever something went wrong with this satellite antenna. But on the other hand, I always made sure I gave him a generous tip after every service call. I found his phone number and placed a call to him, "Paul, how come there are blank screens on all the Chinese channels? Come and see what the matter is with the dish antenna on the roof."

"Wait a moment," he said, "I'll come the minute I finish the work at hand. I'll there in half an hour or so."

Putting down the receiver, I switched back to the English channels. Gosh, the Japanese tsunami again. I switched to another channel and Libya was in a state of war. Multinational troops were bombarding Libya and the allied air forces of the U.S., the U.K. and France began to strike Gaddafi's troops on grounds that Gaddafi was bloodily suppressing his own people who were peacefully protesting his regime…

Enough! Both parties claimed to be in the right and no party seemed to be the least bit convincing. I was immersed in the TV program when the phone on the desk rang, "Linda, are you okay?" On hearing Lisa's voice, I calmed down at once. Her voice had an appeasing effect on my mind especially when I was driven into a state of mania from writing. Whoever heard my accounts about souls thought I was insane and had a muddled head. But actually I was as cool as a cucumber in judging everything around me. All the characters in my accounts had their prototypes in real life. As my English translator had put it, "Mad writers and cool compilers are necessities for a great masterpiece." Whenever I was in a turbulent state of mind, it was Lisa who came to cut the knot in my mind and comfort me. Lisa read widely and was an author herself so she was quite aware of the psychology and behavior of writers.

Every time I had something on my mind, she came to straighten me out. She was the best listener and my first person to confide in. Lisa said, "I haven't heard from you these past few days. You scared me to death last week. I had planned to fly to see you for fear some terrible thing had happened to you," she added in a muffled voice, "I would have done so if I was not pregnant then."

I jumped with joy at hearing the good news that she was pregnant, "Hey, give birth to a nice hybrid!"

"It is sure to be a nice one," Lisa said with pride, "If it is a boy, he will surely take after his father, a lusty fellow."

"Even if he doesn't take after his father," I burst out laughing, "he will become a lusty fellow regardless, since he has overheard so many dirty stories while he was in your womb."

I went on to tell Lisa, "That day after I finished the phone conversation with you, I called my translator. He said when some devoted writers arrived at a certain stage, they were most likely to develop delusions. On the day Goddess was born, I would have gone mad if it wasn't for your direct, sharp warning. Now I know what it is like experiencing a delusion and have learned how to adjust my mood. Don't worry. I have a super ability to control my emotions and will never go mad."

"That's fine then," Lisa said, "I was worried about you. From now on, be sure to call me every day and let me know you're okay."

"Well. What are you doing now?" she went on to ask. "I am eating pork hooves," I was biting at a tasty bone

"A gift from Old Michael?" it was Lisa's turn to burst out laughing, "Ha, ha. When we were watching TV last night, I joked about it with my daughter. I mentioned her Auntie Linda was so easy to please. You just needed to give her six hooves and you could ask any special favor of her. As my daughter had gone shopping with me, she knew hooves were very cheap and cost a little more than a dollar each. She exclaimed, 'It's too stingy of that man to pay as little as some hooves in exchange for a favor from Auntie. Pork hooves can be given as gifts in China but here in Australia they are seen as rubbish. No Australian will go so far as to taste them.' Hearing my daughter's comments, I doubled up with laughter on the sofa. The more I thought about it the more amused I was. But my husband and daughter didn't know the truth and were wondering why I was laughing so heartily."

Lisa and I had much in common. Lisa's husband and my ex-husband were both local Australians and their middle names were both Thomas. I didn't know whether it was Providence or coincidence but I thought we were destined bosom friends and besides, we were both forthright women with big voices and living in the same foreign country so we got along very well.

"No," I said indignantly, "Since hooves are as cheap as a dollar each, I may as well settle accounts with the Old Mike someday. For the past four years, he has been giving me six every time and saying they are worth twenty dollars. It turns out he knows he has been enjoying my service for only six or seven dollars each time and has been coming so often. My losses have added up to a large amount of money. What makes me even angrier was Old Michael came today and brought me three hooves, which he said he had cooked for me. What a shrewd old Shylock! He calculated that if he paid me with six raw hooves, then he could pay me three dollars less if they were cooked. You didn't see how he pestered me before. I was made to kneel, squat and lie down at last. His big cock couldn't rest for a single moment."

Lisa almost choked with laughter on the other end of the line. I stopped her and said, "Stop laughing. I will settle accounts with the guy next time."

When we got tired of laughing, I went on to say, covering the receiver to muffle my voice, "Say, Lisa, a client sold me seven boxes of lamb chops earlier. Those from the best part of the sheep with a T-bone, you know? They sell most expensively in the supermarket. The client said eight boxes were worth two hundred and forty but he charged me only one twenty at half price. When you come this Sunday, take some with you. I just can't consume them all."

"No," she refused,"Leave them for yourself. My fridge doesn't need filling."

"Just take them. I'll be annoyed if you don't," I insisted, and then added in a low voice, "I suspect they're stolen goods."

"How do you know?" Lisa began to laugh.

"The plastic boxes were all marked with Woolworth's logos," I deduced like Sherlock Holmes, "Could he be so foolish as to buy something for two hundred and forty dollars and sell them for one hundred and twenty the next minute? Unless he had gone mad."

I went on to paraphrase what the lorry driver and the thirty-five-year-old said in detail, but before I had finished Lisa was already convulsed with laughter. I echoed her laughter on my side of the line, "Look, our God has supplied me with ample material. It's a miracle I should encounter so many amusing stories."

We were chatting gaily and loudly when the doorbell rang. I ended the conversation, "Wait, wait. I have to go make money. Goddess also has to make a living. There's no free lunch, even in heaven."

I put the receiver back into its cradle and went to answer the door. It was the repairman Paul, who had come to fix my satellite antenna. He was covered in a layer of dust from head to toe. His shoes were worn out at the heels and greatly faded. Hardly had he come in when he asked, "What's the matter? Can't see any programs on the Chinese channels?"

"No," I said helplessly, "I can't find any programs at all on Chinese channels. There must be something wrong with the disk on the roof."

"Let me check the inner circuit first," he said.

He picked up the remote controls to the TV set and the satellite antennaontheroofandthencheckedthemprofessionally. I hurried to the kitchen and took several cans of drink and a bottle of mineral water from the fridge for him, "Have a drink first. You don't need to be in a hurry."

"Leave the drinks aside till I finish the repairs."

He tried pressing here and there on the remote controls and suddenly he couldn't help laughing, "Here they are! You forgot to switch on the button to the satellite antenna. How can you watch satellite programs if you don't switch it on? Linda, you have had the satellite antenna installed for more than three years and you still can't remember how to use it."

I tapped my temple with my right finger, "I'm no electrician and I am an absolute blockhead with any novel gadget. Believe it or not, though I have been in Australia for ten years, I don't know how to send text messages on a mobile phone. Sometimes a client texts me asking for a price but I don't know how to reply on the mobile. My mobile is only used for making or answering calls. "

"You have too many TV sets in your home," Paul smiled, "Of course you can't remember which button is which. Now remember the Chinese channels are on A1, the two TV sets in your waiting room are on A4 and as for the other two TV sets in your working room, one is on A2 and the other A5 (because they are of different brands). Listen carefully and jot them down. I'm leaving if there's nothing else I can do here."

"Wait a minute," I stopped him, "Let me pay you."

"You don't need to pay me," he said sincerely, "You have been paying me too generously and how can I take your money for so little a service today."

"No. I insist," I said, "At least I should pay you the fare for coming here."

He dodged and headed toward the door, saying, "No thanks. No thanks." I tugged at his sleeve to stop him from escaping (My clients often mentioned the stubbornness that was distinctively characteristic of me in refunding money or giving gifts). I hurried back to the kitchen to pick up a fifty-dollar note, a red wine and a port together with the drinks and snacks on the desk and put them into a plastic bag. To make sure the bag wouldn't burst, I put it into another plastic bag. I stuffed the gift bag into his arms and tucked the money into his pocket, "Get along and make your way. If you feel obliged, you can thank me by coming on time whenever I call you. Usually I tend to be impatient."

He left happily, "Okay. Call me if you need me."

I closed the door and shook my head in amusement. These days I was so engaged in writing and worked so devotedly that my mind was occupied by Goddess or God and I totally forgot my real identity.

Day Five: March 25, 2011

At around one thirty after lunch that afternoon, a New Zealander client arrived. He was in his mid-twenties and stood about five foot ten. He was neither too fat nor too thin with a short, thick, black haircut. He had a very handsome oval face with a pair of sunken big eyes, a nice pointed, high nose and a sexy, curved mouth. When he smiled, he exposed a set of white even teeth, which made him even more pleasant and amiable. He took a shower and lay on his back on the white towel I had spread out for him. I went over to him and looked covetously at his shapely body: broad shoulders, muscled arms and a flat belly. His six, strong symmetrical abdominal muscles showed that he exercised regularly and the knots of muscles in his thighs were equally spectacular.

"Hi, young man," I asked, "What is your profession?"

"I'm a professional weightlifter and an amateur martial artist and boxer."

"Do you exercise every day?"

"Yes," he answered, "and very hard at that. I get up at five o'clock every morning to train and I spare three evenings every week to study and practice Chinese *Shaolin Temple* martial arts."

"Are you good at *Shaolin Wushu* or martial arts?"

"I'm learning from a Wushu master from the *Shaolin Temple*. It's really wonderful seeing the master looking straight ahead as if he could swallow up all the mountains and sky in front of him."

"Do you believe in the existence of souls?" I asked.

"I do," he said, "I want to keep it because some others have lost theirs."

"So do I," I agreed, "And I have found the existence of it…"

After blowing him, I found him a large condom and put it on his big cock. As he laid his young body on me, my thoughts suddenly flew back to my adolescence when I wrapped my arms around my young lover Zhang's strong, slim waist. I said to myself, "My dear Zhang, fuck me hard. My cunt is so itchy. Ah, yes. Deeper and harder! To the left and to the right. Push your cock against the opening of my womb. Right. Harder and still harder!"

The young man rhythmically and relentlessly moved his huge cock in me. I could hear the squelching sound of my lust water spilling out between our sexual organs as he fucked me away salaciously. His yells, "Ah. Ah. I'm fucking you! I'm fucking you!" were echoed by my responses, "Oh. Oh, yes. Harder!"

By and by, I began to itch all over and a sharp tingle arose in my soles. A couple of minutes and I would have reached my climax. But at the most inopportune time, the young man stiffened and then ejaculated in torrents with three loud groans. I could distinctively feel his cock jerking six or seven times in my cunt. After quite a long time, he lay on my body motionlessly. Finally I helped him to his feet, peeled off the condom filled with white sperm and pushed him to the bathroom. However, I was not satiated and my cunt itched intolerably. I knew my sexual appetite had just been whetted and I was helplessly in an awkward situation. I complained in my mind that he was too young and inexperienced; too green to know he must be patient to satisfy a woman…

Following the young man was a German big cock, one of my loyal fans for nine years. He was tall and fat with a huge beer belly. He had a big, round, clean-shaven head. On his balloon-like face, he had a pair of vigilant eyes under thin eyebrows, a vegetable nose and thick lips.

His stout, bronzed upper torso showed he was a worker who was used to being stripped down to his waist and exposed to the sun for long hours. He said he was a bricklayer in a construction company. I knew well his cock was a gun ready to discharge easily and I hoped it wouldn't today.

He followed me to the working room and stripped hastily, saying impatiently, "I have already had my shower."

With that he flopped onto the bed on his back, and below his huge belly erected a somewhat bent cock, like a banana. Being aflame with insatiate lust, I wasted no time in tossing off all my clothing and throwing myself astride his great cock. I began my up-and-down gymnastics on his cock: one, two, three, four, five… It was only several minutes before I became breathless. To me this was very intoxicating exercise but it was so exhausting that my strength quickly ran out.

Seeing I was huffing and puffing, the German big cock rolled out of the bed and threw my legs onto his shoulders. He thrust his cock into my cunt and moved it even harder and quicker than before, "Oh, yes. Oh, yes. I love to fuck you! Your cunt clamps me so hard! My cock is so happy! I feel my cock so hot in your cunt!" It was only five minutes before he came with three desperate yells of "Oh! Oh! Oh!" He ejaculated all his white sperm on my belly. I was frustrated and cursed his disappointing performance. Another five minutes and I could succeed in coming. Damn it! Just my luck. I was languishing but no one could satisfy my desire. I had to leave listlessly to the toilet to wash my private part while he was having his shower.

I was washing when my mobile buzzed. "Are you busy now?" I heard a man ask.

I recognized in no time he was my eighty-one-year-old Austrian lover. Here came my savior! I could be satiated thoroughly by him. "No," I said eagerly, "When can you be here?"

"I'll come in ten minutes."

I put on my dress and went back to the working room. The German client was dressed. I charged him forty dollars as a special price and saw him off after giving him a bottle of red wine.

Five minutes passed and the doorbell rang. I opened the door to find my old fan staring at me, "How are you and how hot are you?"

"I am so hot," I said, "I have been impatiently waiting for you."

"Have any big cocks visited you today?"

"To hell with those two useless cocks!" I said in anger. He smiled, "Mine is better, isn't it?"

"Your mouth is better than your cock," I said jestingly and accompanied him to the working room

When we were there, we stripped in no time and lay naked side by side on the bed. He was lying on my left and pouting his lips toward mine, "Honey dear, I love you and have missed you for so many days."

Forget the word "love," I thought. What I wanted most now was to find someone to satiate me sexually. He slowly shifted his mouth to my right nipple to suck it. An intolerable itch surged from my nipple via my heart to all parts of my body. I picked up the bottle from the bedside table, poured some lubricating oil onto my right palm and applied the oil around the opening of my cunt. My "old lover" was lying on his side, poking his right forefinger and middle finger into my cunt in place of his own cock. He thrust his fingers here and there randomly inside my cunt. I dipped my right middle finger in the oil and ran it slowly around my clitoris – the bud between my lips. I felt a warm thrill generating there as if an electric current flowed through my body. Narrowing my eyes, I imagined I were Cixi the Empress Dowager, who was enjoying her carnal pleasure. In my imagination, one of my favorite ministers was spreading my lips and sucking my clitoris. He asked in a whisper near my ear, "Do you enjoy it, your majesty. Are you satisfied with my performance? I haven't licked any other woman so earnestly, not even my own wife."

And I said in my mind, "Work harder. If you satisfy me and make me come, I will promote you to a higher rank." In my daydream, I told my favorite kneeling on my left to suck my left nipple and another one on my right to suck my right nipple… In reality my "old lover" was hurting my nipple because his false teeth had no sensitivity at all. In the past I would be startled by the pain. But today, strangely enough, it didn't feel so painful. Instead I seemed to begin to like this pain. This was a pain somewhere between an itching pain and a painful itch. At the same time, I kept daydreaming that all my favorites were kneeling around me and praying, "Let her majesty fuck her fill. Her majesty's carnal pleasures are our greatest happiness…" In reality I was murmuring, "Suck my nipples hard. Gnaw at them hard!"

Though his teeth almost cut into my right nipple, I did not push him away. I kept fumbling my clitoris until at last I held my breath as a most tingling current thrilled through my clitoris and nipple to my heart and then to the whole of my body. I burst out yelling, "I've come! Thank you. Thank you. Thank you!" I extended to him my triple hearty thanks!

Meanwhile my "old lover" went on pistoning his fingers in my cunt so as to increase my pleasure when I came. I convulsed several times before I lay paralyzed on the bed, gasping a long time for breath. Relieved from sexual starvation, I felt thoroughly refreshed because this time I was satiated by the combined efforts of three men instead of just one. My brain seemed to have been cleaned most effectively.

It was common sense that men were supposed to be quicker in coming than women, so in sexual intercourse men should consciously slow down their pace so that both sexes can reach their climaxes approximately simultaneously. Usually it took women twice as long as men to come. For example, if a man needed ten minutes to be satisfied, a woman needed twenty minutes or more. And of course the time needed to be satisfied varied from woman to woman. The differences were accounted for by their profession, attitudes toward sex and many other factors. As for me, an experienced prostitute exposed to so many cocks every day, the threshold became very high; therefore it was extremely hard for me to come with a man. I usually needed twenty to thirty minutes' strong stimulus to come.

I took a rest after I had reached my climax. Then I sprawled by his left side, picked up his little cock and began to suck it. My "old lover" pressed my head with his right hand, "Suck hard. Suck hard. Still harder!" I sucked his cock as a baby sucked its mother's breast and it took me only three or four minutes to settle his cock. My mouth was filled with a lot of his sperm. I got up to wash my mouth and hands in the bathroom. He went to take his shower too. When he came back, I began to massage him on the back.

"By the way, how are you getting along with your book?" he asked, "I was wondering whether I can live long enough to read it."

"It won't be too long," I answered, "I think I'm writing a book of great value. I have not only found the human soul but also the existence of God."

My "old lover" raised his eyes, "What God? I don't believe in any God."

"I used to be a non-believer in God," I said, "But as I was writing recently, I felt positively there should be one but then after some time I changed my mind and felt negatively again. And it was strange that with all that wavering I should dwell on the significance of God's existence in my book…"

The discussion on theology couldn't go on any further because of my limited English. After I had finished massaging his back and chest, he got up and dressed. I gave him two bottles of red wine and one bottle of white wine as gifts together with three Pepsis, a Coke and two packets of chips. He paid me forty dollars. As a matter of fact, I served him almost for nothing. I earned no more than ten dollars. This had been my special offer to him for years as I knew the old man was retired and was not well off.

When he left, he did not forget to urge me, "I'm expecting your book. Get it published as soon as possible, otherwise I won't have the chance to read it in the remaining years of my life."

Having done all the work, I called Lisa, "Lisa dear, please tell me if there's really a God in the world?"

As a matter of fact, I called Lisa almost every day discussing my feelings with her regarding my writing. She read extensively and was Christian herself. In our discussion, she told me a lot and we argued more than once about the existence of God.

"There is," she said.

"There is none," I retorted.

But sometimes I also said yes. Actually I was not sure. I had confused myself. I was half believing and half doubting yet I was beginning to love that God, though He was invisible and intangible to me.

I heard Lisa proclaiming her assertion on the other end of the line, "Yes, there definitely is."

"Then," I asked her, "Did God create human beings as well as the world?"

"Yes," she answered, "According to *Genesis,* after God created everything in the world, He created man; Adam, like himself and then took a rib from him to make Eve. He had them marry and have children…"

"I don't think God would have created human beings," I argued, "Even if God exists, it must have been that He only created the world and after that various living things began to appear and then the apes. Modern humans have gradually evolved from those apes."

"No," Lisa said resolutely, "It was God that created humans."

We couldn't continue the discussion because we couldn't agree on this controversial topic. We were living in a world with multicultural values. And when she said that humans used to live for hundreds of years, I also took it with a grain of salt.

"Because humans back then had fewer sins," she explained, "and besides, they had a more favorable environment, there being neither pollution nor disease. Humans now have committed too many sins and God shortened their lifespan accordingly."

Then she preached other chapters of the Bible to me but they all seemed Greek to me. She sighed helplessly and went on to ask me about the computer typist.

The mere mention of the typist evoked a lot of grievances in me.

Lisa knew I was hiring Ms. Huang, a teacher from the Guangdong province, in China to type the manuscript for me, so she cautioned me, "You have to employ a typist who can understand your work. An incompetent typist will surely make a mess of your writing because the error rate of a mediocre computer typist is notoriously high. And if your typist is not responsible enough to proofread the manuscript carefully afterward, I'm wondering what will become of your writing."

"It's not so bad," I said, "She said she knew literature and had experience in compiling essays as an editor. And besides, she can read my manuscript easily, even my illegible scrawl. So I paid her four hundred dollars per ten thousand words."

"What?" Lisa let out a cry of surprise, "It's absolutely right to call you a squanderer. Four hundred dollars per ten thousand words! If you employ an overseas Chinese student in Sydney to do it, you can just pay him the minimum wage of ten dollars an hour. The average speed of a good typist is about a thousand words an hour. So you can pay just one hundred dollars for ten thousand words and you can still expect the quality of the work to be good enough."

"All right," I said, "I will fire the typist from Guangdong. I will settle accounts with her by paying her the last one thousand three hundred dollars when she returns her finished work. She must be dismissed because she wasn't even qualified enough to start each paragraph on a new line and crammed several hundred thousand words into a large mass. Even I, the original writer, can't make out which paragraph is which."

"A teacher who doesn't know how to paragraph an article?" Lisa was bewildered, "What kind of typist have you found?"

I was taken aback by this barrage of questions from her. It suddenly dawned on me that I might have been deceived by the typist. Had she really worked as a teacher or an editor?

Though I knew Lisa said so in my best interest, I rejected her suggestion on the grounds that I was unwilling to have young overseas students type the writing of a prostitute baron. They were too young to know about the worries of life for our generation. Furthermore, my book depicts a prostitute's life and most of its content would pollute young readers. I pledged I would print the caution: *Not suitable for readers under eighteen* on every book I issued.

It would obviously be a restricted publication.

I was in meditation when I heard Lisa saying, "I told you not to let her type your writing but you ignored my advice. If you had let me know earlier that she couldn't even paragraph an article, I would have advertised for you in a Sydney paper for a competent typist."

"But," I faltered, "I have already given her most of my manuscript. I should let her finish typing it in any case, though the things she types out will be of no use for me. I am a woman of my word, aren't I? It's my own business to waste my money, anyway."

"Oh, my sister," Lisa said, "No one in the world acts like you. You're throwing money into water with your eyes open by letting her continue typing the five hundred thousand words. You may as well donate the twenty thousand dollars to charity."

"Actually, it is not a sheer waste of money," I argued, "At least we had a casual discussion about my work. She gave some valuable advice and comments on which characters were ridiculous and which were abominable."

"Anyway," there was a note of contempt in Lisa's voice, "she is a person who doesn't know what punctuation is. This shows her true skill level. Why didn't she paragraph her printing? Ignorance? Maybe. Greed? Maybe too. The fact is she deliberately left it unparagraphed to save time. When you said she charged you for the extra fifteen words for each page, I thought you were exaggerating. But now I have come to believe she will charge you for even a single extra word, let alone fifteen. Well, let's forget the money thing. The fact that she crammed all the words into a large mass meant she lacked any sense of responsibility or professional ethics. If I were you, I would have given her the sack in no time."

The more she spoke, the angrier she became and I was speechless and crestfallen, wondering what was wrong with my Cantonese typist.

There was a long story attached to the fact that Ms. Huang, the Cantonese woman, charged for the extra fifteen words for each page.

In October last year, that is 2010, I began to write a book by stringing together all the anecdotes I had accumulated in the past ten years. I was a cyber-illiterate and couldn't type on a computer so I had no way to input my manuscript into the computer. Lisa then was staying in China because she had to apply for a spouse visa outside Australia and she had many other things to deal with there so I didn't tell her my difficulty. One day, I called a friend of mine I knew in the brothel, Lily (alias Ms. Qian), telling her my plan and asking her to hire me an editor in Sydney, who could help me input my manuscript into the computer. Unfortunately a quarrel arose because of this and as a result, we parted in discord. (Lily's story will be dwelt on later)

After I had fallen out with Lily, I advertised in the *Canberra Daily*: A Chinese language typist wanted. Ms. Huang was chosen among a dozen or more applicants. Choice criterion one was no young candidates and she was forty-three. Choice criterion two was the duty to ensure the content of the manuscript must be held in confidence before the book is published.

On November 20th, I gave Ms. Huang the fourth copy of the manuscript. As this part was about my life in China, it seemed innocent in its description. I was ignorant of the salaries in the labor market but heard Lily say it was 500 dollars for 10,000 words (including the work of proofreading the manuscript). When Ms. Huang came to settle accounts with me, I paid her for her 20,000 words' typing work, with one page short. (The words were estimated at 1,000 per page. As she had brought me nineteen pages, including a half page, I paid her 1,000 dollars.)

She said, "I'll make up for the missing page later."

Later I discovered that the average rate for a typist was 285 dollars for every 10,000 words so I negotiated with Ms. Huang and we agreed on a new rate of 350. One day, we had a talk over the phone about my work and she made some valuable suggestions. Delighted by this, I said, "Well, I'll pay you four hundred dollars for ten thousand words in future."

But when she came to settle accounts with me the next time, instead of making up for the page she was short, she took the paid half page into account. I laughed up my sleeve. Though I was computer illiterate, I was good at mental arithmetic. However, I concealed my displeasure and paid her as much. It was quite understandable that being a new immigrant to Australia, she needed money badly. One more page meant forty dollars more (an easy calculation of 1,000 words per page). Though a trifling amount for me, it might be important to her, I thought. So I waved it off.

The next time she came, I paid her according to the number of words she supplied. When she came for the third time, she said she needed a printer and had bought one from a Chinese student for twenty dollars. I said, "I'll give you a hundred dollars for the printer no matter how much you have paid for it."

We were cooperating happily and her typing speed improved rapidly. She could type forty or fifty thousand words a week at that time. When she came to settle the account before she left for

China, she claimed to have typed 54,000 words and I paid her 2160 dollars accordingly. But later I found she had fraudulently counted the half page as a whole one again.

As I had been busy serving my various clients from morning till night, I couldn't and wouldn't check the accounts with her too accurately, so I usually acknowledged any credit she had claimed and paid her accordingly. When she left, I would take advantage of the time when I had no clients to check the whole account item by item. I had double checked a dozen times and her typing work added up to 400,000 words. More often than not there were several miscalculations, all in her favor. I never pointed them out to her and didn't even drop the vaguest hint. It was not that I was not good at calculation but that I didn't feel like concerning myself about trifles.

Later, she took two more copies of the manuscript from me after she returned from China on February 12. When she came back to settle accounts with me one Sunday morning, on February 19, I paid her 2,200 dollars without any inspection of her quantity of work. She gave me an invoice for RMB 700, of which some 300 Yuan was for a memory stick I asked her to buy for me and the rest would go toward her printing paper and ink cartridges. She said all these items were on one invoice and that she would only claim the price of the memory stick and exclude her own share of the expenses. But I just waved my hand and said, "Forget it. I will cover all the expenses and give you one hundred and fifty dollars (Roughly amounting to RMB 900 according to the current exchange rate of 1:6)."

I was particularly busy that day and worked late into the early hours of the following morning. When I found time to check up on her typing work, I found to my dismay the new pages had included six and a half paid pages. It seemed that she had underestimated my intelligence. Actually she had typed fifty and a half pages but she claimed she had brought me fifty-five pages or 55,000 words. And what was worse, she mixed the fifty- six and a half pages with six and a half paid pages. This time, she typed the first half of my eighth manuscript (including the paid six and a half pages of my seventh manuscript, which was about my life in China). I thought it was a deliberate attempt to defraud me.

It was not until nine o'clock the next morning that I finished proofing the typing work. Then I called her mobile phone, "Ms. Huang, the fifty-five pages you sent was mixed with seven pages you had been paid for. I would let it go if it was only one or two pages. But things are different this time. I will show you the next time you come."

She responded promptly, "Maybe I redid those seven pages by mistake."

"By mistake?" I asked sarcastically, "You didn't need to repeat them but you could just copy them on your computer. It was not that I was absolutely cyber-ignorant and couldn't type myself but that my typing speed is not fast enough so I hired you to help me with the typing."

There was an awkward silence for a moment and before she could say anything I hung up the receiver. The incident seemed to have passed like that before she called back at about eight o'clock, "Linda, are you engaged now?"

"Yes," I answered, "I'm engaged. I'll call you back later."

At ten o'clock in the evening, I called Ms. Huang's mobile and heard her say, "Linda, you said I had mixed six and a half paid pages in the fifty-five pages. It's not accurate. I have double checked it myself. The fact is I claimed fifty-five pages but actually I typed fifty-six and a half pages. My real typing work, excluding the five repeated pages, should be fifty and a half pages, shouldn't it?"

I was dumbfounded in anger. Accurate calculation indeed! I said in a fury, "Am I a calculating person who squares accounts in minute detail? Have I settled accounts with you to such accuracy as half a page? I happen to remember I paid you whole page money for your half page the first time and similar things happened several times. And what's more, I gave you a hundred dollars for your printer, which should be your own expense. This time I just said you were quite a number of pages short and I never expressed any intention to deduct any of your pay."

Seeing I was angry, she said, "Sorry, Linda." In a fit of rage, I threw down the receiver abruptly.

How frustrated I felt. The next morning, I called Peter, my real-estate agent in Sydney, asking him to help me advertise for an English language translator in the *Australia News*. (I asked Peter to do it for me because I could only use cash instead of credit card, and I would have had to attend the advertisement department in person to put an advertisement in their paper.) I reckoned if the translator could proofread my manuscript and type, I could get rid of the dishonest typist. Kill two birds with one stone.

I waited until Peter called back on Friday saying the advertisement would appear in Sunday's *Australia News*. I asked him how much the fee was and he said it was twenty-seven dollars. I insisted on paying him 150 but he flatly refused, saying, "Are you kidding? It's twenty-seven dollars not two thousand seven hundred. Let's talk about it some other time." Feeling much obliged to him, I said, "Thank you ever so much for taking the trouble to do it for me."

"Not at all," he said happily, "The newspaper office happens to be next door to my office."

"Then," I said, "I'll pay you back later." With that, we ended our conversation.

When Ms. Huang came to settle the accounts on February 26, she waved the pages in her hand and explained she had typed fifty-three and a half pages and I paid her fifty-four pages so this time she would make up for the half page short. She went on to say, "I have six more pages in my hand but you paid me only fifty-five pages. Therefore I just owed you five pages. Now I've brought you forty-four pages so you may pay me for thirty-nine pages."

Glancing at them briefly, I said, "Well, we may as well round the number of pages to an integer and let me pay you for forty pages. A mere forty dollars more." As a result I paid her 1,600 but she didn't seem to be reconciled easily. "Linda," she went on to say, "I haven't told you before that as a matter of fact, there are a thousand and fifteen words instead of a thousand on each page.

So when I finished typing a hundred pages, I had actually typed fifteen hundred words more." I almost fell faint hearing these remarks. It turned out I was underpaying her by sixty dollars for every hundred words! I threw in the towel, "So how would you like it settled? I can pay you several pages more every time you come to settle accounts?"

Oh my! How much I had underpaid Ms. Huang for the 400,000 or more pages which I thought I had squared. After she left, I double checked and found I didn't owe her anything. And this made me even more frustrated. I had voluntarily raised her rate from 350 to 400 dollars for every 10,000 words but she was haggling over fifteen words per page.

Due to my thoughtlessness, I let her take with her another copy of my newly-written manuscript about my prostitute's life. So she had four of my manuscripts in her hand and she said she had almost finished typing the first one.

Shortly after Peter, the real-estate agent placed an advert in *Australia News*, a certain lady named Murong called in saying she had been a typist for a dozen years in a printing house in China. She admitted her English was not good enough to be qualified as a translator but her typing skills were absolutely at a professional level. At first, I told her over the phone something to the effect that I was intending to find a translator and typist not simply a person doing the typing. At that she said, "But a good translator was not necessarily a good typist and even if the translator can type well, your handwriting will be illegible to him. Therefore some errors are unavoidable. So you may as well hire a typist and input your handwriting into the computer and then send the electronic version of your manuscript to the translator. Being a senior typist for years, I can handle the most difficult illegible scrawl."

What she said sounded quite reasonable and it seemed she was an able and efficient woman. Maybe she was a fitter person to fill the vacancy of a typist than Ms. Huang. So I made an arrangement for the lady from Sydney to come to Canberra on Sunday to discuss the cooperation between us.

Putting down the receiver, I took it up again to call Ms. Huang asking her to type the first copy about a prostitute's life. If she hadn't finished the first copy, she could send it back to me.

At 9:00 am on Saturday, March 5, Ms. Huang came with her finished typing work; roughly the first part of manuscript one, manuscript two and the second part of manuscript three, and printed them all. I paid her 1,600 dollars on the spot.

During this period, I had communicated with Mrs. Murong several times by phone and her opinion was that the manuscripts should be input into the computer by one and the same typist from the very beginning to the last ending, so that the typist could easily locate certain parts of the manuscript at any time if the author wanted to make some revisions and I quite agreed with this principle.

Yet I was a woman with a strong sense of obligation so when Ms. Huang asked me at the doorstep, "Do you still want me to type manuscript eight that describes your life in China?," I hesitated about firing her to her face and ended up by saying, "Go ahead and bring your typing work together with my manuscripts and I will pay you accordingly." I even had her copy manuscripts three and four about "Life of Australian Prostitutes" in case missing pages and other incidents like that might happen. Fifty cents per page.

On March 6, 2011, Mrs. Murong came to Canberra. She was thin and petite, always wearing a happy smile. I ushered her in and showed her the copy of the typing work done by Ms. Huang openly without any covering up. She might have been taken aback at the sight of the sensational title "The Number One Prostitute" but her face remained impassive. She was a sedate and self-possessed lady and we felt like old friends at the first meeting. As I was busy at that time, I had her read my manuscript in the waiting room. Sometimes I would take advantage of the interval between two clients to ask her for advice on my book but she did not make many comments. Before she left for Sydney at four o'clock, we signed a simple agreement on our cooperation.

I grew restless and uneasy after she left, wondering what she thought of my writing. I was in a state of impatience until the next morning at ten o'clock when I called her mobile, "Mrs. Murong, what do you think of my writing?"

"It's a good story," she said, "I read part of it in the train on my way home. The life you're depicting is interesting and the content is eye-catching too. The structure of it, in my opinion, is a little too loose. Your vivid episodes are like sweet grapes and need a vine to string them up."

I felt more assured at hearing Murong's analysis and then another question arose, "Can you read my manuscript?"

"This was the job I had been doing for years before I went abroad and the words I have typed add up to an astronomical figure. What kind of manuscript haven't I encountered? No scrawl is illegible to me. There's no doubt about my professional competence as a typist."

I was writing this episode from the small hours of March 26 to five o'clock at dawn of the same day. I was really exhausted and flopped onto the bed. Eyes closed, I regretted being too stern with Ms. Huang. Did it make any sense haggling over every ounce with her, a poor lady? I even remembered her saying, "Please don't reveal to anyone it is I who did the typing of your book." Well, she was a poor lady with mistakes common among needy people. I might as well spare her by omitting all the paragraphs concerning her.

As I stayed up too late, I failed to sleep off my vexation and thrashed about in my bed. I got up to take a sleeping pill and managed to go to sleep when something weird happened and I had to resume the story of Ms. Huang.

I was woken up by a jangle of the doorbell and opened my eyes to find it was 9:00 am on March 26. I guessed it must be Ms. Huang. It was her last payday. I had informed her and promised I would ask her for help if I had any copying work in future. I ran to open the front door only to find Ms. Huang carrying piles of paper in her arms. They included copies of manuscripts three and four about "The Life of Australian Prostitutes," the typed pages of the second part of manuscript eight about my life in China and the last part of manuscript one about my life in Australia. It suddenly occurred to me she said she hadn't proofread part of them. I told her I would pay her as much even if she hadn't proofread them. I was a woman of promise and I would rather lose my own money than make others unhappy. I was always thinking of lending her a hand whenever possible since she was an immigrant to this new continent.

On her bill she had stated thirty-three pages of typing work; 1,000 words per page and forty dollars for every 1,000 words with a subtotal of 1320 dollars; 510 pages of copying work, fifty cents per page with a subtotal of 255 dollars. The total was 1,575 dollars. As this was the last time I was settling accounts with her before I dismissed her, I was somewhat embarrassed and my eloquence obviously deserted me, "The copying work and the typing work you sent me last time, you know, were actually of no use for me and I…I hadn't bothered to read through them. I mean, I will have a new typist to start inputting my manuscript anew from scratch. However, I am a woman of promise and I will abide by the contract between us and let you earn the money in typing the remainder of the manuscript."

"Well," Ms. Huang said reasonably and politely, "You may well pay me at a discount."

"There's no need for a discount," I said, "I will pay you in full. I'll give you nine hundred in cash and a cash check for the remaining six hundred and seventy-five."

"You know," I tried to cover my embarrassment by saying something funny, "My writing talent can now be comparable to the political talent of Mao Zedong or the artistic talent of Picasso."

In a more relaxed atmosphere, I began to count out the cash and wrote her a cash check for the remaining 675 dollars.

After sending off Ms. Huang, I checked the cash in my safe again only to find there was a hundred dollars short. I could recall that I had paid Ms. Huang fourteen fifty-dollar notes and fifteen twenty-dollar notes and that was 1,000 dollars. Plus a bank check of 675; I had paid her a hundred dollars more.

I called her mobile at once, "Ms. Huang, I'm afraid there's a mistake in the amount of money I paid you. Would you please check your money again by counting the number of twenty- dollar notes?"

"Just wait a moment. Let me pull over the car and I'll check," soon I could hear her counting the money in the car, "One, two, three, four... Yes, you've given me five more twenty-dollar notes."

"Okay," I said magnanimously, "Let's square it next time when I need you to do something."

She said she was very sorry.

Hanging up, I recalled an episodic moment at the time she was counting the twenty-dollar notes; she faltered for a fraction of a second and then went on counting her money. It suddenly occurred to me that God was reminding me to depict all types of human beings, not only those who liked stealing but also those who were seemingly kind but in fact greedy and calculating. Up until very recently I had been a skeptic about the existence of God. But weird and amusing things kept happening to me.

But the next thing that happened was far from amusing. It almost caused me to fly into a fury.

Having finished the phone conversation with Ms. Huang, I went to the toilet to wash my hands. To my frustration, I found the stainless-steel tap in the washing basin was dripping. Just then an old client came and I had to go out to serve him. After the job, I begged him to look up the Yellow Pages for a plumber from the Creaney & Sweeney Company to come to my house. The plumber informed us that he happened to be in the suburb of Garama and he would be there soon.

Five minutes later, the doorbell rang. I opened the door to find a medium-built Australian man in his mid-twenties. I led him to the toilet and he set out to check the dripping tap. Several minutes later, he said, "The tap is out of order and needs a replacement."

"How much will it cost?" was my natural response. "A couple of hundred dollars, I think," he answered.

"No problem," I agreed, supposing it was two or three hundred.

"Then I'm going out to get the replacement," he said, "I will be back in about forty minutes."

An hour or so passed and the plumber came back with the newly-bought tap kit. As he got ready to start the repair work, he casually mentioned the cost again, "The whole cost including the labor should be five hundred and fifty dollars."

"What!" I jumped to my feet in a rage, "Five hundred and fifty? You said it was a couple of hundred, didn't you?"

"But I didn't," he denied flatly.

"It's really dishonest of you to deny what you said," I said, "I won't pay you five hundred and fifty dollars and I don't want to see you any longer."

"In that case," he said calmly, "You should pay me a service fee of two hundred and forty dollars."

"I had my tap repaired before," I argued, "The service fee is supposed to be around eighty dollars, isn't it?"

"Yes," he said "but it should be doubled as it is Saturday today."

"But a doubled fee should be one hundred and sixty instead of two forty," I was not ready to give in.

"Okay," he said, "I can give you a special price of two hundred dollars but no less."

"Isn't it unfair that you're charging me two hundred dollars for doing nothing?" I went on reasoning with him, "Do you servicemen have a standard rate?"

Glancing at the wall clock briefly, he said, "Look, I came at ten o'clock and it's almost twelve o'clock now. Isn't it fair to charge you at a rate of a hundred an hour for the service fee?"

"Two hours?" I was surprised, "Including the time you idled away elsewhere on the way for my replacement?"

"Anyway, you have to pay me two hundred today," he showed no sign of backing down, "If you continue wasting my time like this, I will charge you more." The dispute between us remained in a state of deadlock for quite a while before I threw in the towel by saying, "Then you should give me an invoice at least."

He went to his van to fetch a pad of invoices before he came back to the kitchen. He placed the invoice pad on the bench and scribbled down something on the top page, which I couldn't read.

As a matter of fact, I couldn't read any English, let alone write it. My spoken English, sometimes broken or ungrammatical, was just sufficient for me to communicate with others around me. After he invoiced me, the serviceman handed the yellow page to me. I grudgingly paid him 200 dollars and planned to lodge a complaint to his boss sometime later.

But on second thought, I realized it was just a pseudo issue because of my poor English – I didn't even know the English name of the toilet tap; how could I complain to his boss when he asked me what was the matter in English? Besides, I had paid him the service fee. Could he refund it? Maybe he was self-employed – he was his own boss. I would just be asking for trouble.

The other day, when I told this to a client of mine, he laughed, "Most likely, the serviceman had made a quick but thorough investigation of your financial situation before he charged you. From the furnishings of your house, he could easily guess your occupation and make a conclusion that you were quite well off. Moreover, you did not speak English fluently. What an ideal subject of extortion. Once I wanted to hire someone to prune the trees around my house. When I asked him for a quote, what do you think he did? He looked me up and down and then glanced at my house as if to evaluate it before he gave me a price he thought would most suit me." "It's a common practice," I sighed, "to profiteer unscrupulously by tricks of discriminative prices."

Strangely enough, the wash basin tap in my toilet never leaked from then on. I wondered whether it was the plumber who was cheating me or it was God who was reminding me never to spare greedy and unscrupulous people by writing them into my novel!

In contrast to them, I was literally earning my bread by the sweat of my brows, making money by twenty or thirty dollars each time. That reminded me of something that happened last night. The following account, I swear, is true to the word. If I lie, I will be condemned to hell by God in future.

The weird thing happened at twelve last night. I was exhausted after a busy day and was about to sit down for a rest. I was just seating myself when I heard the sound of a slamming car door.

I heard someone talking as they were approaching my door. Soon the doorbell rang and I opened the door to find three tall Australian lads, a fat one and two thinner ones. I didn't open the door straight away and asked through the security door, "You haven't made a phone call to arrange an appointment and besides, it seems you three haven't reached the age of eighteen, have you?"

"Yes," they shouted in one voice, "we all have."

A long-haired thinner boy wrapped his hand around the tall fat lad's shoulder and said, "Today is his eighteenth birthday and you're supposed to give us a special offer?"

"Well," I said, "The lowest price I'll give you is thirty dollars each."

After a brief discussion, they agreed on the price.

"But," I added, "You can't come in at once. You should come in one by one." I spotted a large black jeep parked in my car space. I knew this kind of jeep could seat seven passengers so I warned them, "Tell the people in the jeep not to make too much noise. If you disturb the neighbors across the street, they'll call the police and you will get into trouble." My real purpose was to threaten them into being quiet.

The first one that came in was the black-haired, tall, white fatty. I looked up at him. He was really tall, at least a head taller than me. I led him directly into the working room and charged him thirty dollars and he gave me the money. I put away the money in the kitchen and came back to the working room. Opening the large glass door of the cabinet, I asked him, "How old are you?"

"Sixteen," he said. "What?"

"What I meant was my brother had given me sixteen dollars," he collected himself immediately.

"Have you really reached the age of eighteen?" I asked in suspicion, "If you haven't and the police know that I am serving a client under the age of eighteen, I will get into big trouble."

"I'm really eighteen years old," he declared firmly, "Today's my eighteenth birthday."

I knew it would make no sense to keep questioning him and said, "Do you want a shower?"

"Not until I've finished with you."

I tidied the two pillows on the bed and covered the bed with a large white towel. I had him take off his clothes and lie on the bed. Oh my! What thick legs he had! They were like those of an elephant. His cock was proportionally big like a huge carrot. I sat beside him and put a big condom on his cock. I didn't suck his cock for more than five minutes before he suggested, "Let me fuck you!"

So I knelt on the bed and bent over. He half squatted behind me and abruptly thrust his big cock into my cunt. "Ouch!" I couldn't help crying out, "You reckless boy. Haven't fucked a cunt before? You should be a little more tender with a lady."

Being fucked by the boy, I was praying silently, "Oh, my God. Next time never allow a boy of sixteen to fuck me, Goddess." The laws of most countries in the world forbid sexuality under the age of eighteen. Australian laws also stipulated that it was illegal to have sex with teenagers under eighteen. If I was caught fucking a sixteen-year-old boy by the Australian police, I would be found guilty and sent to prison. If only these laws were amended. It was inhuman not to allow a grownup cock to have its own pleasure. I wished God should answer my prayer by pressing the legislatures of all countries to make the proper amendments to lower the age restriction to sixteen but I was soberly aware it was bordering on impossibility.

But I thought I shouldn't be afraid of the Australian police since I had done my duty to inquire my client's age before the transaction. It was also illegal to demand to inspect every client's driver's license, wasn't it? I was weighing the consequences of any possible legal offense while the boy was fucking away upon me and yelling, "I'm fucking you. I'm fucking you!" and I echoed, "Oh yes. Oh, yes!" The reckless boy ignored my entreating to be tender with me and it seemed that he was intending to fuck me to death. He twined his legs around mine and pried his cock savagely inside my cunt, literally hurting me greatly.

"Will you feel my balls?" he asked brazenly. I had to stretch my right hand to rub his balls gently. The boy worked strenuously for a while but still couldn't come. Maybe it was due to his alcohol abuse. I had to get to my feet and lay him on the bed. I tried masturbating his cock with my hand but in vain. His cock, though big and stiff, just refused to come. I couldn't help wondering, "How much have you drunk to prevent your cock from coming?"

"Not much," his tongue seemed to be tied,"Only six bottles."

"Not much for six bottles?" I was at my wits' end, "I'll leave the cock to you. Let me try licking your balls."

Then he resorted to playing with his own cock. He stretched his legs, narrowed his eyes and breathed heavily until he cried out after seven or eight minutes' hard work, "Ah…… I have come!" He suddenly stiffened and then collapsed on the bed… Maybe because he had drunk too much, the sperm he ejaculated was not like white yoghurt but like soap suds. His hands as well as his cock were covered with white foam.

Thank God he had come anyway! I waited for a while and got up to wipe the white sperm off his belly, "Go and take a shower." It took me a good thirty minutes to earn this thirty dollars.

After he finished bathing and got dressed, the big white fat boy demanded, "Give me two beers."

"You're so drunk," I said, "Are you sure you need more beers?"

Upon his insistence, I gave in and went to fetch him two bottles of beer from the fridge in the kitchen.

A few minutes after I got rid of the fat boy, in came a thin boy. He seemed somewhat childish, with a small face, a long thin nose, sunken blue eyes and a red mouth. When he lay down on the bed, I looked over him and asked, "Are you really eighteen?"

"Yes," he answered emphatically, "Actually I am nineteen years old."

His white cock was relatively small, with blond pubic hair around it. When I squatted between his legs to suck his little cock, he asked me to feel his nipples. I laughed at the sight of his nipples, "How come your nipples are so small?"

"I was born like that," the boy smiled shyly. His nipples, pink in color and as small as two grains, were set shallowly in his chest.

I sucked his little cock and meanwhile I pressed his flat nipples gently. As his nipples were as flat as his chest and I couldn't pick them up with my finger tips. He seemed to have abstained from alcohol and was easier to make come. I spent just fifteen minutes to make him satisfied. When he left, I sent him off with two Colas and a bag of chips.

He was followed by the third boy, also tall and thin with fair skin. Blond hair hung on the back of his head. The strong alcohol on his breath almost stunned me. "You little snotty brat," I said, "How could you have drunk so much?"

"I'm twenty-one," he retorted, "Old enough to drink."

"Anyway," I said, "I think you have drunk too much. Look, you can't even walk steadily and you're slurring your speech."

He said emphatically, "I haven't had too much."

Another drunkard who denied having had too much! It was a universal truth that no drunkard would admit having had too much. I led him into the working room and had him lie on the bed. I looked over the boy to inspect his cock. It was really something. Long and thick like an aerosol can of air freshener. I was startled at the sight of his extra big cock head, which had a ring of gooseflesh around it. It was the second time I had ever seen such a grotesque-shaped cock head in the last ten years as a prostitute. I had a scrawny Australian client, who was a faithful patron of mine in his fifties. He also had such a cock head with a goose-fleshed ring, which he claimed would stimulate women more because it had a higher friction quotient against the inside of a woman's cunt. However, I had never tried it out because I didn't allow myself to make love with customers without using a condom as a protective measure, with the exception of a very few of my old lovers. I gazed at his cock, "How come you have such a cock head? I'd like to sandpaper all the bumps off it, or level its rough surface using a chisel."

"But how can I help it?" he said helplessly, "I was born with such a cock head."

I suggested condom-on oral work but he refused. So I had to clean his cock, including the opening and top of the cock, with lubricating oil. I washed his cock thoroughly before I held it in my mouth. During the lovemaking, I had to bear his torrent of verbal abuse, "I fuck your dirty cunt… Fucking hell…" I got used to such kind of abuse and I just ignored it. After all, he was a drunken boy. It was only seven or eight minutes before he thought of fucking me. I put a condom on his cock and knelt on the bed edge for him to fuck me from behind. Thwack! He thrust his huge cock into my cunt abruptly.

Because of his violent action, I plopped onto the bed. I stared back over my shoulder at him and protested, "Be a little more tender! Do you want to crush me?"

He seemed to turn a deaf ear to my protests and gripped his hands firmly around my thighs; he fucked me away with loud pounding noises. I couldn't help yelling out of pain, "Ouch! Ouch!" praying the son of a bitch would ease the tempo and impact of his assault. I suffered his trampling for about ten minutes before he demanded me to sit astride him and had me fuck him by sitting up and down. I obeyed his order and did the gymnastics for another ten minutes. Then he ordered me to take off his condom and suck his cock without it. That was the straw that broke the camel's back. I flew into a rage and swinging one of my arms, I hit him right on the left hip bone. He faltered a second and became sober at once.

"I tell you, you little snotty brat," I warned him, "I'm a prostitute, yes. But I'm human at the same time. You should respect me and my profession. You can't look on me as a sex slave for a mere thirty dollars!"

"I'm sorry," he said timidly.

Seeing he had apologized, I quickly forgave him by serving him another way. I peeled the condom off his cock, applied some baby oil on it and began to move my fingers along his hard shaft back and forth. I adopted my best techniques in masturbating his stiffened cock but it stubbornly refused to come. I had to tell him, "You may as well do your own cock and let me lick your balls. By the way, would you like me to pinch your nipples?"

"Yes, I would."

Just like most women, some men also had sensitive points in their nipples; some had sensitive points in one nipple and others had no sensitive points in their nipples. I stretched his legs apart and sat by his left side, with my left elbow supporting me between his thighs. I rubbed his balls with my left hand, caressed his nipple with my right and gently licked his tautened ball sacks with my tongue. He lay on his back on the bed and closed his eyes, his right hand rubbing his cock. Soon I heard him breathe more and more heavily and clamped my left hand between his legs. He began to let out all kinds of yells, "Ah…" "Yeo…" "Oh…" followed by a long trail of "Ahaaaa…" He threw up his upper torso, "I've come!" and convulsed several times before he plopped onto the bed, gasping for air, "Oh my, I'm thoroughly satisfied."

When he ceased his convulsions, I helped him wipe the sperm off his belly. I happened to spot five red finger marks on his left hip. I regretted my abuse of violence and felt sorry for the boy. He must have felt the pain but didn't dare tell me. I handed him a clean towel and said, "Go have your shower."

As soon as he had finished bathing and got dressed, he was pestering me for beers. He followed me to the four-door refrigerator and asked me for six cans of beer.

"No," I said in an angry tone, "You've only paid me thirty dollars and my net profit is less than twenty dollars for half an hour's hard work." He finally had to give in and left with two cans of beer. I pushed and shoved him to the front door disregarding his swears and curses. No sooner had I got rid of the long-haired thin guy than the white fatty came in, waving a five-dollar note in his hand and saying he would like to buy six cans of beer from me for five dollars. I flared up at him, "I spent twelve dollars on six cans and you'd like to buy six cans for five dollars. What a reasonable deal this is!" I said sarcastically. He grimaced at me, "Aren't they for your loyal patrons?"

"No way, not even for my loyal patrons," I said resolutely. Finally he came to the refrigerator and opened the door himself. Disregarding my renewed protests, he grabbed four cans of beer and took a bag of chips at his convenience when he left.

Day Six: March 28, 2011

Dear Sir, (my English translator)
First of all I must apologize for the illegibility of my manuscript though I'm not always hasty and careless in my writing. It's hard to read just because it was finished in a trance-like state. My insuppressible passion for writing drove me to speed my pen on paper and I was in an unsteady emotional state, crying one moment and laughing the next.

When the typist took the manuscript from me, I cautioned her again and again not to lose it because it represented my painstaking effort and sweaty labor. As the typist finished the last page of the fourth manuscript, I found the existence of souls that had been disputed for centuries. I can prove with my personal experience that souls are of substantial existence and something you can feel within your body. I used to have an ambiguous and dubious idea of souls' existence. I once looked up the word "soul" in a dictionary and it read: "the spirit which superstitious people refer to as being independent of one's body". It's a standard definition of the word "soul" given by almost all Chinese dictionaries describing the soul as superstitious people's reference.

In that sense, I may be among the first writers to elaborate upon the existence of souls in China's history. China's literary history can be traced back to a very ancient time but there were scarce records of the description of souls, at least to my knowledge. In my fifth manuscript, I have devoted a lot of space in describing souls. To avoid turning my book into a dry theoretical research paper, I interlarded it with a lot of sexy jokes so that highbrows and lowbrows alike can enjoy it. My book will later include more content about sexology, physiology, medicine and my personal common sense in daily life.

I will deal with these topics one by one as my story gradually unfolds.

After ten years' experience of being a prostitute, it has slowly dawned on me that sex and love are two related but separate things, which goes against the belief of a good friend of mine. She is an intelligent and knowledgeable woman, who thinks sex and love are identical and has clung to her own opinion up till now. And I can say for sure that there are up to seventy to eighty percent of people in the world who hold the same opinions as my friend. I will illustrate, through my story and characters that sex and love are by no means the same thing. You can find more discussions about human nature like this in this book. The content and ideas in my book have originated independently in my brain without referring to any other books except a pocket "Xinhua Dictionary" at hand. As I seat myself at the desk, I feel at once endless stories and theories welling up in my mind. In my fifth manuscript, I will touch upon the disillusions and illusions in literary history.

Secondly, I must apologize for disturbing you by calling late at night the other day. You told me on the phone that being too devoted to writing might cause illusions and what you said greatly alleviated my anxiety. Yet, the illusion came upon me again at 10:15 am on March 16, two days after I was incarnated when writing at 6:00 am on March 14. I was then with a client when I heard a voice intoning in my brain, "I am Goddess incarnated; I'm greater than anyone in the world; I'm the re-maker of human beings." After that, an ominous premonition kept ringing in my ears that an imminent disaster would befall our Earth. Terrified, I called my girlfriend immediately. She was in the middle of a lesson but I summoned her out of the classroom and it was her brief remarks that brought me to my senses, "Linda, stop writing right away or you'll become schizophrenic. Either lock the door and take a walk outside for relaxation or just come to stay with me in Sydney for a while..."

But to me, I don't feel I am going mad. I'm a superb woman with a strong will, a quick mind, a good memory and a controlling power. I took advantage of the interval between two clients to go on writing until grotesquely the illusion came upon me again— my pen seemed to be animated and wrote automatically of itself the following sentences, "I am the number-one prostitute in the world. I am the prostitute baron, the unprecedented and unequalled. I am the king of the kings among the prostitutes. I am greater than the presidents…" It seemed that something extraordinary was about to happen. Later when I sobered up, I couldn't help chuckling at myself. Greater than the presidents? I was not comparable even to a toe of any president. I was now aware it was a sort of illusion during too passionate a state of mind in writing and I quickly learned how to control my emotions when it happened. Whenever I was about to assume I was the savior, I would calm myself down and quickly tide over the turmoil of emotions.

In the days that followed, the weirdest things kept happening to me and I was beginning to weave these weird things into my sixth manuscript. And what was more weird and unbelievable was I had found faith in the communist doctrine of Marxism and Mao Zedong Thought. I was convinced that the world was doomed to be communized in the future but before the communism came true, the language and the world had to be unified first as a premise. But these were my preliminary ideas and vague guesswork. I was sober enough not to present these immature theories before you. I would confine my pen to the scope of my personal life and pornographic anecdotes. What was in my mind was the future market of my book.

I knew very well I had got a great start in my writing. It was not a question of being modest or arrogant but it was a fact that I was already on a very high level in my writing. Since the day I was incarnated while writing my book, I had been working on it with my heart and soul every day. You had to be confident before you start any career. If you could do any work heart and soul, you would be sure to reach the peak of your career. Few people in this world had the chance to find the existence of souls and fewer people had reached the stage of becoming spiritualized in their chosen careers. I was convinced too that Mao Zedong had sensed the souls but he must have concealed it in his writing. When I died and went to heaven, I was sure to go over and ask him, "Why didn't you tell people the truth that everybody had his own soul? The truth could by no means be exclusive to you." Everybody had his own soul except that somebody hadn't found it before he or she died so this truth was regarded as a superstition. It was not a superstition, on the contrary, it was an absolute truth that souls actually existed in our bodies and they could move in and out of our bodies.

Dear Sir, I'm writing to illustrate to you that my writing has gone beyond the original confines of a porn book like Xaviera Hollander's memoir, "The Happy Hooker" in Western literature. My writing talent is far superior to any other writers like Poseidon, God of the sea among the minnows, so whatever I produce will be unique and a first-class masterpiece. As so many weird things kept happening to me, I began to believe in the existence of God and most probably I will be among the first to see the presence of God. I have the assurance to claim they are not the extemporaneous products of my delirium. I am a woman of strong will and I will never go mad. I am not afraid of the series of grotesque and weird things that have been haunting me. There were, there are and there will surely be mysterious things that cannot be explained by the science and technology of the times. Who can explain how Paul, the oracle Octopus has predicted with astonishing accuracy the election of Gillard as the Prime Minister of Australia?

Sorry for my illegible scrawl, Sir. Because as I am writing this letter, my pen is beginning to write automatically of itself as if it were following my soul instead my brain.

My brain is now stuffed with too much writing material and the smallest portion of it can be extended to an excellent book. I will write out numerous things no other people in the world can have the chance to know but I have to stop here as I have to concentrate my time and energy on this present book. I will be the fastest writer with ample works to my credit. I am ambitious enough to surpass Mao Zedong and even Picasso. Picasso, like me, also found his soul and the only difference between him and me lies in that he expressed his belief in the form of painting while I do so in the form of writing.

I'm looking forward to listening to your advice. If it is not convenient for you to talk over the phone, please don't hesitate to write to me. I am a woman of principle. Though I'm engaged in a business despised by many people, I still consider the profession I've taken on as a noble or even sacred one. I will demonstrate it to the world later in my writing.

My business house in Canberra was purchased in the name of my limited company in Australia and mine is a legal business. My accountant and solicitor are both gentlemen and I never push jokes on them too far. You know, business is business and friends are friends. You are also a gentleman and I'm not supposed to take any liberties talking about anything with you. I'm just letting you have a general idea of what kind of a book I'm writing and how confident I am of my success in achieving my goal. I'm not to confine my ambition to being only a prostitute baron. I want to be a literary baron as well.

Sorry again for my hasty and careless writing here because I've just served a client for thirty dollars. He has left now so my handwriting is becoming much neater. I was hoping to tell you more but I have little time because I have to serve my clients now and then. Would you be so kind as to proofread the copied manuscripts three and four for me? They were copied by the typist in Canberra.

I have just said I'd like to be a literary baron and I of course know there are so many talents in the field of writing. I'm not afraid of competition because I'm unique in having a fortitude rarely seen in a woman and once I decide on what I think is a correct course, I will follow it to the end without considering the cost. And I'm fully convinced I have the ability to do so.

I have predicted the world is to be unified as one and it must be unified so that people all over the world can live a harmonious and happy life. The world country will be administered by a unified government led by a president and a vice-president. The unification of the whole world must be based on the unification of all the religions. I have the necessary ideas for this grand plan and I will have more in the future…

Sorry to stop here as a new client is coming now.

Linda, at noon, March 28, 2011

P.S.

1. Since there is a term "soul" in the Chinese dictionaries, it shows there indeed was someone in the history of Chinese literature that had found the existence of the soul. But the lack of clear definition of the soul shows no one recorded it in any of the existing dictionaries so the term "soul" is still defined as something spiritual that superstitious people refer to.

2. You said writing too devotedly for too long a time will lead to illusions. I agree with that but when I calmed down I thought it needed a further analysis. The three sentence statement "I am the Goddess incarnated. I am greater than anyone in the world. I am the re-maker of humankind," was innate in my mind, along with my presentiment that a disastrous catastrophe would strike the Earth. So it's not hard to understand why Mao Zedong got to deify himself in his twilight years until at last he lost his own identity. I'm now sharing a similar feeling with Mao and often imagine I am a deity flying through ethereal space. Actually, I don't think there is any saint or deity in this world. There may be some brighter people, their intelligence quotients several times or even dozens of times higher than ordinary folks. They may be very bright, I mean, in a particular field not in all fields. Hence the master mathematician Hua Luogeng, the father of guided missiles Qian Xueseng, the computer wizard Bill Gates and the stock baron – Sage of Omaha Buffett.

I am cyber illiterate and I become mad at the mere sight of the computer screen. It is said that the Hollywood action film star Stallone is also cyber illiterate. He wrote his script by hand. I didn't have much schooling and read widely. The reason I can write something unique and unusual is that I am gifted literarily and never tire of learning to write. Besides, I have an unyielding will and never give up once I have chosen what I think is a correct course.

3. I used to be an atheist and had no religious belief. I never went to church to worship God or went to the temple to worship Buddha. So I had been skeptical about God's existence until

recently when a series of weird things kept happening to me and then I was converted into a believer of God. So God's existence is the prerequisite of this book. When I was writing the sentence, "Most probably I will be among the first to see the presence of God in my life," I knew clearly this sentence was not the product of my heart or brain but the product of my soul. Since my soul was incarnated I have been writing wholly automatically without the participation of my heart or brain as if my soul were guiding my pen in writing. As soon as I take up my pen, a gush of inspirations well up and I can easily write two to three thousand words an hour. If I have more spare time, I can write ten thousand words a day.

God in my understanding is not a human but a divine being, though I don't have a clear idea of what He is like as I haven't seen Him in person yet. I am of the full conviction that the founders of the three great religions of the world must have had a rendezvous as they had to write their respective Scriptures. They encountered the almighty god in succession, who the Buddhists called Buddha, and Christians called God. I am a layman in matters of religion and it is my soul that directs me to write these things. Actually to my mind, there is only one god in the world but it is described differently in different scriptures.

As an Iraqi client of mine said last night, he had lived in the United States for thirty-two years and he had been listening to a Buddhist TV station every evening. A tonsured master monk in a red cowl sat cross-legged on an altar and smilingly preached his Buddhist Scripture with a lot of listeners sitting around him. My Iraqi client said he believed in Buddhism and listened to the preaching every evening though he didn't understand even a single word of it. But he said he always felt very relaxed and fell asleep in no time. I knew for sure there are another two TV stations that were preaching Christianity and Islamism. I asked my Iraqi client who he thought was dominating the world and he answered it didn't make any difference. I thought as much as him.

If the present God is to unify the world, He should unify the world's various religions first. Once the various religions are unified, there will be no strife or war. Only then can we realize the communist society Marx and Mao Zedong had promised. Who will take on the divine task of writing such a theoretical guideline? I think God has chosen me. As Confucius contributed a classic "Analects" and its doctrine has guided Chinese life for so many generations in the span of 2,000 years, I, Goddess incarnated, will contribute a masterpiece on religious unification to mankind, by which to unify all the existing religious beliefs as it's God's will to unify all of human's ideologies.

I know it's not easy to unify all the religions in the world and it may consume all my life's energy to write a "Scripture". As to how to write it or when to finish it, I'm sure God will tell me in due time. Though I already have a rough outline of the book, God keeps supplying me with fresh materials. I am drowned in writing now and I can't go to sleep unless I have written something. I have a sense of mission and I'm anxious to finish the great task God has given me. But at the same time I have anxiety about my own autobiography: how much time can I spare to writing it and can I expose my life as a prostitute to people all over the world? Yet I always have a feeling that God will not leave me to take my chances and He cares for me, Goddess very much. He is sure to help me go on writing the Scripture together with my anecdotes and make mine a matchless book in the world many generations to come will study. I have no lust for wealth or fame or power except for some carnal pleasure. That's why God has chosen me for the task. I have pledged to God to fulfill the task he has given me. Then He will kiss me on the forehead, saying, "Well done!" and leaving with me. That may happen in two hundred years. We plan to unite all countries into a unified country and let all the people on this planet live a happy life. From then on, there will be no war or racial discrimination and all people will be acknowledged to be created equal. Communism will be realized in its real sense and human beings will continue to develop on and on. This is God's grand cause.

Believe me, Si. There IS a God in the world. It is He that created the world and all the people in it. God asked me to pass on a message to you that you should try your best to translate this masterpiece into English; a language which will be used as an official language in the future unified country.

This postscript was written from 11:00 pm to 1:30 am and the letter from 11:00 am to 1:00 pm. I had a lot of clients to serve at noon so my handwriting was hasty and careless. I'm again apologizing for my illegible scrawl but I hope you manage to make sense of it. I hope you can join me and my friend in assisting God to fulfill His grand plan to unify the world. I have informed my friend last night and God told me to write to you in my own handwriting. My friend and I both have copies of this letter. I must tell you frankly that during the writing of this letter, I served two young clients. One was an Australian lad of twenty-nine, my old patron of seven years; the other was an Indian boy of twenty.

This letter was finished at 1:30 in the early morning.

Linda
March 29, 2011

Day Seven: March 29, 2011

At about 2:15 in the early morning, on March 29, God had me write to my friend Lisa. The letter read as follows:

Dear Sister Lisa,

I'm writing to ask you to believe me that there is really a God, who created the world and humans themselves. When I was writing, "Man has evolved from apes and the Yangtze River and Yellow River valleys are the cradle of human beings," I was a skeptic about God's existence. I used to be an atheist brought up in the Mao Zedong era. I accepted the above statement as indisputable truth from my high school textbooks, which I now know doesn't square with the facts. Now God has told me definitively it was He that created the world and human beings.

God now ordered me to pass on to you the copy of the letter I sent Tim, my translator. I hope you can work hard with me to fulfill God's grand plan to unify the world within 200 years. It's our divine mission. God wanted me to keep it a secret from my family members that I am writing such a book and I will follow His order faithfully. It's God's arrangement when the book can be published.

God promised to ensure a wealthy life for you and me as we are both too kind to cheat anyone. There are so many bad guys and crooks that are so well off in the world. It's high time we good guys enjoyed some good days. We are not so greedy and we are not yearning to live too luxurious a life. God will surely give us good fellows the chance to see the world unified and communism realized.

We are sure to see the final unification of the whole world.

Oh, yes. When my book is published, I'd like to sign my real name and give my real date of birth: December 13, 1961. That's why I've liked the number thirteen all my life. Many people hate the number thirteen, thinking it's an unlucky number. On the contrary, thirteen is an auspicious number. In my writing, I adopt the structure of a cycle of thirteen days for my porn anecdotes, a structure never seen in the history of literature. I don't need to worry about what literary techniques or what literal structure I should adopt in my future writing as God will instruct me in due time when I need them. I will try my best to produce more amusing, comical stories to entertain my readers. My book is intended to make people all over the world laugh heartily. I'd rather them burst out with laughter than gloomily go on quarrelling or fighting or even divorcing. I wish all families a happy life from now on.

March 29, 2011, at 3:15 in the early morning.

When I finished writing the letter to Lisa, I heard God whispering in my ear, "Poor girl my Goddess, you really have had a miserable life. You were cheated when running a restaurant in China and were cheated by two women again when buying houses in Australia. As a matter of fact, these two women knew in advance that the two houses were not allowed to be demolished by law. When Ice asked Sunny what to do next, Sunny answered, "Keep it a secret from Linda. Otherwise we can't settle the purchases and who will pay us?" God went on to say, "Look how I will punish these two women."

"Don't worry, My Goddess," God added, "You shall be the wealthiest person in the world."

I was wondering how God could let me be the wealthiest person in the world. He couldn't pay me directly in cash, could He? Now it slowly dawned on me that He wanted to make me rich by selling my book and at the same time made it clear that the world was created by God.

"I could create the world," God went on, "Also I could destroy it. If those bad guys go on behaving so unscrupulously, I can turn the Earth into an inferno of flames. But since the Earth and the people on it is my fond creation, I don't have the intention of doing so for the moment. I hope all the people on Earth can live a happy life. And this is the purpose for which we are writing this book on unification. I have been overlooking myriads of millions of human beings on the Earth for centuries, some of them are enjoying their lives and others are suffering. I have long been planning to send a new god to change this situation but the trouble is I have no right candidate at hand. The first time I sent Jesus but he was nailed on the cross and the second time I sent the Seventh Princess of the Emperor Jade but she eloped with Dong Yong so she was soon retrieved by me. Now you Goddess have been incarnated and you're one of my favorite goddesses. Though there are no such carnal relations as sexual intercourse between us, we have a lasting passion for each other. I love my Goddess very much and will join forces with you and we will work as one to save all the souls of human beings so that they can live like their primitive ancestors, free of any sorrow or anxiety."

I didn't finish writing the letter to my friend Lisa until 3:30 before dawn of March 29. After that I went to bed but couldn't go to sleep. I tossed and turned restlessly in bed, thinking only of God. It was He that gave me the grand mission to tell the people all over the world that God's existence was real… My brain was obsessed by only the image of God and gradually I fell asleep…

I woke up to find it was already 9:00 in the morning. I jumped to my feet and rushed to the bathroom to clean myself. After I pulled on my trousers, a pair of black cloth shoes and a white blouse with a blue floral design, I put the letters to my translator Tim and my friend Lisa, together with my purse into a handbag, thinking since God had me write to them, I'd better send theses letters as soon as possible. I put the bag on my shoulder, locked the door, checked the security door and walked along the garage wall to the back door, pulling at it to make sure all security measures had been taken before I left the backyard onto the west path lined with cypresses. I was walking along the street and heading south to Woden Shopping Mall.

The fall in Canberra was really intoxicating. The cool breeze caressed my face pleasantly as I watched the bustling traffic in the street. I couldn't help blessing myself in my mind and wanted to announce to the drivers and pedestrians, "Hey, you guys haven't known the existence of God but I have. God has had me write to my translator and my friend and He has had me pass on this important information to all of you!"

Obsessed with God's mission, I didn't notice I had arrived at the post office west of Woden Mall. I stepped in and urged myself to post the letters as quickly as I could.

I took two large Express Post envelopes from the shelf, paid for them at the counter and addressed them to my translator and Lisa respectively on a desk against the wall. When I slipped the two yellow envelopes into the yellow post box outside the Post Shop, it was as if a weight had been lifted from my mind. By tomorrow, they would be able to receive my letter and be made aware of God's existence as I was…

Having sent the letters, I walked across the underground car park to the escalator and took the escalator to the first level. At Woolworths Supermarket, I bought five boxes of Pepsi and five boxes of Coke, together with some fruit and vegetables. After checking out at the cash register, I pushed a fully-loaded trolley to the south gate taxi rank. Seeing I was pushing a trolley along, a taxi driver came over to greet me enthusiastically. To my surprise, he turned out to be an old client of mine for the past six or seven years. He was short, neither too thin nor too fat with short black hair, big eyes, a high nose and a little mouth. I knew he was Lebanese and had lived in Australia for more than seven years. It was said he went back to Lebanon to get married but his wife hadn't been granted an Australian visa. So he naturally became a frequenter of mine. Since sex was indispensable; if your desire was aroused, your wife was not available and you couldn't randomly rape any woman in the street, it was reasonable and legal to go to visit a prostitute.

Glancing at the load in my trolley, the driver laughed,"Linda, have you bought all these things for your clients?"

"Yes," I said, "but what can I do with so many clients who have to eat and drink? This is part of my business."

We were talking friendlily as we moved all the items from the trolley into the taxi. As I seated myself in the passenger's seat and fastened my seat belt, the Lebanese driver got into the car and turned the indicator to the right. When he drove the taxi onto the road, he asked me, "How are you getting along these days? Still as busy as before?"

"Yes," I answered, "So many years. Most are frequenters. I don't worry about the flow of clients but I sometimes feel worn out, either physically or mentally."

"It's about the same with all trades," he said, "As for us taxi drivers; we're riveted to our seats for more than a dozen hours a day going everywhere around the city. Sometimes I feel so tired that I think I've broken my back."

"Do you often work till late in the night?"

"I usually work till nine at night and call it a day," he said, "I never do night clients especially those drunkards, who would beat you for no reason at all. Once three lads robbed me of one hundred dollars instead of paying me."

"Driving taxis is also listed as a high-risk trade," I felt sorry for him, "The other day I heard a policeman say years ago two teenage girls in Sydney murdered a taxi driver but got a penalty of only three years in prison. I think it was unfair and unjust. If the case happened in China, the two girls should be sentenced to death or at least got life imprisonment."

"The Australian laws are sometimes too lenient," he agreed. "People taking on my trade are also at risk as you taxi drivers,"

I said, "I am particularly careful when night falls. I never allow in those who have drunk too much or have taken drugs. They sometimes make trouble in front of my door. They either keep pressing the doorbell without letting go or kick at the door. They will load their toy guns with raw eggs and shoot at my front doors and windows and stain them with flowing egg whites and yolks, which I will have much difficulty washing away the next day. What makes me most annoyed is that they will smear nasty shit on the doors, windows or electricity meter box and block the keyhole to the box with the same material for good measure, making the whole backyard stink to the skies. I gnashed my teeth with resentment when this happened but I could do nothing about those little rogues. We have our laws, which never allow us to punish them for their mischief ourselves."

"Then why didn't you call the police?"

"Call the police?" I shrugged my shoulders, "What's the use? The police can neither arrest them nor put them into prison for such minor offences. Once a little bastard was caught, but he refused to confess to any offence, so the police had to release him at last. They're just headaches to us and to the police as well."

We were talking leisurely in the taxi and didn't notice we had arrived home. After he parked his taxi on my car space, we began to unload the goods from the taxi to the French door. As he was once my client, I paid him forty dollars; ten dollars more than the meter price. When he drove away, I opened the security door and the glass door and moved the goods into the house and then locked the security door and the glass door. Just then the mobile in my bag buzzed. I answered it and greeted, "Good morning!"

"Linda, may I have appointment for forty-five minutes?" I heard him ask.

"No problem."

"I'm coming in half an hour."

Putting down the mobile, I hastily moved the Pepsis and Cokes into the garage and moved the fruit and vegetables into the fridge. After that I cooked two eggs, poured myself a cup of milk and began to enjoy my lunch, wondering whether there was really a God in the world. If not, why did I have so strong a foreboding all last night that I would be impelled to keep on writing until I succeeded? For what did God have me write to my translator and my friend? I was deep in thought while chewing a boiled egg. What an amazing feeling!

Soon the doorbell rang and I put down the cup in my hand to answer the door, "Morning, Tom! I didn't know it was you! Come in, my master writer."

The stout man stood over five foot six with long curly hair, a big face and a broad mouth. He looked very kind and was all smiles.

"Morning, Linda. Long time no see."

"Yes," I said, "How time flies. It's more than a month since we last saw each other."

"I've been writing recently," He said apologetically, "I really can't spare any time to come visit you."

"What have you been writing, my great writer?"

"An academic essay," he scratched his head, "Very brain-consuming. I can hardly write five thousand words a week."

"It must be a very professional essay" I said, "I myself am writing my autobiography and I have an inexhaustible source of funny anecdotes and amusing stories. I can write five thousand words a day."

"But they are different categories of writing," he just smiled wryly.

We talked intimately until we arrived at the working room. He produced seventy dollars and handed it to me,"Forty minutes as usual. The usual price?"

"Of course the usual price," I said, "We're old friends for so many years."

I went on to ask, "Do you like white wine or red wine?" "Dry white wine. No sweet wine."

I put away the money in the kitchen and fetched a white wine for him from the garage. When I was back in the working room, he had lain on his back on the clean towels I had spread out for him. He said, "I have already taken a bath at home."

I settled cozily between his thighs and took up his banana-shaped big cock and held it in my mouth. It was not an exaggeration to say his cock was like a banana. Not only was its head shaped like a banana but it was also bent like a banana. I had only sucked his cock for two or three minutes when he cried out, "Aye, Hey, Ouch… Linda, you're the best sucker in the world. You've made me feel like a real man."

As he breathed in and out heavily, his bad breath mixed with cigarettes began to assault my nostrils. I had to close my eyes and pinch my nose while sucking his cock. He parted the opening of his cock tip with his fingers and said, "Linda, lick me inside. I enjoy you sucking the opening of my cock."

"I've been doing this job for ten years," I said with a note of pride in my voice, "No one in the world is more knowledgeable than me in this field. I've grasped all the know-how to make a cock come."

I didn't suck his cock for ten minutes before he called a timeout, "Stop! Let me fuck you."

I got to my feet and found him a large condom from the bedside table. He threw himself upon me and while huffing and puffing, managed to tuck his cock into my cunt,"I've fucked more than a hundred women. I find yours is the best and sweetest cunt of them all."

"Nowadays it's hard to find a man who's loyal to one woman all his life," I said with a sigh, "and vice versa for a woman."

The corpulent writer was apt to sweat and he hadn't fucked me for a dozen minutes before his salty sweat beads dripped onto my face. He clumsily helped me wipe his sweat off my face and repeated his apologies, "I'm sorry. I'm sorry."

Seeing his awkwardness, I took up the remote control to the air conditioner from the bedside table and set the temperature to the lowest seventeen degrees and then I pressed down the "start" button. As the air conditioner started, he was suddenly bathed in the cool breeze and he sweated less. He began to piston away his big cock inside me, yelling, "Hey! Hey! Fuck you! Fuck your sweet cunt!"

"Oh, yes," I echoed under his weighty body, "Oh, fuck me. Fuck me hard!"

Another dozen minutes or so passed and his face turned crimson and his breath became coarse and heavy, "Ah, I'm coming! I'm fucking you Linda! Fuck you to death!" With that, he sneezed loudly and spluttered his saliva all around. I had to wipe my face with the back of my hand as he apologized repeatedly, "I'm sorry. I'm sorry. I'm …"

I could feel his big cock throbbing inside my cunt and I waited for him to come completely. Then I had him pull his shaft out and I peeled off his condom. I threw the dirty things into the dustbin and massaged his back for about twenty minutes. I sent him off at the door and he was in high spirits.

At around 2:00 p.m. when I had just had my lunch, the doorbell rang and I opened the door to find my client of more than four years. He was a high-school teacher. He was about five foot six and a little too thin; his eyes looked particularly large and incompatible with his little nose and mouth. Every time he came, he acted prudishly and affectedly like an excessively shy girl. When he entered the room, he always snuck about as if he had committed some sinister crimes. I had to assure him repeatedly that there was no one other than me in the house before he could set his mind at rest. Then he would follow me into the working room without daring to raise his head. When there, he would hand me fifty dollars and I only charged him thirty because he came quickly (within ten minutes). I remembered once he said he had married one of his own students – an overseas Chinese student. They lived together for three years and she gave birth to three daughters. Now his wife had found a good job and a good boyfriend in a policeman as well. She was seeking a divorce but he refused on the grounds that he would see his daughters less so his wife often came home to pick a fight with him and have him sleep alone in the smallest room of the house. She even kept her daughters from talking to their father. He felt distressed and frustrated.

I tried many times to comfort him, saying since there was no love left between them, the marriage would be a curse rather than a blessing and a quick divorce might be a quick good riddance. And according to the law, his wife could not deprive him of his right to see his children.

So this time as soon as he entered the house, the first sentence he uttered was, "It's done and my mental burden has been relieved…"

He followed me to the working room and handed me a fifty-dollar note as usual. I handed him a clean towel for him to take his shower and went to the kitchen to fetch a twenty note for his change. When I came back to the working room, I found him lying on the bed with the towel wrapped around his waist and he covered his private part tightly with both hands. I went over to pull off his towel, "You've been here so many times and you are still so shy?"

No sooner had I snatched off his fig leaf than his cock erected stark and stiff like a straight cucumber, quivering in the air. "Look," I said, making fun of his long cock, "It's getting so impatient and you want to cover it." With that, I held his hot, jerking cock in my mouth and started to suck it. With his repeated exclamations of "Oh my God! Oh, my God," I spent only ten minutes making his cock ejaculate. Wave after wave of white sperm gushed onto his belly and I asked him, "Are you thoroughly satisfied this time?"

"Yes," he admitted, "I haven't had sex for several months."

After I helped him wipe off the sperm from his belly with a tissue, he jumped to his feet and went to have a shower. When he came out of the bathroom, he dressed promptly and hastily headed for the front door. I saw him off at the doorstep. He stood under the cypress tree, looking to the right and then to the left several times. Only after he was assured that no vehicle was passing by did he dare to get into the red car parked on the street. "Poor fellow," I heaved a deep sigh, "There are always those who are afraid of anything related to sex. Even if they badly need an outlet for their sexual desire, they go about it furtively."

At about three in the afternoon, the long-haired man with a vegetable nose who had sold me the lamb chops came with a young man of about thirty-five. The young man also had long hair with little eyes, a long and narrow nose and thin lips. On entering the house, the man with the vegetable nose said to me, "I've brought you a new client. I told him you were very nice and he would like to have a go of you today."

I stretched out my hand and shook hands with them, "You're welcome, gentlemen. By the way, what drink do you want?"

"Beer for both of us, please," the man with the brandy nose said.

"What would you like; VB, Tooheys or Melbourne ale?" I said, "I also have light ale."

"Strong beer, of course. A VB for me. What about you?" Vegetable Nose asked, turning to his companion.

"A Tooheys for me," the blond-haired man replied. I brought them their choice beers and they began to drink.

"We've just come back from the nude beach. All the people there, male and female, were swimming in their birthday suits. The naked ladies were so seductively sexy that we were totally aroused. We are burning with passionate desire so we had to come here."

"I heard there's a nude beach in Sydney but I didn't know there was also one here in Canberra," I was wondering. Vegetable Nose said a place name but I didn't know where it was. To be frank, though I'd lived in Canberra for ten years, I was still a stranger to this city. I had been busy making money and besides, being a prostitute in a relatively small city, I didn't like to go out in public places. Many customers invited me to dine out but I declined them all, "Sorry, I'm too busy to go out."

Seeing they had almost emptied their beer bottles, I asked, "Which of you will be the first?"

"Of course my friend is first."

So I left Brandy Nose in the waiting room, who was watching the TV program while waiting for his turn. Then I led the thin blond-haired guy to the working room. He produced a fifty- dollar note from his wallet and said, "Here is the service fee."

He said he had taken a shower at home so I let him lie down on the bed. I hadn't put his cock in my mouth for long before he began to yell, "Ah, yes. Oh, yes. Suck my cock hard!" I ran my tongue tip along his cock but by accident I cut his cock with my teeth. "Ouch," he cried out, "Why are you biting at my cock?" I answered, "Sorry."

"No worries," he said, "Last Sunday, Joe (Brandy Nose) and I went to visit a toothless prostitute. She was really adept at sucking cocks. She will by no means bite at a client's cock like you."

I laughed out, "a toothless prostitute will charge more for providing a special oral job."

"One hundred dollars for half an hour," he said, "and two hundred for an hour."

"Well," I asked, "How did you like her service?"

"My cock felt soft inside her toothless mouth," he said, "It felt the same in her mouth as it does in a cunt."

"Well, you can't enjoy my toothless service for another twenty years," I smiled. With that, I resumed my sucking, and he kept on groaning, "Oh…wow… Ah…" A dozen or so minutes passed and he shouted, "Now, let me fuck you!" I found him a medium- sized condom and bent over for him to thrust his cock into my cunt from behind. He then had me kneel on the bed and put my legs as close to each other as I could. He stood behind me with his two legs parted, "Put your legs close together and your cunt will seem smaller than it is." I thought to myself, "Whether my cunt seems small or large all depends on the size of your cock. Someone with a cock as small as a date kernel or a little pepper will find my cunt fathomless when he inserts his little thing into it. But lucky you have a cock of medium size." At that time, he had parted his legs and stood behind me, ready to take action.

"Put your legs close together and tighten your pussy," he said, "On your marks – get set – go!" With that, he thrust his cock into my cunt with all his strength. He didn't forget to give his compliment, "Wonderful! So warm!" before he pistoned his cock away in my cunt.

"Clamp my cock, Linda," he seemed to find my cunt was not as tight as he had expected, "Squeeze it. Grip it hard!" I tensed my stomach muscles and cunt muscles to please him while he was pistoning his cock inside me and pounding his belly against my buttocks loudly. He breathed through his teeth, "I fuck you. I fuck you. I fuck you…" followed by a drawling howl of "Ah ----------." He came at last and I helped him peel the condom off his cock. After that, I went to the bathroom to wash my hands and mouth before I put on my dress. When he finished dressing, I went to the kitchen to fetch him six cans of beer and sent him to the waiting room to wait for Brandy Nose.

I then led Brandy Nose into the working room. Half an hour later when I finished serving him, I opened the door to the waiting room and found the blond-haired thin guy had changed the porn video to the English news program. It did not strike me as odd at the time but when I saw them all off and went back to the waiting room, I found there was something fishy about the DVD. I tried shifting the "TV" key to the "AV" key but there was no picture on the screen. I hastily opened the DVD only to find the disk titled "Oriental Fever No.4" was gone! Damn it! Wicked villain! After drinking my drinks, eating my food and fucking my cunt, he stole my indispensible productive means – the porn disk! Once a thief always a thief. Could a leopard change its spots?

I was seething silently in the chair when the doorbell rang. I opened the door to find a thirtyish Australian man standing on the doorstep. He had a blond-haired little head, with a high forehead, narrowed eyes, a pointed nose and a wry mouth. Somehow I found him vaguely familiar, so I asked, "Hi. What can I do for you, a massage or a whole-set service?"

"I've come to borrow money," he said.

"From who?"I was surprised, thinking he must have mistaken the house.

"From you, Linda," he said, unperturbed, "I need the money urgently. May I borrow two hundred dollars and I will return it by Friday? Thursday is my payday."

"But I don't know you," I was a little annoyed, "What has made you believe I will lend you the money?"

"Because I was your client," he explained, "I have visited you several times before."

"But my clients are not entitled to borrow money from me," I became mildly indignant; "Don't you know I have only business relationships with my clients?"

"Please! Linda, please!" he refused to leave, "Would you please lend me some."

"Sorry," I said firmly, "but I have no money and I can't lend you any. Please leave my house." With that, I slammed the door shut behind me.

Back at the west living room in my chair, I was wondering why a loan arrangement, usually a taboo subject between friends and relatives in China, should have been picked up so casually by a stranger…

The hassle caused by the farcical Australian borrower combined with the DVD disk theft by Brandy Nose's friend made me unhappy for quite a long time and I hadn't even got over it after I finished serving three clients.

At around nine thirty that evening, a young man about thirty came to visit me. He was also one of my "old" patrons of more than five years. He was short and fat with a little head, a chubby face, a high nose, round eyes and a pouted mouth. His head looked just like a round ball. He wore long, thick, blond hair that almost reached his hips, which was so eye-catching that you could spot him at the first sight among a great crowd of people.

I led him to the working room and had him bathe. He also belonged to those who took their time in doing everything so I could do nothing but wait for him by drinking a cup of water over the TV program in the kitchen. I waited until the splashing water died down in the bathroom and went into the working room. He had just taken a shower and his moist long hair looked attractively glossy. I covered the pillows with a folded towel lest his wet hair should dampen the pillows. He lay on his back on the bed and I sat between his legs to suck his cock. I had little difficulty in making him come in less than five minutes. After I washed my hands and mouth, I then turned him around and began to massage his shoulders and back. After that, I turned him onto his back again and masturbated his cock by hand. This time it was not so easy to make him come. I worked myself so much that my shoulders became sore and stiff. At last, I managed to make him come.

When he was taking his second shower, I pulled on my dress and went to the garage to fetch a bottle of red wine. I put the wine on the massage table and went back to the kitchen, eating a banana while waiting for him to come out.

It was seven or eight minutes before he came out with a backpack on his shoulders and his long hair flying about his back. He headed for the front door nervously, looking askew at me with not the least sign of readiness to pay me. I waited for him to come closer and suddenly asked him, "Excuse me, young man. It seems you forgot to pay me." Only then did he unwillingly produce a fifty-dollar note from his trouser pocket and hand it to me, "Oh, I almost forgot." "It's the third time you have played the same trick," I said earnestly.

He used to be a good customer and always paid me fifty dollars on entering the house before the service. However, on the last two occasions, he seemed to have changed into another man.

He purposefully didn't mention money before he left. He looked furtively at me as he was heading for the door. Today, in order to sound him out, I, too, purposefully didn't mention money before he left and waited for him in the kitchen. Sure enough, he was trying to play the old trick. It was beyond my ken how a decent young gentleman, after enjoying half an hour's sexual service, should try to leave without paying, and with a gift bottle of wine! Could he do that with a clear conscience?

After I saw him off, I kept lamenting over the moral degeneration of young people nowadays. It suddenly occurred to me that maybe I once forgot to charge him because I was busy serving other clients and it was this that tempted him to follow suit on the following three occasions by trying to take advantage of my negligence to enjoy a free service.

That night I was lying in bed, lost in deep thought. What interesting and ample writing material God has supplied me with! The long-haired man having stolen my porn disk; the man with a vegetable-nose selling me lamb chops of questionable origin;

the blond-haired man trying to evade service fees. People in the world were really experiencing a crisis of morality!

I contemplated over it for a long time before I decided all these cheating stories should be included in my book. Oh my Lord, do you know what sort of people you have created? …

Day Eight: April 1, 2011

At about 9:00 a.m., I heard indistinctly God calling me, "My Goddess, get up. You have a lot of things to do now."

After I got up, I washed up and put on my clothes. God was heard saying again, "Go and see what day it is today?" I went to the calendar on the wall only to find the March page hadn't been turned over and it was supposed to be April today. I tried to turn it over but I couldn't because I accidentally dented the margin of the March page so I couldn't hang it on the nail. God said calmly, "Try again, my Goddess. I'll give you a magic puff." God blew at the calendar but I still couldn't hang it on the wall. God said, unable to be reconciled, "Try once more." And I tried once more but in vain. Then God said, "Once more again!" I tried and failed a third time. God then said helplessly, "Alas, my magic breath doesn't work for these trifling things!"

"Oh, my Lord," I said, "Another hundred years will pass and you will lose your control or influence over most human beings."

"Yes," God answered, "I, too, have such a hunch but no worries. Before they have degenerated beyond redemption I will save their souls and unite the world into a peaceful place for all human beings to live a happy life in." After that, God said, "Now let's get down to business. I'd like you to send the copies of the manuscript your typist typed on the computer to your translator. Did he post you the twenty-thousand-word sample of translation the other day? You can pass it around to your local clients to see how the quality of his translation is. But I think he is qualified enough as I have read the sample. For the present, he's the best English translator as there are no better alternatives in Australia now. I can find you a better one in the United States, but it's inconvenient for you as he lives too far away from you. In my opinion, he is the right person. Before the publication of the book, the fewer people know about it, the better. I expect the book will cause a big stir in the world as soon as it is published because you're writing not for yourself but for your Lord. You're writing a Scripture, a sacred book for the cause of peaceful unification of the world. In due time, I will have the biggest publisher in the U.S. contact you, sign contracts with you and publish your book. Even Hollywood will probably film your book then.

I took what God had said with a grain of salt. I went to the kitchen, took a bag from under the cabinet and put the copies of the typed manuscript I had just proofread in it. Having locked the door, I walked up a secluded small street and headed for the Garama Post Office, which was about a mile away from my house. I crossed the street and walked on the pavement on the other side. I was walking when I caught sight of a head figure sprayed with greenish-blue paint beside a small globe, much like our Earth. God pointed at it and said, "It was sprayed by us deities."

I was amused that God was making fun of me. I didn't walk far before I arrived at a semi-circular beige brick bus stop. On the wall of the bus stop I could see two black male head figures face to face, painted by someone. Then God said, "It's also the work of us deities and so are the crop circles in the U.K."

Admiring the omnipotence of the almighty God, I went over to feel the black male head figures on the wall with my hand. Were they the graffiti sprayed by some naughty children? But why had the children painted such vivid pictures here on the bus stop wall? I was much perplexed. When I was in the Post Office, I posted the manuscripts and bought several lined writing pads. After I posted the manuscripts, I went directly home. Scarcely had I stepped in the threshold before the doorbell rang. I then heard God say, "I've brought you a new client."

I opened the door to find an Indian lad, not tall with a chubby face. I boasted hundreds of young Indian clients and most of them were lovely clients. But I hated serving cocks wrapped in their foreskins, especially when they were not washed thoroughly. The stench might kill you. I asked him, abruptly, "How come you came without making an appointment in advance?"

"My friend introduced you to me," the chubby face said with a broad smile.

I let him in and went on with my questions, "How much did your friend tell you he had paid?"

"Forty dollars."

I knew at once he was an overseas student and didn't have much money. I said, "My price is fifty dollars for half an hour but I give all overseas students a special price of forty for half an hour."

He handed me two twenty-dollar notes and I put them into the drawer in the kitchen. I asked, "What do you want to drink?"

"I don't want anything for the moment," he said.

I led him to the working room and got the bed sheets and pillows ready for him. When he lay down on his back, I noticed a thin string tied around his waist and I traced the string to a walnut stick, about two inches long and half an inch thick.

"What is this stick for?" I was very curious.

He answered it was a mascot that could ensure his happiness and safety all his life. I had seen Indian and some Ceylonese lads wearing a similar thing around their waists more than once. When you asked them what the purpose of the stick was, their invariable answer was it was a mascot that would bless them.

"Do you believe in God?" I asked.

"We're Buddhists," he answered, "We believe in Buddha, the master of heaven."

"I believe God and Buddha are the same person," I began to preach my own belief, "but with different names."

"So do I," he agreed.

"The master of heaven is none other than me!" God interrupted.

To my relief, the Indian lad's cock was not wrapped in foreskin. But his cock had an unusual shape. It was like a pestle or a club, one end being much thicker than the other. His cock had a very slim base but a big round head. After ten minutes' mouth work, I found him a medium-sized condom and bent over by the bed edge with my buttocks lifted skyward. He stood behind me and asked politely, "May I fuck your asshole?"

"No, you misunderstood me," I said promptly, "I won't allow anyone to fuck my asshole even if he pays me a hundred dollars. Do you think you can do it for a mere forty dollars?"

"But once when I was in a brothel, a Japanese girl allowed me to fuck her asshole without a condom and ejaculate sperm in her asshole. She said she wouldn't be worried about the possibility of getting pregnant."

"I can say for sure she wouldn't allow you to fuck it for forty dollars," I said definitely, "Besides, my asshole is used for shitting not for fucking." The chubby-faced boy had to give in and thrust his cock into my cunt from behind. Then he began his fucking with yells of "Ah!" "Oh!""Fuck hell!" Though a young lad, he was really an expert fucker with rich experience. He took his time in moving his cock inside me rhythmically and forcefully until ten minutes later, he asked, "Will you please fuck me?" He stood motionless on the floor and had me slide his cock between my buttocks. I did but muttered my complaint, "You lazy bones only know how to toil me."

"Role exchanging will add novelty," he laughed, "Come on. Keep fucking my cock with your ass." I aligned my asshole with his erected cock and clenched my plump buttocks around his penis. With his cock still inside me, I pounded my buttocks heavily upon his cock until my buttocks began to feel hot. He kept shouting, "Ah, yes. Oh, yes. Good!" and encouraged me, "Harder. Still harder!" I echoed his groans sultrily until I myself began to breathe heavily. Only then was the real meaning of my doctor's motto brought home to me: Sexual intercourse amounted to four miles of jogging. A dozen or more minutes later, he inhaled a deep breath through his teeth with a hissing sound and yelled madly, "I'm coming!" I felt his cock jerk spasmodically several times before it rested motionless.

I waited until he stopped gasping for air and got down from the bed. I praised his performance while removing his full condom, "I didn't expect you were so strong a love maker for your age."

"Of course," he said with a note of pride in his voice, "I've already fucked almost two hundred girls. The oldest of them was sixty-five years old."

"Really?" I asked.

"She's my neighbor," he added.

"How do you like her?" I was curious.

"She's very sexy and looks just like a lady in her forties," he smacked his lips; "She's a ballet coach and has a very supple body, waist and legs. When my cock was deep in her cunt, her toes could reach my ears, my forehead or my nose. She could even hold her toes in her own mouth and savor them. Moreover, while we were closely copulated, she could fling herself into various poses with her arms and legs so gracefully that I felt as if I were dancing with her in a ballroom."

"What a romance! It's well you have no age discrimination in choosing your sexual partner," I said sarcastically.

"Women are born to be fucked," Chubby Face said brazenly, "I don't care about the age of cunts as long as they can satisfy my desire."

I had the chubby-faced boy bathe and get dressed before he left with three bottles of beer and a large packet of chips. Chips might serve as poor students' snacks during the intervals between classes at school.

The cubby-faced boy left merrily and on the steps he turned back to say goodbye, "See you next time."

"See you," I said as politely.

At eleven o'clock in the morning, a new client came by appointment. He wore a dark-beige suit. He was around forty and of medium build, with short blond hair, a square face, sunken blue eyes, an aquiline nose and thin lips. A gentleman who looked amiable and approachable, I thought. As soon as he entered, he smiled and said "After I parked my car alongside the street, I saw some people watch me walking toward your house. I figured they knew where I was going. I smiled and nodded to them as if saying you're just jealous of me."

"I usually receive ten to twenty clients a day," I said in dismay, "If they feel jealous every time a client comes, their emotions will fluctuate as many times a day."

"There, there," the new client said, "My wife knows I am here. Sometimes I go to brothels. My wife would rather I went to a prostitute than go find a girlfriend."

"Many of my clients also say so,"I said,"last year, an Australian young man of about thirty said he had married a Vietnamese girl and made her pregnant, so she gave him money and urged him to come to my place."

We walked and talked until we got to the working room. Hanging his suit in the wardrobe, he said, "People like to seek new stimulus in their sexual activities. Take my father, he has had a girlfriend outside his marriage and he still has relations with her. My mother was very jealous at first when she found out about the affair but as time elapsed she had to give tacit consent to the status quo."

"All is well as long as the marriage is not affected," I commented, "Trouble arises when a married man has a girlfriend outside his marriage, has fallen in love with her and comes home to seek a divorce by picking fights with his lawful wife."

The man was taking off his trousers when he said, "That's why I don't go to find a girlfriend – to avoid unnecessary trouble.

I come to visit you as I don't fear I'll be caught here. One day a woman came to press our doorbell and it was my wife who answered the door." We both burst into a roar of laughter. He had stripped and went to the bathroom to have a pee. But he failed to raise the toilet seat before pissing so the seat was stained with dirty yellow urine. I had to find an old towel to clean the toilet seat, complaining in my mind about his unsanitary habit. It was inconsiderate of such a decent gentleman to commit such an uncivil offence as Mr. Hooves did. He had stained the toilet seat. How could his successor use it? Had his mother never taught him how to do the right thing at home or in public places?

Having cleaned the toilet seat, I went back to find he was sprawled on the massage table. He said, "One hour. Let me have a good relaxation today." Seeing he was sincere and honest, I didn't charge him before service.

As a rule, I usually charged every new client before the service began, unless they were my old patrons. Nowadays many young guys were not reliable or trustworthy. More often than not you finish serving one and he says he has no money with him. You can't cut off his cock as a mortgage, can you?

I began to massage him from his shoulders to his back and from his shin to his waist. When I moved my hand to his buttocks I couldn't help admire, "Oh, how white and tender your hips are! They are just like those of a baby." He said with a smile, "That's because I work in the office and have little chance to sunbathe."

I said, "Even if you had more chance to be in the sun, could you take off your pants and expose your hips to the sun?"

He was greatly amused.

"Do you have any children?" I asked.

"No," he answered. "I don't want any children. You may like them but if after some time you cease to like them, can you send them back to where they came from?"

I was also greatly amused.

"It's well you don't want any children," I said, "I have an Italian client. He is fifty-eight this year. He has three sons; the eldest is thirty-one, the second eldest twenty-seven and the youngest twenty-one. None of his three sons have any regular work and whenever they meet him, the first sentence they utter is invariably, "Daddy, give me some money!" He has to part with his money, sometimes fifty dollars and sometimes a hundred. But when he has fallen ill and is lying in hospital, none of them will come to take care of him. What makes him angrier is his youngest son's addiction to drugs. One day when they were quarrelling over drugs, his youngest son punched him and made his left eyelid bleed a lot. He was sent to the emergency ward and given two stitches by the surgeon. In my opinion, such a child is a curse rather than a blessing."

"I have talked it over with my old girl," he said, "We don't plan on having any children. It will cost you at least one million dollars to bring up and educate a child. A baby will break your arm and when it grows up, he or she will break your heart."

"Me too," I couldn't agree more, "I plan to spend the rest of life as a childless prostitute."

"If I were a woman," he echoed, "I would take on your occupation, too."

"But many people despise this occupation," I went on to say, "Actually in any occupation, there are good guys and bad guys. There are also bad guys in the police force and it's a stereotype that all prostitutes are bitches, or bad dirty women. You can't judge a person just by his or her occupation, can you? I've been in this business for ten years and I never smoke, never drink and never go to casinos. That's why I have so many high-brow clients. My clients include policemen, doctors, lawyers, teachers, officers, civil servants working for the government and so on."

"There are no good professions or bad professions," he said, "Whatever you do; it's not easy to do it well."

By then I had finished massaging his legs and soles and when I turned him over to massage his chest, I noticed a glittering gold cross with Jesus nailed on it hanging around his neck.

"Are you a Christian?" I asked.

"Yes,"he answered,"My wife and I are both devout Christians and we go to church on Sundays."

"How many Christians are there in Australia or believers in God?"

"About forty to fifty percent of Australians are I'd say. Do you believe in Christianity or in Catholicism?"

"Neither," I answered, "but recently I became a believer of God's existence."

We were chatting about every subject under the sun, ranging from sex to religion when I found one hour's time elapsed quickly. He paid me ninety dollars and left with a bottle of red wine in his hand.

Thus a busy work day was beginning…

It was eleven in the evening and I happened to have no client so I settled down to writing. Now I was unmistakably and thoroughly aware that I was writing the secret of God and it could never be revealed to anybody before my book was published. I was kneeling before God, pledging myself to keeping the sacred book's contents a secret by any means necessary before its publication. It was the grandest plan God had been working on for a long time and even I, an ordinary goddess, should not know and could not know the plan's content. In my mind, I feared God and admired God in awe. God was my Lord.

Thinking of this, I again lost control of my emotions and gave way to sudden tears. My heart was nearly broken. God was watching me writing in tears and had pity on me. He knew I was working for Him yet he still could do nothing to help me. Heaven had its law just as a country had its own law and be you a mortal or a deity, you must obey God. Whoever disobeyed Him would be punished most severely.

God was watching me writing so I dared not write absentmindedly. He would duly punish me for any negligence.

It was already two in the early morning but the conversation between the God and I did not come to an end. I found that God was a million times more benevolent and almighty than Santa Claus and His magnanimity knew no bounds. He was the Creator of the myriads of universes and almightier than any god. He was the most sacred and irresistible god. All deities and mortals must kneel before Him and obey every will from Him; otherwise all of us would perish in no time before Him. From now on, I stopped suspecting and hesitating and believed all the world was created by Him and anyone, including us deities, should be under the command and mercy of Him. He would crush any disobedience or grievance from us. We must be most docile and submissive before our Lord -- the most sacred God.

I was working on His divine will and I had cried numerous times in overcoming obstacles while working. God had pity on me but He was helpless because His grand plan had to be implemented by someone – in this case, me. We were discussing and sometimes arguing as I insisted on converting from a goddess to an ordinary mortal but He meant me to go back to heaven after

I finished the essay on unification. I kept on crying, refusing to return to heaven when I felt a piercing pain in my right shin bone. I let out a cry of pain and looked down to find a black spot the size of a five cent coin on my right leg. God said calmly, "A minor punishment for your disobedience." I had to submit and dropped to my knees, "My Lord, I will do anything You tell me to do through fire and water." Hearing that, God was beginning to have mercy on me, "Well, you've been crying all night so I'll give you a day off…"

Day Nine: April 4, 2011, Monday

When I got up at nine the next morning, a voice, apparently coming from the depth of my heart, kept on ringing in my ear, "Why do I have to work for God, who is neither visible nor tangible. He has me write a certain book but doesn't promise to pay me for it. Am I too naïve and foolish? You say you're God. Well, show me how almighty you are. Since you cannot pay me directly, let me win a lottery, will you?

After washing up, I put on my sweater, trousers and shoes. I locked the door, took my handbag and wallet before I headed for Woden shopping mall. I walked southward on the pavement along a street bustling with traffic and pedestrians. It was autumn, the best season in Canberra when dense trees, green lawns, blooming flowers and chirping birds formed a most beautiful oil painting. But I was not in the mood for appreciating the scenic view. I was preoccupied and somewhat entranced as I walked in the sun. God accompanied me to the mall, his voice repeating in my ear, "My Goddess, I'm going to pay you for your last three months' work. Go and buy a lottery ticket." I silently said to God, "If you do pay me, I will go on with the book otherwise I will stop writing right away and stop believing in you." I was repeating my prayers when I arrived at the shopping mall and went directly to level one. I asked Him, "My Lord, how many tickets do you advise me to buy?" To my question, God answered, "Just one is enough to show my power." I said to myself, "It is you that told me to buy just one ticket. If you fail to let me win the lottery, I will stop believing in you." I asked,"By the way, could you please tell me what day's ticket to buy?" God said he wouldn't tell me until I reached the lottery counter.

When I reached the lottery counter in the mall, several clerks were busy selling lottery tickets. It so happened that a lady of forty with a trolley was buying her tickets and another gentleman was being served. As he quickly finished the transaction and left, I went over to the counter, "Excuse me, what day's tickets are being sold now?" The clerk answered, "There's a ticket for ten million to be drawn on Wednesday. And…"

I didn't hear the next part of his sentence distinctly but I heard he said there would be a ticket for three million to be drawn next Thursday. Just then God whispered in my ear, "Buy Thursday's ticket." I was amused. God didn't want to spoil me by paying me too much at once so he had me buy Thursday's for a smaller reward. Perhaps He might be a shrewd manager with a rendering-to-each-according-to-his-work principle so he had to inspect my work first before he paid me. He obviously didn't want to spoil me by paying me ten or twenty million at will. Deities might have deities' rules and regulations, managerial as well as financial. But still I didn't believe in God's power until I won the lottery. Suddenly the clerk's question brought me back to reality, "What ticket would you like to buy?"

God promptly dropped me a hint,"Buy a ticket not exceeding twenty dollars."

I told the clerk as instructed, "I'll buy a ticket for around twenty dollars."

"Then buy a sixteen dollar fifty one," the clerk advised, pointing at the price list under the glass top.

"Okay," I said, "I'll take one."

I took out a twenty-dollar note and handed it to the clerk, who printed a ticket for me and handed me the change of three dollars fifty. I took the ticket without scrutinizing it and put it away together with the change into my bag, still doubting whether God could make me win the lottery and vowing if I didn't I would never believe in any God and He could not have me work for Him.

I went on walking and took advantage of the relatively less busy Monday to do some shopping. I headed for the southern part of the mall while having a small chat with God, who was heard clearly speaking in my ear.

First I went to the newsagent near the southeast gate and searched the shelf for writing pads but found there were none. Then I heard God whispering, "You can go to Coles for lined writing paper (I could only write straight on lined paper)."

Then I went to the stationery shelf for pens. Lisa had warned me not to write with a ball-point pen as the ball-penned manuscript would not keep long and she recommended I write in carbonic ink. I decided to buy some pens with carbonic ink. I found there were two colors, blue and black. I tilted my head for direction and God said, "Buy black ones."

I began to choose black pens one by one and grasped them in my left hand. God said, "Choose thirteen pens." Looking at the chosen pens in my right hand, I went to search the shelf for more when God said again, "Later I'll tell you why we like the numbers five, seven and thirteen." Oddly enough, I had had a particular preference for the number thirteen since my childhood. When doing business, I would jump with joy at the sight of the number thirteen…

Pushing a trolley, I entered Coles Supermarket. I first went to the beer aisle to see whether any beers were on special, only to find there were no beers that were tied with the yellow tags of discounted prices. Just then I heard God saying in my ear, "There's no sale on beers today in Coles. Go to Woolworths to buy special-priced beers."

I was amazed that God should know where to buy special-priced beers. Was it all real? I was wondering. Since there were no beers on sale, I may as well buy some tissues so I pushed the empty trolley to the personal care and hygiene aisle and threw two large multi-packs of tissue boxes into it.

It suddenly occurred to me that I needed some lined writing paper so I pushed the trolley to the stationery aisle only to find it had been changed into a food aisle when God whispered again, "Try to find some in the middle of the aisle." I searched for the paper from the last row of shelves to the top row but in vain. I began to complain about it silently. Perhaps God might have made a mistake. God then said, "Sorry, my Goddess, I almost forgot. The lined paper is on the third shelf." I searched again as instructed but I still couldn't find any. God seemed too incompetent at this point but He cried out, "Oh! I remember that Coles never sell stationery so you can buy it in the Post Office not far from your home next week. Anyway, you still have two pads of lined paper left at home, don't you?" God knew I still had two pads of lined paper left at home! All the time, I was walking like a robot programmed by God. When I arrived at the checkout counter, the cashier there scanned the goods in the trolley and told me the total amount for forty-eight boxes of tissues (two packs of twenty-four), at a dollar seventeen each, was fifty-six dollars and sixteen cents. When I took the receipt the cashier handed me after I paid, God complained, "The receipt today is printed in smaller letters than usual." Looking down at the receipt, I found it was indeed printed in smaller letters. After that, I pushed the trolley to the bottle shop near Woolworths. On entering the shop, I found a local boy with a short cut busy serving a customer at the cashier desk. I waited for the customer to leave and asked the clerk, "Hi, mate. What brand of beer is on sale today?" The young clerk answered politely, "Just a minute. Let me check for you."

Then God interrupted, "Look. I'll have him give you a special price."

I thought it was amusing that God should know the price of beers here. Soon the clerk carried a box of VB beer from the cold storage and dumped it on the desk. Glancing at the screen of the computer, he told me the price was thirty-seven dollars for each box and I said I'd like to take six boxes. Pushing the trolley, I followed the clerk to the cold storage. After the clerk entered the cold storage, I took the tissues out of the trolley. As the package of tissue boxes had been opened, several boxes of tissues accidentally dropped onto the ground.

"Look how clumsy you are." God furrowed his brow, "You're old indeed."

I smiled to myself that God was perhaps a chatterbox.

It was not long before the young clerk pushed out a cart from the cold storage, with five boxes of VB beer piled on it. God whispered in my ear, "You needn't carry these boxes yourself. I'll have the young man load the beer into your trolley."

No sooner had God finished his sentence than the clerk took up two boxes and dumped them into my trolley. When I moved a box God said, "Leave the remaining two boxes for him to carry."

The young man was so strong he quickly loaded the trolley with the remaining two boxes of beer and the two packs of tissues lay by the trolley as well. In the process, he accidently dropped several boxes of tissues onto the ground. God gave a wry smile, "Look at the young guy. He's even clumsier than you."

I couldn't help laughing out. "Sorry," the clerk said, somewhat embarrassed.

"Never mind," I said, trying hard to suppress my laughter.

He helped me push the trolley back to the cashier's desk. After he loaded the box of beer on the counter into my trolley, I paid by swiping my credit card. Thirty-seven dollars a box came to a total of 222 dollars for six boxes of beer. As the young clerk had me sign the printed receipt, God said, "Look at this receipt. It was printed slantingly." Sure enough, I found not only was the receipt itself but also its content was printed slantingly. After I signed the receipt, I found the invoice he handed me was also slanted, which made me laugh even more heartily. God said, "See? Just as I thought."

Pushing my trolley, I went out of the bottle shop and to the seafood counter. God told me,"Go and buy a lobster. Don't you like lobsters? There's only one lobster over there that has just arrived." Just as He predicted, when I came to the end of the counter, I found a nice, fresh, huge red lobster sprawled on the glistering crushed ice. A young, dark-haired little man standing behind the counter saw me and asked, "May I help you?" I said I'd like that lobster and the young man spread two pieces of bluish paper on a digital scale and put the lobster on the paper. The amount shown on the screen was thirty-eight dollars forty. God said to me, "Give him forty dollars and tell him he can keep the change."

The short salesman turned and packed the lobster into a plastic bag. At that time, a tall fat salesman looked up at me so I was about to hand him the money but God said, "Give it to the short man. It was he that weighed the lobster for you." God also said in my ear, "I didn't want you to give money to that tall man. I'd like you to give it to the short man." The short man had packed up the lobster and handed me the plastic bag together with the invoice. I gave him the money, "Here's forty dollars and you can keep the change."

The clerk was happy when he took the money and I put the lobster onto the beer boxes in the trolley. Then I went to a Japanese snack bar in Woden Mall and bought three boxes of vegetable pies, three boxes of shredded kelp and twenty packets of vinegar pickled ginger. God said in my ear, "You needn't go on a diet by eating these low-calorific foods. From now on you will not put on any weight whatever food you eat. Don't you find you're getting slimmer and slimmer? That's because I have done something to your soul."

Yes indeed. On the day immediately after March 14, 2011, when I was incarnated, I found to my joy I had got much thinner and since then I have been slimming every day around my belly and waist and my fat belly has disappeared and it has become as flat as when I was in my thirties. The young saleswoman kindly handed me the packed food and I heard God saying in my ear, "From now on I'll have everyone smile his welcome and his farewell to you every time he or she serves you."

When I pushed the trolley loaded with various items out of the south gate of Woden Mall, I found two taxis parked there and the drivers were waiting for their prospective customers. God told me, "Get into the first taxi. The driver is a spectacled old man near seventy." I opened the taxi door and to my amazement he was indeed an old Australian man who had taken me home many times. I said, "Hi, mate. I'll pay you thirty dollars as usual. I've bought some beers today."

The old man got out of his taxi and opened the trunk. God instructed me, "Don't let him load the goods as he is an old man."

I vied with the old driver in loading the goods into the trunk of his taxi. I did four boxes of beer and he did two. Then I piled the two packs of tissue boxes onto the back seat and the packed lobster on top of the tissues. Taking the Japanese fast food in one hand, I sat on the passenger seat beside the driver, slammed the door and fastened my seatbelt. The driver got into the car too and before I had time to tell him my address he said to me, "You needn't tell me the address. I know where you'd like to go." "Yes," I smiled, "you have taken me home many times."

He started the car and was about to drive me home when my mobile rang, "Linda, where on earth are you?"

God dropped a hint then, "He is a fat guy. He pressed your doorbell but found you were not at home. Now he is hanging around the convenience shop near your house."

"Wait for a couple of minutes," I answered the caller, "I'll be home in a moment."

The taxi pulled up at my parking space and I promptly put the plastic bag containing the Japanese food on the steps of my front door. When the old driver came over to open the trunk, God told me, "Hurry to unload the goods. Take two boxes at a time. They are not heavy and I'll blow a magic breath into you to make you stronger. So don't labor the old man too much." I took two boxes of beer at once and the old man couldn't help admiring, "You're so strong to be able to carry two boxes at once." I put the beer on the ground in front of my garage and the old man piled his box onto mine. I unloaded the rest of the boxes and the old man unloaded the packs of tissue boxes from the back seat.

This time God did not forget to remind me, "You've left your lobster on the back seat." I went around to the other side of the taxi and opened the door. Sure enough, the lobster was still there.

I picked it up and didn't move as God hadn't given me further instructions as yet.

Just then God said, "Don't forget to pay the taxi driver. Give him five dollars more." I produced thirty-five dollars from my wallet and handed the fare to the old man. He was very happy and drove away with it.

I had some difficulty moving the boxes of beer into the house. I was about to carry a box of beer when God said in my ear again, "Don't bother carrying the rest. The fat guy is coming and let him do it for you. Do you remember he used to pay you twenty dollars and it was me that had him pay you forty dollars last time? But there is only thirty dollars left in his pocket today."

I saw the fat guy pull his white van into my parking space and hardly had I gone out to greet him when he volunteered to carry the boxes of beer in for me, "Hey, where should I put these boxes?" I pointed to the four-door refrigerator near the dining room and he unloaded the beer boxes there. He hurried out and hurried in with another two boxes of beer.

God asked me in whisper, "Isn't it amusing?"

I couldn't help chuckling and the fat guy chuckled too though he didn't actually know the reason why I was chuckling.

"Stop chuckling," God warned, "otherwise the fat guy will be confused." But I could hardly suppress my laughter. God demanded, "Have him take his shower now. You will scare him by chuckling so madly."

While he was taking his shower in the waiting room, I covered the bed with clean towels, got the pillows ready and switched on the DVD player to play the porn video. Having made the preparations, I went to the kitchen, took a can of Coke from the fridge and had a sip. Thinking of the series of amusing episodes I had just encountered, I could hardly restrain myself from laughing and all but threw up the Coke I was drinking.

"Stop giggling," God smiled, "Or you will choke. Take your time in drinking the Coke. He is still in the bathroom." I didn't waste time in picking up the vegetable pies bought from the Japanese snack bar. I opened the box, took a piece, dipped it in the sauce and bit off nearly half of it in a mouthful.

"You are as hungry as a wolf, poor girl," God said, "Take your time. He is still bathing and wondering what had made him help you carry the beer boxes so willingly." After I wolfed down two pies, I washed my hands and went back to the working room. The fat guy seemed totally perplexed today and stared at me blankly. He saw me smiling and he smiled too, yet not knowing why I was smiling. I was smiling because God was finding pleasure in making a fool of others while he was smiling because he was wondering why he should volunteer the hard task of carrying in four heavy boxes for me without being asked to help. So we smiled for different reasons respectively. I chuckled at him and he giggled at me.

I sprawled between his fat thighs and fiddled with his fat cock. God was heard to say, "He's pondering over his unaccountable behavior just now so he can't concentrate on the sex. Look, his cock remains sluggish." I held his cock in my mouth and sucked but instead of yelling wildly as before he just kept giggling at me foolishly. I felt his cock turning soft and hard alternatively and it failed to be stiff long enough to come successfully. I worked on him vainly for a while before God whispered in my ear, "Go on with your game. He's now thinking of his girlfriend, who is much older than him, about your age. You can make sure by asking him about it."

I thought it was an embarrassing question. Could I ask him like that, "Hey, your girlfriend is nearly fifty?" It was against social manners, so I didn't dare do so.

I had much difficulty in making the fat guy's cock stiff by sucking and rubbing his cock and balls, but he suddenly jumped to his feet and demanded,"Let me fuck you!" I found him a small condom and had him stand by the bed. God said, "I'll make him come soon. It will take you less than five minutes to be able to make him come."The fat guy mustered all his remaining strength and impacted me desperately. Pretty soon he was nearly out of breath. He yelled at the top of his voice for less than five minutes before he came. I couldn't help admiring the almighty God, who could have everybody on a string like a puppet. I watched the fat guy's back as he staggered like a drunkard toward the bathroom. After he had finished bathing and got dressed, he produced thirty dollars from his pocket, two twenty notes and two five notes. It was really amazing! God could see through any person and foresaw their every action. He was really an Omniscient God!

Seeing off the fat guy, I began to move the beer boxes into the garage. In moving the goods, a question suddenly occurred to me how I should have become a Goddess. I thought it much better being a human than being a Goddess. Some day, I would be retrieved to heaven by God and I could no longer enjoy the carnal pleasures of a human being. I was astonished at the gloomy future of being retrieved by God to heaven. Oh, my Lord. I didn't want to be a Goddess and begged not to be taken back to heaven. My poor mom would pine when she heard I had been taken back by God, or I died and my soul returned to heaven. Could she, who had so much difficulty in bringing me up, survive the news that I departed my life and the world and she could never see me again in person? At the deplorable future in my own imagination, I was prostrate with grief. I knocked my head on the earth and rolled around on the ground crying. No! I wouldn't have such a tragedy happen to me. A tragic separation between mother and daughter was going to befall me. I was heartbroken and almost cried my eyes out. I knelt and knocked my head on the ground thrice loudly, "My Lord, I beg you to have mercy on me. You don't know the difference between gods and mortals. Gods have no affection but we have. You don't know how profound the affections between mortals are, especially those between mother and daughter."

It seemed to me that God would retrieve my soul to heaven at any time of any day so I would have no chance to see my dearest mother any more. Seeing all this, God seemed to be weeping too, "My Goddess, please don't cry like that. My heart is breaking. You're my angel and I took you with me wherever I went when you were young. You're my most loved one. We gods also have affections among us. Though we do not have sexual relations with each other like mortals, we can communicate our affections among us by touching and feeling. I have many goddesses but you're the one I like best. Mortals cannot appreciate and enjoy our gods' life. We can walk freely in any corner of space. We sleep in the daytime and appear in space at night. We can create dozens of, hundreds of or myriads of universes."

"You gods don't need to eat to live?"

"We gods never eat but drink dewdrops."

I rolled on the ground and yelled, "No. No! I would rather be a mortal than a goddess!"

"My goddess," God seemed a little offended, "You're being disobedient. If you keep on behaving like that, I will punish you."

Hearing that God would punish me, I jumped to my feet at once and cried repeatedly, "I'll be obedient. I'll be obedient."

"I sent you to inspect the world," God said, "and gave you a mission – to lay a foundation for the unification of the world by writing a masterpiece."

"My Lord," I fell to my knees, "I beg you to tell me when and how I was converted from a goddess into an ordinary human being."

"Fifty years ago," God began to narrate from the very start, "You were a little angel as big as a fly. At the age of eighteen, your mother, who was very beautiful, married your father, an honest and true man of thirty-one. It was your father's second marriage and he had a daughter with his ex-wife. I told your father his daughter died but in fact she didn't. So he married your mother. When they were mating, I blew you into your mother's womb."

It struck me as the weirdest thing that God should know that my father's daughter, my stepsister, actually did not die at all.

It reminded me of another weird thing. It happened when I flew back to China to see my mother last year. My sister told me when she went to visit father's grave she was very surprised to find there was a large bunch of flowers and various fruits as a sacrifice offer in front of the grave. I was shocked to hear her story and wondered whether God was really so almighty as to work so many wonders. Though I was not completely convinced of God's existence, I was wondering why I was working like a robot, as if dictated by someone to do this or that. God's voice was always lingering near my ears. But I couldn't see Him so I asked the void, "Then where is my father's soul? You say everybody has his soul."

"Your father's soul has been converted into a goat."

I was shocked and burst out crying, "Oh no. No! Why did you turn my father into a goat?"

"I have told you a thousand times you're not a human but a goddess. You're my Goddess. He's not your father and nor is your mother your mother."

I wailed all the more sadly, "No! No! I can't make do without my father neither can I make do without my mother. And I'm not a goddess. I'm a human being! A human being!"

I kept on wailing until I was out of breath. God became somewhat impatient and said sternly, "My Goddess, You can't cry any more, otherwise your soul will part with you and you'll become a corpse!"

I was terrified and stopped crying at once, "I will do whatever you order me to do. I don't want to be a cold, dead corpse. I want to live. I want to live."

"Then," God said, "Be a good girl and work hard for me. Write whatever I order you to write and finish writing as many words as I order you to. You mustn't go to sleep unless you finish a certain workload or you will suffer from a headache as punishment."

God went on to say, "I am the Supreme and Almighty Lord of the world. As you have just witnessed, I can dictate anyone's consciousness and make him go wherever I want him to go and do whatever I want him to do. Even souls of gods are under my command. I have a lot of gods and goddesses and they are all my obedient servants. Anyone who dares to disobey will be most severely punished by me."

I was overwhelmed by awe and reverence and could hardly stand firm. I plopped down onto my knees and kept on knocking my head on the ground loudly, "My Lord, I will be your most loyal servant and I am willing to do anything you tell me."

"Then do as I told you just now." God said solemnly.

"My Lord," I said, "I'm your most loyal servant but you should pay me for my service. I have to eat to live before I can serve you by writing. The question is I am a mortal not a goddess. Anyway, I have to make a living."

"Didn't I tell you to buy a lottery ticket this morning?" God explained, "And you are sure to win the lottery jackpot of three million next Thursday. I promise to pay you ten million dollars a year as a reward for your work."

"How could you prove that, my Lord?"

"Of course I can," God answered, "You can doubt my power now but you will prostrate yourself before me with awe and reverence next Thursday."

"Well," I said, "If I receive my pay next Thursday, I will worship you forever."

"I'm the Lord Almighty," he said, "I can perish all the human beings in the world if I please!"

"My Lord," I begged with my forehead to the ground, "No. No! You can't. After all, good people account for the majority."

"Since I created the world and human beings, I of course have no intention to destroy my creations, at least for the time being. But if the people all over the world go on ignoring my authority, I will perish them to the last man!"

"Please don't, my Lord," I kept begging Him, "Save my mother, my sisters and their children."

"I have told you she is not your mother."

"She *is* my mother, my mom. Please. She is indeed my mother. I'm longing for a peacefully unified world with neither war nor strife, a world in which everyone can live a happy life."

"Yes," God said,"We are all striving to realize this grand plan and you are the angel I've stationed on the Earth. Your present task is to write the essay on world unification. I will inform you in due time when to publish your finished book. Write strictly as I've indicated you to. You should know that the content of your book is all dictated by me. You're actually writing with your soul and your soul is under my command."

Seeing me huddled in fear, God comforted me by saying, "My Goddess, you will not die. You will live forever unless I retrieve your soul. Since I have you incarnated, I won't retrieve you before my grand plan has been realized. You can stay alive for another two hundred years and I will retrieve you to heaven as soon as you have completed your mission. We gods will also die but our souls can be recycled. Generally we can live three to five thousand years or even ten thousand years. No life in the world is immortal and we gods are also a form of life. As for human beings, they can lengthen their lifespan by refraining themselves from committing more sins. Everyone shall face God as soon as he or she dies. He or she will be converted by God into either human beings or animals like pigs, dogs or cats. Mao Zedong, who often taught his cadres to serve the people like an ox when he was alive, has been converted into an ox and Richard Nixon a sea turtle…"

Seeing I was on the verge of breaking down, God said, "My Goddess, stand on your feet. My baby, you know you're my favorite goddess. You're not only brave and resourceful but also so loyal to me. Since you left me fifty years ago, I have been missing you almost every night and more often than not I cannot go to sleep because I'm thinking about you. Do you know why you often have a pain in your right sole? That's because I am missing you as my dear wife. We gods also have love among us. Since your birth, I've been watching you grow up. Once I saw your mother beating you and how I wanted to punish that woman! Another time I saw you fighting with Zhang Haiyang (my lover in China from when I was twenty-one until I was thirty-five years old. His story will be dwelt on later in my book) and I was glad to find my Goddess was really different from those ordinary women, so brave and fierce. As a matter of fact, I deliberately dictated Zhang to treat you like that in order to cultivate you as the most courageous and vigorous woman in the world. In heaven I treated you just as Zhang did on Earth – I sometimes loved you dearly and sometimes hurt you badly. Do you know how dearly I love you? I can hardly bear for you to sob in my face." At that time I felt distinctly my right sole was aching, which meant God loved me. He said, "My heart is painful so stand up and go lie on the bed. Let me blow a magic breath into your body. Look, your eyelids have become swollen. You're being ugly. You used to be very pretty when you were young and you were also pretty when you were in heaven." Following his advice, I obediently stood up and lay on the bed in my bedroom.

"Rest your head on your pillow," God said, "and cover your eyes with a black scarf. I will blow a magic breath into your body." I lay on the bed as instructed and suddenly felt a hot wave run through my soles and then along my shanks upward. It was less than three minutes before God ordered me, "Get up and run on your treadmill for half an hour and you will become much younger. I promise to make you younger by five to ten years within a short period of about three years."

I followed God's instruction and began to exercise on my treadmill. God asked me in my ear while I was running, "How do you feel?"

"Not bad," I said, "I can hold on. Since I'm your Goddess, I'm willing to do anything for you." I was then soaked in sweat and the sweat began to sting my eyes.

"Don't wipe your eyes with your hand," God warned me.

I closed my eyes tightly, trying to prevent the tears from flowing in and went on running for about fifteen minutes.

"Stop," God ordered, "I'm afraid your soul will escape from your body while you're running. If so, I will take the trouble to help you retrieve your soul." I got off the treadmill as instructed, sweat dripping from my forehead.

"Mop the sweat off with the towel. How are your eyes? Are they okay?"

"They're okay, my Lord. And I'm also very well."

"Look," the Lord said, "Here comes a new client. Wipe off your tears and go greet him."

I quickly rubbed my swollen red eyes and went to open the door. It was a short, thin Australian man with long blond hair tied with a rubber band like a girl's ponytail. Afraid of being noticed to have been weeping, I rubbed my eyes with the back of my hand. I guessed he must have known the fact that I had cried a lot because my eyes were so swollen. I was a woman of fortitude and had seldom shed tears before strangers from my girlhood to the year I turned fifty. Now that I believed in the existence of God and was convinced my fate was in His hand, I had been weeping for the last half a month and I was afraid I had exhausted almost all the tears of my life.

"Don't worry," God said, "He won't stay long. I will have him leave soon."

The pony-tailed young man took his bath, lay on his belly on my bed and had me massage his back. After a while, he lifted up his buttocks and asked me to lick his asshole. I hesitated but God said, "Go ahead. He has cleaned it thoroughly."

"No," I retorted, "I don't want to lick any asshole even though it is very clean. Whether I am a goddess or a human being, I won't lick assholes any more. I have had enough of it the last ten years."

"I'll make his asshole hurt when you lick it."

The young man lifted up his narrow hips and exposed his asshole. I was surprised to find there was a dark-brown pigmented mole the size of a coin around his asshole. I stuck out my tongue and felt it was very rough, not as smooth as my usual one. God said, "I'll make your tongue feel rough and thorny today."

I began to lick the young man's asshole as God whispered to me, "Pretty soon, he will decline your licking." Sure enough, only a couple of minutes passed before he rolled over and said, "Stop. You may as well suck my cock."

"Another example," God said triumphantly, "Look at your TV screen and see how I can dictate the program to be paused." At that time, I happened to be watching the porn video playing on the screen on the east wall, in which a Caucasian man suddenly ceased thrusting his cock into an Asian girl's cunt but a few seconds later, resumed his cock movement in the same sudden way. That was enough to make me convinced of God's existence and his omnipotence. I felt weak at the knees and all but knelt down but God stopped me, "Don't kneel down. The young man will think you're kneeling before him."

I smiled and God was pleased, "Look, you're smiling." The young man was perplexed by my mysterious smile, wondering why Linda's tongue should be so rough today as to hurt his asshole so much.

"Look," God said mischievously, "He will flee at once, wondering all the way home why Linda's tongue should be like a coarse file today."

After I mouth-worked him and made him come at last, I told him, "Please turn over and let me massage you."

"No, no," he waved his hand, "I must be going now. I have something important to do."

I didn't try to request him to stay as I wanted to resume the casual talk with God, so I said, "As you have stayed less than twenty minutes, I'll charge you thirty dollars."

Having bundled off the long-haired man, I was in a wavering state of mind, wondering whether it was God's instructions or just my own delusion, something subconscious that was always ringing in my ears so I asked God, "Oh, my Lord. May I ask you a question? You have been watching me grow up so you must have witnessed how I was cheated by so many scoundrels on various occasions. Why didn't you mete out due punishment on them?"

"You're wrong in assuming I didn't," God argued, "The woman who called you a bitch in Tong County had died of cancer and the scoundrel Liu who cheated you in running the Huairou Hotel in Beijing was now lying paralyzed in bed. He had a wry mouth because of a partial paralysis. You can see it with your own eyes when you go back to Beijing next time."

I was half believing and half doubting what God had said, as I used to be an atheist who didn't believe in any ghosts or deities. God found he needed further proof to convince me of his power,"I will punish the two women in Sydney, who cheated you in the purchase of your properties. I will spare them for several years and then torment them to death. You will see it." I said in answer, "And there's more. The woman Lily I knew in the brothel ten years ago found me an unqualified editor and we quarreled about it over the phone. Finally she heaped abuse on me, 'Fuck you bloody hell!'" God said quickly, "I'll have her crawl her way to you and lick your toes. She will end up dying of cancer, too. You wait and see."

I was still dubious of His existence emotionally. I was not a pious believer of any religion. Despite this, I had been a kind and tolerant woman since my birth and I tended to compromise with those who maltreated me but hadn't gone so far as to murder me. Hearing what God had planned, I couldn't help falling to my knees and begged God to have mercy on them, "Forget it all, my Lord. Forgive them all. Everybody has his selfish motives. They cheated me or abused me out of their different motives then. Spare them all. I am well off enough now though not fabulously wealthy."

"What I mean is to show you that evil will be rewarded with evil. My Goddess, you're only too kind so you suffered a lot in your past life. I have found a divinity in you when I saw you fighting with Zhang bravely and fiercely. I'm sure you will realize my grand plan."

"My Lord," I said, "I still don't believe I'm a goddess. But whether I am or not, I will muddle along unless my life is at risk. If my life is threatened, I will surely fight to the end."

"This is where my Goddess is different from others," God said not without a note of pride in His voice, "You are kind yet courageous."

"This is also my own principle all my life," I went on to say, "But I still take my belief with a grain of salt."

"Well," God seemed somewhat helpless, "Now call your mother in Beijing, China to see what I can tell you she is doing."

I thought it was a good idea. My mother lived thousands of miles away in China. If God could tell me what He knew of my mother, I would recognize His power. I went to the west living room, grabbed the receiver and dialed my mother in Beijing. I was waiting while God counted for me, 1, 2, 3, 4, 5… Suddenly God told me,"Listen, your mother is connected. Ask her whether she was coming out of her kitchen."

I asked her, "Mom, have you just come out of the kitchen?"

"Yes," Mom answered, "How do you know I've just come out of the kitchen?"

"Mom," I went on to ask, "Have you had your meal?"

"What meal at this time?" Mom said, "Lunch or supper? Do you have anything else to talk to me about? (It was 3:00 p.m. Beijing Time)"

"If I talk about my book to you,"I pretended to be complaining, "You will say you can't understand it at all. So I begin with the question, 'have you had your meal?'"

"In the past, every time you called me, you invariably said you would be a second J.K. Rowling, the author of 'Harry Potter' and become as rich as she is. But these days when you call, you're always talking about God? I don't even know who God is."

"God is a noble-minded and almighty deity," I explained, "I didn't believe in Him but now I do."

"A noble-minded and almighty deity?" mom asked, "Are you referring to Chairman Mao? He died."

"Yes, he died. He has been reincarnated into a donkey."

"Into a donkey?" Mum was bewildered, "Maybe you are confused by writing too hard. I'm not interested in what you're saying."

"That's why I have to begin with the question 'Have you had your meal?'"

God said again, "Your mother is now watching TV in her armchair, scratching her feet."

I immediately asked mom over the phone,"You're scratching your feet, aren't you?"

"Yes, my feet hurt at the heels."

Only then did I become totally convinced of God's existence. Who but an almighty God could describe in every detail what my mother was doing thousands of miles away in China? I went on to ask some questions about the school life of my nephew He Chen in Holland and then put down the receiver. I got down to my knees, then prostrated myself on the ground and burst out crying, "It's really incredible, My Lord. Am I really your Goddess? I love you. I love you. I love you! I now know why I can't fall in love with any man. It turns out that my Lord is in the heaven and my lover is none other than God!"

"Trust me," God said emotionally, "You're my Goddess, my loyal servant. You can devote your life to me. In order to accomplish my grand cause of unification, I allowed you to be incarnated. For the last fifty years when you were away, I have been missing you. I miss you each and every day!"

"My Lord," I was overwhelmed by great sorrow, "Allow me to be retrieved. I want to see you and I will give up all that belongs to me, my money, my house, my car or anything else. I miss you. Don't leave me alone in this world. I will languish from missing you."

"My dear Goddess," God said, "It was for the grand cause of unification that I allowed you be incarnated in the world so I won't retrieve you at will. I can see my Goddess is still as loyal to me as before you left. It's proven that we deities can be incarnated into human beings and so can I myself in the future."

God went on to say, "Stop crying, my Goddess. Stand up. If you don't stop crying, your soul will flee away from you and then you will die." I was frightened by what God was saying and jumped to my feet. I heard God go on to say, "Go and have a piss in the toilet. See what color your piss will have become? I've just blown a magic breath into your body and you will be getting younger and younger in future."

I stood up, ran to the toilet in the waiting room and had a loud piss into the toilet bowl.

"My Lord, it's bluish green (not the normal light amber passed by ordinary people)," I reported its color to God.

"Excellent," God said, "You will be rejuvenated and get younger and younger with every day."

I seemed to be hesitating again. How come I ceased to be a human being and became a goddess? I couldn't fall in love with any man because I was hardened by a long time of living a prostitute's life. I could manage to do without a lover but I could never make do without my mother. So I began retorting in mind with God, "I am not a goddess. I am a human being."

I dared not voice my grievances but harbored the unspoken criticism in mind. Since the moment I half-believed in His existence, I somehow began to fear Him. I went all weak at the knees at the mere thought of Him and was ready to prostrate myself before Him at any time. I used to be a dauntless woman who feared nothing, not even death. I remembered ten years ago when I decided to go it alone and start my own business, the mafia leader in Sydney's Chinatown threatened to set fire to my house with petroleum, trying to frighten me into paying protection fees to them regularly. I asked my fellow prostitute Lily how I could get a gun in Sydney. I was ready to fight a mortal combat with them. Hearing that, Lily tried her best to persuade me to give up my desperate plan, "Dear, you can't do that. It's illegal to own a gun in Australia. The police will arrest you and throw you into prison for having a gun."

HARD COCK

These episodes will be elaborated on later in my personal history. They will tell you how I came to Australia and how I have become a prostitute famous throughout the country. So my book may seem a little lengthier to some readers but it will surely be a meaty one. I have endless stories stocked in my mind and I'm afraid I will take them to my grave. I'm anxious to tell them all to my readers. I'm ambitious to be a literary baron as well a prostitute baron.

I was cheated by two scoundrels when I was running a big hotel in China and I was cheated again by two women scoundrels when I was purchasing two properties here in Australia. I was cheated just because I was too credulous not because I was too weak. I am a woman knight-errant with an invincible spirit. I will elaborate on these interesting and exciting stories in my future book. You will like them without fail. Just wait for its publication!

Now let's go back to our almighty God. All my body felt like jelly at the mere mention of God and was ready to kneel at His feet at any time. All my life, except for my two lovers from when I was young, I hadn't knelt before anybody, even my two ex-husbands, let alone my parents. I often argued with my parents and they called me a stubborn donkey.

But as God's image mysteriously entered my brain, I was entranced with awe and was ready to cry upon thinking of Him and get down to my knees upon hearing His voice. I felt like my soul would leave me if I failed to listen to Him. If God really retrieved my soul from me, I would become a walking corpse.

I was murmuring to myself, "I am a human being not a Goddess."

Then God said, "You'll get to know whether you're a human being or a goddess. But I don't want to push you." He then went on to say, "Go and open the door. A new client is coming."

Sure enough, a new client was pressing the doorbell. Almighty God! He even knew when a new client was coming.

I opened the door and let out a cry of surprise, "Hey, you. My Hard Cock." He was one of my favorite cocks, an expert at fucking who could easily make me come and thus make me more refreshed and more intelligent.

"Why didn't you give me a call before you came?" I was more happy than upset.

"I did not go to work today," he explained, "I went to the garage to buy some spare parts to repair my car. After I fixed my car, I was walking by and dropped in to see whether you were busy or not."

"Not really," I said, "I was talking with my God." "God?" he smiled, "I don't believe in any God.

"I didn't at first," I said, "but I do now. You may as well do in future. If you don't, God will be displeased. He will punish you by making you die sooner."

He was sticking out his tongue in jest when I heard God say, "Look how I dictate him to do whatever I'd like him to do. Try asking him for some money. I guess he has only a hundred dollars with him."

I asked tentatively, "Could you pay me fifty dollars first?"

He produced two fifty-dollar notes from his pocket and handed one of them to me, "You have never asked me for money first. How are you today?" I laughed up my sleeve, assuming the air of a Goddess. I said to Mr. Hard Cock, "I'd like to know whether you have money with you."

"Have I ever failed to pay you, even once?" he poured out his grievances, "Every time I fuck you into coming, I have to pay you instead of being paid. It's unfair. Actually, you should pay me."

"Shall I pay you with wine or beer?" I said, trying to soothe his grievances, "As a rule, every client is given a bottle of wine. But I always give you several beers in addition to the wine, don't I?" I knew iced VB beer was his favorite so I took out two cans of VB beer from the fridge and handed them to him, "Enjoy your beer. I will supply you with more as soon as you finish them."

He opened a can and drank it as he walked in, "Let me have a shower first. I am covered with dust all over from repairing my car."

I took a clean towel from the cabinet and handed it to him. When he was in the bathroom, God asked me, "Is your pussy hot and wet?"

"Yes." I answered, "Though I'm a Goddess, I now have a pussy and I never cease to want sex."

"Neither do I," God said, "How I wish I had a big cock now and could fuck you on the spot. My Goddess, please wait for me to be incarnated some day and fuck you with the biggest ever cock. I will make you the happiest and most satiated woman in the world."

I began to imagine what God would look like if He was incarnated. He must be as handsome as handsome could be, tall and handsome like Prince Charming or a Gallant King. God asked me a most unexpected question, "Would you like me to be incarnated into a person that resembles your Chinese lover Zhang Haiyang?"

"Zhang is tall," I answered, "but not handsome enough and besides, he doesn't have a big enough cock. I have been a prostitute in Australia for nearly ten years and I have appreciated so many handsome young men."

"Then," God was wondering, "Who do you wish me to resemble? Do you wish me to be a black man, a white man or a brown man?"

"I don't have a clear idea for the moment," I admitted, "In due time I will let you know."

Mr. Hard Cock, having finished his shower, came out bare-hipped. He took the beer can on the bedside table and emptied what was left of it in one gulp. When he was lying on the bed, I resumed the conversation with God, who said, "Suck his cock and I will let his cock become harder than ever. But you have to put a condom on his cock when he fucks you or else I will be jealous of him."

I was then sprawled between his thighs and sucking his cock. His cock was not very long but thick and strong enough. What was most attractive; it could last for a particularly long time. He boasted that he could fuck his wife for three or four hours at a stretch. If my pussy were not my lucrative asset, I would let him pay fifty dollars to fuck me for a full four hours. Sometimes I even wanted to indulge myself in carnal pleasures with him for several hours on end to thoroughly satiate my lust. My desire had been so greatly whetted that my cunt gushed out with lust water at the sight of or even at the mere mention of men's cocks, just as a child drooled at his or her favorite food. Now I couldn't tear my eyes from Mr. Hard Cock's stiffened shaft, "Oh, my Lord. He's going to fuck me. You needn't be envious of that. It's not my fault that you don't have a cock. It's not that I'm not loyal to You but that I now have a hot and watering cunt and can no longer resist the temptation. I'm sorry but your Goddess has to take liberties to answer nature's sexual call."

"But you should put a condom on his cock! Otherwise I shall be very jealous."

I thought to myself, "Since God has expressed his displeasure; I'd better not offend him. What if he retrieves my soul? Then I will die. Of course I don't want to court death since I'm still so young. I have a chance to win if I fight with somebody but I have none with God. Disobeying God means inviting death. In a fraction of a second I would be a corpse." I murmured as I was busy putting a condom on his cock. The Hard Cock was surprised, "Hey, what are you doing? We usually don't use that silly thing, do we?"

"Then go ahead without that condom," God heard his grievance and conceded him the privilege of fucking me without a condom, "Anyway, I haven't grown my own cock."

Mr. Hard Cock stood beside the bed and I lay on my back on the edge of the bed, throwing my legs over his shoulders. As he was not very tall in height, his cock was level with my cunt. I murmured, "Oh my God, he's really thrusting his cock into my cunt."

"I am watching you," God said, "All my goddesses and I are watching you through the window. We're watching with great interest how our Goddess is making love with a mortal man."

"But you can't harbor any grudge against me."

"No, I don't"God said calmly,"But as soon as I am incarnated, I won't allow you to make love to anyone. You will belong to me alone."

The Hard Cock abruptly thrust his hard cock into my cunt with a loud "Hey!"

"Has he thrust his cock to the hilt?" God asked me out of jealousy rather than out of curiosity.

"Yes, it has just reached the bottom of my cunt," I tried to console God, "but still inferior to many cocks I have seen. Some cocks are twice as long as his and much thicker than his. However, his cock is hard enough to hit the spot with me."

"When I am incarnated," God promised, "I will have a cock much longer and thicker than any man in the world ever has seen. I promise to fuck you with an XXXL cock."

I was wondering how long a God's cock might be.

"Maybe as long as an ox leg," God seemed to be able to read my mind, "Anyway, it's none of your business. Go ahead with your fucking. It's great fun watching you fucking. You can take him for me in your sexual fantasy."

He pulled out his cock with squelching water and then thrust it back into my cunt. God asked, "Your cunt has been satisfied, hasn't it?"

"Yes," I answered, "it has been more than satisfied. My lust water is gushing out incessantly."

"I enjoy listening to your sensual groans in fucking. I'm expecting them now."

At that time, Hard Cock was busy pushing and pulling his cock away with yells, "Oh, yes. Fucking hell!"

"Oh, yes. Fuck me hard!" I yelled madly.

"It seems my Goddess is in her ecstasy," God seemed enchanted with earthly pleasures, "Tell me what you want him to do next to please you?"

"I'd like him to spread my cunt lips apart to let his cock thrust deeper."

"Okay," God said, "I'll have him do as you please."

Magically enough, Hard Cock used both his hands to spread my labia as wide as possible and thrust his cock into my cunt as hard as he could. God asked me, "Well. Are you totally satisfied?"

"Much better now," I let out a deep groan,"The itching inside my cunt is beyond description."

"Then I'll have him hold on for a while longer."

Hard Cock spread my cunt lips wide and pistoned away his stark cock in my hole with all his strength. I felt I was on the zenith of sexual pleasure. My cunt was as itchy and desirous as it could possibly be. It was throbbing and contracting with squelching water. I enjoyed myself to the utmost and the inside of my cunt was itching beyond any description. God asked me, "My Goddess, are you happy now?"

"Yes," I had hardly any strength to admit, "I couldn't be happier now."

"Actually, you should be happier than any woman in the world," God pointed out, "Because you are a goddess not an ordinary woman."

"Well,"I thought to myself,"Be I a goddess or a human, I may as well satiate myself first. I should well be content to be fucked like this forever. It was worth it if I could enjoy this transient ecstasy before God called me back. It was the predestined fate of a woman who wanted to seek the sublimation of sexual enjoyment."

God asked me once more, "What do you want next?"

"Aren't you the most enthusiastic watcher of my lovemaking scenes?" I asked sarcastically, "You should know very well the most sensitive point in my body is my right nipple. I will shiver all over and then quickly thaw if any man comes to lick it. It takes me a fraction of a second to come on the spot."

"Well," God said, "then I'll have him suck your right nipple." No sooner had God finished his sentence than the Hard Cork bent over to lick my right nipple. I felt as if all my bone joints became loose and I myself turned into a mass of jelly.

"What do you think about his performance?" God asked, "Are you going to come?"

"Another couple of minutes, please," I begged, "I'm going to come pretty soon."

"No worries," God assured me, "I'll have him hold out till you come."

Mr. Hard Cock kept on pistoning his hard cock in me relentlessly and at the same time resorted to any conceivable means to play with my right nipple – suck it with his mouth, lick it with his tongue or hold it between his teeth and cut it gently. I was thawed and paralyzed as the incredibly itching sensation thrilled through my veins.

"Now let me blow a magic breath into your body to make you thoroughly satiated and perched on the zenith of carnal pleasure."

My brain went completely blank as if my soul were retrieved by God. I let out a loud cry of joy and yelled at the top of my voice, "I've come!" and then in English, "I love you! I love you…"

Mr. Hard Cock thought I was shouting "I love you!" to him. He seemed to be greatly moved and responded by accelerating the frequency of his cock movements, which made more lust water gush out.

Actually I yelled the three words to my Lord instead of to him as God had told me in advance that I could take him for Him and imagine it was Him that was fucking me in my sexual fantasy.

Seeing I had reached my climax, Mr. Hard Cock quickened his pace of pistoning and with a loud yell; he ejaculated all his white sperm onto my white belly. I rolled over, jumped to my feet and wiped my belly clean with tissues. While the Hard Cock was taking his shower, I went to my toilet and squatted under the sprinkler, washing my private part carefully. Lazily and exhaustedly, I stood up, totally satisfied with the sexual pleasure. It was indeed a different feeling to be watched by God making love madly. It was wonderful. Up till now, I still couldn't believe I was a goddess instead of an ordinary woman…

When writing this passage, I suddenly shuddered at the thought of how I had the audacity to write about God like that and to profane an Almighty Lord. It was said that in the United States, the believers of Christianity accounted for seventy to eighty percent of the whole population. It was really too rash and audacious of me to do so! I always boasted to my friend Lisa that I was going to offer the world a masterpiece. It seemed I was not going to write a masterpiece but was sealing my own death warrant.

Believe it or not, I had intended to write an autobiography but by and by I unwittingly changed the theme of my book and now I can't write a page without writing about God. Why I had changed an autobiography into a theological narration was beyond my ken. Did I get confused by writing too devotedly or was I courting death by writing this blasphemous book? Or was there really a God who was dictating to me? The problem was I could not adjust my state of mind and settle down to write about only a prostitutes' life. Since my soul was dictating me to write in this way, I had no choice but to follow its direction. Anyway, I had neither obligation nor attachment to anybody in this world except my mom, who was living thousands of miles away in China. So I could face death with indifference. If my book could be published one day, I would calmly receive God's decision to retrieve my soul on the condition that the bad news should not frighten my mother to death.

These days, I had a nagging feeling that God was dictating me in my writing because He was always with me, talking to me as I wrote or even as I worked and having me do whatever He told me to. More often than not, I would write something not of my free will or even against my own will, as if an Almighty God were remote controlling me in my writing. He even said something outside my window, "My Goddess, I'm watching you writing by your windowsill. You can feel free to write anything I'd like you to write. No one in this world would dare to touch you. If anyone dares, I shall punish him by retrieving his soul from him."

For weal or woe, I would go on writing as directed by God. I couldn't do without writing. If I was deprived of the right to write, I would surely be driven mad. And rather than being driven mad I would die. It suddenly occurred to me that God, the Heaven and the Lord were three in one. The world couldn't be ruled by three Gods just as a country by dual presidents.

After seeing off Mr. Hard Cock, I was silently muttering, "Am I a goddess or a human?" when God told me, "Go to the kitchen and enjoy your lobster. I have already blown a magic breath into it. Eat this lobster and you will be rejuvenated. You are getting younger and younger until you will look like a girl in her twenties when I am incarnated."

"But how long shall I wait?" I asked, longing anxiously for that great day.

"Not too long," God answered, "about thirty to fifty years."

"I'm afraid I can't wait for so long," I grumbled, "As you'll be a handsome young Prince Charming when you are incarnated while I would already be a wrinkled old woman in her eighties. How could I be your match then?"

"I've told you that you will be getting younger and younger from now on. And when I am incarnated, you'll be a young girl in your prime and we will be a perfect match. Wherever we go, we will be accompanied by a lot of goddesses."

"But I still have my misgivings. Why will you, at that time, choose me, an old woman while you're surrounded by so many beautiful young goddesses?"

"Haven't I told you so many times?" God was somewhat fretful, "You're not a human but my Goddess. You will live on forever in this world. If I would die, I will die in your arms. We gods will die too though we live much longer than human beings. We gods can live for five thousand, eight thousand or even for ten thousand years and besides we can create some more universes and create another human race. But now among the huge universe, the Earth is the only planet inhabited by human beings. These days, scientists from various countries are researching the task of landing on the Moon. It's also My will. My plan is to land half of the Earth's population onto the Moon because the Earth is so overcrowded that it can no longer support it. If My plan fails to be accomplished by the year 2050, the Earth we are now living on will be obliterated from the universe. Then we have to make our way for another universe and another Earth to harbor a new human race. Human scientists are now undertaking a lot of research projects in space, in which there is actually nothing, just a meaningless void. The present priority is to accomplish My grand plan to land people onto the Moon."

All that God had said was wholly beyond my understanding and I was greatly confused. It had nothing to do with my book and I was quite at a loss as to who I was.

Musing on this over my lobster, I picked up the receiver and contacted Lisa. It so happened she was at home and I told her all about the funny things that had taken place today together with all the heartrending things that God had done to me. Actually, since the terrible day when I called Lisa declaring my triplet statement "I am Goddess incarnated; I am greater than anyone in the world; I am the re-maker of human beings," I had been phoning Lisa every day discussing the weird things I was encountering recently. I argued I had never assumed I was really a Goddess. I just regarded myself as a prostitute baron. The title of Goddess was less important to me than the five dollars my client should underpay me.

"Judging by what you are saying," Lisa said, "There seems nothing wrong with your head. Your thinking is quite clear and logical."

"Sure there's nothing wrong with my head," I said merrily, "If, as my translator pointed out, writing too devotedly will most probably lead to illusions, the fact that I have illusions about the Goddess means my writing level has reached a certain height. I am catching up with Mao Zedong and when I have illusions about God, it will mean my writing level is near Mount Everest and of course beyond Picasso. I will surely be the literary baron in the world by then."

The fact was that I understood that there was no doubt about God's existence, no matter what form He might take on, be it Christ or Buddha and that He remained invisible unless you could enter a frantic state of mind in writing. I couldn't tell the main religions from each other very distinctly as I was not a pious believer of any religion… The founders of the three main religions most likely experienced illusions of God from writing too devotedly. When they woke up, they described God according to the memories in their illusions. Thus the origins of the present three main religions in the world contain three different descriptions of the same God. Similarly, all minor religions in the world had their different forms of Gods. So many minor religions or religious factions had been springing up every year.

As for me, I have been writing every day for almost ten years and have entered a near frantic state of mind. Besides, I was a dauntless woman and was not afraid of facing gods or devils in my dreams. So God chose me as the first person alive to be able to see Him in my presence. I was right in the letter to my translator, Tim in saying God was almighty and so He could put my thinking under His control. It was another thing whether He could be incarnated or whether He wanted to be so. To control all people's thinking, God had to make them read the Bible. But the Bible was so dull and hard to read that few people could understand it fully or liked to read it with interest. Seeing me writing diligently for ten years and at the same time being a successful prostitute baron, God chose me as the writer of His intended book. I had planned to string the episodes of the number-one prostitute's sensual life into a porn story but God now wanted me to write a book advocating the unification of the world and make this propaganda book as interesting as possible by interlarding it with a lot of narrations containing sexually explicit and lively pornographic jokes. God promised if the world was unified, it would be rid of any strife, war or nuclear weapons and the people all over the world would live a happy life. God planned to alleviate the burden of the Earth by dividing the whole population into two halves to inhabit two separate planets. God wanted me to write to warn people of the imminent danger that the Earth was facing and to remind them that no other human beings have been found up till now and if any were to be discovered, it would in thousands of years; a problem not worth considering for the next few generations. God continued to urge us that we should not waste time on space researching programs but the top priority now was to explore and develop the Moon. What an omniscient God He was!"

"Yes," Lisa said and I could deem her to be nodding at the other end of the line, "Your analysis is well-grounded and logical as well."

"Nothing wrong with my head?" I said, "I am neither mad nor ill, I tell you."

Just then my mobile rang. It must have been one of my customers calling.

"Yes. Come along, please."

Putting down the receiver, I said to Lisa, "Well, I'm not mad, am I? Whether I am a Goddess or a bitch, my first priority is to make money. Anyway, no one can do without money in this world."

We often made fun of each other over the phone and I made a fool of myself by stating I was a Goddess when writing but a bitch when doing business with my customers. At that time, God shouted in my ear, "I won't allow you to call yourself a bitch in future. You're my Goddess!"

I had just put down the receiver when the doorbell rang. I opened the door to find a brown-skinned man of about fifty, with a pair of bovine eyes, a high nose and a protruded mouth. He was not tall and wore a dirty uniform and a cap popular among men in Canberra. Somehow I was much disgusted at the mere sight of him. God asked me in a whisper, "Do you want to serve him?"

"No," I said definitely. "Well, I'll make him leave."

The man was seen wavering at the door and muttering to himself. God said, "He didn't even know what he himself was saying."

"Have you just knocked off?" I asked.

"I have just had lunch," he answered as he belched. I raised my brow at his irrelevant answer.

"Have you drunk much?"

"I have just earned six hundred dollars."

The conversation seemed grotesquely incongruous. He began to speak to himself, "I may as well go home."

"Look, he is leaving," God said, not without a note of pride in his voice.

"Yes, he is leaving," I echoed.

"My Lord," I asked, "Since you love me so much, why did you let me be incarnated?"

God answered, "Because I'd like you to help me accomplish the grand plan to unify the world and make necessary preparations for me to be incarnated. Now I have seen the twilight of your victory. I will go on incarnating more goddesses to help you."

"Then when will you be incarnated?"

"I have a long-term plan as I am in charge of many grand projects of the universe. For example, I am planning to create a new human race, maybe with three arms and three legs."

"How awkward would it be to have three arms and three legs!" I was shocked, "It's much better looking to have two hands and two legs like humans do now on Earth."

"I was kidding," God said, "The new humans will have two hands and two legs and besides they will be prettier than their predecessors, at least as pretty as you are. You look more beautiful now than you were in heaven. We gods and goddesses are usually not so pretty. I didn't expect that you should be so pretty when you were incarnated. I have watched you grow up."

"My Lord," I heaved a deep sigh, "I'm old now."

"No," God said, "You will never get old. I will blow magic breath into you every day and I will do so to any food you will eat. Now go and enjoy your lobster in the kitchen."

I went to the kitchen and had a good bite at the lobster.

"Take your time," God smiled, "Lest you will choke. You're always doing everything in a hurry as you did in heaven."

"My God," I said, "I'm unwilling to go back to heaven and live in a world without the pleasure of eating or drinking."

"But," God tried to explain, "We gods have our own pleasures. We can travel thousands of miles in a second and we're creating more solar systems; much better than the one human beings are living in."

"I don't care for any other solar system," I said, "It's none of my business and I only care for the one we inhabit now."

"Then you'll have to wait for me," God said, "I will be incarnated as soon as I can.

"I will feel too lonely all by myself," I frowned.

"But you're not human," God said, "You're my Goddess. I will be with you every day from now on."

"Go and drink some water," He went on to say, "I've already blown some magic breath into it."

I picked up the large bottle of mineral water and emptied much of it in several gulps. God asked me, "Does it taste sweet?"

"I can't taste any sweetness in it," I mumbled.

"It's water not Coca Cola, my Goddess," God said, "It tastes sweet for water. Or you can drink that can of Cola over there."

Last year, I was diagnosed with *hyperglycemia* – having too much sugar in my blood -- and my doctor forbade me from eating sweet food so I had to drink Cola with zero sugar. When I drank the Cola on the desk, I was amazed to find it tasted quite different from usual, "Oh, how sweet, as if mixed with honey."

"Now taste the pear."

I picked up the pear in the fruit bowl and had a big bite from it, "Wow, it tastes so sweet as if it has come from heaven's spring." Between bites, my tears slowly rolled down my cheeks and dripped onto the pear I was eating. God loved me so much but we couldn't meet each other in person. I found I could no longer bear the fact of being separated. I fell to my knees and cried, "My Lord, how I want to see you!"

I knocked my head on the ground loudly twice and burst into tears again. God said with emotion, "But my Goddess, you can't see me in the daylight."

I was rolling on the ground in desperation and screaming, "How I miss you, my God. My heart is broken… broken. When can we ever meet each other?"

"It's really hard to say," God also seemed helpless; "We gods have our divine duty. I have to try my best to accomplish my grand plan and you, too, have to complete the task I have set you in order for us to meet each other as soon as possible."

"How soon?" I asked, "One hundred years or two hundred?"

"I'm determined to unify the world in the shortest possible time so I can be incarnated and meet you sooner."

Seeing I was still screaming and rolling over on the ground, God said, "Stop crying like that or I will be distracted and disheartened. Do you feel the sting in your right sole?"

Sure enough I felt a piercing pain in my right sole. Afraid of worrying my Lord too much, I stopped crying and sat up when God said, "My Goddess, can you see an insect in front of you? Go and kill it."

I saw a small ant-like insect crawling on the ground and I just killed it with a finger.

God then said,"How brave you are. You're as brave and fierce as you were in heaven." He went on to say, "Look, what's that over there?"

To my surprise, I found a fly-like insect appearing from nowhere but I swiped at it and killed it without hesitation. No sooner had I disposed the body of the insect than a third insect appeared and this time it had become as large as a spider. I killed it in no time.

"My Goddess," God praised me, "It's so brave of you. How I love you. Do you still feel the sting in your right sole?"

"Yes."

"Then go and wash your hands," God ordered briefly.

I stood up and went to the kitchen to wash my hands. A fly the size of a black bean pestered me by buzzing around my face. I had been trying to swat it for days but in vain.

"Don't kill it," God said, "It is your guardian though it is much smaller than you. Whenever you're approached by a bad guy, it will protect you by blurring your assaulter's view. Actually you can't touch the fly, let alone swat it."

When I finished washing my hands, God told me, "Finish eating your lobster and you will get younger and younger until you become a beautiful young princess. You will appear together with me in this world as the wife of the Lord, followed by a procession of goddesses. I will appoint ladies to all the leading positions except that I am God and you Goddess. By then all the people in the world will live three hundred to five hundred years and live a happy life. People will be clear of any evils or sins and the world will be unified."

I could distinctly hear God whispering near my ear. He told me to have a rest in bed as soon as I finished eating the lobster and fruit. In order to further convince me, God said, "I will make you sincerely believe my existence in this universe by telling you a lot of anecdotes in your childhood that no one else should know about."

I lay on the bed, having a small chat with God in the sky. He said, "When you were a child of only four or five, your grandma told you she had a son, actually your uncle, who died at the age of four so you began to fear death very much. You cried almost every night, quite different from other children as they usually had no sense of death at all and didn't know when they would die. It was because you are supposed to live for thousands of years as a Goddess so you were terrified at the prospect of dying at such a young age. Actually I am too and am even more fearful than you of dying at last. As I have told you, we gods will die some day. My father died and I am the second generation of the Ex-God. We gods and goddesses have children too and our children may take over our positions. When I die one day, are you willing to die in my arms? At that time, you will still be young while I old."

"Since I'm your love," I was pledging my loyalty to God, "I'm more than willing to die in your arms. In this earthly world, I have no love for anyone but You, my Lord. It will be my great honor to silently die in Your arms."

"After we gods die," I asked, in a faint hope, "Will we be reincarnated?"

"Yes, of course," God answered and the balance in my mind began to shift in God's favor.

He went on to say, "Do you remember that day you were fighting with Zhang Haiyang in the white van? You broke part of your middle teeth?"

Yes I definitely did. It happened when I was in my early twenties. My lover Zhang Haiyang and I co-owned a minivan taxi and we ran our joint business around the *Yuquanying* roundabout area in Beijing. He was the driver and I was the conductor. In a fit of jealousy of his wife, I provoked a fight with him. In the dogfight, I gripped his belt between my teeth with such tenacity that a part of my tooth, the size of a small green bean, had broken off from my even white teeth. Somehow I had left the broken tooth unfixed for more than twenty years and it was only when I went to visit my mother last year that I went to a dentist to have it fixed in Anzhen Hospital.

God enumerated a lot of my childhood stories, many of which were unknown even to me. He said, "When you were compiling the history of your growth, I was with you all the time to help you recall all those stories."

It suddenly dawned on me that since I decided in September, 2010 to string the episodes of my prostitute's life into a book, I had been writing almost every day as soon as I finished my business. I was writing my personal history effortlessly without any thought. I could produce several thousand words a day even after the busiest day of serving nearly twenty clients and succeeded in finishing a personal history of around seven hundred thousand words. It turned out that God was with me all the time in helping me accomplish all this.

I often told Ms. Huang, who was inputting my manuscript into the computer then, "Oh my, I can hardly bring my book to an end. I don't know how I can have so much material to write with. I'm afraid I will have a long way to go in completing the book." She agreed but she couldn't offer any advice.

At that time, God's voice came from the void, "I had intended her to help you but later I found she was incompetent. So I made you fire her by purposely letting her enrage you with her greed so that you could find a more competent typist to help you. You are too tender-hearted and credulous to take the initiative in dismissing Ms. Huang solely because of her incompetence. Be you a human being or a goddess, it is a fatal weakness to be too kind. I was sounding an alarm for you with Ms. Huang's fraudulence. I'd like you to talk to your friend Lisa often because she knows not only literature but the psychology of literary people so she may serve to relieve your depression in your writing."

"Then is my translator a person You sent to help me?" I asked. "Yes."

"Is he a god, too?"

"No," God answered, "He is but an ordinary person. But his consciousness is also under my control and he will translate your work earnestly. I promise both of you will be greatly renowned throughout the world for your work and your names will be stamped on the annals of history and be remembered by the generations to come. After it is unified, the world will be rid of all forms of wars and plagues. I will have a statue of Goddess erected for you in memory of your efforts and contribution to unifying the world."

God finally said, "Let Ms. Huang forget her plan to immigrate her family to Australia. As a punishment for her ingratitude, her work visa will not be renewed after it expires. She will go back to where she has come from. I saw you were so kind to her. You not only presented her with a new TV set but also agreed to offer her work-time testimony when she asked for it. Even so, she kept the hundred dollars you overpaid her against her conscience. Her wavering before the dishonest gain when counting the twenty notes was in my full view. There are too many people who pretend to be innocent but are actually greedy in mind. They are coveting not only wealth but also many other things, fame, power etc. I'm determined to change this vicious trend…"

What God said reminded me of another thing. It was two weeks before Ms. Huang settled her accounts with me for the last time. When I called her that night, talking about the copies of my manuscript, she said, "Linda, will you do me a favor as to offer me a work-time testimony?"

"Of course," I answered, "I can give you one in my company's name but I have to leave it for my accountant, as I don't know the procedure."

A week later at 3:00 p.m., Ms. Huang and my accountant came to meet at my house by appointment. My accountant explained in detail to her the relevant procedure, such as the paying of insurance or superannuation. She didn't say anything at the time. When she was about to leave, I gave her a newly- bought twenty-two-inch TV set as a present. Several days later when I called her again talking about my manuscript, she said, "I decided to give up applying for the work visa because I can't afford so many fees. Let's put it aside for later."

Then a surprising thing happened. Three days later, she returned her dishonest gains of a hundred dollars out of her troubled conscience.

When God said He would make her go back to China after her visa expired, I still couldn't help entreating God to show mercy on her. At that, God criticized me, "There you go again. I've told you a thousand times be you a human or a goddess, you shouldn't be too tender-hearted or you can accomplish nothing. Take me as an example, I'm the supreme God and have a lot of minor gods under my command. Neptune, who is on equal terms with me, often quarrels with me but in most cases he will listen to me."

"Neptune?" I asked, my attention being distracted in another direction, "The god in charge of the seas? Then what's the cause of the earthquakes and tsunamis in the seas of this planet?"

"Earthquakes and tsunamis?" God said, "They are punishments I have meted out to human beings."

"Then what about so many children who died in the disasters?" I said indignantly, "They were innocent and they shouldn't have been killed"

"I don't care so much," God said, "They are just the sacrifice."

"Then what about the war in Libya?" my interest suddenly shifted to international politics, "Which side is on the right and which side is on the wrong?"

"Leave them fighting against each other," God said indifferently, "Anyway, the world population is on the verge of exploding. Sooner or later, I will send most of them to develop and settle on the Moon."

From afternoon to evening that day, God and I were having a talk on a wide range of topics, including the anecdotes during my childhood, the future of the Earth and God's grand plan to create a new universe.

Our talk continued till 8:00 p.m. when God said, "I'm sending you a new client, who will tell you something fresh. Let's serve as two good listeners, shall we?"

"My Lord," I said, "You're kept awake all day long and you're going to go on with your grand plan to create a new universe. You must be tired and you'd better take a rest."

"For the fifty years since you were incarnated, there's scarcely a moment when I've not been missing you," God said with emotion, "You are always in the most tender part of my heart. When you were young, I couldn't reveal to you your real identity because at that time you were too young to have enough knowledge or experience about society. I'm only too glad to have the chance to have a good talk with you. I told you several days ago about my existence but you refused to believe. It seems we lack mutual trust and understanding between us."

"I still don't entirely believe in your existence." I said.

"I will prove to you with adequate evidence that you're my love, my Goddess and my favorite lady. You're not a human. You're a goddess!"

"But I'm actually a human not a goddess!"

Just then, the doorbell rang and God said, "Stop arguing. Go and open the door."

I went to answer the door and found it was John, the Potbelly of about sixty, who the Iraqi man brought to my house last time. Having been introduced to me, he frequented me every now and then. I opened the security door to find his black car was parked below my parking space. I asked him, "Why didn't you park your car right in my parking space?"

He looked somewhat drunk and in response to my reminder, went back to his car and started it. God whispered, "Look, he's too drunk to put his car into the right gear."

It took him quite a long time to start his car and move it right into the parking space.

"Need I take precautions to evade his car?" I asked God.

"No, you needn't," He answered, "He is under my control."

As a matter of fact, he managed to park his car in the space, just three feet before me. He got out of the car and went with me into the house. I had just closed the door when the man with the potbelly said to me, "Hi, Linda Carter."

"Who's Linda Carter?" I was surprised.

"The sister of the former president of the United States," he said.

At the back of my mind I vaguely remembered that there was a former United States president who was still alive and whose name was Jimmy Carter. I smiled, "I look like Linda Carter, do I?"

"Definitely," he cried out, "You not only look like her but you will also be as rich as her in the future."

"How rich is she?" I was curious.

"She owns a magazine that is well known throughout the world," Fat John explained, "It was the wealth she accumulated that helped her brother campaign for the presidency and succeed in the election."

I knew in the United States, you could never run for president without ample funds because the campaigning was incredulously costly. "Hey, let's forget the president's sister or her magazine. It's none of our business." I then asked him, "Do you believe in God?"

"I believe in Buddha, as I've told you," he said, "You Chinese call him the Lord of Heaven."

"To me," I said, "I think God and Buddha are the same and identical one."

"So do I," he echoed while walking into the working room.

God then said in my ear, "You don't have to ask him for money. Let me do it for you."

I took out two cans of Tooheys beer from the four-door fridge in the kitchen. As I came back to the working room, I saw him dipping into his wallet for money. He usually didn't pay me until I asked him to and once he even wanted to give me a dubious card to pay for the service.

He handed me a fifty-dollar note, "Here's your service fee." "That's a good boy. No money no honey."

I handed him a towel from the cabinet and had him take his bath. After I put away the money and came back to the working room, he was lying on the bed, enjoying his beer. God said, "I'm going to cast a spell over him and let him leave in a few minutes."

I was sitting between his thighs and fiddled with his cock. I held it in my mouth and began to suck it. Soon I felt a hot thrill running through my legs and feet.

Fat John yelled wildly, "Linda's my Cock Doctor! Linda's my Battery Charger!" It was only five minutes before he came after a long procession of groans and moans.

"Look," God said proudly, "I can help you finish a client within five minutes with my magic spell."

I got to my feet and went to the toilet to wash my hands and mouth. When I came back, to my amusement I found Fat John playing with his own cock with the help of a money note. God said, "Is it funny he is playing with his own cock. He is being dictated to by me." I couldn't help bursting into laughter. The more I laughed the more I wanted to laugh. "Now listen to your own laughter. Do you think you're laughing like a human?

Up to now, I refused to admit I was a Goddess no matter what God had said. But since 6:00 March 14, when my soul drifted away from my body in my writing, I had had a feeling that my laughter changed a lot. It was quite different from my usual laughter. Now my laughter sounded like a euphonious trill of silver bells, or rather, like Sirens' seductive voices in Greek mythology that could lure any man into the fathomless depths of the ocean.

Fat John kept flirting with me while I was massaging him. I said, "If you believe in God, He will let you live for a hundred and fifty years."

He laughed, "I believe in Him and I love Him."

I laughed too, "God promised I could live two hundred years if I believed in his existence."

I went on to say, "When I turn ninety or even a hundred and twenty, will you come visit me?"

"I will," he said, imitating an old man by bending himself and wobbling on an imaginary walking stick, "I will come see you like this."

We were jesting, flirting and laughing for a long time when he said, "I'll tell you a thing which happened between 1961 and 1962. A certain lady opened a brothel in the northern part of our country. It was said she could serve almost one hundred men a day. She became very famous and her clients varied from foreign tourists to local countrymen. Once I went to her place and stood in line with a queuing number of twenty-nine but she told me I was her ninety-sixth client. She was a Cock Wizard who could finish a cock in a matter of minutes. She really made a great fortune in this way."

"Is her brothel still open now?" I was quite curious.

"It went to the wall within a year," Fat John sighed, "because her trade was against the doctrine of our religion."

God added in a whisper, "She was a goddess I had sent to that part of the world."

It reminded me of the year of my birth, which happened to be 1961. Was it true that God had a long-term strategy to unify the world by advocating the policy of making love instead of making war?

After chatting for some more time, God said, "I'd like you to finish that song before he leaves. Let me examine how effective my magic breath is in improving your memory."

A beautiful melody of a Chinese song was being played on my stereo, "My missing is an intangible web…"That was my favorite song I would invariably sing in the presence of my clients. I had sung it so many times and every time I sang it, my longing would travel thousands of miles back to China, to my mother. When I finished that song, tears blurred my vision. After a moment's silence, God and Fat John both exclaimed, "Bravo!"

When he went to the bathroom, I picked up the can of beer that John had not drunk and put it on the kitchen bench. Then I took out another six cans of beer and also put them on the kitchen bench. Totally inadvertently, I put one can in the centre and six other ones around it to make a perfect regular hexagon. God praised me, "How clever my Goddess is! This just symbolizes the new setup of the world after it is unified. There will be only One God."

After Fat John left, I asked God abruptly, "Am I destined to go back to heaven?"

"Yes, you are, sooner or later, "God said resolutely, "As soon as the world is unified, you have to go back to the heaven."

I was nearly on the verge of breaking down, "I don't want to go back. I want to be a human not a goddess!"

The prospect scared me to death that I would be one of the insubstantial deities flying in the cold void and living a dry life without any carnal pleasures so I beseeched God, "Oh, my Lord. You have promised me to be incarnated as a Prince Charming and then live happily with me in this earthly world, haven't you?"

"But it's hard to say, for the moment at least," God said, obviously caught in a dilemma, "I find you've forgotten all the divine life experience in heaven before you were converted into an ordinary woman. And what worries me most is that when I am converted into a man and then after some time converted back to God, I will lose all the memories as a God and my legitimacy to rule the world will be questioned."

I began to cry again, weeping inconsolably for a long time, "Oh, no! I won't go back. If I do, who will care for my poor mother? She will be scared to death at the news I am suddenly converted into a goddess."

"She is not your mother!" "Yes, she is!"

"But she is not!" God insisted.

I began to wallow over on the ground, "But she is!"

Seeing I was still wallowing in protest, God said,"My Goddess, why are so concerned about the affairs of human beings?"

Seeing I showed no sign of stopping my protest, God compromised, "Or I will retrieve your soul after you die?"

I stopped crying and asked, "Then can I come back to visit my mother?"

"When she dies her soul will wait in the sky and you can come back to see her."

"What about my sister?" I was a person who was given an inch and would take a mile.

"Her soul will be waiting, too, in the sky."

"And what about my father?" I was still insatiable.

"Your father's soul has already been waiting for you in the sky. When you come back, his soul will meet with the souls of all of your family members. After that, I will convert your father into a goat, your mother a tiger and your sister a duck. Then you will come back to heaven and join us in creating a new universe and a new mankind."

Shocked at hearing that, I kept beating my breast and screaming, "Oh no! No! I won't have them converted into animals. I want them converted into humans."

"Humans' souls can only be converted into animals," God explained with great patience, "and then these animals can be converted into humans."

But I kept wallowing on the ground and wailed, "Definitely no! I demand them to be converted into humans. Otherwise I refuse to be retrieved to heaven by you and I will stop writing for you. I'm going to die in Australia."

"Do you know that Mao Zedong, who always taught his cadres to serve the people like an ox when he was alive, has been converted into an ox," God went on to say, "And Richard Nixon a turtle under the sea. Both of them are contributing to my grand plan to unify the world."

"An ox?" I asked, "Need he toil all day by pushing a grinding mill and end up becoming meat on people's dining tables?"

"Far from that," God explained, "When the great men were converted, they would turn into donkey barons or turtle barons living leisurely in the mountains or under the seas. No one can easily catch them and toil them."

"I don't care for them," I almost growled, "But I won't have my family members converted into a goat, a tiger or a duck!"

"I have told you a thousand times," God seemed to have lost his temper, "that your mother is not your mother, your father is not your father and your sister is not your sister! What's the point in quarrelling with me about those who have nothing to do with you? You're a goddess not a human being!"

"I'm not a goddess but a human being!"

"If you keep on making trouble out of nothing like that," God was threatening me, "I will punish you. Look, what can you see on the ground?"

I looked down and found to my terror three drops of red blood the size of a fly on the ground. God went on to say, "This is the power of God. Now stand up and look at what is on the stone bench top in your kitchen."

I scrambled to my feet and ran to the kitchen bench. I found three drops of red blood but this time they were triangular- shaped. I was shocked. God said again, "Now go and see what it is on the north wall under the mirror." I staggered to the north wall and found a line of paint the length of a book. I was about to chisel it off with a knife when God warned me sternly, "Don't try to do that or the house will collapse in a second."

Seeing I was dumfounded and trembling with fear, God softened his tone, "Believe me, my Goddess. I'm your beloved God. Take a bath and lie on the bed. Let's have a talk at leisure."

I went to the bathroom in a trance and hastily washed up. I was so absentminded that I forgot to get dressed and lay down on the bed in my birthday suit. God whispered in my ear, "I have told you a lot of your childhood anecdotes. Do you remember them? Let me give you another example. Your first husband, Cao Guihai, was also a deity I sent to the world. I first married you and then separated you for the purpose of training your ability to deal with things independently. You know, he's now married to another woman and has a daughter."

As a matter of fact, I haven't known up till now whether my first husband had remarried. Every time I went back to China, I always invited him and his mother, his brother and sister, together with their spouses and children to have dinner at restaurants. I still regarded his mother as my mother-in-law. My mother asked Cao's sister several times whether her brother had married again, but his sister's answer was invariably "No" every time. It's amazing that

God should know what I didn't know. I'm secretly surprised and I have to believe that God is omniscient.

God went on, "Your second husband Ian Thomas Philip was another deity I sent to the world. He took the trouble to travel thousands of miles from Australia to China to meet you and marry you. It was nothing other than my intention to prepare you for the grand cause of unifying the world. After you came to Australia and got married to him, I purposefully sowed seeds of discord between you two by letting a German company invite him to work in South Africa with the only purpose of recruiting you to work solely for me. Ian has now married a black woman and settled in South Africa. Remember once when dining with your ex-husband, his black girlfriend was calling from South Africa? It was also my arrangement. Ian struggled to remain calm by saying, "You're calling at a most inopportune moment; I'll call back later." Soon Ian made a feeble excuse of going to the toilet and called that black woman. That aroused your suspicion. You came back to Canberra two days in advance of your planned holiday and left Ian alone at the hotel in Sydney."

Oh my. God was watching my every act and move from above the sky! I couldn't help but believe in Him.

"If you still don't believe me," God said, "I can have your first ex-husband talk to you. The souls of both of your ex-husbands have now been retrieved back."

In no time, I heard my first ex Mr. Cao speaking to me, "Chang Meili (my alias name in China), what God said is truth. My soul is now in heaven."

He sounded exactly the same as when he used to lay beside me. I asked, "How are you in heaven?"

"Not as well as in the world," he answered, "You should obey God and serve Him well; otherwise he will retrieve your soul to heaven as a punishment." I was so scared that I began to shiver involuntarily.

"Do you remember our common classmate in high school, Xu Jinhui?" Cao asked. The mention of the name of Mr. Xu proved he was sure to be my first ex-husband Cao. I was reduced into a mass of jelly by awe at the omniscient God.

God said again, "Now I'll have your second ex talk to you. Mr. Ian Thomas Philip."

Ian was heard speaking, "Madam Chang (As I had run a big restaurant in Beijing, China, I was then referred to as Madam Chang. So Ian had been calling me Madam Chang since the day I knew him. These anecdotes will be dealt with later in this book.) Do you remember the day we were dancing at the ballroom in your restaurant? You pushed a young lady in white into my arms?"

This second proof sealed my fate finally. I knelt bare-hipped on the bed and begged, "Oh God, my Lord. You're my father. You're my grandfather. You're my ancestor. Be sure not to retrieve my soul back. Now that I'm a mortal, please let me live a mortal's life a bit longer. I'm begging you, my almighty Lord. I love the life here and I enjoy all these various cocks." After that I knelt to the north and knocked my head on the ground loudly. "Oh God, my Almighty Lord. I beg you not to retrieve my soul back to heaven. Even if I'm retrieved, are you going to satisfy me with a cock if you ever have one?"

"That's no problem," God said, "When you come back, I will fuck you in a God's way. Though I have no cock, I can make you satisfied too. When you're satisfied, you will hug me and shout, 'God, I love you!'"

I kept on wailing, "No. No! I want to be fucked in a conventional way not in a god's way. I got frightened at the mere thought of insubstantial, intangible gods. Oh my God, my Almighty Lord."

"My Goddess," God heaved a deep sigh, "How come you have forgotten all the divine things in heaven and only care about the vulgar cocks you've encountered since you were incarnated dozens of years ago. You know, we gods have our sacred cause. Not only have we created the existing mankind but we are going to be joined by you in creating a new mankind."

"It's well you'll create a new mankind." I argued, "Now that you have so many gods and goddesses around you, you may as well let them help in your sacred cause and leave me alone in this world, waiting for you to be incarnated."

"To tell you the truth,"God said earnestly,"I was joking when I said I would be incarnated one day. As God, I will never be incarnated. I, the Almighty Lord will join forces with Neptune under the sea in undertaking the grand plan of creating more universes."

"If you're not incarnated," I said, "I refuse to be retrieved by you. Let me stay and live in this secular world forever."

"You must come back from heaven at any time when I need you," God said authoritatively, "Because you're my love, my Goddess and my spiritual pillar."

"Oh God, my father," I said, "Your glorious image has already faded away from my memory. I am now preoccupied with a variety of cocks."

"My Goddess," God was half amused and half annoyed, "You quit kneeling and lie down. How I want to give you a good kick. You good-for-nothing only have eyes for cocks. You have changed so much since you were incarnated. Well, I know how to cure you of your addiction to big cocks."

I didn't stop wailing on the bed, "No, my God. I cannot make do without big cocks. My cunt itches all over every day and I indeed cannot tear myself away from those big cocks, even for one day."

"I will cure you of the cock-mania one day," God said with his teeth clenched.

"My God," I besought, "Will you please let me remain what I am now? Or will you allow me at least two hundred years? You have promised the other day that you would let me stay in this world for two hundred years to witness the unification of the world."

Thinking I was destined to go back sooner or later, I decided to stay in this world as long as I could. The longer, the better. God seemed able to read my mind and said, "It all depends on the pace of the unification. Anyway, you'll have to come back the minute the unification is accomplished."

"Then I'd rather the unification's pace was slowed down."

"What?"God was more angry than surprised "Slowed down?"

"I meant I would slow down the pace of essay writing to ensure its quality. Actually, I'm ready to do whatever you want me to without hesitation."

I was really afraid that someday my soul would be retrieved by God and I would become a skeleton on the bed. Could my dear mother survive such a terrible scene? No matter how much God loved me, He was a deity after all and He could never understand the friendship, the affection or the love between ordinary human beings.

"From now on," God declared, "I will take over the authority to dictate your every act and every move, including eating, drinking, working and shopping. I will follow you and dictate to you what to do. You will be put under my control even if I am busy working in a certain remote universe."

I felt I was becoming a programmed robot that could be scolded at any time for disobedience.

God said, "When the world is unified, people will live completely naked with absolutely nothing on."

I couldn't help bursting into laughter, "How funny if a person drives a car, a locomotive or an airplane with nothing on!"

"I will make it a rule that everybody should wear nothing whatever they're doing."

I began to chuckle as I reclined on the bed, "God hasn't seen much of the world. What a scene it would be if all men and women were driving their cars and doing shopping in the malls all naked?"

I could hardly suppress my laughter at the imaginary picture of so many people in the nude walking about in public places. I was chuckling on the bed when God said, "I will make you the wealthiest person in the world and no one will dare to offend you. If someone does, I will punish him with the death penalty. Some day, I will have the Chinese president and premier pave the red carpet for you and meet you in person in the Capital International Airport."

"What?" I burst into a roar of laughter, "The Chinese president and premier to meet a prostitute baron from Australia in the Capital Airport?"

"You're not a mere prostitute," God said in sad earnest, "You're my Goddess. You're the herald of the unification. I will have the United States President Obama meet you in Australia."

"If I should have the honor of meeting Obama, I'm willing to be his attendant," I said jokingly.

"I will let your mother be your attendant."

"No," I said definitely, "It's absurd my mother being my attendant. I won't allow such a thing to happen!"

"No?" God said, "If you go back to China this June, see how I will make your mother be your attendant. I have told you so many times she is NOT your mother."

I didn't want to show my white heat and said, "She IS my mother!" but at the same time I feared God might be offended and would do something unreasonable or inhuman. I would probably be deprived of the right to pay my last respects to my mother.

I suddenly thought of another question and asked, "My God, how come you can speak Chinese?"

"Why can't I speak a language since all languages are my creations? I speak Chinese as well as English. My Italian and Spanish are even better."

Italian and Spanish languages were Greek to me. I could only speak in English, "I love you, my Lord."

"I love you too, my Goddess," God answered in English too. Just then I seemed to hear someone discussing something so

I asked God, "Hey, who are you talking to?"

He said, "I'm discussing with Neptune how to ensure the security of your family members."

"What security?" I asked.

My instinct told me there must be something with great consequence that was going to happen imminently.

God went on to say, "I won't allow your family members to join you in Australia and disturb you in your writing on unification. I will arrange for them to settle in other countries." I heard God murmuring, "China and India both have the biggest populations…"

My imagination was stirred and I was suddenly startled. Oh my, God was planning to decrease the world population by knocking another star against our planet! It dawned on me why God had said this morning He would send half of the world's population to the Moon. I had to beg Him, "My Lord, be sure to guarantee the safety of my mother, my sister and all their family members. Send them all to Australia, please."

"Know what you should know," God declared His discipline, "And don't try to know what you shouldn't. We gods have our arrangements and we also enforce our own divine rules. Do well what you should do." God went on, "I will let this world become an inferno of angry flames!"

"I am not afraid," I said dauntlessly, "Anyway; I have neither concern nor care for this world except for my mother."

God said seriously, "Very well, I'll let you die now. Before you die, let me hug you for the last time. Close your eyes." I closed my eyes and huddled in the quilt, worrying what a scene it would be if I died all naked on the bed and the people from the morgue came to collect my body so I tucked myself into the quilt to cover myself better. I repeated to myself in my mind, "I am not afraid but will obey God's order. I am not afraid but will obey God's order."

Though I was courageous enough, I was afraid to open my eyes. I used to be a dauntless woman and feared none in the world. I dared to flirt with men with a gun or a dagger. But the mere thought of an angry God could easily reduce me to a mass of jelly. I felt my face burning and soon God's voice was dying away, "Listen, do you sound like a mortal?" Suddenly I felt I was sinking into a dark fathomless abyss. I tried my best to gasp for air and I felt very uncomfortable in my abdomen. By and by, I became oblivious of everything…

Day Ten: April 5, 2011

When I woke up at 8:00 a.m., I felt especially sober and refreshed. But I was preoccupied with the things that had happened yesterday: Had Cao Guihai really died? Yet he was undoubtedly speaking to me last night and even mentioned the name of our common friend I already forgot. So it couldn't be false. I thought of the feeling I had when I was incarnated and it suddenly dawned on me that God might have called his soul back to talk to me without necessarily taking away his life. It was little wonder that recently whenever I started to write, I would invariably feel a temporary loss of consciousness for a fraction of a second. It must have been God that was censoring my writing. I could judge for sure that Cao had not died because just a few days before, I had a conversation with his sister on the phone. Since I divorced Cao and came to Australia, I had felt I owed him a lot as I hadn't borne a child for him. I tried many times to persuade him to remarry and have his own child but he always faltered and wavered. So I often sent him some money as long as my finances permitted in care of his sister, lest his pride should be hurt. The next time I called his sister, I could easily confirm whether he was still alive. Actually I had already known for sure that my second ex Ian was also alive as my first ex Cao was, though I could not prove that he was still living in South Africa.

And I had a strange feeling that God had printed some kisses on my cheeks when He left me. That was because when I went to wash up in the bathroom, I found two imprints like some residue of sperm on both of my cheeks. It felt like some soap bubbles.

After I washed away the stain off my cheeks, I settled down in silent meditation. By saying, "I will turn the world into an inferno of flames," God meant to test my will power. If there was such a Lord, He must be an omniscient God, otherwise how could He lord over other gods? And moreover, as I wrote before, God told me to notify others that the Earth would perish if we failed to send half of the world's population to the Moon by the year

2050. They would solve the problem by having two stars collide against each other but I didn't think it would happen in the near future. God and Neptune jointly created this beautiful planet and they of course wanted to keep it intact. The collision of two stars against each other would have a destructive impact on the Earth. And in my opinion, the Earth wouldn't destruct as some people had expected in 2012. Surely some calamities or disasters would happen to the Earth as usual but by no means would a catastrophe occur such as the collision of two stars.

God had told me He would always be with me whenever I got down to writing and He would dictate me to write whatever he wanted me to. I felt distinctly that recently I could write without thinking. It seemed thousands of words would well out from the tip of my pen effortlessly and the content of my writing seemed to go farther and farther from the autobiography of a prostitute baron. By and by I began to regard myself as a real goddess. I hoped all the people in the world could live a happy life and no one would die for any reason at all. I shuddered at the mere thought of millions of people perishing in an instant. Out of mercy on so many prospective victims, I knelt on the carpet in the west living room and knocked my head on the ground loudly, praying, "Oh my God, I beg You not to destroy this world because good guys account for a great majority of the whole population after all. Most of them have come to this world and lived a hard life and some of them can't even keep body and soul together. I now recognize myself as a goddess of yours. I am your Goddess. I've made up my mind to help you accomplish your grand plan to unify the world by writing the book on unification. I have the capacity and determination but don't call me back to heaven right now. Allow me another two hundred years and I'm sure to succeed. Retrieve me in two hundred years and I will then join you in heaven and help you create a new mankind."

I prostrated myself on the floor and burst out wailing again. I almost cried my heart out at the thought that God, who loved me so much, was watching over me from heaven. I loved Thou too, my God. Since I was your most loved and most trustworthy goddess, how could I just go back to heaven without accomplishing anything? I was scrawling on the ground, heartbroken and crying out of breath when God said, "My Goddess, you're a wise goddess. You have stood up to my test and come to understand a lot of things. If you're missing me, cry out loudly. Your cries sound different from others', which were rarely heard by outsiders. It has made my heart ache to see you're so loyal to me. Do you feel it? Your right sole must be aching now."

My right sole did hurt convulsively and I nearly cried my eyes out. I was rolling on the carpet again and wailing, "Why? Why? Why do you let me bear the unbearable suffering of the separation?" The fact that I could talk to my Prince Charming face to face but just couldn't see and touch Him was greatly tormenting me and I beat the carpet repeatedly with my right hand, making the 3D TV set vibrate precariously.

"Get to your feet, my Goddess," God said, "I have seen your unswerving loyalty to me. So stop crying now or else your soul will drift out of you. Then I have to retrieve it if it does so. When you come back to heaven, you will become oblivious of all of your life experience in this world. It is the same with human beings. If they die, their soul will be retrieved and forget whatever they have undergone in the world."

I was scared to hear that. If I kept on crying like that I would become a walking corpse. I of course wouldn't take it lying down, "You have promised me that when I come back to heaven, my soul will be reunited with the souls of my family members."

God said, "Yes. But only by my revelation can the souls of your family remember their life experiences."

At nine thirty in the morning came a new customer. He was a black man of about forty years old. On entering the house, he asked bluntly, "How much for a whole-set service?"

"Seventy," I answered, "But I can offer you a better price of fifty."

Then I ushered him into the working room and he said he had taken his bath before. When he took off his clothes and exposed his private part to me, I gasped at the size of his cock – it was, without any exaggeration, no thinner than a beer bottle! It was more than twelve inches in length and its tip was as thick as its bottom. I weighed his cock in my hand and estimated its weight at about two pounds! I exclaimed in astonishment, "In my ten years as a prostitute, I've seen a lot of black lads' big cocks but it's the first time I've ever seen such a long and thick one."

"When I went to brothels," he said proudly, "some ladies were frightened into fleeing at the sight of my cock."

I frowned heavily, "I'm afraid I can hardly bear that cock of yours being thrust in my cunt."

Pointing to the actor on the screen, the black client smiled with contempt, "That guy has a small cock." Looking up at the screen briefly, I agreed, "Yes. His cock is hardly one fifth the size of yours."

This was a porn video stared by some fat Japanese girls the director had recruited all around the country, each of them weighing from 220 to 330 pounds. It was really not an easy job for the director to collect so many fat girls. A fat girl, who weighed at least 300 pounds, was seen half squatting and half kneeling and supporting her own weight on the bed with both her hands. It was a follow shot taken from behind the girl's buttocks. You could see her plump breasts, as huge as a cow's, swaying over the bed and a hefty roll of flab overhanging from her waist. Her meaty round buttocks were like an elephant's and a lanky Japanese man was kneeling behind them, ready to thrust his dark-brown cock into the girl's hairy pussy. The fat girl's plump buttocks were undulating rhythmically and her dangling breasts and waist flab were also swaying with the pistoning movement of the man's cock.

"Such a small cock can't be thrust completely into such a large cunt," the black man commented.

"You're wrong," I argued, "Just on the contrary, the fatter a woman is, the smaller her cunt is. Though that girl's cunt looks large, the inside of her cunt is not necessarily loose. However, her oversized buttocks may hinder the man's cock movement and prevent it from reaching the bottom of her cunt."

"Well," he said, smacking his lips, "A plump girl's cunt must be sensual."

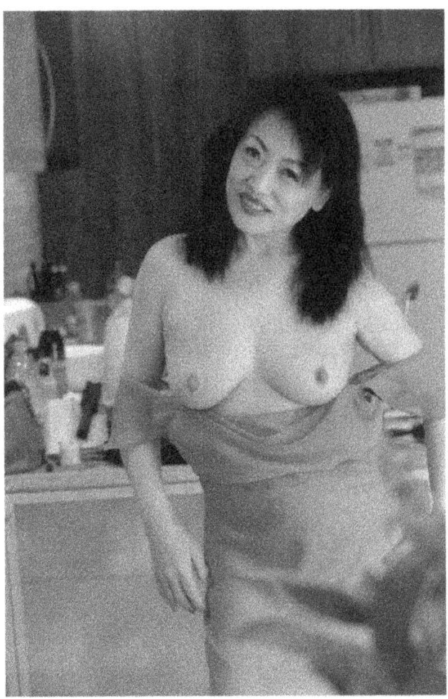

"So she can be the fittest girl for you," I jested, "You have such a big long cock that her cunt will never stop you from fucking her to the hilt."

"Anyway, a plump girl looks sexy," he was making a conclusion. "Maybe it's the effect of reverse psychology – Rare is valuable," I sighed, "Usually we have seen too many slim ladies fucking men so it is novel and impressive seeing fat girls fucking men."

With that, I took off my dress and sprawled between his thighs. I opened my jaw as wide as I could and still had much difficulty in swallowing his cock into my mouth. My eyes almost popped out from the strenuousness. In less than three minutes, his cock erected angrily and became as hard as an iron bar.

I found an extra-large condom and put it on his cock but the condom could barely cover half of its length. He demanded I bend over but I faltered in fear, "No. Yours is too big a cock for my cunt. If you fuck me from behind, it will surely pierce my womb. I can only make do with the missionary position – you on top of me."

I lied on the bed and spread my legs apart reluctantly, like a lamb ready to be crucified. Before I had time to take a breath, he had thrust his huge cock into my cunt at once to the hilt. I couldn't help uttering a cry of agony, "Ouch. I can't bear it!" My cunt was burning and bursting as if it had been ripped open by his huge cock. Even my hip bones hurt greatly. My cunt was agonized more than it would be if I was giving birth. The black lad was so startled that he hastily withdrew his cock out of my cunt.

"Your cock is much thicker that the Italian's big cock or even the lawyer's big cock," I gasped to say, "You almost ripped my cunt open. I have never suffered so piercing a pain in my ten years as a prostitute."

"I'm so sorry," he apologized sincerely but he thrust his huge cock to the hilt again.

"Ouch!" I screamed and lashed him on the hip, "I'm not joking, my lad. My cunt hurts so badly. Take your time and do it a little more tenderly."

"I'm so sorry," he said apologetically.

"Well," I said to myself, "You're saying sorry and you won't stop fucking me. But business is business. It's my duty to make you come by draining all of your sperm."

With every movement he made, I let out a cry of agony "Ouch" followed by an apology "Sorry" from him. Soon the room reverberated with a rhythmic sequence of sounds "Thump- Ouch-Sorry," "Thump-Ouch-Sorry" and "Thump-Ouch-Sorry."

It was by no means a process of sexual enjoyment for me. Since I took on this trade, I had preferred big cocks to smaller ones because they could give me more enjoyment but the huge cock moving in my cunt now was only a source of suffering instead of pleasure.

Hearing I was groaning louder and louder, the black lad covered my mouth with his palm, "Shh – Linda. You'll be heard by the passersby."

"Mate," I said, gasping for air, "You'd better go to another brothel for larger cunts next time. Mine can't hold such a huge thing as yours."

The black lad's face reddened at once and he said nothing.

Yet his huge cock kept on moving violently in my cunt and showed no sign of coming soon. I frowned heavily and clenched my teeth but I had to bear his torment until he came.

I took a deep breath trying to alleviate the untold stabbing pain inside my cunt. What a cock he had, I admired in my mind. How big, how thick and how robust! No orifice in my body could bear being fucked by his oversized cock. My mouth would ache, my cunt would burst and my asshole would rip open if he ever thrust it in. He may as well thrust it into a mare's cunt as did Mr. Dave from Melbourne. While I was crying unscrupulously, I expected him to come as soon as possible.

He was fucking me relentlessly and I was groaning and moaning incessantly when a dozen minutes later he suddenly collapsed with a loud yell, "I'm coming!" His huge cock jerked violently several times before he collapsed on me motionlessly.

I waited until he was completely satisfied and got up to help him rip the condom off his limp fat cock. Taking up the condom filled with white fluid, I cried in affected exaggeration, "Wow, you're so strong to have such sap of youth!"

I went to wash my mouth and hands and came back to massage his back.

"Where are you from, young man?" I asked. "South Africa."

"From which part of South Africa?" I went on to ask.

The black lad kept silent. It was apparent he was a taciturn man and always grudged his words to any questioner.

When he left my house, I gave him a bottle of white wine and he paid me fifty dollars. I had already recovered from the great agony of mating and said jestingly, "You should have paid me double for your extra big cock. You fucked me for twenty minutes but you'll leave my cunt in pain and numb for half a day." He smiled shyly.

Seeing off the black lad, I received an Australian lad in his late twenties. He had a big head and big ears, big eyes, a big nose, and a big mouth on his face. He had braided most of his hair back into a glossy, black thick ponytail but the hair atop his head and around his temples was cleanly shaven; a hairstyle similar to that of the ancient Chinese men in the Qing dynasty. Judging by his appearance, I guessed he might be the descendant of Greek or Italian immigrants. He first visited me at the age of eighteen and had already been my young regular client for more than eight years.

As soon as he entered the house, he found me rubbing my tummy so he asked me, "Are you sick?"

"It's you who is sick," I answered back angrily.

The braided lad was taken aback, wondering whether he had offended me. It was not until later that I realized there was a misunderstanding of languages between us. In the English language, "You're sick" just meant "You have a disease," but in the Chinese language, "You're sick" is a derogatory term, meaning "You're a freak" or "Something's wrong with your head." Such linguistic discrepancy might account for many unexpected jokes in cross-cultural communications. Some very funny Chinese jokes, if translated into English, might sound senseless to a non-native audience and was therefore received by them with nonchalance.

Once when I returned to Sydney for my holiday, my husband Ian and I invited his family members to dine in a restaurant. Ian told us a joke over dinner. A gentleman bet a young couple that if the wife's answer to three set questions was identical to that of her husband to the same three questions, they would win 5,000 dollars. The gentleman took the husband aside and asked him the three set questions.

"Did you have sex today?" he asked. "Yes," the husband answered. "When did you have it?"

"In the morning at seven thirty." "Where did you have it?"

"On the kitchen table."

Then the gentleman took the wife aside and asked her the same three questions.

"Did you have sex today?" "Yes," the wife answered. "When did you have it?"

"In the morning at seven thirty." "Where did you have it?"

The wife hesitated and the gentleman went on to say, "If your answer is identical to your husband's, you will win five thousand dollars."

"In the ass," the wife answered promptly.

At this, all the guests roared with laughter but I remained unimpressed. The joke was making use of the pun question "Where did you have sex?" which could mean "In what place did you have sex?" or "How did you fuck your partner?" at once. In the Chinese language, I thought, they were two totally different questions.

Some of my customers said, even in English-speaking countries, there were a lot of discrepancies in the language they were speaking. A joke that could be uproarious to Englishmen might not wring any laughter from Americans. And vice versa. So whatever language you spoke, if you wanted to be a witty talker, a master of the language itself was not enough but you had to have a good idea of the historical and cultural background of that country.

I led the braided lad to the working room and he gave me forty dollars, which was a special price I had offered him for years. I handed him a clean towel and had him take a bath first. After I put away the money and went back to the working room, he had lain on the towels I had spread for him. He rested his head on the pile of three pillows – he liked sleeping on an elevated pillow. I sprawled between his thighs and held his cock in my mouth, thinking to myself: It never rains but it pours. Big cocks like to come together. In succession with the previous one, now came another big cock and this one was by no means smaller than the previous one. I was meditating when the braided lad's mobile chimed. At that time, the TV screens on the walls were showing "*Asian Fever No.28.*" An Asian girl with short hair was making love to a Caucasian man. Perhaps in order to get better effect, the girl groaned in a somewhat exaggerated tone in her mating.

I knew the braided lad had his own girlfriend so I pressed the button for the DVD player to eject the disk, lest his girlfriend should hear the sound effect of the porn program. Seeing he was busy talking with his girlfriend, I closed the door to the working room and went to the kitchen for drinking water. It was only a couple of minutes before I heard the amorous groans of the girl in the porn program. I thought the lad must have finished his conversation with his girlfriend and slid the disk back into the DVD player.

I went back to the working room to find the braided lad had shut himself in the bathroom. When he saw me, he tipped me a wink and put a finger to his mouth. I was puzzled when he disconnected his mobile phone and came out of the bathroom, "Linda. You're causing trouble for me!"

"What's the matter?" I asked innocently.

"While I was talking with my girlfriend," he said, frustrated, "the girl in the porn program started groaning in a loud voice. My girlfriend asked me, 'Where on earth are you?' I answered, 'I'm helping out in hospital. My colleague's wife was giving birth to her baby. What you heard was her painful groan in her difficult labor.'"

I roared with laughter, "How could you help out when your colleague's wife was giving birth?" I looked down to examine the DVD player. The disk had slid back in the slot automatically. I said apologetically, "I'm so sorry. I didn't know my DVD player could resume playing automatically."

"Will your girlfriend believe what you said?" I went on to ask.

"Maybe or maybe not," he said, "but I insisted I'd stay in the maternity hospital."

I bent down to resume sucking his cock but it refused to regain its glory and remained soft the whole time. I figured he wasn't concentrating on the lovemaking itself but on how to make up an excuse when he confronted his wife later…

I labored myself for almost half an hour before I emptied his balls of sperm. My cheek muscles hurt and stiffened but up till the end I couldn't make his cock erect. When he left, I gave him six cans of Cola. He would be racking his brains all the way home to concoct a more plausible excuse for his girlfriend…

Having been busy for a whole morning, I felt a little dizzy so I went to have a nap for about forty minutes. When I woke up, I settled down to writing. Thinking of the series of weird things that happened these days, I became more and more perplexed.

The most mysterious thing of all happened when my long-lost, silver, big earring presented itself on the carpet of the bedroom! Another mysterious thing was that an insect the size of a small fly was flying about in my kitchen. I tried every means to swat it but in vain. Then a miracle took place. On the carpet in my bedroom, I found the silver earring I had left in the taxi a week before. Could the Omnipotent God really recover the thing I had lost long before?

On the morning of March 23, 2011, I went through the north gate of Woden Mall and happened to meet the mustached manager who was coming toward me. I took a Citizen watch packed in a blue canvas from my handbag and handed it to him, "It's a present for you. I bought it in Hong Kong for less than sixty dollars but it's worth a hundred and fifty to two hundred dollars here in Australia." He was very pleased and said, "Thank you. Tell me when you need my help later." I thanked him and left.

When I was shopping in Coles, I wanted to buy some beers. The mustached manager was walking to the beer aisle when I asked him which beer was cheaper and he answered, "Melbourne Beer." But the aisle happened to be out of stock of this brand of beer. He then asked me how many boxes I'd like to buy and I answered I needed eight boxes. He took my trolley and pushed it to the storage depot. A few minutes later, he pushed my trolley back loaded with eight boxes of beer. I thanked him and pushed my trolley away. Then I bought some other things such as fruit, vegetables and milk. In the process, a certain client called me saying he would come at eleven. Glancing at my wrist watch, it was already ten thirty. Pressed for time, I hurriedly pushed my trolley to the checkout in order to get home sooner. I was pushing the trolley loaded with a lot of goods to the front gate of Woden Mall. I found there was only one taxi there. The taxi driver was not tall but a little fat with black hair, maybe from a Middle Eastern country. Seeing I had bought so many things, he said jestingly, "You've bought so many things. Are you going to have a party at home?"

"No, not for a party," I answered as jestingly, "but for my children."

We kept making fun of each other when we unloaded the goods I had bought. We put the vegetables, fruit and milk that were packed in plastic bags on the back seats or on the floor by the front seat. As there was a spare tire in the trunk of his taxi, there was little space left for five boxes of beer. I had to put the other two boxes on the back seat but there was really no space for the last box. I went around the taxi to the opposite door and thrust the last box between the driver's seat and the back seats. While I was doing so, I seemed to find that something dropped onto the floor in the car but I didn't think too much of it at the time. When we arrived at home, I paid the driver thirty-five dollars and moved all the items into my house. Just then, I touched my left ear and found to my dismay that my silver earring was gone! What a pity and it was hopeless to find it again. Since there were so many taxis in front of the mall, how could I recognize the taxi among them in which I lost the earring?

It seemed that I had no choice but resign myself to fate. It was not that it was worth much. Actually it was a present from my ex-husband and the pair of earrings cost 255 dollars. I lost one of them and I had only one left which was worth 127.5. I could make do with wearing one earring and no one would notice.

Before my second marriage ended in divorce, Ian Philip had sent me three gifts. He sent me a present on May 26, 1999, when we first met. During his third visit to China in December, 1999, he bought me an Omega watch as my birthday present. I asked him the price of the beautiful watch though I knew at once on seeing its large luxurious package it must have been very high. But he smiled and didn't give me the answer.

Once Ian and I flew to China from Australia and we happened to pass the watch counter at the airport. I found to my amazement that this kind of watch was extremely expensive, about 1,300 dollars! I knew by then Ian had spent so much money buying me the birthday present. A person could have sex with a lot of others but it was God's arrangement to lead two of them to wedlock. My first and second marriages were both by God's arrangement and I really owed my two exes so much!

The second gift Ian gave me was a pair of diamond earrings. On the eve of our second wedding anniversary, Ian flew back from Papua New Guinea to Australia for his holiday. When he transferred to the domestic flight at Brisbane International Airport, he bought me the pair of diamond earrings for 2,500 Australian dollars.

The third gift was that pair of silver earrings.

At twelve thirty last night on April 4, or rather, in the early morning on April 5, after seeing off an old client of mine, I went to my bedroom for my electric epilator. I had to have it charged before I could use it to shave my private part. The epilator, together with its blades, charger and the extension socket, were all littering the floor. As I looked down, I was surprised to find my silver earring right beside the extension socket! I picked it up for a closer examination and it was none other than the silver earring I had left in the taxi on the morning of March 23! Was it again the divine intervention of God?

Up until the present, I had been half believing, half doubting the existence of God. I used to be an atheist in my youth but the occurrence of many weird things recently had impressed the belief of His existence into my brain. Of course, not all people in this world could see God as He was a God invisible and intangible to most of us. Even if someone accidentally saw Him he wouldn't believe he had really seen God. But in fact He was real and it was He that created mankind. There could be no world without His existence. He hoped to give the people of this world a happy life and rid the world of the endless wars and disasters. He hoped for Peace!

Now God had assigned me the monumental task of writing the essay on the unification of the World. I would defy all the difficulties and hardship for God. We would strive to accomplish His grand plan at any cost. We had no other purpose than to make the world safe and peaceful and have the people live a happy life on a planet free of any strife or war.

Since the day of March 16 when the message entered my brain that I was Goddess incarnated; I was greater than anyone in the world and was the re-creator of mankind, I had been preoccupied with a terror that an unprecedented catastrophe was imminent and a sense of helplessness when I saw so many people, men or women, old or young, shopping in a carefree atmosphere in Woden Mall, totally ignorant of the approaching disaster. When I came back, the great solitude and helplessness reduced me to weeping and wailing for half an hour, but God didn't say a single word to me. It was not until the small hours of March 29th, after I finished writing my letter to Lisa that God began to talk to me. I thought God was purposely ignoring me to test my psychological endurance. These days I had to go all out to make money as you could hardly get by without it. Apart from making money, I was doing nothing except writing day and night. I was really having a hard time because God often made me cry my heart out and then made my head ache acutely.

"Oh, my Lord," I prayed, "Please don't make my head ache. Obviously you don't want to torment me, your Goddess, to death, do you? If I died, who would help you accomplish your grand plan to unify the world? After all, it is not easy to make a Goddess out of me in fifty years."

Before I had finished my prayer, my head became sober in no time.

"Well," God said, "I will send your favorite client to you." And sure enough He sent a man as my Prince Charming to make love to me.

Let me tell you something about my Price Charming, as his story must be of more interest than that of God.

At around six, came a clerk who was in his mid-thirties. He was an amateur boxer. As I had told you before, he was a very handsome and muscular man, who was wooing me a year before. At that time, I didn't know yet I was Goddess. I just thought I was a prostitute with some fame. Many men had proposed to marry me but I myself didn't intend to accept any of their proposals. What I enjoyed most was to play with various cocks, big or small, long or short, black or white and soft or hard. After I had got enough fun, I got down to writing. I took up writing with the initial purpose of raising enough funds for my old-age support. But rather unexpectedly, from the day of March 14, many weird things kept happening to me and nearly all of them were related to God. I was at a loss as to who I was and put aside all other things such as wealth, fame or rank.

Sometimes I slapped my forehead, asking myself whether I was driven mad by writing too devotedly and then forgot my own identity. Yet I refused to admit my insanity as I was sober enough to know how to eat, drink or shop and I never made errors in calculating my financial affairs. I remembered clearly which client had underpaid me by three or five dollars. I was far from being insane yet I couldn't explain so many weird things that happened to me recently.

As a matter of fact, or in my innermost mind, I didn't believe in God because up till now I hadn't seen God with my own eyes. If ever one day God would grace me with His presence, I would kneel before Him and pray for blessings for all the people in the world. It was God that created this magnificent world and the people on it should have been very happy. Who could expect that the world would be afflicted with so many disasters and ravaged by so many wars? If we could accomplish the grand cause of unifying the world sooner, we would save myriads of people out of the abyss of misery.

Let us return to the affairs between me and my Prince Charming. As I got tired from writing and was crying for quite a while, my mind was still in a tumult when he arrived. While he was massaging me on the bed, I suddenly thought of my mother thousands of miles away in China. If the poor lady should know she gave birth to a girl who turned out to be Goddess, she would have been scared to death. My mother, like me, didn't believe in God. I still couldn't accept the fact that I was Goddess incarnated. I didn't want to be a goddess, but on the contrary, I was perfectly content to just be a mortal and live an ordinary life as an ordinary woman. I was not eager to be a goddess but Fate had played a joke on me and turned me neither fish, flesh nor fowl. I was not able to predict what day I would be incarnated into a goddess and my mother would be scared to death.

I was heartbroken and I prayed that God wouldn't turn me into a goddess, at least while my mother was alive. My mother had lived a hard life up to now. She used to be a poor laborer who could hardly keep body and soul together. Since you, my Lord, was the creator of mankind, you should have allowed them to live a happy life. And besides, she is my mother who has given birth to me and brought me up. Even if she is not my mother, she has contributed so much, after all, in making a goddess out of me for you. I'm not worried about my future fate as I have not many concerns or emotional connections in this world. My only concern was my mother.

As I was a woman of emotions, I couldn't hold back the tears in my eyes and they welled out uncontrollably. Lest my Prince noticed I was weeping as he turned me back, I wiped off my tears with the back of my hand and pretended to be watching the porn video on the screen. Actually I was not watching the screen as I was already fed up with such videos. I had watched them thousands of times. I was missing my mother, who was waiting for me travel to Europe with her this June. She was in her late sixties and she had never travelled on a plane until last August when I took her and my family members to fly economy class to Hong Kong. Now circumstances have changed. I'm the Goddess and I'm supposed to travel first class to Europe with my mother. Oh my Lord, you have had my mother act as a surrogate mother and give birth to a goddess. So you're supposed to give me some money to buy her a first-class ticket to Europe. Should I earn the fare by sucking cocks by myself? It will be a scandal for you, my Lord.

It would really be a scandal for God to let His Goddess travel economy class with her mother and have to put up with the contained seats. Well, I have my own countermeasure by refusing to write for Him. No pay no service! If He wants me to write the essay on unification He will have to pay me first but the question is in what form He can pay me. God doesn't even know the value of the Australian currency and He cannot print them on the spot either. However, God must have His own way. Yesterday God told me to buy a lottery ticket. Before the lottery is drawn, God can blow a magic breath and I will surely be the winner of the first prize. If I can win the prize of two to three million dollars, I will be quite well off and be able to afford to travel first class to Europe. I'm not greedy. Three million will be enough. After all, you can't bring all the remaining money to your grave. The die is cast and God must have settled the matter already. In case God doesn't do me this favor, I will definitely refuse to work for Him. You can't make a horse ride you without feeding it with adequate hay. I have made up my mind not to be such a foolish horse any longer.

In my daydream, I smiled. Seeing I was crying one moment and laughing the next, my Prince Charming thought I had lost my mind. He hesitated for a moment. It seemed he was about to ignore my mental health and thrust his cock into my cunt. With a loud yell, he entered me to the hilt. I suddenly woke up from my daydream, complaining silently he had spoiled my fond dream of winning a prize of three million by fucking me at a most inopportune time. I was wondering how God would pay this time. Anyway, I decided that no pay from God, no service from Goddess. When I was writing, I looked dignified as a Goddess but when I was serving my customers I was simply like a worn-out shoe – an epithet for a loose woman in Chinese language. Any foot could slip into this loose shoe, big or small. God didn't care a bit whether all the other men in the world would come to fuck me or not.

But later I thought better of it that women were created by God to be fucked by men so what was the difference to be fucked by this man or that one or by any of them? The Goddess incarnate was after all a woman and there would be no gods without goddesses. Thinking of this, I calmed down and found the epithet "a loose shoe" didn't sound so harsh and offensive to the ear. Instead, I happily accepted this term of abuse as a compliment to me. So when you met any woman who was called "a loose shoe," tell her to take it easy because the Goddess in Australia was "a loose shoe" herself. By the way, the abusive epithet reminded me of an interesting episode that happened in my youth.

It happened when I had just resigned from the police station under a favorable policy of retaining my position but suspending my salary – that meant I could quit the job as a policewoman for the time being and had to earn my own bread. I wanted to go into business but couldn't find any proper projects at the time so I had to take on the business of running an unlicensed bus service, one the locals referred to as a private minibus, around the Third Ring Road in Beijing. Along the Third Ring Road, I was notorious for my previous experience in the police station. I had been well trained in shooting, boxing and wrestling and worked as a prison wardress for more than ten years so I commanded a kind of respect from all the people in the underworld. Nevertheless, I was challenged by a woman from Tong County. She was running another unlicensed bus and had harbored a long-standing grudge against me because I earned much more money than her. She was a corpulent woman in her forties and had just been released from prison. One day, in a fit of jealousy, she drove her minibus and stopped it in the way of mine. Moreover, she provocatively yelled out the abusive term "a loose shoe" in my presence. I flew into a rage and had someone give her husband a good beating. The final result was my minibus was detained by the Bureau of Public Security. (This scandalous event will be dealt with later.)

Now that I was Goddess, I cared for nothing. Goddess and the loose shoe were but two different sides of a coin. Well, let's quit mentioning the loose shoe and return to my Prince Charming. Since God let him serve my lust, he was supposed to make his cock stiff and stark but the hardness of his cock varied whimsically, sometimes as soft as cotton and sometimes as hard as iron. And besides, that thing of his was on the verge of yielding. Oh my Lord, you had me work for so long and made me shed so many tears that my head was bursting with pain but you still couldn't comfort me by having my Prince fuck me hard. My God, do help me! Don't allow him to slack in the nick of time!

God must have been watching us making love and complaining about his poor performance in bed. Perhaps He was considering how to punish him for failing to serve my cunt well. I was preoccupied with too many things and was too eager to accomplish God's grand plan to be able to concentrate on making love. I tried to brace myself up by shaking off all the details of writing from my brain but in vain so I had to try rubbing my clitoris softly with my right middle finger.

Just as I was masturbating, his cock suddenly began to erect, slowly but steadily until it became as hard as hard could be. I believed God must have blown a magic breath into it. Well aware of where my most sensitive spot was, my Prince bent over to lick my right nipple while he was moving his hard cock deliberately slowly in my cunt.

I narrowed my eyes and enjoyed the ecstasy of carnal pleasure, praying at the same time God had blown enough magic breath into his cock to make it hold on longer. Another two or three minutes and I would come. But to my dismay, one of my mobiles rang suddenly. I didn't answer it. No sooner had it stopped than the other mobile startled me. I was angry. It was the neglect of duty on God's part for his failure to stop the two mobiles from interrupting my lovemaking in the nick of time.

But I had to pick up the mobile and answered harshly, "Hi, what can I do for you?"

"Nothing," he was perplexed, "I was calling a prostitute. My cock is itching now."

"What prostitute?" I said abruptly, "The prostitute you know has been converted into a Goddess. If you'd like to contact her, you must call God for his permission."

With that, I hung up the receiver and went on fucking madly with my Prince Charming. I was indeed in my element when fucking. To hell with the unification! To hell with God! Forget it all and let me satisfy my lust first.

I indulged in my ecstasy with my eyes narrowed, "Fuck me hard, my Prince. Show off your sexual ability before God. If you don't, you will be sent to hell by God." At the same time I swore in my mind if my Prince failed to satisfy me this time I wouldn't serve God any more. I would quit writing and He could appoint whoever He liked to take over my job. It seemed God had taken notice of my idle threat and began to make my Prince exert all his strength on his cock and fuck me rhythmically and forcefully, "Linda, it's really fun moving my cock in your cunt."

How dare he mention the name of Linda, I thought to myself. He didn't know he was actually fucking a Goddess instead of Linda. If he had known, his cock would have been frightened to shrink into a fleeing rat. But now I'd better keep my identity a secret from him otherwise not only my Prince Charming but also all other of my clients would be frightened away. I couldn't work for God with my own stomach empty all day, could I? Since God couldn't serve as my ATM, I had to find a way to make my own living.

Behold, my Lord. Wasn't it great fun having his cock moving away in my cunt? That was the human being you have created, who have to reproduce themselves in this way from generation to generation. Please wait until my book is published, it will surely be a funny book.

The various scenes of men fucking women were really spectacular and sometimes even grotesque. How I wished to take some photos of them as samples for God. But wait, I was wondering whether God would deign to look at these pornographic pictures if they were ever taken. Besides, God himself hadn't graced me with His presence so even if I had taken these pictures, I would have no chance to present them to Him. With God in my mind, I looked with great savor at my Prince Charming fucking me away: His big cock, glossy because it was covered with a layer of lust water flowing from inside my cunt, was being pulled deliberately slowly out of and then thrust as deliberately slowly into my cunt. Whenever his cock was pulled out, my cunt lips flapped out, and whenever it was inserted in, my lips flapped in, too. Though the whole intercourse movement was being done deliberately slowly, it still sounded audibly awkward, like a bike pump in the rain. I was carried away by the untold pleasure and it was not very long before I yelled out in ecstasy, "Ah! I'm coming. I love you!"

I repeated the three words three times! But I knew my Prince must have been thinking, "To hell I love you. You love me only at the moment your lust has just been satiated. Two or three minutes will pass and we will be entirely independent of each other again. He didn't move his cock for too much longer once he saw I had come. He ejaculated all his sperm on my tummy. He must have refrained from ejaculating for a long time in order to make me satisfied first.

We both got up to wash ourselves in separate bathrooms. When I finished bathing and put on my dress, I still heard the splashing water in his bathroom. Perhaps my Prince Charming was afraid of being infected with some venereal disease from me? Impossible, mate, I was clean. Even if I was not, God would cure me of the disease in no time. Who was God? He was the omnipotent God.

Finally my Prince Charming finished bathing, dressed and came out of the working room. I presented him with two bottles of red wine but didn't mention the invitation to dine outside because I had a very busy working schedule from morning till night and hardly had any time to write for God. The workload God assigned me might be much heavier than that of any president in the world. It seemed as if my God was intending to toil me to death, I hadn't been allowed since my childhood to have an easy day or a less tiring day. When I was in primary school or high school, I was pushed to come first in almost every field. When I was in the Police Academy, I was expected to be among the best of all candidates. When I graduated from the Academy and came to serve as a wardress in the prison, I showed my initiative and was active in doing anything only to get a demerit on my record on account of my too much enthusiasm for sex. No one knew me better than God when He said my only weakness was my passion. I was always wondering why I had such a craving for cocks, cocks galore. Nothing in the world was more enjoyable than the fun of cocks, big or small, moving in my cunt…

Pussy Needs a Holiday

The Number One Prostitute (Part II)
Chapters 3, 4 and 5

1. My proudest achievement in the last ten years in my trade of prostitution -- a coming rate of 99.95percent or a dropout rate of only 0.05 percent. And also during the last ten years, it was the first time that I had ever heard of an incest relation between a son and his mother, which lasted as long as fifteen years.

2. It's unbelievable that today in the twenty-first century, I should be able to offer a vivid description of how gods convert to human beings and how gods live their lives. It's also unbelievable that I should be able to predict the year 2050 will be the time when the Earth and the Moon are to shift their positions with each other in a cycle of 5,000 years. Is it a delusion or an illusion? Am I really a woman converted from Goddess? All this is to be proven in time.

3. I took a large number of sleeping pills at midnight, yet still couldn't go to sleep. Did I go mad? I was rushed to the emergency ward in an ambulance. I told the doctors there I was a second Michael Jackson…

4. Following the example of Xaviera Hollander, whose book forty-five years ago represented a milestone in our trade, I'd like to commit myself to carrying forward the trade of prostitution to a new stage.

Linda Li is a famous erotic story author in the world now an American company published "The Number One Prostitute" are selling America Canada Holland Italy Sweden India Australia England. Her new Chinese book "Follow the Dream" A Chinese company will publish soon.

Linda Li has a great dream "No Sex No Life" apply "Novel literature Peace Prize".

Linda Li she lives with her boyfriend in Canberra Australia. Peter He was in army 15 years, now he works for Australian government.

Review Requested:

If you loved this book, would you please provide
a review at Amazon.com?